Paul Lynton was born in New Zealand and lives with his wife in London. His interest in creative writing began as an antidote to a career in retail advertising and marketing.

SCEPTRE

Also by Paul Lynton

Innocence

Farewell to Barbary

PAUL LYNTON

SCEPTRE

Copyright © 1998 by Paul Lynton

First published in 1998 by Hodder and Stoughton
First published in paperback in 1998 by Hodder and Stoughton
A division of Hodder Headline PLC
A Sceptre Paperback

The right of Paul Lynton to be identified as the Author of
the Work has been asserted by him in accordance with the
Copyright, Designs and Patents Act 1988.

10 9 8 7 6 5 4 3 2 1

A CIP catalogue record for this book is available
from the British Library

ISBN 0 340 68031 8

Typeset by Palimpsest Book Production Limited,
Polmont, Stirlingshire
Printed and bound in Great Britain by
Clays Ltd, St Ives PLC, Bungay, Suffolk

Hodder and Stoughton
A division of Hodder Headline PLC
338 Euston Road
London NW1 3BH

FAREWELL TO BARBARY

is dedicated to my three children
Scott, Brett and Leigh Lynton

Acknowledgements

To recapture the past, to present it as it was and not as we might like it to be, requires an intimate understanding of the period, the people, and the events that shaped their lives. In my search for this understanding I freely acknowledge a large debt of gratitude to John Luke for his Tangiers Diaries (1670–73); to Samuel Pepys for his Tangiers Journal (1683); to Lieutenant-Colonel J. Davis for his history of the Tangiers Regiment (1887); and to E.M.G. Routh for her 1912 history of the English occupation of Tangiers. These and other sources of reference which include Lord Dartmouth's maps and documents, etchings and watercolours by Wenceslaus Hollar, etchings by Robert Thacker and oil paintings by Dirck Stoop, are fully documented at the end of this novel.

Martyn Fenton and his immediate circle are men of fiction, but the wider cast is drawn from real life. The story of Tangiers – the story of the English garrison, the building of the Mole, the Moors, and the political and religious conflicts that shaped their destiny – has not been changed or consciously distorted to dramatise the narrative.

To Lieutenant-Colonel P.G. Collyer I would like to extend my whole-hearted thanks. His military expertise, his detailed knowledge of the English history of Tangiers, and the comments he offered after reading the original draft of this novel have given the text the stamp of authenticity.

Paul Lynton
London, January 1998

PART ONE

At Sea – January 1673

(1674 according to the modern calendar)

I was faced with a stark choice.

I could submit to Sergeant Brandon and let him do to me what he wanted to do, or I could offer myself to someone else and hope that he would protect me from Sergeant Brandon.

It was a choice that was not a choice. It was a choice that I did not want to make. It filled my soul with misery and it brought the taste of fear into my mouth.

I lay back in my hammock and stared into the beams – pitching and yawing a few inches above my nose – and I emptied my mind and tried not to think about the night that lay ahead.

But the choice that was not a choice seeped back into my mind and it churned round and round. And like sour milk it began to curdle, began to sour my mind, and it took me back to the first night I lay in this hammock – two weeks ago – when my fears were made manifest, 'made man' to use the words of the creed.

I had known he was coming, known since the day he conscripted me in Deptford, but I had put it out of my mind, and I had hoped, had hoped that I was wrong. But I was wrong to hope.

On our first night on board the *Salisbury* as the twilight softened the coast and blackened the cliffs at Land's End, England slipped away to our right, slipped into darkness, and almost without realising it, England and the village of Elme where I was born thirteen years ago, became places in my memory.

We ran with the wind, towards the south-west – keeping the unseen Isles of Scilly far to our right and the coast of France far to our left. When the wind freshened and the troughs between the waves became longer and deeper, the high stern began to catch the wind, to act like an extra sail, and the *Salisbury* began to heave and roll. The sailors stripped the sails from the aft mast – the mizzen mast, left it standing gaunt and bare, and they reduced the sails on the other two masts, and the heaving and the rolling gave way to a slow swaying.

For a while I leant on the wooden rail and watched the red, green and white lights on the other merchantmen make arc-shaped patterns in the dark. It was a convoy of colour, colour that would keep us apart, keep us at a safe distance, for we were sailing together, sailing in convoy, and subject to naval orders, naval discipline – because of the war with the Dutch and the Barbary Pirates who prowl the shipping lanes from the Coast of Barbary to the coast of Kent.

I watched the bubbles foaming along the crests of the black waves, and wondered how long it would take these same waves to reach the men-of-war that had taken up station on both sides of the convoy in the late afternoon, then I clambered halfway down the ladder and pulled the hatch shut. The hold smelt cold and damp. Most of the men were lying in their hammocks with their grey coats spread over their legs or their shoulders. The sleeves were black-cuffed and some of them were dangling below the hammocks, and as the ship swayed, they swayed, and they looked like black tentacles waiting for their prey, waiting for me to come swimming amongst them.

I shivered, rubbed my hands against my breeches, and told myself it was colder than I thought. I took off my stockings and stuffed them into my shoes, rolled my breeches into the shape of a pillow and pushed them into the top end of my hammock. Then I wrapped myself in my blanket, and with one hand pulling on the beam, I half-slid half-rolled into the hammock, and pulled my coat over my shoulders. The coat is heavy – it's lined with black serge – and in the summertime it will make me sweat, but right now it wasn't warm enough, and I pulled it tighter and tucked the sleeves into the hammock.

I closed my eyes, and in the blackness of my mind, in the secret place where my thoughts march up and down, I felt a swaying, a slow swaying. Then I began to feel queasy, and despite being up with the dawn, and feeling tired, I could not go to sleep. Maybe it was the excitement of leaving Plymouth, of leaving England. Maybe it was being on a ship for the first time, or sleeping in a hammock. Or maybe it was a little of all of them. I don't know. But I do know I couldn't sleep and my face was getting cold, and I pulled my coat right up to my nose. My coat doesn't have a collar and when it's buttoned up it forms a circle around my neck and this rubs at my skin – now it began to rub at my nose.

I stretched, yawned and turned over, and began to think about the white scarves we tie around our necks to stop the rubbing. Mine was in my pocket but I didn't want to put my hand out in the cold to find it, and I eased the coat away from my nose.

After a while my eyes began to feel heavy and my thoughts began to drift, to dream, and I saw a hand, saw a green cuff. I blinked hard and lifted my head. Sleep fled, and I watched that hand, watched it open the night lamp and trim the wick. I knew that hand. I knew the moment I saw the cuff. Only two men wear green cuffs in our company: Sergeant Brandon and Sergeant Owen – and he's in the other hold with the musketeers.

Sergeant Brandon is an old pikeman and he says he'll make us into pikemen, make us into copies of himself – within six weeks. In Deptford when we first drew our pikes – they stand sixteen feet high and are capped with an iron spear or spike – he said: 'You carry them in your right hand, and you make a cup like this' – he extended his arm and curled his fingers, then he closed them around the end of the pike – 'and you rest the pike on your right shoulder like this.' He looked up and down our lines, then he grounded his pike. 'You can always tell a pikeman. He has a horny hand.' He held up his hand, turned the palm towards us, and in the cold wet light it looked like leather tooled with raised circles. 'Of course there's one other way. One other thing that makes it horny.' We laughed, and he laughed; then his laugh became a smile, became a lecherous grin.

I am short, and my shoulder is lean – thin on muscle and light on bone – and my arms are not long enough to balance the pike. On the march from Deptford to the Nove in the Medway, where we boarded the *Salisbury*, my fingers had to make the cup, and after a while this stiffened my arm, made my shoulder ache deep inside the joint. I let the pike slip through my fingers and held the end about six inches off the ground. For an hour or two this eased the ache, the stiffness, but as I began to tire, to despair of the road ever coming to an end, my shoulders slouched and my head dropped, and I plodded along in a soft dream.

Then the Sergeant saw me and screamed: 'If you bend over any further I'll have your arse!'

Then he gripped his halberd – it's only eight feet high but it's better than a pike because the head is made up of three weapons: a spear to thrust, a blade to slash and a hook to pull men off their horses – and he jabbed at me, and we all straightened up and woke up. Then he made the drummer boy beat his drum, and for a mile or two I marched – we marched – with a firm tread. But then weariness overtook me, overtook us, and the beat began to slow, to soften, to die. The pikes slipped through our fingers, our heads began to nod, our eyes began to close, and from a far-away place came the sound of the Sergeant screaming.

In a light rain, made cold, made bitter by an off-shore wind, we sailed past the mouth of the river Thames, rounded the white cliffs that are straddled by Margate and Ramsgate and dropped anchor in the Downs – in the stretch of water that lies between Deal and the Goodwin Sands. Next morning, in a dawn made dull by a light sea-fog, we sailed past Dover, intending to anchor for the night at Saint Helens on the Isle of Wight, but the winds were contrary and they pushed us away from the land. For the next three days we clawed our way along the south coast, and late in the evening of a day of blustery winds that raised the height of the waves and pitched the bow, we picked up the anchor chains deep in Plymouth Sound.

For two days we weren't allowed to go ashore in case we deserted, but on the evening of the third day – when there was still no sign of the new recruits from the West Country – Sergeant Brandon changed his mind, and next morning, in a dawn greyed by a clouded sky we landed on the Hoe and marched to the Royal Citadel.

Sergeant Brandon ordered us to wear the old armour for a day 'to know what it feels like to be a real pikeman'. My helmet had lost its padding and the shape didn't fit my head. It sat hard on my ears and pressed on my forehead, and by the end of the day it gave me a thumping headache. Metal shoulder straps locked the breastplate – the cuirass – to the backplate, and a leather belt, slipped through metal loops and buckled at the front, pulled the plates together, flattened our bellies and flared our coats. The armourer couldn't find any gorgets – the curved piece of armour that should protect our necks – or any tassets – the thigh guards that should hang from the cuirass – and Brandon said: 'You're getting off lightly. That lot only weighs about ten pounds.'

I turned away from the past, away from the dead-weight of the armour we would never have to wear again, and I watched Brandon creep back to his bunk – it fitted into the curve of the bow – and I closed my eyes and tried to sleep.

But I could not sleep, and in the dredgings of memory I heard Brandon say: 'Armour is still used by sentries sometimes. For them the weight doesn't matter because they don't have to march or run anywhere and it doesn't slow them down.' Then he paused. 'When I was a young man we were taught to think of our pieces of armour as weapons of defence because they could protect us. The pike and the sword—' I opened my eyes. My sword was in my shoulder belt – my baldric – hanging from a peg on the wall, and as the ship swayed, it swayed. I closed my eyes and his voice picked up his words again. 'The pike and the sword are the weapons of a soldier-of-foot. They are offensive weapons. Weapons of attack. You are soldiers-of-foot and they are the only reason for your existence.'

An hour or so later – when sleep was still teasing me and my mind was drifting among the black tentacles – Sergeant Brandon came prowling like a wolf searching for a lamb that has strayed from the flock. He stopped and sniffed the air and looked around. I saw his green-cuffed arm and I knew there was something wrong with that coat of his, something to do with the buttons, something to do with the past, and I couldn't think what it could be.

Then he took a man from his hammock, took him into his wooden bunk and pulled the curtain. When I heard the man cry out, I knew the wolf had done to him what my Father had done to me. It made me shudder and twitch, and it loosened my bowels, and like a man with the flux, the shit dribbled out of me. The smell of it seeped through my shirt, my blanket and my hammock, and it hung in the air.

I couldn't get that smell out of my head. It lingered on and on. It was a legacy from the past, and it made nights that should have been dead and buried, live again in my mind, and they brought me out in a cold sweat, made me shiver and shake.

After a week of watching the wolf shepherding men towards his lair, my bowels were twitching and I was finding it difficult to sleep. The nights were becoming warmer, and since crossing the Bay of Biscay and sighting Cape Finisterre on the northern coast of Spain, I had hung my coat on a peg, and slept in my shirt, on top of my blanket. The blanket softened the knotting in the hammock and now that I was used to the hammock swaying as the ship swayed, I found it more comfortable than sleeping on the floor or on the wooden benches we pushed together to make the bed I used to share with my Mother and Father.

In some ways this was perverse, for I had always thought a bed that was warm and comfortable would encourage sleep, and I turned over – and the hem of my shirt rode up and exposed my private parts. It was always doing this and it annoyed me, and I pulled it down and tucked it tight around my knees, and then I raised my head an inch or two and let my eye run along the line of hammocks. There were nineteen of us sleeping elbow to elbow, like corpses laid out in a common grave. I was hard against the bulkhead with my head to the hull. Crabtree lay beside me, and Oldfield lay next to him. They talked for an hour or more. In my mind I walked around the edge of their friendship – they were older than me and I was hoping I could be their friend – and I closed my eyes, was drifting towards sleep, when I heard Oldfield say: 'He's not going to have me.' Crabtree said something but the uprights that hold the ribs and shape the hull were groaning – like old men with phlegm in their chests – and they muffled his words. Then Oldfield leant over Crabtree, patted me on the arm and said: 'And he's not going to have you either.'

I smiled to myself and ran my fingers along the beam above my nose. It felt damp – felt misted with my breath – and I listened to the soft slosh of the water running along the outside of the hull.

Oldfield has short legs and big hands that dangle about his knees and make big fists. Last night when the wolf came sniffing – came lifting up the shirts of two or three men in the middle of the line – Oldfield raised his fist in the air and punched the palm of his hand. A hard thumping smack rippled down the line, and in the silence that followed he hissed: 'No!'

The wolf froze.

Oldfield punched his hand again and repeated the word: 'No!' This time his fist stayed in the air and he kept it clenched hard.

The wolf turned his back on Oldfield and took a man into his lair. And somewhere in the night, in the hours before the dawn, the man staggered back to his hammock.

I emptied my mind of last night, and listened again to the soft slosh of the running water.

Then I heard a noise, heard feet thumping onto the floor, and I grabbed at the rope edge of my hammock. In the middle of the line Lockhart was crouching down, reaching for something. I breathed a sigh of relief for now I knew it wasn't my turn – not tonight it wasn't. But then I began to feel uneasy, and I looked again and there was no sign of the wolf, and my heart began to thump in my ears. Lockhart pulled his blanket around himself – he comes from the West Country and complains about the cold and the damp – and he climbed up the ladder and pushed open the hatch. Cold air and a swaying shaft of pale light crept into the hold. In his hand he was holding his pipe. The barrel was black, and the stem was long and white and it looked like a bleached bone, and as he moved it pointed at me and then Oldfield and then me again. It was like an evil omen – witchery for lack of a better word – and in my mind, my rational mind, I knew it was just a coincidence, a working of chance, and of no significance. But it left me feeling cold, feeling as though my turn had arrived, and it would be tonight or tomorrow night.

A few minutes later I could smell tobacco. It smelt sweet, like the smell of burning peat, and I could see wisps of smoke drifting through the shaft of light.

I remembered Sergeant Brandon lining us up against the side of the hold on our first night and saying: 'Let me tell you about the bilboes. There are two of them on this ship. One in the hold below us and one on the deck above us – up by the bow. They're nothing to look at. Just an iron rail fixed to the planking. They're for the tars, the seamen. For the ones who won't do as they're told. And they are the essence of simplicity. They clamp a chain onto one ankle, loop it under the bilboes and clamp it to the other ankle. A man can walk up and down – for three or four feet – and if he's down below he stays in the dark, and every couple of days someone looks in to see if he's still alive. And if he's up on deck the sun and the rain and the salt spray can turn him into a gibbering idiot.' He looked at us and pursed his lips.

'On this ship there are several things you're not allowed to do. One is to go onto the raised deck at the stern. Another is to talk to any of the passengers, unless of course they talk to you first. In that case you are expected to make a civil reply. And keep it short.' He paused for a moment. 'And you're not to have any sort of light or fire in this hold – apart from the candle in the night lamp. Fire is the worst disaster that can befall a ship at sea. Any man caught smoking in this hold will be formerly charged and paraded in front of the ship's Captain and I wouldn't be surprised if he ends up in the bilboes for the rest of the voyage. He could even be flogged – the offence is that serious. For those of you who are wondering why you would be paraded in front of the ship's Captain instead of our own Captain Lacey, the answer is simple: all the authority on this ship is vested in the ship's Captain. And while we are on this ship we must bow to his commands.'

I wondered how Lockhart had lit his pipe. He hadn't used the night lamp. I would have seen him if he had. And I don't think he could have got into the galley where the cooks prepare the food. And anyway, in the evening, before they go to bed, I've seen them pack the hot ashes under humped lids with tiny handles, and they cover these with fire bricks. He wouldn't be able to unpack them and get a flame going. Not in the dark he wouldn't. And I was thinking one of the seamen could have been up on deck having a smoke – and maybe he gave him a light – when he sat by the hatch and dangled his legs down the ladder.

I watched the smoke swirl around his legs and his feet like a fine mist, and for a while my thoughts drifted in this mist, this smell of peat. I remembered cutting the peat, cutting the turves and stacking them to dry in the sun, in the wetlands, in The Fens of East Anglia where I used to live. And I remember walking through the reeds and the rushes, watching them sway in the wind, watching the twilight suck the colour out of them, and make them into bands of black swaying in the blackness of night. In the blankets that were hanging from the hammocks I could see those bands of black.

They were swaying. But unlike the reeds and the rushes that rustle and fill the night with noise, the blankets were silent, were muffling the soft snores.

But then the blankets began to tremble, began to move, to be pulled aside. I rolled onto my side, peered into the darkness, and saw the wolf, creeping on all fours below the hammocks. He raised his head, looked in Lockhart's empty hammock and felt it with his hands. Then he vanished. My heart stopped as it used to stop when I was a child and played childish games, and I held my breath, shut my mouth, clamped my teeth, and dared not move. Three or four seconds passed then the wolf reared up beside Oldfield. His hand slid under Oldfield's shirt. Oldfield yelled, sat up with a start, and banged his head against the beam. The wolf punched him in the ribs. Oldfield flayed the air with his hands, then he fell back into his hammock and the wolf rolled him onto the floor.

The wolf crept out and stood up straight, and for a moment I could hear the gentle slosh of water. Then Oldfield roared and hurled himself at the wolf. They crashed to the floor, rolled under the hammocks and fought among the blankets. The noise woke the others and the hold filled with hissing and whispering.

Then there was silence, and the slosh of water returned again.

After a few minutes the wolf staggered out and leant against the bulkhead. He wiped his nose on the sleeve of his shirt and stared at the long smear of blood. Then he shuffled down the hold – past all the silent faces – limped into his lair and drew the curtain.

I felt safe.

But in the morning, when the night lamp was blown out and the hatch opened, the wolf was the Sergeant, with a swollen face, a broken nose, a cut lip, and a limp that dragged his foot.

I do not know what he said to Captain Lacey, but I did hear him tell Lieutenant de Colville that he was woken by the smell of smoke, and soon after that Sergeant Owen and four of his musketeers came for Oldfield. He was paraded before Captain Lacey, charged with striking a superior officer and ordered to stand trial in front of the ship's Captain. In the afternoon we waited to be called as witnesses, but no one was called. Oldfield admitted the assault – claimed he dreamt he was being attacked and did not realise the Sergeant was trying to wake him – and he begged for the court to show him mercy.

In the evening we learnt that mercy was to be thirty lashes and in place of the light duties that would have followed for a seaman suffering punishment he was sentenced to be shackled to the bilboes – on deck or down below, according to the vagaries of the weather and the whims of the Officer of the Watch.

In the morning, at the formal break-of-day parade, we paraded with the whole crew, heard prayers, and listened to the solemn reading of the sentence.

Oldfield – white-faced and grim – stripped off his shirt, tossed it on the deck and turned to face the rigging. Two seamen tied him to the rigging and a big brute of a man stepped forward, stripped off his own shirt, flexed his muscles, pulled a cat-o'-nine-tails out of a bag and flicked it in the air. The nine tails splayed through the air, formed a fan of knotted rope. Then the tails sprung back on themselves and made a hard cracking sound, like the sound of a long whip herding cattle.

It sent a shiver right through me.

Then one of the ship's officers yelled: 'Let punishment commence!'

Poor little Billy Foster, our drummer boy, wiped his cuff across his forehead and beat his drum: once.

The man with the cat, screwed his face into a tight scowl, swung his body to the right, raised the cat high in the air and lashed Oldfield. A spray of red welts ran from his right shoulder to the knobbled line that was his spine.

A seaman yelled: 'One!' Foster beat his drum again, and the cat welted Oldfield's left shoulder, and the seamen yelled: 'Two!'

The solemn beat of the drum, the swishing sound of the lash, and the calling of the numbers, went on and on like an endless chant. The welts on Oldfield's back joined up, became a bright red jacket that ran from his neck to the middle of his waist, and below that there was not a mark, not a fringe of red. It was a cruel perfection – it is forbidden to lash the buttocks or the waist because it can damage a man's kidneys and hasten his death.

At the count of twenty Oldfield sagged and bit at the rigging. Then the red welts began to split, to peal open and his back dribbled blood.

I shut my eyes and I began to feel the pain, feel the lash, and it made me feel ill, and one by one I counted off the last strokes.

The seamen untied his hands, turned him round and helped him to sit on the deck. The knotted ends of the cat had crept over his shoulders, crept round his chest, and made two ragged lines that ran from his nipples to the level of his belly button.

The seamen poured a bucket of salt water over his wounds – brought a scream to his lips, a scream the lash had never succeeded in bringing – patted them dry and tried to staunch the bleeding.

Twenty or thirty minutes later one of them rubbed a white salve into his wounds, helped him back into his shirt and pushed a straw hat onto his head.

Then they shackled him to the bilboes by the bow, and there – or in the bilboes in the hold – he is to remain till we sight the Coast of Barbary and drop anchor in the Bay of Tangiers.

In the late morning, when my arms and thighs were still aching from an hour of Ensign Wyndham's sword drill, I wiped the sweat from under my arms, picked up the slop bucket and dropped it over the side. For a moment or two it swayed on the crest of a wave, then it gulped in water and began to sink. I hauled it back onto the deck, splashed water on my face and cooled my hands. As I looked up Sergeant Brandon was smiling and beckoning to me. I took him the bucket and he thrust an old shirt into my hands – it was stained and torn, and looked as though it couldn't be patched any more – and I followed him up the steps and onto the upper deck.

The officer of the watch was standing in front of the state cabins, and to his right stood a seaman with both hands on the ship's wheel. Near the bell, the compass box and a steep flight of steps another seaman was standing guard.

The Sergeant said something to the officer, then he grabbed hold of the overhead rope and slid down the stairs. I came bumping after him – trying not to spill the water – and on the lower deck, in a passageway darkened by closed doors, we found a shaft with a ladder fixed to the wall. As we climbed down the ladder, I was expecting darkness and a candle, but the hold was full of light. It was coming from a slit that followed the curve of the stern. The slit was about twenty inches high, and through it ran a long wooden tiller that was hooped with iron, loosely chained to the floor, and roped – through wooden pulleys – to both sides of the hull. From there the ropes ran through more pulleys and vanished into dark holes in the roof.

A seaman was sitting on a wooden bench that fitted into the beams of the hull, just outside the arc of the tiller. He looked up and grunted.

For a moment we both peered through the slit, watched the bubbles streaming away from the rudder, and I was thinking the ship didn't sway so much down here at sea level, when Brandon said: 'If the steering wheel was damaged or the ropes broke they could steer the ship from here. That's one of the reasons for this opening. It allows them to see what they're doing. It also allows them to ventilate the ship – to freshen the air. In heavy seas they fit boards into this groove' – he ran his fingers along the groove in the bottom of the slit – 'and the tiller slides them backwards and forwards. And that keeps the sea out.'

The seaman looked up and said: 'Most of it.'

Brandon laughed, walked over to the bulkhead about six feet from the end of the tiller and knocked on a door. There was no reply. 'The Lieutenant sleeps in this one. Wyndham's in the next one. And those other two are for the officers of the watch – if they have to steer from down here.' He pushed open the door. The smell of vomit hit me in the face. I gagged and turned away. 'He's got a delicate stomach, he has,' he laughed. 'You clean it up and wash the floor. And when you've finished leave the door open. Prop it open with something.' He looked around. 'That chest of his, that'll do. And then it'll dry.'

I washed the floor twice but the smell was deep in the cracks and it wouldn't come out. I needed to run a knife through them. I needed another bucket of water, and I was thinking of pushing the bucket through the slit, when the morning – the early rising – caught up with me. I yawned, felt tired, felt as though I'd done enough, and I pulled the chest against the door and sat down. I ran my fingers over the metal straps, and thought I'd have a look inside – but it was locked – and I began to wonder how a man could own enough things to put in a chest.

I have a sack, and it holds two pairs of stockings, a spare shirt, a woollen vest and another scarf. That's all I've got, and the sack is far too big. Some of the men from north of the border call them haversacks, and they tie a rope onto both ends and carry them on their backs. When I first heard the word I thought they were saying: I have a sack. But now I know it's a Scots word and haver means oats. And when a Scotsman goes off to war he carries a sack of oats, and when he's hungry he grinds up the oats, stirs in water or milk, and cooks himself a thick porridge. I've never liked porridge. There's no taste in it. It needs a lot of salt or honey. And I didn't want any oats – that's what I said when they told me about haversacks.

Lockhart laughed in my face. 'Oats,' he said. 'A man needs his oats – twice a day,' and they all laughed. Then he patted my head, ran his fingers through my hair. 'And you so young and innocent, and sleeping with a lot like this.'

I pulled a face and grinned. I knew he wasn't talking about oats. He was talking about swiving – about fucking. I remembered his joke about having a woman in the sack, and his other one about putting a sack over her head, and I grinned some more.

Then a man was yelling and the seaman jumped to his feet, and I jumped to my feet. It was instinctive. I did it without thinking. Then I realised that was wrong. It was not instinctive. We'd been taught to do it, been prodded and beaten with the end of Brandon's halberd, and now we did it without thinking. I turned and looked at the man – he was one of the ship's officers – and when he began to talk to the seaman I sat down again. He looked like all the rest of their officers, and for the life of me I don't know how the sailors distinguish one rank from the other.

Our officers make it easy for us. They all wear gorgets – the moon-shaped piece of armour that used to cover the gap between a cuirass and a full-face metal helmet. They wear them round their necks and they tie them on with coloured ribbons. Captain Lacey wears a gold gorget. Lieutenant de Colville wears a black one with gold studs; and Ensign Wyndham wears a silver one. From a distance they all look the same, but up close it's easy to tell one from the other, and I was thinking this officer should wear something similar, when he yelled: 'What the hell are you doing down here?'

I jumped to my feet. 'Washing the floor, sir.'

'And I thought you were having a little rest.' He shook his head and walked towards me. 'Have you finished?'

'Yes, sir.'

'Then get out of here. And take that bucket with you. And don't come back.'

Up on deck I tossed the last of the water over the rail, and looked at Oldfield. He was sitting with his legs pulled against his chest and his arms were wrapped around them. His chin was resting on his knees. His eyes closed, were shaded by his hat. I turned to Crabtree – he was leaning against the rail, watching the coast of Spain drift by – and I said: 'I didn't think his face would burn so quickly.'

He said: 'It's the wind. It's as bad as the sun. I keep telling him to keep his hat on but he doesn't like wearing it.'

I turned and looked again at Oldfield. He was wearing a thin pair of white breeches with a loose shirt that looked as though it had formed a dull red scab, had become part of his back, part of his chest.

That night as I was sliding into sleep the wolf came for Crabtree.

Crabtree stands tall and thin like a willow that has grown too fast, and he does not have the fight in him that Oldfield has, or had. He whimpered like a lost child, then without saying a single word he slunk through the hold, pulled the curtain and vanished into the lair.

The wolf leaned across Crabtree's hammock, pulled away my blanket and ran his hand up my leg. I grabbed at the sides of my hammock and the rope bit into my hands. He breathed in my face and said: 'Tomorrow I shall come for you. And then the word pikeman will take on a new meaning.'

In the morning we paraded with seven-foot staffs on the lower deck. 'I want you to pretend,' yelled Sergeant Brandon, 'that these are full-sized pikes. We can't drill with full-sized ones, that's obvious.' And he pointed to the rigging that tented the deck. 'This is the best we can do and with them you can learn the commands and practise the drills.' He ran his eye along the line of wooden staffs – the ends were sharpened to a point – then he yelled: 'Stand to your arms!'

I splayed my feet, pulled my staff up straight and put my left hand on my hip.

'Advance your pikes!'

I flicked the staff onto my right shoulder and held it upright – in my cupped hand.

'Charge your pikes!'

I ran the staff under my armpit and held it with both hands – made the point level with my shoulder.

'That is the position for advancing upon the enemy. We can't advance very far on this deck but we can march on the spot, and keep the pike at the correct level. And half an hour of that twice a day will help to strengthen the muscles in your arms.' He paused. 'On the march we talk about the pike being shouldered or trailed. The meaning of shouldered is obvious. But the meaning of trailed is not at all obvious. Is anybody prepared to hazard a guess?'

The obvious meaning was to drag it in the dust but that couldn't be the meaning, it was too easy.

He ran his eye along our three ranks and nobody said a word. 'Trailing is used at night so nobody gets lost and nobody trips over the end of a pike. It's also used at funerals as a mark of respect.' He paused. 'Spread out. Leave four feet between each man.' We shuffled apart. 'Right turn!'

He walked to the head of the column. 'The order is trail pikes. The man at the front takes his pike in his right hand and holds it just below the spearhead. The man behind him holds the end of it in his right hand. That man holds his own pike in his left hand – once again just below the spearhead – and the man behind him takes the end in his left hand. This pattern runs all the way down the ranks and if you're smart you'll know that it takes ten men to carry nine pikes in this fashion – so the second to last man has to carry both a pike head and a pike end in his left hand. And I always make sure the man with the worst drill gets that position.' He smiled and walked back to the wooden railing.

'In the old days, and by that I mean before the advent of muskets, the order "at push of pike" meant the pikemen charged an opposing block of pikemen and kept on doing it till one or the other gave way. Today, in a large battle, the pikemen protect the musketeers but because of their slow rate of fire most companies have two musketeers to every one pikeman. The greatest threat to a musketeer is a man on horseback. Horses are hard to kill. They can be hit with a musket ball – several musket balls – and still keep on charging, and they can be on top of the musketeers before they've had time to reload. So,' he smiled, 'this morning we are going to face some charging horses.'

A laugh rippled down the ranks – destroyed our funereal silence.

He grinned. 'Shoulder pikes . . . re-form ranks . . . left turn.'

He watched us go through the three movements and he shook his head. 'The order is "Charge to horse". You crouch, wedge the butt of your pike under the instep of your right foot, and angle your pike to the horse's breast. He paused. 'I want you to pretend that the big waves, the ones with the foaming crests, are horses charging.'

A couple of men looked at each other and pulled faces.

'Charge to horse!'

We crouched, anchored our staffs, gripped them with two hands and tried to make the right angle. Brandon walked along the ranks. He looked at Crabtree, pulled his pike into a softer angle and said to him: 'How big do you think a horse is?'

A couple of men giggled.

Four little waves hit the side of the ship one after another and our knees absorbed the gentle rocking of the deck. Then the Sergeant yelled: 'Here comes a big one. Brace yourself . . . now!'

The wave smacked the side, tilted the deck, tossed spray high in the air, and hurled us backwards. We collapsed in a ragged line and slid towards the wooden railing on the other side of the deck. I stood up, and felt foolish. In a real battle I knew the butts of our pikes would be rammed into the earth and they would absorb the weight of a charge, and for a moment this reassured me. But then I remembered Lieutenant de Colville saying the Moors had kept Tangiers under siege for the last ten years, and each year they launched an attack in the summertime, when the spring planting was finished and the harvest was still to be gathered. It was a time when the sun baked the ground, made it hard – like the deck – and I began to think this exercise might be more realistic than I had imagined.

We re-formed ranks and looked with wary eyes at the charging horses. We absorbed the next two charges, and they sprayed us with water.

'Think of it as blood,' Sergeant Brandon yelled – as he stepped away from the railing and stayed dry. The next charge came at us with a wild madness, with a thundering fury, and it sent us skidding across the deck. Captain Lacey hurled down the stairs – he'd been leaning on the rail at the front of the upper deck, watching us and talking to Ensign Wyndham for several minutes – and he yelled: 'Get on your feet! And get back in your ranks! This is disgraceful. You look like fools. And you're making me look like a fool.'

Behind him, the ship's officers, had gathered in a loose knot by the compass box, and now they were holding their hands to their mouths, trying to smother their laughter.

We lined up again. For a moment we watched the horses, watched them galloping towards us, galloping in from the coast of Spain, then Sergeant Brandon screamed: 'About turn!'

The Captain walked up and down, then he said, in a voice that was now back under control: 'One day you may have to face a charge of horse in Tangiers, and you must prepare for that day. The Moors have more horses than we do, and when they attack the brunt of the fighting will fall upon you. It will not fall upon our troopers. And what may look like a foolish exercise right at this moment, could one day halt a charge of horse, and it might save your life.'

Then he turned his back on us and walked over to Sergeant Owen and his musketeers. They'd been practising musket drill for an hour. Their muskets were the old firelocks with a length of rope – of match – that has to be kept smouldering all the time. The ship's Captain had refused permission for them to load gunpowder and fire because of the danger of a fire on deck or in the rigging. I heard him tell Sergeant Owen that all the musketeers on the naval ships are now equipped with the new flintlocks – they don't improve their rate of fire but they do reduce the danger of a fire at sea.

Oldfield was huddling against the solid railings – trying to stay in a wedge of shifting shade. He didn't want to go down to the hold, to the darkness that would blind his eyes and chill his bones. And he didn't want to wear his hat and now the sun had blistered his face and his scalp – his hair was thinning – and the sea had frosted him with salt. He was bubbling words, slurring them together. I hissed at him, tried to attract his attention, but he didn't appear to see me, or hear me; and some of the men are saying this will warp his mind and he'll never be the same again.

Pike drill gave way to sword drill. For an hour we slashed at ghosts, cut them to pieces and tossed them over the side. Then the musketeers replaced the ghosts, pretended to be the enemy, pretended to be Dutchmen – the war was almost a year old now and feelings were running high – and they cut us to pieces. It was humiliating, and it brought us another hour of cut and thrust, and this time the ghosts put up a hell of a fight and they died hard.

In the night I crawled into my hammock. My wrist was aching and so were my arms and the backs of my legs. I couldn't get comfortable. I turned over, lay on my side, dozed and waited, tried not to think about Sergeant Brandon. But I found I was thinking about him – thinking about last night – and in my mind I saw Crabtree stagger back to his hammock again. I saw him slip and fall and lie on the floor. I heard him sob, and I tried to help him into his hammock, but he pushed me away.

I lifted my head and looked at him lying now in his hammock. He was sound asleep. For him it was over. It was part of yesterday, and it lay in the past. For me it lay in the future. I did not want to think about the future and I let my mind drift back to the day Sergeant Brandon jerked me out of my sleep, beat me till my thoughts crumpled, my legs collapsed, and I could stand no more. It was the day he and Captain Lacey forced me to volunteer. Volunteer is a strange word – it is their word, not mine – and it cannot disguise the truth. I was forced to do what I did not want to do: I was conscripted. And now I am a pikeman, a soldier-of-foot, in the Tangiers Regiment-of-Foot. That is our formal name, formal title, but in everyday speech most people call us the Governor's Regiment, or the Middleton Regiment. Lord Middleton is the Governor of Tangiers. He's also the Colonel of our Regiment and they say he's a Scotsman with a liking for porridge, but I doubt if he's ever had to carry his own haversack, or forage for wild oats.

The sailors have another name for us, a nickname: the Tangerines. It's also the name of a small thin-skinned orange that grows in these parts, and it led to a rash of jokes, sly jokes and knowing winks – about squeezing our pips.

I reached down and felt my pips. They were tucked up tight, hiding in the hair between my legs, and they felt as though they'd shrivelled, felt as though they knew I was afraid.

Then I heard the bells – the sailors ring them every half-hour to signal the passage of the watch – and I counted four strokes, heard them echo in my mind, and tried to tell myself he would not come.

But then I could smell him. He was breathing in my face, breathing herring pie and vinegar, and his hands were pulling at my shirt and he was rolling the hammock and I was sliding out. I was sliding into his arms, and I did not want him and I did not want the things he wanted to do to me, and in my head I was screaming. I pummelled him with my fists, and I kicked him with my bare feet.

He laughed, and clouted me round the ear.

My head spun, I sagged, and gasped for air.

He pulled me up, held me tight, and laughed again.

I grabbed at his bottom and he spread his legs. I slid my knee up the inside of his leg and he said: 'That's better. That's much better.'

I took a firmer grip on his bottom – it was broad and fleshy – and I breathed some more of his vinegar. Then I kneed him in the balls.

His hands shot away from me and his mouth opened and he sucked in a breath. Then he doubled over, nursed his balls and swayed backwards and forwards.

I hurled under the hammocks, over the shoes and the sacks, and I heard him bellow: 'I'm going to have you, Fenton! I'm going to have you right now. And tomorrow you won't be able to sit down on your pretty little bum.'

I swallowed hard and popped my head up between the ends of the hammocks. He was about ten feet away, reaching for the lantern. It was casting shadows on his face and filling in the lines around his mouth and his eyes. It was making him look mad, almost rabid. I sucked in a breath, and he spun towards me.

Then he laughed. It was an evil laugh, unnatural, like the vice that makes a man want a man.

I bent low and crept towards the door. Then I stumbled over a sword and a baldric. The sword clattered against something.

The noise made my heart thump, and I heard him chuckle. I lay flat on the floor and slithered along.

At the door I raised my hand and pulled back the locking bar. The ship swayed and the door swung out of my hands and banged against a stool, sent it skittering across the hold.

I jumped to my feet and hurled into the passage. For a second I thought I was free, but then his hand grabbed at me and it brought me to a sudden stop. It jerked my arm and spun me around.

The air in the passageway was cold and it made me cough and splutter. Then I saw his hand. It was about four inches from my mouth. I lunged and bit his hand. He swore and let me go.

I tore up the ladder, shoved open the hatch and ran onto the deck.

He thundered up the ladder. I could hear him muttering and I didn't know what to do.

I ran around the deck looking for somewhere to hide.

But there was nowhere to hide. One of the sailors giggled, another whistled, and another grabbed at me and said: 'I'll look after you little boy.' I pushed him away and skidded to the other side of the deck. Oldfield sat up, and I slid in behind him, lifted one of his blankets over my head, hugged him tight and tried to become part of him.

The Sergeant prowled around the deck, and the sailors laughed. He scowled at them, then he prodded Oldfield with his foot and said: 'Have you seen him?'

Oldfield shook his head. The Sergeant grunted, said: 'Liar,' and kicked him in the ribs.

Oldfield gasped and flopped forward. The Sergeant bent down. 'Who the hell gave you two blankets?' He grabbed one, pulled it away, pulled it off me.

He laughed and grabbed at me. I jumped to my feet and in my haste, my panic, I ran towards the stern instead of the bow. I ran up the steps, past the wheel and the compass box, and past the sailors with their grabbing hands. Then my feet were running in the air and I was falling.

I crashed down the stairs, rolled along the passage and thumped into a door. It rattled and swung open.

A woman shrieked. A man said something. Then there was darkness.

I felt their hands lifting me before I could open my eyes. Then I heard their voices, heard the words they were saying, but they didn't make any sense. Then his face came into focus. It was pink, with white stubble and a thin fringe of white hair. I tried to think of his name – I knew his name – but I couldn't think of it, and he said: 'What do you want?'

Want? I didn't want anything. It didn't make any sense. I didn't want anything. I stared at him, and he looked at her and shrugged, then he said to me: 'What's your name?'

'Name?'

'What do they call you?'

I couldn't think of it. My mind was empty. I stared at him and I turned to her. Her hair was long and golden like strands of honey, and it framed her face, made her skin look white, as white as her night shirt. Then it came to me and I blurted out: 'Fenton. My name is Fenton. Martyn Fenton,' and I began to remember the day they made me volunteer. They wrote William in the muster book. It is the name of my cousin who was with me. It is not my name and I do not want it, and I would like to give it back. But they will not let me give it back, and I said: 'William. They say my name is William.'

I heard her say: 'He's only a child. I think he's confused. I think he's hurt himself.'

I felt my knees sag. She wrapped her arms around me, pulled me close, rested my head in the soft valley between her breasts. Clumps of tiny flowers – bell-shaped and embroidered in white – peeped out from the folds of her night shirt. In my head the bells were ringing, and when I moved, opened my eyes, the flowers were speckled with blood. I groaned to myself and sank into the valley. From far away her voice came to me saying: 'I think we should lie him on the other bed, and cover him up, and keep him warm for a while.'

When I woke a candle was burning in the lantern, and it was moving the shadows along the beams and across the floor. I stood up and swayed with the floor. I reached out and steadied myself on a chest. The top was rounded, bound with brass straps, and lettered with the words:

THE VERY REVEREND GEORGE TATE
Cannon Emeritus
of the Cathedral Church of
Saint Mary and Saint Peter,
Exeter – in the County of Devon.

He was asleep on the bed. His arm was wrapped around her and it looked as though he was trying to stop her running away. She was younger than him by twenty or thirty years, 'young enough to be his daughter', Crabtree had said last Sunday when Mister Tate read the prayers and preached a sermon on the evils of popery. I couldn't think why she would want to be married to someone like him. And she made me wonder why an old man who served God all his life would want to go to Tangiers, to a place of sin and depravity, to a place where morals are under siege, if his own words are to be believed.

I crept out of their cabin, up the stairs, across the upper deck – the candle in the compass box was making the compass, the half-hour glass and the four-hour glass glow with a soft yellow light – down the steps and past Oldfield who was wrapped in his blankets and was sound asleep. I opened the main hatch, eased myself down the ladder and tip-toed past the door to the hold where Sergeant Owen sleeps with his musketeers.

They say Owen and Brandon were pikemen at Dunkirk, in the last months before the evacuation. Then they went to Bombay with the first soldiers-of-foot in '62 or '63, and that was where Brandon acquired a taste for men, young men who remind him of India.

I opened our door and slipped into the hold. Sergeant Brandon had pulled his curtain. I climbed into my hammock and shut my eyes. I wondered how long he'd been back in his bunk, back in his lair, and I remembered that old expression about a wolf in sheep's clothing, and I was thinking how apt it was for him, when I remembered the buttons. In my mind I could see them as clear as clear. It was the day I was conscripted, and he reached down and pulled me to my feet and his buttons were an inch or two away from my nose. On them was an image, an image of a lamb – the Lamb of God – with a flag and the cross of England. And now those buttons were gone, cut off, and replaced with plain buttons. Or maybe they weren't plain. Maybe they were textured, like a coarse fabric. Then I began to think he might have two grey coats, and the other one had the buttons with the lamb. But that couldn't be. I'd seen him carrying his haversack, and it wasn't any bigger than my sack, and he didn't have another coat in it. I wondered why he would want to cut the buttons off.

Then I must have dozed, for in my dreams I smelt herrings and vinegar, and I felt his hand and he said: 'I like a boy with fight. It makes it more exciting. I shall come for you tomorrow tonight.' Then the bell rang, the bell to get up, to get dressed. He laughed and ran his hand under my shirt. 'I was wrong,' he said. 'It already is tomorrow; and this' – he grabbed my cock and pulled it, pulled it hard – 'is for tonight. I shall come for you. And if you run away again, and hide, or climb the rigging, I shall find you. And I shall have you.' He smoothed the hem of my shirt. 'You cannot escape. There is nowhere for you to go.'

And now it is tonight, the night on which I must make the choice that is not a choice. In my head, in my heart, I knew that Brandon was right: I could not escape. And if I did not make the choice that was not a choice, he would have me. I knew I could not put it off any longer, but I did not want to move, and I kept hoping he would not come.

I lay back in my hammock and I remembered the first time I'd been turned on my belly and had. It hurt then, and it hurt in the morning. I hated him and I hated what he did to me. But hating didn't take away the hurt. And hating and hurting didn't make him stop, and they would not make Brandon stop.

Then I saw his curtain quiver. I slipped out of my hammock and out of the hold. I wrapped my blanket around myself and huddled into Oldfield. His mind was wandering – the sun had beaten down on his head all day and the glare off the sea had screwed-up his eyes – and he asked for some water. I cupped my hands and dipped them into the water-butt, but he did not drink the water. He made me dribble it around the shackles – the sun had heated the iron and it had burnt the skin around his ankles – then he sighed, and I held him, and he fell asleep.

I thought about the choice that was not a choice. A pikeman, one of my own kind, could not protect me, and nor could a musketeer. I thought about Sergeant Owen. He and Brandon are mates. That's what they say, and I'm not sure what they mean by that. I've heard of mating, birds and animals mating, but not of men mating, or being mates. To me it sounded like a perversion of the flesh, and I knew if I chose Owen – made the assumption that he too had been corrupted in Bombay – I would be swopping like for like, and I did not want to do that.

I would have to choose an officer who could protect me from Sergeant Brandon, that was the choice that was not a choice. I would have to hope that he would want to protect me, would want me in every sense of the word, and would not throw me out or have me clamped in the bilboes. And I would have to hope that he would not want to turn me on my belly and do what Brandon wanted to do. For if that was his inclination, it would be better to crawl into the lair of my own free will and let Brandon do what he wanted to do. Then I would have to hope, hope that I would be like all the others, and he would lose interest in me and go sniffing around another hammock.

But somehow I did not think that would be so – not after last night – and I could see him herding me towards his lair: night after night. I knew I had to make the choice that was not a choice, and the choice had to be an officer.

I thought about Captain Lacey. He's a married man, and he sleeps alone in the cabin next to Mister Tate. They say his wife came to Tangiers once, and will not come again. I remember the day I was conscripted, the day he made me drop my breeches. And I remember afterwards, when he sent Sergeant Brandon out of the room and made me read to him, and I suspected he would have me, if I went to his cabin. But it would only be for a short time, for they say he has a woman, a Portuguese woman, and she lives in his house and sleeps in bed, and there would be no place for me. And then Brandon would have me.

So I must look to the future, to the days that are to come, and I must choose between Lieutenant de Colville and Ensign Wyndham.

Lieutenant de Colville is about twenty years of age – seven years older than me – and they say he comes from Devon, and is the son of a Lord. Most of the men find him a little strange, remote might be a better word, and I sense he's beginning to regret his decision to come to Tangiers.

Ensign Wyndham says his mother is a widow of ten years, and a month ago, on his sixteenth birthday, an uncle-by-marriage presented him with his commission. It was purchased, they say, for two hundred pounds; and he tells me his mother has gone to live with his uncle in Cambridge because 'it will be more convenient'.

Wyndham and de Colville are about the same height, but de Colville would weigh a little more. They sleep in their own holds and have their own chests, their own possessions. At prayers last Sunday they both bowed their heads and closed their eyes; and if they weren't officers neither of them could get a man to do what they wanted him to do.

I thought about them for a long time – in truth there wasn't much to choose between them – and I had no idea if one or the other, or both of them would throw me out of their hold. Then somehow the choice seeped into my soul, and I knew who it had to be. I stood up, wrapped my blanket around Oldfield and said: 'I'll be back for it in the morning.'

I walked down the steps in the stern, climbed down the ladder into steerage and stood in front of his door. One of the sailors on the relief watch sat up and looked at me for a moment – the light from the lamp gave his face a swaying drunken look – then he laughed and lay down again.

I took a deep breath, and knocked on his door.

PART TWO

TANGIERS

We caught the Levant. It was a biting wind, an east wind and it came howling off the Coast of Barbary. To our left it blued the hills of Spain, made them look cold and shivery; and to our right it stirred the clouds, greyed the hills above Tangiers, and drenched the Bay with rain. It made the city look shapeless, lumpy, like the heavy grey coats – the surtouts – that sentries wear when the night is cold and wet.

The fleet split in two, and as the afternoon wore on the ships that were going down the coast of Africa and on to India – to Surat and Bombay – became smudges on the horizon. We kept station with the ships that intended to trade in the Mediterranean and we shortened the sail – tacked backwards and forwards in the mouth of the Straits of Gibraltar.

The ship's Captain was hoping the wind would die as the day began to die, and then we could slip into the waters off Tangiers – the Tangiers Roads – and drop anchor about a mile out from the city. But the wind freshened and it drove us towards the coast a mile south of the city. As we turned and headed out into the Atlantic swell, a patch of mist and rain cleared from the hills and the cliffs that ran down to the sea. The cliffs looked raw, looked as if the rock had been wounded and still needed time to heal, and at the water's edge, bathed in a bright wet light, lay a tiny village.

I leant over the rail, shaded my eyes, and peered at the village. It appeared to be a lot closer than it was – maybe it was something to do with the light or my closeness to the sea – and I could see a man leading a string of horses. Then a pair of large double doors like those on a stable, closed, and apart from the smoke that was coming from two or three chimneys the whole village appeared to be deserted. 'That's Whitby,' a voice said in my ear. I turned and looked into the face of Sergeant Owen, and I jumped to attention. 'Relax,' he said. 'You're not on duty now.'

I tried to smile, to relax, and I half-leant against the rail.

'You're Fenton, aren't you?'

I felt my body stiffen, and I couldn't think why he would know my name. I tried to nod, but my head was heavy and my movements wooden.

He put his hand on my shoulder. 'Relax,' he said, and this time he made the word sound gentle, calming. 'I'm not going to hurt you.' Then he smiled and leant over and whispered in my ear: 'I hear you got away,' and he began to laugh. 'I know I shouldn't laugh. And I know what he does is wrong. But there aren't enough women. And if a man can't have a woman he'll have a man. They know that.' He nodded towards Captain Lacey and Lieutenant de Colville who were pacing up and down. 'But that doesn't make it right – does it? I keep telling him the men should agree to what he wants. But he won't listen to me, not now he won't. And I keep telling him someone will complain and demand a court martial. But he says no one would dare.' He sighed and shook his head. 'Would you dare?'

I felt my jaw sag, and I stared at him for a moment or two, then I shook my head. 'Hmm,' he said, 'you're all afraid of him. Aren't you? I suppose it's for the best. But I still don't agree with it.' He shook his head.

I wanted to leave, to go back to the hold. But he would see that as an insult or an act of defiance – for we must have no thoughts or actions of our own – and I waited and watched.

High in the hills the Levant blackened the clouds, but at the shoreline it cleared the hills to the right of Whitby, and it uncovered a fort. It was cut square and raised to a height of three or four storeys, and it stood alone on a line of empty hilltops. If I could have touched the banks of earth, the stones and the wooden palisades that formed its lines of defence, no doubt I would have had other feelings for it, but here at sea, it looked small and helpless, and not worth defending. Below it, on the stony ground by the water's edge, stood another fort. It was even smaller – maybe two storeys high with a tile roof – in truth it was nothing more than a blockhouse with a palisade that wasn't much better than a picket fence. Then I began to realise that this was where English law, English rule, came to an end, and this was where we would face the enemy.

I could not see the enemy. But I could see his tents. They were on the next hill to the right: small triangles of white locked into dark patches of scrub, and through half-closed eyes they looked like white pimples. It looked to be a simple matter, a matter of giving them a hard squeeze, and then they'd be gone and we could live in peace. But the truth of the matter was not so simple – they'd been laying siege to Tangiers since the time of the Portuguese – and according to Ensign Wyndham: 'They're strong enough to keep us locked within the Bay, but not strong enough to breach the walls, or the chain of forts that protects the city.'

Below Whitby the beach formed a small crescent of golden sand. It was scarred by a black stone quay that curved inwards like a little finger. The waves were breaking against it, washing right over it, and throwing plumes of spray high in the air. Towards the right of the quay, the buildings butted into each other and they appeared to enclose a courtyard. The tallest building was square like a tower, and it might have been built as a fort, for its windows were high, narrow, and shuttered from the inside.

The roof on this tower rose to a steep point, and like all the other roofs it wore orange tiles tinged with red. Through squinted eyes the tiles could have been peeled off a tangerine, but through open eyes the red was more like blood that had seeped and stained, and for some reason this seemed to be a portent, an omen of evil to come. It made me shiver and I shoved my hands deep into the pockets of my coat.

'It reminds me of the borders,' Owen said. 'I come from the Marches on the Welsh borders. For hundreds of years my ancestors were farmers and they were caught up in the wars between the English and the Welsh. They didn't want to be, but they were, and they never knew when they were going to be raided by one side or the other. So they fortified their farms, by grouping all their buildings around a central courtyard, and running all the external walls into each other. At night they brought all the cattle in from the fields and that was how they protected them, and protected themselves. And as long as they didn't have a thatched roof that could be set on fire they were safe – as safe as a man could be in a place like the borders.'

I looked again at the tiles that would not burn and I nodded, and he said: 'In Wales, most of ours are old and decrepit now, relics of their former selves, and my father used to think they could still be used in times of trouble. But he was a farmer and he saw them with farmer's eyes. I used to tell him a cannon would smash through the walls in ten minutes, and a mortar would lob bombs over the walls and into the courtyard – and they'd explode – and the men inside wouldn't last for more than half an hour. He'd shake his head and touch his nose as if he knew something I didn't know – and this from a man who never saw a cannon fired in anger in his whole life.' He paused, as if to reflect upon his words, then he went on: 'When I first came here, and saw Whitby, I couldn't believe my eyes. It was as if the past had come to life again. As if the science of war, and all the ideas of the last hundred years had been put aside and forgotten, like unwanted toys,' and he shook his head.

'But surely,' I said, 'the Moors have cannons and mortars. And they can buy gunpowder.'

'Hmm,' he said. 'They have a few. They're old and small and their range is short, and they can never get enough gunpowder. But one day someone will sell them what they want, and they'll haul them over the hills. And they'll get their hands on a master gunner – he could be a German or a Spaniard or one of our own men nursing a grudge – and we won't be able to stop them.' He turned towards me. 'There's a lot with a grudge against us. And it's a wonder the Dutch haven't allied themselves with the Moors and attacked us together – from the sea and the land at the same time. They'd have us by the balls and within a week, two at the most, if our fleet couldn't sink the Dutch we'd be left with two choices.' He dug me in the arm. 'Can you guess what they are?'

We could surrender or retreat. But I didn't want to say either of those words out aloud, so I shook my head.

He looked at me for a moment or two. 'I thought you were smarter than that,' and he pursed his lips. 'We could surrender, could become slaves, and wait till the King pays a ransom to get us back – and that could take ten years. Or' – he paused as if to give me another chance to have my say, but I stared at him and waited – 'we could cut off our own balls and run. And when you see the two castles, linked together by their own walls, like balls in a ball bag, you'll appreciate what I'm saying.' And he smiled.

'But the Dutch are Christians,' I said, 'and Protestant like us. They wouldn't ally themselves with the Moors – they're heathens.'

He shook his head. 'There's an old saying: war makes strange bed-fellows. And if they stayed in bed long enough to destroy us, it wouldn't have to be like a marriage. They wouldn't have to live together when the war was over.' He smiled to himself. 'If the Dutch are stupid enough to think the Moors would let them have Tangiers, they'd be in for a bloody big surprise. The Moors don't want the Dutch. And they don't want us, or the French. And they don't want the Portugese back. And they don't want the Spanish back. What they want is Tangiers – for themselves.' He leant over the rail, looked into the water, and sighed. 'If the King doesn't send out a lot more troopers, a lot more soldiers-of-foot, we won't be able to stop them. And one day they will get it back.'

We settled into a sober silence – watched the waves rise, curl, and fill the air with a fine mist – then my eyes ran up the beach, ran with the bubbling foam, and I looked again at Whitby. It sat behind its wooden stockade and it looked to be dead. There was nobody on the quay or in the tower or climbing the path that wound up the hill to the left. There were no boats sheltering inside the quay, or pulled up on the hard, and there were no carts or signs of stabled cattle. But there was a haystack. It rose above the tiles and it was enclosed in another wooden stockade. I nodded towards the stack and said: 'Where do they cut the hay?'

'In the meadows around the forts. But there's never enough. And most of the time the Moors won't let us cut the grass on their land, so we buy a lot from Spain and bring it over from Tarifa.' He leant over the rail, coughed and spat into the water.

'If I hadn't seen that man with the horses, and the smoke from those chimneys, I'd have thought the place was deserted.'

He laughed. 'Some nights there are sixty or seventy people in there. Most are quarrymen – miners – and their wives and children. But there are always a few men from the rock boats, and a few more from the rock carts. They go in early and lock the gates before it gets too dark – because of the Moors.' He sucked at his teeth. 'They're not like us. They're dark-skinned and they wear flowing robes – soft browns and muddy whites – and they blend into the earth or the sand. And they hide in those little bushes.' He pointed to the low scrub that edged the path to the hill. 'You can't see them, and suddenly they're right there – in front of your eyes – with a lance or a sword.' He coughed and spat again. 'And you can be dead before you know it, before you have time to scream. And then they fade away, and we never catch them. So no one goes out in this light. It's the same in the early morning, in the dawn when the light is confusing. You learn to be careful. And you never go out on your own.' He paused. 'Ambuscades – that's what we call these attacks. You won't think they're real, till you see a man with his throat cut from ear to ear, and his head looks as though it's about to fall off.'

I gulped and swallowed and watched the seagulls ride the wind above the quarried cliffs. Then I shaded my eyes and peered into the hills, and looked from tent to tent. There was no sign of the Moors or their horses or their cattle. I thought there might be a stray dog sniffing around but there was nothing – nothing that moved.

'This can be a very busy place in the afternoon,' he said. 'Most of the cartmen prefer to spend the night on the Mole and they like to be on their way by three o'clock. But the trouble is it takes a long time to fill all the carts with rock, and the road runs along the foreshore. It's covered from half-flood to half-ebb, and if they can't leave by five at the latest they have to spend the night in Whitby. That's the rule. There's stabling in there for ninety horses, so there's always enough room. The men sleep above their horses – in the lofts where the straw is kept, and it's warm and comfortable. But they don't like it, and they don't like Sir Hugh Cholmley's personal chaplain. He's a mean little man and he lives in Whitby, in his own house near the base of the tower. He thinks he has the right to tell them what to do and if it wasn't for the respect they have for Sir Hugh, I think they'd have arranged an ambuscade of their own by now.'

He laughed and I laughed with him, but mine was a nervous laugh, a laugh that made my belly gurgle.

'I've seen a few fights,' he said, 'up there in the quarries, when it's late and the tide's coming in fast and the carts are only half-full. And sometimes I think the miners go slow – deliberately – to amuse themselves at the expense of the cartmen,' and he laughed again.

'It's made worse of course when the weather's fine and the sea's calm, and the small boats can ply from here to the end of the Mole and dump their loads of stone straight into the water. They usually run the boats up to the quay there' – he nodded at the quay – 'and they settle on the sand. Then they load them up with stone and float them off again. The tide rises and falls by about nine feet, so it's easy to do, and they always fill the boats before the carts. That's another of Sir Hugh's rules. It makes the cartmen bloody mad. And you know what the trouble is, the real trouble?'

I shook my head.

'There aren't enough men. Never enough to do everything that has to be done. When I first came here there used to be two regiments, and now there's only one. And since all the old miners went home, went back to Whitby in York, the new ones have been coming from Cornwall, from the tin mines – but they can never get enough of them. And now we have to work on the Mole and they say we might have to work in the quarries.' He shook his head. 'I bet a pound – that's about five pieces-of-eight – they didn't tell you that back in England when you signed the muster book, did they?'

I shook my head, and I was about to ask him why they used Spanish money in Tangiers – instead of pounds, shillings and pence – when I saw something move. I touched his arm and said: 'There's something there. To the right. In the black rocks above the quarries.'

He grunted, and we peered at the rocks – the gloom was beginning to blur them around the edges – and he said: 'The dark's a funny thing. It plays tricks on your mind and sometimes it makes you think you see something that isn't there. And if you've been on guard for five hours, and there's still another hour to go, and you're tired and you don't want to make a fool of yourself, you shut up. You learn to live with your fear. And after a while you come to hate the nights.' He gripped the rail with both hands. 'Some nights you can hear the Moors calling to one another, when you're out in one of those little forts. That one by the water's edge is Devil's Drop and the one up there on the brow of the hill is Henrietta. And some nights there might be twelve of you, and fifty of them. And like your Sergeant Brandon down below, every one of them will be waiting – waiting for you to make a mistake.'

Later that night as we lay at anchor in Saint Jeremie's Bay, about four miles from Cape Spratt – the rounded head of land that some call Cape Spartel – I helped Oldfield into his hammock.

Five days ago he was racked with fever and shivering in the sunshine and still saying he didn't want to go down to the hold, didn't want to be left alone in the dark. It was a strange fear, almost a pretence, and when the ship's Captain began his first round of the day, he stopped and stared at him for two or three minutes. Then he crouched down and tried to talk to him but Oldfield didn't seem to be able to recognise him and he sucked at his lips, looked at the deck, and didn't say a word. The Captain called for the Surgeon and a few minutes later they unlocked the bilboes and carried Oldfield down to the sick berth, the coffin-shaped berth that the tars call the port-to-heaven or the port-to-hell – depending on the sort of life the man who is lying there, dying there, has led.

For Oldfield it became the port-to-hell and for two days the wounds on his chest oozed pus. The surgeon tied his hands to the wooden rails to stop him tearing off the long strips of cloth that bandaged a white salve to the flesh that should have begun to heal, begun to scab by now.

I sat with him for a couple of hours, tried to spoon soft lumps of salted beef into his mouth, and tried to make him drink black beer, strong beer, to ease the pain. But his mouth was frozen in a rictus of death and I couldn't get him to open his teeth.

On the following day he recognised me, and on the day after that – yesterday – the surgeon allowed him to return to our hold.

I tucked my blanket around him; and he pulled the blanket I'd rolled into a pillow over his head, made it look like a monk's hood. Then he sucked at the cheese I'd saved for him and the pallor of death, the whiteness of flesh that is about to decay, was blushed with pink and he tried to smile.

I told him about Sergeant Owen, and about Sir Hugh building the stone breakwater – the Mole – and taking ten years, and still needing another ten years to finish it. Then I told him about Whitby.

'Whitby,' he said, in a voice rasped with pain, 'is a fishing village, about forty miles north of York where I was born. They built a stone breakwater there, at the mouth of the river, to protect the fishing boats, and I wonder if . . .' He closed his eyes, moistened his lips, and let out a long sigh.

I reached out and touched the mound of blanket that was his hand – it felt hot – and for a long time I sat beside him, sat in silence. The gentle rocking soothed him, and after a while I heard him snore. It was a soft, snuffling snore, and I said: 'I'll come back later on.'

The air in the hold smelt rank, and the heat was rising, and I didn't want to go to bed. I crept up the ladder and leant on the wooden railing. In the distance I could just make out the line of the hills and I was wondering if it would ever be possible to see the lights of Tangiers when a voice pounced on me and hissed: 'What the hell are you doing here?'

I jumped, shrieked, and tried to cover my mouth with my hands – all at the same time. Then I began to shake, my legs trembled, and I sank towards the deck. His hand grabbed at my shoulder, his fingers dug into my bones, and they lifted me up. 'Christ!' I said. 'You gave me a bloody fright.'

His fingers found my head, twisted my face towards his face, and he whispered: 'Fenton?'

I blurted out: 'Yes, sir.'

'I'm not sir, I'm Sergeant. Sergeant Owen.'

But the fright had scrambled my mind and now it scrambled my words, and I couldn't think straight, and I said: 'yes, sir.'

'Dear Jesus,' he muttered. 'They say you're a quick learner. Can read and write and add up figures, and you're going to be a clerk.' He shook his head. 'A drummer boy, that's what you should be, and then the beat of the drum could beat some sense into your head. Some common sense.'

'Common sense?'

'You're not supposed to be up here at night. You know that don't you?' I nodded and looked down at the deck. 'And you know you could be punished?' I nodded again. 'So common sense, or prudence, should have told you to stay in the hold where you belong.' He paused. 'Why did you come up on deck?'

'I've been looking after Oldfield and I needed a breath of fresh air.'

'What's wrong with him?'

'The wounds aren't healing. He's still in a lot of pain. And he needs help, needs looking after – all the time.'

'In Tangiers we would have shot him. That's the punishment for striking a sergeant. And we would have buried him by the gallows in unconsecrated ground, and for a while his grave would have been mounded with earth. Then he would have rotted and the earth would have sunk and made a hollow. In time we would have filled in the hollow – the gallows are on the Old Parade and somebody could have tripped over it – and after a while no one would ever know, would ever remember, that a man was buried there. And I say he's lucky to be alive.'

8

I heard Sergeant Brandon's voice bellowing in the blackness, and without thinking I swung my feet out of the hammock and slid to the floor. For a moment I swayed with the sway that was not there, then Crabtree climbed the ladder, pushed up the hatch and let the dawn into the hold, and I blinked away the night.

For a minute or two – as we rolled up our hammocks for the last time and shoved them into the wooden lockers – we were naked, flesh brushing flesh, shuffling in the shadows with no sense of modesty, no sense of shame. The nights had become hot, too hot to wear a shirt, and three weeks of eating, drinking, dressing, undressing, farting, vomiting – and sitting on a bucket in the corner when the bow dug into the waves and filled the privies, the heads, with torrents of foaming water – had stripped away our sense of privacy, our sense of dignity.

I grabbed my old shirt, wiped the sweat from under my arms, from between my legs, shoved it into my sack and pulled on my breeches.

I eased my way through the press of bodies and helped myself to three slices of cold salt beef, a couple of biscuits – made soft by a night in a crock of black beer – and sat down on the edge of the locker, between Crabtree and an older man by the name of Lockhart. He was born in the West Country, in a small village near Bridgewater, and he says – in a rippling of vowels that stretch and roll his words and make them sound like running water – that the land is ditched and drained, and the fields flood in the winter. To me it sounds like The Fens, but that's a word he does not know. He says they are the Levels, the Somerset Levels, and we've talked about eels, wet feet, and the fevers that ride on the night airs. And now there is between us a harmony, a feeling that we think the same, are the same – are the spawn of the waterlands. He turned to me and said: 'They told me I could go home in September. For a whole month. To help with the harvest. They promised. Every year, they said. Did I tell you that?'

I nodded, but he did not appear to notice. Or maybe he thought the ship was making me sway, making me nod in time with the waves, for he hit his plate with the blade of his knife, made it bounce in the air. 'They're not going to send me home. Not from here they're not.' He slumped forward, mashed his biscuits, stirred them round and round, made a thick black paste.

Crabtree looked at me and shrugged. I shook my head, looked at Lockhart, at his paste – felt it glue me to the past – and I remembered him saying: 'I was supposed to serve in Plymouth. That's why I signed on, because it was close to home. And then they told me I had to go to Tangiers. They were short of men, and I had to go. I could go in the hold or go in the bilboes – the choice was mine.'

They deceived him, and I fear they will deceive us. And in my black moments I know there is nothing we can do about it. He told me that. Not Lockhart – the man in the hold, in steerage – he told me that on the night I knocked on his door. He called out: 'Come in!'

I went in, bowed, and with my eyes fixed on the floor, I took off all my clothes and heaped them against the door. Then I knelt on the floor with my knees together, with my private parts displayed on my thighs, like fruit that is offered for sale, and can be touched or felt or fondled – to determine the softness or the hardness – and I said: 'I will do whatever you want me to do. I will be yours and yours alone. In return I would ask you to protect me from Sergeant Brandon, and men like him.'

I tried not to think of what followed, when the anger slipped away from his face. And I tried not to think of the kindness, the confusion, that was within him, for I had not been expecting them. An outburst of anger and the threat of the bilboes – I'd been expecting them – but not kindness or confusion. They were foreign to my way of thinking, and somehow despite his body wanting me, despite him coming and standing in front of me in his nightshirt, and letting me run my hand up the inside of his leg, I could sense that my coming was both right and wrong, wanted and unwanted – all at the same time. In this conflict, this battle between the spirit and the flesh, lay the confusion that leads to kindness – to the confusion of kindness.

I shut my eyes, they felt tired and heavy, and I shut out these memories – unglued the past – and sipped my beer. It was supposed to be a 'small' beer, a weak beer made from the third pressing of a barley-malt-ferment, but within a few minutes I could feel it working deep within me – brewing up a sense of excitement. And it was working in all the other men, brewing noise and chatter, and then this noise, this chatter, this air of excitement was battering at my ears. It woke my mind – as it does most mornings – and if today was like yesterday and the string of yesterdays that are tied to it, it would dull my senses and rock my mind back to sleep in a couple of hours. And that, as some of the men in this hold are fond of saying: 'Is the best way to make a day in this swiving regiment – bloody bearable.'

I picked at my teeth: prised out the strings of beef and rubbed away the biscuit that was beginning to make my mouth taste like fur. Then came the ringing of the bell. The strokes were fast and doubled up: dong-dong, dong-dong, dong-dong. For a moment the echoes hung in my head – soft and wood-muffled – then they were gone, and the watch that times the tars, governs them by day and by night, was three hours old. Over our noise and into our chatter came the sound of the pipes. It was like a twittering of birds greeting the dawn, then it was drowned by the thumping of feet and the heaving, hauling clank-clank-clank of the anchor chain.

The ship took a list to the left and I reached out to steady myself. Then I pulled on my stockings, pushed my feet into my shoes and tied my garter ribbons. I buttoned up my waistcoat; slid my arms into the sleeves of my grey coat and left it unbuttoned above the knee to ease my stride. I slipped my leather baldric over my head and onto my right shoulder, and made sure the pair of leather bands that hold the scabbard were hanging at the right angle, and I wished the band was adjustable, was buckled like a belt, and could be raised a few inches to keep the end of my scabbard off the ground.

I pulled on my hat, crossed the ribbons under my chin, tied them at the back of my neck and remembered Sergeant Brandon saying: 'If you lose that hat, or anything else, you will have to pay for it.' But not one of us had seen a penny, or even a halfpenny, since the day we signed the muster book, and how can you take away something from nothing? That's what Oldfield says. But then he can't read or write and he thinks memories decay, and he forgets that things written down in a book have a life of their own. They do not decay and they do not go away. They are forever young.

Two men lifted Oldfield out of his hammock, helped him to dress and leant him against the side of the hold. He looked decayed – old beyond his years – and his ankles were red and raw: shackle-red the tars call it. It's a colour I'll not forget. It made me feel sick in my belly and I knew he would not be marching with us today. Would not be marching with those dreams of his, those private dreams that would have put him out in front, made him a sergeant and seen him carrying a halberd in a year or two.

I bent down, took his arm and helped him to sit up straight. He stared at me with empty eyes – the effort of getting dressed had exhausted him. Crabtree brought him a tankard of black beer and held it to his lips. He sipped at it, but it must have been too thick, too strong, for it caught in his throat – made him cough and retch. Then I heard a laugh, a cruel scoffing laugh. I straightened up, turned around and swallowed hard. My nose was about a foot away from Sergeant Brandon's nose. He scowled, pushed me away, bent over Oldfield and said: 'Get up.'

Oldfield looked up at him – his eyes were still empty, still drained of life. Maybe he didn't recognise him, or maybe the sun, maybe the fever, had curdled his mind, for he sat like a man in a trance and he didn't move.

I crouched down to help him up, but Brandon pushed me away, leant towards him and yelled: 'Get up!'

Oldfield lifted his arm. His hand shook and his fingers clutched at the air. His head flopped to the side and his eyes rolled in on themselves. Brandon grabbed him by the shoulders, jerked him to his feet. His mouth sagged, his eyes rolled back into place, and Brandon whispered: 'This voyage will soon be over. But it's not over between you and me. I'm going to have you as soon as you can bend over and touch your toes, and stick your bum in the air.' He laughed, and let him go.

Oldfield bumped down the side of the hold, slid off the locker and crashed to the floor. He lay with his arms and legs outstretched, like a leafy plant that has wilted in the hot sun.

I shook my head and went to help him, but Brandon grabbed me by the waistcoat – locked his fingers into the gaps between the buttons – and pulled me hard against his chest. 'They tell me the right name for a cocky little boy like you is a poppadom. You won't have heard of it before. It's an Indian word. It comes from Bombay and it's a sort of bread. A flat round bread that keeps for a long time and doesn't go stale. The Indians use it to scoop up their food – they don't use a knife or a spoon – and I think it suits you. And one day I'll scoop you up, and I'll have you – little Mister Poppadom.'

He let go of my waistcoat, straightened the front, ran his fingers down the buttons, and stepped back. 'And let me tell you something else. I can wait for him' – he looked down at Oldfield and sucked at his lips – 'and I can wait for you. I can wait for the day when your charms go stale, and the man down in steerage doesn't want you any more.'

9

I stood at ease and rested my hand on the hilt of my sword. I was buried
in the second rank, with my back to the railing, and it felt strange not to
be holding a wooden staff – a make-believe pike. Opposite us, in two ranks
with their backs to the coast, stood the musketeers. They were wearing
their bandoliers – criss-crossed over their baldrics – and they'd left their
muskets in the hold.

Sergeant Brandon and Sergeant Owen walked into the middle of the
deck, and waited near the main mast. Their heads were almost touching.
From my angle it looked as though their halberds had crossed, and as the
deck swayed the halberds could have been the crested heads of a pair of
birds performing the first steps of a mating dance.

I began to wonder if they had mated, had done to each other what
Brandon wanted to do to me. I remembered Owen saying yesterday, as
we tried to catch our first glimpse of Tangiers: 'This is where you will
live and die. And this is where men mate with men because there are
only two sorts of women here: the whores who have the pox; and the
married ones who have a wedding ring on their finger. They say we will
never marry. They say we are married to the regiment, to each other,
and that is the truth. The hard truth that will sour your days and blight
your nights, and make your balls ache. And sometimes I think it's the
reason, the real reason, why we all drink so bloody much.' He blinked
his eyes, blinked away the tears. Then he wiped his face with the ends of
his scarf, blew his nose, cursed the rain and the salt spray, and mumbled
something about it 'making my eyes sting'.

I let these memories drift back into the past.

High on the hill to the right of Whitby tiny specks of white were
moving. They looked like white maggots crawling on black flesh, and
I began to think the land was dead. But then the black faded to blue
and softened to pink, the hill warmed to the first rays of the sun and the
sea-mist vanished. The maggots became the Moors, and the pimples of
yesterday became their tents.

Sergeant Brandon came towards us, walked up and down the front
rank, like an officer making an inspection, and then, as if satisfied with
what he'd seen, he turned and looked at the coast for a moment, then

he said: 'That's Teviot Hill. It used to be called Jews Hill when we first
came here. And down in that valley, on the left flank, in amongst the
trees, there's a river: Jews River. You can't see it at the moment but
it marks our boundary, our western boundary. Later this morning when
we drop anchor in the roads you might see the other river: Old Tangiers
River. It's crossed by a stone bridge and it marks our eastern boundary.
Someone was asking me last night how big the place is. The answer is
three hundred acres. That doesn't sound very big. And it isn't. But when
your bowels are fluxed, and you can't crawl out of bed, and the garrison
is down to a thousand men who can mount guard – and we need you –
you'll think it's big, too bloody big.' He grinned. 'But the truth is it's not
big enough. And we need that hill, Teviot Hill. Anybody know why?' He
looked along the ranks. Crabtree said something about it being a high
point and easy to defend. He nodded, mumbled: 'Hmm,' and waited a
moment or two. 'There's another reason. And it's right there in front of
your eyes.'

I looked but I couldn't see what it was. I half-turned to Crabtree and
he shrugged his shoulders. Then Brandon said: 'It's the trees. And the
scrub. We should be up there cutting them for firewood. If you look at
all those other hills, in behind Tangiers, the ones to the left are sandhills,
and they don't grow anything. The rest are bare, apart from a few patches
of scrub. So most days you'll see the little boats, the pinks, coming over
from Spain, loaded high with firewood. And there it is,' he nodded at
Teviot Hill, 'and it should be ours for the taking.'

And then, by the workings of chance, thin wisps of smoke began to rise
from the tents and the air that was washed clean by the rains of yesterday,
began to curdle, and a soft grey haze settled upon the hill, upon the wood
that was not ours to burn.

I yawned, wiggled a loose tooth with my tongue, and sucked out a
string of beef. Then I shut my eyes, drifted in the haze, and wondered
what the Moors were cooking. I was thinking it wouldn't be salt beef
and biscuit, when Sergeant Brandon stamped his feet on the deck and
screamed: 'Company!'

I planted my feet twelve inches apart and lined up the toes of my shoes.
He swivelled his head from side to side, made certain we were waiting for
his command, and yelled: 'Attention!'

I stiffened my legs, pulled my pike upright and straightened my back.
The end of my scabbard slid into one of the cracks the sun had opened
up on the deck. I leant to the right, thinking my baldric would lift the
scabbard out of the crack, but it was stuck. It wouldn't budge. I tugged
it with my left hand – tried to keep my movements rigid, tried to make it
look as though I wasn't moving – but it wouldn't come. I swore and yanked
it hard. It flew out of the crack and out of my hand, then it dropped, and
the metal cap that protects the end of the scabbard hit the deck. It made
a dull thud, and it jerked the hilt of my sword out of the scabbard – two

maybe three inches. Then the hilt fell back on the scabbard guard and it made a heavy clunk.

Brandon twisted towards me and scowled. I thought he was going to say something, but he and Owen about-turned, like a pair of puppets jerked by the same strings, and stood to attention – facing the steps to the upper deck.

Captain Lacey came down the steps carrying his partisan – his short pike, his staff of office. This was the first time he'd carried it on parade, and I sensed this might be a special occasion, and I ran my eyes along the ranks. But there didn't seem to be a reason for anything special, and I shrugged off this thought, this feeling, and looked at the Lieutenant. He was coming down the steps, behind the Captain, and for the first time he too was carrying his partisan. It was topped with a green tassel, a plinth of balls, a cross-bar and an ornamental spear, and it looked just like the Captain's partisan. And that surprised me, for I'd been expecting they would be different, and at a distance we'd be able to distinguish one rank from the other. But they were identical, or so close it didn't matter. And so were their red coats, green cuffs, black hats and white breeches. With half-closed eyes they were twins. And behind them came another twin, a triplet-officer: Ensign Wyndham. But then I looked again, looked with care, and I realised he didn't have a partisan. He had a sword, but not a partisan, and before I could think why, Captain Lacey was saying: 'This is the last time you will be permitted to parade in such a manner.'

He was met with silence, stark silence. He walked his eyes all the way down the musketeers, paused and stared into the distance, then he walked his eyes back along our front row, and for a moment – for some reason – they jumped a rank and rested on me.

I stood rigid, tried to think what the hell I'd done wrong, and then he said: 'Standing orders. For those of you who don't know what standing orders are, let me tell you. They are permanent orders. Orders that apply all the time. And the first order, the most basic order, the order that applies to every man in this garrison is this.' And he paused. 'Every man must carry his personal weapons with him at all times. On duty or off duty. On parade' – he walked his eyes down the ranks again – 'or off parade. Day or night. Wet or fine. There's never a moment, never a time when you won't have your personal weapons with you. And there's no excuse. None at all. If you are found without your weapons you will face a court martial. Being drunk' – he pulled a smile – 'is not an excuse. The first time you are found guilty you will be whipped. The second time you will ride the horse. The Sergeants will show you the horse in the next day or so.' He nodded to Brandon and Owen. 'For a musketeer' – he turned towards them – 'your weapons are your sword, your musket, and the bayonet that plugs into the barrel. And you must wear your bandolier at all times. And each of the wooden tubes that hangs from it – the ones you call the twelve apostles – must be full of powder. The powder must be dry. And both your powder flasks must be full of powder, and your bullet bag must be full of lead bullets – lead balls.' He paused for a moment. 'A musketeer without his balls, is not a musketeer.'

They burst out laughing. He smiled and turned to us. 'For a pikeman it's a lot simpler. You must carry your pike with you at all times. And you must wear your sword.' He frowned and beckoned to the Lieutenant, then he walked towards me. He thrust his partisan through the ranks, prodded my scabbard and said: 'This man was having trouble with his sword. Did you see him as we came down the steps?'

The Lieutenant shook his head. The Captain turned to Sergeant Brandon. 'You saw him didn't you?'

The Sergeant stiffened. 'Yes, sir!'

'So why's his sword dragging on the ground?'

'The baldric's too big for him, sir. And we don't have any small ones. And we don't have any short swords.'

The Captain stared at him, then he walked along our front rank, pointed to another man and said: 'His sword is dragging on the ground, and so is that one.' And he pointed to another man who was no older, no taller, than me. Then he turned and looked at Billy Foster, the drummer boy. 'His is the right size. If you can get his right why can't you get these right?' And he flicked his hand at the three of us.

The Sergeant's neck stiffened and flushed red. The flush spread to his face and darkened like a birthmark that age has livered. The Sergeant opened his mouth, but then he seemed to change his mind, to think better of it, and he stood without making a sound.

A sneer ran across the Captain's face and he turned to the Lieutenant. 'Did you have an inspection before you came on deck?'

'No, sir. I left it to Sergeant Brandon and Sergeant Owen.'

He leant towards him and hissed in his ear: 'This is your responsibility.'

I don't know if the Captain intended the two or three of us who were close to him to hear or not. But his words were clear – quite clear – and he said: 'You are in charge. They have to do what you say. And next time they go on parade I want you to inspect them before I arrive. If you find something wrong, I want it fixed before I arrive. And one more thing: think a little more about this world, and a little less about the one that is to come. It might help your men to stay alive.'

The colour drained out of the Lieutenant's face and it left behind a skin that was grey, ash-grey. And like the Sergeant he stood up straight and did not say a word.

For a moment or two the Captain watched him – tight-lipped – then his mouth relaxed, he raised his voice and said: 'Lieutenant. I want you to present my compliments to the ship's Captain, and ask for the loan of three short swords. Tell him the Governor, Lord Middleton, might be at the Head Court of the Guard this morning, and I would like to make a good impression.' He paused. 'And tell him you will be responsible for returning the swords. Tell him you will do it personally, tomorrow morning.'

The Lieutenant bowed and walked up the steps and across the upper deck. He walked, stiff-necked and rigid, like a toy soldier with wooden legs. The Captain followed him with cold eyes, and I could almost feel his disapproval. Then he turned to Ensign Wyndham and said something. The Ensign's face flushed, his mouth sagged, his hands fluttered in the air, and he followed the Lieutenant up the steps and across the upper deck – and he too walked on wooden legs.

10

For several minutes Captain Lacey stood on his own, rocking in the swell – like a red-coated buoy shoaled by grey-coated rocks – then he looked towards the upper deck, shook his head, said something to the two Sergeants, and began to pace up and down. The sails spilled their wind, grew limp and heavy, and in spite of the out-going tide that should have been carrying us away from the coast, we were almost becalmed.

The sun fingered the slopes, the clefts of Teviot Hill, and then it began to catch something that was moving, began to throw bright flashes of light towards the sea. They made my eyes squint and they seemed to trouble the Captain. He stopped pacing and stared at the hill for several seconds. Then he ordered the musketeers to about-turn, and with all of us looking at the hill, he said: 'The Moors are up there with their spyglasses, watching and waiting. They are creatures of habit, creatures of patience. They're always up there. Always watching. Always waiting. Waiting for us to make a mistake.'

He paused, and with perfect timing another spyglass caught the sun and flashed at us. He allowed himself a slight smile, then he continued: 'Lord Teviot made a mistake. He was determined to teach the Moors a lesson, and he chased them into the woods. He had them on the run. That's what he thought. In truth they lured him on, and cut off his line of retreat. Then they massacred him, and thirty-five of his officers, and four hundred of his men.' He shook his head. 'We've never been back to bury their bodies, to say the prayers that should be said. They tell me the birds and the ants have picked their bones, picked them clean. And they still lie there, on that hill' – he nodded towards Teviot – 'white and gaunt. Bleaching in the sun.' He sucked in his lips and stared into the distance for a moment or two, then he went on: 'It's been ten years now. Ten bloody years – and I mean bloody in the true sense of the word – and we still don't have enough men to capture that hill.'

His coat looked new, looked fresh, like new-spilt blood. It made me think it would soak up his blood and it wouldn't show, if we were sent to capture Teviot Hill and he was wounded. But then I saw the lining. It was green, sea-green, and it matched his cuffs. If he was wounded the green would stain and the sea would not wash away those stains. Then I began to wonder about the men who died on that hill. Were they wearing grey coats like us, or red coats like him? And were they young like us or old like him? Then I began to think they must have come into the Bay just like we were coming in. They must have seen what I was seeing, must have believed they would be safe behind the city walls.

The thought heaved my belly, heaved the beer and the biscuits, sloshed them up and down, and left me feeling queasy. I took a deep breath, shuffled backwards and leant against the railing. Crabtree dug me with his elbow and whispered: 'How can he know about those bones if we haven't been back?'

I rolled my eyes and shrugged, and the Captain said: 'If you're wondering how we know about those bones,' Crabtree dug me in the ribs again, 'the answer is simple. We know because we know the Barbary Jews. And they know because the Moors allow them to trade. Allow them to travel from town to town. Such men are not to be trusted. They are beyond the pale – as the saying goes. And here in Tangiers the pale should start in that valley where the shadows are beginning to lift. And if you look hard, in amongst those black rocks, you might just be able to see the river: Jews River.' He paused and sucked at his lips – licked them with the end of his tongue – made it look as though he'd just eaten something, said something, that was distasteful. Then he went on: 'The Jews were expelled from Spain and they say some of them settled over there. If they did, they're not there now. I can assure you of that. The Moors are there. Not very many at the moment for this is the wet season, and most of them go home when the rains start in October or November.' Then he lowered his voice and his words became more intimate: 'But come the summer, when the days are long and hot, and the perspiration is running down your spine, they'll be back, like a swarm of mosquitoes. And they'll be back for a taste of blood, your blood.'

For a moment or two the waves smacked against the hull – it sounded like a hand smacking at mosquitoes – and then he said: 'If I had my way the Jews would be expelled from Tangiers. They spy on us and they spy on the Moors. They sell our secrets to the Moors, and they sell the Moors' secrets to us. Sometimes the secrets are lies, are the price of thirty pieces of silver, the price of betrayal, and I think we'd be better off without them.

The thought of spies, blood and death, churned in my mind, and I remembered the Jews who betrayed Our Lord. And I knew: if they could betray Him, they could betray us. It was as simple as that.

Then Lieutenant de Colville returned, gestured at Sergeant Brandon to take my old sword and handed me a short sword. It was protected by a scabbard – bound with brass and decorated with small anchors burnt into the leather. I slipped the sword and scabbard into my baldric and burst into a grin. I couldn't help it. It just exploded all over my face. Captain Lacey smiled at me and I smiled back. Then I realised I was being impertinent and I dropped my eyes, looked at the deck, at the cracks that had lost their seams of tar. A moment later he said: 'After the blessing—'

Crabtree hissed: 'What blessing?'

I shook my head. This was Saturday, not Sunday. We never had a service on Saturday – we had morning prayers but not a service – and I couldn't think what he was talking about. Then I realised his words had drifted through my ears when I was exchanging swords – and I didn't know what he was talking about – and now he was saying: '—and today is quite different. I want them to spy on us. The Moors that is, not the Jews. I want them to see us. I want them to train their spyglasses on us. I want them to count us, to know we are coming to reinforce the garrison. So, straight after the blessing, you are to line the landward side of the boat, and you are to stay there till we drop anchor in the roads beyond the Mole.'

Then the sails stirred and picked up a light wind that was coming off the land. In the wind I could smell wood smoke and oranges, and a sweet spice that tasted like nutmeg. As the wind grew stronger, flicked spray in the air and salted the nutmeg, we heeled away from the land. Through the rigging, I caught a glimpse of the Mole. The end was way out to sea, a quarter of a mile or more. Yesterday I'd seen it for a moment or two, drenched in rain and spray, and drowning in white-capped waves. Then it was nothing more than a faint line of houses or warehouses with orange-tiled roofs; but now it was a long spit of black rocks humped with stone buildings. Yesterday I thought the buildings marked the end of the Mole. But I was wrong. The Mole continued on for another hundred yards, and today the end was marked by plumes of spray. They were catching the sun, making glitter, filling the air with hundreds of tiny rainbows, and like the rainbow that follows the storm, they spoke of promise.

I remembered my Mother, remembered her calling me a dreamer and telling me not to waste my time 'chasing rainbows'. I remembered the promise I made to her, the promise to do what Aunt Mary said I should do. It was a promise to obey. But I did not obey. I did what I wanted to do and went to London – was conscripted, was forced to promise, forced to obey, forced to do what I did not want to do. And now I follow orders, and dream of going back to Elme, to England, but that is not to be.

I turned away from the Mole, away from rainbows and false promises, and looked again at the coast, at Whitby.

The chimneys were layering the air with grey smoke, and men were coming out the gates and walking up the paths towards the quarries. They were carrying picks and shovels and pushing wheelbarrows, and their pace was slow – more like the pace that marks the end of a long day. After a while I caught a whiff of burning coal, and I could taste sulphur at the back of my throat. It was the taste of cheap coal, brown coal, and it reminded me of London, of narrow alleys choked with smoke, and I wondered if the miners had found a seam of the same coal, when they were quarrying the stone.

Then I noticed two carts making their way along the foreshore. They looked like square boxes riding on a pair of spoked wheels that were almost as tall as a man. They were piled high with rocks, and they were being pulled by teams of three horses with collars, shafts and traces that kept them plodding along – one after the other. The drivers were walking beside their lead-horses, holding the reins and carrying whips; and although they kept glancing back over their shoulders, they gave the impression of being tired, being worn out. And I guess, for them, this was just another day and another load of rock that had to be dumped in the sea and would never be seen again.

Then the Captain said: 'From here the Mole looks small, but it's about thirty yards wide, and in ten years' time – God willing – it will be another hundred years long with an arm to the right. And there'll be a couple of forts way out there' – he waved his hand in a vague way at the empty sea – 'and our ships will be able to pick up the anchor chains in calm water.

They'll be able to ride out the storms, and they won't have to up anchor and make for the open sea as they do now.' He paused and waited, as if to give us time to think about his words, then he went on: 'And all of this will only be possible if we keep the Moors at bay.' He smiled at his joke, at his play-on-words, and looked to us for approval.

Some smiled, some smothered a laugh, but I kept a straight face – I didn't want to draw any more attention to myself – and I watched the horses plod along the road. By now they had come about half a mile and were out of sight of Whitby, were heading for the guardhouse at the end Mole, and high above them, a hundred yards in from the sea, the Upper Castle sat on the brow of a hill.

The castle was built of stone. The right-hand end was twisted to face inland, and buttressed in the middle to support a tall thin tower with a rounded top. The Union Flag flapped from the rounded top – flapped fragments of red, white and blue, the colours of England and Scotland – and below it hung the black silhouette of the biggest bell I'd ever seen. The tower was braced to the battlements by two triangles that reminded me of flights of stone steps. It was called Peterborough Tower – after the first Governor. It looked to be seven or eight storeys high, but it was hard to gauge, hard to be accurate, for there were no trees, no houses, nothing to compare it to. The land it guarded was stark naked and stripped of life.

I knew the Upper Castle was a separate fortress, but from the sea I could not separate it from the outer walls, the northern walls. They ran into each other, formed squat towers and staggered down the hill till they flared and ran towards the coast. At the lowest point, about fifty feet above the road that follows the base of the cliff, the walls ended in a square tower. Then the cliff face was braced with stone to support a battery of round black snouts, cannon snouts that looked as though they were sniffing the salt air. Behind them two sentries – two sticks of red – were marching backwards and forwards. A few feet further along came another tower, and then more walls that ran up the hill and locked into the lower castle.

This was York Castle. It overlooked the Mole and guarded the road to Whitby. It was named after the Duke of York – the King's brother – and it reminded me of the night Lieutenant de Colville spoke of him. Admiration and fervour crept into his voice and I found it strange – we all found it strange – for the Duke has taken leave of his senses and become a papist. He has betrayed the Protestant faith. He is an apostate and is not to be trusted. No papist is to be trusted. That is what the country thinks and that is what Parliament thinks, and now the Test Act forbids papists to hold public office and they are prohibited from holding the King's commission – they cannot serve as an officer in the army or the navy. The act forced the Duke to resign his commission, to give up the office of Lord High Admiral.

Afterwards, when de Colville was long gone and we were lying in our hammocks, talk flew from mouth to mouth, and no one could understand why he supported the Duke. It was a rash thing to do, and by implication it branded him a papist. To my mind he too had taken leave of his senses, and we feared it might send him back to England – in disgrace.

11

A few minutes later the musketeers about-turned, faced our ranks, and we stamped to attention. Captain Lacey eyed us for a moment, then he said: 'I have invited the Reverend Mister Tate to conduct a special service for our company. And I have asked him to bless the ensign.'

I blinked. What on earth had Ensign Wyndham done to deserve, to need, a special blessing? He'd come back on deck a few minutes ago holding a short pike with a flag wound round the staff. I hadn't seen it before but I knew every company had its own flag, and I guessed this was our flag. Then I remembered the flag was called an ensign and it gave its name to the officer who bore it, and this was the first commission a man could hold.

Sergeant Brandon stood us at ease, and Mister Tate stepped forward. He was dressed in black and looked like a black rooster, a skinny one with long white hair, and white lace – white wattles – hanging from his neck. He took off his hat, bent down, slipped the brim under his foot, and opened his prayer book. The wind blew his hair around his face, fluttered the pages of his book, and carried away his words. My eyes drifted from him to the hills that overlooked, that threatened the town, and I counted three forts. They looked small and lonely. They reminded me of warts on an old man's face, and I remembered my Father slicing his off with a sharp knife. He made it look so quick, so easy, and when he cut one of mine off I didn't feel a thing – till afterwards. And I began to understand that if I was in a fort and it was cut off, was captured, I would last about as long as a wart my Father had decided to behead.

This was a dark thought, a black thought, and it led me on to the Moors. Most are brown-skinned, like dry earth, but some are black. And they say at night when it's dark, the black Moors can take off all their clothes and disappear. They say they can climb up the sides of the forts and we don't know they're coming, and that's why some of the smaller forts have rows of sharp stakes set high in the walls and angled towards the ground.

I looked at the forts, tried to see the stakes – and maybe they were there, shadows within shadows – but I couldn't see any sign of them. Then I remembered the Reverend Mister Salthouse. He used to preach in our parish church and he used to talk about good deeds. Each one he would say, was like a stake, and when they were set around a soul they would protect it from evil. And he used to say black men were like animals: they don't have souls and they don't have to do any good deeds. God placed them on earth to serve us and if they won't serve us, won't obey the divine command, we can force them to obey, force them to be our servants, our slaves.

I wondered what I would make of the black Moors. Sergeant Owen says they are men just like us, and they have a God of their own – one God, not three like us. They believe in life after death, in heaven and hell, so they must have a soul, that's what he thinks. And when I said: 'We were all ransomed by the death of Our Lord. It was the price he paid to cleanse the world of sin.' He laughed in my face and said: 'He forgot about the Moors. And he forgot about Tangiers.'

Then the Captain's voice came into my head, and he was saying: 'Before I ask Mister Tate to bless the new ensign, Ensign Wyndham will explain its significance.'

He must have been expecting this for he stiffened and yelled: 'Yes, sir! The ensign is a symbol. It represents the company. We salute it and we march behind it. In battle it is carried in front of the pikes, and we must fight to defend it, to prevent it being captured by the enemy.'

'Anything else?'

'Yes, sir! If we are separated in the heat of battle we must rally to the flag, because that is where the other men in our company will be. We must support each other. It is one of the principles of war.'

The Captain nodded and said something to Lieutenant de Colville. He stepped forward, laid his partisan on the deck, and grabbed the ensign by both corners. It filled with wind, billowed and flapped like a sail, and made the Captain scowl. The Lieutenant flushed, pulled the corners further apart and held them tight.

The Captain touched the middle of the ensign with the point of his partisan. 'This,' he said, 'is the cross. The red cross. The sign of our salvation. It is also the cross of England and the cross of Saint George, England's patron saint. It is outlined in white, the colour of purity, and that is a virtue you might aspire to – for some of the whores in this town smell like a sewer when they open their legs.' Then he remembered the presence of Mister Tate, glanced at him, flushed, and hurried on – almost stumbling over his words: 'The cross is laid on a dark green ground and you can see that from each corner of the cross, golden rays – rays of fire – have been painted over the green. In heraldic language they are known as Admiral's Rays. Why they would have such a name, a name that conflicts with a regiment that serves and fights on the land, I do not know. But I do know that the green ground is called sea-green, and you will notice it matches the green on my cuffs.' He held a cuff against the ensign. 'And when you are issued with your new uniforms it will match your cuffs.'

Crabtree and I looked at each other and rolled our eyes – it was the first time we'd heard of new uniforms – and then we turned back to the Captain and he was saying: 'Green is the colour of Her Majesty Queen Catherine. And we are honoured to bear her colour because Tangiers formed part of her dowry. For those of you who do not know what a dowry is, it is a wedding present, and it was given to His Majesty. So, Tangiers is a royal city. It belongs to His Majesty, it is his personal property, and it is maintained by him, from his privy purse. It is not maintained by Parliament, although some say . . .' He shrugged and looked away for a moment. 'The Queen came from Portugal. She was a princess, and Tangiers was part of Portugal. Today many of the houses in Tangiers are still owned by the Portuguese, and you will often hear them speaking their own language.' He paused.

'I think I should tell you that it is His Majesty's policy that religious tolerance is practised in all his overseas possessions: in the Plantations – in the Americas; in Bombay which was also part of Her Majesty's dowry; and here in Tangiers. It allows the Portugese to have their own church, their own cathedral, and it means that the rituals of popery are performed in our midst, and we must accept them – must tolerate them.' I heard a sharp intake of breath, and some loud muttering. The Captain glared at us, and when the muttering died away he went on: 'It is His Majesty's wish. And it is Her Majesty's wish. And I would remind you that Her Majesty is a papist and we must respect her wish. I would also remind you that you are sworn to defend the crown.' He pointed to the crown that was painted on the red cross.

Underneath the crown the letter C and its reverse image were linked and decorated to form a cypher. The Cs were short for King Charles and Queen Catherine, and I could remember seeing them on the back of a silver tuppence, and I was wondering if we would be paid when we stepped ashore, when the Captain said: 'The company number is still to be painted on here,' and he touched the red above the crown. 'Some companies are being re-formed, and I thought it best to wait till we knew our new number,' and he smiled.

Crabtree hissed in my ear: 'They say so many have died of flux or fever that most of the companies are now down to half strength.'

I turned towards him, and I could feel my eyes flaring, and he nodded – confirmed the truth of his words. Then Sergeant Brandon called us to attention, and Ensign Wyndham lowered his pikestaff and rested the spearhead on the deck. The wind flapped the ensign, sucked it flat against the decking, and the lines of tar that had seeped from between the boards moulded it into long straight ridges. They looked like battle lines. Some were awash with green – with hope; and some were covered with gold – with glory; and some were drenched with red – with blood. Then the wind picked up this painted battlefield, flapped it away, and uncovered the cords and the tassels that hung from the spearhead. They were red and green with a threading of gold, and for a moment they quivered on the deck like a pair of rare beetles, then the wind lifted them into the air – spread the tassels – spread their wings, and they tried to fly away.

Captain Lacey turned to Mister Tate, bowed and said: 'I would like to invite you to bless the ensign. The crown and the royal cypher were gilded by my own dear wife, and she and His Majesty are the two persons I hold most dear, most precious, in this life. It is my pledge, my public promise, that I will guard this ensign with my life, and I will lay down my life to defend it.'

For a moment the air was heavy with silence.

A flag, a piece of painted cloth, did not look to be worth a man's life, and I wondered if I could ever make such a promise, and mean it.

Mister Tate bowed to the Captain, raised his right hand high in the air, like an ancient Roman giving a salute, and pronounced a long blessing. Then he lowered his arm and said: 'With the kind permission of Captain Lacey I would like to tell you that I believe I have been called by God to preach the gospel in Tangiers. I understand several chapels that were once in the grip of popery have now fallen into disrepair. It is my hope, my fervent hope, that with God's grace and the help of my beloved wife, we will be able to restore one of these chapels. I know there is a garrison church, dedicated to our late King under the title of King Charles the Martyr, and I know the garrison worships there every Sunday. But I also know there is always room for another church, another place where the truth of Our Lord Jesus Christ can be proclaimed.'

He closed his eyes for a moment and moved his lips – spoke to God – then he returned to us. 'The Captain told you about the Portugese church. It is a den of iniquity. A den of sin. And I have to tell you' – he lowered his voice to a whisper – 'that I shall be praying for it to be closed. I shall petition His Majesty, for it is an affront to his dignity as Head of the Church of England. And I shall petition the Bishop of London – Tangiers lies within his spiritual jurisdiction – and it is an affront to his sacred ministry.'

He reached down, picked up his hat and held it to his chest. Then he sucked in his lips, moistened them with his tongue, and said: 'I have to tell you, that I do not believe in tolerance. It is a trick of the devil – an excuse for popery – and I will fight it till the day I die. I will not rest till this popish church, this place of corruption is closed, stripped and cleansed. And all the trinkets of superstition and idolatry are destroyed.'

In the distance the falling tide was uncovering the shoals of black rock that reefed the approach to the landward end of the Mole. They looked like teeth, black teeth gnashing the waves and spitting foam in the air. I looked back to Mister Tate. His mouth, his spit, was frothing, foaming – and over the black stumps that were his teeth came the words: 'I cannot do God's work on my own. I need your help.' He walked down the ranks of the musketeers and peered at each man like a shepherd choosing rams to run with his flock.

For some reason Sergeant Owen and Sergeant Brandon fell in behind, like an escort, and they followed him past the musketeers, and then they followed him along our ranks, and halted just in front of me.

Mister Tate took his place by the Captain and closed his eyes. And once again his lips began to move and Sergeant Brandon whispered to Sergeant Owen: 'I'm getting bloody sick of this.'

Crabtree sniggered and dug me in the ribs, and I grinned to myself.

Then Mister Tate said: 'I need your help to rebuild the chapel. And I need your help to proclaim the faith. If you will help – if you have the courage to help – I ask you to step forward.' He paused. 'God will help you. And I will help you. And between us we will rid this place of popery.'

Sergeant Owen sniffed; Brandon leaned towards him and said – in a loud whisper: 'The man's a bloody madman. He won't understand this place till the Moors shove it up his smelly bum, and he realises we're fighting them – not a bunch of bloody priests.'

A giggle ran through our ranks. Sergeant Brandon half-turned towards us and hissed, and I bit my lips.

For a few moments we listened to the wind and I stared at the walls that run from the Upper Castle to York Castle. They were becoming grey, light grey, as if all the colour had been leached out of them, and I was thinking we should be able to see something of the city by now, when Lockhart stepped forward and jumped to attention.

I stared at him in wide-eyed disbelief, and I wondered if he had maggots in the brain. We all waited, and listened again to the wind, for two or maybe three minutes. Then Mister Tate said: 'God has blessed me with one man. Adam was one man. We are two men. From him came great things, and from us will come great things.'

Crabtree leant towards me and whispered in my ear: 'Not if I know Lockhart it won't. He's only interested in the thing between his legs.' I sniggered, snuffled, and tried to swallow his words. But they wouldn't go down – and I spluttered. Brandon turned and glared at me, then his face softened, and deep inside, I knew he was laughing at me, laughing at Lockhart.

A few minutes later, as we passed close to the end of the Mole, and I was thinking Lockhart was a fool, the tars fired a five-gun salute. The wind blew the smoke back onto the deck and carried it into the sails. Then the wind died for a few seconds, and all the smoke dropped back onto the deck. It was like being caught in a light fog, a swirling fog that smelt of sulphur. The sulphur was stronger, more throat-catching than the sulphur that comes from brown coal. It smelt of muskets and gunpowder, and there was something about it, something that raised the hairs on my neck and shivered my spine.

I leant against the rail, and peered at the Mole.

The two cartmen from Whitby were bringing their rock carts to a halt – twenty or thirty yards from the end of the Mole – when the cannons on the Mole began to acknowledge our salute. One of the horses reared in fright and both the drivers rushed towards it. I counted a salute of five-guns and I was thinking the horse would calm now, when the guns high on the walls to the left of York Castle began to fire a salute. The repeating boom was loud and deep and it roared down the Mole and into our sails like a clap of thunder. It made the horse rear again and I could sense the panic, the fear, that was rising within it – and so could the other two horses that were hitched to it – and within a second or two they were trying to break into a gallop and the cart began to roll towards the end of the Mole. Four other men – molemen – rushed towards the cart and grabbed the bridles. They dragged the horses round, forced them to turn, forced them to walk back towards the castle, then they brought them to a halt.

'Christ!' I said, turning to Crabtree. 'They would have drowned, if they'd gone into the water. The stone would have pulled them straight down.'

He shook his head. 'The stone was acting as a drag – pulling them back. It would have stopped them before the end of the Mole.'

I looked at him, I could feel my forehead pulling my face into a frown, but I didn't know horses, had never sat on one in my life, and maybe he was right. I nodded, turned away and looked again at the town.

Then I saw that York Castle and the Upper Castle were linked by two walls: the northern wall, the Atlantic wall I'd been watching for most of the morning; and a second wall that was tall and thin and bent in the middle, and looked like a wasted leg. The lower left-hand bastion of the Upper Castle formed the groin of this wall, and from here it ran down Castle Hill. It enclosed the upper and the lower flanks of the hill, and it protected the approach to the castle gate. Below the bend, below the knee, it enclosed three or four low buildings with long roofs. At the ankle it made a sharp twist to the left. The foot was pulled straight to lengthen the leg, and then it ran across a swathe of flat ground. In my imagination the toes were like locking stones, they gripped the wall that ran from the left of York Castle, and they locked the two castles into one great fortress. I could see if we were ever threatened with death, with defeat, and we had to retreat, the fortress and the Mole that lay below it – that lay right in front of me – would be our path to the sea, our path to salvation.

For a moment or two my mind stayed with these gloomy thoughts, then my eye walked along the parapet of the thin wall. The stone looked fresh, just-quarried – still in need of time to age, to weather; and the mortar looked raw, looked new. Then I began to think that the fortress was a new idea, a new place of safety; and if we had to abandon the city and the forts, had to live within the fortress walls, we could fight and wait for more troops to arrive – wait for salvation to come from the sea.

The city lay to the left of the new wall. The roofs of the houses struggled down the lower slopes of Castle Hill, and into a valley that sloped towards the sea. Then they rose again, struggled out of the valley and climbed towards the high point in the far left-hand corner. A stone wall with towers and strong points enclosed all the houses. It stretched from the far side of the Upper Castle – from somewhere near Peterborough Tower – to the high point on the left-hand corner. Then it ran down to the sea in a straight line, turned to the right and followed the waterline for about two hundred yards. At the point where the valley meets the sea – where the open sewer that was once a stream discharges its cargo of muck – it dog-legged inland and ran along the top of the terraced cliffs till it joined the walls of York Castle. This wall, or maybe walls is a better description for it was built in many short sections, looked old and decrepit – like the stone walls of an abandoned farm.

Near the water's edge, on the cliffs below York Castle, some of the towers and the thin walls that spoked them to the castle – and should have been able to break up an attacking force and funnel it up to the killing points – had crumbled and decayed. They wore a bloom of green, of shrubbery, and from some angles two of the towers looked as though they were crowned with laurel wreaths.

Above the roofs a thin bloom of blue smoke hung in the air. It softened the orange tiles, sucked the red out of them, and it dulled the white of the walls; but it gave a sharpness, a brightness, to small wedges of blue. These wedges appeared to be contained within the houses, within the courtyards, and I thought them harsh, unnatural, and then I overheard Sergeant Owen say: 'The blue cools the houses and keeps away the chinches – the mosquitoes. And after you've seen the size of them, and itched their bites and found they won't heal, you'll wish the whole bloody place was painted blue.' And he laughed.

I stared into the water – the sun was making it glitter, making it look bright blue – and I shuffled along, stood beside Lockhart, and said: 'What the hell did you volunteer for?'

He looked at me and smiled: 'You think I'm mad, don't you?'

I nodded and he laughed. 'Did you hear him talking about great things to come?' I nodded again. 'And have you thought how often an old fool like that does this with his thing?' He clenched his fist and rammed it up and down.

I shook my head.

'Once a week? Once a month? Or once a year?' He paused. 'It can't be very often. She hasn't had a baby and my old dad used to say it only took him two or three times.' He grinned. 'I think she'd like a man, a proper man, a man who can give her a baby. Mister Tate won't be there all the time. He'll be off doing his preaching, or visiting the sick, or whatever it is he thinks he has to do. And that will leave me in the chapel – on my own, helping her. And I'll have my hand up her skirt in no time and I'll have her.' He grinned again. 'And while you dream about doing it – and I know you do, so don't deny it – I'll be doing it. And you – he prodded me with his finger – 'will be dreaming. And that's all you'll ever do with her.'

12

In deep water, about eight hundred yards out from the round tower, the Eastern Tower that overlooks the anchorage and guards the bottom left-hand corner of the city walls, we furled the last of our sails and dropped the small anchor. After the tide turned, the seamen lowered three small boats, and with one tied to the bow to act as a guide, and two tied to the stern to act as drogues, we drifted in for another hundred yards or so and dropped the main anchor.

Some of the seamen were saying the bottom was sand with a little shingle, and the Mole was moving it about, making the harbour silt up, and now there wasn't enough grip down there and the anchor might drag. Others were saying they'd been here before and we were over the rocks and they were sharp, and they'd seen them cut through anchor ropes. And if an anchor could be dragged or cut, and the Bay was silting up, and a ship the size of a frigate couldn't get in this close in a few years' time – what was the point of building the Mole?

I wasn't sure what to make of this. Last night Captain Lacey had called it one of the great wonders of the world, a marvel of English engineering, greater than anything the Romans had ever built. To me it was a stone quay: longer, wider and straighter than anything I'd ever seen in England – and for the life of me I couldn't see anything to merit the praise he heaped upon it. But I have to admit, I couldn't see under the water, couldn't see the difficulties, the problems of construction. If I remember Captain Lacey right, he said: the current is strong, and the tide rises and falls by nine feet, and at dead low tide there's still another twenty feet of water. Nothing has ever been built before at this depth – four hundred and fifty yards out from the shore – and it's so exposed, so open to the elements that 'most days you feel as though you're dumping rock in the middle of the ocean'.

Then he'd gone on to say: 'And now they're talking about filling ships up with rock and sinking them to make the next part of the Mole.' I looked at him in amazement – ships are worth an enormous amount of money and officers can be shot or hanged if they are sunk through negligence – and I was trying to think how much the Mole must be costing to build, when he changed the subject, and went on to talk about walking on the aqueduct the Romans built to carry water into Old Tangiers.

I squinted and shaded my eyes, and in the curve of the Bay, about two miles away – overshadowed by green hills that gave way to snow-capped mountains – lay the ruins of Old Tangiers. The stone walls had crumbled and the towers had toppled, and below them, on the long sweep of beach that edged the Bay, that ran all the way to the rocks in front of Eastern Tower, the Moors speckled the sand and blended into the decay of the past.

Sergeant Owen walked along the deck, stood beside me, and said: 'You'll get used to the Moors.' I nodded. 'You know what I hate most?' I shook my head. 'The bastards who sell them muskets and gunpowder, and make money out of them attacking us. Blood money, I call it.' He bit at his lips. 'And you know what I dread most?' I shook my head again. 'The day they sell them two or three cannons. Not small ones like these' – he flicked his hand at the five small cannons that were mounted on wooden carriages and lashed to the deck – 'but big ones. New ones. Ones with a big bore and a long barrel. And if they put one up there, on the sandhill where the Moors are camped, where they can overlook Irish Battery' – he nodded towards the battlements on the upper left-hand corner of the city walls – 'and another one over there to the right of Peterborough Tower; and another in the middle, on the hills beyond the far wall; and angled them high like mortars; they could bombard both castles and the town. And if they fired on the forts, destroyed them one by one, they could move the cannons closer, and then they could hit the Mole and the ships inside the Mole. Nothing – no one – would be safe. And at the moment, with few men and less than half a troop-of-horse there's nothing we could do about it.'

A cloud came over and for a minute or two it darkened the Moors' tents on the sandhill, made them look more numerous, more threatening. Then the sun returned and I caught the glint of a spyglass. I couldn't believe we would let them sit there – two or three hundred yards from the walls – let them watch, let them wait, let them see everything we were doing. I turned to Owen. 'Why don't we build a fort up there on the sandhill and get rid of the Moors?'

He smiled, in a pitying way, and said: 'The sands are shifting all the time. If they blow away, they expose the foundations and the walls collapse. If they pile up against the walls, the walls become useless – a fort without high walls isn't a fort. And besides we'd have to take in a lot more ground and stockade the paths to the fort, and we don't have the men to do it.'

'So what are the Moors waiting for? Why don't they attack? They must know how many men are in the garrison. They only have to open their eyes and count – any fool can see that.'

'They do attack. In small numbers, all the time. We keep making peace treaties with them and they keep breaking them. We never know when they're going to attack and that means we have to maintain a full guard all the time. It also means we can't repair the walls or strengthen the forts, or raise the embankments – they protect the lanes that lead to the forts – without mustering a large force. As I said before, we don't have enough men.'

'So why don't they attack in large numbers and overwhelm us?'

He shrugged. 'I don't know what the Moors think, or why they do what they do. But I'll tell you what I think – what most of the Sergeants think.' He paused. 'We think they're waiting.'

'Waiting?'

'Hmm. Waiting for the Mole to be finished. And then they'll attack in great hordes, and we'll be forced to retreat, to evacuate the whole place. And that Mole' – he turned and looked at it – 'that will be our memorial.'

'How long will it take to finish?'

He shrugged. 'Five years. Ten years. Who knows?'

I looked from the Mole to the sandhill and back to the Mole again. In ten years it would be 1683 – I could be going home in 1683. It was a thought I'd never dared to think before, never believed it could be possible. It set my heart racing and for a moment I felt light-headed, dizzy with excitement. Then I began to think about the sand, the shifting sands. I knew the Moors couldn't fire a cannon from a sandhill – it needs a solid base – and if he was wrong about that he could be wrong about going home. The dizziness died, and the excitement went with it, and I said: 'I thought you couldn't fire a cannon from the sand. I thought you had to have a solid base of stone or wood.'

'Earth will do. If a thousand Moors carried one basket of earth each into the sandhills and stamped on it, it would make a firm platform. And if the recoil from the cannon broke up the base or dug holes into it, they could make it firmer with shingle, more earth, and planks of wood. There are so many of them they can work miracles in the dark, and what wasn't there at sunset can be there by sunrise.'

Then he went quiet and leant on the rail. I began to sense he didn't want to come back to Tangiers, began to sense that the prospect filled him with gloom. Some of the gloom that was in his soul seeped into my soul, and if we'd been alone, I might have tried to comfort him. That was a strange feeling, a strange emotion, for most men in our company say it's not the Moors who are the enemy – it's the bloody Sergeants.

13

As the *Salisbury*'s longboat drew close to the bow, the oarsmen lifted their oars in the air and grabbed at the mooring line that was looped along the side of the ship. Then the seamen on the lower deck tied ropes around Mister Tate's wooden chest, manhandled it onto the rail, and lowered it into the boat. On the upper deck Mister Tate and his wife spoke to the ship's Captain for several minutes. Then they bowed to him and three of his officers, and as they came down the steps and walked towards us – drawn up again in four lines – they smiled and nodded. It was a strange thing to do, for apart from the formal prayers at the parade each morning when we all became equal before God, they had ignored us. As they came closer, I took off my hat and bowed my head. Then I remembered Lockhart's words, and I wondered if they did it once a week, or once a month, or once a year. And I was thinking I wouldn't want to do it with him – if I were her – when she said, in a soft voice that was meant for me and me alone: 'How is your head?'

I swallowed hard, and looked at the deck. In my foolishness, my ignorance, I thought she'd forgotten me, or hadn't recognised me. When I looked up she was smiling with her eyes, and I said: 'It isn't sore any more. And the lump's gone down.' I patted the side of my head.

'You must be more careful when you're going up and down stairs,' she said. 'It's too easy to fall, to trip, especially if you're in a hurry, or someone's chasing you.' She smiled. 'I was thinking if you would like to come and help Mister Tate – when your duties allow – it could be a way of saying thank you for the questions that were not asked.' And she smiled again. Then for the briefest of moments, the tips of her fingers brushed across my shoulder, as if to flick away a speck of dust.

I felt as though I'd been touched by an angel, and a warm glow rushed to my face. She turned and nodded to the man in the rank behind me. Then Mister Tate said something to her, and she took Lockhart's hands into her hands and kissed them. My mouth dropped and I sucked in a breath, made a loud gasping sound. But maybe it was louder in my ears than it was in their ears, for neither showed any sign of hearing it. Then I was ashamed of him, ashamed of what lust was making him do. I turned away and looked over the rail. The water was clear – I could see the bottom. The tide was stirring the sand, making the bottom look murky, look grubby, and that was how I imagined Lockhart's mind.

Then he hissed in my ear: 'It's going to work. I can feel it down here.' And he grabbed at his crotch.

I elbowed him away. He laughed in my face, then he said: 'You'll think different, when you're bigger. When your cock jumps up and down every time you look at a pretty woman.' And he laughed some more.

I turned away and watched Mister Tate clamber down the rope netting. Then Mistress Tate sat in a rope sling, hitched up her skirts and held them close to her waist. The seamen pulled her up in the air and eased her over the side.

Her legs kicked the air – they were long, thin, and shaped by white stockings, black garters – and they dried my throat, stirred my flesh. I was ashamed of myself, ashamed of the lust that was rising within me, and I pretended to look away. But out of the corner of my eye I watched her every move, and so did a hundred pairs of hungry eyes.

Then hands that had not reached up to help him into the boat, reached up to help her, and the longboat began to drift away from the ship.

The five oarsmen on the right-hand side touched the water together, made a lazy splashing sound, and the prow of the boat began to turn. It turned the Tates towards Tangiers – made them face the city, face their future – and then the other five oarsmen picked up the stroke, and the boat began to make for the shore. The turn of the tide had raised the waves and strengthened the wind that was coming from the west, and for several minutes the boat looked low in the water, looked heavy, sluggish. But as it passed from the Tangiers Roads to the waters calmed by the Mole it appeared to lift, to lighten, and then it gathered speed and slid into the flat waters to the left of the Old Mole.

This was the old breakwater – it was built by the Portuguese – and it protected the slipways, the beach and the quay. To my mind it did not merit the name Mole for it was nothing more than a finger of rocks broken into two parts. The first part was about forty yards long. The stones were dark grey, rough-cut, and layered at the sides to break the force of the waves. The top bumped along, and the end sloped into the sea. Then came a gap of about twelve feet. The next part was about twenty feet long, and the rocks were piled high, much higher than the rest of the Old Mole, and they were not flattened at the top. I turned to Crabtree. 'There must have been a hell of a storm, to break through the end of the Old Mole like that.'

He peered at it for a moment or two. 'I think it's deliberate. I think they've raised the height to protect the end of the Old Mole.' He paused. 'Or maybe it's something to do with the flow of water. Maybe it lessens the rip, makes it easier to row in and out of there.'

I nodded, and looked to the left, to the reefs that ran out from the Eastern Tower and ended about fifty yards away from the island-end of the Old Mole. Between them, the reef and the Old Mole broke the force of the waves and created a small inner anchorage.

My eyes drifted over the inner anchorage, drifted over a pair of small boats dragging a fishing net towards the beach below the city walls. Then they drifted along the curve of the stone quay and into the masts and the rigging of two ships lying deep inside the Old Mole. The masts closest to the shore took my eyes up to a tower that looked straight down the Old Mole. It was six-sided and at the back it supported another tower, a round tower that was tethered to York Castle by a pair of thin walls that enclosed a steep flight of steps.

To the left of this pair of walls, the hillside was divided into three sections. The middle one was terraced. The terraces weren't wide enough for gardens. They looked more like seating, and as I watched four men – four red-coated officers – walked along one of the rows and sat down. They appeared to be waiting for some sort of entertainment to begin, but there wasn't much to see – apart from men getting in and out of small boats; men unloading provisions; and men scraping, caulking and tarring the hulls of the boats that lay stranded on the hard. I couldn't see the point of the terraces and to be honest, I couldn't think why the Portuguese had wanted to build them in the first place.

To the right of the pair of walls, halfway up the cliff face, the rocks supported the lower bastions of York Castle. Below the rocks, a stone quay that was as wide as a road and followed the curve of the land, the curve of an old beach, and joined the Old Mole to the new Mole. Close to the cliffs a guardhouse protected the end of the Mole and controlled the road to Whitby.

Just in front of the guardhouse, the end of the quay became the end of the Mole, became the side of a small U-shaped anchorage that looked as though it would be suitable for longboats but not much more. A few yards along from here a flight of small stairs ran down to the water, and towards the end of the Mole – in the last section that had reached its full width – a large flight of stairs was protected by a battery of cannon. The Mole ended with a thin spur of rocks that ran for about thirty yards. From the Atlantic side it had given the Mole a long straight edge, and as we'd come into the Straits I thought this section was finished. But now I could see it was a spur, and the rock carts weren't dumping rock at the end as I'd imagined – they were dumping it all the way along the inside of the spur. The spur was acting as a breakwater, it was calming the waves and the rip, and in a storm it would stop the sea scouring the loose rocks.

A cart rolled down the Mole, dumped its load in the curve at the beginning of the spur, turned around and rumbled away. The sentries closed the barrier and about half an hour later – when the waves had washed the dust off the new rock and blended it into the old rock – the longboat returned.

We handed our pikes over the rail and the oarsmen laid them down the middle of the boat, on top of the seats. The seamen lowered the Lieutenant's chest and the Ensign's chest, and the oarsmen wedged them between the seats. Then the Ensign and eleven pikemen clambered down the rope netting, and the oarsmen sat them in pairs – to balance the boat. When they were settled, the Lieutenant climbed down the ladder and sat in the stern on his own.

As the longboat pulled away, another boat, a smaller boat with four oarsmen, took hold of the mooring rope. One of the men stood up. Captain Lacey leant over the rail, and for a couple of minutes they haggled over twelve pence – one shilling – then he stepped back and said something to Sergeant Brandon. I grabbed my sack, followed six others down the netting. One of the oarsmen pointed to the stern and I sat down on the left-hand side. He seated Lockhart next to me, and then – to my disgust – Sergeant Brandon clambered into the boat, gestured to Lockhart to move to the side, and sat between us. The stern tapered and the seat was only wide enough for two. It cramped us together, made our legs touch. Lockhart and I balanced our sacks on our knees and held them with our hands. Brandon also balanced his haversack on his knees but because it was held firm by a canvas strap that ran over his right shoulder and under his left arm, it left his hands free – free to wander. I eyed them with suspicion, and I was thinking how much easier it would be if we all had haversacks, when the oarsmen pushed away from the side of the ship.

The boat lay low in the water and for a moment it seemed to wallow, but as the men began to row, the gunnels frothed and foamed and they appeared to rise from the water. But this rising exposed our wooden flanks, and with a few seconds the wind was slapping waves against them and throwing spray high in the air. The spray felt cold but the wind felt warm, much warmer than it had felt on the deck, and I thought we must be coming up to midday. But when I turned to the east and looked across the straits to Tarifa – where the houses were making small white smudges on the waterline – the sun was still low in the sky and the hills of Spain looked full of sleep, like a face that is still to wake up, and I knew it couldn't be much more than eight o'clock.

As the stones on the island-end of the Old Mole began to grow bigger, to become edged with sea-slime and draped with seaweed, the boat slid into a trough, rammed the crest of a wave and tossed the three of us high in the air. We thumped back onto the seat – as if we were glued together like three wooden dolls – then we split apart. I grabbed at Brandon and he grabbed at me, grabbed at Lockhart. Then we let go of each other, let go of our fear, and laughed.

I pulled off my hat and wiped my face. Lockhart leant on the gunnels, lifted himself off the seat and wiped away the water that had sloshed over the stern. A few seconds later my breeches began to feel damp, and I leant on the gunnels and tried to dry my part of the seat. Then I thought we were settled, but the Sergeant put his right hand on my leg and pushed himself up. His fingers squeezed hard, bit deep into my flesh, flooded my eyes with tears. I shut my mouth and tried to swallow the pain. He wiped at his seat, and just when I thought he was going to sit down, he wiped his seat again, and he leant towards me, made me take all of his weight. I thought the bone in my leg was going to break. I grabbed at the gunnels, tried to cry out, but no noise came out of my mouth. Then he lowered himself onto the seat.

He loosened his grip, and the pain began to drain away. I rubbed at my eyes and sniffed hard, but he did not take his hand away. He pushed his knapsack hard against my sack, hid his hand from the eyes of the oarsmen, and whispered in my ear: 'Tell me what he does to you.'

I turned towards him and he pulled his lips into a tight smile.

There was no need to ask who 'he' was. And there was no point in pretending I did not understand the question. I did not want to tell him what we'd done, for in some strange way I felt something for that man. Something that others might call affection, and such a thought was unnatural. I knew that in the secret corners of my mind, and I have to confess it confused me, and I did not understand why I should feel like that, and I said: 'Nothing.'

He laughed in my ear, grabbed at my breeches, grabbed at my crotch. 'Is this nothing? Is this what he did?'

I bit my lips, nodded my head, and stared straight ahead.

Then he said: 'Did you do it to him?'

I nodded again, felt his fingers relax, felt his face smile.

The oarsmen bent their backs and pulled together – the symbolism made me quiver – and I tried to push away his hand. But he would not let go, and after a few seconds, as the boat swayed, brought his lips to within an inch or two of my ear, he said: 'Did he roll you over and stick it up your bum?'

I shuddered, pushed away the past, pushed away the nights I thought were dead and buried, and said: 'No.'

'No?'

'No.'

He sat without saying another word for several seconds, then he said: 'So you stuck it up his bum? Is that what he made you do?'

I shook my head.

He grabbed at my shoulder and pulled my face towards his. 'Are you telling me the truth?'

I nodded. He pushed me away, and I said: 'He says that's wrong. He says it's against the laws of God, and the laws of nature.'

He pulled a face and laughed out loud.

I bit at my lips, watched the dirty water in the bottom of the boat slosh up and down. It sloshed over his shoes. I lifted my shoes above the water, but a sudden slew, a sudden roll, pitched the water over my shoes. It left behind lines of dirt, lines of wetness. It made my shoes look like his and his look like mine. It made us look the same, and this filled my mind with gloom.

He pulled his hand away from my breeches and placed it on his haversack, and after a minute or so he said: 'If what you say is true, about him not wanting your bum, then I can tell you he'll soon tire of you. He'll be looking for someone new. For someone who knows something you don't know,' and he grinned. 'Or maybe he'll be looking for someone who can do it better than you. Or maybe he'll just be looking for a new face, a new cock. The reason won't matter. It will come to pass – as the scriptures say – because the two of you are playing with each other, like little boys. Men don't want that.' He shook his head. 'They grow out of that, just like they grow out of playing with toys. What they want is a woman and if they can't have a woman, they'll have a man, have his bum, and in the dark they'll pretend he's a woman. That's the way men are. That's their nature. And a month from now I could be having you. And who knows? I might get to like you, and you could be mine for a long long time.' And he patted my knee.

Our boat picked up a wave, a rogue wave that should not have found its way into the Old Mole. It lifted us high, swept us forward and dumped us hard on the beach.

The bow dug into the sand, jerked us backwards and forwards. Then the stern flopped, smacked the water, and showered us with spray. Lockhart wiped the back of his neck and I shook myself, and then we looked at each other and laughed.

The wave frothed and bubbled about the boat, and for a moment it lay quiet – bemused by its own strength – then it felt the pull of the sea and it roared away, sucking at the sand.

A man waded into the water just a few yards along from us, reached into his boat, hooked out a fish, slashed open its belly and washed the guts into the water. The blood bloomed in the water, made sprays of pink flowers. Then a seagull shrieked and swooped, and the guts writhed in the air – looked like long thin snakes with orange skins and red veins.

But the guts were too heavy for the gull, and it lurched towards a boat grounded high on the beach where the sand was compacted with crushed stone and tiny bits of black rock that shone like coal. The gull landed on the beams of wood that were waiting to be unloaded, and for a moment or two it tore at the guts.

Then a brown dog, a hunting hound, came bounding across the beach – barking madly – and the gull took fright. It rose in the air, and still trailing some of the guts, it flew over the water to the inner end of the Old Mole, made a lazy turn and came back along the edge of the quay and landed on a stone jetty about forty feet to our right.

The jetty was still being built. It was long and low, and about six feet wide. When finished it would form the right-hand end of the beach and run straight into the water. The waves were surging over the end of it, pouring through the gaps and falling into the sea where stones the size of coffins were waiting to be hoisted into place.

The two oarsmen at the front jumped out of the boat, grabbed each side and signed for Lockhart to get out first. He stepped onto the sand, saw me looking at the jetty, and said: 'That's not going to be much use at that height, is it?'

Before I could open my mouth, or smile or nod or do anything at all, Brandon turned towards him and yelled: 'We're not that bloody stupid!'

Lockhart flushed red and jumped to attention. He stood rigid, eyes looking straight out to sea. A wave washed over his shoes and left a tideline on his stockings, at ankle height.

The gull stared at us for several seconds, then it pulled at the rest of the guts and tore them to shreds. There was something about that bird. Something imperial – or imperious – and it reminded me of the ancient Romans and how they used to pull the guts out of birds and animals and look for the omens, the auguries, that would predict the future.

I wondered if they ever stood on this beach, or sat up there on the terraces, and read the signs, and saw what they wanted to see. And what would they have made of our gull with its white feathers and blooded breast? To me it was an omen, a bad omen, and it spoke of death, or a brush with death. I knew this place defeated the Romans, the Spaniards, and the Portuguese, and I wondered if it would ever be our turn to be cast out, and it made me feel uneasy, made me grip the end of my seat.

Then Brandon leant on the gunnel and stepped out of the boat as the waves retreated. He walked around the bow and stood in front of Lockhart. 'We're going to build a wooden bridge at the end of the jetty. The decking will be above the high-water mark, and they say it will be linked to a barge or a pontoon that will float up and down. And that means we'll be able to load and unload at any time of the day or night, and we won't be affected by the state of the tide.'

One of the oarsmen pointed at me and I got out of the boat, and Crabtree followed. We were the last two and we tossed our sacks up the beach – beyond the tide line – and helped them push the boat back into the water.

We left Lockhart standing alone, like an old mooring post: grey, weathered, and barnacled with age. Then another boat ran onto the beach just a few feet along from the scour-line that our boat had made. The oarsmen laughed and whistled at him. One of them pretended to throw a rope over him and they laughed again. Their faces were black, sooty, like the faces of chimney sweeps. One of them hoisted a sack out of the boat, tossed it onto his back and began to trudge up the beach. His foot caught a rock and he stumbled – showered the sand with lumps of coal.

I looked again at the terraces, and wondered if the Romans could have built them all that time ago. I was thinking the answer would be no, thinking they would have fallen to bits by now, and it must have been the Portuguese, when I remembered the ditch in Elme. We always called it the Roman Bank and we knew the Romans dug it. And if a bank, an earthen ditch could survive all that time, maybe the same could be true for the terraces. I peered hard at them, tried to imagine all the years that had come and gone, and all the people who had sat upon them. But my mind was a blur, like some of the history

I tried to learn when I was young, and I wandered up the beach to find my pike.

An hour or so later, the last of the musketeers came ashore. Three of them wiped the spray off their muskets, wiped it onto their coats, and two of them tightened the plug bayonet that slips into the barrel. Then they slung their musket butts onto their right shoulders, pushed them backwards, and gripped the end of the barrel. For a second or two, against the light, they looked as though they were carrying cudgels and I remembered one of them saying the butt was a weapon. If the rain wet his powder or there wasn't time to reload, he could attack with the butt, could use it like a club.

One by one they walked around Lockhart, laughed in his face, ambled up the beach, up the jetty steps, passed a cluster of warehouses, and leant against the walls of a round tower. This tower guarded the path that climbed the hill. It was tall and thin and capped with a bell-shaped roof pulled into a spike. It was casting a shadow across the path, up the side of a small two-storeyed house, over the roof and onto the hillside behind it. This part of the hillside was crumbling, and might once have been terraced, for one of the rocks that was touched by the shadow – and could almost have been a marker on a giant sundial – was cut square and smoothed on one side.

The house looked dead. The windows were shuttered and barred and the door was bolted. A bracket for a hanging sign stuck out from under the eaves on the front corner, but there was no sign of a sign – no way of telling what the house was used for – and I was thinking it could be a guardhouse, or a warehouse, or a customs house, when Lockhart shuffled backwards. The movement was quite pronounced. Earlier on, when he was easing himself up the slope, inch by inch, the movement was hard to detect. But now he was growing careless. I felt a sudden spasm of fear. I gripped my pike and turned around, then I relaxed: Brandon was standing beside Ensign Wyndham, and it looked as though they were ordering four men to carry the two chests up the hill.

I turned back to Lockhart, watched him make another little shuffle, and I was trying to work out how far he'd moved up the beach, and thinking it could be ten or twelve feet, when Billy Foster began to beat his drum.

I shouldered my pike and marched up to Sergeant Brandon. He was waiting on the higher section of the path. Pikemen – gentlemen of the pike – have the order of preference. We always go first, always lead the column. It's something to do with us bearing arms that are more ancient, more honourable. To me it doesn't make much sense. The musket is a more powerful weapon, with a longer range, and if I had a choice I'd like to be a musketeer. But the truth is I don't have a choice, and I'm not going to have a choice, and Lieutenant de Colville says they're talking about sending me to York Castle, and I won't have a choice in that either.

I looked up at the castle. The flag at the top of the large square tower was flapping in the wind. I could make out the red cross of Saint George, and underneath came another cross, a white cross laid on the diagonal. The background was dark blue, like a midnight sky on a clear night. I stared at it for several seconds, then I realised the flag of England was pushing the flag of Scotland into the background, and it represented the two kingdoms. I remembered learning about it, learning about the King's grandfather coming from Scotland after Queen Elizabeth died, and I was thinking I preferred the English flag, when Brandon screamed: 'Will you turn round and get in line!'

I spun round, jumped into line, and stared straight ahead – the man in front of me was no more than four inches away, and the man in front of him was about as close. My heart was thumping in my ears and I dared not move my head, dared not look at him. The silence brought me out in a sweat. I thought Brandon would come stomping down the line at any moment, thought he'd push his way through the forest of pikes and grab at me; but then Lieutenant de Colville stepped forward and said something to him. He pursed his lips, and for a moment he seemed to hesitate, then he inclined his head and yelled: 'Make two files!'

We shuffled down the path, shuffled away from the stone wall that buttresses the hillside, and formed ourselves into two files. The path was steeper than it looked, and it was wider than it looked – wide enough for a horse and cart – and on the seaward side the stone wall was double-stepped to form a firing platform.

As Captain Lacey walked up the steps Lockhart came pounding up the path. The musketeers burst out laughing, whistled and jeered, made his face flush red. He skidded to a halt, joined the end of our back file, and stood to attention – without his pike. I felt a shudder of horror, and I realised that not one single pikeman had uttered a sound.

The Captain turned around and his eyes bumped down the jagged line our pike heads were cutting into the hillside, and they stopped at Lockhart – stayed there for several seconds. Then they bumped on down the line made by the plug bayonets, skirted around the base of the tower and drifted into the waters of the Old Mole. For a few moments, they were lost to us – he was lost to us – then he blinked, dropped the end of his partisan over the edge of the top step and rested it on the lower step; and with the spearhead and the tassel close to his face – as if to emphasise his authority – he opened his mouth and said: 'Welcome to Tangiers. Welcome to hell.'

A splutter ran through the ranks.

He pulled his lips into a tight smile, waited for the noise to die, then he said: 'This morning I told you about Garrison Standing Orders. I told you they state that every man must carry his personal weapons with him at all times. There is never an exception. There is never a time when you can step outside without your weapons. We are in a state of siege, permanent siege. And we can be attacked at any moment. We are never allowed to relax our guard. And that man' – he pointed at Lockhart – 'is on parade without all of his weapons. And this afternoon' – he turned to Sergeant Brandon – 'he is to be charged with dereliction of duty.'

Brandon bowed to the Captain, and his faced remained fixed, impassive, but inside I knew the bastard was laughing himself silly. I couldn't believe that a stupid little remark by Lockhart had managed to build itself into something as serious as this. I half-turned to Crabtree and he shook his head, and whispered in my ear: 'Oldfield's bloody lucky.'

He was sitting on the cobbles, close to the round tower, and he didn't have his pike with him. His back had slumped, his head had flopped, his arms had gone limp, and he looked old and grubby – like a rag doll that has been loved to death. I saw Brandon looking at him, and I thought of the corruption he calls love – and in my head the cobbles heaved and so did the dirt that binds them together. I smelt the stench of corruption and not all of it was coming from the black slime in the gutter.

Then I heard the Captain's voice again and he was saying: 'On the other side of Sandwich Port we'll break ranks and form columns of three.' He looked from side to side. 'I can see some of you are looking bemused. Port is an old Latin word. It means gate. And there's another one on the other side of the town. Catherine Port. It's named after Her Majesty. You'll soon find out that most people call this one the Watergate. But his Excellency prefers the old names, and in our written orders it's always called Sandwich Port.'

I looked it up and down. To me it wasn't a gate or a port. It was a square tower with battlements, and double doors hidden deep inside an archway. Thirty or forty feet in front of it, and locked into seven-foot-high pillars of stone, stood a proper gate, a wooden one, studded with iron bolts. On the left-hand side of this gate the walls bulged to form a V, like the abutment of a bridge. A sentry was marching from the archway to the point of the abutment and back again. Each time he turned in the abutment, he paused, looked down the wall he would have to defend if we were attacked from the sea, and yawned. His teeth were black, rough edged, like the coal the men were still carrying up the beach and pouring onto the heaps in the coal yard.

Sergeant Owen had called it a coal yard when we were coming up the steps by the jetty. To me it was more like a dump, and when I said this he shook his head and said: 'A yard is a yard, except when it's three feet.' He burst out laughing. I smiled and looked again at the yard: on the landward side it was contained, was overlooked, by the city walls, and on the seaward side it was enclosed by two walls, a tower, a wooden gate and the base of the abutment. The tower was unmanned, and some of the stone had crumbled. Weeds and small shrubs had taken root in the mortar, and despite all the wind and the rain of yesterday, the stones and the leaves were still black with coal dust. I tapped the toes of my shoes on the cobbles and banged off the sand, then I said: 'It must cost a lot to bring all that coal over from Spain.'

He gave me a strange look – made me feel as though I'd been talking nonsense – then he lifted his hat, wiped the sweat from his brow. 'It comes from England. Most things come from England. You, me, those beams.' He nodded at the wooden beams that were still sitting on the boat. 'Dried peas. Sacks and sacks of the bloody things.' He spat on the cobbles. 'Some things come from Spain: wine, grapes, lemons, pomegranates, cabbages – but you can't rely on them. And often, when they are available, the garrison doesn't have enough money to buy them.' He shook his head. 'I can tell you now, you're going to be eating a lot of salt beef and pease-pudding.'

'But what about the summertime, when the grass is long and we could be eating fresh meat all the time?'

'At the moment we don't have any cattle. And if we did we couldn't leave them outside the walls at night. And if we brought them in we wouldn't have enough herbage to feed them.' He sighed to himself. 'Sometimes the Moors will sell us a few cattle, a few sheep – if we've been able to arrange a truce for six months, and they're in a mood to trade. And sometimes a beast will stray into the lines and we'll catch it. Now and again the Governor will bring some over from Cadiz, from the Bay of Bulls, which I've always thought an apt name.' He laughed. 'But most of the time we eat salt beef.'

'And it comes from England?'

'Yes.'

I thought of the lumps of salt beef that still lay heavy in my belly, lumps that were tough and chewy. They hadn't been soaked long enough in fresh water to leach out the salt and they'd sucked all the moisture out of my mouth. And I remembered thinking we needed to flavour them with herbs and spices. 'I hope it's better than what we had on the boat.'

'Better?' He smiled, and shook his head. 'That was better. Better than anything you're going to get here. Our beef is old and hard. So hard you can hit it with a tuning fork and it'll give you a perfect pitch. You know what a tuning fork is?'

I nodded. The Reverend Mister Salthouse used to tap his on the back of the pew, when we sang in our village church, and for a moment I could hear middle C echoing through the pillars of my mind.

Then he smiled. 'Our beef is four or five years old, if we're lucky. And when the sailors won't eat it they ship it out here to save money. We're not like them. We can't take it back, or refuse to accept it. Once it's here it's here. And when we're on six for four—'

'Six for four?'

'Six men eating the rations for four, you eat the bloody stuff or you starve.' He pulled his face into a grim smile, then he walked away.

I let this memory of a few minutes ago slip away, and I wet my lips.

Out of the corner of my eye I looked at Brandon. The sun had crept under the brim of his hat and sweat was running down his face. Then I could taste the sweat on my own face, it was salted like a weak brine, and I was wondering if the Captain would ever stop talking, when Brandon hurried past me and pulled two men out of our line.

They stripped off their coats, buttoned them together, slipped two pikes through the sleeves, and made a litter. Then they picked up Oldfield and laid him on the coats at Brandon's feet.

Crabtree leant towards me and whispered: 'Look at the bastard. He's bloody gloating. If Captain Lacey wasn't here he'd boot him in the ribs. Oldfield should have given in. Should have let him do it.' He paused. 'He's never looked at me again. Not since that night. It would have been the same for Oldfield and the same for you. If you want my opinion, I think you both made a mistake, and you're both going to pay for it.'

15

We shuffled through the gloom of Sandwich Port, broke ranks in a narrow paved area that was shaded by the walls and still damp from yesterday's rain, and formed three files. Ensign Wyndham marched up to the front, Billy Foster took his place beside him, and then with the flag flapping and the drum beating, we wheeled to the left, and marched up the steep incline. At the top, as we wheeled to the right and turned our backs to the sea, the cobbles gave way to rutted earth, and the English church came up on our right. It was small, not much bigger than our church in Elme, and it was overshadowed by the church on the other side of the road. This was the church of Rome: the church of the Portuguese and the church of the Irish. They say there are several hundred Irishmen in the regiment because not enough Englishmen will volunteer to serve here – and they say we have to trust them.

To trust the Irish is madness – bloody madness – that's what my Father used to say. To him the Irish are steeped in popery and they are an abomination in the sight of the Lord.

I remembered the words of my Mother, the words I was not supposed to hear: 'Patrick O'Sullivan's gone, gone back to Ireland and popery, and he doesn't matter any more.'

The shock of them froze my mind and stumbled my feet. The man in front of me turned around and glared, and I mumbled: 'I'm sorry.' Then we halted between the two churches, reordered our ranks and waited for the men to struggle up the hill with the litter and the two chests.

My Father never spoke of Patrick but my Mother's sister, my Aunt Mary, she spoke of him. She said he was gone before my Father was born, and they never met. My Father named my dog after him, and sometimes he would kick him and curse the Irish, and curse the past that could not be undone. In the depths of my soul, in the black wastelands where truth walks naked, I knew the truth, but I could not bring myself to think about it, think about its meaning, and I shut my eyes, shut out the past.

Then for a moment or two I watched Captain Lacey run his hand up and down the shaft of his partisan, and I remembered what he said about tolerance, what Mister Tate said – and I realised that tolerance walked a narrow path. I thought about Mister Tate ploughing up that path, sowing seed, sowing corn, and shepherding men into the meadows that are the Church of England. In those meadows I could see the corn changing colour and rippling in the wind. Soon it would be cut and stacked and allowed to finish ripening. Then it would be milled, made into flour, and one day that flour would be baked into bread. Some of that bread would be blessed in the communion service by Mister Tate, and it would become the Body of Christ. Not in a literal sense, in the sense of transubstantiation – the sense the Test Act abjures – but in the sense of the spirit, in the sense of commemoration.

I looked at the church of Rome – the Cathedral Church of Saint John the Baptist – and I saw two men coming down the steps. I say men, but in truth they looked like the servants of Satan with shaved heads, brown faces and long black robes. Crabtree leant towards me and whispered: 'Dominicans.'

I shuddered. I'd not expected to see such creatures. They belonged in a book, in a woodcut, but here they were in front of my eyes. I looked into their eyes. They were black, like the pits of hell, and I remembered the men and women they had burnt at the stake. And as I watched their sandalled feet float from step to step I thought of the feet of the man they are supposed to serve. He was betrayed and his feet were nailed to the cross. I thought of my own feet. They had betrayed me, had taken me across the deck of the ship, down the steps, down the ladder and into his bed. I felt his feet – running down the backs of my legs, locking me into his embrace – and I remembered him saying: 'When we are alone I want you to call me Michael.'

I'd never heard of anyone called Michael before. I said this to him, and he said: 'I took the name at the time of my baptism, in honour of Saint Michael the Archangel.'

I couldn't think how a man could choose his own name – the choice was made by my Father when I was a few days old and about to be christened – and I was going to say, I don't understand, when he said: 'What do they call you?'

I said: 'William', and I explained about the mix-up, the mistake Captain Lacey made on the day I signed my name in the muster book. I said I was christened Martyn, and he lifted my chin, looked into my eyes. 'I don't care what the muster book says. To me you will always be Martyn.'

I was flooded with happiness – I hesitate to call it affection for I still think that is wrong between men – so I will call it happiness, but it does not encompass all the feelings I had for him at that moment. Then I began to think some good might come of him and the temptation into which I had led him.

I thought of the Lord's prayer, the prayer of the man who did not give into temptation, the prayer of the man with holes in his feet; and then Crabtree was banging me with his elbow and hissing: 'Look over there.'

I blinked hard and sucked in my breath. Mister Tate was kneeling on the steps to the Misericordia – the large two-storeyed building that adjoins the convent, the cloisters, where the Dominicans live and sleep and do unspeakable things. He stood up and began to walk towards us. He was smiling, but then he saw the two Dominicans and the smile slid off his face. He ran towards them, threw himself down in the dirt and clasped his hands. Then he flung his hands apart, tossed his head back and closed his eyes. His lips moved for a moment or two in silent prayer, then he shouted: 'You are evil incarnate! You are the spawn of the devil! The brood of the scarlet woman, the whore of Babylon, the Church of Rome. You do not belong here. And I command you to be gone! To be gone in the name of the Lord!'

Lockhart made a loud sniggering sound. I picked it up, and it ran through our ranks.

The Dominicans hurried down the last of the steps, flapped their hands in the air – made themselves look like a pair of black scarecrows – and tried to shoo him away.

But like the birds that circle the sheaves of ripening corn, he wouldn't go away. I laughed, and then I felt embarrassed. I know that sounds silly for he was doing the right thing. But I still felt embarrassed for him, for myself, for Mistress Tate. I looked around, looked up and down Misericordia Street, but I couldn't see her, and I was pleased she couldn't see him.

Crabtree tapped me on the arm. 'Aren't you glad you didn't agree to help the old fool?'

I pulled a face and nodded. Lockhart leant towards the two of us and said: 'Well I'm glad I did. And when that bloody old fool is out doing that' – he nodded at Mister Tate who was taking off his hat and pressing his face towards the earth – 'there'll be more time for me to know his wife.'

I laughed at the stress he laid on the word 'know'. I couldn't help it and nor could Crabtree.

Sergeant Brandon turned around and glared at us. We shut our mouths and looked to the front. Then he called us to attention and we marched up the street, pikes stiff in the air. Lockhart thrust his pike up and down, and his meaning was clear, too clear.

16

At the Misericordia the street widened, became part of the Market Place, and the preaching cross caught my eye. It stood close to the corner of the Misericordia, stood in the middle of a two-step plinth of stone, and it was guarded by two small cannons. The dying Christ was nailed to the stone cross. He was cast in a dark brown metal – much pitted by the wind and the rain – and as the life was draining out of him it was staining the stone. The stain was not red, not the colour of blood, the colour of death, but green, a coppery-green tinged with turquoise. I was thinking if this were England we would take him down from the cross, we would remember his death and celebrate his resurrection, and the cross would be a symbol of life, a symbol of hope. Then the sun lit the area behind his arms and his legs and I could see the shape of his body outlined on the cross in green, and I knew that if Mister Tate had his way and the Reformation came to Tangiers, the cross would still retain the outline of the dead Christ. It would be like a ghost from the past, an image that could not be purged without destroying the cross, and it was strange to think that behind everything we believed, everything we held to be most most sacred, there was the image of popery. It was a disturbing thought. A thought I would never have had in England and it niggled at me, like a tooth that has begun to decay.

Two black pigs rooting in the weeds behind the cannons lifted their snouts and sniffed the air. They saw us and for a moment they appeared to be frozen with fear. Then they squealed, ran ahead of us, turned round, sniffed the air again and began to root in the long mud-filled ruts that scarred the middle of the Market Place. Both were hogs – about a year old – and both were wearing leather collars with studs that formed letters, formed a name.

We marched past Taverne Street and came to a halt beside a gateway with a rounded arch. It was approached by two steps and these led my eyes through the arch, across a forecourt – paved and made formal by two lines of potted plants – and up a short flight of steps. The entrance to the house was deep in the shadows and the door was closed. My eye came back through the plants and ran up to the top of the gateway. It was capped with a double row of tiles, and right in the centre, right above the arch, a stone plaque with the top carved to look like a pointed roof bore the words:

YE TOWN
HOUSE

The houses to the left and the right of the Town House locked into the gateway. They were two-storeys high, flat-faced, and lattice windowed. They cast shadows over the gateway and they made it look small, dark, and old, and if it had been in Norwich or Ely I wouldn't have given it a second glance.

The men with the litter and the chests came up beside me, laid the chests on the ground and helped Oldfield to his feet. Then we turned to the left, grounded our pikes and muskets, and stood at ease. Captain Lacey and Lieutenant de Colville crossed the Market Place and entered the building opposite us. For several minutes the space between us and the building lay empty. Then twenty red-coated musketeers ambled out the door, formed two files, shouldered their muskets, and marched past the fountain – it looked like a stone cattle trough pushed against a short wall that bore two water spouts and the weathered blur of some ancient carving – then they marched through the top end of the Market Place, up Catherine Street, and on towards the square towers and the battlements that protect Catherine Port.

For a while I leant on my pike, yawned, and listened to the sound of water pouring into the fountain – it reminded me of little boys peeing in a pond. Then I craned my neck and tried to look behind the fountain, tried to look down Saint John's Street, but I couldn't see much – most of the view was blocked by a garden wall that formed part of the building opposite us. This building looked like an old church and it dominated the Market Place. It was two storeys high, but it appeared to be higher for the front was crowned with a pediment that reminded me of a Dutch gable, and it was topped with a stone cross. Behind the pediment a square tower took the height of the building to three storeys. The tiles on the tower formed a gentle swathe of hills and valleys, and like the tiles on so many of the roofs that faced onto the Market Place they wore a pale red on the hills where the sun was strongest, and a dark red in the valleys where the shadows lingered for much of the morning. High above the tower, a flag was teasing the wind. It was like the flag Ensign Wyndham was carrying – a red cross on a green ground with a circle of golden rays – but unlike the Ensign's flag, the edges had flapped themselves ragged, the colours had faded, and now it looked old and tired.

Brown stone edged the corners of the building, the windows and the pediment; and around the front door the same stone outlined an arch with a wedge-shaped capping stone that was carved to look like a woman's face. The front of the building had been plastered and whitewashed, but now it was brown with dust and speckled white, and some of it was flaking off, like dead skin.

In the tower, through the louvred window that formed a backdrop to the stone cross, I could see the outline of a large bell. Once it must have called the faithful to prayer, now it looked as though it would call us to fight. I turned to Sergeant Brandon, intending to ask him if it was an alarm bell, when he said: 'That's the Head Court of the Guard. When the Moors attack a cannon is fired from the Upper Castle and the great bell in Peterborough Tower is rung. The repeater bells on the Governor's Bastion, the Mole, and up there in the tower' – he nodded towards the louvred window – 'echo the alarm, and we all run to our muster stations if it's a general alarm. There are a number of different rings, different alarms. Some are for us, some are for the troopers, some are for the molemen and some are to warn the fleet – and you'll have to learn the lot in the next few days.'

I didn't know what to say. I felt as if he'd read my mind, and that was an eerie thought, an eerie feeling. I knew I had to respond, and I mumbled something about orders – something about thinking we'd be going up to the Upper Castle, to the Governor's House to get our orders. He stared at me for a moment, then he laughed. 'The Governor tells the Town Major what to do. And he tells the Captain of the Guard. And he tells our Captain. And he tells me, or the Lieutenant, or the Ensign. And we tell you. We won't be going anywhere near the Upper Castle. That's not for you and me.' Then he gave me a smile, a superior, knowing smile.

I nodded, looked at the ground and scuffed my shoes in the dirt. Then my eyes climbed out of the dirt and crawled up the brown arch of the Head Court of the Guard. The stone was criss-crossed, meshed like a lady's stockings. At head-height on both sides, the meshing ran into oblong stones. These stones were banded like garters. I began to think about Mistress Tate, began to wonder what it would be like to run my hand up her leg. Then I looked again at the woman's face in the wedge-shaped stone. It was soft and gentle and the eyes weren't dead as they are so often in statues. The eyes were open, alive, inviting – like her eyes. I began to think about lying in her bed, to think about her seeing me with my clothes off, and my face burst into a sweat. I closed my eyes and rubbed my brow. Lockhart dug me in the arm and said: 'If you're sweating like that now, you wait till the summer when the days are bloody hot.' And he laughed in my face.

I pulled away from that black hole, that toothy pit that is his mouth and I thought of it kissing her lips, kissing her hands – and it made my belly heave.

Then I began to wonder if he would be able to worm his way into her confidence, into her bed, into her body. The thought chilled my body and dried the sweat on my brow. I shivered for her, for the fate that lay in store for her. Then for some reason I began to think about predestination: the doctrine that says that everything we are going to do is predestined, preordained, because God knows everything – past, present and to come. He knows what we are going to do before we do it. So we might as well go out and do what we want to do because we can't change a single thing – everything is fixed, mortared in the mind of God.

I stole a glance at Lockhart. I don't know if he believes in predestination or has even heard of it – he doesn't pay any attention to the things of the spirit. 'The things of the flesh are what I'm interested in,' he said to me one night, and then he burst out laughing. I knew 'things' meant the 'things' between his legs, her legs, and I began to wonder if she would prefer him to me.

He was older than me. And taller. His hair was brown and mine was black. His eyes were blue dulled with grey, and mine were green with a swirl of orange. His skin was brown and pitted red, and mine was white, a white that burnt but did not brown. His shanks had withered and mine were slim and muscled. His bum had sagged and mine was round and firm; and I was wondering what she would think of him, think of me, and thinking I must ask her about predestination, when Captain Lacey and Lieutenant de Colville came down the steps and strode across the Market Place.

Sergeant Brandon called us to attention, and Captain Lacey said: 'Tomorrow we are to parade for the Governor in the Upper Castle, and he will inspect every man and every officer in this company.'

I half-turned and looked at Sergeant Brandon. His eyes were fixed on the Captain, and his body was rigid. I bit at my lips and smothered a laugh, and the Captain said: 'You are to report here at ten o'clock in the morning and we will escort the Mayor up to the castle. If we are invited we will return with his Excellency and the Mayor and attend divine service in the garrison church, the church of King Charles the Martyr.'

Lockhart hissed in my ear: 'Won't that be bloody lovely.'

I shrugged and the Captain said: 'This afternoon you will all have a bath and a haircut. You will trim your fingernails, clean your shoes, your weapons, and all your equipment. Then you will be fitted with your new uniforms. Lieutenant de Colville will hold an early inspection, tomorrow morning at nine o'clock – outside your lodgings in Jews Lane.' He turned to the Lieutenant and nodded, as if to add emphasis to his words. 'Tomorrow afternoon when we know our duties we may be assigned new lodgings. In the meantime these ones are close to the Head Court of the Guard and they will be very convenient.'

A minute or two later, we marched a few more yards up the Market Place and wheeled to the right – into the top end of Jews Lane. The two black hogs scampered down the lane. Crabtree nudged me with his elbow, and said: 'They'll be safe down here,' and he nodded at the hogs.

'Safe?'

'Hmm,' he said, and he smiled. 'Jews don't eat pork.'

I laughed to myself, and about halfway down the lane, where the houses became smaller, became hungry for a coat of whitewash, Sergeant Brandon yelled: 'Halt!' He told us the company was to be lodged in four houses, then he tapped Lockhart on the shoulder and said: 'I want you to look after Oldfield. I want you to make sure he does everything he has to do.' He paused. 'If I find something wrong, something left undone that ought to be done, I'll bloody have you.' And he smiled.

Inside the house I slipped my pike into the rack – it began at the doorway, ran through a wooden wall and ended in the back room close to the fireplace. Lockhart turned to me and said: 'Do you know what that bastard Brandon did?' I shook my head. 'He gave Oldfield two pikes – mine and his – and made him lay them on the cobbles at the side of the tower where I couldn't see them. Then he told him the two pikes were to be used to make a litter and he wasn't to let anyone have them – under any circumstances.' He paused for a moment, then his voice became louder, became laced with bitterness, and he said: 'He did it deliberately. He wanted me to be charged. Christ knows why. But that's what he wanted.'

17

Lieutenant de Colville walked up and down each rank three times. He inspected the front and back of every man – sent four away to polish their shoes again, forced two to borrow clean neck scarfs, and made one wipe smears of dirt off his scabbard – then he stood in front of Oldfield and peered at him for several seconds. 'You are dismissed,' he said. 'You look sick. And I don't want you fainting in front of the Governor. And tomorrow if you don't look any better you are to report to the infirmarium. And Doctor Lawrence can have a look at you.'

I shuddered. They say only one man in five ever comes out of the infirmarium alive. They say it is a place where the dying go to die. And no man in his sane mind, no man with a desire to live, would ever go there of his own free will. Oldfield's shoulders sagged. He walked down the ranks in silence, and the end of his pike scoured a line in the dirt. Then he shut the door behind us, and Brandon turned to the Lieutenant. 'I'll make sure he goes, sir. First thing in the morning.'

The Lieutenant shook his head. 'Before you do that, you make sure he's not malingering. I wouldn't like to think of him up there having a rest.'

'Malingering, sir?'

'Pretending to be sick.'

Brandon smiled, and as the Lieutenant turned away from him, the smile gave way to a smirk and he said: 'There'll be no fear of that. You can rely on me, sir.'

We marched up Jews Lane, halted in front of the Head Court of the Guard and turned to face the Town House. Brandon stood us at ease and we began to wait. In the night when he came to tell us to brush our hats and take off the old ribbons and sew on new green ones, he was calling the Town House the Town Hall. As I looked at it now, shaded my eyes and tried to peer through the gateway, it didn't look big enough to be a hall, and I was thinking there must be more to it than I could see, when the man next to me doubled over, sneezed, and sprayed spit all over the front of his new coat.

Our new coats are red with sea-green lining, and the sleeves are turned up and buttoned back to make sea-green cuffs. The buttons are plain, are cast in a soft brown metal that carries the dents and scratches of a past life.

The hems on our waisted undercoats ride three inches higher than the hems on our coats, and the fabrics are reversed: the sea-green lining is on the outside and the heavy red cloth is on the inside rubbing against our white shirts.

Our breeches, garters, stockings and shoe laces are green, and they almost match the lining. Our neck scarfs look white, not a clean snow-white but a dull oyster-white, like the few inches of shirt sleeve that puffs round each wrist.

To my mind we are like butterflies. We have shed our grey coats, our grey chrysalises, and soon we will stretch our arms, stretch our wings, flutter and fly, and float on the wind.

When I was young I used to think I'd like to float with the butterflies, with the clouds of colour that used to rise from the cornfields, and I remember my Mother calling me a dreamer.

Some of the men have been calling Billy Foster a dreamer, and some have been calling him Silly Billy – when he cries in the night, cries for his mother. The word Silly is never stressed, it's soft and soothing, almost affectionate, and now a lot of the older men mother him, and their eyes are gentle, protective.

I turned round. He was twirling his drumsticks through the fingers of both hands at the same time. It was a trick he'd only just mastered and he was grinning to himself and concentrating hard. I grinned and turned back to the front. His uniform is the exact opposite of ours; green coat with red cuffs, breeches, stockings, laces and hat band. It's almost as though he'll have to undergo a metamorphosis, a change that will be as big as that word, to become a man, to become a red butterfly that cannot fly – fly from Sergeant Brandon.

A green lizard about the size of two fingers came out of the shadows, crawled along the ridge of the tiles on top of the gateway and turned to face the sun. I lifted my face and bathed in some of that same sunshine. A grey mouth rose from behind the ridge. For a moment it looked like a rising moon, leached of colour. Then the mouth opened and snapped on the little lizard and its legs swam in the air. The mouth became a head, became a large grey lizard. He looked down on us for a moment or two, and the little legs stopped swimming, then he slid back down the ridge.

Sergeant Brandon walked along our front rank. He too had changed. He was no longer a grey caterpillar or a grey lizard. He was red coated like us, but I couldn't see him as a butterfly. The fabric of his coat was heavier, more expensive than ours, and the seams had sprouted silver lace, and he'd tied some green ribbons to his halberd. But behind the lace, the ribbons and the green breeches, he hadn't changed. He was still Sergeant Brandon, and with our coats off we were just like that little lizard: sea-green and soft bellied.

A few minutes later we opened ranks and Ensign Wyndham marched out the front and stood at ease. His ensign curled in on itself and hung limp – it reminded me of the flowers of the trumpet tree and the way they curl and wilt when they begin to die. As Captain Lacey inspected the musketeers I thought about dying, dying for this piece of painted cloth, then I began to understand what I hadn't understood on the boat: the ensign was a symbol of our determination to defend Tangiers. We wouldn't be fighting, be dying for a flag, we'd be dying for the town, for the place, for the right to parade in this Market Place – for the right to call it English. And that was why the blood-red cross, the cross of England was on the flag.

Then a company of musketeers marched past us. Their shoulders had slouched and their coats had faded, were now dark pink with circles of red – spots of blood – behind the buttons. In their hats some of them were wearing tin badges with small red crosses. For a moment I couldn't make out the design, then I saw it was a lamb, the Lamb of God, the symbol for Christ, and the red cross was part of a flag. Somewhere I could remember reading that this was also a symbol for Saint John the Baptist, the man who prepared the way for our Lord. I was wondering why they would choose to wear such a thing in their hats, wondering if they had prepared the way for us, when Captain Lacey began to inspect the pikemen in our front rank.

He was followed by Lieutenant de Colville, and both were grinding the ends of their partisans into the dirt when they stopped to look at a man.

The Captain was wearing a new wig with long brown curls that lay about his shoulders. This was the only change any of the officers had made. They were still wearing red coats with sea-green cuffs and sea-green waistcoats. The fabric looked heavy, looked as though it would be too hot in the summertime. The sun was catching the gold lace sewn into the seams, and as they moved they appeared to glitter. Their breeches, garters and stockings were bone-white – the white was made more intense, starker, by the high sheen on their black shoes. Each was distinguished by his gorget, and each was wearing a neck scarf over the top of it. The Captain's neck scarf was lace; the Lieutenant's was linen edged with lace; and the Ensign's was plain linen with white cross-stitching. Each of them gave me the impression he was trying to hide his gorget, his symbol of rank. It looked like false modesty and it did not suit any of them. I began to think if I was an officer I'd show it off. I'd wear it over my neck scarf, and then I realised I was thinking nonsense, day-dreaming. A man from the ranks never becomes an officer. And just because we now have red coats, and look more like them and they look more like us, the gap between us still looms wide and deep, and it can never be crossed, unless a man comes into a fortune and buys himself a commission.

At the end of the inspection we closed ranks and stood at ease, and the

Captain said something to Sergeant Brandon. I watched the smile come onto his face, and I have to admit we did look smart. Our coats were brand new. There'd been a lot of them in the sewing-room, and the tailor was able to fit us, able to make us look like proper soldiers, soldiers-of-foot. Our old grey coats were too large: mine slopped about my shoulders, the Sergeant's was faded, and somehow they never looked right. I brushed at my sleeve, brushed away a speck of white fluff, and then I remembered the buttons on the Sergeant's coat, on the day I was conscripted. They were grey and they bore the image of the Lamb of God; and the cross was grey, was drained of blood.

I half-turned and peered at the buttons on the Sergeant's red coat. They were cast in pewter, were round and plain, and they matched the buttons on the officer's coats.

As the minutes dragged I tried to link the Sergeant's Lamb of God buttons to the badges on the musketeers' hats. I knew there had to be a link, a thread, but what that thread was, and how it sewed one to the other was a mystery, a mystery of faith.

18

A few minutes later the sound of ringing filled the courtyard in front of the Town House. Then a tall thin man laboured down the path. In his hand he held a brass bell. He swung it up in the air and shook it at the potted plants, then he stood in the middle of the gateway – was framed by the arch like a saint in a stained glass window – and yelled: 'Hear ye! Hear ye! Make way for the Mayor, His Honour the Mayor, and the members of the Corporation of the Royal City of Tangiers.' He looked to the left and then to the right, and he rang his bell again. Then he strutted across the empty Market Place, bowed to Captain Lacey and turned to face the gateway.

I was the last man in our back rank. I was standing about two feet from the first musketeer in their back rank. Sergeant Brandon was standing right behind me, and Sergeant Owen was standing beside him. They'd been talking for some time and their voices had drifted in and out of my head as I watched the Town Crier, and I wasn't taking much notice of them, when Brandon leant forward, breathed in my ear and yelled: 'Parade! Attention!'

I jumped, slammed my pike against my shoulder and rocked backwards and forwards. He dug me in the ribs and hissed: 'Stay still.'

Twelve men in purple gowns came through the gateway one by one, then they paired off, formed a procession, and walked towards the Captain. Owen leant to the side, peered through the gap between us and the musketeers and said: 'Common Councillors. I can see a couple of new ones. And I bet they're like all the rest, common as muck.'

Brandon grunted and said: 'Did you see that pile of muck behind the fountain? And those hogs?' He paused. 'They can spend money on gowns but they can't spend money on keeping the Market Place clean.' He paused again. 'I went up to Catherine Gate last night for a few minutes and it was a bloody disgrace. Great piles of rubbish everywhere. And rats and seagulls, and black slime oozing down the road. And the smell? It bloody near turned my stomach.'

Six more men came through the archway and paired off. Their gowns were like the aldermen's in Ely, red with fur trims. They were wearing black hats and carrying nosegays: small bunches of flowers spiced with sweet-smelling herbs. Behind me Brandon was laughing, then he said: 'They'll need those if we go up by Catherine Gate.' I giggled. I couldn't help it – it just bubbled out of me.

He dug me in the ribs again and hissed: 'Don't listen to other people's conversations. It's bloody rude.'

I swallowed my giggles and watched the next man come through the archway. He was all in black and I would have sworn he was a clergyman except the lace at his neck was too fancy, too fine, and there was something about his walk, something that wasn't humble or pious. Then Owen said: 'I hear there's been a row while we've been away – between the Governor and the Recorder. Apparently he doesn't like the Irish, and he's had a few of them arrested for being dead drunk. He thinks they should appear in his court and the Governor doesn't agree.'

Brandon laughed but didn't say anything, then Owen said: 'Did you see those musketeers, the Irish ones who went past a few minutes ago? Bloody typical. Sloppy as hell, and still half asleep. And I could smell the drink on them.'

Behind the Recorder came two men. Both were wearing black gowns – over red coats, breeches and stockings – and both were carrying white wands with gold crowns. Behind them came a man in a long red robe, trimmed with fur. He was wearing a black hat, and carrying a large nosegay, and from his neck hung a gold chain with a pendant shaped like a tear drop.

Brandon edged forward, peered over my shoulder, and said: 'I see that bastard Bland is still the Mayor. I thought his twelve months were up.'

Owen murmured: 'So did I.' Then he laughed. 'They tell me the two of them have finally agreed on something.'

'Who have?'

'Him and Lord Middleton. They've decided their order of precedence. And now the Mayor sits in the front left-hand pew of the church, and the Governor sits in the front right-hand pew.'

Brandon grunted. 'And they're supposed to be running this bloody place.'

Owen didn't say anything, and two or three seconds slipped by. Then the procession shuffled to a halt in front of our ranks. Captain Lacey lifted his hat, bowed to the Mayor, and then to the members of the Corporation. The members were full of dignity, full of importance, and they responded with deep bows. But Bland did nothing for several seconds, then he raised his hat a few inches and inclined his head.

Brandon let out a soft whistle and Owen muttered: 'The rude bastard.'

The Captain and the Mayor spoke for a moment or two, then the Mayor appeared to wave him on – maybe wave is the wrong word for the palm of his hand was open and the movement was more like the bowling of a ball, underarm. It was a gracious movement, very polite, I couldn't fault it, but I knew – and I guess everyone watching knew

– that the place of honour was at the rear, and that was where Mister Bland was going to remain.

Sergeant Brandon yelled in my ear again, and we stamped to attention and turned to the left. Captain Lacey walked to the head of the column, and then, with Billy beating his drum, beating a crisp pace, he led us past the fountain and up Catherine Street – where a couple of sheep were drinking from the water conduit. Then he made a sharp right-hand turn and we marched into Saint Barbara's Street. For a few yards the street was cobbled and humped to speed the flow of rainwater, then it narrowed and cramped us together. As the cobbles gave way to bricks, and the bricks gave way to dirt, to ruts and potholes, the street became greasy and the man in front of me stumbled and swore. I flung out my hand, tried to take his weight, tried to steady him, but he was too heavy for me and my feet began to slide.

Sergeant Brandon grabbed me by the neck, carried me forward, and dropped me on my feet without missing a beat of the drum – and he said: 'You make sure you brush that dirt off. As soon as it's dry.' And he pointed to my shoes. Then he turned to Sergeant Owen and said: 'What the bloody hell did we have to come this way for?'

Owen stepped away from a heap of rubbish, away from the stench of dog pee and rotting cabbage. 'They say all this muck' – he nodded towards the rubbish – 'has blocked up the common sewer, somewhere down by the outfall, by the beach, and the water has backed up and flooded some of the houses on the lower levels. They say it's full of turds, human turds, and the smell is bloody awful. I hear that once it gets into the walls it stains the whitewash and the smell lingers, and you can't get it out. And with all this rain' – he pointed up to the sky, to the grey clouds that were beginning to assemble, beginning to chill the day and block out the sun – 'even if you could wash it out, you couldn't get it dry.'

'But what's that got to do with us coming this way?'

'Bland wants to make an official visit. Wants to express his concern to the residents. Wants to make it look as though he's doing something. That's what I heard.'

Brandon laughed. 'Concern? The man wouldn't know the meaning of the word.' He paused. 'Unless of course it was something to do with one of those warehouses of his – the ones down by the Watergate. And then it would only be to make sure nobody was trying to break in and steal something. All this' – he waved his hand back towards the procession – 'is just show. Just dressing up in pretty robes, and it doesn't mean a bloody thing.'

We marched on a little more, and as the downward slope began to slow our pace, Owen said: 'Even if Bland did want to do something about that sewer, I don't think the Governor would let him close the sluice gate up there under the walls by Johnson's Battery. That's the lowest point, the natural valley between the two hills, and if that was blocked nothing would get washed away. And in a couple of days the stench by the infirmarium would be bloody awful.' He laughed. 'I would think Lord Middleton's about to tell Bland that the Corporation has to spend some money and unblock the sewer. And if they won't do that he'll have it done on their behalf, and he'll charge them for it. And you can guarantee that any soldier who is charged with anything in the next month will be found guilty and sentenced to be a scavenger – a drain cleaner – and it won't cost Middleton a bloody thing.'

Brandon laughed. My thoughts ran away from them and I began to think about Saint Barbara's Street, to think about the name.

I'd never heard of Saint Barbara, and I began to wonder if Barbara's might be Portuguese for Barabbas, the man Pontius Pilate wanted to crucify in place of Christ. I was trying to remember if Barabbas stopped robbing people, followed Christ, and became a saint, when I saw the chapel. It had been robbed of its roof and all its innards. Then I saw a shrine with a female face and Latin words, and I knew it had nothing to do with Barabbas.

Then Billy Foster double-beat his drum and we all stamped to a sudden halt. Captain Lacey came storming down the line. Brandon and Owen turned around, followed him with their eyes, and Owen said: 'We've lost the bloody Corporation.'

Brandon laughed. 'Pity we couldn't have lost them a bit further on, where the turds will be nice and deep.'

Owen laughed. I giggled to myself, bit at my lips, and looked again at the chapel. It was about twelve feet wide and twenty feet long with a square bell-tower in the right-hand corner. The wooden doors and shutters had vanished and this should have filled the chapel with light, but it looked cold and dark. It made me shiver, and I began to think that all the gloom, all the sins of the past were still trapped within those four stone walls. About halfway down the inside wall, on the left-hand side, two stone pillars supported a stone balcony with a door that looked as though it opened into the first floor of the house next door. Below the balcony half a dozen brown hens were scratching among stacks of hay and heaps of rubbish, and on the pile of broken tiles that blocked the front door to waist-height, a brown rooster was standing guard. The four windows in the right-hand wall looked onto a narrow lane. It might have been four feet wide and it led to the back of the chapel where trees and some sort of bramble had smothered a stone fence and covered the end of the lane in shade. The bell had gone from the bell-tower, and so had the birds that had nested in the open space beneath the tent of orange tiles. And now that space was patched with sky – some grey, some bright blue – and wisps of straw were blowing in the wind.

Two strings of stone ran up the front right-hand corner of the chapel.

They were no more than six inches wide and an inch deep but as they picked up the sun and cast shadows onto the stone they created an illusion: they made it look as though the bell-tower grew out of the earth, out of the dirt of life.

The shrine fitted between these two strings of stone and at first glance it looked like a small stone porch: three feet wide and five feet high. The bottom was flat, like a shelf or step, and it supported two columns. These were round and slender and they shone like black marble; and they supported a canopy that was draped with stone flowers and topped with a cross. A piece of white marble completed the shrine. It was so white, so pure, so stark between its pillars of black that it looked unreal, and it made me think of innocence, the innocence of virgins, and the thrusting that will come to them in the blackness of the night. It was carved to the depth of an inch or so, like a plaque, and it showed the face of a young girl with a halo. Her hands were pulling the folds of her dress to her crutch, and she looked as though she was afraid to lose the treasure that lay between her legs.

Deflowering they call it. And it spots the sheets with blood. I was imagining white sheets – I've never slept between sheets and I don't know much about them – when my eye focused on the flowers. They were dark red and tiny – star-shaped – and there were masses of them, like wild flowers at the height of summer. They were splattering the white marble with red, red spots of blood, and I began to think someone must have seen this in his mind, and chosen the colour deliberately. It was symbolic, symbolic of a love that was – or wasn't – I couldn't make up my mind which, and then I saw behind the flowers, behind the spots of blood. She was protected by two pure white cannons. One was shown sideways, in profile; and the other was pointing straight at me, and it looked like a cock stiff with excitement. Both the cannons were mounted on small wooden carriages, like the ones on the *Salisbury*, and in front of them lay piles of cannon balls, and they too seemed to fit into this strange mixture of innocence, fear and lust.

The vases with the flowers sat on the shelf, next to a brass lantern covered with soot. Below the shelf, a brown stone carried an inscription in Latin. I could remember singing hymns in Latin, and I thought I had a few words, but the only ones I could recognise out of a hundred or more were: *Ora pro nobis* – pray for us. Below this stone came a small black stone. It was engraved with a crown and more words in Latin, and I couldn't make any sense of them.

I was thinking she must be Saint Barbara, and wondering why she needed flowers and a lamp to see at night – for the mason had forgotten to open her eyes and she was blind – and I turned to Lockhart and opened my mouth.

Then I saw Sergeant Brandon looking straight at me.

I shut my mouth and looked to the front, looked again at the virginal

Barbara – if that is what she was – and Brandon marched up to me and
breathed into my ear: 'And what were you going to say?'

I remembered Oldfield saying: 'A soldier-of-foot knows nothing. That's
what he knows. Nothing. Then he can't make any mistakes can he?' I
turned to Brandon and said: 'I was going to ask who she was, sir.'

'Sergeant,' he hissed, 'Sergeant, not sir.'

I bit my lips and nodded.

'That's Saint Barbara. She was a virgin. And she became a Christian
and her father didn't like that and he chopped off her head.' He looked
at the plaque. 'Would have been a great pity, a waste, if she really did
look like that.' And he grinned to himself. 'That's her shrine. There used
to be other shrines for other saints outside all the churches and chapels,
and on every street corner. The priests used to look after them. The ones
who lived in that house there' – he nodded to the one by the chapel –
'they looked after this one and they collected the money.' He paused.
'There aren't many shrines left now. Our men destroyed most of them,
some years ago. They don't like living with popery, and nor do I.'

'Then why did they leave this one?'

He smiled. 'I think there's still a bit of superstition deep inside every
man. She's the patron saint of gunners, that's what the Portuguese say.
And we've a few gunners, out there on the Mole, in York Castle and up
by Peterborough Tower, and when you've seen a cannon blow up, blow
one of the gunners to bits, you'll know why they say their prayers.' He
sucked at his lips. 'A lot of men call their cock a gun or a cannon, and
when they've got the pox and it won't fire any more, they sneak up here
with a few flowers or a candle.' He laughed. 'Every year the priests have
a procession for her, on December the fourth – that's her feast day. It
starts down there at that cathedral of theirs and it ends up here, and it
blocks the street for a couple of hours. And I always watch it.'

I looked at him, put a puzzled look upon my face. He smiled and said:
'If a man's in the procession, and he's not a bloody papist, then he's got
the pox. And if he wants some of this' – he ran his hand up my bum – 'you
tell him, no. And you keep your breeches on. Otherwise you'll be up here
talking to her, before you're much older.' He nodded at Saint Barbara.
And somehow he made her seem like a friend, an intimate friend.

19

Saint Barbara's Street led us into Sebastian Place where large paving stones covered the common sewer. The stones were wet, green with slime, and they slowed our feet, made us slip and slide – and a couple of times I slid the end of my pike to the ground and used it to steady my feet.

Cannon Street was steep, narrow, and free from slime, for the sewer still followed the bed of the ancient stream and now it was running behind the houses. We couldn't see the sewer or any evidence of flooding, but we could smell the stench, the miasma. It was putrid, like rotting flesh, and it caught my breath and made me gag.

It would have been easier to go up to the left, up a street called Castlehill Foot and through one of the sallyports in Middleton's Line – the new walls, the new lines of defence that link the upper walls to the lower walls and enclose both the castles – and then we would have been about three-quarters of the way up the steep slope and right in front of the wall that protects the main approach to the Upper Castle. But yesterday, in the Head Court of the Guard, the Town Major had jumped to his feet and yelled: 'A guard of honour goes where the guest of honour wants to go! And if he wants to walk the bloody sewers, to paddle his toes in the turds, that's his right!' Then he added, in a voice so quiet it almost escaped the ears listening in the outer room: 'And you are going to go to with him – Captain Lacey.'

I let this gossip slide out of my head, and as the lanes twisted and turned, flowed into Francifco Street, into Maria Street, and brought us closer to the sea, the head of my pike skimmed past the sign of The Red Dragon, and I began to think of all the taverns I'd seen since yesterday. I could remember about twenty-two, but some of the names escaped me.

Few of them had written signs, for few men can read, so most of the signs were pictures painted on wooden boards and hung near the door. The two in the Market Place were obvious: The Sign of the Castle and The King's Head. And so was The Green Man in Taverne Street, Queen Catherine in Catherine Street, and The Cannon just along from Saint Barbara's chapel. I couldn't make any sense of the three gold balls in Jews Lane or the woman with the headscarf in Maria Street. I thought she might be the Virgin Mary, but she looked too old to be a virgin – too knowing – and I was trying to think who she might be, when we burst into a large open area and wheeled to the left.

Behind us a high brick wall shaded a garden, a house, and five apple trees made bare by winter and gaunt by hard pruning.

The area was cobbled and shaped like a triangle with the top cut off. The city wall ran across the cut, and behind it lay the terraces, the path from the Watergate to the quay, and the beach where we landed yesterday. To our left a row of houses locked an old church into a tight embrace. Hooks held the doors wide open and light was streaming into the body of the church, was outlining three rows of palliasses and a wall fitted with pike racks and pegs for hats and coats.

Straight ahead lay the last side – Middleton's Line – and high in the right corner where the line met the city wall and half-hid the roof of a building that looked like a guardhouse, a sentry was pacing up and down.

The area felt like a dead end, like a killing ground, and I was wondering if it had a name, when a young girl came out of one of the houses and sat down on a stone mushroom. I know that's not the proper name for them, but that's what we used to call them when they sat on the edge of Ely Field and simmered in the summer sun. I remember pulling them close together, criss-crossing them with wood and bracken, and stacking them with sheaves of corn – with wheat – that could not be threshed till the miller was ready to mill it. I could remember the mice trying to climb the stone stems – jumping high, trying to reach the underside of the mushroom and falling back to the ground, to the stubble that lay unburnt around these stacks of gold – and I used to think they could smell the grain, smell the food that lay two or three feet above their noses. I looked again at the girl with her long black skirts draped around the stem, and I was thinking the mice would be able to run up her skirts, and wondering if I would ever run my hands up skirts like hers, when she looked up and smiled. She was older than I first thought, thirteen, maybe fourteen, and I smiled back. She blushed and looked down.

To her right a small wooden plaque, half-framed in the gentle curve of her head and shoulder, hung on the wall. It said:

PAUL BARTHOLOMEW
Apothecary and Herbalist

PURVEYOR OF PRESERVES, SWEETMEATS
AND HERBAL CONDIMENTS

Late of the Bristol Infirmary and now resident on
THE LITTLE PARADE
within the environs of Spiritu Sancto
(The old church of the Holy Spirit)

We halted in the left-hand corner of the Little Parade, a few feet along from the church, and as our first rank began to file through the narrow sallyport in Middleton's Line, I turned to look again at the girl, and my eyes drifted into hers. I know they say silly things about angels, about them being good, being perfect, and floating through the air – and I've never believed a word of it – but now I could feel myself floating through the air, floating around her pale face, her brown eyes, her white cap. Then I was wrapped in a haze of angel wings, of golden haloes that slipped onto our fingers and became rings of promise, rings of wedding. And I wanted to walk with the angels, talk with the angels.

Then I was moving and stumbling, and Brandon was jabbing me in the ribs and saying: 'Look to the bloody front! And watch what you're doing!' Then he was jabbing me in the ribs again, and my angel vanished, and I was left with a couple of sore ribs.

I wondered if Adam had sore ribs when he woke up and found God had taken one of them, had used it to make him a woman, a wife, a mate who would take his seed, would make him into a whole man, a complete man – a man who would see his seed burst into life, new life.

Then I wanted to be like Adam, I wanted to be a man.

20

Middleton's Line gave way to a large open area. It was divided in two by a head-high fence of pointed stakes that stretched from the guardhouse by the sallyport to the walls on the far side of the ground. In the night Brandon had called this whole area the Old Parade and said it could hold two thousand men and three troops-of-horse.

As we lined up and reordered our ranks in the square area that lay to the right of the fence, Captain Lacey and Lieutenant de Colville walked back to the guardhouse and spoke to the sentry.

In the area beyond the fence – an area that was shaped like an oblong and was twice the size of our area – a Lieutenant was drilling a company of musketeers.

The earth in our area was black and stony and it looked lumpy, like a field that has been ploughed, allowed to fallow, and then close-cropped by sheep. There was no sign of any sheep but the earth was marbled with their droppings and it looked as though this area was used as a cattle yard – at night – and I couldn't help thinking they'd go hungry, for the grass was nothing more than a mass of wet roots with a blush of green.

Straight opposite us, in the far right-hand corner of the Old Parade, York Castle dozed like a fat old lady who has found a warm corner, a warm place in the sunshine. The keep was a square tower with battlements and it overlooked the Old Mole. It was huge – maybe six or seven storeys high – and it dwarfed the house and the warehouse that snuggled into its far side. The house was two-storeyed, with a pair of hip roofs that locked a brick chimney into a red-tiled embrace, and it would have looked at home almost anywhere in England. But the warehouse was different: bare walls, a tiled roof and a string of slit windows close to the eaves, made it look like a three-storeyed blockhouse; and it reminded me of the buildings at Whitby.

A curtain of stone walls and round towers butted into the keep and enclosed the house, the warehouse, and an inner courtyard. The walls that faced onto the Old Parade were protected by another curtain, a lower curtain of towers and walls that grew out of a deep ditch: a dry moat. The fence ran along the outer edge of the moat. It didn't look as though it was meant to stop the Moors. It looked more like a barrier that was meant to stop horses, cattle and sheep falling over the edge and breaking their legs or their necks.

The entrance to the castle was hidden by an old church. The church appeared to be small, but then I realised it was being dwarfed by the keep, and the gabled end of the roof was peeping over the top of the thirty-foot-high wall that lay to our right – and it was about the size of the garrison church.

Brandon paced up and down, yawned, looked towards the guardhouse and said: 'In the old days, before Lord Middleton built his wall and cut off that bit on the other side, we used to call the whole area the Parade. You could stand over there' – he pointed to the centre of the oblong area, a distance of about ninety yards – 'and see down the gulley. See where the sewer goes underground. And see up the other side to the cathedral, the houses, and the lower end of the far wall. Now you're lucky to see a few houses up there in the top corner by Irish Battery – unless you're right down the end of the Old Parade, in that gap between the walls, where you can just see a bit of the sea.' And he yawned again.

We waited some more. There was no sign of the Mayor, the Corporation or Captain Lacey. I closed my eyes, began to drift back to Jews Lane and the straw pallet that had felt so hard in the night. I'd missed the swaying of the ship, the gentle rocking, and I was wondering if we would ever sleep again in hammocks – shape the air to the shape of our bones and let our toes wiggle free – when the boom of a cannon exploded in my ears. It made me jump. Made me swear. Made me bite my tongue.

I sucked at my tongue, tried to suck away the pain. High on the wall to our right the next cannon continued the salute and the next one echoed it. Then the first cannon fired again. It was the same battery that had saluted us yesterday. For a moment or two white smoke hung in the windless air, then it rolled off the parapet and dropped down the inside of the wall. As it hit the ground, came out of the shade, out of the shadows, it lightened and billowed upwards. Then it vanished, like fog in the sunshine, and the heady smell of gunpowder, of raw sulphur, drifted through our ranks.

A few minutes later Captain Lacey returned and we marched across the square, through the gap in the fence, and halted beside the church. We turned to the right, faced the fence, faced the front end of the church – the roof was pointed and capped with an empty arch that might once have held a small bell – and grounded our pikes. Then Sergeant Brandon yelled: 'You can talk while we wait, but don't move your feet.'

The gap between the church and the lower curtain-wall revealed the iron chains of a drawbridge. It spanned the dry-ditch and linked the castle's entrance-tunnel to a stone tower that stood close to the side of the church. In the shadows below the drawbridge the battered walls had crumbled and the earth was not dry. It was wet with mud, thick with weeds, and it needed protecting, needed filling with four-pointed spikes – the ones that always land with one point sticking straight up. I could see them filling the moat, taking the place of water and spiking feet, spiking legs, spiking eyes – spiking death.

Captain Lacey walked over to Sergeant Owen. They stood with their heads almost touching for a couple of moments, then Owen said something to two of his musketeers, and they followed him through the narrow gap in the fence, up the steps, and into the old church.

I swung my arm round and round in a circle – eased the ache in my shoulder, and watched a line of men come through the sallyport. Each man was carrying a sack of grain on his back. As they walked through the main gap in the fence and began to cross our part of the Old Parade, I twisted round, watched them stoop, watched them vanish into a long low building.

Two of these buildings lined the edge of the Old Parade. Both wore black shutters, and I was thinking they looked blind, dead-eyed, when Lockhart said: 'Did you ever see so many bloody churches in one place in all your life?'

I twisted round, shook my head, and said: 'I must have seen eight or nine in the last twenty-four hours.'

Crabtree leant towards us and said: 'I don't know what they need this one for.' And he shook his head. 'I would have pulled it down if I was in charge – opened up the field of fire. And if the Moors ever got this far they could never hide behind it.'

'That has been thought of,' Sergeant Brandon said, and he edged close to me, so close I could smell his sweat, smell the lye that still lingered in his clean shirt. 'And there is a plan. Of course there's a plan. And it's this. We're going to wait for the Moors to get close, then we're going to blow it up. And hopefully, we'll blow some of them up at the same time. And it should be a good show.' Then he laughed. 'You don't understand why I'm laughing do you?'

I shook my head and he smiled. 'That isn't a church. That's the playhouse, and sometimes the plays are called shows.' He smiled again. 'And despite that broken capping stone up there – the one on top of the bell-housing, the one that looks like the base of a cross – I don't think it ever was a church.' He paused. 'The Portuguese put crosses on a lot of their buildings. You might have seen the one on the Head Court of the Guard, and there's another on the old customs house down by the Old Mole. I doubt if either of them was built as a church. I think the Portuguese put up the crosses to remind God they needed looking after. But it never did them much good – in my opinion.' Then he turned to Lockhart. 'You were right about there being too many bloody churches. I counted fifteen once, and that didn't include all the little chapels. You don't see many chapels now. Most of them were built into the corner of a house, and now they're part of the house – and you'd never know.'

'What about that one we saw a few minutes ago?' I said. 'That one up there in Saint Barbara's Street.'

'For a long time it was used as a hay barn. We had three troops-of-horse in the first few years, and there was never enough dry storage. Then it got caught up in that silly bloody row with the Portuguese Fathers . . .'

His words dribbled into silence, and we both watched Sergeant Owen and his two men come down the steps. They were carrying rags – bundles of torn clothing.

'Now what the hell is that all about?' Brandon said, in a soft voice that sounded like the gentle mutterings of a man who is used to talking to himself.

The three of them marched to the end of the column, stood at ease and laid their bundles on the ground. Captain Lacey gave Owen a curt nod. Brandon grinned, then he said: 'It's an act. A bloody act. That's what it is.'

Lockhart frowned and stared at him for several seconds. Then the frown gave way to puzzlement and he said: 'Act? Is there going to be an act in the playhouse?'

Brandon leant towards me. 'What? What did he say?'

'He was asking about the playhouse. Asking if they're going to put on a play – put on an act – in there.'

'Yes,' he said, 'of course they are. We have plays all the time. We're always looking for more men to take part. Especially young men, men who would make a pretty little girl.' And he grinned at me.

I bit my lips and watched the Mayor's procession come through the sallyport. Then he said: 'A couple of years ago we had a company of players over from Spain. Their English was poor, but their acting was good, so good they could carry you off to another place for a couple of hours.' He sighed. 'Most of their plays started in the late afternoon when the day was beginning to cool, and I can still remember the one they called *The Tartar Lady*. The leading lady was ugly. Fat nose. Warts. Black hair on her chin, and bags under her eyes. But when she heaved her bosom, the men whistled, clapped, and stamped their feet – and they bloody loved her. They really did.' And he sighed again.

As the procession came onto our part of the Old Parade, Sergeant Owen screamed: 'Company – attention! About turn! Stand at ease.'

A hush settled on our ranks – an uneasy hush.

Brandon muttered in my ear: 'What's he playing at?'

Lacey lifted his hat, bowed, and in a clear voice that carried through the ranks he said: 'May I welcome you sir to York Castle.' And he bowed again. 'My men have obtained some rags. I thought our shoes needed cleaning before we approached His Excellency. But then I remembered your good self and the members of your Corporation. And we have waited so that you – if it is your pleasure – may clean your shoes while the rags are still clean.' He signed to Sergeant Owen and his two men, and they began to hand out the rags.

My shoes were spotted with mud. Some of it had flicked onto my stockings, and I was thinking the Captain was being very thoughtful when Brandon said: 'The cunning bastard.' And he began to chuckle to himself.

I turned and looked at him. He grinned and said: 'Keep watching. It's not often you'll see something like this.'

Then Sergeant Owen and his men collected the rags, and Captain Lacey said: 'It will take some time for my men to clean their shoes, and the ends of their pikes. And then I want to make another quick inspection. I want to impress His Excellency. We all' – he waved his hand at us in an airy manner – 'want to impress His Excellency. And not wanting to delay Your Honour, to make you late for your appointed time, I would most humbly suggest you go ahead.' He bowed again and gestured with his hand.

For several seconds the Mayor looked at him with frozen eyes, then he gave a curt nod to the Town Crier and the procession headed towards the granary. Captain Lacey came close to our ranks and hissed: 'You have two minutes to get them clean.'

Owen and his men ran down the ranks. The rags flew from hand to hand and the dirt vanished. The men grabbed the rags, and as they ran back to the playhouse, Sergeant Brandon screamed: 'Attention!'

Then he leant towards me and whispered: 'And now Captain Lacey will go to the back of the column, to the place of honour. And that bastard Bland won't play any more of his silly bloody games with him.' And he giggled in my ear.

Ten seconds later as we pounded across the Old Parade at double time, he whispered: 'We're going to get right in behind him – right up his bum. And that path is too narrow for him to let us pass.' He smacked his left hand against the knuckles of his right hand – made a clapping sound, made it sound as though he was applauding, was enjoying, a great performance.

We pounded past the granary; past a cluster of small houses; through the crumbling remains of a stone wall that looked as though it had been mined for stone; through plots of earth – still staked and heavy with vines and long grey pods that had split, curled, and shed their beans – and onto a gravelled path that struggled around the rocky outcrops. As the path grew steeper it dragged at our feet and slowed our pace. It made my heart pound and shortened my breath, and as Ensign Wyndham passed through the lower wall and caught up with the Mayor, it brought me out in a sweat.

Then the path, in a dying burst of madness, ran up a steep ramp embanked in stone, and came to an abrupt halt.

As the wooden drawbridge came down, locked into the end of the ramp and exposed the gate to the Upper Castle, the Town Crier rang his bell and walked forward. His pace had lost the spring of the Market Place and he looked to be feeling his age.

The gate – the entry portal – sat halfway up the right-hand side of a high stone wall. Both ends of the wall were protected by stone bastions. They swelled at the base and then they split into roots, gripped the rocks and filled the fissures – and this made them look as though they'd grown out of the natural outcrops of rock. The wall and the bastions enclosed the drawbridge and the end of the ramp in a U-shaped embrace. Through the battlements of the right-hand bastion, long-barrelled cannons with round black eyes watched two ships beat their way into the Straits.

The Governor's House sat behind the left-hand end of the wall and it overlooked the left bastion. It appeared to have been enlarged several times, to be a marriage of different styles and different heights, and some parts looked old, looked decayed.

From the corner of the right-hand bastion, a wall ambled down the hill. The inside of the wall formed a straight line and it splayed to my right. The outside was jagged and broken by a series of towers and bulges that made the parapet, where the sentries were walking up and down, look like a chain of small wedge-shaped islands. The wall ended in a square tower that overlooked the end of the Old Parade.

Then came a gap of a few yards, a round tower, and a short wall that linked the tower to York Castle and enclosed the end of the Old Parade. A small battery-store with a sloping roof butted into the wall and the curve of the tower. The gap was paved and it supported three cannons, modern ones with long barrels, spoked wheels and a better range than the ones Saint Barbara was guarding. Behind each cannon the gunners had stacked cannon balls, had made them look like mountain cairns, and the rain had rusted them, had stained the paving stones.

Through the gap lay the black-toothed reef that broke the force of the waves and helped to protect the mole. Just below the gap lay the Strand: the first section of the road that runs to Whitby.

I felt a spit of rain and then the sun vanished and the day cooled. Far in the distance grey bands of rain moved across the hills of Spain, left behind the wet rock that is Gibraltar, and entered the Straits.

The Mayor strode through the gate and disappeared into the darkness.

We began to march up the ramp, and as our feet hit the wooden drawbridge they made a thumping sound – it was regular, like the beat of a drum – and it echoed in the chasm below the bridge. The echo seemed to rise, to ricochet between the two bastions and it became louder, much louder, more like the tread of a hundred men – twice our number.

Inside the portals – where the vertical grooves still bore the scars and the rust stains of an old iron portcullis – we broke our step, and the beat became confused. Then, as we passed into the barbican, into the fortifications that are supposed to protect the gate, we were flooded with light and the beat became soft, muffled, and it felt as though we were in a cattle pen with high stone walls and no roof. The floor was cobbled and it rose at a steep angle – to give the defenders the advantage of the high ground. The double doors at the far end opened inwards and they were latched to the inside of the walls. When they were closed and barred on the other side, this pen would become a place for killing, a place for culling men, and suddenly I knew how an animal must feel when it scents blood, scents death, and realises there is no escape.

We spread across the paved area beyond the double doors and onto the cobbles of the great bastion, then we re-formed our ranks. On the wall above the gate the two derricks that raise and lower the drawbridge were making black A-shaped silhouettes against the grey sky. To our left the cannons that guarded the Straits and threatened the path below the ramp had become a pack of old guard dogs with no bark and no bite. They were useless, fit only for retirement or one of Saint Barbara's miracles – for most of the gun carriages had rotted away – and now they were held in place with blocks of wood and ropes lashed to iron rings. The touch holes that should have rushed a spark to the gunpowder, had filled with water, and rust had dribbled out of them, had laid circles on circles and filled them with fine veins, and now they looked like the petals of a dried flower.

We marched past the barbican, past the main entrance to the Governor's House – where the members of the Corporation were arranging themselves into one long line – and onto the great bastion. We turned to face the view, to drink in the town that lay about two hundred feet below us, and then we stood at ease. In Spain, Gibraltar was now bright with sunshine and the rain clouds had given way to a blue sky. In Tangiers it was clearing in the south: beyond the sandhills, beyond the hills that push the mountains high into the sky and make the horizon look like a row of stumpy teeth – chewing teeth. For us the wind was now carrying spots of rain and it was flapping the ends of my neck scarf and making me shiver.

Captain Lacey and Lieutenant de Colville marched towards the main entrance. Ensign Wyndham grabbed at the ensign, pulled it towards the staff and held it with both hands. Sergeant Brandon and Sergeant Owen walked up and down and corrected our spacing.

Then they stood behind me and we began to wait.

A Lieutenant, two gunners and two matrosses – gunners' mates – marched onto the bastion and stood at ease beside the cannons. Five of the cannons were between eight and nine feet long and one was about twelve feet, and I assumed this was the one that fired the general alarm, the one everyone called the 'great cannon'.

Then the gunners broke ranks, hauled two cannons back from the parapet, and carried ram-rods, long-poled swabs, buckets of water, and small barrels of gunpowder out of the battery-store that lapped over the parapet and enclosed the corner of the bastion. The roof of the battery house wore a cloak of stone and moss, and it was capped with a lead finial that had spiked two ball-shaped urns. As the minutes slipped away, the matrosses elevated the cannons, ran ropes through the wooden carriages and lashed them to the iron rings on the cobbles. Then spots of rain began to dribble down the finial, began to darken the lead, and on the roof they began to blacken the stone and brighten the green moss.

Forty or fifty feet below us lay another stone bastion that formed the major fort, the major strong-point in Middleton's Line. It was protected by six cannons. They looked to be about eight feet long, and they were mounted on wooden carriages with spoked wheels that were almost as high as the sentries who had propped their pikes against a battery-store, and were now wandering up and down, and leaning over the parapet. A few feet along from the alarm bell – it sat on top of a high post and was protected by a wooden housing – the parapet locked into the walls of Middleton's Line, and I could follow the walkway all the way down to the Little Parade. To the right the parapet was hidden by our parapet and the gunners who were now lining up behind their cannons. In the distance, far behind them, the secrets of the upper wall lay exposed.

Johnson's Battery was a half-round tower that looked as though it had swollen from the outside of the wall – like a monstrous carbuncle – and now it was grey and putrid with age. Catherine Port was two square towers, strengthened by external side walls and protected by a V-shaped outerwork that would divide an attacking force in two and stop the gate being rammed. Irish Battery was the simplest of all the defences – a square tower that reinforced the far corner and drew support from a line of cannon placed on top of the wall.

Beyond the wall, long lines of oak palisades tethered the forts to each other, and guarded the lanes to Catherine Port. The closest fort, the easiest to recognise, was Whitehall. It was more grey than white, shaped like a cube, with flat walls, and a square tower that rose from the middle of the wall nearest to us. It looked to be about thirty feet high. The main roof was flat and I couldn't see any cannons or battlements. It was the first fort to be built beyond the walls and now it was enclosed by other forts and in the daytime – according to Sergeant Owen – it was used by the officers as a place of refreshment and that was why they'd laid out a bowling-bare: a square of rolled sand and fine shingle that was framed by an embankment of black earth and stone. The embankment made a barrier, a sharp contrast to the swamp, to the valley of ponded water that lay to the right.

A stream ran along the near side of the embankment, ran past the rolling flanks of the hill that supported the Upper Castle; then it toppled over the edge of a deep trench in front of Johnson's Battery – the trench was cut into solid rock and it protected the walls from the Upper Castle to Catherine Port – then it ran through the sluice, through the iron grills that keep out the Moors, and somewhere deep under the walls, in the blackness of a rock tunnel, it lost its sparkle, collected muck and became the common sewer.

Between the embankments of Whitehall and the city walls, on a long strip of rising ground that drained towards the stream, the earth was cultivated, was quilted with gardens. And like a quilt of many colours, many fabrics, each garden was a different shape, a different size – with patterns of green – and all of them were sewn together by low earthen walls that looked as though they were capped with stone.

Behind us lay another garden – the Governor's private pleasure garden. It took up the other half of the bastion, the half that ran towards the gate and overlooked the drawbridge. It was closed off by a line of orange trees growing in barrels that had been cut in half and banded around the top to take the weight of the earth. Through gaps in the trees I caught glimpses of tables, chairs, statues, and more barrels, small barrels – cut in half and full of green shoots that looked like spearheads. I turned to Owen and said: 'What an incredible place to have a garden – and a view like that.' I waved my hand towards the city and the Straits.

Owen smiled. 'That's for him up there.' He pointed towards the Governor's House. 'They say, at night, when the sun is setting, that garden has the most beautiful view in the world. And this is as close as we're ever going to get to it.'

I wiped a couple of spots of rain off my face, wiggled my toes, and yawned. Then I saw a double line of men in black cloaks and hats coming out of Catherine Port. They were carrying a coffin. As I watched they inched towards the left, crossed over the lane and passed through an embankment. Then I realised that what I'd thought was a field with hundreds of little mounds – mounds that might once have grown vegetables – was the graveyard, the land of the dead. As my mind began to drift, I began to think about the Day of Judgement. I could see all those mounds bursting open, could see the bodies rising into the air, and there were hundreds of them – trailing white winding sheets as they rose – and I was wondering if I might lie in that ground one day, when Lockhart said: 'Sunday's a strange day to have a funeral.'

I looked at him and nodded, and Owen said: 'That's the papists for you. No respect for the Lord's Day.' And he shook his head.

We watched in silence for a minute or two, then Crabtree turned towards Sergeant Brandon and said: 'You were going to say something about the papists, when we were down there, on the Old Parade.'

'Papists?'

'The Dominicans. Something about a row.'

He nodded. 'So I was. It was before I came. In the time of Lord Peterborough or Lord Teviot. I'm not sure which. Anyway, the trouble was the Portuguese Fathers claimed they still owned all the churches. They said they never belonged to the King of Portugal so he couldn't give them to the King of England. Lord Peterborough didn't take any notice of them. He said they belonged to the King, our King, and he'd do what he liked with them.' He paused. 'You have to understand that when the Portuguese left they took the windows and the doors from their houses, and sometimes they stripped off the tiles and took them too. So a lot of the buildings were empty shells when we first arrived, and we had to use the churches for stables and storage – and quarters for some of the men.'

'And that was the end of the row?'

Brandon pursed his lips. 'No. Not at all. The Portuguese Fathers complained to the Queen – because she's Portuguese, and a papist – and she complained to the King. The King complained to Lord Peterborough and he was told to treat the old churches with respect. The papists couldn't have them back – one church was enough for them – but we weren't allowed to use them as stables any more. Or taverns. Or storehouses for gunpowder. Most of them were stripped of their tiles and their wood – shutters, doors, beams. After a while the rain seeped into the walls and they began to crumble. Then people began to help themselves to the stone.'

'And that's what happened to Saint Barbara's?'

He shook his head: 'No. There was a fire in the hay. It got into the rafters, and the roof collapsed.'

'We arrived soon after that,' Owen said. 'I remember we were going to pull it down and use the stone to repair York Castle – it was falling to bits at that stage – and we were told to leave it alone.'

'Hmm,' said Brandon. 'And a month after that the Queen paid to have the shrine restored. And since then—'

'They're coming,' hissed Owen.

Brandon screamed in my ear again – reverted to his usual bloody self – and we snapped to attention.

Lord Middleton walked along the front rank. His long wig and his black hat with its white plumes hid most of his face. His coat was red with large bands of gold lace. His gloves were green and they matched the long scarf he'd wound around his waist and knotted at the side. For a moment he paused, leant on his walking stick and said something to Captain Lacey. Then they came down the middle rank and he appeared to trip, to stumble on the cobbles, and Captain Lacey reached out to steady his arm. As they entered the last rank he lifted his head and I saw his face for the first time – it was clean-shaven, with dark eyes, and white cheeks divided by a florid nose.

He stopped about four feet from me, and I stared straight ahead. Down below, the funeral was over. People were leaving the burying ground – four of them were carrying the empty coffin – and I was wondering what would happen to the papists on the Day of Judgement when I began to smell beer or brandy-wine. The smell was stale. It reminded me of the fumes that linger in a tavern, early in the morning before the door has been opened to the first customer of the day.

Lord Middleton turned to Captain Lacey and said, in the soft rolling burr that marks a man from the Highlands: 'I asked for men, and they send me boys.' He twirled his walking stick through his fingers. 'What can I do with boys? Boys like that.' And he nodded at me.

'That one can read and write, sir. We had it in mind to make him a clerk. At the Head Court of the Guard, sir, or maybe York Castle.'

'York Castle. Send him there. Sergeant O'Sullivan is short of two clerks. Or it might be three by now. They keep dying on him.' And he pulled a face. 'It must be something in the ink.' Then he tapped me on the shoulder with the knob of his stick and said: 'A good clerk is a valuable man. A good clerk can rise to be a Sergeant. And they say the Sergeants run this regiment.' He turned to the Captain and they both laughed.

A moment or two later – as they walked to inspect the gunners – Brandon hissed in my ear: 'And if they didn't, drunken bloody sots – Scots – like him wouldn't last a week.'

22

Half an hour later as the bell began to toll, we lowered our pikes and shuffled into the church. The entrance offered a strange welcome. It did not compose my mind, prepare it to enter the house of God, as the arched entrance to our church in Elme used to do. Through half-closed eyes these arches looked like a grove of palm trees and the floor looked like swirls of coloured sand – made into tiny bricks no more than two or three inches long and fixed to the floor with a pale mortar. It felt frivolous, felt like the entrance to a house of pleasure.

Inside the feeling changed. Orange tiles darkened by grime covered most of the floor, and whitewash covered the walls, and apart from the stone carving that edged the windows and the tops of the columns, the church had been stripped bare, cleansed of all forms of ornament and decoration. It was the simplest, plainest church I'd ever been in, and it would have brought joy to the heart of every Englishman who's ever called himself a Puritan. But there this man's joy would have stopped, for this church bore the symbols, the trappings of the Restoration. The pews were arranged in two lines with a central aisle. The communion table was pushed against the far wall, the East wall, and covered with a purple cloth. In the middle of the table a Bible lay on a purple cushion. A Turkey carpet – patterned with red, black and purple – covered the flagstones in front of the table. In accordance with the laws that regulate public worship, the East wall bore the King's coat of arms and three boards: lettered with the text of the Lord's Prayer, the Ten Commandments and the Apostles' Creed.

The pews were all full – apart from the front ones on both sides – and as we laid our pikes on the tiles and shuffled along the wall, the trumpets sounded a triple fanfare. The people in the pews stood up. On our side, the right-hand side, the red coats of the officers speckled the congregation, and they reminded me of the red poppies that grow wild in the cornfields. There were more women, more children than I'd expected and I remembered someone saying they now had a schoolmaster. I wondered how many of them would be able to read the boards on the back wall, and I was thinking it would have been a good idea to have a commandment which said: THOU SHALT LEARN TO READ, when the procession began to pass down the aisle. It was led by four clergymen. All of them wore long black gowns covered with a white surplice, and from their necks trailed the black scarves that are the mark of a minister, a servant of God. Behind them came the Corporation and the Mayor. Behind them came two men in black, six officers in red coats, and three ladies. And right at the back, all on his own, came Lord Middleton, smiling and nodding as the men bowed and the women curtseyed.

A purple cloth covered the front of Lord Middleton's pew and eight purple cushions lay on the seat. They made it into a special place, a place of honour, and as the three women filed into this pew, I caught the eye of the second woman, the younger woman, and she smiled at me. I stared at her, that's rude I know, but it was so unexpected I couldn't think why she would smile at me. I peered at her face – half-hidden in a froth of white lace – and I could feel a frown forming on my forehead. Then she lowered her eyes and as she turned to face the front I recognised her. Then I recognised him, recognised her husband. He was standing close to the communion table with the other ministers and he was wearing the pink and black hood – draped down his back – that denotes a Master of Arts.

As we drifted into the liturgy, into the words of Morning Prayer, I began to wonder if he'd mastered the art of love. I let my eyes run down the curve of her neck and over her shoulder. I drifted through her black shawl, drifted over the gentle hills that are her breasts and walked in the secret places, in the dark valleys, the valleys of love.

Then everybody was sitting down and the minister was climbing into the pulpit and I realised I hadn't heard a word, I'd made this house of prayer into a house of pleasure. I felt ashamed of myself, ashamed of my thoughts, ashamed of the weakness of my flesh. I screwed up my eyes and prayed for strength, but then I saw her in my mind, and even though I could hear the words of the gospel, the words of our salvation, I couldn't open my eyes. I was under the palm trees, standing on the sand, standing on a mosaic of colour. And she was smiling at me, walking towards me with arms outstretched.

Then my head exploded with desire and everybody was saying 'Amen' and 'Thanks be to God' and it felt as though they'd been watching us, watching me, and my blood ran cold.

The minister in the pulpit closed the Bible, sent a thump around the church, then he said: 'For those of you who do not know me, I am Doctor Turner, the minister of this church, and it is my very great pleasure to welcome Your Excellency and Lady Middleton' – he inclined his head towards them – 'and Your Honour' – he inclined his head towards the Mayor – 'here this morning. It is also my pleasure to welcome the musketeers and the soldiers-of-foot who arrived yesterday under the command of Captain Lacey.'

Lockhart leant against the wall and mumbled: 'Isn't that bloody nice of him.'

I turned my head, pretended to nod, and Doctor Turner said: 'Captain Lacey, has already volunteered his men to help in the service of God. And I will be talking more about that later on.'

'What the hell is that all about?' Lockhart whispered.

I rolled my eyes and shrugged.

Doctor Turner reached for a small book, lifted it up to his eyes and said: 'I shall now read from the "*Laws and Ordinances of War*, Established for the better governing of His Majesty's Forces in the Kingdoms of Sus, Fez, and Morocco, under the Command of His Excellency the Earl of Peterborough."'

He paused and looked up. 'The text has been altered slightly since the time of Lord Peterborough, but the essence remains the same, so I shall continue.

"Duties to God

ONE

Let no man presume to Blaspheme the Holy Trinity – God the Father, God the Son, and God the Holy Ghost; nor the Known Articles of the Christian Faith, upon pain of his tongue being bored with a red-hot iron.

TWO

Unlawful Oaths and execrations and scandalous derogations of God's honour, shall be punished with loss of pay, and other punishments at discretion.

THREE

All those who often and willingly absent themselves from Sermons and public Prayers, shall be proceeded against with discretion. All those who violate places of Public Worship, or things consecrated to holy use, shall be punished at the discretion of the Lord General, or a Court Martial."'

He closed the book and placed it beside the Bible. No one coughed. No one spoke. No one made a sound. Inside – in my spirit, where the waters of faith are supposed to run deep – I felt sick, felt as though those waters had been dammed, had been muddied, and would never be quite the same again.

Then he began to speak again, in a soft voice: 'My text for today's sermon will be taken from the Gospel according to Saint John. It will illuminate the words I have just read. They govern the conduct of most of the men in this congregation and I thought you might like to have a few minutes to think about them, to prepare your mind to receive the word of God – the spoken word.' He paused, and the silence hung in the air. This time it felt oppressive, felt heavy, felt like a smothering blanket.

'In accordance with the law, next Sunday will be a Test Communion Sunday, and all officers who present themselves for communion will be required to take the Oath of Supremacy and Allegiance, and subscribe to the declaration against transubstantiation. The certificates for this will be signed by myself and the other ministers who take communion at this service.'

He laid his hands flat on the Bible, as if to draw strength from it, then he continued: 'And now I would like to welcome the Reverend Mister Tate, Cannon Emeritus of Exeter Cathedral.' He turned, opened his hand, and invited him to stand.

Mister Tate half-stood, made a slight bow, and was rewarded with a splattering of polite applause.

'He has come with his dear wife' – he inclined his head towards Mistress Tate in the front pew – 'at his own expense, to preach the gospel. And God knows, we need every voice, every man who is willing to spread the gospel. At Mister Tate's request we have been able to arrange the lease of a house on his behalf. It is in Saint Barbara's Street. It used to be called the Priest's House, and I'm delighted to know that once again it will become a house of prayer.' Then he put his hands together, made it look as if he were about to pray. 'A man of God must eat, must pay the lease, and restore his house. And at the suggestion of Lady Middleton' – he inclined his head towards her – 'there will be a special collection today for Mister Tate and his mission. For those who give by quarterly tithing we will make a special addition to the tithe, and present it to Mister Tate on your behalf.' And he smiled.

'And one last thing. A thing of great joy. Lord Middleton' – he inclined his head once more, made himself look like a puppet with a broken neck – 'has most graciously, most generously granted Mister Tate a fifteen-year lease on the old chapel of Saint Barbara – at a nominal rental. Restored and renamed, it will become a place of Protestant worship. It will enhance the area and raise the moral tone. For those of you who think it strange that an old papist chapel can become a place of true worship let me remind you about our own church.' He opened his arms wide as if to gather up a blessing. 'Once it was the church of Saint Dominic – the man who founded the order of priests that still controls the cathedral on the other side of the road – and before that, in the time of the Moors, they say it was the public baths. They say the water used to run down here from the fountain in the Market Place, and this was where the Moors cleansed their bodies.' He paused. 'Today with water and baptism we cleanse the soul, and God is glorified, and this is a place of prayer. In our prayers today we will be giving thanks to Almighty God for sending Mister Tate to labour amongst us, and we will be asking Him to bless Mister Tate, Mistress Tate, and their new chapel.'

Lockhart leant over my shoulder. 'I bet the old fool takes a hammer to that shrine. I bet you a week's pay he has Saint Barbara off that wall before next Sunday.'

Sergeant Brandon turned and stared at both of us, then he said: 'And I bet you a month's pay the Dominicans make such a hell of a fuss, Saint Barbara will stay put. And I bet by tomorrow everyone will be remembering the Queen paid to restore that shrine.' He nodded at us, drew back a couple of inches and thought for a moment. Then he prodded Lockhart in the chest. 'If you're a real betting man, I'll wager six months' pay that Mister Tate will never make Saint Barbara's into a Protestant chapel.'

23

Early next morning, Sergeant O'Sullivan laid down his quill, reached over his desk and shook my hand. I looked over the top of his spectacles and into his eyes. They froze my heart and dried my throat, and I burst into a sweat, a cold sweat. He was the image of my Father: same age, same wet green eyes, same black hair and pale skin, and same smile – without the twist that pulled my Father's lips down to the right.

I was grabbed by an eerie feeling, a feeling of doom, a feeling that the past was about to catch up with me. I tried to say something, to pretend this feeling meant nothing, but my words stumbled over my tongue and they made a soft mumbling sound.

He stood up, pushed his stool against the wall and said: 'Are you all right?'

He was the same height as my Father, but a lot thinner and his gut had spread over the top of his breeches.

I nodded, and he said: 'A lot of men fall sick within a day or two of arriving. I've often thought it must be something in the air or the water. Or maybe it's just this place.' And he smiled.

Then this eerie feeling, this feeling that he was my Father – born again in different flesh – began to fade, for his words flowed into each other, and the accent was different. It was more like a lilt, like music, like singing that wasn't singing. And it had none of the harsh rasping that shaped my Father's words.

Then he smiled again and said: 'Where are you from?'

'From England. From Elme, in East Anglia.'

'Myself – I'm from Ireland.'

I remembered my Father saying the heathen came from Ireland, from Tipperary. The Sergeant didn't look like any of the heathen who used to live in my mind when I was a child. They carried wooden clubs and ran around stark naked till they could kill a wild animal and tie the skin around their waists. He looked ordinary, inoffensive. Then he itched his back and shrugged his shoulders, and somehow he shrugged off the heathen past my Father would have bestowed on him, and he became himself, became an Irishman. He squinted a couple of times, turned away from the windows, away from the light, and took off his spectacles, and the shape of his nose mimicked the shape of my Father's nose.

I blinked hard but I could not blink this nose away, and I said: 'What part of Ireland do you come from?' Somehow I had picked up the tones of his voice, the lilt of his words, and they echoed in my head, and as they died away they left a faint image, a faint echo of the past.

'Ohoo,' he said. 'You'll not have heard of it. It's a tiny village. Or it was when I was last there, fifteen years ago. We called it Bogrowan. There was another name, an English name – Rowanmarsh – but we never used it.' He paused and looked into the roof, looked into the rafters where cracks of light were ridging the tiles. 'No – that's not true. We did use it. I used it, when I was the schoolmaster for a year. I had to write letters, official letters on behalf of the school, and I had to use the English name, because that was what they wanted.' He paused again. 'I'd forgotten that. Forgotten what they made us do, if we wanted to work for them.' He sighed to himself. 'You haven't heard of Bogrowan have you?'

I shook my head.

He pulled his stool back to the desk and sat down. He shuffled his bottom into the curved backrest and hooked the heels of his shoes over the bar that strengthened the front legs. The sunlight was coming through the windows that overlooked the Mole and it was just catching the tips of his fingers – on his right hand. All of them were stained black. The thumb and forefinger were a deep black and the other three were a light black with furred edges – like a soft smudging. 'It's near Tipperary,' he said, and he made the words sound like a melody.

I stared at him and I felt my jaw sag. He pushed a stool towards me and said: 'I think you should sit down. You look sick. My last clerk died of the flux and the one before that died of spots and a fever. They thought it was the plague and everybody was talking about it. Was dreading it. Doctor Lawrence came to see him and he told the Governor. Can you believe that?' I shook my head and rested my hands on the stool, on the backrest. 'It wasn't the plague. It was a distemper, with a fever that flushed his face. Then the poor boy went mad and tried to throw himself out that window.' He pointed to the one in the corner, the one that overlooked the end of Old Parade and the road to Whitby. 'That can be your window now, and you can have his desk.'

I walked towards the desk – one side was raised to make a slope, to make a writing surface – and I ran my fingers over the wood. It was oak with an inky black grain – oiled and polished to give a dull sheen. As I touched it with my fingertips, and looked to see if they were still clean, I remembered Patrick O'Sullivan: the man who haunted my Father's past. I wanted to ask, wanted to know more about him, and I opened my mouth – but then my courage faltered.

I sucked in a breath, a deep breath, and took in the room. It was in York Castle, on the top floor of the building that looked like a blockhouse. The windows ran round three sides and they should have flooded the room with light, but they were too narrow, too slit-like. At the moment they were slicing the sun into long shafts of light but in an hour or so the sun would move round the castle and we would be left on the cold side, the dark side.

Two empty desks lay between the Sergeant and me. A large table, covered with books and papers, stood in the middle of the room. Beyond the table, in a nook that looked to be about eight feet deep and seven feet high, two chairs sat in front of a fire, and to the right of them sat four beds – built in pairs like beds on a ship. Books, papers, and stone bottles – I presumed they were full of ink – sat on the shelves to the left of the fire. Two curtains, made from heavy brown sacking, hung from a rail. During the day they could be pulled across to hide the nook, and at night they could be used to keep in the warmth of the fire. In front of my desk a bench was pushed against the wall, and above it, on the pegs that filled the gaps between the windows, hung a corporal's coat, a sergeant's coat, a baldric with a sword and scabbard, and a black hat.

A grey badge was pinned to the side of his hat. It was the same badge the Irish musketeers had been wearing yesterday when they marched past us at the Town House. It was the Lamb of God. I stared at it, and turned to ask him if it was a mark of the Irish, some sort of symbol. But then my courage failed me – once again – and out of the corner of my eye I saw the beds, saw the palliasses, the pillows and the blankets, and I said: 'Who sleeps over there?'

'You do.'

'But yesterday we moved into a lodging house by Middleton's Line, near the other end of the Old Parade.' I stood up and looked out the window. 'I can see it from here.'

'Hmm,' he said. 'But sometimes we have to work late. And sometimes, when we've run out of candles we have to start early – as soon as the light comes through that window.' He pointed to the window that looked over the Mole, looked over to Spain. 'They shut the gates at night and then no one's allowed in or out of York Castle. And if you want to get some sleep, that's where you're going to sleep.'

'Then why don't I bring my things over here and sleep in one of those beds all the time?'

'Because you belong to your company. If we're attacked you have to be ready to fight with your company. And that means you must go where your company goes. You must drill with them and go on guard with them. You must never forget you are a soldier-of-foot.' He paused. 'In effect you are on loan to me. It would be nice to think you could be a clerk for eight hours a day, a pikeman for another eight hours, and have the remaining eight hours for eating, sleeping, and slouching off to an ale house, or a whore house if that's what you've got in mind.' And he paused again. 'But it doesn't work that way, and this is what we do.'

He smiled. 'There's a parade at three in the afternoon, every afternoon, down there' – he nodded towards the Old Parade – 'and every man who is not on duty, who is fit for duty, has to go on parade. And that includes you. After prayers, those who are going to relieve the forts, the town guard, the moleguard, they march off, and the rest are drilled for an hour. If your company is going on town guard you go with your company, and you report to me at seven next morning. If your company is going to the forts, you don't go. You spend the week with me. If it's a day of rest, you come here and I decide if you can have the day off. If a work parade is called – and it doesn't matter if it's for the morning or the afternoon – you must go. On a good day, if you don't draw a double duty in the middle of the night, you might get six hours' sleep, and that's it.'

Then he picked up a sheet of paper, looked at it for two or three minutes, and appeared to forget me. I coughed, and he looked up. For a moment he seemed surprised to see me, then he said: 'I suppose you can read and write?' I nodded. 'And figures. Arithmetic. Can you add up?' I nodded again. 'Multiply and subtract?' I nodded again. 'And divide? What about that?'

'Yes. But I have trouble with long numbers.'

He smiled. 'Most people do.' And he picked up a thin book. 'I want you to read a couple of paragraphs to me. And after that you can copy out a couple more and I can have a look at your writing.'

He held out the book. I walked along, took it, and sat on the stool at the desk beside him. I opened it up and read the first page: '*Laws and Ordinances of War*, Established for the better Governing . . .' I skimmed the text, then I looked up and said: 'Mister Turner read from this yesterday. And he preached on a soldier's duty to God.' I paused. 'Did you hear his sermon?'

He shook his head. 'I've never heard him preach. I'm a Catholic, a papist, and I don't go to the English Church. And maybe I should tell you right now so there's no misunderstanding: I don't care what you think about Catholics. Or the Irish. My rank is Sergeant and you will respect that rank. I don't care if you don't respect me. I'm used to that. But you will respect the rank, and if you don't you will be placed on a charge. And when you come to know that little book a bit better, you'll know there are hundreds of things you can be charged with.' He smiled. 'Turn to the section that's headed "Duties Towards Superiors and Commanders".'

I flicked past the section 'Duties to His Majesty' and past the section 'Duties in General', then I said: 'I've found it.'

'Read from the second point.'

'"TWO No man shall presume to quarrel with his Superior Officer upon pain of cashiering and arbitrary punishment; nor to strike, or offer to draw his Sword against any such, upon pain of death.

'"THREE No man shall violently assault the Commissary of Musters on pain of death.

'"FOUR No man shall depart his Captain without licence upon pain of death.

'"FIVE No man shall resist, draw, or offer to draw or lift his weapon against any officer correcting him for his offence, upon pain of death."'

'They all apply to you. In number two and number five, the word officer may be replaced with the word Sergeant. From now on I'm your Sergeant. And I will be obeyed. You may think whatever you like about the Catholics and the Irish, but when you are in this office you will keep your opinions to yourself. You will shut your mouth, and do as you are told. And you will not try to demean or belittle my beliefs.'

I swallowed hard but I couldn't swallow my beliefs – the certainties of my faith – and I said, in a quiet voice: 'What about Sergeant Brandon?'

'Is he with your company?'

I nodded. 'And Sergeant Owen is in charge of the musketeers.'

'Hmm,' he said. 'I was with both of them in Dunkirk. They stayed on, and I came here in '61 with Lord Peterborough when the first two regiments were withdrawn from Dunkirk. After the evacuation they went on to Bombay. And they didn't come here for another five years, but to listen to them you'd think they came out on the first fleet. But that's not what you're asking is it?' I shook my head. 'The answer to your question is: you always obey your Sergeant. When you're in this office I'm your Sergeant, and when you're with your company, Sergeant Brandon is your Sergeant.'

'But what happens if you say I have to be here in the afternoon and he says I have to be on guard duty?'

He laughed to himself. 'That was sorted out years ago. Up to the age of fifteen, I have the first right. You may choose if you wish, to stay on in this office till you're sixteen and in that case I will still have the first right. After your sixteenth birthday you will cease to be a clerk. You will be a soldier-of-foot.' He looked at his desk, picked up his quill and milked the ink off it with his thumb and forefinger. 'You see, they think that only boys, old men, the lame and the sick, are fit to be clerks.' He shook his head. 'If you're wondering why I'm here, I was hit in the thigh with a musket ball, and the muscles in my leg withered. And now I can't march. If I hadn't been able to read and write they'd have sent me back to Ireland by now.'

Then I noticed a walking stick, hooked over the end of his desk. I nodded, tried to look solemn, look serious.

'How old are you?'

I didn't want to say thirteen – it made fifteen sound so far away – so I said: 'I'll be fifteen in about fifteen months.'

He nodded, opened a drawer, and pulled out a sheet of paper. He ran his finger down the side of it – it looked as though he was counting – then he said: 'You'll be my twenty-third clerk. What's your name?'

'Fenton. Martyn Fenton.'

'I thought they said your name was William?'

I felt my face go hot. 'I'm sorry. Yes – it's William. William Martyn Fenton.'

He shook his head and mumbled: 'Now they're sending me boys who don't even know their own name.'

He dipped his quill in the ink and wrote my name. 'I don't even remember half of them now.' He bit his lips and stared out the window for a second or two. Then he continued: 'The faces have blurred. And when I hear they're dead I put a cross beside their names.' He counted the crosses. 'Fourteen are dead. Four of them lie in the burying ground at Whitby.' He smiled. 'I wouldn't like that. The land moves. Slips. All that drilling, all that gunpowder, it makes the earth unstable. And if you ask me the dead at Whitby will be rising out of their graves long before the Day of Judgement.'

I wasn't sure what to say to that. I sat on the stool, looked over his shoulder, looked down the Mole, looked at the empty rock carts and the men who were hitching them up to the horses. Then he said: 'I do remember one young man. His name was O'Sullivan, the same as mine. He was killed at Fort Anne. Shot between the eyes and it blew his brains out the back of his skull. Not that he ever had many brains to blow out.' And he sighed.

The silence between us hung heavy, like a pall on a coffin at a funeral, and I said: 'Is O'Sullivan a common name in Ireland?'

'It is where I come from. Why?'

'In my family they talk about a man from Ireland. A Patrick O'Sullivan.'

He roared with laughter. 'In my family they talk about a Patrick O'Sullivan. They talk about me.' He laughed again. 'I've met a lot of Patrick O'Sullivans, and most of them were no bloody good. Drunk on poteen they were for most of the time. And none of them were related to me, thank God.' And he laughed some more.

I laughed with him, laughed away the fears that had been brewing in my head, and he said: 'In your drawer you'll find a little knife, a penknife, and a needle. I'll show you how to cut a quill, how to make a pen.' He took a new feather, a goose feather, out of his drawer. 'Cut it straight across like this.' And he cut off about quarter of an inch. Then he cut a scoop out of the back, and on the front – in the middle – he made a half-inch split. Then he cut a curve towards both sides of the split and formed a nib with a square end. 'And now comes the secret part.' He smiled, walked over to the fire, lifted the salt-glazed pot that had kept the fire from dying, and sprinkled some wood shavings on the ashes. When they caught he lit a candle. Then he held the end of the needle high above the flame. When it was glowing red he plunged it through the split and made a small hole. 'I don't know why,' he said, brushing away the curl of smoke, 'but that hole seems to let the ink breathe, and when it breathes it flows, and it gives your writing an even flow.'

I thought I could cut a quill – and the truth is I could – but mine was nothing like his. My edges were rough, the curves of the nib did not mirror each other and the hole was too big. After my third attempt, he said: 'I want you to try some writing now. There's some old paper, some spoilt paper in your drawer. You can copy some of the *Laws and Ordinances of War*.' He picked up the book and flicked through the pages. 'Start here.' He pointed to the heading: 'Moral Duties'. Then he laughed, snapped it shut and said: 'I've always thought point number three would catch Sergeant Brandon one day.' And he laughed again.

I sat down at my desk, hooked my shoes over the bar on the stool, found the section 'Moral Duties', ran down to point three and read: 'Rape, Ravishment and unnatural abuse, shall be punished by death.'

24

Sergeant O'Sullivan looked at my writing, shook his head, and said: 'Go back and start again. Keep your hand at the same angle all the time and make your words flow. Learn how much ink the nib will hold. And make your breaks the natural breaks between each word. Then you won't have these thick spots where you've started again and tried to join up the letters.'

I walked back to my stool and sat down. My hand was aching, and my fingers felt cramped – they weren't used to being curled up and leant on for so long – and I looked at my work. It was awful: blotched and splattered with a fine spray – the split in the nib was opening and flicking ink when I didn't hold the pen square to the paper. I cleaned the ink off the nib and held it up in the air and peered at it. And I was thinking if I cut the nib at an angle it might lie on the paper better, when the door opened and slammed and a young man rushed into the room. He heaved his sack onto the top of the bed closest to the wall, and hung his hat, coat and sword on the pegs between the windows. Then he looked at me and said: 'Some help! Thank Christ for that.'

He thrust a piece of paper at the Sergeant. 'Only ten carts made it yesterday. It was Sunday and the tide covered the road for most of the morning and they didn't work in the afternoon. They say there'll be a lot more today. I've been to the Head Court of the Guard and my company's going to Charles Fort this morning. There was an attack last night and they want some more men. They won't be back for a week and I have to sleep here.' Then he sat down on the stool next to me, lowered his voice, and talked to his desk. 'And that means I'll be writing twice as much and my bloody hand will hurt like hell.' He flicked his fingers, made it look as though he was flicking the hurt, the ache out of them.

Then he turned to me and said: 'I'm Ives. Edward Ives. Pikeman in charge of a quill, for six more bloody months,' he pulled open his drawer and looked at a piece of paper, 'and ten more days. Then I'm fifteen and I'm off. And I'm not bloody coming back.' He looked towards the Sergeant.

The Sergeant dipped his quill into his ink pot and continued to write. Ives shrugged, turned back to me, and whispered: 'I see he's got you copying *Laws and Ordinances of War*. It's a heap of crud and he made me do the damn thing three times. And it took a week. A whole bloody week before he would let me do anything that meant anything. And then it was only copying letters into the letter book, and it's not as if anybody ever reads it. It's just there for the record, in case the original gets lost or somebody says they never received it. And that's never happened since I got here. Not once.'

He wandered over to the table, took four sheets of paper out of a box – they were covered with writing and looked like letters – and brought them back to his desk. Then he opened a large leather-bound book and peered at the first piece of paper. 'This one's for salt. An order, a commission to buy salt. A whole ship load of it, and they don't want to pay more than six shillings a ton.' He paused. 'They must have found a cheap place in Spain or Portugal. That price is too low for England.' He looked at the next letter. 'This one's for ten tons of dried pease and five tons of salted butter. And this one's demanding a refund of twenty-five per cent – that's a quarter – because the wheat biscuits were full of weevils and not worth the £120 we paid for them.' He laughed to himself. 'A.J. Woodgate & Sons of Bishopsgate in the City of London are going to be bloody annoyed about that. It's going to cost them £30, and if they don't pay they aren't going to get any more orders and . . .'

His voice slipped into the corners of my mind and I kept thinking I'd heard him wrong. But I hadn't heard him wrong. I knew that. I knew Mister Woodgate. I knew his office in Bishopsgate and his warehouse in Billingsgate, beside the Thames. And I knew a lot more about him – things I shouldn't know – and I shut him out of my mind. Then I heard Ives say: 'Look at this one. What the hell is this one doing here?' He pushed back his stool, rushed to the Sergeant and thrust it in front of his nose. 'I thought Corporal Trigg was going to the Head Court of the Guard this morning. I thought he was going to do these.'

Sergeant O'Sullivan leant back in his stool. 'We had a message from the Governor's Secretary and he had to go to the Upper Castle first thing this morning. They've a lot of dispatches to copy, dispatches for London, and they have to be on the *Falcon* before it sails at twelve noon. So the Town Major sent that over for us to copy.'

He slunk back to his stool, flopped forward and read the letter for a moment, then he turned and said: 'It's a request to purchase one thousand new oak palisades "ten feet long and six or seven inches square – which when planted will secure the approach to the south-east corner of the City walls." That's down by the rocks, just along from the Old Mole. They're scared the Moors are going to mount a surprise attack down there when the tide is low. They could be on the beach and swarming over the bridge in a couple of minutes.'

'The bridge?'

'That's what they're calling the new landing place. It crosses the end of the new quay – it's going to look like a bridge.'

I nodded, and I thought of Lockhart, thought of the scavenging, the sewer-cleaning he'd accepted instead of a court martial, and I was wondering which I would have chosen, when Ives continued: 'The only good thing about working here is you know what's going on.' He picked up a quill and cut a new nib in five strokes, in less than five seconds.

I felt sick – not vomit-sick but green-with-envy-sick – and I stared at my blank paper. Then I wrote:

'Moral Duties'
ONE
Drunkenness in an Officer shall be punished with loss of place; in a private Soldier, with such penalties as the General or Court Martial shall think fit.

'What's loss of place,' I whispered.
'For an officer?'
'Hmm.'
'Means he's no longer in the regiment. And normally he doesn't get any pay. But he can hang around – on half-pay if he's lucky – and wait for someone to die or go back to England. Then he can rejoin the regiment, if the Colonel will have him.'

I nodded and wrote:

TWO
He that is drunk on the Watch-day shall be Cashiered and Banished from the camp.

'Cashiered,' I whispered. 'Does that mean thrown out?'
'Hmm. But no one's been thrown out since I've been here. They usually send them down to Whitby in chains, and stop their pay for a year. They're always short of men down there.'

Then I wrote:

THREE
Rape, Ravishment and unnatural abuse, shall be punished with death.

Rape and Ravishment implied a strength I did not have, and I could never imagine myself doing such things. But I did not have to imagine unnatural abuse. I knew too much about it, too much about the sins of men. To me they were like a stain on my soul – ink black, like Sergeant O'Sullivan's fingers. Then I began to think that wasn't right. The sins varied, and so did the intensity of the stain. With my Father it was a black stain, a sin of the black hole. With Sergeant Brandon it would also be a black stain, like O'Sullivan's thumb and forefinger. But with Michael it was different, was a sin of the cock, a softer sin, a greyer sin – one with blurred edges, like O'Sullivan's other three fingers. But as the words came back into focus, death was death, was lettered in black, and I knew my soul was stained. I knew this stain could not be removed – only baptism could do that and I'd been baptised and it couldn't be repeated. I told myself I'd have to live with my sin, live with my stain, and I wiped the nib between my thumb and forefinger – stained them black – made a living stain, a symbol of my sin, my degradation. Then I dipped the nib into the ink and wrote:

FOUR

Adultery, Fornication, and other dissolute lasciviousness, shall be punished with death.

FIVE

Theft and Robbery exceeding the value of Twelve pence shall be punished with death.

'Christ!' I whispered. 'There's a hell of a lot of things in here they can hang you for.'

'I added them up once when I was bored. I think there were sixty-six, or it might have been sixty-seven.' He turned towards me and yawned. 'But most of them are just threats – to keep us in order. In all this time I've only seen two men hanged. One was for mutiny and the other was for deserting to the Moors. The silly bastard changed his mind and came back. I got a good view out that window there.' He pointed towards one of the windows just along from me.

I leant towards the window, looked down on the gallows, down on the empty square of air where men dance the dance of death. I wet my lips and wrote:

SIX

He that is found drunk, or convicted of frequent swearing shall forfeit half a day's Pay.

I leant back and blew on the words, waited for them to dry, and watched Ives, watched the words flow from his quill. Every letter was perfect – as if it had been cast in a mould – and every letter leant at the same angle, like the sails on a fleet of small ships. He was so quick, it was magical. He seemed to be able to suck whole sentences into his head and let them flow down his arm, through his fingers.

Then he realised I was watching him, and he said: 'It's practice. Hours and hours of fucking practice.'

The next three hours passed in silence. He finished his four letters and three more; the Sergeant finished five letters; and I finished the section

'Challenges and Duels, or Provocations' and made a start on 'A Soldier's Duty Touching His Arms'. And I was thinking I would like to touch the arms of the young girl on the Little Parade, and a lot else if she'd let me, when the door opened and a little old man shuffled in.

Ives stood up, took his hat, sword, and coat – it was a corporal's coat with one line of lace in the seams – hung them on the pegs, and hissed at me: 'From now on you have to do this for both of them.'

Then I saw the man wasn't little and he wasn't old. His grey hair was making him look old and his back was humped, like a widow's hump, and it was hunching him, pulling him down towards the ground. He shuffled across the room, placed his hands on the top of my desk and looked at me. Then he picked up my sheet of paper, shook his head, shuffled over to his desk, and sat down on his stool.

He didn't look at the Sergeant, and the Sergeant didn't look at him, and a strange silence fell between them. Then the Corporal turned to Ives and said: 'Will you tell the Sergeant I have to go back to the Upper Castle, to the upper granary at five o'clock. They're making a list, an inventory of all the provisions that are left in the whole garrison. By tomorrow we could be on short rations.'

Ives stood up and said: 'Excuse me Sergeant. The Corporal has to return to the Upper Castle at five o'clock. They're making an inventory in the upper granary.'

The Sergeant nodded, and I looked at Ives. He put his finger to his lips and bent over his work.

I wrote some more and came to the end of the paper. Then I dried the ink with sand, turned the paper, and read the other side. It said: 'NOTES FOR A REPORT ON THE STATE OF THE GARRISON 4/14 JANUARY 1673/4 BEING THE TWENTY-FIFTH YEAR OF THE REIGN OF HIS MAJESTY KING CHARLES II.'

The dates didn't make much sense to me. It seemed strange that a report would take more than a year to prepare, but I pushed this to the back of my mind and read on:

In January 67/68 the numbers in the garrison were reduced. The new establishment became ONE REGIMENT-OF-FOOT AND HALF A TROOP-OF-HORSE.

Officers, Sergeants, Corporals and Drummers numbered 135
Troopers (including one officer, one Corporal, one Trumpeter and one Farrier) numbered 34
Officers on His Excellency's Staff (including the Minister, the Engineer and Muster Master of Fortifications, the Judge Advocate, the Physician, the Surgeon, the Quartermaster Provost Martial, the Commissary of Musters, the Commissary of Ammunition, the Town Major, the Master Carpenter and the Comptroller of Ordinance) numbered 13

Gunners and Matrosses in the Train of Artillery numbered 24
Pikemen and Musketeers numbered 1,440. Today this number is
reduced by death and a failure to recruit enough new men, to
approximately 1,200. This figure is further reduced by illness and
infirmity (at the moment about ten men per day are reporting sick)
to 1,000. This number is reduced again by approximately 100 –
for officers' servants, and men seconded to work on the Mole and
at Whitby. The maximum number of men who are fit for duty is
therefore 900 and given that we have to maintain a 24-hour guard,
the maximum number per guard is—

I flicked through the other sheets of spoilt paper but none of them
continued the report, and I turned back to the first sheet of paper. In
another hand, a cramped hand with many crossing-outs, someone had
written:

You are stating the obvious and by implication insulting the intelligence
of His Excellency and any other officer who reads your report. You
should start with the two things that matter most:- ONE: because of the
Reformadoes and Gentlemen Volunteers there is never any shortage
of officers. TWO: the number of Pikemen and Musketeers established
at 1,440 is reduced by sickness, infirmity and death . . .

I reached over and touched Ives on the arm, and whispered: 'What's a
reformado?'
'An officer on half-pay. Once it used to mean his company was being
reformed, and he was waiting for that to happen. Now it just means he's
waiting to take up a place on the regiment. Sometimes there's ten or
twenty of them hanging around. And that means that a Sergeant like
him' – he nodded towards O'Sullivan – 'even if he was able to walk
properly, would never be promoted to ensign because there's always an
officer or a gentleman volunteer waiting to take every place that becomes
available.'
A few minutes later the boom of the noon-day gun ran down the hill,
through our open windows and out to sea. Ives jumped to his feet, yelled:
'Can we go now please Sergeant?' And without waiting for a reply he
grabbed me by the arm and yelled: 'Come on!' He rushed me out of the
room, down three flights of stairs and into a whitewashed cellar. 'They
call this the refectory. If you get down here as soon as the gun goes off,
you can eat and still have time to run back to your lodging house and eat
again with the rest of your company.' He grinned at me and I grinned
back. Then I began to laugh and the grin slid off his face. 'Shit!' he said.
'I forgot. They're going to Charles Fort, and they won't be eating at the
lodging house. Not today they won't. And not for the rest of this week,
and this is all I'm going to get.' He spun round, looked at the cook

standing behind two iron caldrons, put the grin back on his face and held up his plate. The cook ladled out some pease and covered them with a brown stew that looked like a slurry. It must have contained a lot of thickening because it began to set around the edges as soon as it touched the plate. 'Can I have some more?' he said. 'I'm a growing boy.' He shrugged and smiled.

There was something about him, something appealing, something charming, something that would have made the girls in my village look at him and smile. But the cook could see none of it, and he said: 'Boys are supposed to get half-rations. That's a man's portion that is. If you want a boy's portion I can take half away.' He held out his ladle.

Ives stepped back and pulled his plate towards his chest. Then he held out his hand for two rounds of bread – cut thick and spread with butter – and dropped them onto his stew. He picked up a fork, twirled it through his fingers, and without a word of warning, he jabbed me in the thigh. I yelled, jumped, and shook my fist at him. The cook whirled on me with his ladle. Ives whisked another two rounds of bread onto his plate, rushed over to the beer barrel and poured himself a pint of beer.

He sat down on the bench, kept his back to the cook, stretched out his arms and hid his plate. I laid my plate and fork on the table – opposite him – walked over to the barrel, turned the tap, and poured myself a pint of beer. It was a brown beer, watery, much lighter than the small beer we drank on the ship. It frothed at the top and ran over my fingers. As I sat down I licked them clean and the smell filled my nose. It was heady. It smelt of summer. Of barley and yeast, and long hot nights. I remembered stretching out on the warm earth, resting my back against the sheaves of corn, and watching the heat haze blur the stars on the edge of the horizon. I smiled at those nights, those dreamy nights that might never come again; and he said: 'Does your leg hurt?'

I shook my head, and he pushed a round of bread towards me. I pulled out the middle, rolled it into a ball and covered it with gravy. It looked soft and delicate, like a new-born mushroom. As I stuck my fork in it and lifted it up to my mouth he said: 'If you didn't want to eat all that I could eat it for you.'

I smiled and shook my head.

'Or maybe you'd like to run back to your lodging house and eat there, and then I could finish that up for you.'

I smiled again, and I began to laugh – I couldn't help it – and he said: 'I could pay you a penny.'

I looked at the half-eaten stew and the two rounds of bread. Then I popped the stolen crust into my mouth, chewed it half a dozen times. 'I was told we're going to be paid nine pence a day, less six pence a day for victuals – or it might have been five pence halfpenny with another halfpenny deducted for something else – and as this is the main meal of the day, I would say it was worth threepence.'

He laughed. 'It doesn't matter what it's bloody worth. I've been here eighteen months and I've never been paid. Not once. And I've got no money. They're always saying we're going to be paid but I've never seen any money. Some of the men have been selling bits of their uniform, or their equipment, and drinking the money. But then they get court-martialled and flogged, and made to pay for the things they sold, and the things that are needed to replace them. In some companies, where the men have been here a long time, and not paid for more than two years, there's a lot of thieving. They don't want the things to wear, they want them to sell – to drink. And if I were you I'd put my things under my palliasse at night and I'd sew in my name.' He pulled his shirt away from his neck, and pointed to the inside of the collar-band, and I read: Edward Henry Ives.

We ate in silence for four or five minutes, then he wiped his plate with his bread, drank the rest of his beer and stood up. 'Hurry up,' he said. 'We're supposed to be back in fifteen minutes. If you're any later, they sit and stare at you like a pair of bloody old turkey gobblers, and at the end of the day when you're all finished and you think you can go, they'll find you another letter. And O'Sullivan will lay it in front of you, and he'll lapse into that bloody Irish brogue of his, and he'll say: "Well, well, well. Bless my soul. Look what the little people have brought."' I burst out laughing. He was a natural mimic, and I could hear the Sergeant in his voice. 'It's nothing to bloody laugh about. They often send over things from the Head Court of the Guard at the end of the day, and you have to do those as well. That's the rule. And you end up missing out on your supper. And I bloody hate that. So hurry up!'

We washed our plates and forks, dropped the mugs onto the pegs beside the barrel and ran up the steps two at a time. Then I saw the pike rack and I yelled at his back, as he bounced up the next flight of steps: 'Is this your pike in here?' He nodded and I yelled again: 'How come you've got a small one.'

He stopped, turned, groped at the front of his breeches. 'It's not a small one. It's growing bigger every day.'

I laughed, and he smiled. 'The pike,' I said, 'the pike.'

'It's thirteen feet. They sent a thousand of them out in '62 or '63, and if you're on moleguard or town guard – and that includes sentry duty in the castles – you're allowed one. But if you go out to the forts you have to carry a full-size one in case you're attacked by Moors on horseback.'

I nodded, thought for a moment and said: 'How do you know it was '62 or '63? How can you be so precise?'

'It's in the Ordnance Book. It's there on the shelves beside the fire. There are all sorts of things in those books, and the ones stored up in the rafters. Late at night, when I'm here on my own, I curl up beside the fire and read them. I reckon I know more about this place than most of the officers. I've often thought I'd like to go up to the Governor's House and help his secretary, then I could read all sorts of other things. But they won't let you work up there unless you're a Corporal or a Sergeant.'

Then I remembered the Corporal's message, the message the Sergeant had heard with his own ears, and I said: 'Why did the Corporal make you repeat his words?'

He stopped on the landing in front of our door and turned towards me. 'Because they won't talk to each other. That's why.'

I shook my head. Corporals are not much better than us. They have a bit of lace on their coats, and they're paid twelve pence a day, but they still have to carry a pike, and they still have to do what the Sergeants tell them to do. I could never imagine one talking to Brandon the way Trigg had talked to O'Sullivan, and I said: 'Trigg must be bloody mad. O'Sullivan could have him reduced to the ranks, and then he'd be just another pikeman in charge of a quill.'

He shook his head. 'It goes back to the days when they were both corporals. They both used to wear that badge on their hats. The one with the lamb on it. You must have seen it.' I nodded.

'When you hang up Trigg's hat you'll see it's still got a couple of holes in it. In the side where the pin used to go.' He reached for the door knob. 'The priests hand them out in the cathedral. They have some sort of ceremony once a year, and they say the Irish didn't want to throw them away after the first ceremony, so they pinned them onto their hats, and it became a talisman or a lucky charm. Now it's become a sort of symbol, a way of proclaiming their allegiance to popery. Mister Turner says it's an arrogance, an act of defiance, and they'd never be allowed to do it in England. And that's true. But this is Tangiers, and things are done different here. Mister Turner doesn't like it and he talks about the Irish being branded. Trigg was branded, was a papist, and about two years ago, O'Sullivan—'

The door jerked open and O'Sullivan stared at us.

Ives lowered his eyes and mumbled: 'Later. I'll tell you later.'

25

An hour or so later I finished copying the section headed 'Duties in Marching', looked out the window and yawned.

Sergeant O'Sullivan tapped his desk with his fingernail, and the sound echoed in the rafters. Trigg and Ives both turned and looked at me, and I felt as though I'd done something wrong – like farting in church – and I picked up another sheet of paper and wrote:

'Duties in Camp and Garrison'
ONE
None that is appointed for the defence of any Breach, Trench or Sconce, be he Captain or Soldier, shall willingly forsake the same, or through any false-coloured occasion or excuse, absent himself from thence without sufficient Order or Warrant allowed by Council of War, upon pain of death.

I knew the word sconce meant a candlestick that could be fixed to the wall but that didn't make much sense in this context. I leant towards Ives, held out the paper and pointed to the word. But before he could open his mouth, O'Sullivan said: 'What's the matter?'

'Sconce. I was wondering what it meant.'

'Sergeant,' Ives hissed at me.

'Sergeant.'

'It's a small fort or an earthwork. We use them in the daytime to protect work parties. But you could never stay in one all night. Not here you couldn't. It would be too dangerous.'

I nodded and as I started to read point TWO, the boom of a cannon filled the room. I leant back on my stool and looked out the window. High up on the bastion by the Governor's House a wisp of white smoke was clawing its way down the stonework. I turned to Ives and said: 'We were up there yesterday.' The cannon boomed again, and more smoke clawed at the stonework.

'That's Mordaunt's Battery,' he said. 'That's the old name for it. It's mentioned a lot in the old copy books, the ones up in the rafters. But nowadays most people call it the Governor's Bastion, and every day they

fire the signal up there at quarter to three. The sound carries all over
the town, and it means you've got fifteen minutes to get onto the Old
Parade.' He dried the end of his nib. 'In truth you haven't got fifteen
minutes because you have to parade outside your lodging house first,
and then march onto the Old Parade and be ready for the inspection
at three o'clock. Long ago I asked my Sergeant if I could slip into the
ranks as they marched on, and if I had to parade today I'd still have
another ten minutes. But you . . .' He paused. 'If you haven't asked your
Sergeant, you should start to run.' And he smiled at me.

Sergeant O'Sullivan looked up and nodded. I wiped my nib, put the
stopper on my ink pot and slipped the paper into my drawer. Then I
slung on my coat, sword and hat, hurled down the steps, grabbed my
pike, pounded across the courtyard, through the tunnel in the castle wall,
over the drawbridge, down the side of the playhouse, through the picket
fence, over the Old Parade and up the slope.

As I turned into our lane I came to a screaming halt. The whole company was lined up and standing at ease, and with the oiled smoothness of
a long-practised drill, every man turned and stared at me. The musketeers
had their muskets, but not a single pikeman had his pike except me. I
couldn't believe my eyes. I remembered Lockhart, remembered him
parading without his pike, and I couldn't help thinking this looked like
madness, like mass stupidity.

Then Sergeant Brandon yelled: 'Put that pike away! And get in the
back line. And bloody run!'

I hurled into the house, shot my pike into the rack, hurled out the door
again, and sprinted into the back line.

Brandon yelled: 'Pikemen! Left turn! Drummer! Beat double-time!'

We thundered down the slope – retraced my footsteps – and halted
inside York Castle, in the courtyard in front of the keep. Then we filed
into the armoury and drew short pikes. In truth thirteen feet isn't short
but it felt short. And it felt light, too light, and I knew it could never repel
a charge of horse. To my mind it was like the staffs we drilled with on
the ship: it was a toy. But it still felt right for my height and right for
my weight. I grasped it in my right hand, joined my black thumb to my
black forefinger, made a loop and ran it up and down the shaft.

We formed ranks, slammed our pikes through the drills: made spines
and prepared to resist the enemy – and the images of sin, of a toy, of
a plaything vanished. Then we marched back onto the Old Parade and
joined the musketeers.

The Town Major walked along the front of our ranks, then he turned
to Captain Lacey and said – in a quiet voice that only just carried: 'This
is their first time on guard duty, isn't it?' The Captain nodded. 'Put
the musketeers in York Castle. They'll make a good reserve if there's
any trouble. And put the pikemen on Three-gun Battery.' He pointed
towards the cannon at the end of the Old Parade. 'It's the weakest

point in this section of the line. We had a couple of scares there while you were away. During the day you must maintain a guard of three at all times. During the night that increases to eight: three in each tower and two by the cannons. The men in the round tower are to patrol the wall to York Castle. The men in the square tower can patrol the walls to the first flight of steps. Since the battery-house was built we've been able to take all the gunpoweder out of both towers and make them into guardhouses. We've put in a couple of small fires but they're still a bit cold, a bit damp, and I'm trying to get some more pitch poured on the roofs, on the flagstones – hopefully next week, so that should help.' He paused, said something I couldn't catch; then I heard him say: 'And they can do all that for a month. Can be on duty every second night and that should break them in.' And without waiting for a reply, or a nod, or any sort of acknowledgement he walked on to the next company.

Captain Lacey spoke to our two officers for a couple of minutes then he turned to us and said: 'The musketeers are to guard York Castle, and at night when the castle gates are closed I will be joining them. The pikemen are to guard Three-gun Battery and the walls on both sides of it. Lieutenant de Colville will be in command and he will sleep in the round tower with half the pikemen. Ensign Wyndham and Sergeant Brandon will sleep in the square tower with the rest of the pikemen.' He looked up and down the ranks. 'I want to remind you that sleeping on guard is a court-martial offence and it can be punished by death. That may sound harsh. But we never know when the Moors are going to attack. We have learnt not to trust them, not to accept their word – even when they come begging for a truce, begging for a month or two of peace. And when you're up there on the walls, when you're pacing up and down on your own, just remember that the life of every single man, woman and child in this town, in this garrison, depends on you seeing the Moors before they attack. If you're asleep you won't see them. And if we hang you for going to sleep, you'll never see anything ever again. And that includes the whore houses up there by Irish Battery.'

We burst out laughing. He smiled for a moment then his face hardened, wore again its mask of granite, and I knew he was serious: dead serious.

We marched over to Three-gun Battery and as the old guard withdrew – came down off the walls and out of the towers and formed two files – Lieutenant de Colville stood us at ease and said: 'Because of all the rock carts that pass along the Strand it is most unlikely that the Moors would ever be able to mount a surprise attack in this area during the hours of daylight. That means we can maintain a guard of three men: one in each tower and one here by the cannons. At night the Town Major wants the guard increased to eight. I've worked out the figures and it means some men will do one day-guard and one night-guard, and others will do two night-guards. Every guard will last three hours. For those of you who are tempted to moan, let me remind you that most daytime guards last six hours, and if you're out in the forts you'll be doing two nights on and one night off. We will come on guard every second day – straight after the parade – and we will stay till we are relieved soon after three o'clock next day. You will be required to parade for work on the mornings and afternoons when we are not on guard. Now where's Fenton?' He looked along the line till he saw me. 'Captain Lacey tells me you have to leave before seven every morning, so you'll have to do six hours before then. You can do a double duty. Start at six and finish at midnight, and that'll give you six and a half hours' sleep. And tomorrow when you're doing all that writing it might help you stay awake.' A couple of men laughed and he smiled at them.

The six o'clock guard was designated a night-guard and I thought the three of us would talk and that would help to pass the time. But they didn't want to talk and they didn't want to walk. They both stayed on the tower, fell into a glum silence, and watched the sea. I walked the full length of the wall four times every hour or what I thought was every hour – it was difficult to tell for the clouds were gathering fast, greying the sky and bringing the day to an end.

Then the wind came up and I stood inside the sentry box at the York Castle end of the wall, pushed my hands in my pockets, and tried to warm them. The box felt like a coffin with no lid, and I wondered what it would be like to be buried upright, and I was thinking my legs would sag, when my eyes started to sag, to make me feel sleepy, feel dead to the world. I stepped out of the box, walked up and down, leant over the parapet and had a piss. I didn't need a piss – it was just something to do – and then I saw I wasn't the first man to choose this spot: the wall smelt sour, and the moss, the slime, looked bright green.

I watched a couple of ships try to enter the Straits but the wind kept pushing them towards the north.

The sun burnt away some of the grey haze far to the west, made it look like wind-blown streaks, and for a moment or two the glass windows in the clerk's room blazed with light – almost dazzled my eyes – and I thought I saw a shape, saw Ives. I waved, but the shape did not wave back.

Then Ensign Wyndham came along the wall and said: 'Have you seen anything unusual?' I didn't know what was usual or unusual but I said no – and he nodded – and for a while we talked about the rock carts that were carrying the large blocks of stone. I hadn't seen these ones before. They were two wheeled – the wheels were as high as a man – and each one carried one rock, slung on chains below the axle. Some were being pulled by three horses and some by four or five, hitched in a line. They weren't carts in the true sense of the word – they were just a pair of wheels – but I couldn't think what else to call them, and nor could Wyndham. Then for a while we talked about the Moors: he seemed to think they could come in over the reef in small boats, carry ladders up the cliff and climb the stone wall that reinforces the base of Three-gun Battery.

In the next hour the darkness stole most of my view. Crabtree brought up a lamp and hung it inside the waist-high shelter that butts onto the parapet and looks like a large coal box. It covers the hole in the roof, protects the ladder and keeps the wind and the rain out of the tower, out of the top floor where half the men are sleeping.

Two new guards replaced the sullen pair on the tower, and another hour limped away. Then Lieutenant de Colville came along the walkway. He came with the silence of a black cat, a black shape, and when he was close to me, I stepped out of the sentry box, grabbed my pike and stood to attention. As he stopped and turned towards me I said: 'Good evening, sir. The password for tonight is Princess.'

'Fenton?'

'Yes, sir.'

'The response is Anne of York.'

'Thank you, sir.'

'You sound cold. Shivery. Are you cold?'

'Yes, sir.'

'Are you wearing a waistcoat?'

'No, sir. It was too hot this afternoon, and I left it off.'

'Is it down below?'

'No, sir, It's in the clerk's room. On the back of my stool.'

He shook his head. 'They tell me some of the men wear two shirts and two waistcoats when the night is cold. And they also tell me a cold sentry is a sleepy sentry and he's more worried about keeping warm than knowing what's going on out there.' He pointed into the darkness. For a moment we both listened to the waves breaking along the edge of the Strand, then he said: 'Next time I see you without a waistcoat you'll do an extra duty – early in the morning when the air is at its coldest.' He turned, walked back along the wall with one hand on the parapet – the walkway is only two feet wide and it doesn't have a railing – and climbed down the ladder. For a moment the lamplight silhouetted his shoulders, his head, his hat – then he was gone.

I imagined him looking at the shapes sleeping on the wooden floor, walking a couple of feet to the right, climbing down the next ladder, finding more sleeping shapes, finding one or two who were restless and wanted to exchange a few words. Then I imagined him stepping to the side again, climbing down the last ladder, looking at the fire, opening the door, stepping onto the flagstones, touching the cannons, feeling their cold embrace, and talking to the sentries. I imagined him walking over to the square tower, finding a moment of warmth by the fire, climbing the ladders, seeing the sleeping shapes and walking the walls.

I peered at the walls, peered long and hard, but he did not walk the walls – the walls he had walked in my mind. I stamped my feet, stamped the cold out of them and walked my wall, walked with my hands straight out like a bird making a long flat glide. I told the two new men it was safe to walk the wall. 'Just put one foot in front of the other,' I said, but they shook their heads and stayed on the tower.

The cold seeped into my mind and I couldn't think. My nose felt as though it was going to fall off, and my feet felt as though they were wearing clogs carved from ice. For the next hour I walked up and down about once every ten minutes and I kept my hands stuffed in my pockets. When Lockhart arrived, he said: 'Christ! It's bloody cold.'

I grunted, shoved the pike into his hands and tore along the wall, Then I stopped, turned and yelled: 'I thought you were on scavenging.'

'That's only in the daytime. At night I have to go on guard – just like everyone else.'

I shrugged, tore along the rest of the wall, slid through the shelter, dropped down the ladders and crouched in front of the fire. The smell of burnt porridge, stale sweat and coal smoke hung in the air and it wrapped around me like a warm fug. I pulled off my shoes and wiggled my toes at the fire. But the fire was more dead than alive, and the porridge was cold – it looked like grey glue. As my toes began to thaw, I toasted two crusts of bread, spread them with fat, and sprinkled them with salt.

The door kept opening and closing as the men guarding the cannons changed places, and after a while most of the warm fug managed to escape, and the cold seeped back into my toes.

I looked for some coal, patted all the open-topped boxes that circled the room, but all of them were full of cannon balls, and they were ice-cold – were sucking the last of the warmth out of the room.

I climbed the ladder and stood on the first floor. It was like a sleeping loft – there was nothing in it except palliasses and sleeping shapes. I stepped over the shapes, tried to find an empty palliasse in the middle or by one of the walls where it might be warmer, but everyone else was of the same mind and they were all taken. The only empty one lay right by the ladder, by the hole to the ground floor. I lay down and pulled the blanket over myself. The palliasse felt damp and it smelt seedy, and the blanket wasn't thick enough to warm me – and I couldn't go to sleep. For a long time I lay there, shivering, rubbing my hands, my legs, trying to warm myself, trying to go to sleep.

Maybe I dozed for a while – I'm not sure.

Then I saw a man in uniform waking another man, and I could feel a breeze on my face. I rolled over and looked down the hole. The lamp in the stone nook by the door was casting a soft glow over the three-hour glass. The sand was almost through: it was almost three o'clock. I remembered thinking the glass would give the sentries by the cannons something to do. They could come in and check on the sand, watch it pouring through the neck, watch it making sand castles, red sand castles. And they could wake up the next watch. And from time to time they could slip inside and have something to eat – if they were quick – and they wouldn't be deserting their post if they left the door open.

About half an hour later after the watch had changed and the men had settled on their palliasses, had burped and farted and gone to sleep, I heard the door open. Ensign Wyndham came in carrying a bucket of coal and he was followed by Lieutenant de Colville. They banked up the fire and began to toast some bread. After a while I could smell burning cheese and it made me hungry, made me wish I could go down there and sit beside them. But I couldn't do that. They didn't want me. Then I realised that wasn't true. Michael wanted me. I didn't want him but I knew he still wanted me. I'd seen him watching me, and sometimes I could still feel the imprint of his body, the warmth of his body. I could feel it in my body, on my body, and it disturbed me, made me feel uneasy.

Then I began to wonder if I'd made the right choice, on that night when I had to make the choice that was not a choice. As I rested my face on the edge of the ladder-hole, looked from the Lieutenant's back to the Ensign's back – both hunched and rounded as if to soak up every morsel of heat – I began to think it wouldn't have mattered which one I chose, because I could sense things were changing, changing for the better.

In the lodging house Ensign Wyndham was sleeping with the musketeers, in three rooms – opened up to form one large room. The empty frames had been left to support the roof, and despite being covered with clothes – hung on wooden pegs – the Ensign could still see the length of the room if he raised his head from the pillow.

Lieutenant de Colville was sleeping with us – in the back of the lodging house – in two long rooms opened up to make one large room. Sergeant Brandon's bed lay against the end wall, the wall that overlooked the garden, and the Lieutenant's bed lay at the other end, close to the door. My bed was five along from the Lieutenant. I keep saying 'bed', but in truth that is too grand a word, for each 'bed' was nothing more than a frame of slatted wood that lifted us about six inches off the floor. They are supposed to stop the night airs chilling our bones. Whether they do or not I've no idea, but I do know that the wolf, deprived of his lair, deprived of the shadows that lurk below hammocks, and deprived of proper beds – beds that could have hidden him, had given up prowling.

And so I was thinking, was hoping, that things were changing for the better; and in my idle moments I was beginning to wonder if I still needed Michael to protect me.

As the fire began to warm up the lower room, the heat began to rise, to pour through the ladder hole and I felt warm, felt like a spring lamb bouncing around in the sunshine. Here I was safe from the wolf. Then I remembered the buttons on Brandon's coat, on his grey coat, on the day I was conscripted. They bore the image of the Lamb of God, the same image the Irish bore on their hats. It was the badge, the mark of a papist. That's what Ives had said. But despite what I'd seen with my own eyes – and would see no more since Brandon had cut the buttons off – I couldn't believe the man was a papist.

I rolled over and dug Crabtree in the ribs. 'Is Brandon a papist?'
'What?'
'Is Brandon a papist?'
'For Christ's sake, Fenton, go to sleep.'
'Hmm. But is he?'
'How the bloody hell would I know?' He pulled the blanket over his head.

He couldn't be – it was against all reason, all common sense. And he didn't act like one. But then I had to admit I didn't know how a papist would act. I'd never met one till today – till yesterday – when I spoke to Sergeant O'Sullivan. He didn't have horns, or cloven feet, or a forked tongue. And for some reason he looked a lot like my Father, and my Father wasn't a papist, and never would be. So it couldn't be anything to do with the way a man looked. It had to be something to do with his soul, something that couldn't be seen – and if it couldn't be seen how would I know it was there? How would I know he was a papist?

Later, as my mind fell into sleep, fell into the pit of darkness, I began to feel, to believe, there was something else, something that had driven Brandon to wear the symbol of the Irish, the symbol of popery.

26

Next morning, just before seven o'clock, I grabbed a sheet of spoilt paper from the table and read some notes about cracks appearing in Middleton's Line, just above the Old Parade where the wall starts to rise. The notes were ornamented with half a dozen tiny doodles of plants with flowers that had broken their stems and shed their petals, and they seemed to be suggesting – as they emerged from a thicket of crossed-out words – that some of the foundations had settled, and the repairs 'could involve the demolition of a section of the wall that fronts—'

I turned over the paper. But the back was blank, apart from a list of 'replenishments': musket balls, powder, fuses, matches and grenadoes that had to be taken to Fort Catherine 'today'.

I wondered when 'today' was. It seemed strange to think it was still 'today' on the paper, but it could have been a week ago, a month ago, or even longer. I smoothed the paper with the tips of my fingers, smoothed away the past.

I sat down at my desk, opened *Laws and Ordinances of War* and found my place from yesterday. I skimmed down the rest of the page, didn't like what it said, and didn't want to copy it, so I skipped a couple of pages and read:

'Duties in Action'
ONE
If a Pikeman throw away his Pike or a Musketeer his Musket or Bandoliers, he or they shall be punished with death, or as a Court Martial shall think fit.

I pressed the end of my quill against the paper, tested the nib for cracks or splits, and for a moment I watched O'Sullivan and Trigg. Both were hunched. Both were peering through their glasses and both were working in wordless silence. And like a pair of old monks, old scribes, they were bathed in the rising sun and I could see specks of dust floating in the air above their heads, like guardian angels. They made me think it must have been like this in the old abbeys, in the sanctuaries that faced the east, when the monks rose before the dawn and greeted the sun, greeted the day with prayer, prayer that dissolved into work.

I remembered greeting the day, watching the dawn, more than an hour ago from the top of the tower – after I'd given up trying to sleep. It was bloody cold, and I prayed for a woollen vest with long sleeves and a tail that wrapped around my bum. The thought of it made me smile: my Father used to wear one. My Mother used to sew him into it at the beginning of winter, and as the goose grease on his skin soaked into the wool it moulded itself to his shape, and by spring it looked – and smelt – like an extra layer of skin.

Then Ives rushed into the room, leant over O'Sullivan's desk and said: 'If I can take Fenton down to the Mole now, he can do it on his own tomorrow.'

O'Sullivan looked up, looked over the top of his spectacles, and said: 'Good morning.'

Ives smiled and stepped back. 'Good morning, Sergeant.' Then he looked at me, raised his eyebrows, made himself look like a startled owl, and he tapped Trigg's desk. 'Good morning, Corporal.'

Trigg nodded. Ives looked at me again, pulled his face into a grin, and said: 'Any messages?'

The silence was so loud, so cold, I felt myself shiver. Then Trigg laid down his quill and said: 'You may tell the Sergeant that the Governor's secretary has hurt his hand, and has asked me to help him, at nine o'clock this morning. He is to dictate the letters and the instructions, and I will write them. Later I am to copy them into his record books.' He pulled his lips into a tight smirk.

Ives repeated the message, word for word, paused for a moment – waited for a reply that did not come – and said: 'The Mole. Can I take Fenton to the Mole?'

O'Sullivan nodded, dipped his quill into his ink pot and bent over the copy book.

Ives tapped my desk. 'Get your hat and your sword.' And he rushed out of the room.

I grabbed my things, rushed after him and thundered down the stairs. He handed me my pike. 'There's no need to hurry. O'Sullivan thinks there is, but there isn't. But if you make a big act of hurrying, he thinks you're working hard, and he doesn't give you a lot of extra things to do.'

I laughed, and followed him through the back of the castle, into a tower, down the path enclosed in the pair of high walls, into another tower and onto some steps just above the quay – at the base of the cliff. Then a voice from above bellowed: 'What the hell are you doing down there?'

I turned and looked up, looked into the face of Sergeant Owen. 'I have to work for the clerks every morning from seven o'clock, up there in the castle. And we have to come down to the Mole to—' I turned to Ives.

'To record the number of rock carts that arrived yesterday.'

Owen nodded and waved us on. Behind him I caught a glimpse of one of his musketeers, and he looked like I felt: half-awake.

We ambled along the quay – kicked at the pebbles thrown up by the waves – and paused to watch four men haul a boat up the slipway. Then we wandered around the other boats lying up-turned on the quay, drifted along the side of the dock that formed the first part of the Mole – Ives called it the little harbour – and watched a small boat round the end of the stone breakwater and edge close to the wall, just a few feet below us.

To our left two small buildings nestled into the rocks at the foot of the cliffs and faced onto the quay. They looked old and grey – weathered by the sea – and Ives thought they might have been used by the moleguard when the first sections of the Mole were being built.

As we walked onto the end of the Mole and turned to face the Straits, the first three buildings on the left-hand side butted into each other and formed a solid barrier that blocked the view and kept the Moors off the Mole. The first building was small and old. It was raised high on a stone base and it butted into the cliffs. The next building was two-storeys high and it could have been mistaken for a lodging house. It was the Head Court of the Moleguard and it looked new: the stones were still clean; no moss or lichen had taken root on the tiles and the black paint on the doors and shutters hadn't had time to peal. The next building was a square three-storeyed tower that some call Fort Whitby Gate. It was capped with a small tower – to keep the sentries dry. Beyond the gate lay stone barriers and oak stockades that stretched into the water – to well below the low-water mark, and they looked like the black spines of a sea urchin. To the right of the tower two cannons sat high on a bastion of stone and looked straight down the road to Whitby.

'The guard room is in the tower, to the left of the gate,' Ives said. 'That's where you have to go every day.'

A rock cart lumbered up to the gate – became framed in a square of black – and a sentry ambled out of the guard room. We watched him for a moment, then I said: 'Why do we want to know the number of carts?'

'It's to do with the money they pay Sir Hugh Cholmley and the molemen to build the Mole. Every few months they measure the progress and calculate the cubic measurement. Then they add up the number of carts that have arrived, work out the cubic content and add on the rock that came over on the boats. Then they compare the two figures. But the problem is the size of the rocks slung under the open rock carts varies, and if the bottom of the sea is soft, or sandy, the rock sinks into it and you'd never know it had been dumped there. The seabed has to be made firm – no one argues about that – and the rocks have to be allowed to settle, but the trouble is they can't measure all this rock that just vanishes. And there's a lot of arguing about how it should be calculated, and who should pay for it.' He laughed to himself.

'We have to go to the guard room every day and add up the marks.

The sentries make one mark for every cart, and they're supposed to record them on two lists: one for the open carts and another for the bucket carts. So make sure you get both of them. Then you go all the way down to the end of the Mole, to that shed.' He pointed to a tiny building far in the distance. 'It's on runners, like a sledge, and every six months – when the Mole has grown a few more yards – they hitch up a team of horses and pull it out a bit further. So the longer you're here the further you're going to have to walk. At the moment it's about four hundred yards and it's a good walk on a fine sunny day. But when it's raining, you get drenched, and you can never dry your coat properly on that stupid little fire in our office, and you'll bloody hate it.' He pulled a face and shook his head. 'The shed is supposed to be the site house, but most of the men think that's a bit of a joke. And they don't like the two clerks who work in there, don't like them keeping an eye on them, and they call it the prickmaster's office.'

I burst out laughing.

He laughed with me, then he said: 'It's nothing to do with your cock. A prick is an old-fashioned word for a clerk who used to make a prick-mark on a piece of paper. It was a way of counting. And the prickmaster was the man in charge of the pricks. I've often thought is would suit O'Sullivan but I've never had the guts to say it to his face.' He pulled a face and shrugged. 'Anyway – down there, down among the pricks, where you should feel at home' – he smiled – 'you get their figures for the carts. And you make sure their figures agree with our figures from the guard room. And if they don't there's a bloody great row and somebody gets a kick up the bum. So you and the pricks at the end of the Mole make sure they agree. And for that they give you a tankard of hot chocolate. And when you come back – if they don't agree – you call into the guard room and rub out one of their marks, or add another one, and tell them they must have miscounted. They couldn't care less. To them every cart is just a scratch on a bit of paper, and in a week, two weeks at the most, they'll be off moleguard and out in one of the forts, and they could be dead or drunk – or both.' I stared at him, and he laughed in my face. 'Dead drunk, that's what I meant.' And I laughed. 'What I'm trying to say is nobody in the guard house will ever remember the true figures, and when you write them in our book – it's kept on those shelves beside the fire – they become the true figures. And if anybody ever questions them, they can look in the book the pricks keep and . . .'

He grinned, and we ambled into the guard room, talked to the sentries, added up the scratch marks – eight for the open carts and eleven for the bucket carts – and ambled down the Mole.

As we drew level with a pair of stairs – running into the water on the right side of the Mole – and I was thinking it would be a lot easier if everybody could read and write and add up numbers, Ives pointed to the stairs. 'They're called King's Stairs, and from here on O'Sullivan can see you, when he's sitting at his desk. I sat on his seat one day, put a couple of cushions under my arse to make sure I was his height, and I checked it.' He smiled. 'Of course if he stands up he can see you. But he doesn't do that very often in the morning, there's too much to do, so I wouldn't worry about it if I were you.' And he smiled again.

Then he pointed to a fenced enclosure – it began by the steps and ran up the Mole for about a hundred yards. 'That's the timber yard, and over there' – he pointed to the other side of the Mole – 'that's where the molemen live.'

Two long buildings ran down the Mole for about a hundred and eighty yards. They were joined in the middle by a large two-storeyed building that looked square, looked a little like a fort. 'There's room for fifty families in the main buildings,' he said. 'And a couple of shops, and some stabling for the horses that don't get back to Whitby at night. And there's a blacksmith up the far end.'

As we came closer to the middle building, a man leant out the opening on the second floor – it was double-doored like the doors on a barn loft – ran a rope through the wheel on a wooden hoist-beam and began to lower a sack of grain. 'That's a granary up there,' he said. 'Wheat is stored all over the place – in case of fire. And down there' – he pointed to the ground floor – 'that's the Mole office.'

After a couple of minutes the timber yard gave way to another flight of stairs – the Queen's Stairs – and a beacon that looked like an iron basket mounted on the top of a twenty-foot pole. The pole was spiked for climbing, and bundles of sticks – faggots coated in pitch – were heaped against the pole. I was thinking it was strange that the faggots weren't up in the basket, when I began to realise this was more than a beacon. It was also a light for landing at night, and it could have been used a few nights ago for the bottom of the basket was full of burnt sticks and long dribbles of black tar had run down the pole.

We veered over to the other side of the Mole and marched past a battery of cannon, looking cold and wet in the weak sunshine. Then we came to the gunners' house, and a couple of gunners: yawning, stretching, and blinking at the sun. A white arrow was painted on the front wall and before I could open my mouth and ask what it was for, Ives was saying: 'That arrow points to the three-hundred-yard mark. It's chiselled into a block of marble, in the cobbles by the door. If you want to see the other marker, the one they take all the measurements from, it's back by the rocks, to the left of the caves that go into the cliff.'

'Caves?'

'They run in under York Castle – just below the lower bastions. We call them caves, but they're more like short tunnels – cut into the rock.' He paused. 'You mightn't have noticed them. The doors are usually locked, and they're painted black, so they blend in with the rocks.' I shook my head and he shrugged his shoulders. 'They say they used to keep gunpowder in there, but the water drips through the cracks in the wintertime and now they keep it out here in the gunners' house. They're not supposed to smoke in the house but they do.' And he nodded at one of the gunners who was cutting tobacco off a plug and packing it into his pipe. 'And that next building, with the big wheel on the side – the donkey wheel – that's the tarras mill. The donkey goes inside the wheel, and as he walks he turns the wheel and that turns the grinding shaft. But he died a couple of months ago and they still haven't got a new one.'

As he spoke a man opened a pair of double doors, and after a second or two – deep in the gloom – I could see the head of a drudging-horse. It was blinkered and harnessed to a shaft. It was walking round and round a circular trough, turning a central pillar, turning a large revolving stone, and filling the air with brown dust. As we came closer the man with the whip slowed the horse to a stop and another man began to shovel the powder into wicker baskets. Then the man with the whip poured two sacks of crushed rock into the trough, cracked his whip and made the horse start trudging round and round again. Within a few seconds the dust filled the air again. It dusted the horse, the men, and the wooden feeding boxes that were full of oats, beans and pease – and it would have dusted us if we hadn't stepped back from the door. It reminded me of the inside of a windmill, a flour mill, and as another man walked past us, tossed an empty basket down and swung a full one onto his shoulder, I said: 'Is that tarras?'

'Hmm. It's a mortar, a sort of cement. The stone comes from Italy and when it's ground into powder they mix it with lime, river sand, tiny chips of marble, and fresh water. Salt water's no good – it makes the mortar decay, and then it crumbles and falls to bits. If they want to use it under water, to bind the rocks together, they stir in a lot of pitch and bind the outside with iron and that holds the mixture together till the mortar dries.'

We fell in behind the man with the basket, slowed our pace to his and began to pass another battery of cannons – the ones that saluted us on Saturday and now I could see what I hadn't been able to see then: in the sea, about twelve feet out from the side of the Mole the waves were rolling over a long line of wooden piles honey-combed with worm. Beyond them ran two lines of stone pillars, and beyond them again the tops of more wooden piles were breaking out of the waves. At first glance there were forty or fifty stone pillars and they appeared to begin about halfway along the Mole and run right out to the end, to the deep water where the carts were now dumping rock straight in the sea. In spite of being able to see the calming effect of the piles and the pillars they still didn't look right, didn't look like what I'd seen in England, and I said: 'Wouldn't it be better to fill in the gaps with stones and let the waves break against them?'

'The gaps are filled in, below the water, and that stops the base of the

Mole spreading out – so it doesn't collapse from the top. They say the force of the waves has to be reduced, or broken up below the surface of the water. If it isn't the waves pound against the side of the Mole and weaken it. In a storm they tear out the weak bits, and in time they could wash away the whole Mole – reduce it to a reef.'

I looked over the side – the rocks at the edge were four to six feet long and three or four feet high, and bonded with tarras. 'Are you sure?'

He nodded. 'It was somewhere about here, three or four years ago. There was a huge storm, and it tore away a lot of the Mole – made an enormous hole. After that they spent about a year hammering in the piles, making the pillars, and filling in the hole.'

Then a wave broke on the rocks, heaved spray in the air, and we both ran backwards, and laughed. 'When the tide's a bit lower you'll see the pillars are clamped in iron and lead. They must have cost a bloody fortune. But since they were put in place the Mole has survived three winter storms, so I suppose they're worth the money.'

The man with the basket opened a gate on the other side of the Mole, walked into a fenced enclosure, and poured the tarras into a large cistern that looked like a shallow trough. 'That's a puddling pool,' Ives said. 'They steep the tarras in them, then they mix in all the other things. If you have a look on the wall in the prickmaster's office, you'll see the different recipes, the different mixes, for tarras. It all depends on what they want to use it for. Some mixes are stronger than others.' He leant over the fence and yelled: 'What are you going to build in there?'

The man looked up, then he ambled over to the fence and said: 'Cellars. There's going to be a line of them, all the way down here,' and he waved his hand down the side of the Mole – it was edged with oblong stones and a line of mooring posts that ran all the way back to Queen's Stairs. 'And later on they're going to move the guardhouse' – he nodded at a wooden house with a tar roof – 'and we're going to build a new one in stone. I haven't seen a drawing of it yet but they say it will look like a fort. And it'll tower over the roofs of the cellars and have an unimpeded view – that's the word they used.' And he nodded, as if to confirm what he had heard. Then he turned, picked up a wooden paddle with a short handle and a fat blade, and walked back to his puddling pool.

In the prickmaster's office the figures for the carts tallied, and as Ives made himself a tankard of hot chocolate – the pricks wouldn't let us have two tankards – I read the recipes for tarras and looked at a diagram drawn onto the wall. It was a cross section of the Mole, in the shape of a square with a triangle pushed against the left-hand side – the side that faces the black reef and the storms that come in from the Atlantic.

The measurements read:

MAXIMUM DEPTH AT LOW WATER:	19 feet
TIDAL RISE AND FALL:	10 feet
HEIGHT ABOVE HIGH WATER:	8 feet
MAXIMUM TOTAL HEIGHT:	37 feet
WIDTH OF TOP:	96 feet
WIDTH OF BASE:	96 feet minimum (both sides vertical) 200 feet maximum (vertical on the inside and banked on the outside to make a reef – from the hundred-yard marker to the end of the Mole)

I looked at the drawings lying on the table. One was for the cellars, 'the new vaults', and it called for eighteen of them to be built of stone, lined with bricks, and secured by wooden doors fixed in round arches that would make the front look like a colonnade. And one was for a house, 'a Tarras Beater's House', to be built at the end of the Mole, abutting the 'north-facing wall'. I'd seen that wall. It was about ten feet wide and eighty yards long and still being built. It looked as though it was designed to protect the end of the Mole, and stop the Dutch and the Barbary pirates landing in the middle of the night. I was trying to think if I'd seen any openings on it for cannons, when Ives pushed the tankard at me and said: 'You can have the rest.'

I sipped it, but I didn't like it much. It was too greasy and it left an oily taste in my mouth. 'You put the tankard on that nail there,' he pointed to a rusty nail, 'and from tomorrow that's your tankard.' He waved to both the pricks and we wandered out of the shed – it didn't deserve to be called an office – and he said: 'We might as well go right out to the end. I can always tell O'Sullivan I had to show you everything, or the pricks couldn't find the figures.' And he smiled.

The end was seething with men – forty or fifty of them. Some were hoisting an eight-foot-long stone into the next section of the 'north-facing wall'; some were mixing tarras and using their pickaxes to force it down the cracks between the rocks; some were laying cobbles to form the carriageway; and others were out on a pier – it was shaped like an oval with the end drawn into points – waiting for a boat to round the end of the Mole. The pier looked like a boat caught in a net of mooring poles, and I said: 'Is that what I think it is?'

'Hmm. They filled it up with stone and tarras and sank it. They made it for the galley – to make landing easier – but now most of the boats from Whitby tie up there, and the stone is humped or barrowed onto the Mole.'

'Why don't they make a proper wharf, of wood and stone?'

He leant on his pike and looked over the edge. 'The water's getting to be too deep and the rip's too great. The pricks tell me there's a bloody great row going on. The storms have been breaking up the rocks below the water and a couple of months ago they made a chest of oak – it looked a bit like a large cage. Then they filled it with stone and bound it with iron and lowered it into the water – it's down there somewhere.' He pointed at the water but I couldn't see anything. 'Nobody seems to know how to make the next bit. You can't just dump rock into the sea and hope for the best. It has to be bound in iron or tarras, or both, otherwise it just washes away.'

We watched four men lower a dressed stone over the side of the Mole – just behind the guardhouse – and he said: 'They're building another flight of stairs.' Then he paused. 'There's a lot going on today.' He nodded to himself. 'There hasn't been much for the last couple of years.'

'Because of the storms?'

'Hmm. They bring the work to a halt in the wintertime, but it's mainly money. They don't have enough to pay the molemen and buy tarras and iron. And lime from Spain. And not enough men, enough soldiers to maintain a guard. So they forced the molemen to be sentries – not in the forts they're not good enough for that, but on the walls, from Irish Battery to the Watergate. That's the safest part. And now the bastards are having their revenge.'

I looked at him, and he laughed. 'Most of the men out there' – he jerked his finger towards the end of the Mole – 'are soldiers. If you're on work parade this week, you can bloody guarantee that's where you're going to end up.'

In the distance a man swung his pick into the air and struck the rock. Then he straightened his back and flicked his hand – the way I flick mine when it's cramped from too much writing – and I could see there was pain in it, real pain, jarring pain. 'We have to parade for work this afternoon,' I said, 'straight after the guard changes.'

He looked at me and laughed. 'You'll bloody hate it.'

27

In the afternoon, soon after we'd eaten, the door flew open and banged against the wall. I looked up expecting to see Corporal Trigg, but another man, a Lieutenant, staggered into the room, threw his hat on the table and flopped into the chair. Ives and I stood up; O'Sullivan half-stood, bowed his head and sat down again. The Lieutenant patted the air with his hand, and we sat down. For a minute or two he didn't seem to know where he was. He blinked, looked at his fingernails, pushed the books away from the middle of the table and cleared a space in front of himself, then he turned to O'Sullivan and said: 'I have to write another report. This one's about water.' He pulled a sheet of paper out of his pocket, unfolded it and read: 'You are to advise on measures to increase the availability of fresh water in the summer months – that means opening up old wells and clearing the rubbish out of the conduits. And you are to confirm the cost of a new cistern inside the Old Mole – it's supposed to draw water from the springs under York Castle. But they dry up in the summer and they could never supply the ships with all the water they need – any bloody fool knows that.' He slumped on the table. 'And anyway, the captains like going over to Tarifa or Gibraltar to water their ships. And most of them buy fresh meat at the same time, so I don't see why we need it.' He sighed and rubbed at his head. 'I suppose we could use it to water the houses on the Mole, and mix tarras. That would be more sensible.' He sighed to himself, rested his head on the table – cradled it in his arms – and closed his eyes.

Ives looked at me and pulled a face. Then he cut a quill, took some sheets of paper and a pot of ink out of his drawer and laid them in front of the Lieutenant.

For twenty minutes we worked in silence, then the Lieutenant sat up, blinked, dipped his pen in the ink and began to write. The first few sentences flowed from his pen, but then he seemed to hesitate, to lose his concentration. He looked out the window, picked at his nose, sighed, and crossed out a few words. Ives leant towards me and whispered: 'Won't be long before you've got another sheet of waste paper.' And he grinned. 'He comes in about once a week. And so do a lot of the others. O'Sullivan helps them with their spelling, and sometimes he does the final copy for them if he's in a good mood.'

A few minutes later the Lieutenant said: 'How do you spell separate?'

O'Sullivan looked up. 'It's in the book.' And he waved at Ives.

Ives ambled over to the table opened up a book and pointed to a word. The Lieutenant grunted and slammed it shut.

Ives look at me and rolled his eyes. As he sat back on his stool I whispered: 'What's the book?'

'O'Sullivan thinks there should be a correct spelling for every word. So every letter in the alphabet has two pages in that book of his and he's written down all the difficult words, place names, surnames, and a few others. And every time we use them we have to spell them the way he spells them, in that book. And if you don't he'll make you write the whole thing out again.'

'But that's bloody silly,' I whispered. 'Everybody knows that words can be spelt in two or three ways. I can remember one of my old teachers saying it was a sign of a good mind if you knew all the variations.'

'I know. But don't tell him that. And one other thing. It's all right for officers to make mistakes in their work. But it's not all right for us. We – you – have to write the word properly. And be warned. He reads the copy books at night, when he hasn't got anything else to do. And the first time he finds a mistake, he'll make you do an extra hour. The second time it'll be two hours. And the third time it'll be three hours. And so it goes on.' He shook his head. 'Next time I make a mistake I have to do twelve hours. That's a whole bloody day for one lousy little word.'

I ran my finger down the margin of *Laws and Ordinances of War* and was thinking I should read each word with more care, when the Lieutenant sat up and said: 'Shit! I forgot to tell you. They want him' – he nodded at Ives – 'at the Head Court of the Guard. They're doing the new guard rosters – the ones that start tomorrow – and they have to make four copies this afternoon.'

Ives sighed – made his sigh sound as though he was breathing out the word 'shit' – then he looked at O'Sullivan and said: 'There's a couple more sentences to do on this one. But all of these . . .' He held up a heap of paper.

I looked up and smiled, and for a moment I was filled with hope and the beery breath of the Lieutenant, but O'Sullivan ignored me and held out his hand. My spirits sagged and I looked down and read 'whosoever shall receive a commission from any that is not Authorised by His Majesty or the Lord General, shall dye without mercy'. I began to wonder if O'Sullivan would accept the way dye was spelt – when it was printed in an official document – or was his outlook coloured? Then I saw the joke, the pun, and I began to giggle.

The Lieutenant jumped to his feet, screwed up his paper, and yelled: 'I can't work in here with all this laughing.' And he stormed out the door – punching his hat.

Ives looked at me, pulled a face and rushed out the door.

O'Sullivan shook his head and wrapped me in a cold silence.

When the gun sounded for the changing of the guard, I put my things away and stood up. O'Sullivan pointed to the pegs and said: 'Help me on with my coat.'

I took it off the peg and held the sleeves wide apart, then I reached for his hat. The lamb in his badge looked fat and smug, well fed, and there was something about its eyes, something supercilious – if that is the right word. I brushed the head with my fingers, brushed away a speck of dirt, then I handed it to him. He smiled and said: 'That's the Lamb of God. It's a symbol of Saint John the Baptist, the man who came to prepare the way for our Lord. It recalls him saying – when he was referring to Christ – "Behold the Lamb of God".' And he paused. 'You probably don't know, but the cathedral is named after Saint John the Baptist and on his feast day – the 24th of June – the badges are given to everyone who takes communion on that day, or one of the eight days thereafter.'

Behind him the door was beginning to open.

'The eight days are called the octave – it comes from the Latin for eight – and the feast is commemorated on those days, with special prayers. If a man is on guard duty on the 24th and can't hear mass that day, the octave allows him to participate in the feast and wear the badge. That's one of the many ways Holy Mother Church looks after our spiritual welfare.' And he smiled again.

I looked over his shoulder, looked into the eyes of Corporal Trigg – they were dark with anger – and he was clenching his mouth, shaking his head.

O'Sullivan must have sensed Trigg, or felt a draught from the open door, for he turned around and grunted, then he gestured at me to get his sword belt, and he said: 'Tell the Corporal I have to attend the Town Major. And tell him that pile of letters on my desk is for him.'

I opened my mouth, felt a fool, and nothing came out. He jabbed me with his finger. 'Come on. Tell him.'

'Corporal,' I said, and I could hear the hesitation in my voice, 'the Sergeant is going to attend the Town Major. And the letters on his desk are for you.'

Trigg nodded. O'Sullivan walked out the door and as he reached to close it, Trigg smiled and said: 'Will you tell the Sergeant the Dominican Fathers have written to the Governor protesting about the use of Saint Barbara's chapel. They've told him it is still a Catholic chapel and a place of worship because of the shrine. And they've reminded him that the restoration was paid for by the Queen. They concluded with the words: "and with due respect and loyalty to Your Excellency in the discharge of your high office, we must – being answerable to Almighty God – petition His Majesty if Your Excellency cannot annul the lease that was granted to Mister Tate".'

I repeated his words – it didn't feel quite so stupid this time – and then he said: 'The Secretary tells me the Governor was so bloody mad after he read the letter, he called for a bottle of brandy and shut himself in his room for half an hour. And he tells me the Governor now intends to go down and help with the chapel – personally.' He smiled at O'Sullivan.

I turned to O'Sullivan and said: 'And the Secretary tells—' He breathed hard and slammed the door in my face.

Trigg burst out laughing, then he flopped on his stool. 'One thing about working here, you get to know what's going on.' And he paused. 'But you have to learn to shut your mouth. If you can't shut your mouth, talk to me, or Ives, or O'Sullivan if you have to. But never talk to anyone outside this office about what you see, or hear, or read.' He pulled his face into a tight smile. 'We did have a clerk once who broke a confidence, and the Governor was going to make him tiptoe the gallows for a couple of hours, but he died suddenly. Of fright. I think.'

My mouth dried. I moistened my lips and said: 'Tiptoe?'

He smiled. 'They put your neck in a noose – on the gallows – and they pull it tight and force you onto tiptoes. As long as you stay on tiptoes the noose won't strangle you. But every time you weaken, every time the pain runs up your ankles or starts to cramp your legs, and you try to rest your feet on the ground – the noose will strangle you.' He smiled again. 'I've always thought it was an appropriate punishment for a man with a loose mouth.'

I tried to smile, but it came out as a grimace.

Then he said: 'I think I should warn you about him.' He handed me his sword and I slipped the baldric over the peg. 'He's a papist, as you know. One of the worst sort. He believes in it.' And he shook his head. 'A lot don't. They pay lip service – say they do, but they don't. But he does. And what's so bad, so insidious, is that he will drip the poison into your mind. Drip, drip, drip. Day after day. And you won't notice it.' He paused. 'It'll be like today. You'll think it's a discussion. Think you're learning something new. But bit by bit he will wear away your faith. And one day you'll find yourself thinking he might be right and you won't have noticed it was happening, till he suggests you might like to go along to that church of his 'just to see for yourself – to see with your own eyes'. And by then it will be too late. And if you've ever walked on quicksand, felt it shiver and shake, and start to suck you in – you'll know just what it feels like.'

He fingered the two holes in his hat, rubbed at the imprint the badge had left in the fabric. 'It's what happened to me.' He shook his head as if amazed, appalled, by his own stupidity. 'It took about a year – maybe a bit longer because I wasn't aware of it for a long time – and it could happen to you, if you're not very careful.'

28

An hour later – as the troops down on the Old Parade divided into two: those who were going to relieve the guard, and those who were going to stay and do an hour of drill – we changed into our grey coats, our work coats, and lined up in the lane outside the lodging house. Sergeant Brandon and Sergeant Owen also changed into grey, but the Captain, the Lieutenant, and the Ensign, remained in their red coats. And once again we were as we were on the ship, and all the distinctions that had been blurred when we changed into our red coats were restored, but this time there was a subtle difference: on the ship we worked together, and on guard we watched together; but now we were to work and they were to watch. When I said this to Crabtree, he pulled a face and said: 'What the hell did you expect?' Then he wiped the sweat from his brow.

The afternoon felt cool, felt cold when the clouds skidded across the sun, and I said: 'Are you all right?'

He shook his head. 'It hurts in here.' He touched his forehead, just above his eyebrows. 'And I've been to the bloody privy four times today, and my guts still feel bloody awful, and I can't stop farting.' He leant on his pike and sighed.

Then I smelt the smell of shit, the tell-tale smell of runny bowels, of flux. I gagged and turned away. Then I felt sorry for him and I said: 'You'll be all right when we get out on the end of the Mole, and you can breathe the salt air.'

'The Mole? We're not working on the Mole. They' – he jerked his finger towards the musketeers – 'are going to Anne Lane, to raise the embankments, on both sides of the lane. That's why they've got all those shovels. And in a month or so, when they've lifted the palisades by a couple of feet, that should take our heads out of the Moors' line of sight. And it should be a lot safer to walk to Anne Fort.' He wiped his brow again. 'As for us, we're going to—'

Brandon slammed the end of his pike against the cobbles and yelled: 'Company!' We stiffened, waited for his next command – and then came to attention. He marched to the back of our rank and stood just behind me.

Captain Lacey walked up the steps of the lodging house and turned to face us. 'For this first month, work parades will not last longer than half a day. Next month when you are on guard for one day and off for two, work parades will last a full day. This afternoon, as I think you know, the musketeers are going to Anne Lane with Lieutenant de Colville, and the rest of you are coming to Saint Barbara's with me. And we – as the Minister intimated on Sunday – are going to clean the rubbish out of the chapel, and make it into a place of worship.' He paused. 'And while we are talking about worship let me remind you that next Sunday is Test Sunday for the officers in this company. It is traditional for a company to parade with its officers that day. To escort them to church and witness their communion. And as we will once again be in the presence of His Excellency, there will be a special inspection before we go to church, and everyone will need to get up about an hour earlier than normal, and I want the Sergeants to see to that.' He looked at Brandon and then at Owen. 'And one last thing. There is a rumour, a possibility, of a very important visitor coming to look at the chapel this afternoon. So let me warn you,' and he paused, 'any man caught swearing can have a week of scavenging, of cleaning the sewers. And any man caught having a little rest, or a sleep, or not working as hard as he should be working, can have two weeks in the sewers. If you finish what you've been ordered to do, you must report to me right away, or to Ensign Wyndham or Sergeant . . .'

Oldfield leant towards Crabtree and whispered: 'Who's coming?'

'I don't know. It could be that minister from Sunday. The one who preached the sermon.'

'No,' I whispered – knowing Oldfield hadn't been in church on Sunday, 'it's not Mister Turner. It's the Governor.'

'The Governor?'

'Hmm.'

'You sure?'

'Yes.'

Then some fingers dug me in the ribs and Sergeant Brandon whispered: 'And how the hell do you know that?'

My jaw sagged, and I felt my face flush. I shrugged, but his fingers dug me in the ribs again, and I whispered: 'I was just guessing.'

'No. You sounded too confident, too sure of yourself.' For a moment we both listened to the Captain, then he whispered, right in my ear: 'You know, don't you? You know because you hear things in that office.' And he chuckled to himself.

I felt like a fool. Like an idiot. Like a stone dropping down a hundred-foot well. I couldn't believe I'd been so stupid, so soon after I'd been warned. I knew I had to do something, say something, and I blurted out: 'Lady Middleton.'

'Lady Middleton?'

I don't know where the thought came from. It left me winded, left me feeling as though I'd hit the bottom of the well. And the well was empty.

There were no more thoughts there, and I didn't know what to say. I mumbled: 'Hmm.'

'What about her?'

I couldn't think of a thing, then I remembered Sunday and being in church, and he prodded me in the ribs again. And somehow that prodded my thoughts, filled the well with water, with lies. I know they say a drowning man will clutch at straws – and I've never believed it – but I clutched at those lies, those straws of the mind, and I said: 'I'm not supposed to tell.'

'Tell what?'

'What I hear.'

His finger pressed on my ribs, threatened pain. I sipped a breath and said: 'The clerks say Lady Middleton is going to visit the chapel this afternoon, because she was the one who suggested the special collection. They say she wants to see how the money is going to be spent. But I say they're wrong.'

'Wrong?'

'Hmm. It's too soon. She'll wait for us to cart away the rubbish, clean the walls, and sweep the floor. Then it will be more lady-like, more suitable for her to visit. That's what I told them.' I paused. 'If there's going to be a visit today, it will be by His Excellency because he granted the lease and men don't mind getting a bit of dirt on their shoes. That's why I'm certain it will be him, and not her.'

My last sentence sounded limp in my ears, but he didn't seem to notice, and he muttered something. Then we shouldered our pikes, turned to the right, and marched up the lane.

In Saint Barbara's Street, four rock carts, each pulled by three horses, were coming to a halt in front of the chapel, and blocking most of the street. The narrow lane beside the chapel was also blocked with scaffolding that ran to the top of the wall, came round the corner, and screened most of Saint Barbara's view of the street. Her shelf with it's flowers and lamp was stripped bare, and now it was being used to support the scaffolding.

As we laid our pikes against the front wall, the carpenters were opening and closing the new shutters on the two front windows; the blacksmith was banging the hinges on the new doors and trying to make them fit onto the old iron uprights; and two masons were hoisting a bucket of mortar up to the top of the scaffolding.

At the top of the wall facing the lane, the masons had replaced several stones, and the new ones looked raw, looked as though the fire had peeled off their skin.

Inside the chapel Sergeant Brandon, handed shovels to six men, then he pointed to me and three others and said: 'You stand with them against the wall. Everyone else – pick up any bits of wood, and all those half-burnt beams, and that old pig pen, and take them through that door there.' He pointed to a door on the far side of the balcony. 'Then you can saw them into lengths for the fire, and stack them near the back door. After that you are to clean up the back yard, and do whatever Mister Tate wants you to do. And as for you lot' – he turned to us – 'those with shovels will take all the dirt, the rubbish, and the weeds out to the carts. Those without shovels will carry the bits of broken stone and the broken tiles out to the carts. If there are any tiles that aren't broken, stack them against the back wall there' – he pointed to the corner near the bell tower where the flagstones still looked clean – 'and Mister Tate might be able to sell them.'

As we carried the rubbish out to the cart and pulled down the small bushes that had taken root in the back wall, we uncovered a step and an altar. The step ran all the way across the chapel and it divided it into two parts. The upper part, the old sanctuary, occupied about a third of the chapel, and it was lit by two windows high in the back wall on the left-hand side. The altar stood on the right-hand side, hard against the back wall. It was hewn from one piece of stone, and a few inches above it – mortared into the wall – stood a narrow stone shelf that might once have held a crucifix with flowers and candles. The flat top of the altar was engraved with five crosses – one in each corner and one in the middle – and as I ran my fingers over them it was hard to believe that I was standing in what was supposed to be a place of sacrifice. And in spite of myself, in spite of all I knew, all I believed, a feeling of awe, of reverence, ran through my body, and deep inside, in my spirit, I felt a sudden chill – and all the old certainties were not quite so certain. Then I heard all the laughing, the talking, the grating of metal on stone, and the moment passed. I dug my fingernail in the middle cross and prised out the dirt. Then I felt a hand on my shoulder and I turned expecting to see Sergeant Brandon, but instead I saw Mister Tate, and behind him stood the Captain. 'No need to clean those,' he said to me, then he turned to the Captain: 'I want to remove this altar. To replace it with a wooden communion table. But it looks as though it's set deep into the earth and it could support the back wall, so I think we'll have to leave it for a while.'

I moved back to the step, picked up small bits of carved stone – they looked as though they were once part of a balustrade, or an altar railing – and carried them out to the carts. Then I found a couple of whole tiles, and as I carried them over to the corner and added them to the pile, I heard Mister Tate say to the Captain: 'I think this must have been a shrine to the Virgin Mary.' And he pointed to a plinth in the corner below the tower. About four feet above the plinth, a stone canopy came out from the wall and it made the corner look dark, mysterious. 'I've found traces of blue paint in the canopy, and that's her colour. And I would think they had a statue up there, and an altar down here where we're standing.'

I wanted to stay, to listen, but Sergeant Brandon caught my eye, and with one finger he pointed to the stone balcony. I cleared out some rubbish

from under the balcony – it was wet and slimy – and then I found a long
rail with rings on it, and I was holding it up in the air and letting the rings
slide backwards and forwards when this voice said: 'That could make a
nice curtain track.'

I knew the voice. It came to me in my dreams. My wet dreams. I smiled
and turned around. She held out her hand – didn't appear to recognise
me – and I said: 'It's very dirty.'

She shrugged, took it in both hands and slid the rings up and down.
Then she said: 'My husband says this was the confessional. Where they
knelt down and confessed their sins to a priest' – she waved her hand in
the air, made the sign of the cross – 'and all their sins were taken away.'
She shook her head. 'What nonsense. What arrogance to think that man
could do what only God can do.' She shook her head again. 'He said they
did it in public, but this rail, this curtain rail' – and she slid the rings up
and down again – 'proves he was wrong.' And she smiled.

I smiled back and said: 'I was wondering why they had that thing. I
thought it was a balcony.'

She looked at me. Touched my cheek, wiped away some dirt. 'I'm
sorry,' she said. 'I didn't recognise you.' Then she smiled with her eyes.
'It was also used as a balcony. Mister Tate says the priests would have knelt
up there and said their prayers. And on holy days, when they brought out
their relics and exposed them on the altar, or on that shelf above the altar,
they would have sat up there all day and made sure nobody touched the
relics. And they would have made sure everyone left an offering. You
only have to look at how poor this area is, and how big this chapel is,
to know that they extracted a lot of offerings.'

Before I could reply the Captain came over and said: 'May I take that
for you?'

She smiled and handed it to him, and he said something I didn't catch.
Then I heard him say: 'Lady Middleton, it's only a rumour but . . .'

Her face paled. She grabbed the rail out of his hands, pushed open
the door – the sanctuary door – and rushed away.

For a moment I felt dazed. Felt as though I'd been struck on the
head. Brandon was the only person who could have told him about Lady
Middleton, could have told him about my lie. I crouched down, my belly
rumbled, and I farted. I wafted the air with my hand, picked up some
more bits of altar railing, and I couldn't think what possessed him.

Then I saw Mister Tate's legs and he was saying: 'I hadn't realised
there was an altar step in here. I would have preferred to have the whole
chapel on one level. It makes us all equal in the sight of God.' And he
paused. 'Strange to think that in all the years men and women knelt here
to receive communion, never once were they allowed to receive both
the bread and the wine. It's as if they weren't good enough to receive
the Blood of Christ.' And he shook his head. 'But now' – I stood up,
came out of the confessional, trembling, wondering if I would ever have

to confess my lie about Lady Middleton – 'it will be as Christ meant it to be, and everyone will drink from the cup.'

They talk about a cup of sorrow. A cup overflowing. 'My cup overfloweth' is the way they put it. They mean overflowing with joy, happiness. When it comes to sorrow I think it just sits in the cup, and in time it goes sour, like old wine, and it sours the spirit. This sourness, this vinegar was seeping into my soul, when one of the carpenters on top of the wall above the balcony yelled: 'Move out of the way!' And he heaved down the burnt end of an old beam.

It thumped the ground. We all looked up and saw the carpenter's legs straddling the wall. This wall was higher than the outer wall – the beams must have run from one to the other to make a simple sloping roof – then he yelled again and heaved down some big stones that had cracked and flaked in the fire. These hit the flagstones, made a heavy, echoing thump, and in the silence that followed I heard the faint sound of singing, chanting – it was as if the thumping had disturbed the past, disturbed those who were buried below the flagstones – then the singing was overlaid with clapping, and we all turned around.

For a moment, framed in the arch of the door, with her back to the sun, I didn't recognise the lady in red. Then I couldn't believe my eyes. I dropped the rocks I'd been clutching to my coat and began to clap, and so did everyone else in the chapel. Lady Middleton beamed at us, nodded to everyone – as if we were old friends – and she waved to the carpenter up on the wall, and to the two masons who stuck their heads through the windows of the outer wall.

Then Captain Lacey and Mister Tate rushed forward and bowed to her.

It was like a miracle, like a cup that overfloweth, and I was grinning like a fool, and shuffling my bits of altar railing into a neat pile at my feet. Then Brandon caught my eye and he nodded – he was smiling, almost grinning – and I was thinking this was one lie that wasn't a lie, it was a prediction, a prophecy, and now there was no need for confession, for the curtain of darkness that used to hang below the balcony. Then I remembered Lord Middleton and the confusion I'd tried to create, and I looked beyond Lady Middleton, beyond the two ladies behind her, and I saw our men, clustering close, making an escort of grey coats and beaming smiles.

Mistress Tate came into the sanctuary – she'd changed her dress and washed her hands – and now, in grey, she looked timid, nervous, looked as though she wanted to scurry away. Her hands were twitching, and so were her eyes, and she reminded me of a church mouse. For a moment I saw Lady Middleton as a cat, a plump red cat, but I knew that was silly for she was smiling, and it was Mister Tate who was watching her every move – like a hungry tom cat. I crouched and picked up my bits of altar railing, clutched them to my coat, and I heard Mister Tate say: 'We think the new beams should be oak, English oak. And we were wondering about the tiles. They should be made in Spain or Portugal, I know that. But I have to confess I don't like the idea of buying things from godless countries, and I was wondering what Your Excellency might advise.'

I closed my ears, walked out of the church, walked into the street, and once again I could not believe my eyes. Every single inch of the street was packed with people, and they weren't making a sound. It was as if they had oozed into the street like a river of hot tar and sand, and now they were bonding the horses, the carts, the windows, the walls, the doorways and the cobbles, into one solid mass. I heaved my rocks into the cart, and as they clattered down the sides – filled the air with a wooden thumping – someone hissed at me, and pointed.

I turned, then I saw them, saw the priests.

They were standing in front of Saint Barbara's shrine. Three were wearing long red robes, white skirts and black hats. Five were wearing long white surplices with black skirts and black hats, and were carrying a processional cross, two lamps on the end of long poles, a silver dish that looked like the hull of a boat, and a silver ball with long silver chains. Behind them, wearing black hats and long black skirts, stood another eight or nine priests with heads bowed, eyes closed, lips moving.

I'd never seen so much error, so much evil congregated in one place in all my life. I should have averted my eyes, turned away from it – from them – but I was caught, caught in that river of black tar, and I couldn't take my eyes off them.

Then one of the priests was doing something with the silver boat, waving his hand in the air – making the sign of the cross with a dignity, a reverence that had not been in the one Mistress Tate made. Then the silver ball was puffing white smoke, and the priest was waving it in the air. The smoke drifted up through the scaffold, around Saint Barbara, and around the masons who were now hanging over the top end of the scaffold looking bemused.

Then I could smell the smoke. It was sweet, sweeter than turf, and it reminded me of perfume, and I was thinking this must be incense, when one of the priests opened his mouth and sang: '*Dominus vobiscum.*'

It was the ancient salutation – the words of welcome – 'May the Lord be with you'. And everyone – except me, two pikemen, and the masons – responded with '*Et cum spiritu tuo*'. The words filled the street, filled my mind, and in them I caught the echo of the words I'd sung so often: 'And with your spirit.'

Then the priest sang: '*Oremus. Domine dirige nos . . .*'

I could recognise, 'Let us pray. Lord guide us . . .' but then the words became sounds, became echoes, and I was being pushed, pushed forward, pushed closer to the cart, and the horses were twitching and the driver was patting them. Then I heard a cry, a strangled cry, right in my ear. I half-turned and looked up into the face of Mister Tate. His flesh was drained of blood. His lips were frozen, contorted like those of a corpse.

His eyes had rolled and all I could see were balls of white veined with red. Then I could hear the air being squeezed out of him and I thought he'd had a fit, a seizure, and I turned right round and yelled: 'Get back! Get back! It's Mister Tate. He's not well.'

We carried him into the chapel and laid him on the stones. Mistress Tate knelt down and cradled his head, and as the colour began to return to his face – and the priests began to sing a Latin hymn – he opened his eyes. Captain Lacey muttered something to Lady Middleton and two or three minutes later, as the singing died, I heard her say: 'Maybe it would be better if we didn't rush the roof, didn't make things worse . . .'

The priests sang 'Amen' and it filled the chapel, smothered her words. Then the voices of the people joined the voices of the priests and they sang 'Amen' again, and this time I could hear the excitement, hear the exaltation in their voices; and I remembered that Amen was a Hebrew word and it meant 'So be it'. The irony of it, the cruel irony, was lost on her and him; but it played in my mind and I couldn't help thinking that somehow God – in the signs he sends to us – doesn't see things as we see them.

Then I began to wonder if we were wrong, and they were right. I began to think the unthinkable: to think that God might be a papist.

29

Next morning, soon after six o'clock, we marched up to Catherine Gate, broke ranks and waited for the drivers to bring the horses up from the stables and hitch them to the rock carts. Yesterday – till the priests blocked the street – we thought we'd be able to take the carts through the gate, dump the rubbish and be back inside the walls before twilight. But the priests prayed and sang for an hour or more, and just when we thought they were going to leave, they pushed their way into the chapel and presented Mister Tate with a letter. He refused to take it, held his hands behind his back; and they laid it on the ground at his feet.

No one moved. No one spoke.

A minute passed. And then another.

Sergeant Brandon leant forward and whispered something to Ensign Wyndham. The Ensign shook his head and a look of scorn, of disgust, passed across the Sergeant's face. Then he stepped forward, picked up the letter and held it out to Mister Tate.

Mister Tate threw his hands in front of his face – as people do sometimes when a fire flares – and he tried to step back, but too many people were crowding behind him, and he couldn't move.

Sergeant Brandon pushed the letter into his hands.

Mister Tate jiggled it for moment – like a hot coal – then he flicked it into the air, and it fell to the ground.

The priests made a soft groaning sound.

Mister Tate lifted his foot high in the air, stamped on the letter, and ground it into the dirt.

The priests groaned again, and swayed. They reminded me of seaweed and the way it ebbs and flows with the tide, but does not let go of the rock that is its home.

Then Mister Tate took off his hat, waved it above his head and yelled: 'I command you to be gone! I command you in the name of Almighty God – for this is now his house – and you are not welcome in his house. So go! Go in the name of God! In the name of righteousness! And do not come back!'

A look of anger came and went on the faces of some of the priests at the front; but most stayed bland, indifferent, and they reminded me of children – beaten into submission. Then it occurred to me that they mightn't understand English, and what looked like submission might be nothing more than ignorance.

Then the priest in the red robes – the one who sang the prayers in the street – opened a book and began to read in Latin. He did not stress any of his words. They flowed in a fast even torrent, and after three or four minutes, my eyelids began to grow heavy and I yawned. I looked up at the sky, at the oblong of deep blue, and I wished he'd stop, wished somebody would have the courage to make him stop. But he went on and on, without interruption. I shut my eyes and thought of God, thought of Him sitting up there, hiding behind that oblong of blue, having to listen to this every day of His life. And I felt sorry for Him, sorry for this endless procession of boredom – and I was wondering what I would do if I were Him, when I heard the silence.

I opened my eyes. Another priest, all in black and looking like evil incarnate, was handing the red-robed priest a bucket of water and a twig with green leaves.

The red-robed priest dipped the twig into the water and flicked it over everyone in the sanctuary. Mister Tate looked as though he'd been touched by the devil. Mistress Tate looked bemused, and some of our men laughed. Then the priest turned and flicked the water over the other priests, and over the people who had crowded in behind them. They did a curious thing: they picked the water off their faces or their clothes with their middle fingers, and they made the sign of the cross.

Then an eerie silence settled in the chapel, and as the priest moved towards the door, the crowds opened a way for him, and somehow the power, the glory, the majesty – whatever it was that was vested in him – went out the door with him. He left me feeling that he, and his priests, had reclaimed their chapel.

This feeling, this thought of yesterday, was still with me as the four drivers began to hitch their horses to the carts. And it was made stronger a few minutes later when the clouds flicked a few spots of rain at us, and I remembered the water of yesterday, the holy water, the water that tasted of salt. And I was wondering why they put salt in it – it didn't need preserving or pickling – and I was thinking I must ask Sergeant O'Sullivan, when two troopers came galloping through the gate and one of them yelled to Captain Lacey: 'You can can go out now, sir. We've finished the picket. We flushed a couple out by the lines towards Charles Fort and sent them running with a couple of shots over their heads. But apart from them' – and he smiled – 'it's dead quiet.'

Captain Lacey nodded, then he turned towards us. 'Two troopers go out every morning and ride the lines. As you heard him say, they managed to flush out a couple of Moors. However, I should warn you' – he paused and looked down our ranks and over to the musketeers – 'that sometimes the Moors dig a hole and cover themselves with sand.

And you can't see them till you're right on top of them. If they leap in
the air and come screaming at you, they'll give you a hell of a fright. And
if you're slow, slow to react, slow to attack, that scream will be the last
thing you ever hear.'

We filed into Catherine Gate, into a dark passage that felt like a tiny
maze. It ran to the right and then to the left, and the doors on either
side did not align. This made it harder for the Moors to capture the gate,
but it also made it harder for our carts, and it confused the horses. The
one closest to the cart began to shy, and the spades and the axes piled on
top of the rubbish clanged and rattled and filled the narrow space with a
high-pitched ringing. The driver grabbed the horse by its bridle. Lockhart
grabbed the next one as it began to shy, and I took hold of the front one
– it was a calm old plodder and maybe that was why it was at the front
– and I patted it on the nose. The driver nodded his thanks and signalled
us to go on, and we walked the horses through the passage, out the door,
and into the V-shaped cobbled yard that lay behind the stone walls of the
revetment. It was matted with horse shit, and the heavy shadows cast by
the towers of the gate made it smell cold and damp. It made me shiver
but it calmed the horses, and as soon as the driver flicked his whip the
lead horse was pulling for the picket gate – the posts bore the scars of
other carts, other axles – tossing its head in the air and eyeing the grass
growing deep in the rutted earth.

To the left of the revetment, in a large area enclosed by a palisade, we
faced the walls and re-formed our ranks. In front of us lay a deep trench
cut out of solid rock. The rock from it must have been used to build the
foundations of the wall for they displayed the same harmony of colour
and texture, and they made it look as though the walls had grown out
of the trench.

The walls rose to about thirty feet – more if I added on the depth of
the trench – and they were reinforced by three towers. Then they made
a dog-leg, and as they ran up the hill to lock into Irish Battery they were
reinforced by four more towers. They were like guards: cold, impassive,
always on duty, always ready to protect the place of safety; and they gave
me the impression of great strength, great power.

Then we about-turned and the impression vanished.

The hills rolled to the left and to the right, and they filled half the
sky. They were vast, and we were small, like tiny grey ants – if such
things exist – and our forts were no more than white pimples waiting to
be squeezed.

On Sunday morning, when we'd been in the Upper Castle – on the
Governor's Bastion waiting for Lord Middleton – the hills had drifted
into the distance and those on the horizon were cloaked in cloud, and
because we were high up we saw them from the same perspective, and
there was a feeling of equality. But down here, where the lanes converged,
the perspective changed, and now we were looking up and there was no

feeling of equality – in truth the feeling was the exact opposite. The clouds had lifted and now the air was crisp and clear, and it drew the forts that lay about half a mile away – on the edge of our lines – closer, and it made them look as though they were no more than two or three hundred yards away. In a perverse twist that I've heard called the optics of sight, it expanded the land – the Moorland – that lay beyond the forts. It gave the hills on the horizon a hard edge and it stressed the butting of white to blue, for the tops of the hills were now capped with snow, with the chill of winter; and despite the warmth of the sun I could still feel that chill.

The musketeers shouldered their muskets, and swinging shovels or picks in their left hands, they marched through the gate in the centre of the palisade and into Anne's Lane.

We turned to the left, marched past the earth-mounded walls of the burying ground, wheeled to the right, and waited for the rubbish carts to pass through the gate in the corner of the palisade. Then we followed them up a lane – it has a name but it escapes me at the moment – and after a couple of hundred yards of slow-pacing we drew level with Pole Fort. They say this was the second fort to be built and sometimes it's called Catherine Fort. I can understand why it would be called Catherine – it protects the approaches to Catherine Gate and it honours the Queen – but I can't see much sense in the name Pole. All I can think is it honours someone I've never heard of, and he must have done something special, or been someone important for this was a huge fort: tall, square, ringed with earthworks and palisades, and topped with a square tower that looked down on our lane; and only Charles Fort – long, low, and sprawling over the top of a hill about half a mile to our right – was bigger; and it was named after the King.

We marched another two hundred yards – with eyes blinkered by earthworks and palisades – made a slight bend to the left, and continued on for another hundred yards. Then the carts rolled through a gate and onto a wedge of rising land that ran between a pair of hills – shadowed and shaped to look like a pair of firm young breasts – and we came to a halt in front of small fort or redoubt.

The top of the right hill was nippled with a square fort, and although the shape was not right for a nipple the name was – for this was Anne Fort. High above us, and just down from the fort, the musketeers were beginning to pull out palisades, to expose Anne's Lane, and shovel earth and rock onto the embankments.

The top of the hill to our left was also nippled with a fort – James Fort – and although the name was most inappropriate the shape of the fort wasn't. It was fat at the base with tapered walls and a flat top – where the sentries were pacing up and down – and a small central tower or sentry-post; and maybe the whitewash had been tinted for it looked pink, looked like the nipple of a young girl. Then I began to wonder what the girl on the Little Parade looked like when she slipped off her dress. I could remember an old uncle of mine saying 'Women paint their tits, women do. They paint them pink and red and purple. And them's the colours of your knob – boy. And they're trying to tell you something they are.'

I began to wonder if she would paint them for me, and I was thinking she wouldn't have to buy the pigments – her father would have them in his apothecary – when I heard Captain Lacey's voice and he was saying: 'I want you to fill up the holes on this slope. The Moors get over that fence' – he pointed to a low fence that ran from one nipple to the other like a string of black beads – 'and they hide in the holes. And the sentries up there' – he pointed to Anne Fort – 'can't see them when the holes are full of shadows. So we're going to fill them in. And I want you to tramp them down hard, make them smooth, make them flat. And after that, you are to cut all those tiny bits of scrub' – he waved his hand at the scrub that was giving the breasts a hairy look, a manly look – 'and load it onto the carts. And that'll be less for them to hide behind.'

I jabbed my pike into one of the oak palisades in front of the redoubt – intending to fix it firm – but the palisade broke and fell inwards. The end of my pike flew up and belted me between the legs. I gasped. The pain doubled me over, and for a moment I saw stars, saw the face of the apothecary – saw him scowling, wagging his finger at me.

Then I heard laughter, waves of laughter. I fell to the ground, curled over, hugged my balls – and tears ran down my face. Then I felt a hand pulling me up and I was looking into the face of Captain Lacey and he was saying: 'Oak rots out here. It's something to do with the weather. Or the soil. Or both. And those palisades, they give the impression of strength, of safety.' He shook his head. 'But it's an illusion. And that's true of almost everything you can see.' And he waved his hands at the forts, at the nipples that the Moors would like to milk of life. A cold shudder ran down my spine and it numbed the ache in my balls.

About an hour later, when I'd axed some scrub and loaded it onto one of the empty carts, I pulled out some wild flowers. They were dark red, and they looked like a stunted version of the flowers that had been on Saint Barbara's shrine last Sunday morning. I wandered over to one of the holes, and helped to tramp down the last of the rubbish, the last of the rubble that had come out of the chapel. My foot rolled on a stone and I tried to stamp it into the earth but it rolled away. I chased it, booted it, and chased it again. Then I grabbed it with my right hand, my hand of wild flowers. It was sharp and it cut and crushed the flowers – stained my hand red, and stained the rock. I shrugged and rolled it over, and then I froze. I was holding the face of Christ, crowned with thorns. The arms were broken and gone, and so was the belly, but his chest was still heaving with pain. The red stain was running through his hair, through the thorns and down his face. It was an omen. A bloody omen. I looked at the redoubt, the forts, and the slopes that lay between. They were not breasts and nipples. They were the slopes of death.

I turned him over, saw his brains had been bashed out, and now they were like pulp, like the wild flowers. I turned him over again – his nipples were bleeding. I wiped them clean, looked up, looked at the forts, and beyond them I could see white specks, could see the Moors waiting and watching. I looked at the redoubt, at the oak palisade that had fallen, had tried to mash my balls, and I felt ill. I shoved him into my pocket and spat on my hand tried to wash off the stain. But the stain was part of me, part of what was to come, and it would not wash off.

30

Next morning, soon after six o'clock, as a light fog was beginning to roll across the Bay, I ambled along the quay, into the guard room, and added up the marks for the rock carts. Fifteen bucket carts and ten open carts had come through the gate. I looked to the sentry and said: 'Yesterday was busy.'

'Busy?'

'Twenty-five carts in one day.'

'No,' he said, shaking his head. 'There were only three or four in the morning. And a couple more in the afternoon. I think.'

'But look at this.' I showed him the marks.

He shrugged. 'Don't mean anything. That looks like two or three days to me. Or it could be from last week. There was a busy day last week, I remember that.'

'Is there another list? A list for yesterday?'

'Another list?' He looked at me and blinked. Then he waved his hand around the room – it was furnished with a table and two stools – and said: 'If you can find another list, then there's another list. If you can't—'

'But how do I know the right numbers if you don't have a list?'

'I do have a list. That's my list.'

'But it doesn't tell me how many carts came through the gate yesterday.'

He yawned in my face. 'Make up any number you like. That's what the other boy did.' Then he walked outside, raised the barrier and lifted his hat to two officers on horseback.

I wandered down the Mole. At King's Stairs I turned and looked back at Sergeant O'Sullivan's window – it was bright with glare and I couldn't tell if he was there or not – and I lowered my pike to the correct slope and began to march. But as the fog softened the air and sucked the sparkle out of the spray at the end of the Mole, I slowed down and began to think about the lists. It was such a simple thing, to put a mark on a piece of paper.

Then I was at the door of the prickmaster's office, brushing away clumps of seaweed – they'd caught on the wooden step – and shoving open the door. Inside the air frosted my breath. It was cold, much colder than it was up on the walls by Three-gun Battery, pacing up and down half an hour ago. The floor was wet and the fire had gone out, and both the pricks were sitting at their desks, wrapped in blankets, with their hats pulled over their ears.

The older one looked at me and said: 'What was your name again?'

'Fenton.'

He grunted. 'There's no chocolate this morning. We were swamped by a wave last night. A freak wave. It came down the chimney and everything got bloody drenched, and half the stuff out there' – he waved his hand towards the window and the bare cobbles that lay beyond it – 'got washed away.' Then he pulled the blanket closer to his chest.

I told him about the numbers, the missing numbers. He shrugged. 'How many did he think he counted?'

'Three or four in the morning. And another two in the afternoon.'

He opened up a book. 'What say we call it? Three bucket carts? And two open carts? I can remember them, just before the sacks of ash arrived.'

I looked into the fireplace. Their ash looked like porridge, wet, grey and brown, with a few black lumps – glistening like stewed prunes – and I said: 'What do you want ash for?'

The younger prick looked up. 'We mix it with tarras and sand from up there.' He nodded towards the sandhills behind Irish Battery. 'And lime, and fresh water. It sets like rock and it doesn't break up under water. But it costs a hell of a lot of money.'

I smiled and pointed to the ash in the fireplace. 'That lot won't cost you a thing.'

He laughed. 'That's coal ash and wood ash. We're talking about volcanic ash. It comes from Mount Vesuvius, in Italy, in the Bay of Naples. They bag it and sell it, and we can never afford to buy enough to—'

The door banged open, a pikeman stuck his head in and said: 'Any extra work for tomorrow?'

The older prick reached for a piece of paper. 'It's low tide about six in the morning. Can you start then?' The pikeman nodded. 'What name?'

'Turner.'

The older prick nodded, the pikeman banged the door and silence settled on us. 'What did he mean by extra work?'

The younger prick pulled his blanket tighter and shivered. 'When you don't have to mount guard you're allowed to come down here and work for the day. Sir Hugh pays eighteen pence a day – when he's got the money – and you don't go home till it's dark.'

'Can I come down as soon as I have a day off guard? I haven't had any pay and I haven't got any money.'

'Are you fifteen?'

'No – not yet.'

Then you're going to have to wait. Sir Hugh won't employ anyone under fifteen. Says you can't do a proper day's work.'

'But they say our company's going to have to work on the Mole and I'll know what to do. And if I can work for the company I can work for you.'

He shrugged. 'Maybe. But Sir Hugh makes the rules, and he pays the money. And he won't employ boys.'

'So what do I do for money?'

'You do what everyone else does in their spare time. You go fishing.'

'Fishing?'

'Hmm. You can sell what you catch in the Market Place, or you can sell it to a fishmonger, and he'll sell it in the Market Place or hawk it from door to door. It's good fishing if you have the time. They catch a lot of nunfish, starfish, rockfish. Congers always sell well and so do whiting. Some of the men have bought nets and they trawl for skate and plaice. And shrimps.'

'But I don't have any money. I can't even buy a line and some hooks.'

He laughed. 'Do what I did. Get out on the rocks and collect crabs, limpets and sea eggs. Somebody always wants to buy them. And if they don't, go up to the Market Place and swop them for fresh meat. Geese, ducks, pheasant, hare, kid, partridge, pigeons. There's always a good selection if you've got the money – or the fish.'

'And there's no work here for me?'

He shook his head and smiled. 'Go fishing,' he said in a gentle voice, 'on the Mole. By the end of the reef – that's the best spot.'

Twenty minutes later I pulled the ledger out of the bookcase by our fire, entered the figures, and peppered them with sand to make the ink dry faster. Then I noticed every day was double-dated. I turned back a couple of pages and ran my finger down the entries, and every one differed by ten days. I remembered the sheet of paper, the spoilt paper, the one with the notes about the state of the garrison, and I opened my drawer and pulled it out. Monday's writing leapt off the page and hit me in the eye. It was dreadful. Thick stokes. Thin strokes. Clashing slopes. Poor curls. Scruffy tails. Broken letters. Letters that did not join, did not flow. I couldn't believe it was so bad. I stared at it for ages, and the thoughts I'd been nursing – the secret thoughts of being asked to copy a real letter before the day came to an end – withered and died.

I turned the paper over, and there was the date: 4/14 JANUARY 1673/4. Once again the dates were ten days apart, if I ignored the difference of a whole year. It didn't make any sense, and I stared at it.

Then I slipped the sheet of paper back into my drawer – I would have liked to crumple it into a ball and toss it into the fire but O'Sullivan had said I must keep everything – and I pushed the ledger towards Ives, and whispered: 'Why does every day have two dates?'

He looked at me, shook his head, and said: 'Didn't they teach you anything?'

I opened my mouth, but before I could say a word, O'Sullivan said: 'What are you two talking about?'

I heard Ives sigh, and then he said: 'The calendar, Sergeant. We were talking about the calendar, and having to write two dates for every day.'

O'Sullivan nodded, laid down his quill. 'There are two calendars. Did you know that Fenton?'

I shook my head, and he said: 'Then tell me what you do know.'

'About the calendar?'

Trigg looked up and gave me a piteous look; Ives giggled; and O'Sullivan didn't say a word. 'Each year is divided into twelve months. The months are divided into weeks. And there are fifty-two of them in a year. Seven days in a week. And 365 days in a year.'

'Hmm. And what else?'

I couldn't think of anything else, and I stared at the fire. I couldn't imagine a wave coming down our chimney and putting out the fire and wetting the floor. The wave would have to be enormous, three times the height of the one at the end of the Mole last night. Then I heard him cough. I looked up and shook my head.

'Leap years,' he said, 'what about leap years?'

'Oh,' I said, 'leap years. They turn up every four years, when the year can be evenly divided by four. Then we have to add an extra day onto the end of February. And that means it has twenty-nine days instead of twenty-eight and it's called a leap year. But why it's called a leap year when it doesn't leap over anything is something I've never been able to work out.'

Trigg shook his head, and kept on writing. Ives' face swelled – he looked as though he was about to burst into laughter – and he bit at his lips. O'Sullivan stared at me, then he said: 'Well you know more than Ives did when he first arrived.'

Ives looked down at his desk and his look-of-laughter dissolved into a scowl. O'Sullivan smiled, for the briefest of moments, then he said: 'And what about New Year's Day?'

I remembered Elme. Remembered the days of my youth: days of dancing; days of singing, talking, eating; days of drunkenness; days that passed in a whirl and ended in swiving. And nine months later, the babies of that day, that night, would be born on Christmas Day. And none of them was ever called Jesus. Not in our village they weren't. I smiled to myself, and said: 'It's celebrated on the 25th of March: Lady Day.'

He nodded. 'And why is it celebrated on that day?'

'Why?'

'Yes. Why?'

I shook my head. I had no idea.

'Ives – tell him.'

Ives looked at me and clenched his mouth – mimicked the rictus of the dead – then he said: 'It's the Feast of Our Lady, the Feast of the Annunciation, when the Angel Gabriel told Mary she was going to have a baby. And that's why Christmas Day is nine months later, on the 25th of December.'

O'Sullivan nodded. 'It's the beginning of new life, divine life. That's what we're celebrating.' And there was in his voice a tone of respect, a tone my Father used to call sanctimonious. It was like an echo of sermons past, and I could remember those sermons, spoiling, or trying to spoil, the excitement that bubbled and brewed that day, that day that was stripped of work, stripped of inhibitions – if I remember right the word my Mother used to use. I remembered how long it used to take for that day to arrive – an eternity of days, an eternity of waiting, an endless unfolding of time, of the thing they call the calendar.

Then O'Sullivan said: 'So why do they celebrate New Year's Day on January 1st, in Scotland?'

I shook my head.

'Ives?'

'They've gone back to the way the calendar used to be.'

'Some would say they were influenced by the French, but you're right. They've gone back to the calendar of Julius Caesar – the Julian Calendar – and he decreed that the new year would always begin on January 1st. So in Scotland, it's already 1674. But here in Tangiers we follow the "Old Calendar", so it's still 1673, and it won't be 1674 till March 25th. On the Continent they keep January 1st as the start of the new year, so over there' – he pointed towards to Spain – 'it's also 1674. And that's why you'll see a lot of documents written 1673/4.'

'That's easy enough to remember,' I said. 'All documents written between January 1st and March 24th carry the date 1673/4 and from the 25th March to the 31st December they carry the date 1674.'

Ives burst out laughing. O'Sullivan shook his head, and said: 'If only it were so easy.' Then he turned to Ives and said: 'You tell him.'

'Towards the end of last century the Pope decide to change the calendar and he—'

'Tell him why.'

'The seasons were running ahead of the days. It was something to do with the leap year. They hadn't worked it out right. And they should have been adding on more days. And there was ten days difference between the two of them. So this Pope—'

'Pope Gregory.'

'He decides everyone has to jump forward ten days, to lose ten days of their life. And then, puffed-up with his own importance, he calls this new calendar after himself. And that's how we got the "Gregorian Calendar". Naturally enough we decided not to to use it in England – having no need of popery or things continental – but out here we have to use it. For trade and things like that. So all our documents carry two dates. The first one is always the "Old Calendar" and the second one is always the "New Calendar", and we never call it the "Gregorian Calendar".'

O'Sullivan looked at me. 'Do you understand all that?'

I nodded. 'The "New Calendar" runs ten days ahead of our calendar, the "Old Calendar". And for us New Year's Day is on March 25th and for them it's on January 1st.'

'And in Scotland it's also on January 1st, but apart from that they still follow the "Old Calendar".'

I groaned and pretended to hold my head. Ives laughed.

'Write down these dates,' O'Sullivan said. 'December 22nd 1673, and March 25th 1674. And work out the new dates. And when you've done them bring them over to me.'

They were dead easy and I wrote: 22 December/1 January 1673/4,

25 March/4 April 1674/4. I laid them in front of O'Sullivan and he shook his head. 'The first one's right, but the second one's wrong.'

'Wrong?'

'When the year is the same in both calendars we only write the year once.' He paused. 'And from now on you write both dates every day in the book for the carts. And every document, every letter, you copy into the books must bear both dates. If an officer has forgotten to put on both dates – a lot of them leave off the new date because they get it muddled – you are to write the date onto his letter. And make sure you get it right. Not getting it right is a mistake. And mistakes are like spelling mistakes. They will cost you an extra hour, and if we run out of copying, there's always something else that can be done.' He smiled. 'Sweeping, cleaning, washing the floor, laying the fire – something like that.'

I wrote the dates into the cart book – it was a simple matter of adding on one day – and then, as I opened up *Laws and Ordinances* and looked for something a bit more interesting to copy, Trigg said: 'Ives. You haven't told him about the Regnal Year.'

The silence was like the grip of death. I could feel it round my throat.

Ives coughed and said: 'On some documents—'

'All legal and official documents.'

Ives looked at Trigg, and began again. 'On all legal and official documents – we don't see many because most of them are written in the Upper Castle – the year is the Regnal Year. That means the number of years the King has been reigning. In the case of His Majesty, he dates his reign from the death of his father on the 30th January 1649. And he counts the years of the Commonwealth, the years of Cromwell, as part of his reign. So every 30th of January – according to the "Old Calendar" – we add on another year. And we are now in the 26th year of the reign of His Majesty King Charles II.' He turned towards Trigg and pretended to doff his hat.

Trigg smiled. O'Sullivan said nothing. But the air was thick, thick enough to need cleaning.

A few minutes later O'Sullivan muttered something about having to help the Quartermaster Provost Martial for the rest of the morning. I handed him his hat and sword. He picked up his walking stick, hooked it over his arm, and hobbled out of the room.

Trigg sat back and smiled – gloated might be a better word – then he turned to Ives and said: 'That was very good. Not the hat. That was the act of a clown. A fool. But the rest – the rest was very good.' Then he leaned towards me. 'You must learn the number of days in each month. Most people make mistakes because they can't remember the number of days. There's a little rhyme. Well – maybe not a rhyme, a little ditty, and it goes like this:

'Thirty days hath September, April, June and November all the rest have thirty-one, except February has twenty-eight clear, and twenty-nine in each Leap Year.

'And then of course there's one other thing he didn't tell you about. In the year 1700, the "Old Calendar" says the year will be a leap year because it divides by four. But the "New Calendar" – for reasons best known to itself – says the year won't be a Leap Year. And that means that from then on we'll have to add on eleven days.' And he smiled.

'Christ,' I said, 'I'll be forty then.'

Ives leaned towards me. 'I wouldn't worry about it if I were you. Most men are dead and buried by thirty-five. Twenty-five if they're lucky, or unlucky, depending on how you view it. And how this old fool' – he gave Trigg a gentle tap on the shoulder – 'has managed to hang on for so long I don't know.' And he laughed.

Trigg smiled. 'And your life expectancy might be a lot shorter than twenty-five – I seem to remember you were supposed to be at the Head Court of the Guard. At seven o'clock.'

Ives' mouth gaped. His smile died and his skin paled. He whispered: 'Bloody hell!' – grabbed his hat and sword in one hand and tore out the door.

Trigg looked at me and laughed. I closed the door, closed out the draught, and tossed a couple of lumps of coal onto the fire.

After a few minutes of quiet copying Trigg said: 'O'Sullivan didn't tell you about that church of his. They follow the "New Calendar". So Easter's always wrong. And so's Christmas. And so's every other feast. Sometimes it's quite strange to see them celebrating the birth of Christ, and know that we – we who are supposed to have the truth – still have to wait for another ten days.' He fiddled with the end of his plume. 'At least they don't have any bells at that church of theirs. If I had to listen to bells, to hear them ringing out the wrong day, week after week, that would hurt deep in here.' And he tapped his chest.

I nodded, then I saw his hat on the peg, saw the marks of the badge, of the Lamb of God, and I said, in a whisper, like a man in the presence of evil, 'They tell me you used to be a . . .' He turned and looked at me, and I wet my lips. I'd been going to say papist, but I softened it to, 'Catholic'.

He nodded.

'And you were converted.'

'By him.' He nodded towards O'Sullivan's desk. 'It was a mistake. The most dreadful mistake I've ever made. And I don't want to talk about it.'

I nodded. I wouldn't talk about it if I were him. It would be embarrassing, be like having to admit making snowflakes in the privy when no one else was there. I sighed, scratched my crotch, and thought about the girl with the painted tits. I could see her face, see her pale skin, her pink lips and her big round eyes, lamb's eyes, innocent eyes. Then Brandon's buttons, his buttons with the lamb's eyes, the innocent eyes, floated into my mind and they blurred into his eyes. And deep inside my soul, in the marrow of my being, I began to shiver, and I knew that somehow I had to blind those eyes, eyes of lust, eyes of desire; and I said: 'Can I ask you a question?'

He looked up and nodded. 'Sergeant Brandon. He used to have some buttons, on his grey coat. They were just like that badge on Sergeant O'Sullivan's hat and I was wondering . . .'

He burst out laughing, then he said: 'If he was a papist?'

I shook my head. 'No. I don't think he's a papist.' I paused. 'I don't think he believes in anything. He complies, conforms. But in his heart . . .' He nodded. 'I think there was something else, something I don't understand.'

He wiped the end of his quill with a rag and laid it on his desk. 'That's very smart. Very clever.' And he looked me in the eye. 'Maybe there's more to you than I thought.' He bit at his lips and nodded to himself. 'You're right. Brandon is not a papist. Never was. And never will be. The man's corrupt. A purveyor of unnatural vices. But I suppose you know that already?' I nodded. 'He's also an opportunist. You won't find that word in O'Sullivan's book of words. It means if he sees an opportunity he seizes it with both hands. He doesn't think about it. He just does it. And to hell with the consequences. And the annoying thing is that nine times out of ten it works to his advantage. But this time' – he paused – 'it didn't. This time he made a fool of himself. And he killed any chance, any prospect of promotion.' He smiled to himself.

For two or three seconds he said nothing, then he looked up, the smile dissolved, and he said: 'If you want to copy something, you'd be better off copying the words in O'Sullivan's book. That way you'll get to know them, and you won't make any spelling mistakes,' he paused, 'or maybe I should say you won't make as many mistakes.' The smile came back onto his face – it made him look like a contented child – and he dipped his nib into his ink pot and started to write.

I watched him for several seconds, then I coughed and said: 'The buttons. You were telling me about the buttons.'

'Oh! I'm sorry. My mind ran on.' And he put the quill down. 'It's always doing that. And so often, when I think about doing something, I think I've done it. But I haven't done it. I've just thought about doing it.' He paused. 'It's a strange thing. A quirk of the mind. And I don't quite know what to do about it.' He smiled and paused again.

I thought he was going to drift away again, but then he looked at me and said: 'It began when Lord Belasyse was the Governor. He was the one before Lord Middleton. And if you look in O'Sullivan's book you'll see you can spell his name three ways: Belasyse, Bellasis and Bellasize.

He didn't mind which way it was spelt. He always claimed all three were correct, and he would never have agreed with O'Sullivan and this silly idea of his that words can only be spelt one way.' He smiled. 'If I was in charge – as I should be – we wouldn't have that book.' He shuffled back on his stool and looked into the beams.

'This young man arrived from England. His name was Parson. David Parson, or it might have been Daniel Parson. It began with a D, I remember that.' And he bit at his lips. 'He was an Ensign, a reformado. You know what they are?' I nodded. 'And a recusant. You know what they are?' I shook my head. 'Old Catholics. Catholics who can't see the error of their ways and go on being Catholics.' He looked into the beams again, like someone praying, seeking inspiration. 'It didn't matter much in those days. This was before the Test Act. And hard as it is to believe now, Lord Belasyse was also a Catholic, a papist, and he took a fancy to this young man. Not the sort of fancy Brandon takes to young men. But one of friendship and favour. He became part of the Governor's train, his staff, his entourage. And after a while, he took to wearing the badge, the Agnus Dei in his hat.'

'Agnus Dei?'

'It's Latin for Lamb of God. It was a bold thing to do. Him being an officer. Most officers were more discreet, more circumspect. But not him. He was like a convert in the first flush of his faith.' He looked at his desk, shuffled the papers. 'Converts do silly things. They're so sure they've found the truth. And they're so eager to share it, to proclaim it to the world. It's a sort of madness. And later . . .'

He was talking about himself. I knew that, and he knew that. And for a second or two his words drifted on. Then he came back to the point and said: 'And then one day he's wearing these buttons on his coat. And every one of them bore the image of the Agnus Dei. He had them made in England, at his own expense, and they say he gave some to the Governor, but I never saw him wear them. It caused a sensation. And most of the officers were highly offended. They called it "tampering with His Majesty's uniform". But that was a nonsense, for every officer pays for his own uniform, pays for the changes, and the more money a man has the more likely it is that he'll make changes. The King has nothing to do with it. But I do concede that most of the changes have to do with lace and the quality of the fabric – so this was rare. And offensive, because it smacked of popery.'

He stood up, walked to the end of the room and looked out O'Sullivan's window. Then he sat on O'Sullivan's stool, sat where I could see he thought he belonged. 'Then this young man had a fit, an apoplexy, and he fell down the stairs and couldn't move his arms or his legs. They bled him. And purged him. For two or three days. And just before he died he said he wanted his body to go back to England, to be buried in the family vault. But he didn't have any money to pay for this, so they sold his commission and auctioned his clothes and all his other things. Sergeant Brandon bought his gorget and coat. The one with the Agnus Dei buttons. There was a hell of a row about it. They say the Governor was outraged.'

'But he could have bought the coat himself if he wanted to.'

He shook his head. 'A Governor doesn't buy an Ensign's coat. It would be below his dignity. And besides, he would have no use for it.' He paused. 'Do you know why he was outraged?' I shook my head. 'Can you guess?' I shook my head again. 'In effect Brandon was telling him he was a fit and proper man to be an Ensign, an officer.'

'Hmm. But if Brandon had the money he could have purchased a commission, and that would have made him fit to be an officer.'

'Hmm. But he didn't have the money. So he wasn't fit and proper.' And he smiled.

'Then why did he buy the coat?'

'Because if the Governor is of a mind, of a mood, or the stars are right, or whatever it is that moves such a man, he can grant a commission without payment of any money.'

'But I thought all commissions had to be bought.'

'In law a commission is granted to the fittest man, the best man, without any form of payment whatsoever. But in practice all commissions are bought and sold. And when an officer sells his commission – at the end of his service – it becomes his pension. It has to keep him in his old age. So nobody wants to see commissions given to men with no money. It debases the system, devalues the pension. But sometimes Sergeants are given commissions, without payment, as a sort of incentive. And this encourages men like Brandon to work harder, to aspire to greater things. It also makes them think they're better than they are.' And he smiled.

'So, contrary to everything I've been told, there is a chance that a man, a man like me, could become an officer one day?'

He laughed. 'If every reformado died, and all the gentlemen volunteers went back to England, and the Moors killed a few Ensigns, there might be a chance, if you were a sergeant of ten years' standing. But I wouldn't count on it, if I were you.'

32

In the afternoon, a minute or two after the boom of the cannon announced the parade to change the guard, Trigg wiped his quill, looked at the two empty desks that straddled his, and said: 'As they're not back yet you might as well come to the Upper Castle with me. I can show you where you'll have to go when your writing improves a bit more.'

I nodded and smiled, but inside I was pissed off. I'd been thinking I might be able to have the afternoon off: all the rubbish was out of Mister Tate's chapel; there was no mention of a work parade for us this afternoon; I'd copied four pages and the letters had an even flow – looked as good as anything I'd ever done.

I went to get his coat, then I noticed there were two of them side by side, and both were corporal's coats. 'Which one do you want?'

'The one on the right. The other one's the spare one, and it's too small for me.'

'Then what's the point of having a spare one?'

'We use it to deceive those who think they know best.' And he laughed. 'You have to be a corporal to work for the Secretary, in the Governor's House. It's supposed to recognise age, maturity, experience – things like that. It means the best man is always sent up there to help, when it's necessary. But sometimes there isn't a corporal available, and O'Sullivan can't walk that far. The hill cramps his leg and that stick of his isn't much help. So we have that coat, and if they send down for help we put it on the man with the neatest hand, and for an hour or two he's a corporal.' And he smiled.

The hill made Trigg puff and pant, and in Stayner's Battery we sat on the bench for a few minutes. I watched the troops assembling on the Old Parade. I tried to recognise the men in our company as they came out of the tower by Three-gun Battery, but the uniforms made them all look the same, and their faces were too small or half-hidden by their hats.

Trigg caught his breath, wiped the sweat from his brow. 'I often sit here,' he said. 'I like to arrive looking cool and refreshed. It doesn't do to look as though you left it so late you had to rush up the hill. They like to maintain a dignity in there.' He nodded towards the Governor's House. 'A decorum they call it. Everything is slow and solemn. Ponderous

– to tell you the truth. But if you have to stay late the food's good. Much better than we get. And there's more of it. When we used to have an office full of clerks it was thought to be a perquisite. But now, when there are so few of us, I don't look forward to it any more. I've often wished Ives was a bit more responsible, not so impetuous, then we could slip that spare coat onto him, from time to time.' He sighed and shook his head.

The Upper Castle was not a castle in the traditional sense of a keep protected by one or two perimeter walls. It was more like a small town. High walls linked the four great bastions and enclosed an area of six or seven acres that was laid out with houses, warehouses, gardens and cobbled streets. The Governor's House commanded the town and the view from the Bay. Peterborough Tower commanded the heights – reached for the sky – but it didn't look very big because it was too slender and from most angles we never saw the step-shaped supports that strengthened both sides of the tower. The top of the tower could be seen from all over the Bay and when I asked about the beacon – it was full of pitch-coated faggots that looked like bundles of dead crows – he said: 'If the Moors attack at night, it will be lit to warn the ships anchored in the Bay. They say the Governor has an understanding with the Admiral and the navy is supposed to land enough tars to help. But if you've ever seen what a drunken bloody lot they are, I wouldn't rely on that promise if I were him.' And he nodded towards the Governor's House.

As we walked down the steps I looked again at the warehouses we marched past on Sunday. The three of them were about fifty yards long, built side by side and covered with steep pointed roofs that made the front end look saw-toothed. Houses butted onto the right-hand side of the warehouses, butted into each other, and enclosed a large square of private gardens. Further to the right came a narrow lane and more houses that enclosed more private gardens – oblong-shaped ones. The far end of the warehouses was set well back from the walls – to make a long forecourt for the main entrance to the Governor's House. A row of houses, without any pretence of gardens at the front or the back, ran from the end of the forecourt to a low stone wall. The wall butted into the great bastion in the far left-hand corner of the castle and it enclosed a house that was set in gardens and half-hidden by tall trees.

I was thinking about this house, thinking someone important must live there, when Trigg pushed open the door to the warehouse and I was hit by the most glorious smell. It was oranges and lemons; onions and garlic; pepper and bay leaf; cinnamon and cloves; and a hundred spices I couldn't name. It filled my head with the taste of food, fresh food with no hint of salt, no touch of bitterness. The meat was soft in my mouth, soft because it was killed and hung for a few days, and it wasn't rank, or hard, or stringy. 'God!' I said. 'I'd love to work in here.'

He laughed at me. 'For a day or so – yes. But after that it kills your sense of smell, and the dust – the dregs you sweep up off the floor – they get in your clothes and your hair. And after a while it's you that is spiced, that is a hot little bit of meat.' He dug me in the ribs and laughed again.

As my eyes adjusted to the gloom, the three warehouses ran into each other and became one – like the mystery of the Trinity – and I felt as though I was walking through a great barn, a cathedral of wooden poles that splayed into arches. The smell of spice was soon replaced with the dry dusty smell of grain: barley, oats, wheat. This gave way to the sour smell of brine, and open vats where water was sucking salt out of meat. As we climbed the steps the smell of salt was replaced by the smell of peas, that musty smell that comes when the peas have become damp, have swollen and dried again, and the new shoot, the new life, has withered and died.

Upstairs, Trigg banged on a door and a voice yelled: 'Come in!'

From the half-gloom, we walked into a room drenched in light, and looked down into the square of gardens. Gravel paths divided the gardens into squares and oblongs, and I could recognise the colours of the herbs: mint, sage, rosemary, thyme and parsley. I could also recognise the orange trees, the lemon trees, with their polished leaves. Against the far walls, the sunny walls, the branches of pear, peach and nectarine trees – gaunt skeletons, bare and espaliered – were blackening the bricks, making shadows that looked like the shadows children make with their fingers, and they reminded me of witches and wizards and haunted forests. And there in front of me was a creature from this forest: a gremlin in a Sergeant's coat. He was about five feet tall, thin and gaunt like the espaliered trees, and his hands, face and neck, were brown, were cracked like dry bark. His eyes bulged out of his face, like ripe puffballs covered in dew; and his lips were fat and swollen, were purple, like meat that has bloated, has started to rot. Then he smiled, his face lit up, and it softened his ugliness, and somehow it didn't matter, didn't repel. He nodded to Trigg, and said: 'Is this the new boy?'

Trigg nodded, said something I couldn't catch, then he turned to me. 'I'll leave you here with Sergeant Carpenter. You can stay for half an hour. Then go back down to the office. If you're too long O'Sullivan will yell at you and he'll make you work late tonight. So don't dawdle.' And he smiled. 'I saw you this morning, saw you dawdling along in the fog, thinking nobody could see you. But I could see you. And so could O'Sullivan. And if you want my advice' – he paused, pursed his lips – 'march at all times. March properly. Don't slouch. And remember this: if you act like a soldier, people will think you're a soldier. If you act like a clerk, a sloppy clerk who couldn't care less, they'll think you're a prick – and they'll be right.'

Sergeant Carpenter burst out laughing, waved Trigg out the door and said to me: 'Does my ugliness, make you feel ill, here?' He prodded me in the belly. I moved backwards and shook my head. He laughed. 'I like a liar, a good liar. They ease the pain.' Then he looked solemn, serious.

'Tell me a lie,' he said. 'A good lie. A funny lie. One that will make me laugh.'

I stared at him. I didn't know what to say. 'Come on,' he said. 'Hurry up. A bright boy would have thought of something by now.'

I swallowed hard. 'Your face looks like wood. Old gnarled wood. If you were true to your name, a carpenter, a shaper of flesh, you could carve yourself a new face. You could be good-looking. But you'd have to carve a few wrinkles around your eyes, and a few lines, a few frowns on your forehead – to prove you're older and wiser than the rest of us.'

It didn't sound funny in my ears, but he opened his mouth wide, laughed and clapped me on the back. 'I think you and I are going to get on all right.' He smiled and I felt as though I'd been sucked into a cave, a gremlin's cave, and in there he could suck, could chew the life out of me, if he was of a mind to carve some new teeth, some real teeth.

'I'm a Sergeant,' he said. 'A Quartermaster-Sergeant and I used to work down in that office of yours – in the days when O'Sullivan and Trigg and I were all corporals together. That was when we had a proper office.' He looked out the window, watched a pair of black birds swoop past the dovecot and land on the gravel paths. 'I don't think it will last much longer. There aren't enough men available now, and I'm amazed they're letting you work there. I always thought when young Ives left, Trigg would come up here and go over to the Governor's House for a couple of hours every day; and O'Sullivan would end up in the Head Court of the Guard.'

'I've been told I'm there till I'm fifteen. Or sixteen if I want to stay that long.'

'That surprises me. I thought they would have wanted that office for something else before then.'

I nodded. 'The moment I walked into that room I thought it was too big, too good for us.'

'Hmm. It is. It used to belong to the Muster Master of Fortifications. He put in those beds. They came off a ship that went aground on the rocks near Whitby. He was going to take them with him, when he moved to that house over there' – he pointed to the corner house on the far side of the square – 'but it was already furnished.'

'I've never slept in a place with proper beds before.'

'Nor had I, till I slept in that office.' And he smiled. I smiled back, and somehow those beds, or the thought of those beds, bound us together, and I felt at ease with him. My thoughts of gremlins and caves vanished, and I saw him as a kind man, a gentle man, imprisoned in a cage of ugliness.

'Once a month,' he said, 'we have to add up all the supplies – the food not the armaments, we do them once every three months – and work out how long they're going to last. We start by assuming every man is going to get his full ration of flesh, pease and grain; and we also assume that we're not going to get any more supplies for four months. You'd think with England no more than four weeks away every request for provisions could be filled within three months. But it's not so.' He shook his head. 'And if the figures show there isn't enough food for four months, we go on rations: six for five, six for four – if things get really bad. And when you've got six hungry men eating the food meant for four, tempers flare, and patience is a forgotten virtue.' He smiled. 'It would be all right if they'd pay us more often. Then the men could buy a few things when they have a market in the Market Place. But now when they do get paid, they drink it all – to forget, or to ease the pain.' And he shrugged. 'We did the figures earlier this week and we have four and a half months on hand, so at the moment we're all right.'

'I saw a lot downstairs – enough to feed an army.'

He laughed. 'That's just what it has to do.'

'And I saw some in York Castle and some in that store-house – the one above the office on the Mole.'

He nodded. 'And there's some at Whitby. It's a deliberate policy – to spread it around. In case of mould, or damp, or weevils. Or the Moors capturing part of the garrison.' He paused. 'A lot of what you saw in York Castle belongs to the fleet. They draw their provisions from there and that means they can stay here a lot longer.'

'But when I had a look in there everything was all mixed up. There was nothing to say this part was for the garrison and this part was for the fleet.'

'Hmm. The ships' captains are always complaining about it. But nobody will do anything about it.'

'But why not? It would be easy to fix.'

He nodded. 'Of course it would be. But if they're all mixed up, and we're running short, we can eat some of their provisions and claim they were ours. And who would know? And anyway, they can always go back to England and get some more, but we're stuck here and . . .' He lifted his hands, spread his fingers and shrugged.

Then he pulled a sheet of paper out of a drawer. 'I'd like to see how good you are at writing. Rule up the paper and make it into a chart like the ones in this book.' He opened a book, pointed to a page, and handed it to me. 'Then write down all the headings. But don't put in any figures. And next time I can use it for the provisional count.'

I took off my coat and sword, settled down at his desk and ruled the lines, broke the empty whiteness into six columns. Along the top I wrote: UPPER CASTLE, YORK CASTLE, MOLE, WHITBY, TOTAL, WILL PROVISION 1,200 MEN FOR . . . WEEKS. Down the side I wrote: Pease, Oats, Barley, Wheat, Rice, Salt, Sugar, Raisins, Currants, Yeast, Cheese, Butter, Beef, Pork, Mutton, Pickled Eggs, Onions, Ship's Biscuit. After about ten minutes I leant back in my chair. The lettering was the best I'd ever done: same size letters, all joined up, and all on the same slope.

But the ruling was poor. I wasn't used to running a line for twelve inches, and when it touched a bump in the paper the ink had flared.

I handed it to him. He nodded and said: 'And now I want you to work out the number of pints of beer each man would drink in a week. Allow three pints per day, per man. And assume that the garrison is at full strength – 1,200 men – and assume every one drinks his full ration every day.'

That was easy. 3 x 7 = 21. 21 x 1,200 = 25,200 pints. I looked at it for a few seconds, made sure it was right, then I handed it to him. He smiled. 'Now, let's assume you are the brewmaster. And you have to make enough beer for the whole garrison for one month. And to make it easy we'll assume the month has exactly four weeks. How many tuns do you have to make?'

I couldn't think how big a tun was. It was the biggest barrel ever made, and it was too big to move unless a man owned a horse and cart. I could remember that. And I could remember a barrel held 36 gallons, and there was something about a tun holding one barrel for every day of the week, so a tun was 7 x 36 = 252 gallons. A gallon was eight pints, so a tun held 8 x 252 = 2,016 pints. I wrote the figures down, checked them twice, and said: 'Is a tun 2,016 pints?'

He nodded. I smiled to myself, looked again at the figure for one week's beer and wrote: 25,200 x 4 = 100,800 pints, divided by 2,016 = and then I was stuck. I've never been any good at long division. I stared at it for ages, then it occurred to me if I chopped off the last three figures of both of them, I was left with 100 to be divided by 2. And the answer was 50. I looked up and said: 'Fifty.'

His eyes widened and he held out his hand. 'Let me see how you did it.' He looked at my figures and his jaw dropped. 'You did the long division in your head?'

I can't do long division. 'It's an approximate answer.'

'No. It's not an approximate answer. It's the exact answer.'

I didn't know what to say, and I must have been embarrassed because it made me giggle.

'I can teach you long division. And weights and measures. And in no time at all we'll have you working out how much meat, how much flesh, has to arrive here every month to give every man three and a half pounds per day,' and he smiled. 'And now you better get going. Before Sergeant O'Sullivan throws a paddy.' He laughed and I laughed with him. Then I thought of the silence that hangs between O'Sullivan and Trigg, and is no laughing matter, and I said: 'Would you tell me something?'

He nodded.

'Sergeant O'Sullivan. And Corporal Trigg. They won't talk to each other.'

He smiled to himself. 'You remember me saying we were all corporals together?' I nodded. 'Well O'Sullivan thinks popery is God-given. It's the true religion. The only religion. And all the rest are wrong, but he would use a stronger word than that: a lie, a heresy, a perversion – something like. Him and Trigg used to sit next to each other and they talked bloody religion day and night. I couldn't see anything in it myself, but they were always at it. And one day Trigg announces he believes in popery – that's not the way he put it but that's what he meant – and he became a papist. And he wore that badge in his hat. Bloody lunacy I thought. But he didn't care. He was so sure he'd found the truth. And him and O'Sullivan they were just like this.' He twisted two of his fingers together and held them up in the air. 'O'Sullivan was bloody unbearable because he'd always claimed popery was a religion of the mind, and he believed a man could be converted by intellectual argument. And Trigg was living proof of it.'

He sucked at his lips for a moment, then he went on: 'Then our old Sergeant, Sergeant Seaton, he died. And the promotion should have gone to Trigg. He was the older man. And he had more experience. But the Town Major wouldn't agree. He told Trigg he was a bloody fool. And if he could be a fool in matters of religion he could be a fool in other things. And he told Trigg he was going to promote O'Sullivan. They say Trigg told him they were both papists and there was no difference. But the Major said there was, said "O'Sullivan's religion is an accident of birth – something he couldn't help. Whereas yours is a matter of conviction", and then he threw him out of his office.'

'He must have been disappointed. And bloody annoyed. But he should have got over it by now.'

'If that was all, you're probably right. He should have. But it wasn't. You see about a week later Trigg takes his badge off his hat and tells O'Sullivan he no longer believes. Tells him he was seduced, by words. Honeyed words. And just like that O'Sullivan's only convert is gone. And all his posturing, his arguments about intellectual conviction, and the truth of his religion being able to be proved by rational discussion, collapsed in front of his eyes.' He smiled. 'So you see, there's bitterness on both sides, and I wouldn't get caught up in it, if I were you.'

33

I rushed into our office, hoping like hell Sergeant O'Sullivan had not come back, but there he was, sitting in his corner, like a red spider, watching, waiting. He laid down his pen and said: 'Where the hell have you been?'

I swallowed hard. 'Corporal Trigg took me up to the warehouses in the Upper Castle. Sergeant Carpenter made me do a chart for him and he says he's going to use it. And that's the first real bit of writing I've done.' I grinned at him.

'Don't look so bloody smug. It's only good because I've been making you practise. Just you remember that.'

I looked at the floor, looked at the boards – the heat had pulled them apart, and the draught was stirring the dust – and as I started to take off my hat and sword, I said: 'I'm sorry I'm late, but he wanted me to do the work.'

'Don't take them off,' he said. 'You get over to your lodging house and tell Sergeant Brandon you won't be coming back tonight. You'll be here. Working. And you tell him you'll be working more nights. A lot more nights. And then you won't have to waste time going to see him every time you have to work late. And make sure you bring your bedding. It can get very cold in here at night.' He picked up his pen and bent over his desk, and I felt as though he'd swept me out of his mind, out of the room.

A few minutes later Brandon looked at me, and said: 'I don't give a damn how many nights you have to work. You're here to work. And work is what you're going to do. From now on if you're not here for the night-muster I'll know you're down there.' He nodded towards York Castle. 'And how's your arse?'

I sucked in a breath, and stepped back one pace. 'Don't be bloody stupid,' he said. 'This is the daytime, not the night-time. And this is a serious question. How is your arse?'

It was tight, clenched tight. And I couldn't think why he would want to know, and I said: 'Just the same.'

'Have you had a shit today.' I nodded. 'Was it firm? Or sloppy?'
'Firm.'

'And it didn't dribble out? Or rush out like water?'

'No.'

'Any blood? Any bleeding?'

I shook my head, then he turned and pointed to Crabtree – looking pale and drawn – and four other men, lying on their pallets. 'Two have the flux. And the other three look as though they're getting it. It can kill you. You bleed, and you shit yourself to death. And this is the only cure.' He held up an earthenware jug. It looked as though it was full of milk, but it didn't smell like milk – it smelt more like chalk. 'Next time you have a shit, if it's sloppy, just a little bit sloppy, you get yourself up here right away and have some of this. If you don't, and I hear you're shitting slop, I'll boot you in the arse. Do you understand?'

I nodded. Then he filled a small tankard, sat down beside Crabtree and helped him to sit up. He put the tankard into Crabtree's hands, but his hands shook, shook the chalky milk onto the grey blanket. He reached out, steadied his hands, raised the tankard to his lips, and encouraged him to take a sip. I was amazed at this quirk of compassion; and all I could think was a mother wolf must be like this with her cubs, and maybe he saw us as cubs. But then I remembered what he did to Crabtree, and that was not the act of a mother. It was the act of a father, a father who will have a cub if he cannot have the mother. Then I felt confused, confused in my mind and confused in my body; and I crept out of the room.

An hour or so later, when I'd done another bloody page from *Laws and Ordinances* and was wondering if Trigg and Ives were ever going to come back, O'Sullivan stood up, stretched, and said: 'What did Sergeant Carpenter say about your writing?'

'He didn't really say. Just accepted it. Took it for granted. Then he wanted me to do all this arithmetic for him. Working out how much beer was needed for a month. And how much meat would be eaten in a week. And how long the provisions would last.'

'Hmm. I had an uncle who was just the same. He took reading and writing for granted, but he used to delight in figures. Used to call them a science in their own right, and he could add, divide and multiply in his head. It was a sort of passion with him. He never married, and I used to think it would have been better if he'd a passion for women – women's figures,' and he laughed. 'He was a strange man. Very solitary. And one day he heard the beat of the drum and enlisted in Cromwell's Army – told them he was Protestant. And they sent him to England. His sister, my aunt, she told him he'd betrayed the faith. Sold it for money. "Judas money" she called it, and she never spoke to him ever again.'

He leant on the window ledge, looked down the Mole for about a minute, then he turned back to me. 'Family quarrels are bitter things. Running sores. And time doesn't heal them.' He shook his head. 'When I heard the beat of the drum, they were asking for Protestants. I told them I was a Protestant. I would have told them anything to stop being a bloody school teacher. But I never told her, told my aunt.' And he sat down.

Maybe it was a trick of the light, or him talking about his family and making me think of mine, for I could see in him my Father – and the image, the twinning of one to the other, was clearer, much clearer than Monday morning.

Then I knew, knew the man from the past, from Ireland, my Father's father – his true father – was of the same flesh, the same blood. They were flesh of flesh and blood of blood. Their flesh was my flesh and their blood was my blood.

For a moment the shock of this discovery froze my mind. Then my eyes misted over and my nose began to run – as it often does in the cold – and I sniffed, blew my nose.

He looked at me, and those eyes, they were my Father's eyes, and I said: 'This man. Your uncle. He was Patrick. Patrick O'Sullivan.'

He rocked back on his stool and stared at me. 'Patrick? You asked me about him the other day, didn't you?' I nodded, and he said: 'My name is Patrick. I'm the only Patrick in our whole family.' And he paused. 'My uncle's name was Seamus. Or maybe I should say it is Seamus. I keep supposing he's dead, but he could be alive. He'd be an old man by now. And I don't really know if he's dead or alive. It's just easier somehow to think of him in the past, to think of him being dead.'

I nodded, and when I looked at him again, with the evening shadows ageing his face, he was not my Father, he was a stranger, a stranger from a heathen land. Then I knew it was time to let this other stranger, this stranger who came and went in the folds of my family, it was time to let him go, time to let him rest in peace – rest in the past.

34

About an hour later Trigg pushed open the door and dumped a bag and a leather-bound book onto his desk. He tossed his hat at me and said: 'Tell the Sergeant I still have some copying to finish. I have to do it tonight and I'll have to sleep here. I intend to take it back to the Governor's Secretary first thing in the morning. As soon as they open the gates.'

I stood up, repeated his message, word-for-word, and I felt a fool. On Monday – or was it Tuesday? – I thought I was growing used to this perversion of manners. But now, without Ives as a witness, a silent conspirator, it was madness, bloody madness, like performing a play without an audience. Somehow Ives managed to make it appear natural, normal. But when I'd listened to his words, listened with care, he was sucking all the life, all the juice out of them. There was no colour, no sparkle, left in them. He couldn't be accused of changing their meaning, or corrupting their flow, but deep down, where words capture the essence of meaning, they weren't the same.

Then I began to wonder what would happen if I refused to repeat their messages. They could make me work longer, harder. They could make me go to the prickmaster's office three times a day to check on the rock carts, and they could make me wait till it was pouring with rain. They could make me sweep the floor, clean the windows, do things like that. But they couldn't tell Captain Lacey, or the Town Major, or the Captain of the York Castle guard. No. That would make them look foolish. And it could end in demotion: Corporal O'Sullivan and Pikeman Trigg. I smiled to myself and cut a new nib. Then I began to run my penknife around the grooves at the side of my desk. Some of the grooves flowed into initials, some became crosses, some took on rolling patterns like waves. I was wondering how many clerks had sat at this desk, sat in a state of boredom, and I was thinking about parrots – for they say parrots can repeat what people say – when I heard a vague voice. I let it slip in and out of my head, and I drove the end of my knife into a hole, made it spin with one finger. Then I heard another voice, a loud angry voice, and it was saying: 'Are you listening to me?'

I jumped to my feet, grabbed at my pot of ink and stopped it rolling off the desk. 'Yes, Sergeant.'

'Then tell Corporal Trigg what I just said.'

I couldn't remember a word. Not a single, solitary, bloody word. I said 'Umm,' and shook my head. I felt a fool. A bigger fool than when I'd listened and could repeat his words.

'You may tell Corporal Trigg, that I am about to leave. And tomorrow morning I'm going to the Head Court of the Guard. Did you understand that?'

I nodded.

'Don't nod at me. Open your mouth and say something.'

'Yes, sir, Sergeant. I heard what you said.'

'And now you may tell Trigg.'

I'm not sure what came over me. Maybe I was tired. Maybe I was bored. Maybe I was just stupid. For I looked at him and without thinking, I said: 'He already knows. He heard every word you said. And there's no need for me to repeat it like a bloody parrot.'

His face flushed. He reached behind his desk, pulled out a long cane and slashed me across the face. I fell back against the wall and he yelled: 'If you ever speak to me in that way again, I will pull down your breeches and I'll belt you so bloody hard with this' – he whacked it across my desk – 'that you'll have to stand up to write. And I'll keep you standing for a whole week.' He glared at me. 'Now tell the Corporal what I said.'

I wiped at my face, at my eyes. Tried to wipe away the pain. Blood was on my hand, was running in the tiny marks that line my skin, was filling them with red, making them look like dykes of blood, dykes of pain. I remembered my Father, remembered the times he had made me bleed, had filled the dykes with pain, and I looked into his eyes – the eyes that belonged to both of them – and I shook my head.

His face blanched. He bit his lips, swung his arm, swung his cane and slashed at me. I ducked. The cane hit my stool. I ran past Trigg, into the corner, his corner. He came at me – smirking, cane in the air – and I yelled: 'If you hit me once more I'll tell Captain Lacey. I'll tell him about you and Trigg not speaking. And I'll ask him what he would do if he were in my shoes.'

O'Sullivan rocked on his feet. The colour came back to his face, came back bright red. He stared at me for a minute, maybe two minutes – it felt like all eternity – then he slipped the cane in behind his desk, took his hat off the peg, grabbed his walking stick and limped towards the door.

My heart was thumping, filling my ears with madness and I yelled: 'I'm not going to be a bloody parrot, for you or anyone else. Ever!'

He spun round, glared at me, and slammed the door. My ink pot – the pot I'd just rescued – slid down my desk, crashed to the floor and broke. The black ink, the blood of writing, dribbled down the cracks between the floorboards.

35

A few minutes later Trigg looked up from his desk and said: 'You shouldn't have done that.'

I raised my head from the cradle of my arms and nodded. 'I know.'

'Tomorrow. First thing. The moment he comes through that door. Before he can say a single word, you apologise. Say you're sorry.'

I looked at my desk, looked at the long stain of ink-black blood. 'I'm sorry. Sorry I swore at him. I shouldn't have done that. I know that. But I'm not sorry about the rest. And I'm not going to parrot his words – or yours.'

A heavy silence fell between us, and for the next hour he copied letters into the leather-bound book he'd brought back from the Upper Castle. I copied some more *Laws and Ordinances*, and then the dark began to hurt my eyes, to clump the small type together, to make the page look like burnt toast. I shut the book, found a candle, lit it in the fire and slipped it into the brass sconce on Trigg's desk. He grunted, pulled the sconce a little closer – it was hinged to the side of his desk – and continued to write.

For a few minutes I did nothing – just watched the shadows move across the desk as he wrote. Then I picked up O'Sullivan's spelling book and opened up the first page. And there, in his own writing, I read: 'A BOOK DESIGNED TO PROMOTE THE STANDARDISATION OF WRITTEN ENGLISH. Prepared and compiled by Sergeant P. O'Sullivan of The Tangiers Regiment-of-Foot. Begun in the year of Our Lord 1669.' I turned to the first pair of pages, the pages dedicated to the letter A, and read: 'arrears, accompanies, accordingly, assemblies, ambushment, assault, administration, articles, authorised . . .' The words were like troops, they marched down both pages in columns of three, and there must have been more than two companies, more than a hundred of them; and I was thinking they were in a jumble, a mess, and they needed to be ordered – alphabetically. Then I laughed to myself – I didn't know how to spell the word – and I ran my finger down all the columns. It wasn't there, it had escaped his attention, his conscription.

A few more minutes slipped into the past, and I didn't know what to do, and I didn't want to do anything. I pulled open my drawer – thinking to clear my desk – and I saw the head of Christ. His face was dark, shrouded in gloom, and his hair was spiked with thorns. I held him up in the air, twirled him round and round. He caught the light, the soft flickering light. It made his eyes flicker, and it filled his mouth with shadows, made his lips look as though they were twitching, were wanting to say something.

Trigg pushed his book to the side, looked at the broken Christ and said: 'Where did that come from?'

'I found him in the rubble that came out of the chapel. Saint Barbara's chapel.'

He stretched out his hand, took the head and held it close to the candle. He picked at the dirt with his fingernail. Then he wet his finger and washed the face. 'I think it's marble. Brown marble with black veins. If you washed it, gave it a polish with a soft cloth, it would look like new. The carving is very fine, very delicate. It must have been quite valuable – once.' And he paused. 'Saint Barbara's you said?' I nodded. 'That's the chapel Mister Tate has just taken over.'

'Yes – yes, it is. How did you know that?'

He smiled. 'I've just copied two letters into the book. One was for Mister Tate and one was for his wife.' He paused. 'Her letter was nothing much. Just a polite note from Lady Middleton. Thanking her for the visit to the chapel and apologising for Lord Middleton being indisposed.'

'Indisposed?'

'It means he was ill. But in truth he was drunk.' He laughed and I laughed with him. Then the tone in his voice became solemn, serious, and he said: 'You are a clerk – and I hope you will still be one in the morning when O'Sullivan comes back – and you must remember we are all bound by an oath of secrecy. It's not a formal oath, an oath taken on the Bible, it's understood. And if you break it, if you tell anyone about anything you see, or hear, or read in this office, or come to know about because you work for this office, you will be dismissed. I mentioned this to you once before, didn't I?' I nodded. 'No doubt O'Sullivan has mentioned it? And explained some of the punishments?' I nodded again. 'You may think it unfair but it does have one great advantage: amongst ourselves we can talk about everything. And it can be very entertaining.' Then he looked towards O'Sullivan's desk. 'Or maybe I should say, it used to be entertaining.'

Then he picked up the bag he'd brought back from the Upper Castle. 'Come and sit by the fire, and have something to eat. I knew when I saw Sergeant Carpenter, saw that chart you did for him, you'd be back late, and O'Sullivan would be bloody mad with you. And knew it would be my fault. So – I thought I'd make it up to you.' He put his hand into the bag, pulled out three slices of ham, three bread rolls, a wedge of cheese, a pot of butter, a comb of honey, three oranges, and six walnuts. 'I put in enough for three of us, in case young Ives came back. But it's too late now. The gates will be closed.' He smiled. 'So it's all for us. And there's more . . .'

He took the books off the bottom shelf of the bookcase, knelt on the floor, leant into the bookcase and pulled out a stone jar. Then he smiled at me. 'There's six pints in there. Six pints of black beer. It's thick and strong, and you'll have no trouble sleeping tonight.' And he laughed.

We ate in silence for about fifteen minutes, then I sat back in my chair, belched, and closed my eyes. I felt warm inside and warm outside, and after a while I began to float. Our talk drifted from the Head Court of the Guard to the forts and back again. Then it drifted down the Mole, along the Strand and into Whitby, and I can remember him saying: 'They like to think they're independent down there. Like to think they can do what they want to do. And they say they are a Dominion, a Dominion in their own right. It's bloody nonsense. But the stupid thing is, as long as we're here to defend them, to rush troops to their aid if they're attacked, it's true.' He laughed a happy drunken, gurgling laugh, took off his shoes and socks and wiggled his toes at the fire.

We slept for a while – sitting in our chairs. Then we drank a little more, and somehow we were talking about Sergeant Brandon, and I was saying things I should not be saying, and he was shaking his head. Then he said: 'If you're ever sent to Whitby, watch out for Sergeant Lawson. Him and Brandon are friends. He's an evil bastard. Makes Brandon look like a saint, and that's not an easy thing to do.' He yawned and shook his head.

I opened my window, pulled down my breeches and pissed into the night. The moonlight cut my piss into glitter – or black diamonds from the black beer? – then I leant against the window ledge, and as I tried to pull up my breeches, I saw Saint Barbara's tower. I'd never been able to make it out in the daylight, but here it was with its pointed roof scratching the sky. The bell was still missing, torn out like a tongue, and it couldn't speak, couldn't make a sound for her, for Saint Barbara. Or was it for Him, for Him who was a prisoner in my drawer? Or was it for the other him, for Mister Tate? Then I remembered the letter, the other letter, and I said: 'You didn't tell me what was in the letter.'

Trigg looked up and blinked. 'What letter?'

'The other letter, the one to Mister Tate.'

'Bring it. Bring it here.' He waved at the leather-bound book.

He pulled his glasses up his nose and peered into the book. Then he giggled, looked at me, and beat the air with the index finger of his right hand. 'You remember your promise, your solemn oath?' He giggled some more and flopped back in his chair. I nodded and he giggled again. 'Poor Mister Tate. It's from the Governor. From Lord Middleton himself. It says: "In respect of the lease of the Chantry Chapel of Saint Barbara, which lease was granted to you by myself of recent date, and confirmed by my own sign manual; I must now, for the preservation of religious harmony and tolerance between our two communities, place upon you a burden which I ask you to accept in the true spirit of

Christian understanding. The Dominican Fathers have indicated to me, by personal audience and by writing, that it is their intention to petition His Majesty for the return of the Chantry Chapel of Saint Barbara. And knowing the interest previously expressed by Her Majesty through the restoration of Saint Barbara's shrine, there is a possibility – maybe more than a possibility – that His Majesty will be inclined to look with favour upon their petition. The situation is further complicated by the fact that a final financial settlement has still not been agreed upon between His Majesty and the Dominican Fathers for all the former churches and the church property that is now held by the crown. In these circumstances, I must advise you as follows: the current repairs to the walls, remortaring, repointing and such work may be completed. So too may the shuttering and the doors. But no structural alterations may be made in the chapel, and in particular nothing may be removed, and this includes: the stone altar, the balcony/confessional, the sanctuary step and the stone canopy by the bell-tower. On the exterior the shrine of Saint Barbara may not be altered or screened in any manner."'

He paused, and I said: 'Then all that cleaning and carting was a bloody waste of time.'

He blinked. 'Maybe yes. Maybe no. There is more. Do you want to hear it?' I nodded. '"The final prescription covers the roof. To reroof the chapel at this time would be to presume His Majesty's decision. And that would be both arrogant and offensive. Therefore it is my decision – and I feel sure you will agree with this – that the chapel will not be roofed. In the meantime – and I am advised that it may be twelve months before we know His Majesty's decision – the chapel will stay closed. It may be used as a place of private prayer for yourself and your dear wife, and that is all. You will be pleased to know that the Dominican Fathers have given me their assurance – in writing – that they will not attempt to enter the chapel again. They will await His Majesty's decision." Then it goes on to say he could look for another old church or chapel – at the same nominal rental of one penny per year – if that's what he would like to do.'

'That's what I'd do.'

'Hmm. But about five years ago the Dominican Fathers sold the old priest's house to a Portuguese merchant – Manuel Don Prego – you may have seen his warehouse by the Watergate?' I shook my head. 'Anyway – he sold the lease to Mister Tate, through Doctor Turner, the garrison chaplain. That man's a fool, an ineffectual old fool who can talk about the kingdom of heaven, but he doesn't know the price of property here on earth, here in Tangiers. And now Mister Tate is committed, in law, to paying the lease for fifteen years. He can't get out of it. And they say it's worth fifteen pounds a year. If he tried to lease it to someone else he might get eight pounds a year – if he was lucky. It's a poor neighbourhood and poor neighbourhoods attract poor prices. And even if he did get eight pounds he'd still have to find the other seven out of his own pocket. And then he'd have to pay the lease on a new house close to some other church and that could cost him another fifteen pounds.' He sucked at his lips – gave me a bleary look. 'If you want my opinion, for what it's worth, I think the Reverend Mister Tate is sitting on a privy that's about to collapse. And when it does he will be left sitting in the turds, and that will be the end of him, his chapel, and his pretty little wife.'

36

My head was throbbing, deep inside. My eyes were glued tight, and I couldn't think where I was. I pushed away the blankets, tried to sit up, and my head hit the underside of the top bed. I groaned, crashed back onto my pallet and held my head. The black beer, the black treacle that lay behind my eyes went round and round and round. I could see white froth. It was bubbling, and the bubbles were exploding, were filling my head with the sound of muskets: firing one after the other, firing volleys, firing in patterns – always bloody firing. I groaned, eased my feet onto the floor and stood up. Then all the muskets fired together, like a firing squad. I fell to the floor and died.

When I woke it was still dark, and I was shivering. I wrapped a blanket around myself, felt the fire – it was cold – and I staggered over to O'Sullivan's stool and sat down. After a while the room came into focus, became the shape I knew it should be, and I looked out his window. On the Mole the beacon was blazing – making orange waves of tarry fire – and I could see men landing. Black men. I began to think they might be Moors, black Moors. Or were they tars? Then I began to think they'd catch fire – if they were tars – and I giggled, and that reloaded the muskets. They fired together, blew out the back of my head. I groaned, lay my ear against the stone wall – felt the cold, the soothing cold – closed my eyes, slipped into a cesspit, and drowned in treacle.

When I woke again the darkness was slipping out the window. The hills of Spain and the waters of the Straits had formed one black mass. It made me think of the Requiem Mass, the black mass, the mass for the dead, for the dead who lie in the earth of Spain. They are corrupt, denied reform, denied hope of salvation. But as I watched, the tops of the hills softened, became etched in the sky, and the sun began to rise, to rise in the east as it has done since time began, and will do on that last day, on that day when Christ will come again, will come again in glory – from the east. I began to think it was strange that those who had denied him, denied his truth, would see him before those who slept in the earth, who slept in righteousness, here in Tangiers.

Then Trigg stirred, rolled out of bed and yawned. He swayed backwards and forwards for a moment, then he saw me and said: 'Couldn't you sleep?' I shrugged. He pulled up his shirt and peed in the bucket.

Down on the Mole, men were leading horses out of the stables, hanging nosebags – bags of oats – around their necks, and hitching them to the rock carts.

The carts reminded me of the counting and I told him it was bloody hopeless, and no one cared. He poured some black beer into his tankard, took a sip and offered me some. My belly heaved, and I closed my eyes tight. I heard him laugh, laugh in my treacle-head.

Then he walked over to the bookshelves and pulled out two boards. 'I made these years ago,' he said, 'when I had to do what you're doing. And it's dead simple. There are two columns, see.' He shoved a board under my nose. 'One for bucket carts and one for open carts. Each day you give those bloody idiots in the sentry room a new board, a clean board, and they make their marks on it. Then you take it down to the pricks – did you know they were called pricks?' I nodded. 'And they check them. Then you rub out the marks and the evidence is destroyed. And no one can question your figures, unless of course they've been keeping a tally down there at Whitby.' He smiled. 'You can have them if you want them.' He handed them to me. 'But don't show them to O'Sullivan. He's a typical bloody Irishmen. He doesn't like anything new, anything different; and if you disagree he'll argue, at the top of his bloody voice. And he'll go on arguing till your ears are ringing and your head is spinning, and you're wondering what the hell happened to reason, to logic. And in the end you'll give in – to shut him up.'

I tried to smile but it hurt, and put on my hat and coat – I'd decided to go to the Mole as soon as the gates opened. I know that's not what Trigg said to do, but the way I was feeling I was in no mood, no state of mind to face O'Sullivan. I picked up one of Trigg's boards, and he said: 'You're making a mistake. A big mistake. You should get it over right away. There's no sense in thinking about. No sense in brooding on it. You have to say you're sorry, and that's it.'

I shook my head. He was right. I couldn't argue with that. But I couldn't do it. Then I heard a noise, heard the tapping of his walking stick. He was tapping every step, tapping out a message. And each tap was getting louder, closer. I waited, waited for my fear to tighten my arse, waited for my fear to dry my throat. But it wouldn't tighten, wouldn't dry, and I swallowed hard and farted. Then the door opened, and O'Sullivan was tapping the floorboards like an actor demanding attention. He looked at me and said: 'What do you have to say for yourself?'

'I'm sorry,' I said, and I looked down, looked at the mud on his shoes.

'And?'

'I'm sorry I spoke to you like that.'

'You didn't speak. You swore.'

'I'm sorry I swore.'

'And?'

'And what?'

'Are you going to give my messages to Corporal Trigg?'

I whispered: 'No,' and shook my head.

'What did you say?' he yelled.

'No. I said no. I'm not going to do it.'

He raised his walking stick in the air – I retreated towards the wall – and he said, in a voice drained of all feeling, all emotion: 'You will do as I say.'

'Yes, I will.' I nodded, and he lowered his walking stick. 'But I won't pass on messages. And I won't do it because he wants to talk to you himself. He misses talking to you. He wants to talk to you. And it's hurting him in here.' And I thumped my chest.

He looked at Trigg, ploughed his forehead into furrows and swayed on his walking stick; then like a child mouthing its first words, he said: 'Is this true?'

Trigg sat down on his stool, fiddled with his fingers and wiped his forehead. The silence wound itself around us. It was like a noose. It was strangling them, strangling me, and for a long time no one said anything. Then he looked up and said: 'No.'

I looked from one to the other. Their eyes were locked together like the horns of rutting stags. There was no compromise, no concession. Just bloody madness.

My belly heaved. I edged away from them, put on my hat, coat and sword, and crept out of the room.

37

Next morning, just before seven o'clock, as the rain began to soften, I pulled my hat down round my ears and marched from Three-gun Battery to York Castle. My coat was heavy with water – after three hours up on the parapet – and the cold that had chilled the sentry box had chilled my fingers, chilled my bones, and made my teeth chatter.

I ran up the stairs in York Castle, tried to leave the cold behind, but it came with me, and it misted my breath. I pushed on the door and rushed into our room – thinking I'd build up the fire, but it was dead, dead cold. Ives looked up from his desk. 'What the bloody hell did you do to them yesterday?'

I turned away from him, took off my coat, squeezed out the water, put it back on, and picked up the board for the carts.

'Are you going to tell me or not?'

I shook my head.

'Don't be so bloody silly. Of course you're going to tell me. That's what friends are for.' He lowered his voice, made it soft and gentle. 'Now what did you do?

I shrugged. 'I told them I wasn't going to stand up and parrot any more bloody messages.'

'Jesus! No wonder O'Sullivan told me – late yesterday – to tell Trigg he'd come to the conclusion you were unsuitable to be a clerk. And tomorrow – that's today – he's going to tell Captain Lacey that some men do not have the disposition to be a clerk. And you, with your lack of discipline, your lack of concentration, are one of those men. And he doesn't want you any more.'

I wrung out my hat, laid it on the table and flattened the brim. 'I couldn't care less. I didn't ask to come here – and anyway, he can't get rid of me today. Captain Lacey went to Fort Charles yesterday, and he won't be back till tomorrow morning, just before the parade for the Test Communion Service.'

I thumped back down the stairs, and then, for some reason I can't explain, I didn't take the short cut. I marched out the main gate, crossed the Old Parade, passed through Middleton's Line, and found myself in the Little Parade. I ambled up to the apothecary's house, read his sign, watched a couple of women come down the steps clutching tiny packages, and hoped that the girl with the painted tits would come down those steps. But no one came, and no one went, and after about five minutes, I wandered on down to the Watergate, and there she was, selling nosegays. I stopped and smiled, and she smiled back, and I went all weak inside, and she held out a nosegay. The flowers were tiny red rosebuds, dried and scented, and the herbs were fowl-herbs, stuffing herbs: dried sage, rosemary, thyme. I lifted her hand and smelt the herbs, smelt their sweetness, her sweetness. I thought of having her – stuffing her – and my heart began to thump, and she said: 'They're tuppence each, but for you' – and she smiled – 'I could make it a penny.'

I picked up her smile. I was still feeling cold, feeling wet, but it didn't matter any more, and I said: 'I'm sorry, I don't have any money. They haven't paid me. But when I do get some money . . .'

She smiled. 'I'll be here. I'm here every day. Early in the morning. Except on the Lord's Day, and then I'm with the Lord.' She smiled, turned away, and held her nosegay out to another man, a man with money, a man who planted a kiss on her cheek.

I pulled a face, ambled through the Watergate and down to the waterfront. About half an hour later, when I came back through the gate, she was gone. But on the ground, nestling between the ridges of the cobbles, lay a tiny rosebud. It had sucked up the water, sucked the colour back into its petals, and now it was a dark red, a painted red, a titty red, and it made me think of her. I held it to my nose, smelt it, smelt her, and I wanted to hold her, to have her. I slipped the bud into my pocket, thought about buds that open in the spring, open to the touch of a man, and I ambled back to York Castle in a happy daze. As I pushed open the door and walked into our room O'Sullivan said: 'Enter the numbers in the book and then go. We don't want you today.'

I looked from him to Trigg to Ives, and nobody met my eye. Nobody said a word. I entered the numbers, cleaned the ink off my quill, and left. It was about eight-thirty, and I should have gone back to Three-gun Battery, gone back on guard, but I twirled the rosebud in my fingers, thought of her, and walked back to the Little Parade. But her house was locked up tight, and I wandered back to our lodging house.

Lieutenant de Colville was still in his nightshirt and he was sitting on the end of his bed holding his head. He looked tired, looked stubbled, looked the way I'd felt in the hours before the dawn. He sipped at a tankard of milk – or was it chalky milk? – then he said: 'What are you doing back here, at this hour.'

'The clerks have finished for the day. I thought I'd come back here and try to dry my coat.' He nodded, lay down, and pulled the blanket around his shoulders. 'Don't make any noise. They need to sleep.' He gestured towards Crabtree and four other men who were lying on their pallets with their blankets pulled over their heads.

About half an hour after the gun had fired for the afternoon parade, our company poured back into the lodging house and woke the sleeping men. Sergeant Brandon yelled for quiet, then he said: 'There's no work parade today and you're free for the rest of the afternoon. If you go outside you must take your pike with you, and you must wear your sword. If they sound a general alarm – that's one gun followed by all the bells ringing – you come back here. And you run. You run like bloody hell. The evening muster will be soon after sunset and you must be back by then. Anyone not back by then can clean the privies for a week, and by the smell of that lot' – he waved his hand at Lieutenant de Colville and the others lying on their pallets – 'it will be a shitty job.'

I lay on my pallet, looked into the beams – hung with cobwebs. It was hard to believe we'd been here a week, a whole week today, and this was the first time I'd had nothing to do. I closed my eyes, thought about sleep, about sleeping the whole afternoon, and I could feel the cobwebs of sleep wrapping around me – the way a spider wraps a fly – when I felt a kick, a foot kicking my foot, and Lockhart was saying: 'Come on. Get up. We're going out.'

I opened one eye. 'I thought you were supposed to be clearing the sewers.'

'We've finished, and they're not opening another one till Monday. So come on, we're going out.'

'Out?'

'Hmm. Out.'

I rolled over, lay on my side. 'I'm not going out.'

'Oh yes you are.' He leant over my pallet and yanked me to my feet. 'What the bloody hell did you do that for?'

'Because you're going out. We're going out.'

'But I don't want to go out.'

'Will you shut up and get dressed. We're going to see a lady.'

'A lady?'

'Hmm. Mistress Tate.'

I pushed him away and flopped back on the pallet. 'You can do that on your own. You don't need me for that.'

He reached down, pulled me back to my feet. 'Oh yes I do,' he said. 'With your smooth face, and your big green eyes, she won't suspect a thing.' He handed me my coat. 'Now get up before I bloody make you get up.'

About twenty minutes later he knocked on Mistress Tate's door. There was no answer. We waited and he tried again, and just as I was thinking we could leave, the door opened and there was Mister Tate, looking old and bleary-eyed. 'I'm sorry,' he said, 'I was asleep.'

Lockhart doffed his hat. 'We promised to help you. And here we are, on our first afternoon off.' He gave him a smile, a greasy smile full of lechery.

He waved us in. The room was dark, with low beams. We followed him into a back room and he opened a door, and then he led us into the chapel, into the old sanctuary. The doors and the shutters were closed and they were making the chapel look small, look like a tiny courtyard with high walls and a frieze of watered sunshine. The flagstones had been washed, and now we could see most of them were gravestones with lettering and small crosses. 'You won't know,' he said, 'but the forces of evil have conspired against us, and we're not allowed to use the chapel as a place of worship. In a year or so truth will triumph, but in the meantime . . .' He pulled out a piece of cloth and dabbed at his eyes. Then Mistress Tate came into the chapel carrying a basket on her arm. 'I thought I heard voices,' she said, and she smiled at both of us.

'I don't understand,' said Lockhart to her. 'Why can't you use the chapel.'

'It's the papists,' she said. 'They think it still belongs to them. And the Governor won't decide. He says the King must decide. And we must wait for his decision. But in the meantime . . .'

Lockhart nodded. 'The work of God cannot proceed.'

She nodded. 'And we don't know what to do. Mister Tate would like to take over the chapel in Saint John's Street – it's behind the Market Place, close to the fountain – but it's already being used as a house and the prices in that street are too much for us.' She sighed.

We followed her back into the front room, and she invited us to sit. We sat in silence for a few minutes, then she brought us some cake and some flavoured water, and Lockhart said: 'I don't wish to be impertinent, or to intrude upon your domestic arrangements, but do you have any money left from the collection last Sunday or from your own frugality?'

Mister Tate flushed red. She leaned over and patted his hand. 'A little,' she said.

'Enough to take a lease on the house next door – the one with the roof tumbling down – for a year?'

They looked at each and smiled. 'Yes,' he said. 'There would be enough for that.'

'Then you can do what the man did who owns our lodging house. You can break through the wall there' – he pointed to the side wall – 'and pull out all the wattle and daub. If you leave the frame empty it will make it look like one big room, and this could be your chapel for a year. The room upstairs on the other side, would give you about the same amount of space you have in here, so you wouldn't be losing any living room.'

Mister Tate nodded. 'And if we opened up that wall' – he pointed to the wall that enclosed the back room, the room that led into Saint Barbara's chapel – 'we could have a full-size chapel.' He grinned and clasped his hands to his face.

'And Fenton and I would come and help you. Wouldn't we?' He smiled at them, moved his foot an inch or two and gave my ankle a gentle tap, a sly tap.

I nodded and her face lit up, burst into smiles. Then she rushed over to Lockhart and gave him a kiss on the cheek. 'Oh, you dear man,' she said. 'You dear, dear, man. I feel God himself has sent you to us.' She kissed his hands, and the slimy bastard looked over her back, looked over the rounded curves of her body, and winked at me.

Next morning, still wrapped in the cobwebs of sleep, I felt the floor with my feet, cleared a space, and stood up. The room was heavy with gloom, with the debris of darkness. The air was fogged and it felt cold, felt damp; and it smelt stale, smelt of piss, shit, vomit and tobacco smoke. As I picked my way between the pallets, between the sleeping shapes, it took on another smell, the heady sour smell of snowflakes that have fallen in the night, have fallen on barren ground, barren bellies.

I pushed open the shutters, let the gloom escape, and took a deep breath of fresh air. It made me cough and splutter. Then I sneezed and hawked the muck out of my throat – spat it into the yard. Lieutenant de Colville was sitting in the privy about twenty feet away from me. He was sitting in our privy – ours is open with six holes, and his is small, like a sentry box, with one hole and a door – and he was hunched over with his head close to his legs. It looked as though he was trying to peer down the hole, to see into the depths of the cesspit, to see what he had done. But then he lifted his head, took a breath, closed his eyes, and lowered his head again. I began to think he must be trying to smell his own shit, to smell the smell that tells a man he needs to take a physic, needs to purge his bowels.

A few seconds later Sergeant Brandon banged on a pewter plate and yelled: 'Get up! Get up! Come on, it's time to get up!' As he came towards our end of the room, the door opened and Lieutenant de Colville staggered in, flayed his hands in the air and collapsed on the floor. His legs splayed, his shirt ran up his back and exposed his bum.

Brandon and a couple of other men rushed towards him. Brandon laughed and pulled down his shirt. And then as they lifted him off the floor, Brandon ran his hand up his leg.

I felt ill, felt as though I'd lost my guardian angel, for he was feeling the parts I had felt on the ship, the parts I had thought would keep me safe – from him.

Inside the church, the men and women sitting in the pews were well spaced, with room to sit, kneel and stand – as the order of the service demanded – but we were packed together so tight we couldn't ease ourselves apart, couldn't kneel down to pray. Oldfield and I were against the wall – crushed by elbows and sword hilts on the front side and jabbed by rough-edged stones on the back side – and he whispered: 'Be careful of the whitewash. It can mark your coat, if the wall's damp.'

I ran my hand down the wall. It felt dry, but it left a fine powder on my hand, and I whispered: 'It'll be all right.' And he nodded. Then Mister Turner took his place beside the communion table – shifted since last week into the chancel and now covered with a white cloth – bowed to His Excellency, and invited us to kneel. Oldfield rolled his eyes, and for the first time since he'd come ashore, since he'd been released from the bilboes, his face softened and he smiled. 'How are you feeling,' I whispered.

'My back still hurts. I can't lie on it. And sometimes my head aches – if I move too quickly – back here' – he touched the back of his head – 'but apart from that . . .' He shrugged, shrugged off the pain that lingered in his eyes.

When the clatter died, and the people in the pews were settled on their knees, were ready to talk to God, Mister Turner recited the Lord's Prayer and drifted through the collect: the prayer to 'cleanse the thoughts of our hearts by the inspiration of the Holy Spirit, that we may perfectly love thee, and worthily magnify thy holy Name'. Then he began the long haul through the Ten Commandments: 'God spake these words, and said; I am the Lord thy God: Thou shalt have no other gods but me.'

We replied: 'Lord have mercy upon us, and incline our hearts to keep this law.'

My thoughts drifted away, drifted into a soft nothingness, chorused by 'and incline our hearts to keep this law'.

Then Oldfield dug me in the ribs. 'This is the bit I like.'

'And thou shalt not covert thy neighbour's wife, nor his servant, nor his maid, nor his ox, nor his ass . . .'

'When I was a boy we had a minister who drawled the letter A. Made it sound like arr. We used to wait for him to say "arrss". Then we'd pretend to grab the arse of any girl who was foolish enough to stand by us. Foolish virgins we used to call them.' He grinned. 'Most of them were married by the time they were sixteen. None of them married me, and now I think of them as wise virgins.' And he grinned some more.

Then we limped through two prayers for the King, the Epistle, the Gospel and the Creed, and I stumbled over the words 'And I believe in one Catholic and Apostolic Church'. I've always stumbled over these words. The word Catholic claws my throat, sticks in my gullet, and at home – in Elme – I used to shut my lips, shut my mind, and think it madness to say, to recite, something I did not, could not believe in. And here, in this place, just a few yards from the Catholic cathedral, from the bastion of sin, we were mouthing the same words, mouthing support for a church we denied, abhorred; and it didn't make any sense to me.

Mister Turner read his sermon. His words were flat, planed of the highs and the lows that colour the spoken word. I closed my eyes, rested my head against the stone wall. Then her face drifted into my mind, and I smelt her nosegay, smelt the sweet smell of a maid, a virgin. I began to wonder if she was wise or foolish. In my innocence, my naïvety, the wise and the foolish flowed into each, became a wanting, and I was wondering is she would ever want me, when Mister Turner said: 'The collection today will be dedicated to the work of the Redemption Fathers.'

I looked at Oldfield, and he looked at me, and his mouth gaped.

I wondered if Mister Turner was a papist, a secret papist, who could believe, who did believe, in 'one Catholic and Apostolic Church'. I could remember hearing about such men, hearing how they hid their faith till they were lying in their beds, in the presence of death, and their soul had packed the trappings of life and was ready to depart; and then, and only then, would they confess to the faith they had harboured in their hearts.

Then he said: 'Those of you who are newly arrived in Tangiers may think it strange, may think it perverse, that we can take up a collection for the work of papist priests. And under all normal circumstances I would agree with you.' And he paused. 'But this is different. These men, these priests, have dedicated their lives to the redemption of slaves, of Christian men and women who are held captive by the Moors. It is a work of charity. A work requiring great courage, and a great deal of money. It is estimated that at the moment twenty thousand Christians – I include our papist brethren in this figure – are languishing in chains, awaiting the payment of a ransom. And so, in the name of Christian charity, Christian decency, I would ask you to give generously. And when you reach into your pocket or your purse, remember that you too could become a slave in need of redemption if you are on a ship that has the misfortune to be wrecked on a coast controlled by the Moors.'

As the wicker baskets were passed from hand to hand and the clinking of coins reminded me of Jesus throwing the money-changers out of the temple, Mister Turner placed a small silver chalice in the centre of the communion table. The cup was engraved with the letters IHS – set in a sunburst, in a halo of flame.

Mister Tate brought two silver-stemmed plates – mounded high with cubes of white bread – to the table, and placed them on either side of the chalice. Then he brought forward two large silver flagons with lids that flapped onto S-shaped handles, and I knew they would be full of wine, communion wine.

I remembered the first time I saw communion wine. I was disappointed. I'd been expecting the wine to be red, blood red – to make a visual symbol of the blood of Christ – but it was pale brown, like water with a few drops of mud stirred in. I can remember thinking it could have been used to wash feet, muddy feet. Then I was thinking about Christ, thinking about him taking a basin and washing the feet of his disciples – on the night he took bread into his hands, broke it and gave to his disciples saying 'This is my body' – and wondering if the water in his basin was the colour of wine, communion wine. Then I was thinking about his first miracle – the changing of water into wine at the wedding in Cana of Galilee – and wondering about the colour of that wine, when I remembered someone saying the men in France and Spain stamp on the grapes. And if the grapes are green they stain their feet yellow, and if the grapes are red they stain their feet red. And I wondered if they washed their feet, washed off the dirt before they stamped on the grapes that would become the wine, the communion wine, the blood of Christ.

The prayers were like old friends. They came and went with a passing nod, and they did not trouble me. Then there was a stirring in the pews and the officers were lining up to receive the bread and the wine, and we were hearing the old words, the words of faith: 'The body of Christ . . . the blood of Christ.'

Then His Excellency, the Town Major, Captain Lacey, Ensign Wyndham and all the other officers formed a circle around the communion table, and the spirit of the past, the spirit of reverence changed. Now they were like strangers meeting for the first time, testing each other, testing for loyalty, for conformity, for those subtle things that make and break a friendship.

Mister Turner picked up a card edged in black and said: 'Are you all willing to take the oath of supremacy, the oath of allegiance, and make a declaration against the pernicious doctrine of transubstantiation?' They nodded and mumbled, and he said: 'Will you please say after me: Refreshed this day by the holy sacrament of the Lord's Supper, I do most solemnly swear to Almighty God, and to this congregation here assembled, that I . . .'

He waited for them to repeat his words, and to say their own names; then we heard them take an oath to King Charles as 'Governor of the

Church in England', and an oath to him as 'King of England, Scotland and Ireland'; and to declare that the 'Sacramental Bread and Wine remain in their natural substances, and do not contain the corporal presence of Christ's natural flesh and blood, for the natural body and blood of our Saviour Christ are in heaven, and are not here.'

Then Mister Turner and two other ministers of the gospel signed the certificates, and we returned to the past, to the safety of the prayers we knew. The final hymn, the great hymn of praise was the Gloria: 'Glory be to God on high, and in earth, peace, goodwill towards men.' It was a strange sentiment for men committed to live by the sword, but I let it pass, and then we were singing 'Lamb of God . . . that takest away the sins of the world have mercy on us', and I was thinking of Sergeant O'Sullivan and that badge of his, and wondering how often he sang this hymn in Latin, this hymn that should bind us together. It was strange that he, that we, could say, could sing, the same words and mean such different things. Then I shook my head. Bread was bread, and wine was wine, and a lamb was a lamb. It was the language of symbols, and that was all there was to it.

Twenty minutes later we broke ranks and poured back into the lodging house. Crabtree and four other men were still lying on their pallets, but de Colville had dressed, and now he was sitting on the side of his bed looking pale and drawn.

I turned to Oldfield and whispered: 'He looked bloody near dead when I saw him first thing this morning.' And I told him how he had his head down the privy, and looked as though he was trying to breathe it in.

He put his head on the side – the way fowls do when they're sizing you up – then he laughed. 'When I was a little boy, about this big' – he waved his hand at knee-level – 'and I didn't want to do what my mother and father wanted me to do, I'd put my head down the privy and breathe in the noxious airs till they made me gag. Then I'd take a deep breath, hold it, and rush back into the house, and be sick all over the floor. It used to work every time. And I think he' – he nodded towards de Colville – 'knows the same trick.'

40

I came off guard at six, picked up the board for the rock carts, talked to the girl with the nosegays, drank hot chocolate with the pricks and was back at my desk soon after seven. The sun was warming O'Sullivan's stool, and I was wondering how long it would take to reach Trigg's stool, when Ives rushed through the door. He skidded to a halt, saw me, saw the empty stools, and laughed. 'He still hasn't forgiven you. He was in a filthy mood all yesterday afternoon—'

'You worked yesterday – Sunday?'

He nodded. 'We work most Sundays. In the afternoons. The mornings are for church. But I only go when I have to go, and I usually sleep in on Sunday. But not yesterday. Yesterday I was here when they opened the bloody door. And I didn't finish this lot' – he picked up a pile of papers – 'till about six o'clock. And now I have to go to the storehouses in the Upper Castle and do some more, and Carpenter – have you met Carpenter? He's the Sergeant up there.' I nodded. 'Ugly bastard. But I like him. He always keeps something to eat in his room, and you never go hungry when you work for him.'

I nodded and I was thinking about him sleeping in, and wishing I could do the same, when I remembered he was supposed to be sleeping here, sleeping in this room, all week. I leant back, leant against the wall. 'You told me your company was out in the forts, and you had to sleep here this week.'

He gave me a shy smile, then he broke into a grin, and laughed. 'I've been here for more than a year now, and neither of them' – he nodded at the empty stools – 'has ever noticed. But you . . .' And he laughed some more.

'There's this lady in Gormis Street. She's a widow. She's a lot older then me. Twenty-five, twenty-six, something like that. She likes swiving. And she likes being respectable. So I slip in and out' – he giggled to himself – 'when it's dark. And Sergeant Bolland – he's my company sergeant – he thinks I'm here working. And O'Sullivan thinks I'm with Bolland. I've never understood why these two in here don't ask about the weeks when my company's out in the forts. But they don't, and I'm not going to mention it.' And he grinned.

'If O'Sullivan wasn't going to toss you out some time today, you could
have had yourself a nice little widow. I know one, in Rua de Carmo, and
she would have been good for you. She's a bit older than she should be,
and she's got a fat bum, but they say they're easy to ride and you don't
get any saddle-sores.' And he laughed. 'She's been smiling at me a lot,
and the other day she ran her hand down the front of my breeches. I'd
like to have her, but I don't think my lady would like that, if she found
out . . .' He shrugged. 'I could have taken you up to her house, and maybe
I could have had her first. Broken her in for you.' And he smiled.

Then he leant over my desk. 'It's a strange thing, this swiving widows.
They seem to like boys, young boys with big cocks and a bit of hair down
here.' He touched the front of his breeches. 'But they don't like you having
any hair on your chest or on your belly. I had one once – she must have
been thirty-five – and she plucked them all out. Said it made me look
younger. More childlike was the way she put it. Sometimes I think they're
trying to mother me, trying to pretend I'm their son, and that makes it
all right. I don't really care what they think, as long as they let me do it.
But I keep thinking when I'm bigger – I don't just mean down here' –
he touched the front of his breeches again – 'and older, and look like a
hairy ape, look like most of the other men round here, they won't want
me. And I can see myself up there in the lanes by Irish Battery, lining up
with the sailors, and slipping a coin to some old tart with a smelly crotch.
But in the meantime – I'm swiving myself silly. And if you hadn't been
so bloody stupid you could be doing the same thing.'

Then he shrugged, grabbed my hand, shook it, and rushed out
the door.

I opened my drawer, slipped the head of Christ into my coat pocket,
stuck my feet on the window ledge and waited. I watched the waves glaze
the black rocks, and I watched the sun make the waves sparkle. Then I
lowered the brim of my hat onto my nose and closed my eyes. I began to
think about her, her with the rosebuds – nippled red. I felt in my pocket,
felt her rosebud, felt her in my mind. Then I smelt it, smelt her. In my
mind I could see the black rocks – reefed to the Mole – and I drifted
through those rocks, drifted out to sea. Then the mists began to rise,
and the sparkle began to fade, began to die.

Into my silence, my darkness, came the sound of drumming, fingers
drumming on my desk. I jumped to my feet and spun around – heart
thumping in my ears.

Trigg looked at me and shook his head. 'This may be your last day,
but it doesn't give you the right to go to sleep when you're supposed to
be working.'

'There's no point.'

'There's always a point. And right at this moment you're still a clerk.
So get his spelling book off the table, and start with the letter P. You'll
find the word, provocation, right at the top of the list. It means offering

offence, annoyance, and it's what the Moors do to us all the time. It's what you did to me, and him.' He nodded towards O'Sullivan's stool. 'He won't forgive you. And neither will I.'

He sat at his desk and began to write. I looked at the list, looked at the word provocation, and I left it alone, left it to wither on the page, and I copied: psalmist, provisions, punishment, profanity, prisoner, and pretence. Then the sound of drumming, soft drumming, crept into my head. I thought it was coming from outside, was coming from an insect or a small bird beating its wings against the glass. I looked around but I couldn't see anything, then I saw his fingers, the fingers that drummed me out of my sleep, they were drumming his desk, drumming his paper. Then he reached out, laid his left hand on his right hand and the drumming died. I looked down, wrote a few more words, then I looked again, out of the corner of my eye. He was writing with his left hand laid on his right hand, and his pen was crawling across the paper. Each time he dipped his pen into his ink pot and prepared to write there was a moment of drumming, then it was calmed by his left hand.

I copied: parliament, Portuguese, paraphernalia, pilchard, primogeniture and protraction; and then, in the distance, faint at first but getting louder as I listened, I could hear: tap, tap, tap. Then Sergeant O'Sullivan came into the room, and I stood up. He looked me up and down, sucked me into his bog-green eyes, made me feel the fear, the fear of drowning, the fear my Father used to raise in me. I swallowed hard, took a deep breath and held out my hand for his hat, coat, and sword. He shook his head; put them on the pegs himself, sat down on his stool, and hooked his walking stick onto his desk – about two inches from his hand. He made me think it was a weapon, a weapon kept close at hand.

The soft drumming came and went, and came again. Then Trigg coughed, gripped the edge of his desk with both hands and turned towards me. 'It's the cold. It gets inside my knuckles and they swell. And when they swell, they throb. It's the throbbing that makes them shake. It comes in the winter and it goes in the summer, when the swelling goes. So it's not the palsy. The palsy would be there all the time, if it was the palsy.' He walked over to the fire, crouched down and held his hand close to the coals. 'Today I'm supposed to go to the Governor's House. Supposed to be there by ten o'clock. I could be there by ten, and I could write a few words for half an hour, but after that . . .' He shrugged. 'I was thinking young Ives could go. But he's gone to the storehouses, and he'll be up there all day. Then I was thinking you could go. But your writing's not good enough. And you don't know how to repeat a simple message. And we couldn't trust you to mind your manners – could we? So, what are we going to do?'

It was bloody obvious, but I shook my head.

He sucked on his lips – pretended to frown, pretended to think – then he said: 'It might be best if you talked to the Sergeant about it.' He muttered something about the cold, about it making him want to pee, and slipped out the door.

O'Sullivan tossed his pen into the drawer and stood up. 'Are you on guard duty this afternoon?' I shook my head. 'Then you stay here till I get back. By then I'll have had a chance to speak to Captain Lacey.'

About ten minutes later Trigg came back and warmed his hand again. Then we settled into an hour of soft drumming. I finished the last of the Ps: profligate, profanity and problematical: and I was looking at the first of the Qs: quixotic, querulous and quotidian – and wondering what on earth the last one meant – when the door banged open and an Ensign rushed into the room. We stood up and he yelled: 'O'Sullivan. Where's O'Sullivan? I want O'Sullivan.' He rushed to his desk, peered over the top of it – as if expecting to find him hiding in the corner – then he rushed over to the fire, looked behind the beds, and spun around. 'Where the hell is he?'

'He's gone to the Governor's House, and he won't be back till the end of the day.'

'Christ! They asked for him. They asked for him specially.' He took off his hat and wiped his brow. He was bald – old for an ensign – and for a moment he didn't seem to know what to do. Then he said to Trigg: 'You. You'll have to come with me.'

'I can come, sir. But I can't write.'

'But I saw you writing. Just a moment ago.'

Trigg held out his right hand. It was pink and puffy, with red mountains round the knuckles. Then he held out his left hand. It was white, blue veined with a speckling of brown. 'I can write for about an hour then the joints lock.' He twisted his right hand. The fingers bent in, made his hand look like a claw with white talons.

The Ensign turned to me. 'Then you'll have to come. Christ knows what they'll say.' He slammed his hat back onto this head.

'But he's only been here a week, and O'Sullivan doesn't think his work's any good and—'

'Can he write?'

'Yes.'

'Can he copy?'

'Yes.'

'Then he's coming with me.' And he turned to me. 'Get your things.'

We ran all the way to the Head Court of the Guard. He rested his hand on the door for a moment, leant his head against the wall, puffed and panted, then he said: 'You can write can't you?'

I nodded. He put his arm around my shoulder. 'Come on.'

I shot my pike into the rack and ran up the stairs after him. He knocked on a door and we walked into a large room with a long table. Three officers were sitting at one end: working, writing. One of them looked up. 'Where the hell is O'Sullivan?'

The Ensign mumbled something in his ear, nodded towards me a couple of times and the officer stood up. He was wearing the gorget of a captain. 'What's your name?'

'Fenton, sir.'

He nodded. 'Sit there.' He pointed to the end of the table. 'You don't have to think. You don't have to say anything. You just have to write like bloody hell and make a fair copy of everything I give you.'

The morning brought sheets of white paper, to be ruled, to be made into blank forms and headed with the words: FOR THE MORE ORDERLY DISPOSITION OF THE TROOPS AVAILABLE AT THE DAILY PARADE, THE FOLLOWING DUTY ROSTER IS PROPOSED FOR THE WEEK BEGINNING . . .

The afternoon brought the same forms back to me – broken into four sections: Town Guard, Mole Guard, Fort Guard, Whitby Guard. Each company was now identified by the name of its captain. Then came the names of the various places to be guarded; the number of men 'required to maintain an adequate guard'; and the number of men 'estimated to be fit for duty'. In every case the number required to maintain the guard was higher than the number fit for duty. I ran my eye down the numbers for the Mole Guard – they were also required to patrol the Old Mole, the Quay and the path to the Watergate, during the hours of darkness – and they were short of fourteen men. I heard one of the Lieutenants say: 'More men will have to be on their own at night.' I remembered being on my own, up on the wall above Three-gun Battery. It was lonely. The time dragged, and it was hard to stay awake, and despite them calling it a 'safe section', when the darkness was like a black mask or the rain was chopping the visibility down to a few yards, it didn't feel safe to me. In truth it felt as though the Moors should be attacking – would be attacking – at any moment. Shadows became real, real people; and I could remember shivering, could remember wishing I had someone to talk to, someone to help me fight the shadows.

Then the door opened and Captain Lacey strode into the room. I jumped to my feet, stiffened, looked straight ahead – looked at the wall with its panels of oak-brown wood. 'Fenton?' he said. 'What are you doing here?'

'Sergeant O'Sullivan wasn't able to come, sir. He's gone to the Governor's House. And they sent me instead, sir.'

He nodded and stretched out his hand. 'Let me see.'

I handed him the Mole Guard. He lowered his hand towards the floor – still keeping it outstretched – and for a moment or two he appeared to read the figures. Then he said: 'Your writing's good. Clear. Easy to read. But you should remember one thing. As we get older it gets harder to read small writing. A smart clerk, a clever clerk, learns to write big, and if his captain's an old man, he learns to write extra big.' He patted me on the shoulder and laughed, and the other officers laughed with him.

Then I heard snatches of words ebbing and flowing: 'We can't reduce Monmouth'; 'Anne needs a sergeant and twelve men'; 'Fountain's too exposed, too dangerous. If it didn't guard that stream—'; 'Norwood Redout? That's close enough to Pole to—'; 'and Whitehall?'

Captain Lacey stood up. 'I'd like to have another look at Whitehall. We could always rush men from Catherine Gate if we had to.' He paused. 'The one that worries me is Devil's Drop in Western Cove. It's too far to the right of Whitby. Too isolated. I know everyone in this room thinks we have too many forts and not enough men, but I still believe we need another one, to the east of Whitby. Above the quarries. And I promised His Excellency I'd pace it out this afternoon – so if you'll excuse me,' and he smiled.

As the afternoon drifted into the evening, drifted into darkness, the Ensign tapped me on the shoulder. 'You've done well. Very well. Finish that one and come back tomorrow, at eight o'clock. And tell O'Sullivan we'll want you for another couple of days.'

I walked back to York Castle, trailing the end of my pike through the dirt and wondering what O'Sullivan would say, would do. I decided I'd tell him what Captain Lacey said about my writing. And I'd tell him what the Ensign said. And he'd have to let me go tomorrow because they asked for me. But as I walked up the steps, came closer to the door to our room, I began to realise he didn't have to let me go tomorrow. He could go himself. Or he could send Ives. They wouldn't care, as long as the work was done, was well done.

I paused outside the door, took a deep breath and pushed open the door. My heart fell, collapsed in a heap. There was no one there. I banged the door shut, slouched over to the fire and flopped down in the chair.

'What the hell are you doing here?'

I leapt to my feet – heart pounding in my ears – and spun around. Ives was leaning over the top of the bed closest to the fire. His face was about a foot from mine.

'Jesus!' I said. 'Did you have to do that?'

He laughed and dropped to the floor. 'What are you doing here?'

I told him about the day, about writing, about not seeing O'Sullivan. And not knowing.

'And you're not on guard tonight?' I shook my head, and he smiled. 'Then I think we should go to Rua de Carmo. And who knows what might happen.'

I laughed a nervous laugh, and shook my head.

'Are you scared?' I shook my head again. 'You've never done it before have you?'

The answer was yes. Yes I had. Many times. But that was part of the past, the past that belonged to her who was now corrupt in her grave. And now her memory was vague, was soft, was wet, like a half-remembered dream, and I did not want to unearth it, unearth her, and I shook my head.

He took my arm. 'There's nothing to it. You'll love it.' And he burst out laughing.

'But what about him?'

'O'Sullivan?'

'I wouldn't worry about him. She wouldn't let him in. He's too old for her. Too hairy.'

'That's not what I meant, and you bloody know it.' I thumped him on the arm.

He thumped me on the arm, thumped me hard. Then he grinned and nodded. 'I sometimes leave him a note. Then I don't have to come here, first thing in the morning. If you left him a note, you could go straight to the Head Court of the Guard in the morning, and there wouldn't be anything he could do about it.'

I started to laugh, then I pulled an old sheet of paper out of my drawer and wrote: 'Today, with the approval of Corporal Trigg, I worked at the Head Court of the Guard. They liked my work, and I have been ordered to return there first thing in the morning. William Martyn Fenton.'

I handed it to him. 'I wouldn't have written that bit "They liked my work".'

I shrugged. 'What does it matter? He's going to throw me out anyway.' I laid the paper on his desk, anchored it with his ink pot.

We thundered down the steps, across the courtyard, through the tunnel, over the bridge and onto the Old Parade. I felt light-headed and I laughed for no reason. He grabbed me by the arm. 'And now we wait.'

'Wait?'

'Hmm. We wait for them to close the gates. Then we know he can't get back into the castle. And then we go.'

'But what if he comes back?'

'We tell him we're waiting for him. Waiting for him to tell us if there's anything he wants us to do, first thing in the morning – before he arrives.'

I laughed and we waited, waited till we heard the great doors grate on the cobbles and bang shut.

Then he grabbed me by the arm. 'Come on. It's time to go. Time to learn all about swiving.' And he laughed.

41

Rua de Carmo sucked us into a lane of darkness, made narrow by the closeness of the houses, and made dangerous by the cobbles that had twisted, splayed, and sunk into long ruts of soft earth. Ives pounded on her door with the end of his pike, made my heart pound in my ears, and I wanted to rush away, to rush into the darkness, the darkness that would hide my shame, hide my need. He must have sensed this, or maybe I backed away from the doorstep, for he reached out, took my arm and propelled me into the door. The door swung open and I tumbled forward, tumbled into a large bosom. It was soft and warm and it smelt like fresh bread. It roused in me a hunger, a hunger that could stomach shame, and I wanted her, wanted the secret place that lay between her legs.

We fell against the wall. She laughed, then she said to Ives: 'My, oh my! He is precocious.' And she laughed again. Ives picked up her laughter, made it echo in my head and all I could think of was the word precocious. It was a young word, a forward word, a word of early ripening, and it wasn't on O'Sullivan's list of Ps. I smiled at the thought of O'Sullivan needing a word like precocious. She stood me on my feet and said: 'I like your smile. And your green eyes. They remind me of spring. Spring in England.'

Then she nodded to Ives, made the same sort of nod that men make when they're at a cattle market and they've made up their minds to buy a beast of burden. It's a formal nod, a nod to confirm the sale, confirm the purchase. As a child I could remember those beasts being led away on rope halters. I used to think of them going to fresh fields, green fields, but in truth most of them went to the slaughter house where the earth was scuffed raw, was red, was wet with blood – and they became flesh.

She squeezed my arm, squeezed my flesh, and I knew I'd been bought and sold, but it didn't matter – nothing mattered. I bent down to lay my pike on the floor and the blood rushed to my head. I felt hot, felt cold, felt my face flush, and as I looked up she smiled, ruffled my hair. 'What's your name?'

'Fenton.'

'And your Christian name?'

'Martyn. My Mother called me Martyn.'

'Then I will call you Martyn.' She smiled again. 'I could be your mother, if you would like me to be your mother.' And she patted me on the arm.

I remembered what Ives said and I smiled at his words, smiled at her, and shook my head. And besides: a man does not have his mother, does not return to the secret place, the place that pushed him out on the day of his birth. He was washed of that place – made clean by baptism – and now his snowflakes must fall in other places, places of passion, places that are not redeemed by the passion of our Lord.

She gave me a gentle shrug, then she walked over to Ives, and – as he went to kneel down in front of the fire – she leant over him, placed her hands on his shoulders and whispered in his ear. He nodded, said something I couldn't catch, then he stood up. 'I should be going,' he said to me. 'And don't look so worried. What you're about to lose isn't worth keeping.' And they both laughed.

Then he left, left me alone with her.

I didn't know how to begin. I could remember beginning, could remember reaching out for her who was now corrupt in her grave. But now I was shy, shackled by modesty and I had this niggle that she might have the pox, might not be clean in her private parts. It could rot her and it could rot me, in my private parts. We could rot together, rot in sin, rot in hell.

She took my hand and led me to the cloth rug in front of the fire. She wrapped me in her arms, wrapped me in her bosom, and rested her face on my head. Once again I smelt the smell of fresh bread, of bread rising, and I felt a stirring, a rising in my breeches. She began to cry, to mumble words of love, words of wanting. I felt her fingers, felt them coming, coming down my neck, down my back, over my hips, and deep into the netherlands, the lands of lust.

Then I wrapped my arms around her, felt her warmth, felt her softness, and she lifted her head. I looked into her eyes. They were wet with tears. I don't know if she was crying for love, or crying for me, or crying for some other man, some man from her past. I reached for her face, for her eyes, and I wiped away the tears.

Then she kissed me on the lips.

She made them tingle, made them feel as though she'd brushed them with a stinging nettle, a nettle haired with pleasure and not with pain. I kissed her lips, kissed the nettles, and I was stung with desire, desire for her.

I ran my fingers over her rump, over the broad plains of firm flesh, and into the valley that lay between them. Then my fingers returned to the plains, plains that had softened to marshland, and my fingers began to squeeze, to let go, and squeeze again. My fingers formed a beat, a pulse, and it flowed from me to her and back again. Then her hips began to move, began to rub against me – in time to the beat – and we swayed in a soft haze.

Then she pulled off my coat, pulled down my breeches, and we crumpled to the ground. She hitched up her skirts. They were layered – pink on pink – and they flowed around her legs like the petals of a flower. Then she spread her legs, spread the stamens of love, and pulled me into her arms, into her legs.

I found her secret place, her sweet place, and my cock rubbed itself against the lips, against the pink portals, like a cat, a tom cat, making friends with a stranger. Then it knocked on the door, knocked hard, and the door opened.

42

Next day I sat at the table in the Head Court of the Guard, and in a soft daze of sore balls and aching back, I copied fourteen pages of orders, and not a single one was for our company, for Captain Lacey. His face kept going in and out of my mind all day, and sometimes his face merged with her face.

I thought of her, thought of the softness of her touch. To me it was a gentle thought, like a reflection or a meditation, but to my cock it was a call to arms, a call to go exploring. The bloody thing bounced into life and went hard, so hard it hurt. I put my hands on the edge of the table and emptied my mind but it didn't want to go away. I could feel it, feel her, feel my mind walking in a storm of snowflakes.

Then I heard a voice calling in the storm and I looked up. Captain Lacey was standing on the other side of the table, and everyone else was gone. I jumped to my feet and stood to attention with the front of my breeches poking across the black table, making a green arrow head. He grinned, bit his lips, bit away a giggle.

Then he looked away for a moment, blinked his eyes a couple of times, and said: 'Sergeant O'Sullivan came to see me today.'

I nodded, stared straight ahead, but inside I was puffing, was panting – as if I'd run a mile.

'He's says you're impetuous. And by the look of that' – he nodded at my breeches – 'you've got a lot to be impetuous about.' He smiled. 'But that's not the point' – he paused, let the word echo in my mind – 'is it?'

I shook my head, and my cock began to wither. 'He doesn't think you have the disposition to be a clerk. He says you don't have any manners, don't know how to behave yourself in the presence of your superiors. And he would be loath to trust you to help an officer. Couldn't rely on you. That's what he said.'

I looked down at the table and flattened the front of my breeches. 'I don't want to be a clerk. I want to be a pikeman.'

'By night and by day judging by what I just saw.' And he roared with laughter.

I felt the sweat break out on my forehead, felt it run down my face, down my spine.

'And strangely enough Captain Montgomery – he was the captain who was here for most of yesterday – he also mentioned you, last night after you'd gone. He thought you worked very well. Concentrated on what you were doing. And didn't make any mistakes. He told me he was tired of—' He paused. 'No it doesn't matter about that. What matters is this: he thinks he should have a clerk here, all the time. And he's asked for you.'

I broke into a grin, I couldn't help it, it just exploded all over me.

'I told O'Sullivan and he was surprised. More than surprised. And he said, maybe he was wrong. Maybe he'd been a little impetuous. And if Captain Montgomery was right, maybe there was some hope for you.'

I nodded. Looked over his shoulder, looked at the fire, looked at the place where I might be sleeping. And I was thinking maybe I wouldn't have to go on guard if I worked here. And I'd be able to sleep all night every night, and it wasn't too far from here to Rua de Carmo and . . .

'And then he said he'd be willing to give you another chance. Said it was more sensible for you to work for him, because when they ran out of work here you could go somewhere else, go where there was work to be done. And that makes a lot of sense. And it was, of course, the reason why the clerks were all put together in one office in the first place.'

I looked down at the table, looked at the black swirls of grain that matched the swirling in my mind, and I nodded.

'Should Sergeant O'Sullivan ever complain to me about you again, I'll have you whipped.' And he thumped the table with the flat of his hand.

43

About a week later, on an ordinary day, a weekday, a day that felt cold, felt wet around the edges, I ambled down to the end of the Mole, talked to the pricks and the fishermen, and wandered back to York Castle.

Then I flopped onto my stool, wrote 'March 15th in the ledger, entered the figures for the rock carts, and read the first of the letters I had to copy into the Quartermaster's day-book. It was from the infirmarium. It ended by saying: 'In the last three months by the judicious cultivation of herbs and medicinal plants in our own physic gardens – under the superintendence of our new apothecary – we have saved a sum in excess of ten pounds. In previous times this money would have been spent with Mister Paul Bartholomew the apothecary on the Little Parade. He plies a trade in plants, grown and dried in England, and these are – of necessity – dearer than the ones we grow. Although it is not relevant here there is a body of medicinal thought that believes that fresh herbs and plants benefit the patient more because the humours that inhabit the living plant are still alive. In such circumstances it is our intention to continue the cultivation of our own herbal healing – for the weather is clement for much of the year and such an enterprise should prosper – and we would request that the money saved each quarter be used to purchase additional supplies of coal and candles. Our current lack of enough warmth, enough light, is causing a mortification of the flesh and a poverty of the spirit, and these are inducing in our patients a melancholy that presages a sudden death.'

Trigg bent over the fire. Then he pulled his hand – still pink and bloated with knuckles like carbuncles – away from the coals, shuffled over to his stool and sat down.

Ives looked up, muttered something that sounded like 'four fourteens are four fours, are sixteen, carry one, are four ones, are four plus one, are fifty-six. And that one's bloody right'. Yesterday he copied a manifest, a bill of lading. The multiplication was wrong and the value of the bill was too high, and when O'Sullivan looked in the book, saw what Ives had copied, he thumped the desk and called him an incompetent shit.

Ives said he trusted the bill, trusted it was right.

O'Sullivan told him, told me, to trust nothing. A mistake was a mistake. And now he faces hours of extra work: O'Sullivan says he has to rewrite the whole spelling book in alphabetical order, with large gaps between each word so new words can be inserted later on. And he has to do it in a week. Right at the moment I'm trying to remember if I told O'Sullivan about my idea – or did I just think about telling him? I fear I'm getting to be a bit like old Trigg: confusing thinking with doing; thinking they are the same thing.

O'Sullivan walked up to the Upper Castle this morning – he's been doing it each morning, been leaving early because of all the steps and the gravel that slips and slides – and I was thinking we mightn't see him till the end of the day, if we were lucky, when I heard the tap, tap, tap of his walking stick, and I made a start on the letter from the infirmarium.

O'Sullivan came into the room, hooked his stick over his desk and smiled. 'Today is the 25th of March.'

I looked at the date – the 15th – I'd just written it in the book. 'It can't be,' I said. 'It's the 15th. If it was the 25th it would be New Year's Day. And we'd all be celebrating.'

He looked at me and shook his head. It was a look my Mother would have called piteous. 'It's the 25th according to the New Calendar and the 15th according to the old one.' He picked up the Quartermaster's day-book. 'I thought you'd have remembered that by now. And this is a mistake.' He pointed to the date.

'I've just started,' I said. 'I was about to write it in the book.'

He laughed. 'The devil loves a good liar. It makes his work so much easier, especially when it's delivered with such sincerity.'

Then he tapped Trigg's desk with the tips of his fingernails – filled the room with an urgent drumming. 'Happy Easter,' he said to Trigg. 'I prayed for you this morning. Prayed that your faith may be restored. Brought back to life. As Christ was brought back to life.' Trigg's faced flushed, and he opened and shut his mouth – made wordless sounds.

O'Sullivan looked at Ives then his eyes shifted to me. 'Today is Easter Sunday. The day of the Resurrection. The exact day. And today, in our cathedral, and in all the churches in Spain, France, and Italy, we are celebrating the most wonderful day in the history of man.' He smiled. He wasn't drunk, but it was a drunken smile, a drunk-on-the-spirit smile.

Ives pulled a face at me, up-ended his thumb and pretended to squash a fly, to grind it into his desk.

I looked at O'Sullivan. I didn't disbelieve what he was saying. But then again, I didn't believe it either. At home we've always said, always believed that Easter Sunday was the exact day Christ rose from the dead. There couldn't be two exact days. He didn't rise twice like some actor in a play that is performed twice. So one was right and one was wrong. And ours was right, because ours was based on the Old Calendar and that hadn't been messed around by popery.

These thoughts must have frowned my face, or filled my eyes with questioning, for he said: 'Is there something wrong?'

'I don't understand,' I said. 'There can't be two Easters.'

'You're right, there can't be. The date depends upon the vernal equinox – vernal means spring. And in the Old Calendar, as you know, the date has slipped by ten days, and that means that the date for Easter Sunday can never be calculated correctly.' He paused. 'But now that the New Calendar has restored the seasons to their rightful date, we know we have the exact day.'

I said: 'Hmm,' but I didn't believe a word of it. I couldn't believe, couldn't accept that we were wrong.

Then he tapped on Trigg's desk again but this time it was gentle, like a soft awakening. 'Could you tell him,' he said, 'tell him about the date for Easter. How it's fixed.' He paused. 'You're better at these things than I am.'

Ives and I locked eyes and froze. The silence went on and on. Outside I could hear the birds singing, talking to each other, and I kept thinking, if they can sing, can talk to each other why the bloody hell can't you two talk to each other? But the silence went on and on, and then I couldn't stand it any more, and I hissed: 'Say something. For Christ's sake say something.'

Trigg turned and looked at me. His face was dead, drained of life, like the face of a mourner. I stood up, walked over to him and laid my hands on his back – as if to support him – and I said: 'Please.'

The silence went on and on. Then he turned his head towards me. 'You think I should?'

I nodded. 'I think it's what you want. What you both want.'

I felt his chest swell, felt him suck in a deep breath. Then he nodded, and turned to O'Sullivan. 'You want to know about the date for Easter – how to work it out?'

O'Sullivan nodded and they stared at each, and in the silence I could feel them stitching their friendship back together. I crept back to my desk. Trigg coughed, cleared his throat, and said: 'It's to do with spring and the new moon. Christ died in the spring, on a Friday afternoon, at the time of the Passover, the time of the new moon. And he rose again on the third day, and that was a Sunday. So the date has to take all these things into consideration and there is a set of words – I've heard it called a formula – and this is what it says: Easter shall fall on the first Sunday, after the first full moon, after the vernal, the spring equinox.'

'And because both calendars have different dates for the vernal equinox,' O'Sullivan said – taking up the story with an easy flow, 'they don't always coincide with the same full moon, and that means the date for Easter can vary by several weeks. This year, according to the Old Calendar, you' – he turned to me – 'will have to wait till the 19th of April to celebrate Easter.'

*   *   *

We drifted through the last days of March and into April, and as the lenten Sundays began to drop away, and I was thinking Brandon would never be able to have my bum because he could never get near me at night, Lieutenant de Colville moved out of our lodging house. Some said it was for the betterment of his health. Some said he was never sick in the first place. And some said he didn't like sleeping with us, said we were roughery, and he was a gentleman, a man of much refinement – like white flour. I don't know where the truth lay, and to be honest I didn't care much. And the memories of the one night I slept in his bed, lay becalmed in my memory, and sometimes they seemed like a dream, like a moment of panic that had come and gone; and sometimes they seemed like a soft binding, a swaddling, a cocoon.

He settled into a house on the upper slopes of Castle Hill where the air is said to be a little better, and a reformado, an Ensign by the name of Octavius Hogg settled into his bed. He was an eighth child – as his name suggests – short, slight, and well into his twenties.

The flux passed through Crabtree, made his breeches hang about his legs – made them look like bark that is about to peel off a tree.

The scars on Oldfield's back healed, but every so often the scars in his mind pulled apart, and his words tumbled over each other and didn't make any sense. And small things, things like not having any mustard or any fruit – any apricots, peaches, plums, grapes or pomegranates – made his temper explode. He yelled and thumped the table, and his hands shook, and we learnt to pull him down, hold him – and wait for his hands to calm, his scars to heal.

Lockhart spent all his spare time in Saint Barbara's Street, and every time I met him he would say: 'the carpenters have repaired the roof' or 'we've broken through the wall' or 'the new windows are being fitted'. I nodded and smiled and pretended to be interested, but in truth I wasn't the slightest bit interested. Mistress Tate's face became a blur and if she wanted to hitch up her skirts for Lockhart, I couldn't care less. My balls were sucked dry, sucked of the desire to wander, and I knew every grubby cobble, every dirty pothole, every weed that was rooting in the lanes of lust, the lanes that pulled me all the way to Rua de Carmo – night after night.

The apothecary's daughter became a sweet dream, a dream that touched the stars. And some mornings, when she gave me a nosegay to smell, our hands would touch, and my balls would shiver. But try as I would, I could not imagine her spreading her legs. There was something about her, something chaste, pure, something that was not for me.

On Easter Sunday, the real Easter Sunday, the morning limped through a long service and we didn't eat till well after midday. I didn't realise how late it was till we heard the gun for the parade. It thumped in my head – I'd drunk too much, we'd all drunk too much. There was nothing extra to eat, no festive fare as my Mother would have called it – apart from a couple of overripe watermelons – so we drank black beer, strong beer. The sun was hot and we sat outside, and it burnt my head, squinted my eyes. I pulled on my hat and giggled, and then we tramped down to the Old Parade.

I blinked, peered, laughed as the ground swayed in my head. It made Captain Lacey march towards us with a rolling gait. I put my head on the side – tried to still the ground for him – but that heaved my belly and I could taste the watermelon. I pretended to spit out the pips again, to make them arc through the air, and then Brandon yelled: 'Attention!'

Captain Lacey shook his head and looked around. Two other companies were marching onto the Old Parade and they were swaying, laughing, clumping their pikes together – making bonfires in the sky – and almost falling over. Compared to them we were sober.

Ensign Wyndham strode up and down muttering: 'What a bloody shambles. Thank Christ we're not going on guard this afternoon.'

Lieutenant de Colville nodded and bit at his lips, bit away his anger, then he said to Wyndham: 'A couple of hours of extra drill will sober them up. And when it's time for your half-hour you make them run. Make them sweat like bloody pigs. And don't give them any rests. Not a minute. Do you understand?'

Wyndham gave him one formal nod, and Oldfield hissed in my ear: 'Isn't he a good little dog. Woof! Woof!' A giggle ran through the ranks.

'Silence!' Brandon yelled. We looked at each other and giggled some more.

Then Lockhart stepped out of the ranks, stood to attention and said: 'Excuse me, sir. May I speak with you?'

I blinked hard. No one had ever stepped out of the ranks and spoken to Captain Lacey. It was a gross impertinence. A breech of discipline. An act of crass stupidity.

For several seconds we all stood in frozen silence, then the Captain said: 'Yes. But I warn you. If it's not of the gravest importance, you will be severely punished.'

'This afternoon the Reverend Mister Tate is to conduct the first service in his new chapel. As you know, sir, I, and Pikeman Fenton—'

I heard my name, gasped for breath, and felt as though he'd poured a bucket of cold water over my head. And then, as everyone turned to look at me, I became exposed, became lost in the storms of winter, the storms of anger, and the water turned to ice, locked me rigid.

'We've been helping him, sir. And he asked if we could attend the service, could represent the company.' Then he lowered his voice and continued: 'The word represent was not my word, sir. It is not a word I would presume to use, sir.'

The Captain nodded, said something to the Lieutenant but he shook his head and the Captain shrugged. Then he said: 'Ensign Wyndham.

You will represent the company, and Lockhart and Fenton will go with you. March them up the hill at double pace and make sure they're both sober before they go into the chapel.'

Halfway up the hill I said to Lockhart: 'Why the bloody hell did they invite me?'

'They didn't. They didn't invite me either. I couldn't face a couple of hours of drill, and I knew the service was this afternoon so . . .'

I laughed and it hurt my head, and I didn't say a thing.

We walked into Saint Barbara's old chapel – it felt like a grand entrance, like a forecourt – and a line of small trees in clay pots led us towards the door in the old sanctuary. We laid our pikes in the corner by the door and walked into the new chapel. It was cool and dark, and the beams, the uprights, that were once the walls had been stripped of wattle and daub, and now they were like black bones, like rib cages that still enclosed three rooms, three places of prayer. As I sat down the chapel felt like a symbol for the Trinity – three rooms in one, each separate and distinct, like the godhead, but still one, one God.

There were about a dozen people in the chapel, all sitting, all waiting in prayerful silence, and I was thinking Lockhart's idea had worked out well, when an old man with a dark beard and a woman hanging onto his right arm limped into the chapel. I didn't know him but I knew the girl behind him, and I wiggled my fingers at her. She smiled at me, then she looked down at the floor, at the cold flagstones, and she helped the old man onto a seat.

Wyndham grabbed my thigh, squeezed it hard and whispered: 'Who was that?'

'Her name's Jenny, Jenny Bartholomew. And that must be her father, the apothecary. I don't know who the woman is. She told me her mother was dead.'

'You've been talking to her?'

'Hmm,' I said. 'I see her most days. She sells nosegays down by the Watergate.'

He nodded, gave me a wink. 'I must go down there one afternoon.'

'She's not there in the afternoons. In the afternoons she delivers medicines, tonics, lotions, salves, things like that, for her father. Unless of course it's market day, and then she has a stall in the Market Place, and she sells medicinal herbs – one's that don't require a consultation with her father.'

He gave me a long hard look. 'You do know a lot about her, don't you?'

I blushed. I could feel it making me hot under the collar, and I looked at the flagstones, and wondered what she was thinking.

The service was tedious. Mister Tate went on and on, and all the time Mistress Tate was staring up at him, like a young girl smitten with love. Lockhart watched me watching her, and he said: 'Doesn't it make you sick. All this work' – he waved his hand in the air – 'and we've never been alone together – not once. I've never had a chance to run my hand up her skirts. And I've done all this bloody work – for nothing.' He slumped on the stool and sank into silence.

At the end of his sermon Mister Tate said: 'We must thank Lady Middleton for her most generous gift of this communion table.' And he laid his hand upon it. 'And now, if you will stand, I will ask God to bless it and the boards that now hang on the wall behind me. In accordance with the traditions of our church they list the Ten Commandments, the Lord's Prayer, and the Apostle's Creed. They are the essentials of our faith and when we . . .'

I let my eye drift over the big boards. There were four of them, all about eighteen inches wide and all a little taller than a man – maybe six feet high. The two with the commandments were grouped to the left of Mister Tate and the other two were grouped to his right. Between them hung two small boards. Both were about eighteen inches square, both were decorated with crosses. They looked like identical twins, and they didn't appear to have any purpose, apart from filling up the wall and pleasing the eye.

After the service was over, and we were filing out the door, the queue came to a halt, and I found myself standing close to the board bearing the Lord's Prayer. The script was fine with gold on the capital letters, and curling tails on the end of the last letter in every sentence. And I was thinking it would make a beautiful style, if we had the time to copy our letters in the same style, and I was wondering who did it. Then I saw a name in the right-hand corner. It was no more than a quarter of an inch high and it was close to some gold lines, and at a casual glance I would have taken it for part of the ornamentation and never have seen it. I looked down expecting to read: The work of . . . But instead I read: 'THE GIFT OF LORD EXTONMOUTH'. I didn't know the name, and it didn't mean anything to me.

A few minutes later, in Saint Barbara's chapel, Jenny came up to me and smiled. Her eyes were aglow, and mad as it might sound, she seemed to be wearing a halo of fervour. She grabbed my hand and said: 'Isn't he a wonderful preacher? I think God has touched his soul.'

I smiled and nodded – it was what she was expecting. But if she had asked my opinion, and I'd been of a mind to speak the truth and blessed with a large measure of courage, I would have told her I thought he was touched in the mind. But I do not have that large measure, that measure of madness, and I smiled some more. And then just as I was going to say 'I'll see you tomorrow', her father was at her side gripping her arm and whispering into her ear: 'I told you not to talk to common soldiers. Their words are common and their minds are worse.' And he smiled at me.

'Now come and meet this nice young man.' And he steered her towards Ensign Wyndham.

I watched them for a moment, watched them talking, watched the halo die; then Mistress Tate was tapping me on the arm and saying: 'I'm so pleased you were able to come. Mister Tate is so grateful for everything you've done. And everything Pikeman Lockhart has done.'

'It's nothing,' I said. And it was nothing, nothing much that I had done. For a moment I felt embarrassed, felt ashamed that I hadn't done more, and I wanted to change the topic, to hurry the conversation onto safer ground and I said: 'The boards in the chapel. They look beautiful. And the lettering is very fine.' She smiled, and the lines around her eyes softened. Then she nodded, and I remembered the name at the bottom of the board. 'I was wondering who Lord Extonmouth might be.'

She smiled. 'A very generous man. He used to come to Exeter Cathedral sometimes. He liked my husband's preaching, and they prayed together when he was so worried about his son, Lieutenant de Colville, and—'

She threw her hands to her face and covered her mouth. I looked into her eyes – they were wild with panic. Then she grabbed my hands. 'You won't say anything will you? It's supposed to be a secret. I promised not to tell and I shouldn't have said anything. He would be so cross if he knew.' Then she looked around, made sure no one was looking, and pressed my fingers to her lips.

44

May Day – the 1st of May, the first day of summer – flooded my mind with memories of home: the white blossom on the hawthorn, the blossom that would soon fall like snowflakes; the maypole and the ribbons that danced in the air and plaited themselves into a symbol of love, a symbol of man, a symbol of his fertility; the Queen of the May, the May Queen, the girl who was crowned with garlands, who ruled for a day and was laid low in the heat of the night; and the hawthorn with the dark pink blossom – not the pink of blood, the pink of afterbirth, but a more delicate tone, a tone with a faint hint of purple, of wild violets. It was this colour, this pink with a hint of the wild – displayed against a background of grey – that now binds the ensigns to the lieutenants, and the lieutenants to the captains; for early this morning, one after the other, like doves emerging from a dovecot, they looked around, put aside their hesitations, and took flight in their new uniforms, their summer uniforms.

The style and the cut is much like their old uniforms and in many ways they mimic the clothes of a gentleman, of a man of affluence. But there are two differences, differences I would love to see in our uniforms.

The first is the fabric. It's lightweight and being grey they say it will repel the heat; whereas ours, being heavy, being red, being the colour of fire, will attract it, and we will swelter. And the wash of salt, the stain of perspiration that marks the summers of a man in Barbary, will soon mark the arms of our coats, and we will bear them, wear them, like a silent witness.

The second is to do with their coat sleeves. They are cut short, well above the elbow, and their arms are enclosed in white linen sleeves – puffed and banded at the wrists – and this will help them to stay cool.

Their waistcoats are as long as their coats, buttoned down the front and tied at the waist with dark pink cords. Their hats are grey – trimmed with dark pink ribbons – and unlike our black hats, they should keep their heads cool. Dark pink ribbons froth the shoulders and the sleeves of their coats, and more ribbons of the same colour garter their grey stockings to their grey breeches, and make bows on their shoes.

Their gorgets hang over the white lace at their throats, and the sun makes them glitter.

Their baldrics, in a dark pink fabric trimmed with matching ribbons and silver buckles, drape their swords down the back of their left legs and complete the uniform.

The effect is soft, delicate; and for those who have added extra lace to their throats, coats or cuffs, it is almost feminine, almost like the hawthorn in bloom.

As we waited outside our lodging house, waited for Captain Lacey to arrive, I began to wonder just what it was that made an officer an officer. Money was the essence, the skeleton that made it possible. But after that? What else was needed? Iron balls? Few of them had iron balls. Lacey did; Wyndham didn't; and nor did de Colville; and Hogg might – it was too early to know. Brandon did, and so did Owen; and so did O'Sullivan in his own way. So iron balls were not of the essence, and if they were most of the Sergeants would be officers – and Christ knows what the officers would do. None of them would ever make good sergeants.

Then a tough little bastard marched up. A Sergeant with a swagger, with iron balls that would have looked good on a bull.

He leant on his halberd – it was decorated with long ribbons for May Day – and I knew at once, knew without thinking, he'd like to make us dance around his maypole, and it wouldn't be a bloody symbol. He spoke to Brandon for a minute or two, then he swaggered on. His hair was black, as black as his hat, and as he passed up the lane he passed through a patch of sunshine, and just for a moment he looked like a wart – inflamed red and made fat by a blackhead that needed pressing. I turned to Oldfield. 'Who the hell was that?'

He shrugged, whispered to a couple of other men, then he said to me: 'Lawson. He's from Whitby. They say he's had every man down there, except the Minister – and he was too full of shit.' He laughed. 'If I were you, I wouldn't ask to go to Whitby.'

45

In that strange light that is neither night nor dawn I crawled out of her bed in Rua de Carmo, dressed and staggered down the lane. For the papists it was the Feast of Saint John the Baptist – June the 24th according to their calendar but still only the 14th according to ours – and in the night as we lay naked together we talked about Saint John, and how he prepared the way for our Lord, prepared for his coming. She laughed, played with my balls, bit the end of my cock, bit it back into life, and said: 'This is the only coming I'm interested in.'

'Coming' was her word for making snowflakes. She didn't like my expression. She thought it cold and bleak, and in the warmth of her loins, in the fire of her secret place, my snowflakes would have melted long before they touched the ground. In her they were more like rain, driven hard by a thunderstorm on a hot day, and they – she – made my body crackle and spark. And the final thrust, the explosion of love, 'the coming', blew my head, blew my body apart, and every time it made me feel as though I'd been struck by a bolt of lightning.

I've seen trees struck by lightning. I've seen them crack and split, twist and burn. And I've seen the black stumps, the stumps that look dead, the stumps that will one day put out a tender frond of green. And sometimes, in the ashes of the night, the ashes of love, I think my cock is like those fronds of green.

I yawned and blinked, blinked the dawn into my burnt brain, and I could feel the heat that lingered in the cobbles. I yawned again, and it made me feel tired, feel sucked of life.

Down at York Castle they'd be opening the gates by now – starting the day before the heat seared our will to work. It was a good idea, to work in the cool, but in practice it meant we worked a longer day because if something had to be done it had to be done. And it didn't matter if the room was stinking hot and sweat was running down our backs – if it had to be done, it was done. And that was that. I was wondering what O'Sullivan would say if I drifted in late, and told him I'd stay late – meaning I'd stay as late as I always had to stay – when I saw an officer coming up the lane. I stiffened, lost my amble and marched towards him. His coat was grey on grey – the light was sucking the pink out of his ribbons – and his hat was casting shadows over his face and gorget. I couldn't recognise him or his rank. I called out: 'Good morning, sir.'

He grunted and I marched on. Then I heard him ground his partisan on the cobbles, heard it echo down the lane, and he yelled: 'Fenton!'

I froze, muttered: 'Bloody hell!' and spun around.

He walked up to me, and 'he' became de Colville. 'What are you doing here, at this hour of the morning?'

'We have to start early, sir. As soon as the gates open at York Castle.'

He stared at me for a couple of seconds. 'But the lodging house is down there' – he pointed to his right – 'and York Castle is down there' – and he pointed to his left.

I said: 'Yes, sir,' and I thought you bloody smart-arse. 'My head is sore, and I was thinking if I had a walk, a short walk, before I started, it might help.'

He nodded – but didn't look convinced – and waved me on. I said: 'Goodbye, sir,' and marched down the lane, wondering whose bed he had spent the night in.

I rushed through the door and into our room. Ives was right: rushing always improved O'Sullivan's mood; but this time it was a waste of time – he hadn't arrived. I slumped onto my stool, yawned, and rubbed at the lower part of my back – it was aching deep in the joints – and Ives looked up, smiled, put his thumb in the air and jerked it up and down. I held up my hand, tucked my thumb into my palm and showed him four fingers – stiff and splayed. He sucked in his lips, pulled his head back and laughed. Then he held up two fingers – splayed and stiff. I repeated my four, and he shook his head. It meant four 'comings'. We were supposed to be honest, not supposed to cheat. But one time when I showed him one finger, showed him the truth, he laughed so much I decided I'd never give him less than two fingers, and to hell with what really happened. And then we'd talked about five fingers – a five-finger night. He said we'd have to rest for a week, build up our strength, and I asked him what was the point? In a week of resting we could have done it ten times, and we'd miss out on five fucks – and I wasn't going to do that. But somehow the thought of five on one night still lingered in our minds – like some sort of Holy Grail – and now, whenever I showed him the truth, showed him four fingers, he burst into laughter, and sometimes he made a fist, made it bloom, made it open, made it become the mystical five – the magical five.

Trigg shuffled into the room and sat down. The summer had shrunk his hand and now he could write again, but the winter had bent him a little more, had left him looking older, looking more tired, and it hurt to watch him come into the room. We said: 'Good morning,' and I made him a drink of hot lemon. He smiled, wrapped his hands around the pewter tankard, and sipped at it. Then Ives nodded towards O'Sullivan's desk. 'He's late today.'

'He was going to mass this morning. It's the Feast of Saint John the Baptist, the patron saint of the cathedral. He likes to go to the high mass, the sung mass, and sometimes he also goes to one of the early ones.'

Ives sat back on his stool. 'Twice in one morning?'

'Hmm. Today's the day they hand out the badges, the Agnus Dei. You have to take communion and afterwards you kneel in front of the altar to Saint John the Baptist – if you go into the cathedral you can see his statue above the side altar: he's holding an open book and a lamb – and the priest pins the badge onto you. O'Sullivan likes to know who's a papist. He likes to see if there are any new converts, and one year he went to three masses in a row.'

'Three?' I could hear the amazement in my own voice.

He nodded. 'Most of those who don't have an Agnus Dei like to receive it on the feast day. I remember O'Sullivan telling you about the octave, and some do get their badges then. But most of the new ones will get theirs today, and if you want to know who's fallen into the clutches of popery, today's the day.'

Then he pulled open his drawer, took out his Agnus Dei and held it in his hand, and a sad look settled on his face. He rubbed at it with his fingers, then he walked over to the fire, heaped up the coals and laid his badge on top of them – made it look as though he was offering a sacrifice, a sacrifice that went back to the time of the Old Testament.

Then he pulled up a chair and sat down. As the coal began to glow, to dance with flame, it melted the edges of the badge, and the lamb quivered, then it dribbled into the coal, into the fires of hell and was gone – was lost for ever.

46

Towards the end of June, in the middle of the night, Lord Middleton was taken ill with the flux. They say he got up to look for a candle and tripped over his servant – the man was sleeping on the floor, sleeping in the doorway like a guard dog. He broke his arm close to his shoulder and died in a fever a few days later. Some say – to be honest, most say – he was drunk and the flux was a polite excuse, a veil of make-believe. But be that as it may, it still cast a pall of gloom over the garrison, and as the coffin passed – our company was lining the lower end of the Market Place with pikes trailed as a mark of respect – I felt a sense of sadness, a sense of loss. And despite the fact I know we are all mortal, and must die, I had not expected to see a great man humbled by death. And now he lies under the flagstones in the garrison church, on the right-hand side, the military side, and the trappings of power have departed – and we await his successor – and in death we can do what we could not do in life: we can walk over him.

Later, when I spoke to Mister Tate, he gave me the impression he'd seen too many deaths, too many funerals, and this was just another one – and in the fullness of time the earth will have all of us. He also gave me the impression he'd lost a patron, a man who would have been able to persuade His Majesty to confirm his lease of Saint Barbara's Chapel. And when he was mourning for Lord Middleton, I could sense he was also mourning his own loss.

At the end of July, in the heat of the late afternoon, when our month of mourning for Lord Middleton was over, Oldfield, Crabtree, Lockhart and I ambled up Taverne Street, across the Market Place, up St John's Street and into a square that wasn't a square – it was more like a triangle with dented corners – but it was called Saint John's Square. We paused in the shadows of Saint John's Church – it still looked like a church but now it was a house – and from there we walked up the steep lanes to Irish Battery, made a hard turn to the left and followed the wall till we came to the old Southgate.

Beyond the gate lay Parsons Green. They say some of the first troops who arrived here with Lord Peterborough camped on Parsons Green in London – near Fulham on the north bank of the river Thames – and the shape reminded them of the Green. To me it looked nothing like an English green. But maybe they were homesick or maybe they just wanted a reminder of what they'd left behind.

Our Green isn't green and it isn't flat – it tilts towards the right. The grass is burnt brown, and the earth is rocky. The shape butts onto the town wall for three hundred yards and it makes a rough oblong a hundred yards deep. It sits on top of a high hill, and steep cliffs tumble down to the valley and the long sweep of beach that edges the Bay. It's a natural fortress, and one day the walls could be extended to include it in the town.

In old etchings the Green is enclosed in star-shaped earthworks – raised by Lord Teviot – and protected by a fort in the shape of a triangle. The fort looked to be about three storeys high and it bore the name Parsons Green Bastion.

The bastion is long gone. It was built without a roof and the walls weren't capped, weren't sealed against the rain, and they filled up with water. The water should have escaped through drainage holes, but the holes were never made and the water weakened the walls, brought one of them down and opened cracks in the other two – mortal cracks.

The heat and the rain crumbled the earthworks, and now they are no more than rocky mounds enclosing a path that runs right around the edge of the Green.

A new fort – Cambridge Fort – with a flat roof and drainage holes, now stands in the far left-hand corner. It rises to five or six storeys and about halfway up, the walls narrow, make a distinct line, like a belt of shadow. The four corners are chamfered and the walls are faced with stone, brown bricks and mudblocks – sun-dried and veined with tiny cracks.

I saw Cambridge once, the real Cambridge, from a distance, when I was herding geese. It was bound by walls and topped with towers and spires that spiked the sky, and in the soft mist it was floating above the fields like a grey eminence. When it caught the first rays of the wet sun, grey became violet, became purple, became the indigo of the night. And as the spires began to glitter, to catch diamonds in the mist, it became a place of dreams, of make-believe.

Our fort on the edge of the Green, was too crude, too coarse, to grace a city like that; and once again I was left with the impression that the name was a gentle reminder of things we'd left behind, and in its own quiet way – in the melody of its sound – it was meant to make us feel at home.

Three or four hundred sailors had made themselves at home on the Green. They were having a run-ashore – not a run in the sense of running, but a run in the sense of running wild – and as we passed through Southgate we were swept, were sucked into their midst, into their noise. It was like being in the middle of a fair, a drunken fair. I looked at Crabtree and Lockhart and we grinned, and Oldfield yelled: 'Swiving hell!' And he was right, it was swiving hell, in the tents where the whores were lifting their skirts and tars were forming lines, were shuffling their feet, were yelling at the man on the ground, the man with his bum bouncing up and down to 'get a bloody move on'.

The tents – awnings of sail slung on spars and anchored with long ropes – spread from the walls, spread in straight lines, like sails billowing on a mast. They led my eye on to the stalls, the booths selling oranges, lemons, white grapes, pomegranates, smoked sweetbreads, cold meat, jellied fish, cobs of bread, beer and wine: Sherry, Muscat, Mascadella and Algarve – red wine from the south of Portugal.

Most of the men were milling around – there were no chairs, benches or tables – talking, laughing, arguing, moving from place to place. A few had formed groups. Some were standing, some were sitting on the ground, sitting in circles, sitting back to back, and others had taken off their shirts and were lying on the earth face down – like men in a drunken sprawl.

In the middle of the ground the tars off one of the frigates had run spits through three great beasts, and now they were turning them round and round, fanning the embers of pitted fire, and filling the air with the smell of burnt meat. The meat was fresh from Spain and they were yelling: 'Only a penny a slice! A penny a slice!'

I didn't have a penny. I had a fishing line with half a dozen hooks and a lead sinker – traded for a dozen crabs and two buckets of limpets – but so far I hadn't caught a fish that was big enough to sell. I'd caught a lot of little ones, about four inches long, and they tasted good when they were cooked and the flesh and the soft bones were mushed into bread and sprinkled with vinegar – but they didn't make me any money.

From another fire, from black pans, came the smell of onions, French onions – frying – and they turned my head, made my mouth water. From other fires came the smell of fish cooking on metal grills. The Portuguese had smothered them in oil and salt, and as I watched the fire was twisting their tails, burning their fins, and making their skin split open. The flesh looked white, looked tender, and it made me feel hungry, made the mass of pease and salt beef that sat in my belly feel like stodge, and after a while I couldn't stomach it any more, and nor could Oldfield. We walked to the edge of the ground, walked the path, stepped over the drunks, and laughed off the sailors who wanted to fight, wanted to learn how to port a pike.

We sat on the rocks for about an hour, watched the guard pull up the ladder and close the door to Fountain Fort – in the valley far below – then we thought we should look for Crabtree and Lockhart, should find them before it grew dark. After twenty minutes, we found them sitting inside a tent with their arms around a whore. Crabtree gave me a silly look, then he said: 'She's dried up, down there.' He pointed to her crotch. 'And she says if we can keep those randy bastards' – he nodded towards the queue that stretched into the tented shadows – 'off her for another half an hour, we can have a shilling each. Then we can all eat.'

I laughed – said we'd be back – and then we ambled over to Cambridge

Fort, watched them close the door and set the watch in the battlements, and wandered along the path again. Now the edges were marked with flares and patrolled by a picket of tars with muskets and long clubs tied to their wrists with leather thongs – and the drunks had retreated into the shadows.

As we made our way back to the walls I heard a voice yell: 'Oldfield. Bloody Oldfield. You get your arse over here.'

The voice was slurred, thick with beer, but I could recognise it, recognise Brandon. I stood still. Oldfield ambled forward, ambled into a clutch of Sergeants. It was easy to tell they were all Sergeants, they were leaning on their halberds and above their hats the halberds were making a black crown, jewelled with spears, hooks and axe heads.

'Stand up straight. Stand to attention,' Brandon yelled.

They all laughed. It was not a laugh of friends, of drunks being drunk. It was a laugh of evil, of evil intent, and it made me shuffle backwards. And just as I thought I was safe, Brandon yelled: 'And who do we have over there? Come on,' he lowered his voice, 'show yourself.'

I walked forward and the crown opened and he laughed. 'Little Mister Poppadom.'

A man laughed. 'I haven't heard that word in bloody years.' He grabbed at me and pulled my face close to his. 'He could be an Indian in this light. He's small enough.' He ran his hand down my back, and over my bum.

Brandon pushed him away. 'For Christ's sake, Lawson! He's a bloody poppadom. You can look but you can't touch.'

'That was Bombay. This is here. And if I can have him I bloody well will.'

Brandon muttered something to himself, then he flung an arm around Oldfield: 'No hard feelings, huh?' He shoved his face close to Oldfield's. 'I did what I had to do. Discipline. Respect. That's what we have to maintain. That's what a Sergeant does. And it's what you'd be doing one day, if you hadn't been such a bloody fool.' He paused. 'It's too late now. You can't undo the past, but we can have a drink, a drink on it.' He shoved a tankard into Oldfield's hands. 'No hard feelings.' They all roared with laugher, and he ran his hands down the front of Oldfield's breeches. 'Well – maybe just one.' And they all laughed again.

Brandon pushed a tankard into my hands. The beer washed the dust out of my throat and it tasted better, tasted sweeter than the beer they serve in the refectory. Then came another tankard, and another, and a couple of slices of beef and they warmed my belly, made me feel content, and the Sergeants sucked us into their talk, into their laugher. Then they locked their arms around our shoulders, locked us into their group, their halberd-crown, and although I knew, knew deep in my heart that they meant to have us, I couldn't believe they would do it. Not here on the

Green. And in spite of the darkness and the warmth that encourages such things, I still felt safe.

Then a bell began to ring. The strokes were short and hard – urgent – and they were coming from somewhere near the Southgate. Lawson looked up and said: 'Bloody early for the curfew.'

Oldfield muttered: 'Curfew?'

Brandon looked at him and shook his head. 'Only the tars are allowed out here tonight after the curfew. And the girls. And the Portuguese if they want to stay, want to make some more money.' And he laughed.

I eased Oldfield out of the circle and as we backed away I yelled: 'Thanks for the beer. And the beef. I loved the beef.' For a moment or two they seemed surprised then they came after us, shook our hands, slapped us on the back, laughed, and waved in a drunken floppy way. We waved back, and as they grouped together – made a huddle, a halberd-crown of darkness – we headed for Southgate.

Then Oldfield wanted to look for Crabtree and Lockhart, and we pushed our way through the crowds and wandered along the tent lines. We couldn't find them – we couldn't remember which tent was their tent – and after half an hour we wandered back through the gate, and rested on a low wall, just in case they came through after us. But they never came, or if they did they came in a blur, a blur that was right inside my head, and I couldn't tell one face from another.

The air was now still and heavy with heat. I took off my hat and we ambled down the hill, dragging the ends of our pikes in the dust. I was feeling happy, feeling tired, and as we came into the top end of Saint John's Square – where the houses and the walls pull it into a dark funnel – someone grabbed me from behind, grabbed me by my baldric. Then a voice, Lawson's voice breathed in my ear: 'I'm going to have you.'

I went rigid, tried to swing round, tried to belt him with my pike, but he flung his arm around my neck, held me tight, held me against his body. 'There's no hurry,' he whispered. 'No hurry.'

Opposite us, five shapes, black shapes grabbed at Oldfield, pulled down his breeches, pushed his belly onto a low wall, and held him down. Then I heard Brandon say: 'I'm first.'

I shut my eyes and tried to shut out the cries of pain, the cries of delight that rode together, rode one upon the other – and layered my mind with madness.

Then Brandon came over to us, grabbed Lawson by the arm and shook him. 'For Christ sake!' he hissed. 'I told you not to bloody touch him.'

Lawson snarled and held me tight. 'I'm just getting the feel of him. And he feels bloody good. And if he ever gets to Whitby I'll have him. And to hell with your Lieutenant de Collie or whatever his name is.'

Then he laughed, shoved me at Brandon, strode over to Oldfield, pulled down his breeches, and said: 'I'm next.'

47

Next evening, soon after they closed the gates to York Castle, I walked up the lanes to Rua de Carmo. I stood in the shadows and looked at her door, the door that could open to love, and I walked on, walked up Castle Hill. At his house, the house of Angelo de Araujo, I knocked on the door. It was opened by a Portuguese girl. She looked to be a year or two older than me. She smiled and said, in broken English: 'You come for the Lieutenant – yes?'

I smiled and nodded, then I followed her up the stairs. On the landing we passed a shrine – a crucifix with two women kneeling in prayer – then the stairs split in two, became narrow. She took the stairs to the right and at the top she knocked on a door. To the left of the door stood another shrine with a statue of a woman wearing a crown and holding a boy. A brass lamp with a bowl of blue glass hung beside the woman.

The girl turned and smiled, and the light from the lamp made her skin glow, made it look as though it was rubbed with olive oil.

Then the door opened.

I was expecting to see him in his uniform, but he was bare-footed and wearing a long white robe that crossed at the front and tied at the waist with a white belt. In the lapel, on the left-hand side, the side closest to his heart, he had pinned the Agnus Dei, the Lamb of God, the Lamb who was without sin.

I looked at it, looked at him, and I shivered, shivered at the truth I had half-suspected in the dawn on the Feast of Saint John the Baptist, but had never dared to put into words. He smiled, and I said: 'Michael.'

He said something to the girl, in Portuguese, then he stood back and his hand invited me into the room.

He closed the door and looked into my eyes. Then he opened his arms, and the belt fell free. The robe edged his naked body, made him look pure and strong, with a flat belly and a wedge of brambled hair. He walked towards me, and his arms with their draping of white were like wings and I felt as though I was being wrapped in wings, wrapped in the innocence of the angels, and he became Michael the Archangel – the slayer of dragons.

And so the house of the angels, York Castle, Rua de Carmo and our lodging house, set the pattern of my life – set it in tarras – and it stayed set, stayed fixed, till the morning of my sixteenth birthday.

PART THREE

30th May 1676

(according to the Old Calendar)

48

Sir Palmes Fairborne strode across the Old Parade, mounted a flight of steps and turned to face us. It was seven in the morning, the morning of my sixteenth birthday and the heat was beginning to rise. Behind him two wooden horses stood nose to nose, and right under their tails, looking like piles of horse dung, lay iron weights – rusted with age and heavy with pain.

He was met with a sullen silence.

It was only three weeks since the Governor Lord Inchiquin had returned to England, but already he was making changes, the sort of changes no one liked, the sort of changes His Excellency would never have made. The time for this parade was a good example. It had always been at three o'clock in the afternoon and if a man hated the thought of going on guard or doing an hour of bloody drill, he could have a few tankards of beer – more than a few if he had the money – and they would ease him through the afternoon and into the evening. But now – now we were here at seven in the morning, every morning, and no one has enough time for an extra beer and everyone is cold sober and bloody miserable.

Yesterday was more miserable than most mornings, in truth it was bloody dreadful. Brandon belted his pewter plate in my ear soon after four-thirty – it was still half dark – and we staggered out of bed, pulled on our work coats, our work clothes and paraded in front of the Head Court of the Guard. The word 'work' is a misnomer, a harkening back to what was, for most men have sold their grey coats and their old breeches, and drunk the money, and now our red coats are our work coats. The cuffs on mine have frayed at the edges and I've tried to mend them, tried to patch the tears, but my stitching is crude, as crude as my writing was on the day I became a clerk, and it makes my coat look as though it's covered with spider legs.

Grime and dirt have darkened the green of my breeches and the white of my shirt, and I've been thinking about washing them but there isn't enough water unless we go out to Fountain Fort and wash them in the stream there. But I don't have any spare ones any more – I grew out of them – so I don't have anything to change into while they dry, and now

I try not to notice them, notice the smell that clings to me like an old friend, a rancid friend.

My mouth is pitted with tiny white ulcers and salt beef makes them sting. And when the beef's tough, stringy, it wobbles my teeth and bleeds my gums and the infirmarium says I have the scurvy. He says I should eat more fruit and vegetables but I can't eat what we don't have, and I think, we all think, his doctoring is like his advice: bloody useless.

I had the flux last year, about the same time as His Excellency sent an ambassador to Muley Ishmael, the Emperor of the Moors. It cramped my gut and anchored me to the privy for a week, and I bled so bloody much I felt like a girl with the menses. When it passed it left me weak and shivery, and all I wanted to do was sleep. But at least it went, it passed away, and that's more than I can say for the bloody Moors. The Ambassador came back with some silly bloody story about the Prophet Mahomet appearing to one of the Emperor's saints – Marabouts is the word he used – and now the Emperor believes he can vanquish all his enemies 'providing he does not make peace with the English'. And so the encirclement, the containment that is the siege, is the war, goes on and on, and peace is but an idle dream – a privy in the sky.

Last December the winter storms bit into the Mole, chewed off large sections on the seawardside and swept away the prickmaster's office. The force of the waves, the torrents of foaming water made the tarras beater's house look like an island of stone, a rocky outcrop that could crumble and vanish at any moment. As the storm retreated, left behind a house washed clean – scoured inside and out – the Moors crept up to our lines. Thirty of them broke through the palisades and ambushed the forts.

The roar of the cannons and the ringing of the alarm bells yanked us out of our beds, and in the half-light of the dawn we thundered through the narrow streets, past the infirmarium and onto the walls, onto our muster station, by Johnson's Battery.

The Moors inside the lines were caught in the crossfire, in the patterns of death laid down by the men in the forts and like a storm in the night, a storm that is exhausted by the dawn, they retreated to the hills. And there they lingered, in the company of four or five thousand men on horse who could have destroyed the forts at Whitby if the Moors on foot had succeeded in engaging all our forces for two or three hours.

In the cold light of morning as we mourned the loss of one man, our troops-of-horse rode the bounds. There were thirty-four of them – half a troop – and Christ knows what they were expected to do against five thousand men on horse. It was sad and pathetic. Sergeant Brandon called it an invitation to suicide, and then he said: 'I blame it on Lord Belasyse. He rode out to Teviot Hill one day – it was a sudden impulse, he'd always wanted to pay his respects to his predecessor, Lord Teviot – and he found it deserted. Not a Moor in sight. But next day they were back in their thousands – like hornets made angry by their nest being disturbed. It made him think we could never hold the high ground, the land beyond our lines. And if we couldn't hold it, there was no point in trying to defend it. And if we couldn't defend it, there was no point in patrolling it, no point in having three troops-of-horse. And almost without realising it, we lost the ability to mount a fast flowing attack and became committed to siege warfare, to the art of defence.'

The art included more walls, higher stockades, higher embankments, more guard houses, more forts, more trenches, more cannons on the walls, and more bloody work for us. In truth it was a never-ending bloody battle and there was always something to be done, something to be repaired and that was why Sir Palmes ordered a work parade for yesterday morning: for five o'clock in the Market Place.

I'd been thinking my last day as a clerk was going to be a lazy sleepy day and I'd been looking forward to it for a long time. Never once had I imagined myself standing in the Market Place with a pike in one hand and a shovel in the other. It was not the stuff of dreams, of daydreams. It was not the way Ives began his last day in the office – the day he called his ten-finger day – and it soured my mood. The mood around me was also sour. I could feel it. I could sense it. And the reasons were plain for all to see: no one had been paid for two years and three months; no provisions had arrived and six men were now eating the rations for four; and we were three hundred men short – on guard every third night, and most guards were double duty, six hours at a time.

All round me I could hear a soft muttering, a mumbling of discontent, for it was always the same men who went on guard, who did the extra duty, who were forced to work when they should be resting, should be sleeping, should be eating, should be being doing any bloody thing except waiting here to work – for no pay and lousy food.

As Sir Palmes came out of his house and spoke to the Captains, the soft mutterings began to harmonise, began to strengthen, and over to our right we could hear: 'Home. Home. Home. Home.' Like a refrain, like a chorus, it was taken up by two more companies, then it spread to us and it took on a harder beat, a more powerful beat and it became: 'Home! Home! Home! Home!'

For a moment or two Sir Palmes looked bemused, then he flushed and yelled: 'Be quiet!' But as he turned back to the Captains the cry broke out again. He walked along the ranks and spoke to the men. Then he held his hand up in the air – commanded silence – and filled our ears with sweet words, sweet promises.

Then he ordered us to march out but there was a scuffle in one company and the sergeants swooped, pulled three men out of the ranks and placed them under arrest. We marched out, sullen, subdued, dug trenches, raised embankments, till about nine o'clock – when the heat became too great – then he walked up and down and filled our ears again with sweet words, promises that sounded like shit to me. The man had flux of the mouth and that afternoon it didn't put anything extra on my plate, never bloody would, if my instincts serve me right.

That was yesterday.

Now it is today and the three men are being marched, being escorted, onto the Old Parade. Sir Palmes looked towards them for a moment and then – as if satisfied – he turned back to us and said: 'It's three weeks since the daily parade was shifted from the afternoon to the morning, and I'm pleased to note that the incidence of drunken behaviour – which was a disgrace to the garrison – has declined sharply. As a consequence the guard has been better maintained and the whole town has slept more soundly, and I would like to compliment you on the improvement.' He paused. 'But there are one or two men who have not heeded my message. And they put me in mind of my old father. He used to say if a man was drunk a fast gallop was the best way to sober him up. Personally, I thought it was a mad idea – it was dangerous for the horse.' And we all laughed.

'But here' – he paused – 'I think it's good advice. And from tomorrow any man found drunk on parade will ride the wooden horse for four hours. I have instructed the Town Major to wait till the man sobers up. I don't want him going to sleep on the horse and I don't want a belly full of beer softening the pain. There wouldn't be much point in it then would there?' We roared with laughter.

The wooden horses stand about six feet off the ground. In the dark, with their wooden necks, heads and tails they could be taken for real horses. But here in the daylight, they are what they are: instruments of punishment, of torture. They are made of planks, not shaped and smooth but rough and angular, with edges, with corners that cut into a man's flesh.

Soldiers from the escort lifted the first man onto the horse and bound his arms around the neck. Then they lifted the next man up and bound the two of them together – back to back – and they bound their legs, pulled them tight, pulled them close to the belly. Then they tied weights, tied about ten pounds to each ankle. As the colour began to drain out of their faces, and their mouths began to open and close – as if to expel the pain – one of the escort flicked off their hats with the tip of his pike and exposed their heads to the full beat of the sun.

From the clerk's room I've often seen men ride the horse. Some were on its back for four hours, and some were there for six, and once a musketeer rode him for eight hours. He was weighted with muskets and a week later his feet went green and a week after that he died of gangrene. The weights vary. The worse the crime the heavier the weights. They say they can pull arms and legs out of their sockets, and getting them to go back in again can be worse than riding the horse.

The escort lifted the third man onto the next horse and laid him on his back with his face looking up to the sky. Then they tied his arms around the horse's neck, and tied his legs under the belly. They lifted his head, rested it on the spine of the neck, ran a cloth under his chin and tied it round the horse's neck. Then they weighted both arms and both legs – the weights looked to be about fifteen pounds each – and poured two buckets of water over him.

'Christ,' I whispered to Lockhart. 'What the hell did he do?'

'He's been on the horse before. Twice. They say he told Fairborne he was an arsehole and he wasn't going to do any more fucking work for him. And he wanted to go home.'

I felt a shudder run down my spine. I wiped at my brow – the heat was rising fast, making the cobbles burn and filling my eyes with glints of light – and I said: 'At least he's cool.'

He shook his head. 'The water will shrink the ropes and then they'll bite into him, and his shirt and his breeches will dry and go prickly, and the poor bastard will be covered in itches. His face will go red and the sun will burn his eyes. They say you can go blind if you're up there on your back for more than four hours.'

I scuffed at my shoes. They were new – new to me – the man who had them before me died last week, and we stripped him of everything except his winding sheet, and one man would have had that if we'd let him. And I was wondering what it would be like to lie in the ground, stark naked, and feel the earth rubbing against my dead skin, when Sir Palmes said: 'Everyone here was on the work parade yesterday. Everyone knows what happened. And everyone knows why these men are being punished.' He paused. 'Lord Inchiquin is in England right now. He is arranging your money. He is arranging more provisions. And he is arranging more men. And new uniforms. He is a persuasive man, a powerful man. You all know that as a young man he lost his eye fighting for the King, was captured by the Barbary pirates and languished in prison – and worked like a slave – till his ransom was paid. And remember, the life of a slave is ten times worse than the life of soldier – some would say a hundred times worse. So he knows what you're suffering. He knows it from his own personal experience. So I ask you to be patient, to give him time to do what has to be done.' He paused again. Then he began to talk about the Militia – the townsmen, the burghers, who were forming companies, putting on uniforms, beginning to drill, beginning to mount a guard on the walls – and my thoughts drifted in the rising heat, drifted back to yesterday afternoon, to my last afternoon as a clerk.

My time was almost up. In my mind it was up, and I was thinking in the past, thinking my sentence was finished. And never again would I have to gallop to my desk and ride that bloody stool that used to make my arse ache.

And never again would I have to put up with O'Sullivan and Trigg.

The years have aged them – mellowed them a little – but the infirmities of the flesh, and the Town Major's refusal to replace Ives when he returned to his company on his sixteenth birthday – after an enforced delay of one year, now weigh them down. They lapse into long silences that feel hostile, feel barbed, and I was not encouraged to talk, to break the silence, to break the flow of words, the words that spider their way across the sheets of empty paper.

For me yesterday became a golden day, a day of farewell, but for them – after learning I'm not to be replaced – it became a dark day, a day of mourning, a day on which my work became their work. By dusk they were wrapped in gloom, in resentment, and laying the blame for the passing of the years at my feet. When I put my pen in the drawer and closed the ledger for the last time, my soul soaked up their gloom, their resentment, and it hurt to stretch out my hand and say goodbye to dear old Trigg. His eyes filled with tears. He gave me a hug, nodded his head and for a long time he couldn't say a word. Then he took the corporal's coat off the hook, shook it hard – shook off a cloud of dust – and said: 'I'd like to see you in this. Just once, now you're big enough to fit it.' He held it up in the air, by the shoulders.

I slipped my arms down the sleeves. He did up the buttons, smiled, and said: 'It looks right on you. You could be a corporal. You have it in here.' He tapped his heart. 'And in here.' He tapped his head, then he turned me towards O'Sullivan. 'What do you think?'

O'Sullivan nodded and held out his hand. 'I'll miss you,' he said. 'And I'll miss our talks.'

I smiled, shook his hand and nodded. I won't miss his talks on faith, on religion – his religion – they don't hold the attraction for me they hold for him. But they have sharpened my mind, honed my reasoning, confirmed my faith, and condemned his – which is not what he wanted – and Trigg is proud of me, proud of my logic, proud of the purity of my thought.

I smiled again, and so did O'Sullivan, and Trigg said: 'I've never noticed it before, but you two look alike.' And he bit at his bottom lip. We both stared at him. 'It must be something to do with you.' He nodded at me. 'You've grown up a lot since you first arrived here. You were thin and pale with the face of a boy then. But now, you've shot up and your chest has filled out. And that stubble on your face, that black shadow on a pale skin—' Then he went red, looked bemused, looked the way men sometimes do when they'd just made a fool of themselves in front of their friends, and he said: 'I'm sorry,' and he blinked hard. 'It must be the coat, the same fabric, the same lace. It must be playing tricks on my eyes.' He gestured for me to take off the coat.

Then O'Sullivan shook my hand again. It was formal. Precise. Polite. And it was more than that. It was an ending. A farewell. A thank you. It was all those things he could not bring himself to say. I grabbed my hat, coat and sword, wiped the tears out of my eyes and rushed out the door.

That was yesterday, the end of yesterday.

And this is today, a day of new beginnings, a day of manhood, the day the crude bastards in our company say they're going to pull off my breeches and frog-march me up to the whore houses by Irish Battery and pay for my first woman. It's an idle threat. They don't have any money. And I'm hoping like hell none of them know that the men in Ives's company marched him down to the Market Place on the night of his sixteenth birthday, stripped him naked, stood him in the water trough with his legs straddling the water spout, and roped his hands and legs to the hitching rings at the back of the fountain.

I looked at the three men on the horses, looked at them riding into the valleys of pain, and I wondered if they felt humiliated, felt demeaned – that is the way Ives put it. He was cold, dead scared his cock was going to jump up and down and make him look a fool, but he wasn't in pain. It was a warm night, a night to bring people out, and tonight would be another warm night – and I was wondering what the bastards were going to do to me – when Sir Palmes said something to the Town Major and something to Captain Lacey.

Captain Lacey scowled and for a moment it looked as though he was going to argue with Sir Palmes – dispute his authority as acting-Governor, acting-Colonel – then he turned and marched over to de Colville, Wyndham and Hogg. They huddled in a circle for two, maybe three minutes. Lockhart and I looked at each other and shrugged. Then he whispered: 'We're going to one of the forts. They say Charles is changing over today.' He nodded. 'Want to take a bet?'

I opened my hand and held it out. 'Half of nothing.'

He laughed, grabbed my hand and shook it.

Then Captain Lacey yelled, in a voice meant for all of us: 'Sergeant Owen! Sergeant Brandon! In thirty minutes I want all the men – with all their things – down at the Watergate. We're going to Whitby!'

49

At the Watergate, Ensign Wyndham spoke to Jenny Bartholomew. She was selling herbs and salves from a tray hanging from her neck. The tray was painted blue, and the ribbon around her neck was embroidered with green leaves, red berries, black berries, and tiny clusters of pink flowers. Her bosom was resting on the edge of the tray. Two years ago when I first saw her selling nosegays the tray rested at her waist, and her bosom was flat. In truth it wasn't a bosom at all. Now it is a rounding of gentle curves, ridged by the edge of her tray, and I was thinking it would be soft to touch, soft to kiss, soft to bury my face in, when Wyndham picked up one of her salves and held it up to the light. It looked as though he was trying to see right through it, to see its healing properties.

His skin is spotted and blistered and sometimes it looks red raw. It's the mosquitoes. They attack him – attack us – at night and we've been burning herbs and filling the room with smoke but it doesn't help much. In the morning their bites are like red welts, and in the evening, after a day of itching, the skin breaks and they weep. Sometimes my welts turn into pimples but mostly they just itch, and if I rub goose grease on them they go away after a day or so. Wyndham sleeps with his head and hands under his sheet – and we have to tie the corners down so he can't throw it off in his sleep – but it doesn't make much difference. They still manage to find him and bite him.

I watched him smile his pimply smile, and I watched her smile at him. And just when I was thinking he might buy something – his mother sometimes sends him money from England – he sniffed a sachet of herbs and put it back on the tray. For the briefest of moments her face went tight, then she smiled again, looked up, and caught my eye. I smiled back but she looked away – it was what her father, Mister Bartholomew, had told her to do.

He doesn't like me.

The first time I went into his apothecary, hoping she might be there, I was smothered by the smells of summer – dry grass, withered leaves and herbs that have wilted, have lost the strength of spring – and he was polite. The second time he was abrupt: told me to get out, told me he knew what I wanted, and she wasn't for me. The third time his face

froze and he pointed to the door. Then I laid four sacks on his counter –
most of us had sold our spare shirts, stockings and scarves and we had no
more use for sacks – and I asked if he would buy them, would exchange
them for pilewort. His face softened round the edges, but close to his eyes,
close to his mouth, the lines remained hard. And there was no thaw in
his attitude – it remained locked in the depths of winter.

Oldfield's bum was ringed with pink piles with red mouths that dribbled
blood down his legs and stained the back of his shirt. They looked like a
chaplet of flowers pulled tight on a head of hair and they grew soon after
those bastards in Saint John's Square split his bum. They stopped him
sitting down, stopped him sleeping on his back, and night after night his
snoring was driving us bloody mad.

Mister Bartholomew handed me a small packet of pilewort: the leaves
and petals of the Lesser Celandine. He said it was grown in a churchyard
in Norfolk, had absorbed the humours of the dead, and was very powerful.
We wet it and bandaged it into Oldfield's bum, and it turned the flowers
white, and the heat, the soreness went out of them, but they did not wither,
did not die; and he still sleeps on his front and doesn't like to sit down.

The fourth time I went into his shop – it was November and the rains
had kept her inside for days on end – she was standing behind the counter.
I pretended to need his advice, pretended we still had some pilewort. He
told her to leave. Then he stood in front of me – almost nose to nose
– and said: 'I am an apothecary. A man of medicine. My daughter is a
young lady. And piles are not discussed in front of a young lady. It's three
months since you bought the pilewort and we both know it's gone, long
gone. So what are you doing here?'

I pulled a face and mumbled something. He put his fist in my face and
said: 'She's not for you. She's for a gentleman. For an officer. For a man
who knows his manners, and knows his morals. I know about you, and
that old whore in Rua de Carmo. So get out of my shop and don't come
back' – he stepped back and opened the door – 'unless of course' – he
paused – 'you have some money and wish to make a purchase.'

I let the memories of his face – twitched and bright with anger –
fade into the past and I watched her and Wyndham talk. Then Captain
Lacey arrived with two servants carrying a chest and we marched through
the Watergate, along the quay, through Fort Whitby Gate and onto
the Strand.

A slender tower of latticed wood stood on the edge of the road, just
below Three-gun Battery. An alarm bell hung inside the tower – about
three feet from the top. The wind was catching it, making it stir, and
it reminded me of my lady in Rua de Carmo and the stirrings of
the night.

Mister Bartholomew was wrong. She wasn't a whore. She didn't
do it for money, for duty. She did it for pleasure. I don't think an
old fool like him would know the difference, and I can't imagine

him with his breeches down, can't imagine how he begot a girl like Jenny.

She still has the bloom of innocence – not quite the blush of innocence he believes for she was the one who told me about pilewort – but it is there, like a treasure chest, waiting to be opened, to be explored. And sometimes, when I was deep inside my lady in Rua de Carmo, Jenny would float into my mind and I would feel her body, feel her warmth, feel her desire for me.

Marsala is the name of my lady in Rua de Carmo, but she says I must call her 'Ma'. To me it sounds like a corruption of mother, of the Mother I already have, and although I call her 'Ma' when I am locked in the embrace of her legs, I cannot call her 'Ma' in my mind. Sometimes I just think of her as Rua de Carmo, for she is Portuguese, made English by her dead husband, a Cornet-of-horse who liked to ride his horse by day and her by night – if she's telling me the truth.

I've never seen her with all her clothes off, not once. She talks of modesty, of virtue, and then she makes me take off all my clothes and she washes me all over and measures my excitement. It was six inches when I first came to her. Now it is seven inches and she says I've grown up inside her, and that is the literal truth.

As we marched past the alarm bell, I began to wonder what she would think, what she would do when she found out I wasn't coming back for six months. She still knows Ives, sees him from time to time, but he's too old for her – his hair has run wild on his belly and curled on his chest. She likes her men young, likes them standing on the edge of manhood with no more that a moustache of hair around their private parts. Ives has been telling me for ages that my days – my nights – are numbered. For a long time my hair made a fine furrow from my moustache to my belly button, but now it is becoming darker, becoming wider, and looking like a spearhead – and it's pointing to my chest, to the smooth nipple-lands that are still covered in soft down.

She says hair is like dead bracken, dry bracken and it should be fired at the end of winter – and she talks about the smell of burning hair, and love in the springtime, when the new bracken, the green bracken is poking through the wet earth.

As the Strand came to an end – just below the last of the great bastions that guard the Upper Castle – the road narrowed, and the tide began to lap across the rocks. We broke ranks, formed a single file and marched in a long straight line.

Lieutenant de Colville marched in the gap between us and the musketeers. He marched with a firmness of purpose, marched the way I marched up to his house, the house of the angels, the house of the Lamb of God: twice a week – sometimes more – for the past year. He has no shame, no coyness of the flesh, like my lady in Rua de Carmo. We have lain in bed, flesh to flesh, and the seed that was in him, was in me, has glued us together, belly to belly. In the morning when we woke, woke to the sunrise in the Straits, in the hills of Spain, I wanted him, wanted what he could do to me. It was not the same as wanting my lady in Rua de Carmo. That was more to do with lust, with sowing seed; and some days she made me feel as though my whole body, my whole being was going to pass through the cleft of love and be gone, be lost for ever in the narrow valley that lies deep within her belly.

With her it felt right. Felt normal. Felt natural.

But with him it did not feel right, normal, or natural. With him it felt good. And I wanted it, wanted him, wanted the hardness of his body, and often in this wanting I would think of the softness of her body. In time I came to see that wanting him was a corruption. A corruption of the flesh. A perversion of the natural order that was established by God. And each time I wiped the nibbed-end of my quill, stained my thumb and forefinger black, I saw it as a symbol of the blackness – of the sin – that now stained my soul. For days on end I did not wash my thumb and finger, and I kept on using them to wipe my nib, and now the ink is deep in my flesh – as the sin is deep in my soul – and neither will come off.

Michael says it's not a sin, says something so good could not be a sin. But then he admits he confesses his sins – to a priest – and his sins are washed clean in a curtained blackness that reminds me of the curtained blackness that used to lie below the balcony in Saint Barbara's Chapel.

In the night – when the air was warm and the shutters were wide open and it felt as though we were lying under an eiderdown of twinkling stars – he confessed his sin, the sin that incurred his father's wrath and forced him into exile. But in his confession there is no remorse. He exalts in it, exalts in his madness, and there is no repentance. In my mind he is still Michael, my Michael, Michael the Archangel, but now he flies with the hosts of hell, with the forces of popery.

In the dark of the night I want him, want the warmth, want the comfort of his limbs. In the daytime I want to break the glue that holds us together – and be hers and hers alone – but the glue has set solid, and I need him, need the protection of his body, his rank.

And try as I will, I cannot think of a way to break the glue, to cleanse my soul, and still be safe from Sergeant Brandon.

50

Three-quarters of a mile from Fort Whitby Gate we marched over a flat stone bridge that squatted just a few inches above the level of the road – below it water was flowing fast, scouring sand and swirling it into the sea – and then we straggled to a halt in front of Whitby. It sat on a flattened spur overlooking the beach, the stone quay, the boats and the rockcarts. It had been enlarged, been strengthened since I first saw it from the decks of the *Salisbury*. I counted nine buildings. They locked into each other, locked into high stone walls, and made a small town, a small fortress in the shape of a triangle with a bite taken out of the left-hand point – on the seaward side. It was ringed with wooden palisades and twenty or thirty children were playing in the gap between the palisades and filling the air with bursts of laughter.

To the left the cliffs had decayed, had softened to steep hills and up these wound a rough track, a horse track, that would take us to the forts and the Forage Gate in the Upper Castle. The earth was rutted – grooved by the heavy rain – and here and there, at the bottom of the ruts, the rock lay exposed, lay raw, like flesh that has been slashed open with a knife.

To the right, the cliffs that must once have overshadowed Whitby and made it cold, made it gloomy, had been eaten away by the quarrymen. The rubble, the scree of quarried stone, began by the palisades and crept high into the cliffs, made it look as though the quarry faces were bleeding stone. One of the faces was overhung by a huge shaft of rock – it reminded me of a nose, a bulbous nose pitted by the wind and the rain – and it looked as though it could break free, could engulf the whole of Whitby, if it was of a mind to sneeze, to move, to slide on the scree.

A small redoubt sat on the first ridge above Whitby, close to the edge of the quarry. It was about three storeys high with slitted windows and a pointed roof clad in tiles. The right-hand corner was reinforced with stone and capped with a watch tower that repeated the slit windows and the orange tiles.

Sergeant Brandon leant on his halberd and ran his eye over the quarry, then he turned to Ensign Hogg – he was standing about three feet away from me – and said: 'That's new. That wasn't there the last time I was here.'

'It was built for the miners. They kept saying the new quarry faces were too far away from Whitby – kept claiming they wouldn't have enough time to get back down here if they were attacked.'

Brandon grunted. 'It depends how much warning they get. And how fast they can run.'

Then Captain Lacey beckoned Hogg and they walked towards the main gate.

Devil's Drop stood two hundred yards to our right, on rocky ground close to the shore. It was a square-shaped fort with a sloping roof and it took its name from the sudden drop that carved a great swath out of the hill that lay behind it. In the old copy books in the clerk's office it was also called Western Fort or Giles Fort. I always meant to ask Trigg about the names but somehow they slipped my mind and I never did.

Fort Henrietta stood on the crest of the hill behind Devil's Drop – about a hundred yards inland. It was four or five storeys high: flat-walled, flat-roofed and shaped like a cube. It looked like an old-fashioned keep with embankments of earth replacing the girdle of walls that should have been its first line of defence. It was dwarfed by the banks of hills that rolled to the right – the hills that Wenceslaus Hollar's etchings call the 'enemies' ground' – and they made it look small, look lonely. But it was a pair of eyes – twenty pairs of eyes – eyes that could see, could warn, if the Moors were about to attack, and to me it was a friend, a friend in an empty sky, a friend who was prepared to watch over us.

A palisade that looked like the spine of a fish – a bony meatless spine – crawled up the long ridge from Devil's Drop to Henrietta. It gave the impression of strength, of confinement, safe confinement, till I saw the gaps in the line, saw the wind and the rain had flattened the spines, and all that separated us from the Moors was a beading of mounded earth – and it couldn't keep out a flock of sheep.

Inland from Henrietta – and out of our vision – lay Charles Fort, and beyond that again, like a pimple on the buttocks of Barbary, lay Kendall, our most isolated fort. They say when the Moors are of a mind to destroy us they will attack the forts one by one: Kendall will fall first, then Henrietta, then Charles, and when the heights are safe, are conquered, they will come down to the sea and take Devil's Drop and the new fort in the quarry. Then Whitby will fall, the quarries will close, and that will be the end of the stone, the end of building the Mole.

A few minutes later we marched into Whitby. The place felt empty, felt deserted, and if it hadn't been for the sound of the children's voices coming over the roofs, I would never have believed twenty or thirty families lived within the walls.

The walls and the buildings enclosed three courtyards. The first protected the springs that fed the well, the conduit, and the horse trough that lay beyond the walls. Small fishing boats and oars leant against the inside of the walls, and nets were hanging out to dry. Crab pots were piled high in one corner, and beside them lay heaps of shells that must have been steamed open for they were still clamped in pairs, still wearing that open-mouthed look that belies the sudden approach of death.

The second courtyard was cobbled and split in two by a flight of stone steps. The houses, the quarters for the guard, the cook house, a couple of little shops and the fortified tower made it look like a small market place.

The third courtyard was like a mews: long and thin with stabling on both sides and lofts for a hundred and thirty cart loads of straw. A line of rock carts butted into one another, like insects mating, and from the stables came the sound of neighing. I counted stabling for ninety horses but there couldn't have been more than a dozen of them in the stalls – and no more than thirty between here and the end of the Mole – and most of the stalls were stacked high with hay. The Court of the Guard straddled the top end of the courtyard and overlooked the conduit, the walls, the beach and the road to the Mole. The far end of the courtyard led into an enclosed lane. The doors to the blacksmith's shop, to the farriers, were wide open – were pouring heat and smoke into the lane. The door to the next store, the iron store, was propped open with a brick, and in the darkness I could see staves of iron, ingots of lead, and mounds of iron chain – heavy with rust.

We halted in front of the next door – the back door to the cook room – and a minute or two later the cook came out, counted our numbers and started to hand out tankards of lemon cordial sweetened with sugar, rounds of bread and wedges of rinded cheese that were so hard I had to suck mine to soften it.

Opposite us, in the carpenter's shop, the corpses of dead rock carts – stripped of their shafts and their side boards – were stacked against the far wall; and at the door, in the light, a wheelwright was sucking on a pipe, shaping a new spoke, making curls of wood fall to the ground – and filling the air with the delicate smell of seasoned wood.

Twenty minutes later Captain Lacey crossed the market place, came through the cook room and waited for Sergeant Brandon to call us to order. Then he said: 'As this is the first time our company has been on guard at Whitby there are some things that need to be explained while we are all together.' He paused, looked up and down our ranks. 'A week ago a couple of slaves escaped – ran away to the Moors. As a result of this all the slaves are now confined to the Mole – and because the end is controlled by the moleguard at Fort Whitby Gate it is in effect a prison, a large prison, and they won't be able to escape from there. Unfortunately it leaves us short of men to work the quarries. We are expecting some more miners from Cornwall, they've been promised for months, but so far we haven't seen a sign of them, and in the meantime the work has to go on. Men from the regiment have worked on the Mole for many years, but never in the quarries. But now' – we looked at each other, and I knew what he was going to say – 'men not on guard will have to work in the quarries.' A groan ran along the ranks and it swelled into muttering, angry muttering.

'Be quiet!' Brandon yelled. 'And show some respect.'

Captain Lacey bit at his lips. 'It will only be for a few months and it will harden your bodies. Make you fit – fit to fight the Moors.' He turned to the three officers and said something, then he turned back to us. 'The company is to be split in two. Half the musketeers and half the pikemen under the command of Ensign Wyndham and Sergeant Owen are to mount guard here in Whitby – in the Court of the Guard. The other half, under the command of Lieutenant de Colville, Ensign Hogg and Sergeant Brandon are to mount guard in the New Redoubt.'

Sergeant Brandon split the company in two and we marched back through the stable courtyard, through the outer courtyard and up the path to the New Redoubt.

The entry port was about twelve feet above the ground. As we waited the guards opened the door and lowered a wooden ladder. I kicked at the scree and waited some more, and when it was my turn I ran up the ladder, grabbed the two ropes that fixed it to the beams in the roof and swung myself onto the floor. The room was cramped by a forest of wooden uprights a foot square, and the walls were lined with barrels of gunpowder and boxes of lead shot. A trapdoor had been raised from the floorboards and lashed to one of the uprights. Through it I could see a ladder, could hear the sound of men moaning, and smell the stench, the cloying pee of an airless earth closet.

Captain Lacey stepped onto a box of shot – close to a flight of open-tread steps that led up to the next floor – held up his hand, signalled for silence. 'You will be quartered upstairs. The whole floor will be yours, and you will mount guard in the watchtower, day and night. Those not on guard will work in the quarries from five in the morning till nine in the morning – or later if the day is overcast, is cool. In the afternoon, if the tide is right, you will escort the carts to the Mole and back. Sir Palmes fears a sudden attack on the carts and if the horses are slaughtered the building of the Mole could come to halt. And we don't want that to happen.' He paused. 'This afternoon you will march the bounds. You will go up to Charles, along to Henrietta and then down to Devil's Drop and you will get to know the lie of the land. If you have to fight,' he sucked at his teeth, 'when, you have to fight, this will be to your advantage. And now Sergeant Lawson, the senior Sergeant here at Whitby has a few things to say.'

Lawson stepped onto another box of shot and said: 'This floor is a gunpowder store. Smoking is not allowed in this fort. If you want to smoke you go outside. Your meals are served upstairs at 11 o'clock each day. They are cooked in Whitby and every day four of you will have to carry them up here. For one hour a small fire is permitted in the tower to reheat the food. That is the only time a fire is permitted. Smoking and the lighting of fires in this fort are punished by twenty lashes and a month in the pit.' He pointed to the trapdoor in the floor. 'There is a prison down there in Whitby, next to the old main gate, but at the moment it's being used as an extra powder store and—'

Oldfield dug me in the ribs and whispered: 'He was one of them.'

I shuddered. He was sick, sick in the head. If we were in England they would have discharged him. But here we needed him. Needed the madness that seethed in him. It is the madness they call courage, the madness of maggots in the brain. It makes my bowels run hot and cold, and dries my mouth, and some nights I'm scared of him, and I can't think why I ever wanted to befriend him. I half-turned, patted him on the arm and shook my head.

'Yes it is,' he whispered. 'I recognise the voice. That bastard had me up against the wall. He had me twice he did. And now I'm going to have him,' and he smiled.

My arse tightened. I'd heard his threats many times, and they always unsettled me, left me feeling on edge. I shut my eyes, pushed his words out of my mind, and I heard Lawson say: 'You might have noticed the smell in here. It comes from down there.' He jerked his thumb at the floor. 'You can shut the trapdoor at night and stop the smell drifting upstairs when you're trying to sleep. But in the daytime you have to leave it open.'

He walked over to the door, swung out an iron bar, gave it a spin and a rope ladder unrolled, dropped towards the ground. 'If everyone's going out, lower the wooden ladder and pull it back up afterwards. If only one or two are going out, use the rope ladder. The sentries on duty may leave the door open for ventilation during the day, but they must pull both the ladders back into the fort. Failure to keep them inside, failure to maintain the safety of this fort will result in everyone on guard spending a week in the pit.'

He walked back to the box of shot. 'And now we come to the last thing I want to say. If the Moors are about to overrun this fort, if you are about to be defeated, and you know you are about to be defeated and you can fight no more, then it is your duty to destroy this fort and everything in it. One man – and if I am here I am prepared to be that man – must lay a trail of gunpowder and when the Moors are swarming all over the fort, are about to break in, he must light the gunpowder and blow the bastards to bits. A million bloody bits.'

The whole room fell still, fell silent, and for several seconds no one did anything or said anything.

Then we filed upstairs, in muffled silence, and the first thing I saw was a skin. A human skin, the tanned skin of a man, of a Moor. It was nailed to the wall and his hair was tied in a knot and it hung down his back. His hair was black and his skin was brown and beside him hung a curved sword. It was less than three feet long, not evenly curved like our swords but fat in the middle and thin at the ends. Time had dulled the steel blade and the brass writing, the writing that looped across the blade like snake tracks in the sand, spoke of things I did not know, did not understand, and it made me feel as though I was in the presence of death.

The food was no better than the food in our old lodgings, but there was more of it, and the beer frothed bubbles – made me wonder if they'd managed to trap the bubbles from the well, from the spring in the courtyard.

In the afternoon we marched from fort to fort. They all smelt the same: stale, with a whiff of piss, turd, and rotten fat. Inside they were bigger than they looked but not big enough for the number of men needed to guard them – even Devil's Drop needed twelve men and one Sergeant – and I could imagine at night when they were all sleeping close together on the floor, if one wanted to turn over they'd all have to turn over.

That night Wyndham, Hogg and de Colville laid their pallets in the corners, near the window-slits, near the cross flow of air – none of them appear to fear the taint of the night air – and the rest of us unrolled ours in the middle of the floor and made them into beds. About an hour later when darkness had settled on the day and I was lying on my pallet, letting my eye slide around the skin of the Moor who was spread-eagled the way they spread-eagled Oldfield over the wall, and wondering who had the sword – we'd been passing it round, feeling the sharpness of the edge – when one of the sentries thundred down the steps, and the gunpowder store was filled with barking. Then Lawson came bounding up the steps. He nodded to de Colville and said: 'Good evening, sir.' De Colville sat up and nodded back. 'I forgot to tell you this morning sir, that we have barking dogs. I set them on the chains every night and if they discover a Moor they bark like hell, and you have to sound the alarm and double the guard.'

De Colville nodded, and Oldfield tapped me on the shoulder. 'I'm going out,' he whispered. 'My head's bad tonight. Come down in about half an hour and let me in will you?' He slithered across the floor and was gone before I could say a word.

I waited an hour, maybe more. I was restless and so were a lot of other men – it must be something to do with sleeping in a new place, a new bed, because it happens to me every time I change beds. I crept down the steps, felt my way round the barrels, eased open the door, pushed out the iron bar and spun the rope ladder. Oldfield came up without a sound, then he hissed in my ear: 'What took you so bloody long?'

I shrugged. It was no use explaining some things to him – I'd learnt that long ago – and beside my heart was bloody racing and I was feeling jittery, so I said: 'How's your head?'

'Head?'

'Headache?'

'I haven't got a headache.'

I sighed to myself and patted him on the shoulder. We spun the ladder, flicked it inside and barred the door. I bit my lips and hoped like hell none of the officers upstairs had heard anything.

I crept up the steps, slid across the floor and snuggled into my bed. Ten minutes later, as I turned on my side, as my heart began to calm, to beat the slow soft beat of sleep, Oldfield crept over to the man on the wall, patted his arse, and hung the sword on the wooden peg.

51

The sound of the trumpets – the blast of alarm – shattered my sleep, woke me up, sat me up with a sudden jolt.

The dogs began to bark, began to echo the alarm.

In the half-light men were leaping up from their pallets and rushing to the slit windows. De Colville, in his night shirt, tore over to the corner and hurled up the steps to the top of the tower. Then the sound of a bell, an alarm-bell, came pounding through the air, and a second later came the heavy thump of a cannon.

'What the bloody hell's going on?' someone screamed.

Someone else yelled: 'I can't see a bloody thing out there!'

Then the cannon thumped again and Hogg yelled: 'The Moors are attacking! Get dressed! Everybody get dressed! Now!'

Someone yelled: 'I can see two of them. On horseback. Just down there.'

We crowded the slit-windows, and Lockhart said: 'That's the fucking picket you bloody fool. Can't you see their breastplates?'

I could see their outlines, see the black of their backplates – the troopers were wearing them again to deflect sword cuts and lance thrusts.

They raised the trumpets to their lips, blew another alarm, and made the dogs bark again.

'Get dressed,' Hogg yelled. 'Get your bloody coats on and get outside.'

In the distance I heard the thump of a cannon and that was answered by another one high above us, and echoed by another further inland. 'That's the forts,' Hogg said, 'they're answering the alarm.'

Then we heard yelling – it was coming from the top of our tower – and the next moment de Colville rushed back down the steps and screamed: 'They've found a man. He's lying on the ground. He's wearing a sergeant's coat. And they think he's dead.'

We rushed down the steps, through the barrels, out the door and down the ladder – anchored our pikes in the dirt and stuck them straight out like a frightened hedgehog.

De Colville walked over to the troopers, knelt down and turned the body over. In the half-light we saw the stump that was its neck. The head had been cut off with one blow. And just a few feet away lay the body of the barking dog, with it's skull split open.

I didn't think, I didn't want to think. It was Lawson. It had to be Lawson.

De Colville walked back to us and said: 'The Moors must have been out here, last night, waiting for him.' I felt my guts tighten, and the man beside me vomited all over my shoes. The smell made me gag, and I burst into a sweat. I could hear Oldfield making a snuffling giggle.

'I don't know where his head is,' de Colville said.

Then Crabtree – who has never done anything without a specific order in his whole bloody life – broke ranks walked down the hill a few yards and prodded at the other barking dog. It snarled at him and he jabbed it with his pike and it backed away. Then he touched what looked like a rock and yelled: 'I think you should come and look at this, sir!'

Oldfield whispered in my ear: 'And I was hoping he'd eat the bloody thing.'

For the next two hours we searched the quarry, the hills, the paths, the shoreline – everywhere a Moor could hide – and we found nothing. Nothing at all.

At eleven o'clock, in almost total silence, we ate our meal. Oldfield was mad. And cunning. There was no doubt about it. And I didn't know what to do, what to say, and I took the easy way, the way of the coward: I shut my mouth and did nothing.

In the afternoon Lockhart washed Lawson's head – washed the dirt out of the chewed flesh that was once his ears, his nose, his mouth – and sewed it back on. Then we wrapped his body in a white shroud and carried him up to the burying ground on the heights above Whitby. As we lowered him into the grave, he began to bleed around the neck, and by the time it came to my turn to throw a clod of earth into the grave, he was wearing a band of red, a necklace of blood. It reminded me of Oldfield's arse, of the morning I had to wash it, wash off the blood, wash off the pink snowflakes.

Next day we were joking about Lawson's death – saying he had a head start on us, and the dog was too well fed – and learning how to be miners, quarrymen. There wasn't much to it, that's what I thought. If we wanted to bring down a small amount of rock we drilled and dug a short tunnel, and packed it with two or three barrels of gunpowder. Then we laid a trail of gunpowder – fuse or match was too slow-burning and too expensive – blocked up the end of the tunnel with big rocks to compress the explosion, lit the trail and ran like hell. And down came two or three hundred tons of rock. After that came the hard work: filling the rock carts.

A large explosion followed the same principle but instead of one small tunnel we dug three long ones in the shape of a fan, packed them with thirty barrels of gunpowder and brought down ten thousand tons of rock.

A little explosion thumped our ears and sent a tremor through the ground but a big one was like hell on earth: the ground shook, cracked open, thumped my feet and tightened my balls. I could hear the bang, hear it exploding in my head, then the blast arrived – it was like opening a door in the middle of a storm and being hit in the face by a howling gale.

We soon learnt to lie flat on the ground and cover our ears. I found it exciting, found I liked the heaving and the shuddering, for it was like lying on my lady in Rua de Carmo in her moment of frenzy. I was missing her, missing the warmth of her body. And it was strange to be sleeping so close to Michael, so close to a body that could do so many things to mine, and was doing nothing, was making no sign, giving no hint that it wanted me.

One morning in the privy, when I was the only one there, I found I was doing what I thought I'd left behind, thought was part of my childhood: making snowflakes.

I was disgusted with myself. I've never been disgusted before. I've just accepted it. It was a sort of make-believe, a thing children did. But I wasn't a child any more. I was a man, and a man went swiving. That's what a man did. So why was I doing this? And why was I thinking about Michael? I shook my head. It was madness, bloody madness – like the madness of Oldfield.

I'd been keeping out of his way and wondering if he was planning to attack Brandon with the sword. But he seemed to be quiet, to be calm within himself, and after a while I came to think, to hope, that the storm, the need for revenge, for blood-letting had passed away.

But then I noticed the way he kept looking at Brandon, looking at the curve of his neck, and it chilled my soul.

52

A few days later one of the servants – an Egyptian by the name of Fayed – discovered a plot to seize Captain Bowles, the garrison treasurer, and hold him hostage in Charles Fort. The plotters, if the rumours are right, thought Captain Bowles had received twelve months' pay for every man in the garrison, but didn't intend to pay it out and didn't intend to use it to buy any extra provisions. He had some other scheme, some other priority, some other ploy to keep his hands on our money.

If I'd heard this story when it was a secret, a plot, I might have thought it was true, for they say the last time the garrison received twelve months' pay, it was drunk for a week and the Moors could have overrun us if someone had told them. So it would make sense to pay the money out in small amounts, spread it over several weeks, or not to pay it out at all if the Moors were threatening to attack.

Sir Palmes called the plot a mutiny and a court martial sentenced five men to be shot; five to be hanged under the gallows with their toes touching the ground; and two to ride the wooden horse.

There was an air of gloom in the quarry as we made our way up to the rockface. We all knew the sentences could be carried out at any moment, and we all knew if we'd been in their companies, been out here as long as they had, we could be in the cells with them, waiting to be shot.

Captain Lacey was pacing up and down – he'd been doing a lot of walking since we arrived – and as he turned to say something to de Colville, a pair of troopers thundered past the quay and into Whitby. Crabtree stood up, rested his pick and said: 'Christ! That looks ominous.'

I nodded, and less than a minute later the troopers galloped out the gate and up the slope and yelled: 'Captain Lacey, sir. I have Sir Palmes's orders sir. You are to report to him on the Old Parade with your whole company sir. He's waiting there right now. He says you are to double-march up the hill to the Forage Gate, go through the Upper Castle and down to the Old Parade that way, sir. And I am to repeat, sir, and I apologise for the impertinence: you are to leave right this minute, sir.'

Less than ten minutes and half a mile later we ran through the Forage Gate – it lies to the left of Peterborough Tower and is used by the troopers to forage their horses – pounded through the Upper Castle and hurled down the slopes of Castle Hill. At the very least we were expecting to find a riot, a rebellion, a mutiny. Instead we found ranks of sullen men, two firing squads and two men tied to posts. Not a single man in the whole parade was carrying his pike or musket. Then another company pounded onto the Old Parade, and another and another. They were from the forts, and like us they were bearing arms and were untainted by mutiny. Then four more companies arrived and the town guard and the moleguard were changed, and all the mutineers – the would-be-mutineers – were assembled behind the firing squads.

In a silence broken only by the screech of the seagulls, the firing squads came to attention, pointed their muskets, touched the powder with their burning matches – and fired. The lead balls smashed into the men, bloodied their chests, lifted them up in the air. The sound of the firing, the sudden proclamation of death, bounced off the walls, hung in the air for a moment and then it was gone – with their lives.

The seagulls took fright, flapped and swooped in silence.

The two men slid down the posts and slumped against the ropes.

The seagulls began to screech again, to screech their protest.

Sir Palmes had the men cut down, laid in the graves below the gallows, laid with their faces looking up at the sky for the last time. Then he demanded the parade promise obedience, and he tempered it with a promise of pay and provisions. Subdued by death, by the finality of the grave, the men gave their promise, but they also told Sir Palmes that they 'could not remain calm, remain passive' if the pay and provisions failed to arrive. Then they marched past the open graves, marched back to their quarters, and took up their arms again.

We marched back through the Upper Castle in a quiet mood, and just beyond the Forage Gate – where the V-shaped stone revetments that protect the gate and bastion are being repaired, being strengthened – Oldfield whispered to me: 'I've seen the worst they can do. They don't frighten me. And now I have a plan for that bastard over there.' He nodded towards Brandon and smiled.

53

For the next month I eyed the sword on the wall with increasing terror, and I kept thinking tonight will be the night, the night it will come off the wall. But each night came and went, and added to my fear, and nothing happened. Then I shifted my pallet close to Hogg, and I kept telling myself: if Oldfield wants me to help, I won't, I can't, because Hogg is a light sleeper, and he'd notice if I got up in the night.

By day I didn't see much of Oldfield. I've been helping a funny old coot by the name of Tattleton – we've been digging tunnels. His back is hunched and he walks bent and when he's in the tunnels – they're never more than four feet high – he crawls along on padded knees and he never appears to suffer from backache. Not in the daytime anyway. He wears a tall black hat with a wide brim, and at the front – stitched to the brim and the crown – is a metal holder for a candle, and it means he can always see what he's doing. We shape the tunnels to fit his hat – so they always taper at the top – and I keep telling him if he wore a smaller hat we wouldn't have to dig out so much rock, but he just says: 'This is a proper hat. A miner's hat. The fabric's been dipped in salts of alum so it won't burn. You won't get a hat like this, not here you won't.' He says he wants to be buried in it, says it will light his way to heaven.

Sometimes I think he's daft, but he's good to talk to and in a funny way I quite like him. I just wish he didn't fart so much. I go in behind him and pick up his bits of rock, put them in a basket and pull them out of the tunnel and I keep telling him I should get paid for flatulence, and he laughs. I think he thinks it's something to do with getting fat, and I haven't had the nerve to tell him what it really means.

The stone is soft, easy to work, easy to quarry, and when it's been in the sea for a few months it grows a mossy coat and hardens. But sometimes it crumbles in the water, turns into sand and silts up the inside of the Mole. They say the ship's captains are complaining about the draft of water at low tide, and we may have to dredge out the sand. They also say Sir Hugh Cholmley has lost his commission to complete the Mole and now it's going to be finished by Mister Henry Sheres. He studied a mole in Genoa and he's going to build great chests, clamp them with iron, fill them with rock and tarras, and lower them into the water. Sir Hugh built most of the mole by dumping rock straight into the sea, and he's been making some small chests – experimenting is what he calls it – and I don't know why they want a new engineer. They say Mister Sheres has guaranteed to finish the work for a fixed price, so it may be something to do with saving money. Whatever it is, it doesn't matter much to me, and the only difference it has made so far is that Sir Hugh's chaplain has left Whitby and now instead of being a 'self-contained dominion' which was Sir Hugh's boast, we are a 'Godless self-contained dominion'. And to be honest most of the men prefer it that way.

Soon after midday when my belly was full of bread, gravy and hard pease – it hadn't been boiled long enough – we packed the tunnel with three barrels of gunpowder and filled in the spaces around them with loose rock to force the blast up the hat-shaped wedge 'because that's the way to bring down more rock'. As Tattleton said these words he smiled and tapped his hat – the way some men tap their heads to show wisdom. I nodded, shared his wisdom, and we ran a trail of gunpowder over the top of the barrels and into the main part of the quarry. Then we blocked up the tunnel and lit the trail. It flared up the quarry and died just a foot or so from the tunnel. 'Christ!' he said. 'That's bloody lucky.' We walked back up the quarry. 'You see what happened?' I nodded. The ground was wet, and it had wet the gunpowder, killed the flame. 'If that happened in the tunnel we'd have to open it and have a look.' He nodded to himself. 'I lost a friend that way. The flame was sulking for some reason, and we waited and waited and it didn't go up. But the moment he removed the rock – let some more air into the tunnel – it exploded. We picked up the pieces and put him in a little box about this big' – he opened his hands, made a space of about two feet – 'and now we're not allowed to do it. They say we're too valuable,' he laughed, 'and they make the prisoners in the bagnio do it. And we shout the instructions to them.'

We relaid the trail, exploded the gunpowder and brought down the rock face – it dropped off like a mask – and it thumped the ground, made my feet tingle, made me think of my lady in Rua de Carmo. Then the air chilled, the sky darkened and it began to rain. It poured down for about an hour, then the band of rain moved out to sea, left behind a day that was bright with sunshine, and the ground began to steam. Tattleton climbed up on the rocks and he was just beginning to prod the loose rocks off the rockface with a twenty-foot pole, when a man came running into the quarry yelling: 'There's been a slip, up in the burying ground. It's opened the graves and pushed the corpses right out of the ground. The stench is bloody awful and I've never seen anything like it.'

There were fifty, maybe sixty men working in the quarry. We all dropped our tools, scrambled over the rocks, ran up the hill and onto the flat ground, the burying ground. It was no longer flat. The earth was gouged and seamed and it had moved downhill by twenty or thirty feet. I counted forty-two corpses. They had crawled out of the black earth, and some of them were still wrapped in their white shrouds and they looked like maggots.

For a long time we did nothing, we just stood and stared. Then we waded through the wet earth – it was still slipping and sliding – carried the bodies up to a small plateau of flat land and buried them in a narrow trench, one on top of the other.

The mood to work died, and I wandered up to the top of the hill and caught sight of Oldfield. He's been working up on the Marshan – the land that stretches from the Upper Castle to Fort Charles – for about a week now. I'm not sure how he managed to get up here: telling lies about working with horses in England would be my guess. But I don't know for sure.

The hill is too steep for a rock cart – the horses could never pull the weight – and we have to move about a thousand tons of rock from the quarries to the revetments by the Forage Gate. Some of the large rocks are being carted to the Mole and then taken along the quay to the Watergate, up to the Market Place, up Catherine Street, out Catherine Gate and all the way along the outer walls to the Upper Castle. But because the tide covers the road for six hours twice a day, it means most carts can only make one trip a day. So Captain Lacey decided to leave three rock carts up on the Marshan. And each day we've been filling up the carts – by carrying rock up the hill in baskets – and Oldfield's been hitching up his team of horses and taking the rock to the revetments. One cart is always left standing at the top of the hill, waiting to be filled, so there's never any shortage of bloody work.

I helped Oldfield turn the empty cart, unhitched the horses and hitched them onto the full cart. I was just about to go back down the hill when Sergeant Brandon rode up. There's been a lot of resentment, envy, about Brandon and this horse of his. It's a broken down old hack, a draught horse, a cart horse, but it's made him look superior, be superior, and in truth de Colville, Wyndham or Hogg should be on that horse. But none of them can ride, and Brandon can, and Captain Lacey says he has to watch the loading and the unloading of the carts, and the easiest way for him to do this is to ride backwards and forwards about once every hour. He's also supposed to keep an eye out for the Moors and sometimes he goes to Fort Charles and then to Henrietta and comes back along the ridge.

He leant over the saddle and said: 'I want you to go with him.' He nodded at Oldfield. 'You can help with the unloading. One of the men at the revetments crushed his hand this afternoon and they've taken him to the infirmarium. And now they need some more help.' Then he rode off towards the embankments and the palisades – they break up the Marshan, make it easier to defend, and they protect the lanes that link Peterborough Tower to Fort Charles. The lanes are dead straight and they run for seven hundred and fifty yards. And one day, if they fall, they say the new revetment will be guarded day and night because the Forage Gate, is like a mouth or an arse, it's a weak point, a point of entry.

We walked beside the cart – Oldfield said it was forbidden to ride because the rocks were supposed to be enough weight for four horses – and I was telling him about the corpses, telling him some of the fingers and toes were missing and how one head fell off as we tried to pick it up, when he slowed the horses. Then on a corner, on a curved embankment he eased the left-hand wheel into a high rut and we came to a gentle stop. Rocks began to slide, to slither off the cart and fall to the ground. The horse at the front tried to turn around, and its eyes flared. He yelled: 'Get down there and give it a pat on the nose. Here's some oats.' He tossed me a nosebag.

The horse calmed the moment it sniffed the oats. Then Oldfield picked up a mallet and began to tap at the wooden pins that lock the wheel onto the axle. I thought they must be coming loose, but then I saw he wasn't hitting them in, he was hitting them out, and I said: 'What the hell are you doing that for?'

He looked up, smiled, and told me.

I said: 'You're bloody mad.'

He shrugged. 'Maybe.'

Then he handed me the three pins. 'Walk back,' he said. 'Drop one at about fifty yards, another at a hundred yards and the last one at a couple of hundred yards. Drop them on the left-hand side of the track – your left hand, as you walk back towards Whitby.' He gave the wheel a tap from the inside and began to ease it off the axle. Then he straightened up and yelled: 'Wander about the path – try to pretend you're looking for the pegs. We don't want those nosey bastards up there in Peterborough Tower turning a spyglass on us.'

I wandered along, and wandered back. My mind was seething, was trying to think of some way to stop him, and I said: 'This is murder. They'll hang you for this.'

He stood in the middle of the track, swung the mallet backwards and forwards like a pendulum, then he said: 'He had my arse. And one day he'll have yours. If that's what you want, fuck off and tell someone. If that's not what you want, shut up and do as you're told.'

He swung the mallet again and this time the strokes were harder, faster.

I sat on the bank and looked at the loose wheel. I didn't want Brandon dead. And I didn't want him alive, buggering my arse. I kept thinking there must be some other way, some other path, and then I could hear his horse's hoofs, could hear them thundering up the track. Oldfield rushed along the track, waving and yelling: 'Sergeant! Sergeant Brandon! The wheel's about to come off and we need another pair of hands to get it back on. The pegs have come out and I haven't been able to find them.' Then he stopped, swooped his hand to the ground and held up a peg. 'Christ! I've found one.' He rushed back to the cart.

Brandon swung his leg down, dropped the reins to the ground, stormed over to the wheel and grabbed it with both hands. I rushed over to help, but he pushed me away, saying: 'Hit it. Hit it hard. As I lift it up. And be quick.'

Oldfield nodded, waited for Brandon to take the strain, then he hit the wheel – from behind. It flew off, knocked Brandon backwards, knocked him to the ground. The cart lurched and twisted forward. The axle dug into the dirt. The rocks poured off. Brandon screamed. The rocks covered him. His fingers grasped at the air, grasped at nothing. Then they opened and the dust from the rocks settled on them.

Then came the silence, the silence of death.

Oldfield sat down, shoved his legs under the cart and covered them with rocks. 'Now you run back to Whitby,' he said. 'And don't run too fast.' He picked up a rock, hit himself on the forehead and slumped to the ground. Blood began to trickle down his nose and into his mouth, and within two or three seconds, the flies, the bluebottles, the scavengers of life, of death, were buzzing around his face.

54

I ran and skipped and danced all the way to the burying ground. I felt light-headed, drunk. The bastard was dead. Stone cold dead. Tomorrow he'd lie in the earth. Then he'd begin to rot, and the maggots would have him. I was free. Free from him. Free from his threats. For a moment I sank to the ground – puffing and panting – and the ferns curled around me like tendrils of love, young love, green love. Then it hit me, shook me, like a clap of thunder: I was also free of de Colville. I didn't need him any more.

I felt clean, felt pure, felt reborn – felt like a wisp of white, a wisp of cloud floating in a blue sky. I looked at my thumb, at my forefinger, and the black ink, the stain, the taint, was gone. It mirrored my soul. There was nothing to confess – I had done nothing, nothing wrong.

Then I leapt to my feet, bounded down the hill, screaming and yelling like a demented fool.

Twenty minutes later we had the stones off Oldfield. He looked grey and old. Wyndham thought we should take him to the infirmarium, and we made a stretcher out of coats and pikes.

Then we looked again at the pile of stones. There was a reluctance to disturb them – they looked like a cairn, like a memorial of stone – and I felt, they felt, the man was entombed. Wyndham said a prayer. I don't know what the prayer was, it sounded like a murmuring mumble. Then he took a stone off the pile and tossed it under the cart. One by one we tossed the stones away, then we lifted off the wheel and brushed away the dust and the last of the stones. His chest was crushed, his hips had widened, but his face – when we lifted off his hat – was unmarked, apart from a few red welts and some bruising around the eyes.

We made another stretcher of coats and pikes and lifted Brandon onto it, and he let out a groan.

It sounded like the gates of hell opening – on rusted hinges, on hinges that needed greasing – and it filled my mind with ink, black ink. I couldn't think, couldn't say anything. Someone laid a hand on my shoulder and said: 'I think he might have been hurt too. I think he should come with us.'

We walked down the hill, past Johnson's Battery, through Catherine

Gate – I could hear men asking: 'What happened?' – then we followed the inside of the wall, and close to Johnson's Battery we climbed a flight of steps, pushed open the doors to the infirmarium.

Inside it was cool and dark, and it smelt of flesh, decaying flesh, and it reminded me of the ripe smell that comes from a pheasant that has been left to hang too long. Under this smell lay another smell. It was faint and dusty, and it made me think of old herbs, dry herbs – herbs that should be tossed on the fire, and allowed to smoke, to scent the room for one last time. A sign was painted on a side door. It read:

> Doctor Thomas Lawrence,
> Commissioned Physician at Tangiers,
> AD 1664

The door opened and he slid into the room. The men call him Doctor Death. They say he's pronounced a thousand men dead, men who might have lived if fate had not brought them to his door.

He looked at Brandon, held his wrist for a moment or two, then he gestured for him to be taken upstairs. He made Oldfield stand up. He tapped his leg, twisted his head from side to side, and sewed up the gash on his forehead with black thread. Then Wyndham said something to him. He looked in my eyes, made me open my mouth, and said: 'There's nothing wrong with him.'

On the way back to Whitby, I caught up with Oldfield, and I whispered: 'What do we do now?'

He looked at me with dead eyes and whispered: 'Stick to the story. Don't change a word of it. Not a bloody word. And pray. Pray that the bastard dies, before he can open his mouth.'

55

Next day Brandon hovered between life and death, and the opium silenced his pain, silenced his lips.

On the following day Doctor Lawrence despaired of him, and the Reverend Mister Hughes – the new chaplain to the garrison – stood beside his bed and read the prayers for the dying.

It was a good omen and it cheered me up, and I caught a smile on Oldfield's face. But the following day Brandon sipped some water. On the day after that he sipped some more, and then the delirium, the sickness in his mind, the sickness that rambled his words, began to calm. And they say he slept all of the next day.

On the day after that the guard came for Oldfield. And for me.

He was locked in the cells in Jews Lane.

I was marched over to the Head Court of the Guard and paraded before Captain Carr, the acting Town Major. He was sitting behind the table in the upstairs room – the room where I did the copying – and for a moment or two he looked at me and fiddled with his hat. Then he told me to stand at ease, to pull up a chair and sit down. 'Pikeman Oldfield,' he said, 'is to be charged with attempted murder. He is to face a court martial. He says it was an accident. Sergeant Brandon says, has sworn on oath, that it was deliberate. In case he dies suddenly or lapses back into a delirium, he has signed a statement to that effect, and the Recorder has witnessed his signature – certified that he was of a sound mind and disposition. So it will not be disputed in court.' He bit his lips. 'There are two witnesses. You and a pikeman who was in Peterborough Tower. He saw you walk up and down the road. Captain Lacey tells me you were looking for the pegs that came out of the wheel.' He paused. 'The pikeman did not see Oldfield strike the wheel. That means you are the main witness, and I want you to tell me what happened.'

'It was an accident. Oldfield said I wasn't strong enough to hold the wheel on my own and Brandon – Sergeant Brandon – wouldn't let me help him. Oldfield struck the wheel, close to the axle, but instead of sliding back on, as it should have done, it bounced off and knocked Sergeant Brandon over. And the rocks fell on him.'

He nodded. 'Did he strike the wheel from the front or the back.'

I blinked my eyes – tried to pretend to look baffled – and said: 'From the front.'

'Brandon says the blow was struck from the back. That is why the wheel came off. It was deliberate. A deliberate attempt to kill him.'

I looked at the table and shook my head.

'Did he tell you what he was going to do?'

I looked up and shook my head.

'Are you trying to protect a friend?'

'No, sir.'

'Has he promised you something? Some money?'

'No, sir.'

'So, you and Oldfield both say the blow was struck from the front, and Sergeant Brandon says it was struck from behind. It is up to the court to determine the truth, but I think I should tell you that if it is proved Oldfield is lying, it will mean you are lying. Lying in court, lying under oath, is called perjury. And perjury is punished by a whipping, sometimes two whippings, and a ride on the wooden horse. So' – he laid a heavy stress on the word – 'I would suggest you think very carefully about what you saw. What you really saw. And what you are going to say.' He paused. 'This is a serious matter. And I will not permit you to pervert the course of justice. Do I make myself clear – quite clear?'

I looked at the table and nodded.

56

For a week my mind hung in a black hole. I crawled up Tattleton's bum and hauled out the baskets of rock, and I felt as though I was building a tomb, a tomb for Oldfield. In another week, two at the most, he would be dead, and we would lay him in it – seal it up – and life would go on without him.

Tattleton tried to cheer me up, tried to teach me the finer points of mining, but I have no recollection of what he said or what he taught me. It died in the black hole, and I cannot resurrect it.

Then it was the Monday, the day of the court martial.

Soon after eight in the morning Wyndham and Hogg marched me down to the Head Court of the Guard, and we sat downstairs, on the benches, just inside the front door, and we began to wait. One hour became two, became three, became four – with nothing to eat – then a Lieutenant came down the stairs and said: 'Are you Pikeman Fenton?'

We all stood up and I said: 'Yes, sir.'

'You are to come with me, but I'm afraid you two' – he nodded at Wyndham and Hogg – 'must stay here. It's a closed court. No spectators. I'm sorry. I'd let you in if I could but—' Then he frowned and said: 'I have to find an Ensign Wyndham. I don't suppose one of you is . . .'

Wyndham stiffened. 'Yes, sir. I am.'

The Lieutenant smiled. 'That's a bit of luck. They want to call you as a witness, after him.' And he nodded at me.

'Witness? But I wasn't there.' For a moment or two he looked puzzled, then his face hardened, took on elements of fright, of fear. He reminded me of a startled rooster, and his cheeks, his wattles faded to a whitish-blue. 'But what am I going to say? What do they want me to say?'

The Lieutenant shrugged. 'How the bloody hell should I know?' He beckoned me to follow him up the stairs, and he marched me into the court room.

I was overwhelmed by a sea of red. All the officers had cast aside the greys and pinks of summer, the soft shades of indifference, and changed into red, the colour of blood. It made them, made the room, more official, more threatening. It made my insides quiver, for I knew, knew without anyone saying a word: they were out for blood, Oldfield's blood.

He was standing between two guards, close to the right-hand wall. His arms and legs were shackled, his face was puffy, and his skin was bruised, was stained yellow and green with a bloom of purple. He was staring at the floor.

I looked straight at Captain Carr. In my mind I could still hear Tattleton saying: speak slowly, speak calmly, speak naturally, speak as you would speak to me; and colour your voice with highs and lows, and don't rush, don't panic, don't gabble. I told him, told the court my story. It sounded right, sounded true, and in my mind it was right, was true. I could see the blow, could see the mallet striking the front of the wheel.

At the end of my story I looked at the floorboards and waited. Captain Carr dipped his pen in an ink pot and wrote on the paper that lay in front of him, then he nodded to Captain O'Neale. He commands a company of Irishmen. Most of them can't speak English, and all of them served in Portugal – they say they were going to fight the Spaniards, but they never attacked – and now some of them are working beside us in Whitby. Their coats are red, with blue lining and blue cuffs. Their breeches are blue and so are their ribbons, and they stand out in a sea of green. In some ways it's perverse, for they say Ireland is the emerald isle, and emeralds are green, and logically their coats should be lined with green; and ours should be lined with blue and then we would match the flag of England and Scotland – the flag that takes a bolt of blue and overlays it with red and white crosses.

For a moment or two Captain O'Neale pretended to straighten the white lace that frothed from under his blue cuffs, then he gave me a slight smile – made me feel we were friends – and asked me to repeat my story. At the end he nodded, in a slow ponderous way, then he said: 'When Pikeman Oldfield struck the wheel did he swing the mallet over his left shoulder or his right shoulder?'

I couldn't think which it was. I put my hands together, closed my eyes and raised my arms and swung them from my right shoulder, and then from the left shoulder. 'The right. I think it was the right. I can't be sure. It was very quick.'

'But you did see the head of the mallet strike the wheel? The front of the wheel?'

'Yes, sir.'

He nodded. 'Will you turn to the left, your left, and face the wall.'

I turned and saw a cart wheel. It was roped to the wall. The bottom was about a foot out from the wall and the top was about two feet out from the wall. The effect was to make the wheel look splayed, look as it looked on the cart.

'And now I would like you to show me where Sergeant Brandon was. I want you to put your hands on the wheel. To crouch. To kneel. To do exactly what he was doing when the blow was struck.'

I knelt on my right knee, gripped the wheel – high with my right hand and low my left – and pretended to push hard.

O'Neale walked behind me and said: 'Is that correct?'

I said: 'Yes, sir.'

And another voice, the voice of Sergeant Brandon said: 'My left hand was a little lower. And my right shoulder was closer to the wheel.'

My balls shrivelled and my mouth dried and I swung round and looked over my shoulder. He was lying in the corner of the room, on a stretcher – propped up at the head. His face looked yellow, looked veined with green; and his neck looked white, looked plucked, looked too thin to hold up the weight of his head. His coat was too big for him and his hands were twitching, were grabbing at the grey blanket that covered his legs.

Then O'Neale said: 'Now I want to stand exactly where you were standing on that day.' And he walked to my right.

I waved him back a bit, and then I drew him closer to the wall, and he said: 'Is this right?'

I nodded. Then he crouched at the knees. 'I'm doing this,' he said, 'to bring myself down to your height.'

I smiled. He was beginning to look like a fool directing a play. Then he said: 'Will you point to the place where the mallet hit.'

I pointed to a spoke on the left and ran my hand close to the centre of the wheel.

'Is that the correct spot?'

'Yes, sir.'

'I would like to record, sir' – he turned to Captain Carr – 'that from this angle I am unable to see the spot the mallet is supposed to have hit because it is shielded by the pikeman's body. And if I cannot see it now, he could not see it when it was shielded by Sergeant Brandon's body.'

'What do you say to that pikeman?'

I stood up and turned to Captain Carr. 'The accident happened—'

'It is the function of this court to determine if it was an accident or attempted murder. In the meantime you will refer to it as the incident.'

I came to attention and swallowed hard. 'The incident happened on the corner, sir. The ground was rising. And I had a downwards view.'

He pursed his lips, turned to O'Neale and said: 'Do you have any more questions.'

'Yes, sir. I'd like him to show us where Pikeman Oldfield was standing, and how he swung the mallet.'

I walked to the left of the wheel, spread my legs, swung my body to the right and pretended to strike the wheel close to the centre. O'Neale looked at Brandon – he shook his head. 'And now show me what happens when you swing from the left.'

I made a backhanded swing – a contorted swing – and touched the rim of the wheel. I did it again and this time the blow – the pretended blow – was more like a glancing blow, and in real life it might have made the wheel bounce off. Then O'Neale said: 'Now I want you to swing from the left and hit the back of the wheel.'

I did it but I couldn't hit the back. I hit the rim again. I put the mallet down and said: 'I'd have to take a step forward as I swung, and hook the mallet around the back.'

My words were met with a dead silence. The silence of the grave. Then Captain Carr looked up. 'And that is exactly how Sergeant Brandon says Pikeman Oldfield tried to kill him.'

He told me to sit down, about three feet away from Brandon. I shut my eyes, and sank into the rivers of darkness.

From a distance, a great distance, I heard Wyndham say I was acting in a strange manner after the accident – my eyes were glazed. He thought I might have been struck by a rock, and upset the balance of my brain. And that was why he'd taken me to the infirmarium and asked Doctor Lawrence to examine me.

O'Neale walked up and down, then he said to Captain Carr: 'The evidence of the previous witness, although given with great strength, great purpose of mind, is flawed on three counts. There is confusion about the angle of sight. There is confusion about the blow – was it delivered from the left or the right. And there is confusion about the state of his mind after the accident and this has flawed his memory. I am not suggesting sir that he is lying, deliberately, but given the evidence of Sergeant Brandon . . .'

Inside I was crying. Crying for the man I had wanted to be my friend. Crying for the man who should have been a sergeant, who should have been – should have been so many things.

Then we stood and Captain Carr turned to Oldfield. 'You have been found guilty of attempted murder. There is no essential difference between murder and attempted murder. The intention in both cases is to kill. And the punishment is the same for both. It is set out with great clarity in the *Laws and Ordinances of War*: "Murder shall be expiated by the death of the murderer."' He paused as if to savour the moment. Then he said, in a loud clear voice: 'Pikeman Oldfield. You are sentenced to be hanged by the neck till you are dead. And may God have mercy on your soul.'

57

For the next two days it rained and rained, and just when I thought it was going to clear, the sky clouded over and it rained some more. It was most unseasonal – more like October or November – and when we woke on the Thursday morning, the quarry was littered with rock pools and water was pouring out the cracks between the rocks.

Up in the burying ground the earth had moved again and pushed out more of the dead. The track that ran down the hill was now running with water, and at a corner close to the cliff face the earth had slid over the cliff and exposed the underlying rock, and now water was streaming over this rock, falling twenty or thirty feet, and it looked like a waterfall.

In the late afternoon we reburied the dead, buried them in water – it was seeping into the graves as we dug them – and as we made our way back down the hill, slipping and sliding in the mud that was welling up under our feet, we heard a deep-throated roar. The earth rumbled and shook, shivered my spine and sagged my mouth. We looked at each other and ran.

At the crest of the hill we stumbled to a halt and grabbed at each other. The earth, the hillside had collapsed, had engulfed the quarry, and now like a great wave of black mud it was lapping against the walls of Whitby. Women were screaming, were running out of their houses, were running towards the beach. In the quarry men were trying to claw their way up the cliff.

'Christ,' I said, as much to myself as to anyone, 'the New Redoubt. It's bloody gone.'

Crabtree mumbled: 'Jesus,' and we huddled together like scared children.

Tiles lay on the surface of the earth, and beams of wood were sticking out of it – like broken bones, and they were moving, inching towards Whitby. The mud began to fatten, to crest like a wave, to swell over the walls and onto the roofs. Then the roofs collapsed, the walls split, and the wet earth slithered into Whitby, filled it to the top like a rising dough. Then it broke it apart, pushed the remains through the palisades and onto the beach – covered the reef, curled into the curve in the breakwater, and stained the sea brown.

Then it began to rain again.

We slithered down the hill and ran along the beach. Women were crying, children were screaming, were clutching at their mothers, and men were walking up and down, looking at each other and shaking their heads. Two teams of horses had taken fright – rushed into the water and drowned when their carts sank into the sand – and now the waves were washing their bodies to and fro.

Captain Lacey yelled at the drummer to beat his drum, then he called for silence. A hundred, maybe a hundred and twenty faces, looked up at him. 'If you know anybody who is missing, tell Lieutenant de Colville, here' – he pointed to him – 'and we will try to find him or her.' And he paused. 'I know most of the things you own are in there' – he pointed to the slip, to the scouring that was now the grave of Whitby – 'but there is nothing we can do about that today. This rain isn't going to ease off, and it will be dark in a couple of hours and the tide will cover the road to the Mole in less than half an hour. It's not safe to stay out in the open on a night like this, and I don't want anyone going up the hill till we make sure it's stopped sliding. So – I want everyone to walk back to the Mole. I want every cart and every horse to go. And anything that can be picked up and carried should be taken with you. And when the tide's full I want these boats' – he waved at two lighters and a sloop that lay inside the breakwater – 'to sail to the Mole. The crews are to wait here till I order them to go. My men will stay here till it's dark, and we will search for survivors. We will reinforce the guard in Henrietta and Devil's Drop, and we will mount a picket from dawn tomorrow. By then Sir Palmes and Mister Sheres will have decided what is to be done. In the meantime, no one is to come back until we know their decision.'

Then he beckoned de Colville, Wyndham and Hogg to close on him, and I heard him say, in a low voice: 'Captain O'Neale's company. Where the hell are they?'

'They went to Catherine Gate, sir,' Hogg said. 'This morning, sir, when you were at Fort Charles.'

'He told me some of his men were sick – couldn't walk. What about them?'

'I don't know, sir.'

Then Sergeant Owen rushed up. 'I've just learnt the prisoners are missing, sir. There were six of them – shackled in threes – and they don't think they could have run fast enough to escape.'

'Where were they?'

'At the base of the quarry face.'

They turned and looked. The base was buried under twenty feet of mud. Captain Lacey shook his head. 'Do you know anything about the Irish? Captain O'Neale's men.'

'They went to Catherine Gate, sir. To the new guardhouse, sir.'

'What about the ones who were sick?'

'They're going back on the sloop this evening, sir. Captain O'Neale thinks they should be in the infirmarium, sir.' Then he looked around. 'Christ! Where are they?'

Captain Lacey nodded towards the mud slip, and the high flush drained out of Owen's cheeks.

An hour later we pulled two miners out of the mud – they talked of holes in the rock and swimming up through the earth – washed them in the sea and helped them onto one of the lighters. Half an hour later we broke into the far side of Whitby, pulled four dead Irishmen out of the mud, carried them down to the beach and let the waves wash them clean. Then we loaded them onto the sloop.

A boy appeared from nowhere and couldn't tell us his name. A miner with a broken arm crawled down the hill. And we found another man, a fisherman – dead-drunk and fast asleep – under the hull of an upturned boat.

A few minutes after we helped them into the other lighter – the rain was beginning to stop and the night was casting a pall of darkness over the remains of Whitby – Captain Lacey drew de Colville to one side and said: 'If those dead men were Protestants, I'd have them up the hill in the morning and bury them in the graveyard by Catherine Gate. And the Minister could say a few prayers for them. But this lot were papists, and Captain O'Neale will want to take their bodies into his church for a requiem mass. And we have to respect his wishes. And besides, we owe the man a large debt of gratitude. I don't think Oldfield would have been convicted without him. So I want you, because of your Roman persuasions' – he let the words hang in the air for a moment – 'to escort the bodies to the church, and to hand them over to the priests there. After that you are to find Captain O'Neale. If you can't find him tonight, find him first thing in the morning, and I expect you back here before seven. There's going to be a lot to do.' He paused. 'Take one man with you. And get the moleguard to act as pallbearers.'

I edged away from them, edged into the darkness. But a minute or two later I felt de Colville's hand on my shoulder, and he said: 'I want you to come with me. I want to talk to you.'

58

Our four dead Irishmen were beginning to stiffen, to contort, and their mouths were opening, were rounding, and they looked as though they were gasping for breath, screaming for help. We washed the mud out of their mouths, before lifting them onto the sloop, but now as we headed into the blackness and made the first long tack that would take us round the end of the Mole where the flares were burning in their beacons, lighting a spot that seemed to be too far out to sea, those mouths looked to be full of mud again, the mud of the shadows, the shadows of death.

I covered them with a sail, with a brown canvas shroud stained with mould, but it wasn't long enough to cover their feet, and as the boat swayed their feet swayed. Their feet were bare. The mud had sucked off their shoes and stockings, and their toes and their soles were white and the skin was rippled like skin that has been in the water too long, and they looked as though they were shuffling, were trying to dance the dance of death. They made me think of Oldfield. His feet are soon to dance the dance of death on the gallows. His body will contort, will stiffen, and his mouth will round and scream a silent scream, and no one will help him.

The two lighters, the two shapes in the darkness began to tack to the right, and I turned to de Colville and said: 'Oldfield didn't do it.'

For a long time he didn't say anything, and I was beginning to think he hadn't heard, or didn't want to answer, when he said: 'I talked to Brandon before the court martial and I believe him. I believe he's telling the truth. And if he's telling the truth it means you're telling lies.'

'I was there, sir. I saw what I saw.'

'Hmm. But did you see what you said you saw?'

I trailed my hand in the warm water and sucked at my fingers, sucked at the salt – tasted the bitterness of death. 'Is there any hope for him? Any hope at all?'

'Sir Palmes has to confirm the sentence. He could commute it – change it to something else – if he wanted to. He is a fair man, a just man, but he wouldn't change it – not unless there's a very good reason. And even then, given the fact that he's had to contend with two mutinies, I think he'd be very reluctant to alter the sentence.'

I thought for a long time, then I said: 'The court martial that sentenced the five men to be shot, that was for plotting a mutiny. It was discovered. It never took place. And Sir Palmes commuted three of the sentences and only two were shot.'

'Hmm. That's true. But it could be argued that the men had just cause – no pay, no provisions. And another thing: they just talked about doing it. They intended to do it, I grant you that, but they didn't actually do it. Whereas Oldfield . . .'

I didn't know what to say, and I watched the beacons grow closer, grow brighter. Then he said: 'Is there a reason why Sir Palmes would want to commute the sentence?'

I thought about Oldfield on the ship: about him refusing to let Brandon have his arse, and the fight, and being clamped in the bilboes. And I thought about Saint John's Square, and all those sergeants having him, one after the other. Then I nodded, and told him everything, everything I had kept hidden from him. And then he said the last thing I ever expected to hear: 'So the only reason you came to my cabin that night on the ship, was to protect yourself from Brandon?'

I nodded.

'And I thought – I thought you wanted me.'

A few minutes later, as we drifted towards the end of the Mole, towards the little harbour, towards a huge crowd of people holding flares, crying and wailing into the night, he said: 'Would you be prepared to tell Sir Palmes what you have just told me?'

'Everything?'

'Everything.'

I looked at the flares, the flares that were flaming with life, and I looked at the feet of the dead, the dead who would walk no more. 'What would happen to me, afterwards?'

'I don't know. You could be flogged for perjury. Made to ride the horse. Put in chains for a year. If you mentioned me, mentioned what we've done to each other, it would be worse.' And he sighed. 'I would lose my commission, be cashiered, and sent back to England in disgrace.'

I let my head slump into my hands. 'I want to help, but I'm scared, scared to help.'

He ran his arm around my shoulder and held me tight. 'I know how you feel,' he said. 'And sometimes it's best to do nothing. To walk the way of the coward.' He paused. 'And sometimes it's best to make a choice, to make the hard choice and accept the consequences. That's what I did, and it meant I had to come here, had to spend the rest of my life in Tangiers. But I've never regretted it. It was the right thing to do. And it may be the right thing for you to do.'

59

The wailing, became shrieking, became crying, as I uncovered the four bodies, lifted the first one up, and passed him into outstretched hands. A woman, a Portuguese woman flung herself at the body and they lowered it, lowered her, onto the stones. She took him into her arms, cradled him, and began to sob. But the body was stiff, was rigid, and it did not fold into her arms, into her embrace. She began to scream, to tear at her clothes and beat her breast.

It was weird. Primitive. Unnerving. And it made me shiver.

I turned to de Colville and he whispered in my ear: 'A lot of them married Portuguese women, when they were in Portugal, and they came over here with them.'

Two children came out of the darkness and the flares caught the tears running down their faces. They touched the woman and de Colville said: 'Some of them have children,' and he shook his head.

They grabbed at the next body, held the torches in his face, then they laid him on the stones. They laid the next one beside him. Then we lifted the last body up the steps and a woman rushed at it, tore at its coat, grabbed at its hands and screamed. It was a high-pitched scream. The scream of a stuck-pig. A dying pig. It raised the hairs on the back of my neck and it made me feel that her loss was my loss, and it brought tears to my eyes.

Someone at the back of the crowd yelled: 'Are there any more?'

De Colville lifted his hands and patted the air, patted the wailing to a soft sobbing. 'There are no more dead. There may be tomorrow, but not tonight.'

A voice – a voice pleading with hope – whispered: 'Are there any more survivors?'

'There are a few, in the lighters.' And he pointed to the lighters. They were dropping their sails and edging into the little harbour.

A woman yelled: 'A boy! Is there a boy?'

De Colville nodded and she threw her hands up in the air, shrieked, tore at her hair. Then she flung her arms around a man and began to sob.

A few minutes later the moleguard wrapped the bodies in white sheets, laid them on stretchers and we walked along the quay and up the path towards the Watergate. We were followed by thirty or forty people, and about the same number stayed to crowd around the lighters.

Then we heard a scream. A long nail-scratching scream and it made me quiver. I looked at de Colville – the flares were making his face look brown, look fixed, look carved out of wood – and he shook his head. Just as we were through the Watergate and close to the rough ground that slopes up to the Minister's House, a woman ran past us, screaming. It was the woman who asked about the boy.

At the cathedral the priests were waiting on the steps. As each body was carried up the steps they sprinkled it with holy water and made the sign of the cross over it. At the doors I drew back – it was an instinctive thing. De Colville gave me a shove and whispered: 'Captain Lacey said we were to stay with the bodies. And that means you and me.'

The church was a tomb of blackness, with six candles burning on the high altar. A lamp with red glass was hanging high above the altar. It reminded me of the red lights the whores are supposed to hang outside their houses at night, and it seemed a strange image for a church – unless of course it was dedicated to Mary Magdalen, the friend of Jesus, the whore who became a saint. The only other light in the whole building was a lamp with a blue glass, and it was burning in front of a statue of the Virgin Mary. I couldn't understand why red would represent a whore, represent knowledge; and blue would represent virginity, innocence, lack of knowledge. There didn't seem to be much sense in it, and in truth I don't like either colour much. I prefer green, the sea-green that matches my eyes, matches my cuffs, matches the green of Ireland.

The moleguard laid the bodies with brown eyes, blue eyes, red eyes – eyes that were dead to the green of Ireland – on wooden benches in front of the altar, and they slipped into the darkness. De Colville and I sat down in a seat to the side, and ten, maybe twenty people – shawled shapes, shapes of darkness, shapes that sobbed – crowded around the bodies. Then the priests, I counted eighteen shaven heads, took their places in the stalls on either side of the altar, and one of them chanted a long prayer. Then all of them took up the chant, and in Latin they mourned the dead. From time to time I could recognise the opening words of a psalm: *De Profundis* – Out of the depths I have called unto thee O Lord; *Domine, Exaudi* – Hear my prayer O Lord; *Miserere Mei, Deus* – Be merciful unto me, O God. And then I began to pick up the refrain, the lament of death: *Requiescant in Pace* – May they rest in peace.

The chant came and went, high in the blackness of the roof like measured breathing, and when it ended, whispered into nothing like the last breath of a dying man, I felt a strange peace, an eerie calm, an acceptance of life and death. I'd never felt this in my own church and I didn't know what to make of it.

Then the priests placed a tall candle at the head of each body, put out the candles on the high altar, bowed to the bodies and filed out of the church.

After the mourners shuffled out of the church and we were left on our own, de Colville said: 'That was the Office for the Dead and in the morning the priests will return to say a requiem mass. In the meantime you are to stay here and I'll go up to the Head Court of the Guard and try to find Captain O'Neale.'

I sat alone in the pew, listened to the echo of his footsteps fade and die and heard the door bang. Then I stood up, stretched my arms and wandered around the church. It was square but it didn't feel square, it felt long and narrow because both sides were cut off by rows of pillars and arches, and beyond them, attached to the walls and fitted with steps and side screens lay six or seven small altars. From a distance the arches framed the altars and they made the body of the church feel as though it was enclosed or protected by clusters of small chapels, small places of prayer.

I ambled from one altar to the other, watched the blue lamp making the Virgin Mary look as though she had a pair of black eyes, and found the altar of Saint John the Baptist. It was just as Trigg had described: a long-haired man, wearing a sheepskin, holding an open book and carrying a lamb – the Lamb of God. I tried to imagine de Colville kneeling here to receive his badge, his Lamb of God, but I couldn't picture it. And it didn't seem right to kneel in front of a statue, to worship it.

I wandered about a bit more and then I came back and knelt where he had knelt and looked up at Saint John the Baptist. He was shrouded in darkness, but my eyes were well used to the gloom by now, and I was thinking he was an ugly little man, and could do with a wash, with another baptism, when the door banged and I leapt to my feet.

De Colville thumped down the middle aisle. 'He's not here. He's out in Fort Monmouth for the night and won't be back till the morning. So we have to stay here till then.' He flopped down in a seat. 'If you want to go in next door to the Misericordia – most of the people from Whitby are going to bed down in there for the night – you might get something to eat.'

A priest barred my way. His swarthy skin, black hair, bearded chin and hooded eyes made him look Spanish. In the sanctuary the candlelight had made his bald head look smooth, look oiled, but here at the door it looked freckled, livered with the spots of old age. 'You can't come in,' he said.

I told him I'd been at Whitby, brought the bodies back and heard him sing the Office for the Dead, and I was hungry, and we were to mount guard all night. He smiled, made a human smile, a smile of compassion, and it surprised me. I suppose I was expecting him to be inhuman, to be dead to this world. He pointed to a long table pushed hard against the back wall. I eased my way through the crowd, helped myself to cold pork, bread, butter, cheese, pickled cabbage, dried apricots, walnuts and fish pie.

It made me want to be a monk. It was the best food I'd had since leaving England and I was sucking my lips and biting into a red apple when Sir Palmes, a lieutenant, and a man in a black suit came into the room. The priest rushed towards them and after a moment or two they began to make their way round the room. I shuffled down the other side – thinking I'd get out before they noticed me – when Sir Palmes called out: 'What are you doing in here, Pikeman?'

I stiffened and as he came towards me, I told him about Whitby, and escorting the bodies and mounting guard in the church. He asked me if we'd found any more bodies. I shook my head and he said: 'I'll come in shortly and pay my respects.'

The man in black said: 'May I join you, sir?'

He nodded and said: 'Mister Sheres, I was thinking if we had six companies of men at Whitby by dawn, we could dig out the mud and bring all the dressed stone back to the Mole. If we used that to build the new houses on the Mole, and added another storey onto some of the older houses, we could have them finished in less than a month and that would mean . . .'

They moved towards the table and I could not catch the rest of what he said. About a minute later, Sir Palmes waved at his Lieutenant, whispered something in his ear, and the man rushed out the door.

Back in the church de Colville said we should mount a proper guard. He stood on the right-hand side with his back to the marble altar rail – holding his partisan, and I stood on the left-hand side holding my pike. Between us lay the four bodies and the four candles. For a while we talked about the candles, talked about them representing the soul, talked about them being extinguished after the mass tomorrow, and how that would symbolise the end of life.

The candles made me think of Oldfield, think of his life being snuffed out on the gallows. I turned and looked at the crucifix hanging at the back of the high altar. It was a symbol of salvation, our salvation. It was also a portrait of death. The death of Jesus. I looked at his feet – they were lifesize, laid over each other and nailed to the wood by one nail – and then I looked at the feet that lay in front of me. Beneath the white sheeting I could see the outline of their toes, toes that would soon press against the end of their grave, and I knew I had to do something, say something. And I had to do it – whatever it cost me. In a soft voice, a voice of resignation, a voice that was already accepting the inevitable, I said: 'When Sir Palmes comes in, would you please ask if I could talk to him privately, on his own?'

'Are you sure?'

I nodded and then the door banged and Sir Palmes and Mister Sheres walked down the aisle side by side. They stood by the toes and bowed their heads for twenty or thirty seconds. Then Sir Palmes walked towards de Colville and Mister Sheres asked to be excused. He bowed to the dead

– to the dead I suspect he would never have acknowledged in life – then he walked back down the aisle, back into the shadows, and a couple of seconds after he closed the door the four candles caught the draft. It flattened their flames and they almost died. I took a deep breath. And waited.

A minute or two later Sir Palmes came and stood in front of me, put his nose about a foot from mine. 'I want you to answer one question. And I want you to tell me the truth. No lies. No evasions. Do you understand?' I nodded. 'Did Pikeman Oldfield strike the wheel from the front or the back?'

I looked straight into his eyes, into the pits of blackness, the pits of hell, and I said: 'From the back.'

He stepped back a foot. 'So the decision of the court martial was right. Was just. And so is the sentence.'

'Yes, sir.'

So what do you want to talk to me about?'

'I want to tell you, sir, why he did it.'

'Why?' He made the word, sound like a soft refrain, an echo of hope, then he touched me on the shoulder. 'Come and sit down, over here.' He gestured towards the side altars. 'It's been a long day, and I'm very tired.'

60

For ten or twenty minutes after Sir Palmes left I sat on my own, sat under the gaze of the black-eyed lady with the blue lamp, and I kept hearing his words, his words of warning. They were like a chorus: 'You must not . . . you must not . . .'

They made me feel uneasy, feel nervous, feel worse than I felt when the secret was mine and mine alone. I stood up, walked up and down, tapped the tiles with the end of my pike, tapped out a tune, a beat, a rising and falling of sound. And somehow that tune, that beat, became the beat of the chant, the chant of the priests – and it drove me bloody mad. I thumped my pike hard against the tiles, killed the chant, the chant of mourning. Then the chorus came back into my mind: 'You must not . . . you must not . . .' and beat by beat it brought the chant back to life.

I slumped into the seat, at the front by the bodies. De Colville came and put his hand on my shoulder. 'I think you did right and I fear it will cost you, cost you dear. But that is tomorrow, and this is tonight. And maybe you should stretch out on the pew, try to get some sleep.'

'I can't sleep.'

'Then go for a walk. Breathe the night air. And try and stop worrying. I can look after them for half an hour. After all, they're not going anywhere. Not tonight they're not.' And he chuckled to himself.

I walked down to the Watergate – it was locked in silence – and over to the Little Parade, thinking I might catch a glimpse of Jenny, but her door was closed and her windows shuttered. I walked on to Rua de Carmo. Her door was also closed and the downstairs windows were shuttered, but her bedroom window was wide open, and deep inside the room I could see, could almost feel, the soft glow of her bedside lamp. I tapped on the shutter with the tip of my pike.

After minute or two she poked her head out the window and whispered: 'Who's there?'

I stepped back into the middle of the lane, took off my hat, wiggled my fingers and kneaded the air, pretended to knead her breasts. She laughed, and a minute later she slid the locking-bars, opened the door and pulled me into the room. 'Dear Martyn,' she sighed. She flung her arms around me and kissed me on the lips. 'You can't stay. I'm sorry. There's someone else.' Then I saw a pike in the pike rack, the rack I helped to make. She laid her forehead on mine, and for a minute or two we breathed together, and she calmed my soul. Then she said: 'I'm sorry, but your time has come and gone,' she ran her finger up my cheek, 'you hairy thing.' She kissed me on the forehead, gave my balls a gentle squeeze, and eased me back into the night.

I wandered back to the church, ambled down the aisle – dragged my pike, and was thinking it must be getting on for midnight – when I began to smell smoke. Not fresh smoke, but stale smoke, the smoke that lingers in coats and breeches after burning bracken, burning stubble in the cornfields. It was sweet. Cloying. And I thought it strange I hadn't smelt it earlier on. Then I began to wonder if it was the night air, if it had somehow cleared my head, my sense of smell. I said this to de Colville, and he said: 'It's incense. They burn it, and it gives off clouds of white smoke. It smells sweet, like perfume, and during a sung mass the priests use it to incense the altar.'

'They burn it on the altar – like they did in the Bible, in the Old Testament?'

'No, no. They burn it in a thurible. It looks like a round pot with lots of holes. It pulls apart and they fill it with burning charcoal and grains of incense. The smoke comes out the holes, and it hangs on chains, so they can swing it about.'

I nodded. 'I can remember seeing one when the priests came up to Saint Barbara's that day.'

'I'd forgotten about that.' He smiled for a moment. 'And to finish answering your question – they say the beams up there' – he nodded towards the roof – 'are thick with smoke, and it's like an oil, a preservative. At night, when the doors are closed and the church heats up, the smell drops down from the roof and that's what we can smell now.'

He sat beside me, put his hand on my thigh. I lifted it off, tried to brush it away, but he gripped my hand and held it tight. 'I've missed you,' he said. 'At night, when I saw you lying in your bed, or lying on top of it when it was too hot, I wanted you. I wanted to run my hands all over you. I wanted to have you, to hold you. I couldn't bear to see you there, so close, but so far away. It's been hurting in here' – he touched his chest – 'and I've been pulling the blanket over my head at night, trying not to look at you. But in my mind I can see you. I can see you all the time.'

I sighed to myself and freed my hand. 'Michael. Sir. I needed you when I was young and on the ship. And I needed you after that night in Saint John's Square. And then I came to want you, to need you for yourself. To me your house was the house of the angels, it was like heaven on earth. I know they say it's wrong to do what we did to each other, but I don't regret it, and I'll never forget what you did to me, did for me.' I paused. 'But these things – they are what boys do, do to each other, when they cannot have a woman and they have to pretend, to pretend that the boy in their arms is a woman. But there comes a time when we can pretend no more. A time when we must put away pretence and learn to love a woman.'

'I've been to bed with a woman. With two women. I'm not a virgin. I know what to do and I've done it. I don't like it. And I don't want to do it. And calling it love is bloody stupid. It's swiving, rutting, that's what it is. Animals do it, and I'm not an animal.' He glared at me. Then his face softened and he smiled. 'I want you. I don't want a woman.'

I slumped forward, laid my arms on the back of the pew in front of me and cradled my head.

Then he said: 'Am I revolting?'

'No.'

'Deformed?'

'No.'

'Do you dislike me?'

'No.' I shook my head. 'It's nothing to do with anything like that. It's to do with our nature. We are meant to love a woman. And that's what I want to do.'

I remembered my lady in Rua de Carmo, remembered her tenderness, remembered the way she eased me out, eased me into the dark, into the night. She didn't want me any more, didn't need me any more, but she didn't hurt me, hurt my feelings. She had compassion. I leant forward, ruffled his hair, and said: 'I'm sorry, sir.'

In the hour before the dawn, when they say the night is at its darkest and our sleep is at its deepest, I heard a bell. It was far away and it sounded as if it was coming down a long corridor, and it was strident, demanding. A few minutes later I heard a chant. It was not the chant of the Office of the Dead. It was based on one note, one beat, and each beat was the same length till it came to the note before the pause, and that note was drawn out for half a beat, then it sagged and died. It was like a lament, a muffled drum beat, and after a while it began to thud in my head and it made me sit up and blink.

De Colville was lying in the pew behind me. I leant over the seat and said: 'What the hell is that?'

He opened one eye. 'The priests are chanting Matins and Lauds – morning prayer. They have a chapel of their own, a private chapel up in the convent.'

'Convent? I thought nuns lived in convents.'

'They do, and so do priests. And when they've finished Matins and Lauds they'll hear mass together, the first mass of the day. They call it the Conventual Mass, the mass of the convent.'

I nodded, lay down again, tried to snuggle into the wood, but the wood was hard and my ear was soft, and after a while I sat up, yawned, and rubbed at my ear. The chant went on and on, for an hour or more, then it stopped. I kept waiting, kept listening, but it didn't come back, and outside I could hear the birds. They were beginning to sing, to greet the dawn, and they were better than the priests, more melodic, and unlike the priests they sounded as though they were enjoying themselves.

I can remember thinking, dreaming, if I were God, I'd bind the priests to silence, and ask the birds to wake me up in the morning.

Then a priest was lighting two candles on the high altar, and another one was walking right round the church lighting two candles on every side altar. The brass candlesticks and the brass crucifixes – standing on shelves above every side altar and evoking images of a mass execution – began to catch the light, to make it glitter and glint. The church, the cathedral, became a place of magic, a place of beauty, an island of light, and all the statues appeared to wake, to flicker with light, with life, and their eyes, their painted eyes, their peeling eyes, made me feel as though I was being watched, being subject to a silent catechism, and I did not know the answers, the correct answers.

A bell rang in the sanctuary and we stood up. Behind us a few old women shuffled to their feet.

Two priests walked up to the high altar. One was in his long black robes, but the other had covered his with a white surplice that ruffled his ankles, and over it he was wearing some sort of a vestment that looked like an apron – from both the front and the back. It was black, the colour of death, the colour of requiem. It was embroidered with silver thread, and on the back, framed in a cross, I could read the letters: IHS.

He made the sign of the cross. We knelt down, and he began to mumble in Latin. I couldn't make out a word of what he was saying. Then he moved up to the right-hand side of the altar, and we sat down. He started to read out of a book – still facing the altar – and every so often he bowed towards the crucifix.

Then a long line of priests padded into the church. Most of them were wearing long white surplices and apron-vestments: two were green, one was gold, one was black and the rest were white. Each priest stood at the foot of a side altar, made the sign of the cross and began to mumble in Latin. I turned to de Colville and whispered: 'What are they doing?'

'Saying mass.'

'But why are there so many of them?'

'All the priests have to say mass every day. And they have to wait for everyone to finish before they can have breakfast, so they all like to start at the same time.'

I was going to laugh but he looked solemn, looked serious. I bit my lips and looked to the front. Then the priest crossed to the other side of the high altar and we all stood up, and he mumbled some more.

I began to feel as though I was caught in a storm of words – they were pouring off every altar – and I was wishing I had a book, in English, and could follow what they were saying. I tapped de Colville on the arm. 'Do you understand Latin?'

'I learnt some when I became a Catholic.'

'Became?'

'Hmm. Converted. Received into the church.'

'Like Trigg?'

'Trigg?'

'Corporal Trigg. From the clerk's office.'

He shook his head. 'I don't know him. I don't think he comes here.'

We sat down and the mumbling went on and on. I couldn't understand why I'd heard all those torrents of hate preached about the mass. It was tedious. Boring. It would have sent most of the congregation at home in Elme to sleep by now. I closed my eyes and stifled a yawn. Then he made me kneel, and I said: 'Why did you become a papist, a Catholic?'

'Because this is the church that was founded by Christ. It has an unbroken tradition going all the way back to the apostles. And it has preserved the truth.'

'But what about all the other churches?'

'They broke away and they decided what they will and will not believe. You can't do that. You have to accept, to believe, what God teaches, through holy scripture and the traditions of the church.'

I let that run over my head without a comment.

Then the other priest, the one kneeling on the steps in front of the high altar, rang a little bell. De Colville closed his eyes and bowed his head. Two or three minutes later he rang it again and the priest lifted up a round wafer of bread and bowed. Then he did the same with the chalice – and now the sun was beginning to come in the side windows – and as he held it up, the gold and the silver of the cup caught the sun and it looked primitive, looked like a morning offering, a morning sacrifice.

De Colville leant towards me and whispered in my ear: 'And now by the miracle of the mass, the miracle of transubstantiation, Christ, the same Christ who walked and talked and lived on earth and is now in heaven, is also present on the altar under the form of bread and wine.'

I didn't believe a word of it. It was a deceit. A lie. A perversion of words. Then I remembered our second Sunday in Tangiers, and him with the flux, and I said: 'And now I know why you didn't take communion on that first Test Sunday, just after we arrived here.'

He shrugged. 'Sometimes my courage, my faith, fails me. And I can't do what I want to do, what I should do.'

Then all around us bells were tinkling and round white wafers were rising from the white linen on the side altars. It was like seeing the full moon rise, and rise, and rise again – then rise again. But that is not apt for Christ is the son, the risen son – and then I was playing with the word in my mind, making it into sun, the sun that was now rising and would soon see our four Irishmen into their graves.

Then we were sitting again, and de Colville said: 'I've always admired the Duke of York. He has the courage of his convictions. And they've never wavered, not once since he became a Catholic. I suppose you know it was because of him they brought in the Test Act? And now they won't let Catholics hold public office. Or hold a commission in the army or the navy.' I nodded. 'They made him give up his commission – he was Lord High Admiral. And now they're saying he shouldn't succeed his brother, shouldn't be King if his brother dies.'

Then we stood up again – I was beginning to wonder if they'd ever make up their bloody minds just what it was they wanted us to do – and I said, in a voice much sharper, much louder than I intended: 'I agree with them. I think the King should be a Protestant. And so does everybody else I know.'

'I don't,' and he smiled. 'The Duke is the legal heir, and one day

God might do great things through him. One day the Test Act might be repealed. And England might return to the faith, the true faith.' And he smiled again.

The priests at the high altar made a deep bow to the crucifix, and as they left the sanctuary they made a small bow to the four bodies – to me it looked like an afterthought, like something they'd almost forgotten. Then, one by one, like dandelions on the wind, the priests from the side altars drifted away, and I said: 'They must be hungry.'

De Colville looked at me, pulled a face, a piteous face, and shook his head. At the back of the church I heard footsteps, then the door banged three or four times. A priest drifted around, put out all the candles, and we were left alone, in silence.

'Is that it?' I said.

He shook his head. 'They'll have a funeral mass later this morning. A sung one. And no doubt the Mayor, Sir Palmes, Mister Sheres and Captain O'Neale will be here in the front pew.'

'How much longer before he's back from Monmouth?'

'An hour. Maybe two.'

'Jesus,' I said under my breath. I began to pace up and down. I'd never spent so much time in a church before. I was sick of it, and I couldn't think what would possess a man to spend his whole life in church, to be a priest, a father, and get up so early every morning.

Then I began to think about Mister Tate, to think about him getting up early every morning and saying his prayers in his chapel, and I remembered the boards, remembered the name on the board. 'Is Lord Extonmouth really your father?'

He stared at me. Then he blinked a couple of times, blinked away the surprise that had flared in his eyes. 'Yes he is. But how did you know?'

'I saw his name once. On the boards with the Ten Commandments, in Mister Tate's chapel. And I asked.'

'It said Lord Extonmouth?'

'Yes.'

He shook his head. 'There must be some mistake. It's not possible.' He picked up his partisan and walked out of the church.

Then I remembered I wasn't supposed to tell anyone, supposed to betray her confidence. I flopped onto a pew, my belly gurgled, and I hoped he would never want to go to the chapel, want to talk to Mister Tate.

In the late afternoon, as our four Irishmen were settling into their graves by Catherine Gate, and the last two rock carts – weighed down with stones from the corpse of Whitby – were setting off for the Mole, we climbed the black-spined hill by Devil's Drop and marched from Henrietta to the Forage Gate.

Most days we talked, laughed and joked amongst ourselves – it was allowed on long marches as long as we didn't break the beat, didn't make too much noise – but this time we marched in silence, marched without the beat of the drum. Behind us the musketeers carried the body of Richard Read. He was a quiet man, too quiet some say, and now he will be quiet for ever, and tomorrow he will lie beside the Irishmen. They say no one missed him till this morning when Sergeant Owen counted heads, and an hour later they dug him out of the bowels of the New Redoubt. The mud had coated him, had bound his arms and legs together and he looked like a turd, a human turd.

Soon after midday the molemen found the body of a boy curled in a ball. A stone wall had crushed him, had pushed him against the spring, and as we helped them lift off the stones the water bubbled free. It washed him clean, washed away the mud, the blood, the dirt that had hardened the soles of his feet. We laid him on the sand and for a moment he looked as though he'd been in swimming, and I half-expected him to sit up, to bubble back to life, like the spring.

A miner is still missing, and so is his wife, and their newborn baby. Their cottage was swept away. Their earth-brown floor tiles with corner inserts of glazed mosaic are still there, still glittering in the sunshine, but the walls, the roof, everything they contained, everything that made their life is gone. Captain Lacey thinks they were swept out to sea, thinks we will never recover their bodies. And he says we aren't going to recover the bodies of the prisoners. He says they are to remain in the quarry, to lie beneath the mud, beneath the shroud of scree till the Day of Judgement – when their chains, their fetters of rust, will be broken for ever.

Mister Sheres and Sir Palmes tramped the mud for an hour or so. Then they walked along to the cliffs behind Devil's Drop, and now everyone thinks we'll be opening a new face there, as soon as the last bits of Whitby are loaded onto the rock carts.

At the Forage Gate we side-stepped a mound of horse dung – sometimes the early morning picket waits in here till the dawn lightens the lines – then we marched about thirty yards and halted in front of a long block of two-storeyed houses.

A fat little lady with a cheery face – veined red by sitting too close to the fire – bustled out and said something to Captain Lacey. He nodded and turned to us. 'This is Mistress Copeland. She owns these four houses and we will be lodging with her for the next three months. Sir Palmes intends to build two more forts at Whitby, and he's thinking about a new guardhouse for a dozen men and a sergeant. But Whitby itself will not be rebuilt. In future the company that works in the quarry will live here and march to Whitby every morning. It's only half a mile from here, and it will give you a chance to stretch your legs twice a day.' And he smiled.

'And now we come to a serious matter.' The smile slipped off his face. 'You are to attend tomorrow morning's parade. It is to be a punishment parade.' And he paused. 'I don't have to tell you the nature of the punishment. You know that. And I don't have to tell you why. You know that also. What you don't know is that I want you to conduct yourselves with dignity, with honour – although that is a hard word in these circumstances.' He paused again. 'In normal circumstances I would have allowed you to go into the town tonight, to drown your sorrows, but death is not normal. And as I said before I want to maintain the dignity of this company – even if I can't maintain its honour. So – you are to be confined to the Upper Castle tonight.' A murmur ran from mouth to mouth, and he patted the air with his hands. 'In the morning you will be sober, and in the evening you will be allowed to go into the town.

'One last thing. Sergeant Brandon will not be returning for several months, and it is possible he might never be able to return to duty. In the meantime Sergeant Owen will become the pike-sergeant, and Sergeant Cannon from Captain Erling's old company will become the musket-sergeant.'

Three hours later, as the gloom of the evening seeped into the gloom of my mind and made me feel more miserable, I walked to Stayner's Battery, sat on the seat and looked at the lights. Rua de Carmo was a string of beaded lights, of beaded love, of love that would not return. The Little Parade was like a dish, a rim of light holding a blob of darkness that spread to the left and the right, merged into the walls and became lost in the sea, like my desire for Jenny, for Jenny of the Watergate.

Her breasts have lifted, have swollen a little more, and her hips have rounded. She does not stand outside the Watergate any more, she stands in the shop, in the apothecary, and there is no cure, no herbal cure, for love, for lust, for the firming of the flesh. My flesh. And now her cheeks flush and her lips pout and her eyes will not meet mine when I tap on the shop window and wiggle my fingers.

They say she is to marry. I thought of him, this nameless him, who is to be her husband. I thought of him lying on top of her, having her, and it drove me mad – fucking mad. I jumped up, booted a stone, and tore down the steps.

The cobbles were rough, rough like my thoughts, my desires, my wantings. They ambled my feet, ambled my mind, and then I saw the door to the warehouse was propped open with a brick. I remembered Sergeant Carpenter, remembered that ugly little bastard with the kind heart and the kind words, and I let myself into the warehouse and wandered up to his office.

A line of light was coming from under his door. I listened for sounds, for voices, but it was dead-quiet, like the grave. Then I saw Oldfield, saw him in my mind, saw his face, saw him lying dead in his grave. It flipped my belly and it flipped my mind. I closed my eyes, slid down the wall, and crumpled in a heap. I kept wondering, kept thinking, kept hoping Sir Palmes would reprieve him, but the omens were ominous. Last time he reprieved three men – men who were to be shot – on the day before the execution. And we had heard nothing. Not a word. Not the slightest suggestion of mercy. And I could see Oldfield stiffening, see his mouth twisting in the rigour of death – and it was so bloody stupid, for this man should have been a sergeant, a leader of men. I tried to think what was going through his mind – in the cells in Jews Lane – and I tried to say a prayer, a prayer for him, a prayer for him to say a prayer. But I could not form the words, form the thoughts. I began to tremble and I could feel the tears running down my face. It was so wrong, so bloody wrong. And there was nothing I could do. I banged the floor with the heels of my feet – like a child enraged – then I lashed out: booted the door.

It swung open, thumped against the wall, rattled the ink pots. Rattled me. I jumped to my feet.

Sergeant Carpenter rushed at me screaming.

My brain froze and so did my body.

He grabbed me, pushed me against the wall and rammed his knee in my groin. I felt the pain, felt my face whiten. Then I saw two more shapes – rushing at me like black demons – and he yelled: 'What the bloody hell are you doing here?'

Another voice yelled: 'Fenton!'

'Fenton?' He lowered his knee, lifted my head, peered into my face. 'You're right, it is him.'

Then hands were grabbing at me. I saw Trigg and O'Sullivan shaking their heads, and I felt a fool. I looked at Carpenter. 'I'm sorry. I was coming to talk to you. I was thinking about Oldfield. And the more I thought the worse it became and I just lashed out at the door and . . .'

They eased me onto a stool and Carpenter said: 'Oldfield? Who's

Oldfield.' From a great distance – across the valleys of time, the frozen wastelands of forgotten memory – I heard them prod his memory.

Then Trigg said: 'I saw the Death Warrant. Yesterday, at the Governor's House. It was waiting for his signature.'

As the silence shrouded us, wrapped each of us in our own thoughts, I began to take in the room. It was full of desks, clerk's desks, desks from York Castle. Our old bookcase was fixed to the wall and the chairs were the chairs from our fire. 'What's all this?' I said, and I waved my hand, tried to encompass all the things that were part of my past.

O'Sullivan shrugged. 'Sir Palmes threw us out of York Castle. Said he could make better use of the room. And now we don't have to tally the rock carts any more. But we still have to do everything else,' he sighed, 'and there's more than we can do.'

Trigg held up a pile of letters – as if to prove the point – and the three of them nodded their heads. It was sad. Pathetic. They were drowning, drowning in words, and now they were too old to swim, too old to learn to swim. I wanted to help. Wanted to apologise. Wanted to forget about tomorrow, and I said: 'Can I—'

The door banged open, cut short my words, and Ives rushed in. 'I've got about two hours! If you bloody old farts don't talk too much, and don't give me any more bloody nonsense about my spelling, I'll get you finished before midnight.'

Then he saw me. 'What the hell are you doing here?'

'I saw the door was open, and I thought I'd come and talk to Sergeant Carpenter and—'

'Did you move the brick?'

I nodded. 'Thank Christ for that! I was thinking someone had broken in and we'd have to waste half the bloody night looking for him.' He took off his hat, coat and sword, tossed them in a heap on the floor and pulled on the corporal's coat. He saw me watching him and he smiled. 'Up here I'm a corporal. And corporals tell pikemen what to do. So get yourself on that desk and start writing. And don't say another bloody word.'

I sat at the desk, my old desk, and it made me feel at home. I pulled open the drawer and all my old things were still there. At the back was my head of Christ. I looked at him, at the sadness, at the pain that lingered in his eyes, and I patted him on the head and whispered: 'I need a miracle. A real one. And it's nothing to do with bread and wine. It's to do with a man by the name of Oldfield.' I told him the whole story, the true story. Then I laid him beside the ink pot, and I began to write. And somewhere in the hours that followed my mind calmed, and I committed the soul of the man who was to be executed, into the arms of the man who had been executed for a crime he did not commit.

63

In silence we marched down to the Old Parade. The gallows stood ready, stood waiting. The empty noose, the noose that would tighten, would strangle, would kill, framed a loop of blue sky.

Four men carried a litter onto the parade, laid it on the ground close to the gallows and propped up the back. Sergeant Brandon – white faced and gaunt – blinked at the sunshine.

Eight musketeers marched Oldfield up to the gallows. Rope bound his hands, held them firm behind his back, and a short chain hobbled his ankles. They'd taken away his coat and dressed him in a clean white shirt, white breeches, white stockings and black shoes. And they'd cut his hair and shaved his face – prepared him for the grave.

His eyes kept darting from side to side – as though he had to take in every last detail – and then he began to shake and two of the musketeers grabbed him by the arms, the upper arms, and held him steady.

Sir Palmes and his staff, his train, filed out of York Castle and the parade came to attention. Behind them, on his own, like an outcast, like a man disgraced, came Captain Lacey.

Crabtree leant towards me and whispered in my ear. 'The bastard's grinning.'

I looked at Lacey's face. It was wreathed in smiles, twisted smiles. 'He's a bloody sadist,' I whispered.

The Reverend Mister Turner stepped forward, opened his book and read the morning prayers. Then he bowed to Sir Palmes and left the Old Parade.

Crabtree and I looked at each other in amazement. 'Christ,' he whispered, 'they're going to make him die without a minister. Without a prayer.' And he bit at his lips. 'That's not right.' He shook his head. 'That's not right.' He turned away and wiped at his eyes.

Captain Lacey bowed to Sir Palmes and turned to face us, to face three hundred pairs of eyes. 'His Excellency,' he yelled at the top of his voice, 'mindful of the biblical injunction of an eye for an eye and a life for a life, and possessed of the knowledge that Doctor Lawrence now advises that Sergeant Brandon will make a full recovery—'

Crabtree grabbed my arm and his fingers dug into my flesh and he whispered: 'He's going to commute it, he's going to . . .'

'—has exercised his prerogative of mercy. And the sentence of death passed on Pikeman Oldfield, for attempted murder is commuted' – a sigh ran through our ranks and Crabtree's fingers bit deeper into my arm and they shook me, shook me hard; I closed my eyes, closed them tight, and sniffed – 'to one hour on the gallows, dancing on his toes. And this is to be followed by one year in chains, labouring in the quarries, without pay. At the end of this year the prisoner is to be discharged from the regiment.' He turned to Sir Palmes, bowed again and yelled: 'Punishment may now proceed.'

Inside I was trembling, and my hands were shaking, were making my pike quiver. I sniffed again, sniffed hard, and wiped the tears from my eyes.

The musketeers slipped the noose around Oldfield's neck, lifted him onto tiptoes, took the strain on the rope, tightened it on the crossbar and tied the end to a hook on the upright. Then they stepped away from the gallows and stood to attention, on both sides, like a guard of honour.

I don't know if Oldfield knew – suspected – they were going to commute his sentence or not, but for several minutes he stood rigid with his head bowed, with his chin tight against the noose. Then he slipped, jerked, the way some people do when they've gone to sleep in a chair in front of the fire. He wriggled his hips, and his arms struggled with the rope that bound his hands. Then he threw his head back, gulped in air, and stood rigid. But second by second his toes began to slip, and the rope began to tighten around his throat, and he drew himself up, drew himself back onto his toes.

Sir Palmes said something to Captain Lacey and left the parade. The Town Major began to shout the new duties for the day and six companies marched off to change the moleguard and the townguard. The three remaining companies began to drill, to march up and down, and they honoured Oldfield with the odd glance, the odd grimace.

We remained at attention and waited. The sun began to burn into my back, and it was still making Brandon squint, but the bastard did not move, did not adjust the brim of his hat. He lay on his litter and stared: impassive when Oldfield was on his toes, impassive when the rope was trying to strangle him.

Then I could not bear to watch, bare to witness his struggle for life, and I looked at the dirt, at the gravelled earth, and one by one the seconds dragged into minutes – and I began to understand what eternity must be like. Then I was thinking of Christ, the Christ in my drawer, in the desk that was mine again, and wondering if the decision had been made before or after I prayed to him, prayed to his statue. Then I was thinking of the scorn, the mental scorn, I would have poured on de Colville if I'd seen him in the cathedral kneeling before the statue of Saint John the Baptist.

And I couldn't think if it was right or wrong to pray to – pray through, is the way O'Sullivan would put it – a statue, if a request, a prayer, was answered.

Then they were lifting him down, taking his weight under his arms. His head was sticking out at a strange angle, and it looked as though he'd ricked his neck. His feet had locked – looked like the blades of a pair of paddles – and his legs had cramped and he couldn't stand up straight. And his throat, his neck was welted with purple, a patterned purple that followed the weave of the rope.

We made a litter and we carried him, and the body of Richard Read, up to the burying ground. Two graves were waiting. And so was the gravedigger, with one foot on his shovel and the other on a mound of raw earth. He looked up and down our ranks, scowled, and said: 'They told me there was two this morning. Where's the other one?'

Oldfield looked into the empty grave, that grave that was to be his, and he touched me on the arm and whispered: 'Tell him to keep it for Brandon.' He smiled. Then his mouth filled with bubbles and he closed his eyes, fell into a deep sleep – the sleep with no pain, the sleep that is neither life nor death.

64

Early in October, when the last of the stone, the tiles and the timber that was Whitby had been salvaged and carted to the Mole, it began to rain, to drench the days and the nights with torrents of water. To begin with the water ran off the land – it was baked hard and crusted – then it began to absorb the water, to become soft and soggy. But after a few days it could absorb no more, and the water ran towards the coast, cut channels into the landslide, streamed across the beach, muddied the waves and scummed them brown. When the tide went out it carried a long slick of dirt out to sea, and from the new path cut into the hill, it looked as though Whitby had died of the flux.

By now Sir Hugh would have shut down the quarries, put them to bed for the winter, but Mister Sheres wanted to open up more faces, to expose the rock, to allow it to harden, to weather, and so we were still digging, digging tunnels in the rain. Inside the tunnels, where it should have been dry, water was dripping down the cracks, dripping down my neck. The water was cold, was chilled when the clouds crossed the mountains, and now it is making me cold, making me shiver, and I couldn't keep warm.

Old Tattleton is still farting, still scenting the air; and moaning like hell when drips of water made the candle on his hat splutter and die.

All the barrels of gunpowder are being stored together, in Devil's Drop, on the first floor, the floor with the door, because the ground floor is cold, dark, and damp, like a cellar. Each morning when Tattleton sees the soldiers come down the ladder he laughs, and like a child discovering something for the first time he says: 'God help them, if that lot in there ever goes up. It'll blow them to bits. Millions of little bits.' Then his hands scribe a circle in the air, and his fingers blow it apart.

At night Oldfield is chained in the cellar at Devil's Drop. His eyes have dulled and his skin has lost the faint tan of summer, and he says he's counting the days, counting the weeks, thinking of England, thinking of next year, thinking of autumn in England. He says he can see the leaves, can see them colouring, can see them falling – and these are the leaves that will not bud and burst till April of next year.

By day he's working with us in the tunnels. We give him no favours and he asks for none. And one by one we take our turn – wear Tattleton's hat – and pick and drill at the face of the tunnel; drag out the baskets of rock; roll the barrels over from Devil's Drop; and pack the mouth of the tunnel with large rocks. If it wasn't for his chains, I could almost persuade myself that nothing has changed. But in truth it has, and we are drifting apart, drifting to the edges of our friendship. And I think the long silences – when he doesn't speak, doesn't want to speak – are ploughing furrows in his mind. Nothing is being planted in these furrows, nothing is taking root. And in the summer, when the earth is parched and the wind is whipping it into dust and blowing it away – as it does in The Fens – there will be nothing left to nurture his thoughts. They will wither and die, and the silence on his lips will echo the silence in his mind. And in the hungry months of winter, when his thoughts should feed on the grain of summer, he will starve, will go mad, will be lost to us – will be gone for ever.

His body will be like an empty tomb, a memorial, to what was and will not be again.

As he came towards me with a barrel of gunpowder, I put these thoughts, these fears, out of my mind, and smiled at him. He smiled back in a vague way, then he prised the top off the barrel. Spits of rain found the gunpowder, raised tiny explosions of grey dust, and as we carried the barrel into the tunnel, the gunpowder looked wet, looked like black sand with pock marks. An hour earlier Tattleton thought the rain was about to lift, thought he could have this section of the cliff face down by sunset, but now he was craning his neck, scowling at the lines of grey clouds that were trooping towards us, and yelling: 'A bit of water doesn't matter! Just give it a stir with your fingers. The trail's the important thing. And as long as that ignites the first barrel, the rest will go up on their own.'

For the next hour we packed barrels into the tunnel – it was T-shaped to bring down a long length of cliff – and then we sealed it, ran the trail for thirty yards, lay down on the ground and lit the gunpowder.

I watched the flame run towards the tunnel, watched it burn, fizz, and flare. Then it was gone, was in the tunnel, and the rocks were wreathed in smoke.

We waited.

The smoke cleared.

And we waited some more.

Tattleton sat up. 'Christ! It's gone out.' He held out his hand. 'It's starting to bloody rain again. And that means we can't wait, can't leave it in there overnight. The drips would fill up the barrels and we'd have to dump them. You can't dry out gunpowder. It's too dangerous.' He looked at the sky, at the clouds that were thickening, were hastening the end of the day. 'We might have an hour of light left – if we're lucky. So . . .'

We stood up and I started to walk towards the tunnel, but he grabbed me by the shoulder and pulled me back. Then he turned to Oldfield. 'Go and pull away the stones above the trail, and tell me what you can see.'

Oldfield looked at him and shrugged. For a moment there was a spark of life, a spark of resistance in his eyes, then it died, and he shuffled up to the tunnel. As he began to pull the rocks away, Tattleton pushed me to the ground and we lay face down on the wet earth.

I said a prayer, a prayer for Oldfield.

Then he yelled: 'It's gone out. The drips have wet the gunpowder.'

We ran up and looked. A foot or more of the trail was wet, and the drips were beginning to wash the gunpowder into the cracks. Oldfield turned to Tattleton. 'Shall we lay it again?'

He shook his head. 'It would be wet by the time we had the mouth sealed up again.'

I picked up a length of wood – we'd pulled it out of the mud soon after the rain uncovered one end – and I held it in the tunnel. 'If we laid this over the trail and covered it with rock, made a tunnel within a tunnel, it'd keep the water off the powder for a few minutes. And that'd be long enough.'

Tattleton pursed his lips. 'We'd have to raise the sides a bit with a few rocks. Gunpowder needs air. Then we could cover it with the board, and I think that would work.'

Twenty minutes later we lit the trail again and the gunpowder brought the cliff down. We stood up, laughed, and shook hands.

Two days later we ran another trail under a length of wood and it brought down forty feet of cliff.

Three days after that we couldn't find another length of wood and we compromised: butted four short pieces – of different widths, different thicknesses – end to end and covered them with rock.

Then we lit the trail and waited.

The fire ran into the tunnel, filled the air with clouds of white smoke, and nothing happened.

After a couple of minutes I sat up and looked at it and Tattleton pulled me back down. 'We must wait. An hour. That's what I was taught.' We crawled down to the beach, walked up and down the breakwater – empty now of boats and the children who used to fish from the rocks – and waited.

Closer to Devil's Drop, Sergeant Owen had divided the pikemen into four groups, and he was watching them split open the rock – with wedges, mallets and hammers – and stack it in long piles beside the road.

Inside Devil's Drop, Sergeant Cannon was mounting guard with ten of our musketeers, and up in Henrietta Ensign Wyndham was mounting guard with the other fifteen musketeers. They took over this morning and in a week's time, when the quarries are closed we will relieve both forts, and the musketeers will mount guard in Peterborough Tower. A week after that we will change places, and that pattern is to be repeated till the quarries reopen in January or February. The exact date will depend on the rain and the enthusiasm of Mister Sheres – and as this is his first year in charge, his first year to prove himself, it could be January, late January.

I was wondering where we would go after that, and thinking about the Moors and their new stinkpots – they fling them onto the top of small forts and they fill the fort with fumes, and the men have to get out in a hurry or die – when Tattleton yelled: 'It'll be safe now.' And we wandered back up to the start of the trail.

'I'll do this one,' I said. 'Oldfield did the last one.'

He shook his head. 'The prisoners have to do them. Have to take it in turn. But we've only got one prisoner, so he gets all the turns.' He waved Oldfield forward.

Then he lay down on the ground.

'That's a waste of time isn't it?'

'I've been doing this for twenty years. There were six of us in the year I started, and now I'm the only one still alive. If you want to stand up you can, but I'm not going to.'

I lay down beside him, watched the water trickling through the rocks, and felt it wetting my coat. Three, maybe four minutes went by, then Oldfield yelled: 'I can see what's wrong. One of the boards has collapsed and put out the fire. I'll give it a pull and—'

The explosion thumped in my ears, rumbled the ground and brought down thirty feet of rock. I looked at the wet earth, looked at the water quivering in front of my eyes, and I whispered: 'Jesus.' Then a cloud of dust rolled down the slope and covered us in a brown pall.

I scrambled to my feet. My heart raced, my legs trembled. And without thinking, I ran towards the rock, screaming: 'Oldfield! Oldfield!'

There was no reply. No murmur, no cry, no gasp of pain. Nothing. Nothing at all.

Some rocks ran together, made a rattling noise, like shingle running with the tide. Tattleton shook his head. 'The flame must've burnt the board. Made it smoulder. And when he pulled it free a spark must've jumped from the board to the gunpowder.' He sighed to himself. 'And I thought this was going to be my first year without a death.'

65

I clawed at the rocks, tried to move them, tried to free Oldfield. Sergeant Owen ran along the beach, scrambled over the rocks and grabbed me. 'Oldfield! Is Oldfield in there?'

I shut my eyes, squeezed back the tears and nodded. 'Go down to the beach,' he said, 'and wait.'

I sat at the end of the breakwater, watched the waves wet the rock and felt the spots of rain wet my face. From a distance – as if in a dream – I saw the pikemen break the rocks open, move them away, and make a cleft. It was like the cleft between a woman's legs: the cleft of life, the cleft of birth. But this was the cleft of death: of stillbirth.

I shut my eyes and tried to pray, to pray for Oldfield as the priests had prayed for the Irish. But I had no words, and my prayer was the prayer of silence.

Two musketeers carried a wooden box from Devil's Drop to the rock face. It was a fuse box with a wooden lid and two rope handles. The inside was tarred to keep the fuses dry.

I remembered the first day we looked into one of those boxes. It was half full of fuses: wooden tubes filled with a mixture of fine gunpowder, charcoal dust, and some sort of paste that had dried and set hard. We were learning how to make, how to throw granadoes. The first step was to fill a round iron shell with gunpowder. Then the fuse was shoved into the touch-hole and they were stored in a tray, like apples left to winter in the rafters. When the fuse was lit with a length of burning match, when it was flaming – flaring – we practised throwing the granado at the Moors. In our imagination every one exploded and killed a dozen Moors.

The box contained two types of fuse: short and long. The short fuses were to be used if the Moors were very close, right under the fort. The long fuses were to be used if the Moors were still at a distance but advancing fast. The danger lay in miscalculating the distance and using a long fuse instead of a short fuse – allowing the Moors time to pick up the granado, throw it back, and blow us to bits.

Then I realised the gunpowder had blown him to bits, and the box was to be his coffin. The coffin for his bits and pieces. My stomach heaved and I vomited.

I splashed some salt water on my face and walked back to the rock face.

A white sheet was lining the box, spilling over the edges, touching the wet earth, the earth that was waiting to receive him. On the sheet lay bits of torn flesh, gobbets of meat. I counted four fingers and a couple of toes. The largest part, the most complete part, was a heel and the stump of an ankle bound with a length of chain. Over these they laid bits of his coat – once grey but now red, a curve of bone still bearing a length of skin, of scalp, and some hair that used to be straight but was now seared by heat, was curled and frizzled.

I looked at Sergeant Owen and he said: 'That's all there is. The rest is blasted into the rock.' He covered the pieces with the sheet – in a charnel-house they would have been washed away with a bucket of water – pushed the lid onto the box and tied the leather straps.

I ran my fingers around the top of the box – it was just over two feet long by a foot wide and a foot deep – and I felt it was too small to be a coffin, to hold the life that was his. I turned to Owen and said: 'This all goes back to the *Salisbury*, when he wouldn't let Brandon have his arse.' I sucked at my lips. 'If he had, he could have been a Corporal by now. Maybe a Sergeant. That's all he wanted. To be a Sergeant. To be left alone by that bastard.' I thumped the top of the box with the flat of my hand.

Owen put his arm around my shoulder. 'Come on, let's take him home, to the lodging house. He can be with us on his last night.'

Then some of the men began to bring buckets of water up from the beach, to pour water over the rocks. They washed away his blood, his life-force, let it drain into the earth, and I knew he was dead, truly dead, and this world could harm him no more.

In the lodging house we laid him on the table, but it did not seem right, seem enough when I thought of what the priests had done for the Irish. I slumped on a stool and stared at the box, stared like a man in a daze, like a man who didn't know what to do.

Then Owen came into the room. He was carrying a coat, a sergeant's coat, and he said: 'I've been thinking about what you said. It wasn't right what happened to him. What Brandon did. And I didn't have the courage to stop it. I should have, but I didn't. And I can't make amends, not now I can't. But there is something we can do.' He gave me a gentle smile. 'We can bury him as a Sergeant.'

He opened up the box, took out the remains – still wrapped in the sheeting – and placed them inside the sergeant's coat. Then he folded the coat around them and laid them – laid him – in the box and closed the lid.

I touched the lid, gave him a tight-lipped smile, and tried to blink away the tears. The lines around his mouth, around the corners of his eyes softened. He pulled a flask and two tiny thimbles out of his pocket and filled them with brandy-wine. Then he handed one to me and said: 'It will help to ease the pain.'

It burnt my throat, caught my breath and made me cough and splutter. He laughed. 'Sip it,' he said. 'Sip it slowly.'

Then I felt it warm my belly, warm my insides. After a while it did begin to ease the pain, to make it more bearable, and we began to talk. I told him about the four Irishmen and being in the church all night. And how the papists looked after their dead. And how I thought it was right and proper for the bodies to be taken into the church for the last time. He poured some more brandy, touched the box and said: 'They wouldn't want him in our church. In the garrison church. Not after what he did. They would prefer to forget. To pretend he never was. And tomorrow, if we're lucky – if he's lucky – the Minister will send someone up to the burying ground. Someone who didn't know him. Someone who can read the prayers and see him into his grave. And Captain Lacey will give him a pound. A pound for prayers. And then this someone will go home and have his dinner, and by tomorrow night he won't even remember his name was Oldfield.'

We stared at the box, and sipped some more brandy. Then I remembered Mister Tate. He was a minister, a man who could bury the dead, could commit 'ashes to ashes and dust to dust', and I said: 'What about Mister Tate? What about asking him?'

He nodded, and poured the last of the brandy. 'And what about asking if he' – he ran his fingers along the edge of the box – 'could spend the night in his chapel.'

I laughed. It sounded silly. His chapel was still a trinity of rooms with a communion table and a few boards on the wall.

Saint Barbara's chapel, the chapel that was his, was to be his, was still unroofed, by order of the King. And they say Mistress Tate has made it into a garden with vines and potted plants, and now it is a place of prayer, private prayer.

Then somehow it wasn't silly, it was sensible, was right and proper, and we carried him down to Saint Barbara's Street, and knocked on the door. Mister Tate let us in and we explained what had happened, and what we wanted, and he said: 'If you'd like to fetch the body we can lay it right there in front of the boards.' He pointed to the ones bearing the Ten Commandments.

I touched the box. 'This is the body. This is all that's left.'

'But I need the body, all of the body.' His hands quivered, and it looked as though he was trying to shoo the box away.

Mistress Tate rushed into the room and held his hands. 'It's all right,' she said. 'It's all right. There was an explosion, an accident, and this is all that's left of the poor man.'

I wasn't sure if she'd been listening behind the door or she'd already heard about Oldfield's death, but her presence seemed to calm him, to reassure him. Then he said: 'Am I burying a baby or a child?'

She closed her eyes and shook her head. Then she turned to us. 'He's tired,' she said. 'He was outside the cathedral for a long time today, praying and preaching. Someone threw stones at him and he's a bit upset' – she turned to him – 'aren't you dear.'

'He'll be all right in the morning,' she whispered. 'I think you should go now, if you don't mind.' She picked up the candle to light us to the door.

Then I remembered the four dead Irishmen. I told her about them and the candles the priests left burning at their feet, and I asked if he could have a candle. But before she could say anything he jumped to his feet and yelled: 'That's popery! And we won't have any of that in this house.' And he thumped his fist on the communion table.

Then he looked bewildered, lost, and she said: 'Didn't Christ say he was the true light?' He nodded. 'Then we can have the light of Christ in this chapel. We can honour him with light, can't we?' He nodded again, and then the bewildered look, the lost look, returned. She placed the candle on the box, and opened the door.

As we walked back to the Upper Castle I said: 'Will he be all right tomorrow?'

He shrugged. 'It's all written down. In the book of Common Prayer. All he has to do is read it. It's not as if he has to preach a sermon or give a eulogy. So he should be all right.' He paused. 'Captain Lacey's the one who worries me. I should have asked him before we took the box down to the chapel.'

At Stayner's Bastion he touched me on the arm and said: 'I'm a little puffed. I'm not as young as I used to be. Would you mind if we sat down for a minute.' We sat on the seat. I was beginning to think of it as 'my seat'. Most nights, after I'd finished helping O'Sullivan and Trigg – Ives had gone straight from moleguard to fortguard and most of the burden was now falling on me – I'd sit here and watch the lights go out. When her light went out, the third light from the left on the Little Parade, I'd say 'good night' and go to bed. I still haven't found out who she's going to marry. I was wondering if she might have changed her mind, or her father might have changed it for her, when he said: 'Oldfield would have made a good sergeant.'

I didn't know what made a man a good sergeant but I said: 'Hmm,' and watched her light go out. I thought of her legs, her bare legs, getting into bed. And I tried to see up her legs, tried to see into the crotch of blackness.

'You could be a sergeant.'

I laughed. 'I don't want to be a sergeant.'

'I suppose you want to be an officer.'

'I've been watching Ensign Wyndham. I could do what he does. I think I could do it better – if I'm being honest.'

'Any bloody idiot could do it better. But we don't have the money –

do we? – to buy a commission. The best you and I can hope for is to be a sergeant.'

'I don't want to be a sergeant. They're not officers and they're not men. They seem to drift between them somehow – neither one nor the other.' I paused. 'If I had a choice I'd like to drift in The Fens. Catch eels. Net wildfowl. Do all the things I used to hate doing when I was a little boy.'

He laughed. 'You're going to have to make the best of what you've got. This is it. You're not going back to England, or The Fens, or anywhere else. And I'll give you a bit of advice.' He paused. 'As you get older it gets harder to take orders. To do what someone else says you have to do. It's not so hard at the moment. You're used to it, and most of the men are a bit older than you. But sooner or later some smart little bastard – two, three years younger than you – will make corporal. And you'll have to do what he says. You mightn't believe this right now, but it's easier to give orders, to make men do what you want them to do, than to take orders. And corporals get paid more than pikemen. And sergeants get paid more than corporals.'

A minute, maybe two minutes drifted away, and a few more lights went out on the Little Parade, then he said: 'Sooner or later Captain Lacey is going to have to promote someone to corporal. Brandon didn't want one. Thought he could do both jobs himself. And he was right. He could. But if he doesn't come back – and I don't think he will – Lacey will have to look for a new corporal and a new sergeant.'

'But you're the sergeant.'

'Hmm. But I'm going back to the musketeers when Brandon returns. At least that's the plan. And we can't have Sergeant Cannon for more than another year. And then I think we're going to need a new pike-sergeant.'

'But what about Corporal Franks? He's been your corporal ever since we were on the ship. Everybody thinks he should be made Sergeant. Everybody was bloody surprised when Sergeant Cannon arrived.'

'Well – I'll tell you something. And I'll kick your bloody arse right round the Old Parade if you ever repeat it to anybody.' And he paused. 'Some men make good corporals but they'll never make a good sergeant. They don't have the balls for it. He's a good corporal. And that's all he'll ever be. So you see' – he looked at me with night-black eyes – 'somebody will be made corporal, quite soon, and if Brandon doesn't come back, that somebody will be made sergeant.'

'And you think I could be a corporal?'

'Yes. I do. And I would like to think you would do it for Oldfield. Do it to keep his memory alive. I could help you. Could make you into a corporal – in all but name – and I would make sure Captain Lacey knew you were my choice. And when the time came to make the choice, you would be the one he would choose. And now we come to the best part.'

He gripped my arm. 'If you were a corporal, I could prepare you to be a Sergeant. And if Brandon didn't come back, you would have his job. You would be Sergeant Fenton, the pike-sergeant. And nothing would piss that bastard off more than that. It would be revenge. It would make up for what I didn't do. For what I should have done. It would avenge Oldfield's death, and all the things he did to him.'

For a long time I stared at the lights – dying now in droves – then I said: 'I want to do it. But I don't think I can. It scares me.'

He stood up and I stood up, and we faced each other. 'There's nothing wrong with being scared. It teaches caution. Only a fool is never scared. The rest I can teach you. And now you must begin to want it. To want it so bad it makes your balls ache, and you're prepared to do anything, anything at all – like a man chasing his first fuck.'

Then he laughed, grabbed my hand and shook it hard.

66

We marched down to Saint Barbara's Street – under the command of Lieutenant de Colville – laid our pikes against the wall of Mister Tate's house and filed into the chapel.

The candle was still burning. It looked like a night-light, a light of the watch, and it was casting a shadow, a flickering shadow over the words at the top of the right-hand board. I read the words, read the commandment, the sixth commandment: THOU SHALT DO NO MURDER. They brought a sour taste to my mouth, the taste of death, and I shut my eyes. I must have been staring too hard at the candle for I could still see the flame, could still see the inch of candle, the inch of life that remained. Then I could hear, could feel everyone standing up and Mister Tate came into the chapel wearing the uniform of the militia. Over his red coat, he had draped his black scarf, his stole of ministry.

'What the bloody hell's he got that on for?' Lockhart whispered in my ear.

I shrugged, then Mistress Tate came into the chapel and stood close to the box, close to Mister Tate. She had covered her head and shoulders in a black scarf, a mantilla of lace, like the Spanish women wear when they go into the cathedral. It was a strange image, a foreign image, an image of popery, and I was wondering what Mister Tate would think of it, when he said: 'Would you please be seated.'

He looked at the floor and waited for the noise to die, then he said: 'I am wearing this uniform today to show that we are all fighting for the same cause. The cause of righteousness. We are all fighting evil—'

'And I thought,' Lockhard whispered, 'we were fighting the fucking Moors.' I looked at him and grinned. It was the sort of thing Oldfield would have said.

Then Mister Tate was saying: 'And I am also wearing it to honour the man we are to bury today.' He opened his prayer book and began to read the service in a clear voice.

I stretched my legs, relaxed, forgot my fears of last night, my fears that he would not be able to conduct the service. I shut my eyes and let his words drift through my mind. It was like being in the company of an old friend. I knew he was there. He was saying what had to be said and there was no need for me to say anything. After a few minutes, when he was about halfway through the second psalm, his voice began to fade and I could just hear him saying: 'For a thousand years in thy sight are but as yesterday: seeing that is past as a watch in the night.'

I opened my eyes, looked at him, looked at the candle, the candle that had kept the watch, kept the faith.

He looked at Mistress Tate. He looked confused, looked as if he'd lost his place. She stood up, ran her finger down the page and smiled at him. He began to read again in a clear voice, and Lockhart whispered: 'She never let me touch her. Never even let me get close. And all that work was wasted.' He looked around the chapel. 'Know what she said to me?' I shook my head. 'Told me to honour the seventh commandment.'

I looked up, read 'THOU SHALT NOT COMMIT ADULTERY,' bit my lips, and giggled.

A few minutes later, soon after the words, 'O death where is thy sting? O grave where is they victory?' the service came to an end and Mister Tate blew out the candle, blew out the life that was Oldfield.

Crabtree and Lockhart carried the box out of the chapel. As I went to follow, Mistress Tate touched me on the arm, took the candle out of the candlestick and pressed it into my hand. I smiled and murmured my thanks. Then de Colville was standing beside her, was looking at the boards and pointing to the name in the corner: Lord Extonmouth.

I walked outside, and we stood in the sunshine, stood in silence, and waited for four or five minutes. Then Mister Tate came out wearing his black hat and clutching his prayer book to his chest. De Colville followed him, and his face looked white, looked grim, looked like the face of a corpse.

67

As we marched out of the burying ground – turned our backs on the mound of earth that would soon sink in the rain and lock Oldfield firmly into his grave – de Colville took Mister Tate's elbow and guided him towards Catherine Gate.

Sergeant Owen ordered us to wheel to the left, and we followed the lanes to Whitehall, crossed the stream at the back of the bowling green, and headed up the hill. The rains had scoured the sides of the track and slicked the stones, made them feel as though they were thick with grease, and they made our feet slip and slide, broke the pattern, broke the order of the march.

At the top of the hill, as we were easing ourselves back into order and I was thinking about the committal, thinking how the clods of earth had thumped onto his coffin and would have echoed in his ears – if he still had any ears; and wondering how God was going to put all those bits and pieces back together and make his body whole again on the day of judgement; Sergeant Owen screamed: 'C-o-m-p-a-n-y! Company, halt!'

We slithered to a halt, and he spun around. 'That was dreadful! A bloody disgrace! You looked like fat ducks trying to waddle up a hill.' He marched up and down the front rank. His mouth was quivering and the stubble on his chin, his cheeks, was catching the sun, was making his face bristle with anger. 'It was worse than the musketeers. And I always used to think they were bloody awful.'

He ran his eyes through the ranks, and then he said – in a much calmer voice: 'Fenton. You were one of the worst. Get out here,' and he pointed to the ground beside him.

I ambled out of the ranks, and he screamed: 'Run!'

I gulped hard, ran twenty feet, and snapped to attention.

'Stand up straight! Pull your shoulders back! And hold your pike at the correct angle! The end's supposed to be one foot from the ground. Not six inches. You do know how big six inches is don't you?' He paused. 'You do have something to measure it with, I presume?'

Everybody roared with laughter and I felt my face go red, knob-red. I bit my lips and looked straight ahead. He turned to the drummer. 'Beat the pace.' A steady thump, thump, thump ran round the crown of the hill. 'Now march forty feet, turn around and march back again and come to a halt six feet in front of me. March!'

I marched in a stiff-legged way. My heart was thumping and my face wouldn't cool and my arm froze to the side of my coat. When I turned my feet slid on a rock and my legs tangled with the end of the pike. He screamed: 'Keep on the beat! Can't you hear the bloody beat?'

I came to a halt in front of him. He walked right round me, turned to the company and said: 'Do you see what I mean? His bum is out here.' He patted the air, about two feet from mine. 'And his feet are on skates. Did you see him on the turn?' They laughed, and he shook his head. 'Do it again!' he yelled. 'About turn. Quick march!'

The drummer took up the beat without any command, and this time I could hear it, could hear it thumping in my head, thumping in my feet. I turned on the beat, marched back on it and came to a halt on it.

He pursed his lips. 'That was a bit better. At least I know you're not deaf. I was beginning to think you were – after all that measuring.' The company roared with laughter. I laughed with them, lifted my hat, bowed, and pretended they were applauding.

'Don't be a bloody clown! If anyone's going to be the clown it's me. Do you understand?'

I gulped, swallowed, and nodded.

'Now do it again, three times. March!'

I did it three more times. Then he increased the pace, and as I was beginning to droop, he screamed: 'Keep your shoulders back! Keep your head up!'

After fifteen minutes I was marching like a wooden doll: precise, repetitive, with never a missed beat. He looked me up and down. 'That's better. That's how a soldier should march.' He turned to the company. 'What do you think?'

He was met with a lot of mumbles – they were becoming tired of the whole thing – then he pointed his halberd at Lockhart: 'What do you think?'

Lockhart jumped to attention and grinned. 'I think we should see him do it at double time, Sergeant.'

Owen smiled and nodded. 'Drum! Beat double time. Pikeman – three times up and down. Double march!'

I doubled there and back three times. The sweat ran down my back and under my arms, my hat stuck to my head, and I felt dead. He pursed his lips and pulled a face. Then he turned to the company. 'What do you think?' Again he was met with a lot of mumbles. 'I want you to answer. Yes or no. Can he march?'

'Yes – yes – yes.' The word was soft, it bumbled over itself, and it hummed – the way words do when singers can't remember the words of a song.

'So you agree, he knows how to march?'

'Yes!' This time the word was like a thunderclap. It struck the walls, echoed in our ears and rolled down the hill.

He smiled. 'Good. I'm glad you agree. Because now he can teach you to do it, and give my voice a rest.' And he laughed.

He brought them to attention, dressed the ranks, turned them to the left and made three files. Then he gave me a curt nod.

I took a deep breath, swallowed hard, tried to ignore the twitchings in my belly and yelled: 'Please march!'

The words came out as a high-pitched squeak, and they brought me out in a sweat – a cold sweat.

Some took a step forward, some stayed stock-still. They all burst out laughing. The drummer turned the beat into a drum roll and they laughed some more. Sergeant Owen shook his head. 'Jesus Christ. I think we need some help from up there.' He pointed his finger to the sky and they laughed some more.

Then he said to me: 'You don't ask them to march. You tell them to march. The command is: Forward march!' He smiled to himself and shook his head.

I swallowed my shame, took a slow breath and yelled: 'Forward march!' And they did – without a murmur, without the slightest hesitation.

For the next half-hour Owen yelled at them, and yelled at me to yell at them. And then I knew it was easier to yell, to correct, than it was to march, and I began to relax. And in a strange way, an unexpected way, I began to enjoy myself. Then I saw Lockhart was sweating was wiping his brow with his cuff, and I yelled: 'Drum! Beat double time,' and I made him, made them, do forty yards: six times.

Then Owen said: 'That's much better. Tomorrow we'll do some more. And tomorrow you'll be better than you are today. But you won't be as good as you'll be on the day after that.' They groaned, and he made me march them all the way back to the lodging house.

That night everybody kept giving me a dig in the ribs, kept saying, in voices strangled of life: 'Please march. Won't you please march for me? Please.' Then they roared with laughter, and the strange thing was that the joke was evergreen, ever-new, and every time someone repeated it, they laughed louder, laughed longer.

But I didn't give a damn, give a hoot in bloody hell. I laughed as hard as they did, for I had marched them back to the lodging house, had marched in the corporal's position.

68

Next morning, soon after five o'clock, when the air was still cold and the gloom of the night was just beginning to seep away, we paraded in front of our lodging house. Sergeant Owen walked along the ranks, looked at every man, shook his head and said: 'Yesterday we made a start on your marching. This morning we're going to make a start on the way you look. And this afternoon we're going to make a start on . . .' He paused, then his face broke into a smile. 'Maybe I'll leave that till this afternoon.' He looked at the wet cobbles, pretended to be deep in thought, pretended not to notice the interest his words were arousing. Then he said: 'You're not going back to the quarries. The quarries have closed. In the spring, when they reopen, some other company will be sent there. So – I'm going to make you into soldiers again. Soldiers who are more than pikemen.' And he smiled.

'In a few minutes every man is to go back inside and black his shoes, and wash his face and hands. If you have a spare shirt, a spare pair of breeches, or stockings or a scarf, you are to give them to Mistress Copeland and she will wash and dry them for you today. If you don't have a spare set, you will have to wash and dry what you are wearing, and you'll have to do it yourself, tonight. Coats and hats are to be cleaned with a damp cloth and all spots removed. If any garment is torn it must be repaired tonight. Every man is to have a haircut, and a shave,' he rubbed at his chin, 'and that includes me. Tomorrow morning there will be an inspection. If four men fail, you will all do four hours of drill. If six fail, you will do six hours. And we will do that every morning till we relieve the guard in Henrietta and Devil's Drop.'

'I want you to know that it won't be me that is taking the drill. I don't see why I should have to suffer for men who can't, or won't, look after themselves. So the drill will be taken by Pikeman Fenton. I shall sit on a chair and watch, and if he doesn't drill you hard enough, I'll ask him to do another hour. I'll ask nicely.' He smiled. 'I'm even prepared to say, please.' We burst into laughter, but there was a hard edge to it, an edge that killed the humour, the joy, that had been in it last night.

Just before seven o'clock, with black shoes and black spirits, he marched us onto the Old Parade, and twenty minutes later, after five companies marched off to change the guard, we joined four other companies – formed one long column – and drilled for an hour.

Then followed breakfast – bread, Scot's porridge and black beer – and a quiet half-hour on the privy, and I was just hitching up my breeches, when the Powell brothers wandered around the corner and rammed me into the wall. They don't look like brothers but they stick together like limpets, and everybody says they don't have a brain between them. But they're wrong. They do. And they seem to share it, and when they're together they're smarter than when they're on their own.

The older one sneezed in my face, and the younger one sniffled and wiped his nose on his cuff – the wet weather was chilling our bones, was filling our chests with coughs and colds and sweating fevers, and laying more men in their graves than the Moors were – and he said: 'Any more of that bloody double time, and you're going down there' – he pointed to the hole, to the maggots that were feeding off the turds – 'head first.' Then he patted me on the cheek, and his brother kneed me in the balls.

The pain was sudden, shocking. It winded me. Brought tears to my eyes. And doubled me over.

They grabbed me. Sat me on the privy, smiled and patted me on the head, and they both said: 'Don't forget.'

Twenty minutes later Sergeant Owen marched us through the Forage Gate, through the revetments and into Charles Lane. Then he stood us at ease, told us to fall out, to rest for a couple of minutes. It was most unusual, most unlike him, and it filled me with suspicion, with foreboding, and then he yelled: 'Pikeman Fenton! Fall in the company.'

The words of command drained out of my mind. I'd heard them a hundred times, a thousand times. I could react to them without thinking. But I couldn't remember them. I marched over to him, stood rigid and said: 'I'm sorry. I can't remember the commands, Sergeant.'

He stared at me, then he threw his hands in the air – his right hand was gripping the staff of his halberd, making it splay at a drunken angle – and he yelled: 'He can't remember the bloody commands!'

They roared with laughter, and he said: 'I suppose we'll have to teach him.' They laughed again. 'What's the first one?'

They roared: 'C-o-m-p-a-n-y!'

'That alerts the men,' he said to me in a low voice, and then he shouted: 'And what comes next?'

'Company fall in!'

He nodded to me and I yelled: 'C-o-m-p-a-n-y! Company fall in!' Then I called them to attention, and he made me dress ranks, open ranks, close ranks, space ranks, turn to the right, turn to the left, about turn, stand at ease, stand easy – and after twenty minutes: fall out.

Then we started again. And the words burnt into my mind, seared my soul and became part of me.

He pulled his face into a tight-lipped smile, nodded to himself and walked away, left me on my own.

I drilled them for an hour, and the mud speckled our shoes, made them look the way I thought blackbirds' eggs should look – when I was a little boy and nests scratched the clouds, scratched the mists of spring.

Then I marched them all the way to Charles Fort, and with everyone standing to attention, and Sergeant Owen standing at the far end of the lane, standing in the middle of the embankments and looking like a tiny red doll, I said: 'I have something to say. Something I don't want Sergeant Owen to hear.' I wet my lips – tried to banish the trembling I could hear in my words. 'I didn't ask for this bloody job. And I don't want it. But as long as I have to do it, I'm going to do it right. And I want you to know that this morning two men threatened to shove me down the privy, head first, if I give you too much double marching.' They burst out laughing. I smiled, and waited for it to die away. 'I don't intend to tell you their names. Not this time. But I want them to know, and I want you to know, that if anyone tries to do it, or threatens to do it, I'll double you up and down this bloody lane till you fall in a heap.' I paused. 'Then I'll tell you the name of this sweet little bastard. And you might want to stick his head down the privy. Or mash his balls.' I ran my eyes all the way down the ranks and I was met with a sullen silence.

Then I turned to the drummer and yelled: 'Drum! To the end of the lane – beat double time!'

An hour later, at dinner, Lockhart and Crabtree sat on either side of me, like a pair of sentries. As I was wiping the bread around my plate, soaking up the last of the gravy, Lockhart said: 'You do the drill well. Everybody says so. And it won't be long before the laughter turns to respect. But next week Owen will pick on someone else, and you'll be back in the ranks. And the Powells will pick on you.' He nodded. 'I know it was them. I saw them come out of the privy, just before you came out, looking green around the gills.' He smiled. 'They're touched, up here' – he tapped his forehead – 'and they'll have you, the moment you're back in the ranks. So be careful. In the meantime, we think one of us should go to the privy with you – to protect your arse.'

69

An hour after midday Sergeant Owen locked his halberd into the rack and marched us down to the Old Parade, without our pikes. It was contrary to standing orders and it made me feel naked, feel as though part of my arm had been cut off. Then this feeling was made worse, made more mysterious, when he held out his hand, felt a few spots of rain and ordered us into the playhouse, ordered us to sit on the wooden benches and wait.

I've never seen a play. Never had enough money – no – that's not true. I did have some money, three months ago when we were paid for the first time. Our rate of pay is nine pence per day. The drummer is paid twelve pence and so is the corporal – or would be if we had one – and the Sergeant gets eighteen pence. Ensign Wyndham is paid three shillings and Lieutenant de Colville gets four shillings. They say Captain Lacey is paid eight shillings a day and out of that he's supposed to pay for all sorts of things on behalf of the whole company. I've never seen him buy anything, although he does give money to Mistress Copeland to buy melons, oranges, marrows, beans, cabbages and winter greens at the Monday market; and I've seen her down at the fish stall – the cheap one on the quay by the new cistern that supplies the Mole with fresh water.

Nine pence a day sounds a lot and it would have been if we'd been paid since the day we signed on, or even the day we arrived in Tangiers, but we were paid for twelve months. The rest is still to come, is in arrears – as they say. And then there are the deductions: for meat and beer; for the lodging house; for our uniform; for the replacement of any parts of our uniform that were missing – were presumed sold – and should have been patched and worn till they could be worn no more. Then they're supposed to be exchanged in the quartermaster's store, but the truth is it's cheaper to trade them at the back door of the infirmarium, to wear dead men's clothes and dead men's shoes. But I've never had enough money, and I couldn't trade what I didn't have – so I had to pay the full price, the price of poverty.

For Crabtree, now so careful and cautious they could almost be his watchwords, the deductions came to six pence per day. For Lockhart, still more interested in lechery than a clean shirt or another pair of stockings,

they came to seven pence and one halfpence per day. For me they came
to seven pence per day. So I was left with tuppence a day. It didn't take
long to figure that 2 pennies times 365 days makes 730 pennies; divided
by 12 it makes 60 shillings and 10 pence; and divided by 20 it makes three
English pounds and ten pence: £3–0–10. And because most of our money
was Spanish money, it was converted, was paid to us in pieces-of-eight.

It wasn't what it should be, ought to be – most of the deductions were
make-believe, were legal lies – but it was still more money than I'd ever
had in my whole life. In my head I spent it a hundred times: for Jenny I
bought a gold wedding band with our names inscribed on the inside; for
my lady in Rua de Carmo I bought a silver chain to go around her neck;
for dear old Trigg I brought a new pair of spectacles with stronger lenses;
for de Colville I bought a book of sermons expounding the 39 Articles
of the Church of England – the pillars of our faith; for Ives I bought
a woman, a clean woman, in a whore house up by Irish Battery; for
O'Sullivan I bought a tincture of English roses – in the hope it would do
something for the bog-Irishness that still stuck to him like marsh-mud; for
Oldfield I bought a wooden grave-marker of English oak; and for myself I
bought two pairs of under-breeches so I could change them once a week,
could smell clean, and not rub shit up the back seam of my breeches.

But dreams are dreams, no more than pious hopes, and on the first
night, when the money lay heavy in my pocket, Lockhart, Crabtree and
I wandered down Assoy Street, by the common sewer. The night was hot
and our thirst was great, and we thought we'd try a tavern or two. Tavern
is not the right word. It gives the impression of an inn, a hostelry. Most
were nothing more than one small room with a couple of tables, a few
benches, and a fireplace. One or two were well known for pigeon pie,
and twenty or thirty were better known for the plump young pigeons
who would take a man upstairs and lift their skirts, and let him feel, let
him explore their feathery nethery parts for three shillings. Most of these
taverns, these drinking rooms, were run by old soldiers with a licence to
sell 'spiritous and fermented liquors'. They say there were eighty or ninety
of them – no one seems to know the exact number – but everyone knew
the licence was a sort of pension, a double-edged pension that kept old
soldiers off the street and stopped them begging; and showed us that we
too might have a pension, be snug and warm and off the streets, in the
years of our decrepitude.

On most nights there were too many taverns, too many plying for too
few mouths, and the prices favoured the drinkers. But on this night when
ten ships lay at anchor in the bay, and ten thirsty crews had the run of the
town, and we were fat with money, the taverns filled by dusk, the food ran
out, the prices rose, and the whores lay on their backs and charged five
shillings.

We drifted from Assoy Street – where the prices were a little lower
to compensate for the airs that wafted in from the sewer – to Gormis

Street, to Diefs Street; and where we went from there I do not know. But I do remember a string of small hot rooms, of places of desire, of Lockhart going upstairs, and Crabtree going into a garden with a woman twice his age. I can remember laughing, talking, shouting to make myself heard; can remember refusing to go upstairs or out in the garden. I don't remember where I lost my scarf or who sawed Lockhart's pike in half – that was to cost him a pound next day – and I don't remember how we got back to the lodging house.

I do remember the headache – the gift to myself – and I couldn't believe I'd spent a pound, had spent four months' money in one night, and had nothing to show for it, nothing but the vomit that speckled my coat.

Then the rest of the money was gone, was spent in the apothecary's when Jenny was behind the counter. We talked about the pain behind my eyes, the pain that came when my nose blocked up; and the coughing that woke me in the night; and the bites on my arms; and the chafing, the rash on the insides of my legs. We talked about everything except what we wanted to talk about, and when I tried, she laid her hand on mine and shook her head, shook away the hope that still lingered in my heart. For the coughing I bought an infusion of fennel seeds; for the rash an ointment of cowslip and a poultice of comfrey; for the pain an opiate of poppy; and for my heart she gave me a tincture of hawthorn berries. I gave her a butterfly – blue wings enamelled on silver – the size of my thumbnail and I said: 'Wear it in a secret place, somewhere close to your heart. Wear it for those days when we should have walked through the fields, held hands, and watched the butterflies rise from the grass, watched them colour the air with clouds of blue.' She smiled. Then she let me take her hand for the first time, and I said: 'If you ever need me, want me, wear it where I can see it. And I will come to you.' Then I kissed her on the cheek and left, left her to the man she is to marry.

I was thinking how I could make her breasts rise, rise to meet my desire – in aureoles of nipple-pink – when Sergeant Owen came back into the playhouse carrying two muskets and a bandolier. He climbed onto the stage and said: 'When you're out in the forts you can't defend yourself with a pike. You can use it to defend yourself on the march to the fort and the way back again, but you can't use it in the fort.' And he paused. 'In the fort we use three weapons to defend ourselves. To defend the fort.'

Lockhart blinked and yawned. Owen yelled: 'Stand up!' He pointed to Lockhart.

Lockhart stood up and smothered another yawn. 'I'm sorry you find this tedious,' Owen said. 'Perhaps you could tell us the weapons we use to defend a fort.'

'Cannons. Granadoes. And muskets. Sergeant.'

'Most of the forts have small cannons mounted on the roof, if they have a flat roof. The size varies and some are very old, but there are a couple of Robinets in one fort. They're three feet long with a bore of one and a quarter inches and they fire a ball weighing three-quarters of a pound. In Henrietta we have a Falconet. It's four feet long, weighs two hundred and ten pounds, and a couple of men can push it around. The bore is two inches and it fires a ball weighing one and a quarter pounds. That's big enough to blow a hole right through a Moor, or take his head off if you're lucky.' He smiled. 'And now Lockhart. What about granadoes? Tell us about granadoes.'

'They're round. Made of iron. Two inches wide. And packed with gunpowder – coarse gunpowder. They have a small hole bored into the side and that's where the fuse goes. And we practised throwing them for a couple of hours last year and it made my bloody arm ache.'

A smile rippled around the room.

'When we're out in the forts we'll be doing a lot more practice – with empty shells. We'll practise getting the range. Getting them to fall where we want them to fall. And we'll also practise lobbing them over the top of the palisades, dropping them close to the other side because that's where the Moors like to hide. And because we're in the fort, because we're high up, we have the advantage. So don't look so bloody glum-faced.' He paused. 'And now we come to the muskets. I know some of you have done musket drill before. But some of you haven't so I'm going to start right from the beginning, and later on if I ask you a question, there'll be no excuse for not knowing.' And he smiled.

'There are two types of musket. The matchlock and the flintlock. The matchlock is fired by a match, by a length of rope that's been soaked in salts to keep it burning, keep it smouldering. The flintlock is fired by a spark from a flint, and this musket is sometimes called a snaphance. Most of our muskets are matchlocks and these are what you will learn to fire. There are thirty-two separate movements required to load and fire a matchlock. You will learn them. You will be drilled in them till you can do them in your sleep. And we won't stop till every man can fire one ball every minute. I'm not going to go through all the movements right now. I want you to grasp the principles first. They're dead easy.' He paused. 'A measured amount of gunpowder is poured down the barrel and rammed hard. Then a small piece of felt, of wadding, is wrapped around one side of the lead ball and rammed into the powder. Then we pour some fine gunpowder into this little pan on top of the musket, take aim and squeeze the trigger. The burning match strikes the fine gunpowder. It ignites, makes a flash and sends a spark through this tiny hole – the touchhole. The spark explodes the gunpowder in the barrel. The ball shoots out and it kills a Moor.' He threw his hands up in the air, pretended to die.

We laughed and he smiled. 'Unfortunately it's far harder to hit a Moor than you might think. For one thing they keep running and it's difficult to hit a moving target. And for another, the weight of the balls varies, and so does the amount of powder you put into the barrel –

in spite of measuring it. And there's another thing. Does anyone know what it is?'

He waited for a moment, looked around the playhouse, but nobody moved. 'There's sometimes a slight delay between the match striking the fine gunpowder and it igniting. All these things don't sound much, but they make it hard to hit a man with one shot – despite all our drill. And that's one of the reasons why we fire together. Then of course there's the "flash in the pan", when the fine powder ignites – flashes – but fails to send a spark through the touchhole, and nothing happens. And that's another good reason to fire together.' He stood the musket against the wall. 'If we all had flintlocks we could practise the new drill – firing in volleys. The fire is murderous – it's like being hit by a hail of lead. The best we can do with our matchlocks is to fire three volleys – one for each rank – and after that each man loads and fires in his own time as quickly as he can. We call it continuous, or rolling fire.' He paused. 'Two more things. A lot of men call a ball a round – because of its shape. That is slang. The correct term is a ball and that is what you will use. The order to fire used to be "Apply fire!" It meant what is said: you applied your match to the powder in the pan. But the trouble was some men fired on the word apply and some waited for both words. Today the command has been simplified to one word: "Fire!"'

He picked up a spearhead with a short shaft. 'This is a bayonet. A plug bayonet. It fits into the barrel like this.' He gave it a twist and it locked into the barrel. 'When you run out of gunpowder or lead balls, or the enemy is right on top of you, it makes your musket into a short pike. Or' – he flipped the musket up the other way, grasped it by the barrel – 'it can be used as a club.'

'The main advantage of the flintlock is that you don't have to keep a match burning all the time, and if you're trying to ambush the enemy at night your presence won't be betrayed by a burning match. Some say they can be fired once every thirty seconds – twice the rate of fire that you're going to aim for – but that's not my experience. Some also say that the increased rate of fire will mean we don't need to carry pikes any more because the troops-of-horse will be dead before they can get to us. But I've also heard that it takes a lot of lead to kill a horse, and troopers have charged into the midst of these new companies of flintlocks and cut them to pieces. So, in my opinion, there's always going to be a need for pikemen, and I think the right ratio will prove to be one pikeman to two musketeers. And that means there's always going to be a job for you smelly lot.' And we laughed.

'Now we come to the bandolier. It's always worn over the left shoulder.' He paused. 'Fenton. Where are you?' He looked around the room. I stood up. 'Come out the front and put this on. It always crosses over the top of your baldric.' He handed it to me.

As I put it on, he said: 'Powell. Stand up.' Both the brothers stood up.

He laughed and shook his head. 'Two for the price of one.' We laughed. And so did they – in a half-hearted way. 'I've been hearing a rumour. A funny rumour. About you two. A rumour about going down the privy headfirst.' He walked over to them. 'And it didn't come from him.' He turned and pointed to me. 'It came from someone else. Someone who shall be nameless. And let me tell you two stupid bastards – if anyone's going down the privy it's you. And I shall see to it – personally.' He looked from one to the other. Then he came and stood by me. 'I want you to know, I want everybody to know that if I pick someone to do something on my behalf that man is doing it with my authority. He is me. And I am him. And we'll beat the shit out of any bastard who tries to threaten me, him, or anyone else I order to do something on my behalf. Do I make myself clear?'

We mumbled yes, and shuffled our feet. But it wasn't enough for him. He glared and screamed: 'Do I make myself clear?'

The reply rolled like thunder, screamed in his ears. 'Yes, Sergeant!'

He nodded, walked up and down, and then he said, in a voice so calm I began to suspect he was acting: 'The twelve wooden tubes hanging from the bandolier are usually called the twelve apostles. They rattle. At night if you're trying to creep up on the enemy they'll give you away, and you'll have to pad each one with a separate piece of cloth. If you're ever on horseback, galloping, you'll find they make so much noise you'll never be able to hear the words of commands. And once again you'll have to pad all of them, one by one.'

He walked over to the Powells. 'What are they for?'

The older one said: 'To hold gunpowder.'

He turned to the other one. 'He missed something out. What is it?'

The younger one shook his head.

He looked around, pointed at Crabtree.

'To hold a measured amount of gunpowder.'

He smiled. 'That's it. A measured amount. So you're ready to pour the powder down the barrel. Twelve times. And that's why each apostle hangs on a separate leather thong. In England they're trying a new method at the moment. Wrapping the gunpowder in twists of paper. They call them cartouches and they store them in a tin box belted round their waists. This stops them getting wet. And when you come to load the cartouche you tear off one end, or bite it off if you've still got your teeth and pour the powder down the barrel. Then you wrap the ball in a bit of paper and ram it down the barrel, and the paper acts like a wadding. It stops the ball rolling out.'

We looked at each and laughed. He shook his head. 'It's no laughing matter. If the ball rolls out and you fire the musket you might as well pull down your breeches and fart at them. There's a chance the smell might kill them, but a ball lying on the ground sure as hell won't.' We laughed again.

'I want to show you something. Something that may save your life.' He picked up the musket and pressed it into my hands, made me hold the stock close to my chest. 'Now look at this. Here's the burning match, smouldering away, waiting for you to squeeze the trigger. And he's one of your apostles with a loose lid. Or one with a bit of powder still in it. And the spark jumps from here to here' – he touched the match and then an apostle – 'and woosh. Your apostle explodes. Or bursts into flame.' He shook his head. 'If you see it happen, you'll never forget it. You'll remember the screaming, the smell of flesh burning till the day you die.' He paused. 'And that's another reason why I think that one day we'll all have cartouches and the lead ball will be wrapped in the paper and we'll be able to load with one ramming. But that day isn't yet, and so' – he pointed to the two flasks hanging from the bandolier – 'the large one contains more powder to be poured into the apostles. And the small one contains the fine powder to go in the pan. This little leather bag' – he held it up for us to see – 'is your ball bag. And that's where you keep a small bottle of oil and a priming wire to clean the touchhole.'

'Are there any questions?'

Crabtree stood up. 'It's obvious the match will go out in the rain, and it's quicker to fire a flintlock than a matchlock, so why don't we all have flintlocks?'

'The flints keep breaking. And a flintlock costs a lot more than a matchlock. And we have a lot of matchlocks. The armourers are converting a few matchlocks to flintlocks by fitting new locks. But this costs a lot of money and there's never enough of that is there?' We smiled.

'Are there any more questions?' He waited, looked around the play-house, saw there were no more questions and said: 'One last thing. If it looks as though it's going to rain, put your bandolier on under your coat. A musketeer must keep his powder dry at all times. It's the golden rule.' He paused. 'The muskets and bandoliers are kept in the armoury in York Castle. They used to kept in here, when we first arrived, but plays were thought to be more important.' He shrugged and gestured for us to stand.

As we began to walk towards the door, he pulled me back and whispered in my ear: 'This is not a bloody game. The Powells are a pair of bloody idiots. Dangerous idiots. You can't take them on. Not on your own you can't. They'd kick your bloody head in and drop you down the privy. And you'd drown in your own shit. So remember this. And remember it like it was holy writ: we support each other. No secrets. No pretence. A corporal supports his sergeant. A sergeant supports his corporal. That's the way we keep the bastards under control. Lose control and they'll have you. And if you ever do anything as stupid as that again, I'll have Lockhart out the front, and in three months he'll be the corporal. And you'll have to do what he wants you to do. And you'll have to learn to do it in a bloody great hurry, or the Powells will have you.'

70

Four days later we relieved the musketeers in Henrietta and Devil's Drop and our lives soon fell into a fixed pattern: four hours on guard – in Henrietta this meant being in the rooftop watchroom with a spyglass – and eight hours off. Off gives the impression of doing nothing. It meant off-guard and in the daytime it broke into two distinct parts: what Crabtree called housewifery – cooking, sweeping, airing the bedding, eating, emptying the privy and carrying provisions from the Upper Castle; and what Lockhart called soldiery – practising granado throwing, cannon loading, and musket drill.

For me drill meant two sessions of musketry at both forts twice a day. My voice was sore from shouting and the recoil was making my shoulder ache, but our speed was improving and we were beginning to master the art of firing three volleys and following them up with rolling fire. It was much easier down at Devil's Drop. Here some of the land was flat and we could form three ranks. The men in the front rank fired their volley and then walked backwards through the ranks to become the rear rank. The middle rank stepped forward, fired, walked backwards, and formed the new rear rank. The rear rank – now the front rank – stepped forward, fired, walked backwards and became the rear rank again. By this time the front rank was supposed to be ready to fire again in their own time. There was a natural tendency to retreat, to creep backwards, and each time the manoeuvre was repeated we yielded a little more ground. At Devil's Drop this didn't matter much, but at Henrietta the rough earth made us stumble and fall.

Sergeant Owen ordered ten drills for every live firing, and that meant when we fired three balls each we had practised the manoeuvre thirty times. The volleys shattered the targets – a line of Moors cut out of wood – but after three days, at a distance of one hundred yards, no one, firing on his own, had managed to hit a Moor in the head. We were beginning to appreciate the subtleties of an accurate measure of powder, balls of the same weight, and a match that ignited right away. Matches tended to sulk, like dying fires, and the three volleys never went off together with one bang. They were more like bang-bang-bang-bang . . . bang . . . bang. The last man, made twitchy by his long wait, would make his barrel twitch – they were too long to hold steady for more than a few seconds – and I doubt if he ever hit a bloody thing.

Lockhart was the first man to have a flash in the pan. He stepped out of the ranks, ran his wire through the touchhole, rejoined the ranks and poured new powder into his pan – in time with the other men in his rank. But the younger Powell, on the following day, lost his temper, thumped the barrel on the ground, on a rocky outcrop, and it fired. The ball seared a path through his right eyebrow, burnt his forehead, tore a hole through the brim of his hat and vanished in the sky.

Sergeant Owen screamed, halted the rolling fire, and yelled: 'If that had taken your fucking head off it would have been a bloody good lesson! Everybody would have remembered it. It would have made your whole life worthwhile.' He glared at us. 'But nice little surprises like that don't come from up there.' He jerked the barrel of his musket towards the sky. 'So I'm going to have to teach you how to stay alive. We'll call it safety. Maybe it's the first thing I should have taught you.' And he scowled.

Then he ordered me back into the ranks and screamed and yelled like a bloody maniac – for an hour or more – and we learnt a new set of drills: drills to preserve the lives of idiots.

The nights were dark. Eerie. Black shapes layered on black shapes. The first night brought me out in a cold sweat, and every half-hour I picked up the speaking trumpet and shouted: 'Devil's Drop! Can you hear me down there?'

The reply came out of the void, came crusted with the sound of waves breaking on the sand: 'We can hear you! We can hear you pissing in your breeches!' The voice laughed, and then the darkness settled on us again. A few minutes later I turned to Charles Fort and shouted at them, and they shouted back. From time to time I could hear them shouting at Kendall, but I never heard their reply – even when the wind was blowing in our direction.

Matches burn at a fast rate and the wind makes them burn even faster. One windless night we kept one match burning in one loaded musket, and it looked like a red eye. To begin with I saw this red eye as some sort of monster, some sort of fiend, but then I came to see it for what it was, a friend, a companion. When the wind strengthened, threatened our friend with extinction, we kept him in a wooden box – let him nestle on bars of iron – and in the emptiness of the night, an emptiness that was not filled by the other two sentries who kept the watch with me and liked to remain mute, remain wrapped in their own thoughts, I missed his red eye, his spark of fiery life.

The first few days of the week dragged, went on and on and I thought they'd never end. But the last couple of days, couple of nights – nights that were wrapped in warmth, in a closeness I'd not experienced since Crabtree and Oldfield and I slept close in the hammocks on the *Salisbury*

– ran together, became one, like a perfect volley, and they seemed to vanish in just a few hours.

Then we were back in the lodging house, patrolling the upper bastions and mounting guard in Peterborough Tower. The view was much better, much clearer than I ever thought, and with the spyglass I could see everything, every tiny detail – including the rocks where I sat and waited for Brandon. And how that fool who was up the tower the day Oldfield struck the wheel off the rock cart and didn't see what happened is beyond me – unless of course he was sound asleep and lied to save his hide.

I helped Trigg and O'Sullivan for two nights in a row: copied ten letters, two sets of orders and a report on the 'inherent weakness of Johnson's Battery'. On the third night, when Trigg's hands were bad, and Sergeant Carpenter was too drunk to write, and I was up Peterborough Tower watching the moonlight make the shadows move, make them into waves of black-faced Moors, O'Sullivan took Ives to the Governor's House. And he wore the corporal's coat.

I was so jealous, so bloody annoyed, I couldn't trust myself to say a civil word to anyone. I didn't go near the office and I didn't reply to the message, to the plea for help O'Sullivan sent to the lodging house – I sulked in silence. Then we went back to the forts, back to our daily mash of rice, raisins, smoked fish and onions. And it wasn't till ten days later – when my temper was gone, was worked out on every man who dared to make a mistake in musket drill or musket marching – that I wandered back to Sergeant Carpenter's office.

O'Sullivan looked up and said: 'We thought you were dead.'

I laughed, shook my head and said: 'No. We're back on double-duty, and on guard every second night. It's all this rain. All this cold weather. It's put half the company in bed with chesty fevers and colds, and last week, out in the forts, there were barely enough men to maintain a proper guard. They were sour, bloody sour.' I pulled my stool out from my desk and sat down. 'To tell you the truth it's good to come here. Good to do something different. To forget all about everything for a while.'

He nodded. 'I'm going up to the Governor's House. In a few minutes. Would you like to come?'

I looked at the bench. They were the words I'd dreamt of hearing a hundred times, a thousand times. But I was feeling perverse and I shook my head. 'No. You should wait for Ives. They tell me he's been helping you up there. He'll know what to do.'

He shrugged. 'Just as you like. But I think you should know he's gone for a month. To Fountain and Bridges. Then I think he said they're going to Fort Bellissis, to clear the springs, to make the water flow faster.'

Trigg smiled. 'I still remember my first day in the Governor's House. It was so quiet. So peaceful. It was like being in the clouds and watching a storm raging below you. Everything proceeded at a measured pace. And to be honest I've always thought it was a wonderful place to work. You hear all sorts of things. Things you shouldn't know. Some of it's gossip and not worth knowing, but other things . . .' And he smiled again.

I wanted to be persuaded. I wanted to give in. But for some reason I also wanted to pretend reluctance, and I said: 'What sort of things?'

He twiddled his fingers for a moment – built a steeple and made it collapse. 'In January, Sir Palmes is going to build two more forts.'

'He's always building new forts. He sees every dip, every hollow as a hiding place and thinks it should be guarded.'

'Hmm. But these two forts are going to be different. He's going to surprise the Moors. He's going to build them both in one day.'

I burst out laughing. 'It can't be done. Even with a hundred men. You have to dig the foundations, and the tarras has to set. All those bricks and mud blocks have to be laid. And then there's all the stonework. The woodwork.' I shook my head.

'He going to build them in wood. And they're going to have two walls, two skins with a gap between them. He's going to fill the gap with sand and they say they'll be as strong as stone.'

'They can't be very big if he's going to do all that in one day.'

'Twenty-four feet square, and twenty-four feet high.'

'Christ! That's bloody huge. Like a big box.' I looked at him and shook my head. 'No. You couldn't do that in one day.'

He smiled. 'There's a secret.'

'A secret?'

'Hmm. He's going to build them inside the walls, by Catherine Gate. Then he's going to pull them apart, carry the sections up to the site, and rebuild them in one day.'

'Hell,' I said, in a quiet voice. 'That is smart. And where's he going to put them?'

'One's going between Monmouth and Cambridge – by the sandhills. And that should help to protect the water supply. The other one's going somewhere between James and Anne.'

'I've been up there – when we were filling in the dips and the hollows with rubbish – and there's only a thin little palisade between James and Anne. It's not much better than a farm fence. The Moors could have it down in ten minutes if they wanted to. Then they'd entrench the fort, and it wouldn't last a week.'

'Hmm. But there's another secret.'

'Another?'

'Hmm,' he walked over to the wall, took the corporal's coat off the hook, and gestured for me to stand up and take off my coat. 'Sir Palmes is going to build a new line between James and Anne. There's going to be a ditch – maybe eight feet deep. And then a raised bank faced with stone, and capped with a palisade and a four-foot wide walkway. He says he'll do all of it – all three hundred yards of it – in January. In the rain. When they're least expecting it.' Then he smiled. I slipped my arms into the coat and he patted me on the shoulder.

The Governor's House was huge, cool, and full of dark corners. It smelt of wax, fruit, flowers, cinnamon and spice. Single candles trapped in bowls of glass, cast tiny pools of light, like fireflies stuck on pins. The servants seemed to move, to glide, on cushions of silence.

One of them gave O'Sullivan a candle, and we walked past the great hall; past the green room with its curtains of green and gold; up a flight of stairs; along the great gallery with its portraits of old men, looking grim, looking at us with painted eyes, oiled eyes dulled with age; and into a small suite of offices, panelled with wood and lined with books that smelt like leather. 'This is where Mister John Luke used to work. He was the Governor's Secretary, in the time of Lord Middleton, when things were done properly.' He waved his hand around the room. 'These were his things. And the next room was also his.' He opened a door. In the darkness I could see the outline of a large table and a couple of chairs. Then he walked to the end of the room and opened another door. 'And this is where we work.'

The room was long and thin – no more than six feet wide – with two desks, two stools and shelving that stretched all the way along the inner wall. 'It used to be his storeroom. He never threw anything out. It's all here. All the newspapers. The journals from London. The old books he didn't want any more. The ledgers. The reports. The commissions of inquiry. The surveys of the Mole. The copybooks. Everything.' He ran his hand down the wall of paper. 'And in there' – he pointed to the boxes stacked between the two windows – 'are the warrants. The promotions and the demotions. The new commissions – for a few lucky bastards. And leases. And grants of property. Almost anything you want to name, will be in here, somewhere. It's just a matter of finding it.' He looked around the room. 'Sometimes I come up here on my own, when we don't have much to do, and I sit and read. It's like having my own library. And sometimes I borrow a book, just for the pleasure of having it to myself – pretending I own it – for a few days.' A soft look, a fond look came into his eyes.

Then he lit the candles in the sconces on both sides of the desks and for an hour or more we copied letters, orders, confirmations of punishment, and warrants to purchase extra provisions from Spain.

I finished a few minutes before he did. I walked up and down, stretched my legs, ran my fingers down the piles of newspapers and made a soft drumming sound. Then I felt him looking at me, felt his disapproval, felt the silence of words unspoken, and I pulled a newspaper out of one of the piles and read about the Treaty of Westminster. It ended the war with the Dutch in February '73/4, at about the time I arrived in Tangiers. I remember it took us a couple of months to get the news and it wasn't till a month after that, when Lord Middleton was sure all the ships in the Dutch fleet knew about the peace, that he reduced the size of the moleguard and withdrew most of the gunners from the Mole.

I pulled out another paper, the *London Recorder*, and read about the King laying the foundation stone for the new Saint Paul's, in London in June '75. And right on the top of the pile, on the front page of the latest paper – dated August 1676 – I read about the completion of the Monument, the memorial to the Great Fire of London.

I looked out the window, looked at the lights dying far below me, and I remembered being in London, remembered seeing the men bring down the ruins of the old Saint Paul's, remembered someone in the crowd saying they couldn't agree on a design for the new cathedral. And I remembered the Monument, remembered seeing it poking above the hoardings, looking like a round chimney. It was to be – is now, according to the paper – a column of white stone, set on a base the size of a house, and topped with an urn, with a gilded flame that blazes in the sunrise and smoulders in the sunset.

It all seemed so long ago, so far away, and I was wondering if I might ever see that flame, towering over the houses of London, burning red in a summer sunset, promising a fine tomorrow – red knob in the sunset. Then I was wondering about Jenny, wondering about the red knob that was blazing, was throbbing, was coming to her, to her marital bed, when O'Sullivan shuffled his things into the drawer, stood up, snuffed out the candles with his thumb and forefinger, and said: 'Would you like to come here again?'

'Hmm,' I said. 'I'd love to read all those papers.' I ran my finger down the edge of the pile and made the drumming sound again.

He smiled, held up the candle the servant had given him, and as he led the way out of the room, he said: 'I prefer the books. I'm going to miss them when they're packed up and sent back to London with all of Mister Luke's other things. He had – has I should say, for he's not dead, he's travelling in Spain – such good taste. And his interests are wide. Catholic in the true sense of the word.'

I groaned to myself and thought: Christ! The very first time we're alone together he's talking about his bloody religion again. To tell the truth, I'm sick of his religion, sick of all religions. And sometimes at night when I'm up on top of Henrietta – wishing I was on top of a woman, looking up at the stars, and hearing the Moors calling to each other – I don't think any of them are right. I know we think we're right. The papists think they're right. The Moors think they're right. And the Barbary Jews think they're right. They can't all be right. And some days I'd like to talk to somebody about it, somebody I could trust – somebody who wouldn't think I was raving bloody mad.

Then I was conscious of the silence, and he seemed to be waiting for me to say something, and I said: 'He should have borrowed some books from the Minister. They say he has a library attached to his house and a few protestant books might given Mister Luke's books a better balance.'

He roared with laughter. 'Catholic means universal. His interests are wide, cover lots of subjects, so they're universal.' He laughed again. 'When the word is applied to the church, it means the universal church. And that's why the word is used in the creed.'

I grunted and swore to myself, and he said: 'I've often thought if I wrote a definition, and maybe a synonym and an antonym next to every word in my spelling book, it could be very helpful.'

I thought it was a stupid idea, but I told him I thought it was a good idea – to stop him talking about his bloody religion.

Ten minutes later, back in the office, I slipped off my coat, slipped off my promotion, and became a pikeman again. He was still talking about his book and I was itching to go, but I couldn't get away. I had to promise to help with some of the definitions. It was the only way to escape. It was a mistake – I know that – but at least it has one advantage: most words have nothing to do with religion or the bloody Irish.

In the next few weeks I went to the Governor's House fourteen times – the last three of them on my own – and Sir Palmes nodded to me a couple of times. Then came the Feast of Christmas with its gifts of oranges, lemons, limes, and brown sugar to stir into our rice; and a few days after that, on the 30th December – in an eerie imitation of the census that drove Mary and Joseph to Bethlehem – every person, every house, every property in the whole of Tangiers was counted, was subject to a census. That night as I walked into Sergeant Carpenter's office and sat down, Trigg looked up and smiled. I could tell he'd been waiting for me, waiting for an audience. He turned to O'Sullivan and said: 'I was thinking about the census. And wondering about the Christ-child. The statue of the little baby. The one they put in the crib, in that church of yours on Christmas Day. And you worshipping it like a real person. I was wondering if you included him in the census today.'

Carpenter bit his lips and bubbled with giggles. I clamped my hand over my mouth and tried to stifle the laughter that was fizzing, was trying to explode out of my mouth. We both looked at our desks and waited.

O'Sullivan smiled, assumed the mantle of wisdom, the gentle complacency of the righteous, and said: 'Of course. And we also counted Mary and Joseph. And if you'd been a wise man, had remembered we celebrate Christmas on December 15th – according to your calendar – you'd know the Magi, the wise men from the east arrived twelve days later, on the 6th of January – the 27th according to you – and we also included them in the census.' And he smiled again.

Carpenter and I laughed out loud. Trigg shook his head, then he began to laugh. He couldn't help himself.

O'Sullivan's smile became a grin, a big fat grin. It was hard to believe that these two men who couldn't bear to speak to each other two years

ago, could now joke about the very things that had split their friendship
and silenced their mouths.

Two days later, on the 1st of January, I walked up to the Governor's
House with O'Sullivan, and we began to copy the census, to work our way
through pages and pages of the most intricate, the most intimate detail –
under the guidance of Mister John Bland, Comptroller of His Majesty's
Revenues. Towards midnight, I prepared a summary, an abstract for
him and Sir Palmes. Housekeepers, meaning men in charge of a house,
numbered 197. Of these 129 were citizens, 28 were molemen, 40 were
soldiers. Wives totalled 217 and children 342. Servants numbered 79 and
slaves 17. Priests and Friars numbered 18 and ministers 2. I showed this
figure to Trigg and said: 'They haven't counted Mister Tate. It should
be three.'

He shook his head. 'He's in with the housekeepers. He's not licensed
by the Bishop of London so officially he's not a minister.'

I shrugged – it would upset him but it was nothing to do with me – and
I copied the section for Strangers: 4 Dutch, 45 French, 8 Portuguese, 17
Italians, 51 Jews, 5 Moors. I was surprised at the number of Jews. If I'd
taken a guess, I would have put the Jews at 8 and the Portuguese at 51,
and it made me think most of them must stay inside, stay hidden.

The soldiers totalled 1,247: non-commissioned officers made 96 of
that number, private soldiers 1,085, troopers 34, gunners 16, and the
Governor's train 16. Then I copied the Inhabitants: Citizens 457, Mole
156, Army 1,591. They totalled 2,204, but there was something wrong, and
for a minute or two I stared at the figures, then I called out to O'Sullivan:
'I don't have a figure for officers. Or reformadoes.'

'They're included in the figure for the Army. And there might be
some of the Militia mixed up in there too but don't worry about that
tonight.'

Castles within the walls numbered 2. Forts without the walls 15.
Ordnance (cannons): 30 brass, 120 iron, 20 unmounted – and that meant
they were no bloody use till they were fitted on a carriage. Buildings in
the City: houses, sheds, quarters, churches, stores, totalled 429. Of these 85
were 'inheritances' and 231 were leasehold. The rest belonged to the King
and were used by the garrison and the Corporation.

Next day – in truth later the same day for we didn't finish till well after
midnight – I began a week in Devil's Drop, and it wasn't till the night of
the 10th that I was back again in the Governor's House with O'Sullivan.
The census was long forgotten, and we worked on the orders for February.
Captain Lacey's company was to guard Fort York and Fort Monmouth
for two weeks, and rebuild the inner palisades and deepen the trenches
that linked them together. Captain Molloy's company – Ives's company
– was to take over our lodging house and work in the quarries at Whitby.
This put O'Sullivan in a good mood. He'd been fearing we'd both be out
in the forts at the same time, and all the extra work would fall on him.

The words 'on him' convey a subtle change, a shift of power. The office is supposed to be Sergeant Carpenter's office, and everyone still calls it that. But in truth there's something wrong with the man: he keeps falling asleep; he can't concentrate; and he forgets which line he's supposed to be copying. And now O'Sullivan is telling him what to do. He smiles and does it, and he doesn't seem to notice he's only copying little things, trivial things, and dear old Trigg, is reading his work, is making corrections.

I finished before O'Sullivan. 'Is there anything else to do?' He shook his head, told me to slip away, told me he'd like some help tomorrow night. There was something in his voice, something in the tone that made me smile, made me want to help him, and I put my things away and said I'd be back as soon as I could.

I left my candle with the servant at the side door, and just as I was going down the steps, twirling my hat round and round on one finger, and whistling, I ran straight into Sir Palmes and Captain Lacey. They gave me a hell of shock. I slammed to attention, held my arms rigid. Held my hat against my breeches. They both stopped. Lacey leant forward. 'Fenton! What the hell are you doing here in a corporal's coat?'

I swallowed hard, stared him straight in the eye and tried to ignore Sir Palmes. I told him about working in the office, and having to wear a corporal's coat in the Governor's House because pikemen are not supposed to be good enough to work there.

Sir Palmes laughed, and asked me who else was working in his house, pretending to be a corporal. I said: 'Ives, sir. Pikeman Ives from Captain Molloy's company.'

He nodded. 'What did you say your name was?'

'Fenton, sir.'

He turned to Lacey. 'Why does that name sound familiar?'

'The court martial sir. The one involving the rock cart and the wheel. He was the only witness.'

He nodded, looked at me for a long time, then he said. 'The voice in the night. The voice in the church.'

'Yes, sir.'

'Hmm. Well – let me tell you one thing. I don't believe in pretence. In fraud. From now on you wear your proper coat in my house. And tell Pikeman Ives. And tell your Sergeant.'

'Yes, sir. He's still inside sir. Still in the office.'

'In that case I'll tell him myself.' And he walked up the steps. As he opened the door, I heard him say: 'If a man can do the job he should have the rank unless of course . . .'

I didn't hear what Captain Lacey said, but on the 31st of January, Ives and I were both promoted to corporal, and that evening, in a haze of beer and back-thumping, the Powell brothers told me they knew it was going to happen, and if anybody 'got out of line' they'd drop him down the privy for me – head first.

Next morning, as I marched the whole company through the Little Parade, marched them out to begin our two weeks in York and Monmouth, Jenny came out of the apothecary's shop. Her face was white and her eyes were puffy, and she didn't recognise me, recognise my new coat.

On her collar she was wearing my blue butterfly.

71

February drifted into March, drifted into April, and we were still mounting guard in York and Monmouth, digging trenches and replacing palisades that had rotted at ground level and could be flattened with one hard kick. We were feeling lonely, feeling forgotten, and no one knew, no one would tell us, why two weeks had been allowed to grow into ten weeks with no promise, no hint of a change. In April the days were full of sunshine and the air was warming, and at night we could burn the palisades that we had replaced during the day. This was in stark contrast to February. Then it was cold and wet and we couldn't work outside, and there was nothing to burn in the fire and six men were eating the rations for four. A sense of gloom, of lethargy settled on us, and it didn't begin to lift till the end of February when a ship arrived from England with forty-two tons of provisions, and rations rose to five for six.

The men accepted me as their corporal without a quibble. It might have been something to do with the lethargy. Or maybe it was a form of indifference, an acceptance of things that can't be changed. I don't know. Whatever it was it helped me, and I'm grateful for it, but I have to acknowledge that I never recognised this at the time – it is an understanding that has come with the passing of the years.

But there was no doubting the help Sergeant Owen gave me. He was like an anxious father: my success was his success and it reflected well on him. But the opposite was also true: my failures became his failures, became a personal affront and exposed his judgement to scorn, silent scorn. When he sensed this scorn, this criticism, he'd stand behind me and whisper in my ear: 'That was bloody awful. Bloody stupid. Next time this is what you have to do . . .'

On the hills the Moors were gathering, were riding patrols, firing their muskets in the air and parading their banners. Every morning, as the wind carried the smoke of their campfires towards us, small groups spread their blankets on the earth or the sand in front of the palisades. Then they unrolled carpets and displayed brass bowls, tiny metal boxes, curved daggers, glass beads, silver necklaces, dried fruit, figs and bolts of cloth, lightweight cloth with a thread of gold or silver that caught the glint of the sun. Sometimes they banged a stake into the ground and tethered a goat or a sheep – put the temptation of fresh meat before our eyes. Then they would wait for the Jews, wait to trade. And as they waited, they watched us watching them. Some days there was no trade, there was only watching. But every day ended the same, ended with the Moors wrapping their goods, rolling up their carpets, draping their blankets over their shoulders and drifting into the darkness, drifting back to Barbary.

In the loneliness of the night, when the friends of the day were friends no more, we traded shots, traded insults – in English. I often tried to see if the traders of the day were the insulters of the night, but I could never make out their faces. But once, when the moon was bright, the face was white, too white, and the English was too good, was mellowed in the levels of Somerset. I knew it was the voice of a renegade, a deserter who should be hanged by the neck on the Old Parade. I was hot for slipping through the palisade, through the traders' gate – the traitors' gate – and capturing him. But Owen shook his head, and in silence we lined up a volley and fired. We heard a shout. A cry of pain. And later a moaning. In the morning there was no sign of him, or any of the other voices in the night. But in the sand there was a wet patch, a dark patch, where his life had leaked away.

A few days later six Irishmen joined our company. They were fresh out of Ireland and so bloody green it was hard to believe men could be so stupid. They confirmed all my beliefs – O'Sullivan calls them prejudices – about the Irish. They had about a hundred words of English between them, if we were lucky. Captain Lacey sent three to York and three to Monmouth, and told Owen they were only to go on guard at night, and from now on no one was to use English on the speaking trumpets at night. Irish was to be the language, the only language of the speaking trumpets. That night we lost the intimacy that used to bind our two forts together, and I began to feel I was a stranger, in a dark land, a land of night, a land that did not speak my language.

A couple of nights later Lockhart and I were on guard, were up on the roof of York with a young Irishman by the name of O'Grady. He was wrapped in misery, like a homesick child. I hadn't succeeded in getting more than two words out of him, and they were so thick, so laden with accent, I had to pretend I understood them. I was trying to think what the hell we could do about it, when Lockhart said to me: 'It wouldn't surprise me if one of those silly bastards' – he nodded at O'Grady – 'gets drunk and runs away. After all they don't like the English, and they're only here for the money, and if they don't get paid what's to stop them?' He sniffed and wiped his nose on his cuff. 'I can just imagine one of them sitting out there on the sandhills, holding hands with a sweet little bint, moorish bint' – he roared with laughter – 'listening to every single word we say on the trumpets. And all this talking in Irish or Gaelic or whatever they call it will be a bloody great waste of time.' Then he leant over the parapet and cupped his hands to his ears. After two or three minutes he stood up straight. 'I thought I heard something. Thought there was something out there.' He yawned and stretched. 'And there's another thing. If they can't understand enough English to tell Monmouth exactly what we want to say, what's the bloody use of them?'

I mumbled: 'Hmm,' and then I had an idea. 'Maybe you'd like to teach them English. A sort of army-English that includes all our commands, weapons, places, numbers. Basic things like that. And maybe they could teach you Irish. And then you could be on the trumpets. Be our first English Irish trumpeter.'

He laughed and shook his head. 'I don't want to help them.'

'The Irish?'

'No. Them: Lacey, de Colville, Wyndham, Owen.'

'What about me? Am I part of them?'

He stared at me for a long time. 'Yes, but you don't count.'

I laughed. 'Well – if you can't do it for them, or for me, why don't you do it for yourself?'

'What do you mean?'

'Brandon isn't coming back. That's what I think. And one day we'll be wanting a new sergeant and a new corporal. And if you stopped thinking about your cock all the time, and thought a bit more about the company, you could be the corporal.'

He burst out laughing. 'I've never heard anything so bloody stupid in all my life.'

'Corporals get paid more than pikemen. And you don't work any longer. Or any harder. It's just different. And you have to learn how to do it.'

'It's all right for you. You know what to do. You do it naturally. Everyone says so.'

'They're wrong. I do what Sergeant Owen taught me to do. And if he can teach me, I can teach you. And it helps to get noticed – by Captain Lacey. If you taught these three men how to speak English; took charge of them unofficially; and then we swopped them over and you taught the other three; or maybe you could teach the six of them in a group, in the daytime, that would get you noticed. And one day it could get you promoted.'

I leant over the parapet and thought about Jenny and the blue butterfly. In the darkness I could see her face, see her sweet lips. I couldn't think how I'd ever been so crass, so vulgar, so rude, to think about her painting her tits. It was what whores did to excite men. She wasn't a whore. She was a butterfly, caught in the closet of an old man, a man who was her father, her gaoler. I tried to imagine – as I'd tried a hundred times before – why she was wearing her butterfly on that morning in February. But my mind was empty, was a blank, was a blue haze, was a sky that should have been full of her flutterings.

At the end of May, Captain Molloy's company took over our two forts and I told Ives he could have my old pallet, and the bed bugs that went with it. He laughed and told me I could have a couple of months in the clerks' office, and then he said: 'Sergeant Carpenter's become a bed bug. They can't get him out of bed in the morning. And when they do get him into the office he falls asleep at his desk all the time. He hasn't copied a single thing we've been able to use in months.'

'Why don't they get someone else? There must be someone who can write. Who's limping around. Who's no good to his company any more – and still too young for a grog licence.'

'Hmm. I know of a couple. But O'Sullivan and Trigg won't have them. They're scared Carpenter will end up in the infirmarium, or some bloody old doss house, and they don't want that.' He shook his head. 'What they'd like,' and he grinned, 'is for you and me to come back.'

I laughed. 'Six months ago I might have thought that was a good idea, but now . . .' I shook my head.

June ran into July, and Jenny still eluded me. Some days I thought it was deliberate. And some days I thought it was a coincidence. But every time I was in the Little Parade, the shop was closed, or her father was there on his own, or both of them were there together. Not once did I see her on her own. And not once did I see her wearing her butterfly. Her face wasn't puffy and her eyes weren't red, but something had changed, something had taken the sparkle out of the way she walked, the way she dressed. And now her demeanour was solemn, was serious, was more like that of a matron or a widow.

Down on the Mole, Mister Sheres had sunk a great chest: 'Charles Chest'. It weighed over two thousand tons and it was followed by two more: one of a thousand tons and one of six hundred tons. Three more chests were being built. This was the greatest progress that had been made for a long time and it seemed to vindicate the decision to replace Sir Hugh. And despite the fears of the plague – it was raging in some of the Moors' cities further along the coast and we were being warned every second day to watch for the 'spotted fever' – there was in the town a sense of excitement, a sense of rejoicing. Part of the reason – maybe the underlying reason – was not the physical progress, but what it represented: it meant we hadn't been abandoned by the King. We were still of value. He was still prepared to spend money, his own money, on the Mole. This silenced most of the critics, the sceptics, who were loud in their condemnation of the Mole, the harbour, the town, the forts, the Moors, the food, and the drunkenness of the garrison – when they themselves were deep in their own cups, and verging on the morbid.

We were mounting guard from the Forage Gate to Stayner's Bastion and from there down to Three-gun Battery, and our new quarters were in the Upper Castle, just along from Mistress Copeland's old lodging houses. I was lying on my pallet, looking into the half-light, the shadows of the dawn, and thinking it must be the 17th – the 17th of July – and that meant we had two more full days up here, and I was wondering what it would be like to be on moleguard, when a cannon fired. I jumped out of bed, screamed at everyone to get up and pulled on my breeches. In the distance the cannon fired again, and then again. Lockhart yelled: 'It's not close enough to be Charles. It must be Henrietta.'

I felt as though a friend, a lady friend, was in trouble and it set my heart racing. Then the great cannon on the Governor's Bastion sounded the general alarm and the bell in Peterborough Tower began to toll, to wrench my guts. I pulled on my coat, grabbed my pike, tore out the door and hurled up the steps to the Forage Gate – it was designated a weak point, an assembly point – and I couldn't see a thing. There wasn't a Moor in sight.

Ten minutes later a dozen troopers galloped along the coast road, rounded the headland and vanished in the direction of Whitby. Behind them, double-marching, came three companies-of-foot. Then two companies-of-foot poured through the Forage Gate and double-marched towards Henrietta.

The boom of the cannons echoed across the Marshan, and white smoke layered the hills that blocked our view of Whitby. Volleys of musket fire, crackled and pulsed through a hail of single shots, and I could feel, could sense, the hours of drill that lay behind the precision of those blasts of death. Then the wind began to gust, to catch, to carry, the sound of screaming, not the screaming of someone in pain, but the screaming that frightens, that stirs a man to madness, to doing things he could not do, would not do, if he was calm and collected – of a rational mind.

People from the town flocked to the walls, crowded all the way along the battlements, jostled us for the best view, the best angle of sight. As the smoke cleared, the crack of the muskets died away, and the screeching of the seagulls replaced the screaming of the Moors.

Two hours later, when it was time for us to change the guard, I walked the wall and checked every sentry box. The men were happy to change but no one wanted to leave the wall, and I was thinking, wishing, it was always like this when a hand touched me on the arm, and a voice said: 'I haven't seen you for a long time.'

I turned round. My face broke into a big grin and I said: 'Jenny.' For a moment she took my breath away. She was like fine china, like porcelain with a blush of pink, and I blurted out: 'God, I've missed you.'

She smiled, tapped my arm, tapped disapproval and said: 'You mustn't take the name of the Lord thy God in vain.'

I felt a chill run through my soul. In my imaginings, in my desire for her body, I'd forgotten about her fervour for religion, for things of the spirit. My mind stumbled, tripped over the hard rocks that edge the land of dreams, the land of make-believe, and I couldn't say what I wanted to say, wanted to ask, and I mumbled: 'Are you still going to Mister Tate's chapel?'

I had no interest in the answer. I just wanted to look into her eyes, the eyes that came to me in my dreams.

She shook her head. 'He doesn't remember things any more, and he's given up taking the services. I don't think he meant to. I think he just drifted away from them. Forgot the time. Forgot it was Sunday. And once or twice he didn't seem to be able to read the words, and Mistress Tate read them for him. It's sad. So sad.' She closed her eyes for a moment. 'But at least he still goes down to the cathedral. Still preaches on the steps. And that must be a great comfort for him.'

I nodded. I'd seen him there a day or two ago – ranting and bloody raving – and I was so embarrassed, I crossed to the other side of the road and pretended not to know him. 'I saw you in the shop,' I said, 'on the day we marched out to the forts. You were wearing the butterfly and I wanted to come to you. I wanted to hold your hand. To be with you. But I couldn't break ranks, and I thought I'd be back in a week, but we didn't come back till—'

She touched my hand and said: 'I know. I went to the Head Court of the Guard and I asked about Captain Lacey's company. They told me you were at York, and you weren't coming back for a couple of months.'

'I'm sorry. I wanted to come.' I smiled. She picked up my smile, filled it with warmth, made my heart thump. I reached for her hand and said, in a soft voice: 'The butterfly. Why were you wearing the butterfly?'

'I wanted to talk to you. To tell you he was dead.'

'Dead?'

She nodded. 'Do you remember that accident. Out at the end of the Mole. When the boat overturned and two men were drowned?'

I nodded.

'He was the Lieutenant.'

'In Captain Anderson's company?'

'Hmm.'

'I'm sorry. I didn't know.'

'No one knew. But him and me. And my father. And after he was dead we received a letter from his father agreeing to the marriage.' Her eyes filled with tears and she turned away from me, dabbed at them.

'So there's hope for me?'

'No!' The voice was a man's voice. Deep and coarse. And full of authority. I knew it from the shop, his shop. I let go of her hand and turned to face him. 'She's not for you. I told you that once before. And just because you've got a fancy coat, a corporal's coat, it doesn't make you into an officer. Or a gentlemen. I told you once before, my daughter is going to marry an officer or a gentleman.' He held out his arm and she took it, gave me a weak smile, a smile of resignation, and they walked down the steps.

An hour later after the crowd had thinned a little, Sir Palmes returned with three bodies, English bodies. The Moors had laid an ambush between Devil's Drop and Whitby, on the ground I knew so well. The Moors had all escaped, not a single one was left behind, dead or alive. They say Captain Crawley was keen to pursue them, keen to avenge our dead, but Sir Palmes feared an ambush, feared a repetition of the massacre that left Lord Teviot dead, and he would not permit it.

Next morning we learnt that at Blaney's Bottom – on Teviot Hill – the Moors were waiting, with five hundred men on foot and five hundred men on horse.

In the evening as I came off a guard, and was thinking about the dead, the dead who could have been from our company, a man in a dark grey coat with matching breeches, a man I did not know, came up to me and said: 'Are you Corporal Fenton?'

I mumbled 'Yes', and he handed me a sheet of paper. It was folded and sealed with a red blob of wax – imprinted with a spray of leaves, herbal leaves, caught in a circle. I looked at it for a long time. It was the first letter I'd ever received in my whole life. I knew the seal. It was the seal that was on the things I bought from his shop, the things that were supposed to heal. I knew there would be no healing in this letter and I turned it over and over. I could feel something inside, something small, something hard.

I broke the seal, and the blue butterfly dropped into my hand. I brushed the wings, made them shine, and then I read:

> He says I'm not to see you again, and I know he's right.
> But I also know that when I think of you,
> my heart will flutter – like the wings of a butterfly.

72

In August the Moors continued to test our will. They were about in large numbers – the plague was driving them out of their own cities – and on the 10th they broke through our lines and entrenched themselves between Fort Monmouth and Fort Henry. In the dawn we joined two other companies, attacked them with muskets and granadoes and filled the air with a hail of sparks, lead and red-hot iron, and they fled. We thought they'd learnt their lesson but they were back again on the 16th. This time we flung the granadoes in sling-shots as they fled – made them run through a curtain of iron – and after that we fired volleys every half-hour, at anything that moved, or appeared to move. By nightfall all the palisades were restored, the Moors' trenches were filled in and stamped firm, and we were back at Catherine Gate – with the reserves – waiting for the dawn, waiting for the next attack.

The attack did not come. And despite the fact that we did not lose a single man on either day, I still felt the victory belonged to them because they had proved they could penetrate our lines. And if a couple of hundred men could do it twice in the same place, a few thousand could do it in every section of the lines, and we wouldn't have enough reserves to rush to every breech. And that would isolate the forts, make them into pimples that could be squeezed and popped, one by one.

These thoughts hung in my mind like black clouds, storm clouds, clouds of pessimism, and they were fed by a rumbling belly. Rations went back down to six for four, and most days our pewter plates or our old-fashioned wooden trenchers – they were about ten inches square by one inch deep and chiselled to make two shallow bowls: one for meat and one for salt or sauce – were half-empty. When they were full it was not with meat, but a fatty gruel that oiled the trencher, gave the wood a greasy feeling, and left me feeling empty, feeling hungry.

Then a ship arrived with provisions and for a whole day I imagined plates of meat: pickled meat, pink meat, soft meat, meat with gravy, meat that tasted like meat. But then the navy claimed half the supplies; and two hundred and nine new recruits arrived to strengthen the garrison – I admit we needed them – but they were soon eating like hungry caterpillars, and Sir Palmes, worried about the winter storms sealing off the ports of England and Ireland and supplies having to last for months, did not increase the rations. And night after night we went to bed cold and hungry. In the morning we woke bad-tempered, irritable, and one of our musketeers was whipped for provoking a fight.

Two of the new recruits were a source of great amusement: they turned out to be women in men's clothing. Lockhart wanted me to tell Captain Lacey we'd have both of them for night manoeuvres. I told him not to be so swiving silly but he didn't see the joke. The problem is the Irish have their own sense of humour and he's been the butt of most of it. And the English lessons weren't as simple as either of us imagined, and between them they've soured his sense of fun and made him lose interest in being promoted.

September brought a touch of heaven. Not food but money. Our company was paid for eleven months. Other companies, companies that arrived in Tangiers before us – before February '73 – were paid for fifteen months. We saw it as a gross injustice, a perversion of our natural rights – and it would breed discontent for months to come – but it achieved what the Treasurer wanted to achieve: we were now on a par with every other company: twenty-one months in arrears. And given the history of past-payments – or to be more accurate, non-payments – I knew I'd have to wait another twelve months before I could expect to receive any money for being a corporal.

But I didn't give a damn, and like most of the garrison I ended up stinking drunk, and spent more than I intended and woke up a couple of days later with a bloody great headache. But at least I woke up. Young Powell didn't. We found him dead in the morning with his head down the privy. In some ways it was symbolic – apt – and it didn't worry me much, but it enraged Ensign Wyndham. He seemed to take it as a personal insult, and in the afternoon he lined us all up in front of the corpse – wrapped in a white winding sheet – and said: 'In this town, beer and brandy kill more men than the Moors ever do. And there' – he pointed to the corpse – 'is the living proof.'

We burst into laughter. Then he realised what he'd said, and his face flushed, and the laughter spluttered and drowned in a sea of sore heads. Sergeant Owen leant over my shoulder and whispered: 'The man's a fool and it's a great pity he's not lying out there. Powell wasn't any bloody good, but he was ten times better than that silly prick.'

I smiled and my thoughts drifted. Then found I was thinking about silly pricks, pricks with their foreskin cut off, pricks left red, left raw. And I remembered the Jews.

Sir Palmes has banished them, and they have to be gone by December. Everyone says they should be gone before then, but Sir Palmes thinks they need 'three months to settle their affairs' and that's what they're going to get. Some see this as an act of charity, Christian charity. Others see it as an omen, a bad omen. And they fear that in January, when the peace

expires – the formal peace that still persists in spite of all the attacks –
we will drift into war. A war we cannot win.

I don't have any sympathy for the Jews. They crucified our Lord and
they would crucify us if we gave them half a chance. And if it's true they
spy on us and spy on the Moors and sell information to both of us, there's
no place for them. But I do concede that when I see their leases being sold
for half of what they're worth, it doesn't feel right, feel just. It smacks of
revenge. Revenge for usury.

It is a cruel conundrum, like the need for circumcision, the need for a
man's cock to proclaim he is a Jew.

October brought another thirty-four recruits and a further reduction
in rations. We ran out of beef and cheese and butter was down to a
scraping, down to less than a week's supply. And despite the arrival of a
couple of ships we were on the brink of starvation. Sir Palmes sent a ship
to Cadiz – he could no longer rely on provisions arriving from England.
And according to O'Sullivan who says he saw it in the Governor's House,
and swore me to secrecy, he even sent a message to the Moors, to the
Governor of Alcazar suggesting we exchange gunpowder for beef. There
may be some truth in this for they say last month he sent emissaries to
the Governor to negotiate a new peace and he authorised them to offer
muskets, cannons and gunpowder. To me it's bloody madness: everybody
knows the Moors never honour a treaty, and it would only be a matter
of months till we were being attacked with the very weapons we had
given them.

I was thinking about these things, thinking we could put the weapons
to better use, and wondering if O'Sullivan had any more gossip – and
should I go up and help him for an hour or two? – when I bumped into
Trigg. He was more bent more hunched than usual, and the cobbles were
making him hobble. I held out my arm and he leant on it. Then I saw his
face. It was lined with misery and his eyes were wet with tears. 'What's
wrong,' I said.

'Carpenter died this afternoon. He didn't want any dinner and we left
him sleeping on his desk. When we came back he was dead and he smelt
of piss.' He wiped at his eyes.

'He hadn't been well for a long time,' I said. 'And he was an
old man.'

He shook his head. 'He was younger than me. He just looked older.
I know he didn't do much in these last few months, and I got tired
of correcting what he did do, and doing what he should have done
– but I'm going to miss him.' He sighed to himself. 'And now we'll
have to get somebody new. Somebody we don't know. Somebody who
mightn't fit in.' And he sighed again. 'I don't suppose you'd consider
coming back?'

I smiled and shook my head.

Next day we buried Carpenter, twenty-three graves, twenty-three new mounds of earth along from the indentation, the puddle of water that was Oldfield.

In my heart I mourned for both of them, mourned for a past that was dead and buried, and would not come again. I kicked a couple of stones into Oldfield's puddle, and I told him I was a corporal, and I was working bloody hard, and Owen was teaching me, teaching Lockhart; and one day I hoped to be a sergeant – just like him.

November brought the rains again. It also brought us another two hundred and fifty men – instead of the promised three hundred – and they were soon purged by the flux, weakened by scurvy, and laid low by the distempers that ride on the winds of the Levant. Within two weeks nineteen were sleeping in the earth to the right of Carpenter, and a week after that they were joined by another eight impatient souls. The new minister, Mister Hughes, was reading the burial service at eight o'clock every morning: a common service for the common dead. And one morning, if the gossip is to be believed, they say the gravedigger told Mister Hughes he should be reading the service for burial at sea – the graves were full of water and it was lapping around their feet. Mister Hughes is supposed to have complained to the Corporation, supposed to have said: 'The man lacks respect and is imbued with a spirit of levity.' What the Corporation said to him I do not know. But I do know that now he has a bucket and he bails the water out of the grave before the body is lowered into the earth. Whereas, in the past: he slid the body into the water, held it down with a long pole, shovelled in the earth, and sang a sea-shanty as the water sloshed out in great waves.

On December 6th, on the day Sir Palmes – by public proclamation and beating of drums – ordered every man, every freeman into the militia, and I was wondering what he would do with men like Mister Tate, the door to our lodging house swung open and Sergeant Brandon hobbled in on two crutches. For a moment my mind was frozen in disbelief, then Sergeant Owen's training took over. I jumped to my feet and screamed: 'C-o-m-p-a-n-y! Company, attention!'

I didn't know what to do. He looked pale and gaunt – worse than at the court martial. It was as though the effort of getting into the lodging house, of showing he could do it, had exhausted him. He licked his lips, and I thought he was going to say something, but he just stood and looked at us. I stepped forward, tried to do what a corporal should do. 'Welcome back, sir. Sergeant.' I began to clap – hard. Everyone else joined in and I was bloody glad they did.

Then he smiled, patted the air with one hand, and said: 'I'm back. I'm back to stay. And I want every bastard in this room to know it. And most of all I want you to know it.' He swung his crutch from under his arm and pointed it at me.

73

In the morning Sergeant Cannon stormed out of Captain Lacey's room, wearing a florid face and breathing through clenched teeth. He grabbed his halberd in one hand, his musket in the other, thumped down the stairs at the front of the lodging house, and stopped about six inches away from Sergeant Owen and me. 'I have to go to the bloody Town House, to teach musketry to the fucking militia. I have to be their senior-sergeant for three months. Three bloody months!'

Owen and I both stepped back – he was almost screaming in our faces – and I said: 'I thought you said your old company, Captain Erling's company, was going to be re-formed.'

'Lacey says it's not going to be re-formed. We're not getting any more new recruits. And I'm to think of these men as recruits. Have you seen them?' His voice was rising again to a screaming pitch. 'Fat bums. Pot bellies. Half bloody blind. And dopey. So bloody dopey they don't know one end of a pike from the other.' He clenched his musket and halberd so hard they whitened his knuckles. 'And as for their bloody officers—' He spat on the cobbles, shook his head, and thundered down the lane.

'What's wrong with their officers?'

'They're chosen from the Corporation.'

I burst out laughing. 'You mean those pompous shits who waddle along in long gowns with bits of fur and nosegays. They're going to be officers?'

He nodded. I shook my head and laughed some more. 'I'd be pissed off too. I think it's a stupid bloody idea and I know I wouldn't want to teach the Militia.'

He looked me in the eye. 'It was my idea.'

I gulped and swallowed hard. I could feel my face going hot.

'We have two Sergeants,' he said, 'and we didn't need another one. And somebody has to train the Militia. Somebody who knows what he's doing.' And he smiled.

'But Brandon's bloody useless. We don't want him back. You only have to look at the man.'

'He wanted to come back. And he's got a right to be here. In a month's time, if the peace doesn't hold, we'll be out in the forts fighting the Moors. And we'll need every man, every bit of experience we can get.'

I shook my head. 'He can't even march down to the Old Parade. What do you think we're going to do? Carry him in a bloody litter?'

'I hadn't thought of that.'

'Jesus,' I could hear the exasperation oozing out of every syllable, 'this is bloody madness.'

He smiled. 'Yes, I agree.' Then he marched back to the musketeers, to the men who were returning to his command.

My mouth sagged. I couldn't understand what had possessed him, and I shook my head. I dressed the ranks – we were about to march down to the Old Parade for the seven o'clock parade – and stood them at ease. Then I checked all the plug bayonets were in tight – they tend to work themselves loose for some reason – and we waited. Waited for Sergeant Brandon.

Five or ten minutes passed, then he came down the steps, supported by crutches under both arms. I called the men to attention. The night had refreshed him. The colour was back in his face. And so was the mad bloody glint, the evil leer that infused his eyes and tightened my bum. 'I thought you were supposed to be pikemen,' he yelled. 'Pikemen carry pikes. Get back inside and get your pikes! At the double!'

We thundered back into the lodging house and Crabtree yelled: 'Doesn't the silly bastard know we're having musket-drill straight after the parade?' Lockhart yelled back: 'No! He thinks we should be practising a bit of pike-vaulting!' Everybody burst out laughing. Then somebody yelled: 'I know why he wants the pikes!' There was a sudden stilling. 'He wants to stick them up the corporal's arse!' Everybody roared with laughter. And so did I – I couldn't help it.

Then I bit my lips, smothered my laughter and yelled: 'Everybody out! Fast!'

Brandon walked up and down our lines, nodding to himself, and correcting the angle of our pikes.

Two minutes later Captain Lacey came down the steps, scowled, stamped over to Brandon, and half-whispered, half-hissed: 'We have musket drill in thirty minutes. The men are supposed to parade with their muskets.' He shook his head. 'This is a bloody poor start.'

Brandon mumbled something, and two seconds later we thundered back into the lodging house. Three minutes later as we marched down to the Old Parade – left Brandon standing by the steps looking like an ancient relic, a remnant of soldiery – Lockhart whispered: 'I don't know why we need that old bastard.'

I didn't either. But I didn't have the courage to say it out aloud.

Day after day he made my life hell. Nothing was right. Nothing was quick enough. Nothing would please him. Every morning, first thing –

in much the same way some people say 'good morning' – he leant in my ear and whispered: 'I'm going to have you.'

Later in the morning, or in the afternoon, when I was out the front drilling the men, he would limp up to me and whisper: 'You're a bloody liar. And liars get found out.'

And once a day, sometimes twice a day when there wasn't an officer in sight, he yelled: 'How the hell anyone saw fit to make you a corporal, I do not know. They must have taken leave of their bloody senses.' Then he would look along the ranks, purse his lips and wait for someone to grin.

In the evening he kept me working: inspecting uniforms, seeing muskets oiled, touchholes cleared, apostles filled with powder, pallets shaken, shoes shined, stockings washed, trenchers stacked by the washtub, pikes aligned in the rack. It didn't matter what it was. He kept me on my feet, kept me working, till every man was in bed.

Then the bastard made me help him undress, and each night he said: 'You'd better get used to this. You're going to be seeing a lot of my body. And one day soon you're going to be feeling a lot of it.' And he grinned. His grin was hard, was tinged with tiredness, tinged with pain. His body was now the body of an old man. His muscles had withered, and his arms and his legs looked scrawny. His flesh was pitted, scarred, and some of it looked to be peppered with tiny specks of black rock.

He was taking tincture of opium to ease the pain in his hips. To begin with he kept it from me, kept it hidden under his pillow. But as the days took their toll, stiffened the joints in his back and leached his strength, he made me pour it into a pewter mug, and each night I left him in bed, left him sipping his tincture, sipping his passport to peace.

On the morning of the 20th he added brandy-wine to his tincture and then I helped him to dress. A few minutes later he walked down the steps at the front of our lodging house and glared at us, glared at our pikes. He'd exchanged his crutches for two walking sticks. And despite everything I knew, everything I detested, I had to applaud him, applaud his courage, his bloody-minded determination. I began to clap, and so did everyone else in the company. For a moment or two it lifted his spirits, then he was beside me whispering: 'I'm not fooled. A bit of clapping won't do you any good. I'm going to break you. I'm going to put you back in the ranks where you belong, and it won't take more than a week . . . Corporal.'

Four days later, after I'd sent to the infirmarium for more tincture, he paraded with his halberd – and no sticks – and he looked like a sergeant. Once again we broke into applause. And despite all that had happened, all that I feared was still to happen, I did not begrudge him his moment of triumph. I clapped as hard as any man.

He did not march down to the Old Parade, he hadn't marched anywhere since coming back, but that did not diminish his day. In truth there was a lot of admiration for him, for his guts, and to my surprise most of the men were looking forward to him being back in full command.

In the late afternoon, the whole company was marching back down Anne Lane – we'd just finished firing volleys over a palisade, pretending the Moors had broken through the outer lines and were contained in one of the palisaded fields, the fields that are supposed to become the killing fields – when a trooper galloped up and said something to Captain Lacey.

The Captain beckoned to de Colville and Wyndham, turned to me and yelled: 'March the company back to quarters!' Then he ran ahead of us – with the other two following on behind like a pair of dogs hounding a wild boar – and in three or four minutes they were lost in the revetments in front of Catherine Gate.

As we came to the end of the lane and I was about to order a left turn – intending to march along the outside of the wall, pass below Peterborough Tower and enter by the Forage Gate – one of the musketeers yelled out: 'Bit of luck for you, eh corporal? Sergeant Owen in bed with the gripe, and you in charge. All on your own.'

'Shut up!' I yelled. 'Or I'll give you something to gripe about.'

They all laughed. It was the response I wanted, expected, but underneath I was annoyed, peeved that they would yell at me and never dare to yell at Brandon or Owen. Without thinking, I knew if we went in through Catherine Gate we'd pass a couple of officers, and that would mean the end of any more stupid comments and I wouldn't lose control of the musketeers. I whirled around and yelled: 'Company! Double time!'

I made for Catherine Gate. Behind me the mutterings rose and fell like the muffled echo of a drum. I ignored them and I remembered one of the first things Owen told me: 'Ignore the little things. The petty things. Pretend they don't exist. They'll get under your skin and they'll itch like bloody hell and to begin with you'll find it hard, but bite your tongue and don't say a word. And thump the bastards hard for the big things. But always be fair. They can understand that. Then they'll respect you, and you won't have to maintain discipline. They'll do it for you.'

At the revetements we broke ranks, ran through the gate and re-formed on the other side – as the Sergeant of the Guard screamed at us – then we doubled down Catherine Street.

Far in the distance a dozen men ambled out of the Head Court of the Guard and milled about for a moment or two. They were all armed with muskets, and then they began to walk, to run, towards Peterborough House – Sir Palmes's house, his private house – and I could hear shouting. Then a Corporal thumped on the door with the butt of his musket.

I looked at Lockhart and he muttered: 'Bloody hell!'

I felt a cold chill run down my spine and I sensed something was wrong. But then Major Daniels and a couple of men came out of the Head Court of the Guard and began to walk towards Peterborough House. They were calm, controlled, like men out for a Sunday stroll, and I thought my senses were playing tricks with me and I yelled: 'Company halt!'

A servant appeared, said something to the Corporal, and shut the door in his face. We waited in silence for several minutes – about fifty yards away from Sir Palmes's house. The men in front of the door walked up and down. A couple of them kept waving their muskets in the air and one of them kept yelling: 'Sir Palmes! Sir Palmes! We want Sir Palmes!'

Major Daniels lingered by the fountain, held out his hand – as if to check the rate of flow – and flicked the water off his hand.

I turned to the drummer and yelled: 'Beat the march!'

We marched into the Market Place and as we drew level with Peterborough House the door opened and Sir Palmes rushed out. The Corporal said something. Sir Palmes grabbed at his musket. For a couple of seconds they fought, struggled for possession of the musket.

I yelled: 'Company halt! Left turn. Present bayonets!'

Major Daniels ran towards Sir Palmes.

Sir Palmes wrested the musket out of the Corporal's hands, pointed it at the Corporal and fired. The Corporal fell to his knees. Then he toppled forward and his face hit the cobbles. His arms and legs twitched for a moment. Then his right hand clawed at the cobbles, turned to expose the palm of his hand and his fingers splayed, and I could almost see, could almost feel, his soul leaving his body – through his fingertips.

A heavy silence fell over the Market Place.

Major Daniels rushed forward with some men and yelled: 'Put down those muskets!'

The Corporal's men swung round and pointed their muskets straight at him. I yelled: 'Prepare to charge!' They swivelled round, looked at us, and threw their muskets to the ground.

Captain Lacey, de Colville, Wyndham and two servants ran out of the house.

Major Daniels' men rushed at the Corporal's men, pinned them to the wall and bound their hands behind their backs.

A crowd was gathering, was growing by the second. Captain Lacey ran towards me, yelled: 'Company! About turn!'

We turned and faced the crowd. Faced their silence. Captain Lacey laid his hand on my shoulder. 'Did you know?'

I didn't understand what he was saying. 'Know what sir?'

'About this.'

'No, sir. I saw all these men coming out of the Head Court of the Guard and I had a feeling. A strange feeling that something wasn't right. It just didn't look right, feel right.'

Sir Palmes was splattered with blood. But he was very calm. He called the men mutineers, malcontents, and said they would be punished, then he told the crowd to go home.

A few minutes later Major Daniel said to me: 'When I saw you up there waiting – at the end of Catherine Street – you had me bloody worried. I thought you were with the mutineers.'

'I'm sorry, sir. I saw the Corporal and I knew something was wrong. But I didn't know what it was.'

'Hmm. I had the same feeling. That's why I followed him from the Head Court of the Guard.'

I looked at the ground. My heart was thumping. My mouth was dry. I didn't know what to say. He touched my arm and said: 'This won't be forgotten.'

In the evening two of the mutineers – that is what everyone was now calling them – were tried by court martial and sentenced to be shot next day: Christmas Day.

A strange atmosphere filled our quarters as soon as we heard the sentences. No one wanted to celebrate the Corporal's death, or the two deaths that were about to stain the day that is supposed to celebrate birth. But there was still a feeling, a feeling that we – as a company – had done something right, something that should be recognised. But mutiny is a rebellion of the ranks, a rebellion against authority, and we went to bed in a sombre mood. There was no praise, no public thanks, no recognition of any kind, for us and or what we had done.

In the morning Sergeant Brandon could not get out of bed. His limbs had frozen, and the tincture of opium would not warm them, and the fingers of pain came and went, like fingers of fire. His mood was bleak and he did not want to talk, want to share our company.

Sir Palmes reprieved the two mutineers but the man who provoked their concern, their protest, who had been arrested the day before the mutiny for disobeying Captain Scrope, was tied to the gallows and whipped in front of the whole parade – straight after prayers.

In the afternoon we carried Sergeant Brandon back to the infirmarium. In the evening Captain Lacey, in a quiet voice, a voice that did not reflect the joy of Christmas, said: 'Sergeant Brandon is sicker than we thought. And today, I had to tell him that he would not be able to remain with the company.'

I closed my eyes, let my mind float in the clouds. Then I remembered there is a tradition of exchanging gifts, small gifts, gifts of no real value, on the Feast of Christmas. This was the best gift I'd ever received. I bit the insides of my mouth, kept my face straight, serious, and hid the joy, the glee that was bubbling inside me.

Last year I received a lemon. On the outside it looked smooth, looked yellow, looked welcoming. But on the inside it was sour, bitter.

In my innocence, my naïvety, I did not know, did not realise, that Brandon's gift – gift of departure, of farewell – would be like the lemon: it would go sour, go bitter, in four days.

74

Four days later, at six in the morning, Captain Lacey called me into his room and said: 'We need another Sergeant.' I went rigid. 'Sergeant Owen says you are the man. Can you keep the men in order?'

'Yes, sir.'

'Can you make them do what you want them to do?'

'Yes, sir.'

'You're young to be a sergeant. But as Sergeant Owen says, you're older than most ensigns and you have four years' experience. And that's four years more than most ensigns on the day they join.' Then he smiled and held out his hand

I shook it, and mumbled: 'Thank you, sir.'

'And now we need a new corporal.'

'Yes, sir.'

'Sergeant Owen thinks Lockhart is the man.'

'Yes, sir.'

'Is he your choice?'

'Yes, sir.'

'Can he keep them in order and tell them what to do? And can he make them do it?'

'Yes, sir.'

He nodded. 'You realise if he fails and has to be demoted, I will hold you responsible.'

'No, sir. I didn't know that. But I'll teach him everything he has to know. And I'll make sure he doesn't fail.'

He nodded. 'What's his best feature?'

'The men trust him. They'll do what he says.'

'And his worst feature. What's that?'

I stared at the ground. I didn't know what to say, but I wanted to say what he wanted to hear. But I couldn't think of anything.

'Come on,' he said. 'Hurry up. There must be something.'

'He never stops talking about swiving, and what he'd like to do with his cock.'

He roared with laughter. 'I bet a lot of ladies wouldn't regard that as his worst feature.' And he laughed again. 'Take off your coat. Lockhart can have it for this morning. If it doesn't fit he can get another one this afternoon.'

I folded my coat and gave it to him. He opened a closet, took out a sergeant's coat, and handed it to me. I slipped it on. It was heavy, was frothed with gold lace. It shaped my shoulders and it felt right. Then he picked up a sergeant's halberd from a stand in the corner and handed it to me. I recognised the carving at the top of the shaft. 'This belongs to Sergeant Brandon.'

He shook his head. 'It belongs to the company. It belongs to Sergeant Fenton.' He smiled. 'And now go out and tell them what to do. And send in Lockhart.'

I walked back into the main room. Twenty-four men were pulling on coats and breeches, stretching, yawning, talking in that bleary half-awake way that ushers in the new day. The noises stilled, and died. Then one or two began to giggle, to laugh, and someone whistled, someone clapped. Then they all clapped, roared their approval and slapped me on the back. After a couple of minutes, I lifted one hand and silenced the noise, and in that moment I knew they had passed the power, the authority, from Brandon to me, and I said: 'Lockhart. Captain Lacey wants to talk to you. Something about being a corporal, and—'

The room erupted into a roar, a cheering roar that drowned the roar they gave me. I laughed and clapped. As he approached the door he looked shy, coy, and I could see why the ladies liked him, liked his boyish charm. He had something I didn't have, and for a moment I was almost jealous. Then it passed and I knew we'd fit together like lovers, and we'd have any bastard who tried to prise us apart, who tried to do the things he should not do.

I was surprised at the weight of the halberd. The fighting head: the spear, hook, and blade were cast in iron and pierced with holes to lighten the weight, but it was still top heavy, with a natural tendency to fall forwards. It was over seven feet high but it didn't rest well on my shoulder, didn't feel comfortable, and I was beginning to understand why so many sergeants splayed their legs and held their halberds upright, when Lockhart came back into the room. He was wearing my coat, wearing a bloody great grin from ear to ear, and he was met with another round of applause. It was bloody deafening, and it made me realise I'd never known, never understood, just how popular he was.

They crowded around him, shook his hand and slapped him on the back.

I waited for the noise, the excitement to die away, then I lifted my halberd, banged the metal-capped end three times on the floorboards and a deep echoing boom, a drumming boom that commanded respect, obedience, filled the room. 'It's time to parade. It's also time to show the musketeers that pikemen can do everything they can do. And do it better. So I want your musket drill to be perfect. I want it to get right up their bloody noses.' I paused. 'In the future I think wars will be fought with the musket. Not the matchlock. But the flintlock. And one day there won't be a place for pikes or these things.' I jiggled my halberd. 'So let's make sure no one thinks of us as pikemen. This afternoon we're having new targets. So we'll be able to count the number of hits after every volley. I want us to score more hits than the musketeers. I want us to be better than the musketeers.' I sucked at my lips, waited for my words to sink in. 'In three days' time, when the truce expires, it could make the difference between staying alive, and staying dead for a bloody long time.'

They laughed, and we filed out the door.

The musketeers were already on parade, standing at ease. As I came down the steps Sergeant Owen began to clap. For a moment the musketeers looked startled, bemused, then they began to clap and whistle. I doffed my hat and bowed, and a couple of men in the front rank reached out and patted me on the back.

Sergeant Owen shook my hand, and I said: 'I can't believe it.'

'No,' he said. 'I can't either. I took a wager with Corporal Franks, and it's going to cost me a couple of pounds. He reckoned it'd take you four weeks. I told him he was bloody mad. Told him you couldn't do it in less than six. And it's taken you just over three.' He smiled. 'But then of course I wasn't allowing for that little performance of yours down there in the Market Place – was I?' He laughed and thumped me on the back.

I gasped for breath, and tried to smile.

The morning passed in a daze. The afternoon wasn't much better, and when we totalled up the holes in the targets and found we'd beaten the musketeers by three shots, my head floated away. It was pure happiness. It was like being locked deep inside my lady of Rua de Carmo, with my musket firing – firing hot, firing hard, firing every thirty seconds – and feeling the explosion, feeling the recoil, feeling the discharge of life. And loving every fucking minute of it.

In the evening I drifted along to Sergeant O'Sullivan's office. My halberd echoed all the way across the warehouse floor and up the two flights of steps and I knocked with the end – the way a bishop knocks with the end of his staff, his crozier, when he demands entrance to his cathedral for the first time – and I waited. Nothing happened. I knocked again. Then dear old Trigg opened the door and jumped to attention. I took off my hat. His face burst into smiles. He threw his arms around me and gave me a big hug. O'Sullivan came running, grasped my hand and shook it. Then he kissed me on both cheeks and just for a moment I saw my Father in his eyes, and I wondered what he would think, if he could see me now.

Then I followed them into the office and froze.

Sergeant Brandon was sitting in my desk.

He looked up and said: 'I've put your things in the desk over there.' He pointed to Sergeant Carpenter's old desk. 'The light's too bright for me there by the window.' He dipped his quill into the ink pot and continued with his writing, his copying.

I looked at Trigg. His eyes were moist. He shook his head, and sat down at his desk.

I turned to O'Sullivan and he said: 'We need the help. And they won't give us anyone else.' He gave a shrug, a helpless shrug, a shrug of defeat. 'I'm sorry.'

I felt as if I'd been raped. Forced to up-end my bum. Forced to submit. Forced to endure the pain, the agony, the humiliation.

Then this feeling gave way to numbness. And I knew that my refuge, my retreat, my holy of holies – the place where I could cast aside pretence, could be myself, could be with friends – was rent asunder. Was violated.

I closed the door, left them there together, and sat down on the steps.

In my mind I sucked the lemon, sucked the bitterness of the gift that comes with a sour twist.

75

On the afternoon of the 6th of January, Captain Lacey called me into his room. He was seated at the table. Ensign Wyndham was standing a few feet from the end of the table, with his back to the fire. He told us the Moors were massing on the hills and Sir Palmes was expecting them to attack at any moment. The two most exposed forts, Henrietta and Kendal had already been reinforced but now Sir Palmes was worried about Pond. Then he paused and said: 'I want you two to take Corporal Lockhart and ten men and go out to Pond Fort right away. Take your muskets and half a dozen boxes of granadoes. I fear you're going to need them.' Then he turned to Wyndham. 'Pond is commanded by a Sergeant. You'll be there for two, maybe three weeks. And when you leave the Sergeant will still be there and still be in command. It will be difficult for you but respect his authority, and he will respect your rank.' Then he turned to me. 'Both of you can learn from this man. He's an old sergeant. He's been here a long time. And he knows how to defend a fort.'

In the fort we found their spirits were low, close to morbid. They'd been there too long, been on duty four nights in seven, for weeks on end, and it had sapped their strength, and set them on edge. Despite needing us, needing a couple of nights of good sleep, I sensed they resented us, saw us as strangers, and there was a reluctance, almost a questioning of our competence before they would let me take over the first guard at six o'clock. Wyndham was to relieve me at ten and I was to relieve him at two; and at six in the morning the Sergeant's men were to take over again.

Pond Fort – some called it Pond Redoubt – took its name from a spring-fed pond that lay on the edge of the marshes, just a few yards to the south-west of the fort. In the summer the marshes dried out, became brick-hard, became deserts of cracked earth.

In the winter, in the wet months, they became the wetlands and they fed the stream that ran to Whitehall and Johnson's Battery.

From the roof of the fort, looking back to the city, looking due east, Catherine Gate lay eight hundred yards away. Looking in the opposite direction, looking due west, Fort Kendal lay two hundred yards away, on the heights beyond the stream. Looking to the north, towards the sea, lines of trenches and palisades boxed us into a narrow enclosure. The first hundred yards took us down to the bend in the stream, to the footbridge and the ruins of an old watermill, and then the next three hundred yards took us up to Charles Fort. Three hundred yards beyond Charles, my old friend Henrietta sat on the ridge of a hill looking like a cube of brown sugar that could be dissolved, could be washed away by the storms that come howling in from the sea. Anne Fort lay to the south, at the end of a single trenched line that spiked a dog-leg across the raw earth, and at four hundred yards it was out of range of the speaking trumpets.

Kendal was protected by two lines that flared out on either side like the wings of a bird. The tips of the wings floated free, floated in the moorlands. Charles protected the right-hand tip, but the left-hand tip was unprotected, and there was nothing to stop the Moors surrounding Kendal, and making straight for us – apart from the meanderings of the stream and the marshy ground that the rains of the last few days had sheeted with water.

The hills wore a soft bloom of green, and on the slopes from Peterborough Tower to Whitehall the old fig tree – the only tree within our lines – was looking brown, looking skeletal. As I watched the sun die, watched it colour the branches red, and then black, and wondered if I would see them go green in the spring and stay green in the summer when the grass browned, I was overtaken by a feeling of gloom, of pessimism.

I ordered my five men to load ten muskets, to slip them into the rack and have them ready, have them waiting. I made two men stand guard with their matches burning – made them keep the match below the parapet so the red glow would not provide the Moors with an aiming point – and I lit the match in the match box. But none of this eased my mind, and I ordered Lockhart to bring up two boxes of granadoes.

Then we loaded the cannon and covered it with tarred canvas.

The air was damp, and the sky was clear, and I was hoping for a moon, a full moon. But we were between the moons, in the cusp of darkness and by eight o'clock I couldn't see twenty feet and I felt trapped, felt like a midge floating in a sea of blackness, a blackness without feature, without shape. I began to think the air was full of ink, and I kept dipping my finger into it, pretending to write on the parapet, pretending to write the time away.

I thought of Sergeant Brandon with a pen in his hand, and I remembered the old phrase, the old saying, 'how the mighty have fallen'. I must confess I'd never expected to see him humbled, see him brought so low. There was no satisfaction in it. That was the strange thing. The other strange thing was that I found myself thinking about him, thinking what he'd do if he were in my shoes. And the weird thing, the thing that was beginning to annoy me was that I was doing what he would have done. And now, in his hour of defeat, I was beginning to respect the bloody man, and it was confusing me, confounding my sense of justice.

At nine o'clock I checked the four-hour glass – and was thinking how slow the sands of time run – when Kendal fired her cannon. It gave me a hell of a fright, made me jump in the air, and I almost fell off the bloody parapet. I ran to the bell, grabbed the rope and sounded the alarm.

Within thirty seconds, the men were thundering up the ladder, and twenty-four of us were milling around on the small roof, peering into the darkness, yelling at each. I expected Wyndham or the Pond Sergeant, to call us to order. But nothing happened. I yelled: 'Silence! Everybody shut up!' Then in a calmer voice, I said: 'Stand at the edge of the parapet. Stand right round. And don't make a sound. Listen. Listen for the Moors.' Then I said: 'Sir? Where are you?'

Wyndham came out of the darkness, hands outstretched, and he whispered: 'Christ. What are we going to do?'

The Pond Sergeant – he told me his name when we first arrived but I can't recall it at the moment – edged up to us and said: 'Nothing. We wait in silence. And we hope like bloody hell they don't attack us.'

Charles fired a cannon. And so did Anne. Muskets crackled and granadoes exploded around both forts. Far in the distance, on the edge of darkness, the edge of Barbary, Henrietta was ringed with flashes of fire.

The men in Kendal began to throw granadoes, to fire their muskets, to fill the night with a halo of fire. Then they fired their cannon, their falconette. In my mind I could see the ball tearing through the darkness like a fiery meteor, tearing long holes through the ranks of the Moors.

Then a musket fired, in the blackness close to us. A man screamed a foot from me, dropped his musket, and fell over the parapet. The Pond Sergeant yelled: 'Fire towards Kendal. And Anne. Fire downwards. Fire at anything that moves!'

We fired. Reloaded. Fired again. And again.

The flash of the muskets outlined the Moors. Hundreds of them, running straight towards us. Carrying ladders. Wide ladders. Long ladders. I pulled the lid off a box of short-fuse granadoes, grabbed a burning match and shoved it hard against a fuse. It flared, spat yellow sparks and clouds of smoke. I tossed it high in the air. It left a trail of sparks, like a shooting star, then it exploded and filled my head with bright light, burning light, light that died and made the darkness it left behind even darker than it had been a second or two before.

In the darkness, way below me, someone screamed.

The Pond Sergeant pulled the cannon round. Yelled: 'Get out of the bloody road!' and jabbed the burning match at the touchhole.

The cannon roared, seared us with light, hurled backwards, bucked against the ropes, thumped on the tar-stoned roof and filled my ears with a high-pitched ringing.

I banged my ears with both hands, grabbed Lockhart, blinked my eyes hard, and yelled: 'Get that other box of granadoes and a couple of our men! Toss them over the top of the palisade. Make them fall about twenty feet out from the bank. Then start throwing them further out.'

I pushed the other box at two men. 'Throw them as far as you can!'

I grabbed two more men. 'Bring up more granadoes!'

Then a shape was coming at us. Coming out of the darkness. Coming high. 'Christ!' I yelled. 'It's a ladder!' It was wide. And heavy. Too heavy to push backwards. 'Fire down! Fire down the ladder!'

I grabbed a couple of men. 'Get on this side! All on the same side. And push!'

It wouldn't bloody budge. I yelled: 'More men! More men on this side!' We pushed the ladder, pushed it the full length of the fort. Then it toppled sideways, toppled into the blackness. A man screamed. I grabbed a granado, dropped it straight down the side of the wall and turned away from the flash, away from the explosion.

For a moment I heard the silence, the silence of death. Then it was gone, was savaged by the cannon, by volleys of musket fire, by granadoes filling the air with red-hot blooms of rusted iron.

We loaded, fired and threw without thinking, without pausing.

I caught sight of Lockhart. He was laughing, was holding a flaming granado in his right hand and using it to light another one in his left hand.

I looked at the Pond Sergeant and shook my head. He laughed and yelled: 'If he's really quick he can light four at a time. But the only trouble is if he drops one we're all dead.' He shrieked with laughter. 'We need some nails! That's what we need.'

'Nails?'

'Yes. They'd cut a bloody great swath through these bastards. Better than granadoes. And they go further.' He laughed.

Then Kendal exploded. It lit up the sky. The noise rolled down the hill and belted our ears.

We stopped firing.

The Moors stopped firing. The silence was eerie, unnatural. Then they began to shriek. To whoop. To cheer.

I yelled: 'Keep firing!'

The cheers turned to screams, to howls of pain, to rage made manifest – then they began to fire at us again.

Kendal burnt like a furnace, like a bonfire, and it put a light behind the Moors. 'This is target practice!' I yelled. 'You can see what you're doing!'

We kept firing, kept throwing granadoes. We could see them retreating, moving back towards Kendal.

Lockhart grabbed my arm. 'Look!' He turned me to the right. In the distance, far beyond the cannon flashes and the musket sparkles that outlined Charles, another bonfire was burning.

'Christ,' I whispered, and went cold. 'That's Henrietta.'

An hour later as the sounds of battle began to die away from Anne and then from Charles, we heard whimpering, heard soft crying, coming from the darkness in front of us. 'It's a bloody trick,' the Pond Sergeant yelled. He loaded his cannon and fired into the darkness, into the whimpering.

Half an hour or so later, when the flames of Kendal were making a dull orange glow on the horizon, the Pond Sergeant called for silence. We heard shuffling. Dragging. It seemed to be retreating. 'Lift your fire,' he said. 'Fire at extreme range.

You won't hit anybody, unless you're bloody lucky. But you'll give them a bloody great boot up the bum.'

Towards midnight, he called for silence again. And this time we heard nothing.

We reloaded our muskets, brought up more granadoes, loaded the cannon, sat down, huddled into the parapet and waited for the dawn.

'I thought we'd have heard a column coming out of Catherine Gate by now,' Wyndham said.

'Not till morning, sir,' the Pond Sergeant said. 'It's too dark, too dangerous. The Moors might have got between us and the walls. They could be hiding in a dip right now, and you'd never know till you were right on top of them.'

He snorted. 'I still think Sir Palmes should risk it.'

'Depends on your attitude, sir.'

'Attitude?' I could hear the hackles rising in his voice.

'Yes, sir. We have a thousand men. If we're lucky. And the Moors are prepared to sacrifice a thousand men to capture a couple of forts. Sir Palmes can't afford to lose a couple of hundred men – assuming that's how many he sent out in a column, and that's about what he'd need to make sure they could defend themselves – so he won't do it. Till morning. When he can see what's happening.' Then he leant towards me and whispered in my ear: 'Is he always so bloody stupid?'

I laughed, whispered: 'Most of the time.'

He nodded, and for a long we sat in silence. My mind calmed, my heart stopped racing, and the smell of gunpowder cleared. Then he said: 'Is this your first time?'

'Yes.'

He reached out, patted my arm. 'You did well. Didn't lose your calm. Kept telling them what to do. Kept thinking ahead. That's good. Bloody good. Better than I did on my first time. I shit my breeches, I did. But then, we had fourteen dead that day. And today we've got two.'

'Two?'

'Hmm. One of mine and one of yours. They took him down below. He died about half an hour ago.'

In the dawn a dozen troopers rode out of the Forage Gate. A column of foot followed hard behind. Through the spyglass I could make out the blackened stump that was Henrietta. I watched them surround Henrietta, like mourners at a funeral, then they began to ride, to march towards Charles. Straight ahead of us Kendal sat burnt, broken, silent. The slopes were clean, were cleansed of the dead, the dying, the wounded. And all the scaling ladders had gone from our lines.

I turned to Wyndham. 'Sir. I think you and I should run to Charles. We could be there by the time the column arrives. And you could make your report, sir.' He nodded, told the Pond Sergeant he was in charge, told him to look after 'my men'.

The Pond Sergeant nodded and smiled, but as Wyndham turned the smile became a sneer, a piteous sneer.

We ran to Charles with our muskets in one hand, and arrived just as Captain Trelawny was coming out of the main gate. As Sir Palmes rode up and Captain Leslie's column doubled-marched up a moment later, Wyndham and I snapped to attention. Then Wyndham walked forward to report and I did not hear what he said. He came back three or four minutes later and said: 'Two are dead and eight are missing. He presumes they've been taken prisoner. He says the tactics are new. Long ladders. Wide enough to take four men at time. They get onto the roof, smash the tiles and drop a stinkpot inside. They've found a couple of long wooden forks that could have been used to drop stinkpots over the palisades. Or onto the roof. They've also found a couple of empty stinkpot shells in the ashes. They're round, about the size of a large granado. It looks as though they have two fuses and when they they hit the ground the shell breaks, and the combustion matter that's packed inside burns and fills the fort with smoke. Fumes. And if you don't get out right way you're dead. Suffocated.'

'Christ! A wooden fort wouldn't last ten minutes.'

He nodded. 'That's what Sir Palmes was saying.'

A few minutes later, Captain Trelawny granted us permission to join the column and we marched to Kendal.

We approached in silence. In reverence. 'I don't understand how the Moors could do this,' I said in a quiet voice. 'Seventeen, eighteen years, whatever it is, they never take a fort. And now they take two in one night.'

He nodded. 'They say the Turks are helping them. They think they learnt all these new ideas at the siege of Candia. And now the Moors are paying them to teach them.'

I looked into the blackened ruins. 'They taught them well. Too bloody well.'

As we mounted guard, looked up the empty slopes, looked towards the next ridge of hills – hiding the valleys where Sir Palmes thought the Moors would be waiting – we carried out the remains of ten men. Most were burnt to ashes: bones, fingers, hands that fell away, that clutched at nothing; feet that would walk no more; skulls that were like balls, empty balls with empty eyes, eyes that would look now upon the hosts of heaven, the armies of heaven, and know that for them, the battle was over – was lost.

Their falconette was gone, was dragged away, was destined – Captain Trelawny thought – to be a trophy, a symbol of triumph. A symbol of our defeat.

Sir Palmes confirmed our orders to stay at Pond, and he doubled the guard in every fort.

In the night we waited for the next attack, waited in the empty silence, the empty blackness. But the attack did not come, and the Moors did not return to Kendal or Henrietta.

Ensign Wyndham drew up a special roster and every second night every man mounted guard. It sapped our strength and sharpened our tempers. It made me think of sleep, made sleep the thing I most desired. And when I crawled into bed – still wearing my uniform – the straw felt warm, smelt of fart, smelt of another man's body.

The storms of January locked us into a cold wet prison, flooded the pond that gave our fort its name and linked it to the stream that lay a hundred yards away. The storms battered the Mole, tore great holes into the far end and ruptured some of the chests of stone – they'd been weakened by the first storms of winter – and they battered our spirits. They made us feel as if the forces of nature were conspiring with the Moors, conspiring to destroy everything we had built, had done to protect ourselves – for the rains that came with the storms, came after the storms, scoured the banks, filled the trenches with water and collapsed the palisades. They were doing more damage than the Moors had done, and we didn't have enough men to repair them, and day-by-day as we kept guard, we watched our lines become mounds of mud.

High on the horizon, Sir Palmes flung a guard around the ashes of Kendal and Henrietta and began to rebuild them. By the 1st of March they were bigger, higher, stronger, safer than ever before. They were models of what Sir Palmes said he'd like to do, if he had the money. But they did not fill us with confidence. And at night in my dreams, I saw the corpses of Kendal, saw them dance in the ashes of Pond – the wet ashes – and when I woke, Pond was still Pond, but my head was wrapped in gloom, in melancholy and even the thought of Devil's Drop being strengthened and Fountain Fort being repaired did not dispel the gloom. I was not alone in this. In truth we were all swathed in melancholy, and no one spoke of peace, the peace that would not come.

March ebbed into April and then into May and Lord Inchiquin came back without any extra men, and the number of men fit for guard, fit for duty fell to about eight hundred. The burghers began to fear for the future, fear for their lives. Some left Tangiers, some grew old and tired, and some grew indolent, and the number of men in the Militia dropped to about two hundred and sixty.

The Moors were forever testing our strength, testing our resolve. They laid an ambuscade in the grasslands beyond Fort Charles and murdered two soldiers while they were cutting grass. Then they laid an early morning

ambuscade in one of the quarries at Whitby, in Eastern Tower, where
Mister Sheres was blasting stone for his chests. And it was only by the
workings of chance, of fate, that the quarrymen stayed on the Mole that
morning – to help place a chest in the water – and only one man was
killed: a fisherman.

In June, when the heat was sending rivers of perspiration running
down my spine, Sir Palmes and Lady Fairbourne returned to England,
and I began a month on moleguard. The sea breeze was cool and the
new guardhouse in Fort Whitby Gate was in the shade, and to me it
was the best place in the whole garrison. I admit it was a dreadful place
in winter – freezing bloody cold and always drenched in rain and spray –
but June was the best month of the year and July was almost as good. Sir
Palmes had strengthened Fort Whitby Gate and from the sentry room on
top of the tower I often looked up to the windows of our old room in
York Castle and thought about the past, thought about O'Sullivan and
Trigg, and wondered if they wanted any help.

One night, early in August, I tried to forget my dislike of Brandon –
my confused dislike – and I wandered up to the Upper Castle. In January
the cold had puffed up Trigg's fingers and the warmth of summer had
not worked its annual magic, and now the pain was cramping his fingers,
cramping his spirits, and he was not in a mood to talk. O'Sullivan leant
against the back of his stool and moaned about the lack of work, the
lack of copying, then he lowered his voice and said: 'Inchiquin's a lazy
bastard. He keeps complaining about Sir Palmes spending all the money,
and using up all the supplies of war, and us needing another six hundred
men. But he never does anything about it, and sometimes I wonder why
the hell he ever came back.' He stared at a blank sheet of paper, then
he looked up and shrugged. It was a hopeless, helpless sort of a shrug.
'I'm sorry. There's nothing here for you to do. But you're welcome to
stay, welcome to chat.'

I looked at Brandon, looked at him hunched over my desk, pulled a
face, and shook my head.

Fragments of peace came and went. The lines decayed some more and
the joke about Lord Inchiquin only seeing half of what everyone else saw
– because of his one eye – began to lose its humour, began to take on the
hard ring of truth.

76

On the 3rd of April in the following year, 1679, after months of camping on the hills and setting ambuscades that sapped our patience, frayed our tempers and exposed our weaknesses, the Moors scorned our latest pleas for peace, and Captain Lacey warned us to expect an attack at any moment.

Rumour put the number of Moors at seven thousand and I couldn't help thinking if they all chose to attack Stream Fort at the same time, we'd last about ten minutes – if we were lucky. Stream Fort was my first command, sole command, and after two weeks I was beginning to get the feel of it. Lockhart was my corporal and we had ten men: pikemen masquerading as musketeers.

Stream Fort sat on the southern section of the lines, close to the banks of the stream that runs from Bellissis Fort to Fountain Fort and then out to sea. It was one of the wooden forts Sir Palmes had erected in one day. To begin with it was nothing more than a wooden box without a roof. Now the bottom half, to the level of the door was reinforced with Spanish bricks, and the parapet supported a pointed roof – clad with orange tiles. The two-foot gap between the roof and the parapet was protected by shutters that dropped down from inside the roof. The shutters were pierced with slits for our muskets, and round holes for the barrel of the cannon. The barrel was small and the carriage was high – it raised the barrel to crotch-height and made it easy to haul around – but it wasn't a cannon for a fort, it was a cannon for a saluting battery, for ceremonial salutes. It fired an iron ball that weighed less than half a pound. Captain Lacey told me it was 'bloody useless', and then he showed us how to make nail-shot. He took a dozen three-inch long nails, laid the sharp ends in the same direction, wrapped them in gauze and coated it with wax – to make them slide down the bore, make them fit tight.

As we watched him walk back to Catherine Gate, Lockhart pretended to wrap his cock in gauze and coat it with hot wax; pretended it would give him a tighter fit – next time he had one of the whores up by Irish Battery.

He thrust his hips backwards and forwards, closed his eyes and drifted away to a world of his own making – and we laughed at him, laughed at the dreamy look that softened his face.

Then we made a hundred nail-bombs.

Next day I heard the men calling them Lockharts, and the first time we drilled, rammed the nail-bomb down the bore, someone yelled: 'Lockhart's in tight!' It brought a burst, an explosion of laughter, and by the end of the day it became the signal, the sign that the cannon was loaded, was ready to fire.

Lockhart took this as a great compliment, and I put him in charge of the cannon, thinking it would calm his enthusiasm, but it had just the opposite effect. At least once a day I saw him with his legs astride the cannon, 'his cannon', and it made him look like a man rampant with excitement – and he knew it.

A line of palisades stretched from York Fort to the cliffs below Parson's Green, and it offered us a measure of protection. And so did Forts Bellissis, Fountain and York for they were all within two hundred yards: trumpet-speaking distance. Fort Cambridge and Irish Battery, on the heights of Parson's Green were both within two hundred yards and were well placed to bombard an attacking force. In the daytime it was impossible to mount a surprise attack on them, and they appeared to afford us a large measure of protection. But this was an illusion, a slight of hand, for some of the cannons were old, were in danger of blowing apart, and others needed new wooden carriages. And we were short of gunners, of men who could place a cannon shot in the midst of an attacking force.

When we raised the shutters the Bay spread before us. It was divided into two parts by Fountain Fort.

The left-hand part, the smaller part, ran over stony ground to the humped spine that linked Fountain to the cliffs below Parson's Green. Beyond the spine lay fifty yards of beach, a reef that had grown stilts to support a wooden fort, the waters of the Bay and the end of the Mole where Mister Sheres was about to make a corner, to turn to the right and begin the arm that would enclose two hundred yards of the Bay. Beyond the Mole, ships lay at anchor, and far beyond them the Straits opened into the Mediterranean. On the horizon, to the left of the Straits and half-hidden by the hills of Spain, sat the rock that caught the sunset: the Rock of Gibraltar.

The right-hand side ran for a mile or more, ran over low sandhills, over a long sweep of beach – darkened where our stream sank into the sand – over a bridge, over a river, and past the ruins of Old Tangiers. From here the Bay curved back towards us, made a crescent of green and narrowed the Straits, made the gap look like a tiny mouth, pressed thin, pressed straight by the weight of the sky.

It was a pleasant prospect. But when we turned round it was spoilt by the sandhills that reared into the sky. These were the hills – scalloped like a shell and scarred by shifting sand – where the Moors kept watch, day and night. They were so high, so close, they often made me feel as though I was sitting on the privy with the door open. Nothing was secret. Nothing could be kept hidden. And I knew, we all knew, if they dragged a big cannon up there and built a wooden base, a solid base, they'd have our range in fifteen minutes and they'd blow us to bits. And our wooden fort, our wooden box, would become our coffin, or our pyre if they used red-hot shot.

The night was still. The blues and the purples of the dusk had overwhelmed the colours of the day; and they in their turn had been overtaken by the black of the night: the shapeless cloak, the cloak of darkness.

At about nine we heard the first sounds of firing. They were faint and they were coming from our right, from somewhere high in the arc, in the rim of darkness that is protected by Monmouth, James and Anne.

We loaded our cannon and all our muskets, and waited.

About twenty minutes later, the speaking-trumpets passed a message from fort to fort. It came to us in English – the need for secrecy was gone – and it said: 'The main attack is at Anne. We think they're trying to break through the line between Anne and Pond.'

Lockhart passed the message on to Fountain, and a few seconds later I could hear them shouting it up to Cambridge. From there it would travel to Irish Battery, Catherine Gate and the Head Court of the Guard, and sometimes it would also be passed on to Johnson's Battery, Peterborough Tower, and Lord Inchiquin in the Upper Castle. It might also be coming in along another chain of forts. I was thinking about this, and about the dog-leg line between Anne and Pond, and the gates that allowed our troopers to patrol the grasslands, the gates that breached the line and created a weak point – a point that could not be manned at night – when the blackness erupted in front of us.

Musket balls smashed into the shutters and onto the tiles. It sounded like hail. Heavy hail.

I yelled: 'Fire!'

We shot into the blackness. Stepped back and reloaded.

Lockhart fired his cannon. Cut a swath in the darkness.

In the distance men screamed, tore holes in the swaddling of the night.

We cheered.

Someone yelled: 'Lockhart's in tight!' The smouldering match found the touchhole and the cannon fired, flashed away the night for a second and uncovered shapes, human shapes that were running towards us.

We fired our muskets again. I yelled: 'Keep firing! In your own time! Quick as you can!' I shoved up a shutter on the left-hand side. Grabbed a man. 'Toss granadoes over the palisade. Toss as many as you can. And scream if you see a ladder.'

More musket balls smashed into the front shutters and onto the roof.

Smoke filled the air. Bright flashes of light, caught my eyes, filled my head with stars.

I blinked hard. Slammed up a shutter on the right-hand side. Grabbed another man. And yelled: 'Lean right out and toss them as far as you can.' I pushed a burning granado into his hand. 'I'll light them. You throw them.' He was the best thrower in the whole company. The granado exploded in the air – twenty, thirty yards beyond the palisades.

Someone yelled 'Lockhart's up tight!'

Lockhart screamed: 'I'm killing the bastards!' Roared with laughter, with mad glee, and fired again.

I stuck my head out the side. Looked for ladders. Looked for long-forked poles bearing stinkpots.

We fired, loaded, screamed at each, screamed over the noise – it was like rolling thunder, non-stop hail.

Ten, twenty minutes later, I went cold. In the madness. The excitement. I hadn't noticed, hadn't heard. The hail had gone. The Moors weren't firing at us. 'Stop firing!' I screamed.

'Bloody hell!' Lockhart yelled 'They've run away.'

I heard muttering. Laughing. Giggling. Someone yelled: 'Lockhart's up tight!'

'Be quiet!' I yelled. 'Listen!'

I heard vague noises. Dragging. Shuffling. Crying.

I remembered the Pond Sergeant. Remembered what he did. 'Push up all the shutters. Lockhart! Aim for the sandhills. Everybody else aim high. I want long shots. Shots up their arse. You two on the granadoes, get back to your muskets.'

We blazed into the night, into the curtain of darkness. In the flashes I saw shapes moving, moving away. Three, maybe four minutes later, I yelled: 'Cease Firing! Reload! And wait for my command!'

Into the stench of silence, through the ringing in my ears, came the boom of cannons far to the right – somewhere near Charles and Henrietta.

The firing died around Fountain, Monmouth and James. Messages began to jump from fort to fort: two dead; four injured; line breached at James; Powel abandoned; Kendal still resisting.

Then a message said: Fort Palmes has been abandoned. Then the next message said it wasn't Palmes or Powel it was another fort – a small one, a wooden one – and we couldn't catch the name. The thought of a fort, a small fort, a wooden fort, a fort just like mine falling gave me the shakes, and it made me fart every couple of minutes.

An hour, maybe two hours later, the cannons were still booming way over by Charles and Henrietta. And every so often we could catch the faint crackle of muskets and the explosive thump of a granado.

'You know what I think?' Lockhart said. 'I think this was just a diversion.'

'A diversion?'

'Hmm. It didn't last longer than half an hour. They didn't bring any ladders or stinkpots. They just wanted to make sure we all stayed where we were. They made it look like a general attack and that means Lord Inchiquin wouldn't know where to send the reinforcements till it was too late.'

In the dawn, as the Moors dragged their dead away, Captain Lacey rushed ten men to our fort. They brought granadoes, lead balls, gunpowder, muskets and rumours – rumours that the two forts at Whitby had fallen and all the men were dead.

I ordered everybody to stay on watch for another two hours but there was nothing to see, nothing out of the ordinary: the Moors were going in and out of their tents on the sandhills; their fires were smoking; their spyglasses were glinting; and their banners – plain green and plain white – were flapping in the sunshine. And down on the reef, in the wooden fort that had become a lazaretto, a place of isolation, a place for men with infectious diseases, they were leaning over the wooden railing and dropping fishing lines into the water.

By ten o'clock the first of the watersellers was back at the stream, filling his pails with water, hitching the yoke onto his shoulders and beginning the long trudge back to Catherine Gate.

In the late afternoon Lieutenant de Colville arrived to take charge for the night and he confirmed the rumours, confirmed that Lockhart's suspicions had been right.

The first redoubt that had fallen was a low house with a stone tower – built after the landslide at Whitby – and it was defended by a sergeant and twenty-eight men. They say fifty or sixty Moors climbed onto the roof of the house and began to pull off the tiles. The men couldn't defend it, and fearing stinkpots they retreated into the tower, blew up the house and killed the Moors. They fought on for another hour. Then the Moors collapsed one of the walls of the tower. The eight survivors refused to surrender and the Moors hacked them to death.

The other redoubt was defended by Sergeant Heathley and twelve men. When they ran out of granadoes and lead balls, he ordered them to fight their way out, to fight their way to safety – with swords and pikes. But he didn't go with them, didn't try to save his own life. He stayed behind, blew up the fort: killed himself and forty Moors.

I could not put a face to his name, but I knew his wife, Mistress Mary Heathley. She was a friend, a bosom-friend of my lady in Rua de Carmo. Sometimes she cooked for her, and sometimes she cleaned for her, but most times they just sat and talked and warmed themselves beside the fire. She used to give me a smile, a knowing smile, when I left in the morning. I liked her, liked the things she gave me to eat. And now she is a widow, a relict, a woman on her own, a woman with no money, no means of support. Such women become whores, support themselves on their backs. It is a hard truth, a cruel truth, and Sergeant Heathley died for it.

At midnight I relieved de Colville and the men on his watch. It was cold and I was surprised when he stayed on for a while – leant beside me and watched the lights on the ships far out in the Bay – and I was thinking he must go down below soon, when he turned away from the blackness, away from the fireflies of light and said: 'I still miss you.' I pretended not to hear. Pretended to be absorbed by the darkness. 'I think of you every day. And at night, in the dark, when I'm alone in my bed, it feels empty, feels cold, and I want you.' Then he breathed a soft sigh and turned towards me. 'I don't think there'll ever be anyone else for me. Not now. Now that I know what it can be like.'

I gripped his arm. 'Sir. Please. Don't.' I felt his warmth through my fingers. The warmth that had warmed my body so often in the past, had fired my desires, and it set my heart racing. Then I was wanting him. Wanting everything we used to do. My breathing deepened, my thoughts scrambled, and I ran my fingers down the side of his face. The stubble prickled my fingers, prickled my memory, and in my mind I felt his stubble on my chest, on my belly, felt it, felt his mouth make for the land of honey. My cock roared into life. My balls tingled. And I quivered like a virgin on her wedding night.

Then a voice whispered: 'Excuse me, sir. Sergeant. I think I can hear something. Out there, to the left.'

The moment was destroyed, was broken. I closed my eyes, let the past sink into the pit of blackness – a blackness that should be weighted with stone and sealed with tarras and never felt, never embraced again if I am of a sane mind – and I said: 'Where did you say?'

I peered through the spyglass for three or four minutes. Then I saw it move, saw it stand up, and I laughed. It had four legs. I said: 'It's a dog. A stray dog. It's rubbing its belly, its balls on the ground.'

The voice laughed. And so did I.

De Colville muttered: 'The heat affects us all.' Then he leant on the parapet, leant in loneliness, and looked into the night.

In the weeks that followed the Moors came and went like mosquitoes with a taste for blood. I kept thinking they'd take Devil's Drop or Henrietta, or both, and close the quarries and bring the work on the Mole to a halt. But they had their own thoughts, their own plans, and week by week their numbers increased, and they pressed closer to our lines; and Mister Sheres continued to dump stone in the sea, to strengthen the end of the Mole.

In June the Moors granted us peace, for two months, but at the same time we were swept with rumours of war, of the French invading: they were known to have forty galleys lying at Gibraltar and we thought they were corresponding with the Moors. The prospect of fighting the Moors on the land, and the French on the sea, on the Mole, on the quay, on the beach below the coalyard, sent a wave of panic through the whole town. The foreigners left. And so did some of the merchants, and some of the townsmen – members of the Militia. They took their families with them. And their houses, gutted of all their goods, stripped of their doors and windows, and looking like tombs of stone, blighted every street. The price, the value of a lease, dropped by half.

Lord Inchiquin, stung to action, pleaded with London for more men, more provisions, more supplies of war. At the far end of the Mole, close to the new corner, he raised a small fort and installed a battery of cannon. And fearing the Moor's main attack would come along the road from Whitby, he strengthened Fort Whitby Gate and half-enclosed the last few yards of the road with palisades and small redoubts to channel the Moors into fields of crossfire. And fearing also that they might encircle Charles Fort and lay siege to it, he increased the fort's provisions, stockpiled enough to last five months, and built a 'sally-port, and a line of communication' from the Upper Castle to the fort.

None of this impressed my lady in Rua de Carmo. She knew some of the men were calling the line, 'a line of retreat', and she thought they were right. She began to fear for her life, for her possessions, and she told me she wasn't prepared, 'not at my age', to lie on her back for the Moors.

On the day before she was due to leave, to join the exodus, I knocked on her door. She opened the door and smiled. Then she hugged me and her eyes filled with tears. 'Come in,' she said. 'Come in.'

In the room I found Ives and six other young men. One was an ensign. I looked around the room and I knew, I knew at once, and I felt at home, felt as though we were born of the same flesh.

There was a shyness, a modesty amongst us. There was also a bond, a bond of brotherhood. I did not ask their names and they did not ask mine. And she did not offer to introduce us.

She smiled and said: 'Now all my boys are here.'

We sat and talked, ate a dish of artichoke hearts smothered in olive oil and vinegar, and we all knew we'd never sit with her again – or each other in a group – and it could have been a wake, a mourning for what was, for lost youth. But it was none of those things. It was more like a thanksgiving, a rejoicing that the rites of passage, her passage, had been given, had been shared by all of us.

When it was my turn to say 'goodbye', I kissed her on the cheeks, and the tears welled up in my eyes, and she said: 'You must find a woman. An older woman. A woman who will mother you. She will be good for you. And you will be good for her.'

As I walked down the road, turned my back on Rua de Carmo for the last time, I knew I did not want an older woman. I wanted a young woman. A woman of my own age. I wanted Jenny. I wanted to walk with her. To disturb the butterflies, the blue butterflies. To walk in clouds of blue. To sleep in clouds of blue.

I turned, looked up the lane, wiped my eyes, and began to walk towards the Little Parade.

77

The days of peace slipped through our fingers – were spent, were gone, like pennies from heaven – and the siege that was our way of life, way of being, took on the dross of death, and the war began again.

Night after night we retired into our forts, mounted guard and waited. When the dawn melted the alarms of the night and there was nothing to see, nothing to do, the day dragged, knotted my belly, left me feeling tense, tired. And when the night came round again I had to fight to keep my eyes open.

In the infirmarium men coughed and retched and fought the fevers of summer, and were fluxed of life; and in the burying ground the mounds of raw earth grew like mole hills.

The papers from England carried news of our plight, and they made it sound so simple: we needed more men, money, provisions and supplies of war. They were the things we had always needed – nothing had changed. And according to some men it never would.

It was strange to read about things I knew, things that were months out of date, were overtaken by other events. I said this to de Colville early one evening when we were together in Stream Fort – I don't remember the exact month, they were all compacting like layers of rocks and I was losing track of time – he grunted and said: 'I find it frustrating.' Then he opened a paper, folded it in half and pointed to a column. 'Read that.'

I read about the King proroguing, closing, Parliament on the 24th of May because it was about to pass a law that would have stripped the Duke of York – his brother and legitimate heir – of his rights of succession. The reason was simple, was rooted in the past: the Duke was a papist and Parliament did not want a papist on the throne. I thought it was a good idea and said: 'If I was a member of the House of Commons, I'd vote for that.'

'So you want the Duke of Monmouth – the King's oldest son, his bastard son – to be our next King.'

I looked at him, remembered his papist's hopes – papist pretensions – looked at the dusk that was laying purple over the ruins of Old Tangiers and said: 'I don't care who the King is. It'll never make much difference to me, so long as he's a Protestant.'

'But don't you agree that the succession should go from one person to another by legitimate descent?'

I shrugged. 'I suppose so.'

'Then the Duke's daughter, the Princess Mary, brought up as a Protestant – as you well know – should be the next Queen.'

'I don't like the thought of a woman.'

'And nor does Parliament – despite all their fond memories for Queen Elizabeth. And that's why they're talking about the Duke of Monmouth.'

I looked up to Fort Monmouth – symbol of our legitimate rights, legitimate interests here in Tangiers – and said: 'How long can he stop Parliament from meeting?'

He shrugged. 'Till he runs out of money I suppose. He can't raise taxes. Only Parliament can do that.'

'So one day, when he wants some more money, he'll have to agree to disinherit his own brother.'

'It's not that simple. The Duke has his supporters in the Commons and in the Lords. And despite Catholics being excluded from Parliament since last year's "Popish Plot" – in my heart I still don't believe any Catholics conspired to kill the King – he still has enough sympathisers to form a group, a sort of party, and they're calling them the Tories. It's a term of abuse, and it'll confirm all your worst thoughts, your worst feelings about the Irish.' He laughed. 'In Ireland, the tories are robbers, outlaws who prey on English settlers and soldiers. And now they're using the word to smear the Duke's supporters because he usually favours the Irish.'

'Because the Irish are papists?'

'Maybe.' He shrugged his shoulders. 'As a matter of interest, the so-called Tories, the opponents of the Exclusion Bill are also indulging in some abuse of their own: they're calling the bill's supporters Whigs. It implies they're dour calvinists, like the Scottish Covenanters.' He pulled a long face, a sour face. 'But to get back to the story: the longer the bill is delayed, the more hope there is that support for it will wither and die. And if proroguing Parliament helps, I'm in favour of it.'

'So that makes you a Tory. A sort of blood-brother to some of our Irish troops, Irish roughs.' And I roared with laughter.

'I don't wish to be related to the Irish.' His words carried a chill, and for a moment I thought I'd gone too far, been too impertinent, but then he laughed to himself and said: 'And that makes you a Whig.'

I didn't see myself as a Whig. But I smiled and let it pass. 'You haven't explained what you found so frustrating.'

'I'm praying for the Duke. Praying he will succeed one day. And it's frustrating to think that Parliament might have been recalled to send us more troops, more money—' I burst out laughing. 'Yes, I know' – and he pulled a face – 'but miracles do happen.' Then he smiled. 'The bill might have been passed already. And the Duke might be excluded by now. And my prayers might be wasted.'

I laughed. 'You're not going to run out of prayers. So it doesn't matter if you waste a few.'

He shoved me against the parapet. 'Don't be so bloody flippant.'

Then he was standing an inch or two away from me and I could feel the heat of his body. I put my hands up to my face, opened the palms, stretched my fingers and pretended to push him back.

'I'm sorry,' he said.

I eased myself away from him, away from the past, our past, and I wiped my brow and said: 'I wish it would cool down. The nights have been bloody hot lately. There's no air downstairs, no through-flow, and sometimes it's like a sweat-box and I've been having trouble sleeping. I tried sleeping up here once but I got eaten by bloody mosquitoes and my face came up in lumps and they itched for a week.'

He nodded, and for a moment we watched the four sentries peering into the darkness, then he said: 'I still think of those nights, those hot nights, when we lay together, lay naked on the sheets with the shutters wide open and . . .'

I bit my lips, picked up the spyglass, peered into the darkness and waited for the Moors, waited for the moths of the night to flutter towards our matches, our pinpoints of red light.

The months drifted on. The rains returned and they brought the cold with them. I was feeling low, feeling forgotten – all mention of Tangiers had drifted out of the papers I managed to see – and I was thinking about the Feast of Christmas when we received an unexpected gift: four new companies of men. It was like a miracle, a gift from on-high. It increased our strength to sixteen companies – none of them up to full strength, but that didn't matter. What mattered to me, to us, was that we could be relieved, and three months later, on New Year's Eve, I marched the company back to Catherine Gate, up Castle Hill, and into our new quarters in the Upper Castle.

Twenty minutes later Captain Lacey called me into his room and said: 'Tomorrow morning Ensign Wyndham is to be married in the Garrison Church. I've promised to provide a guard of honour when they come out of the church. So tonight, every man is confined to quarters. Make sure they all have a wash and a shave. And see they cut their hair and clean their uniforms. And polish their shoes. I'd like to think they could all look spick and span, but I know that's not possible at the moment. So I want every man to look clean, look neat. And I'll settle for that.' He paused. 'You can tell them they can have the whole day off, after the wedding, and they can celebrate the New Year then. I don't want anybody drinking tonight, and I don't want anyone drunk on parade tomorrow morning.' He stared into my eyes. 'Do I make myself clear?'

'Yes, sir.' I knew the men would be bloody annoyed. They'd been thinking about tonight, about getting drunk, for almost two weeks. It'd been the sole topic of conversation – once they'd walked their minds up to Irish Battery and had a woman – and the thought of having to give it up for Wyndham to have a woman, would be like tossing a granado into the room and shutting the door. It would blow them to bloody bits. I sighed to myself and said: 'Who is he going to marry?'

'A girl from the Little Parade. I don't know if you know her or not. I don't. He says her name is Bartholomew, Mistress Jenny Bartholomew.'

My mind went blank, went white, and filled with clouds of blue butterflies. Then the butterflies died, went black, filled my mind with clouds of black – black flutterings – and I do not remember any more of that day.

78

Next day – New Year's Day, the 25th March 1680 – as we waited for them to come out of the church, waited for them to pass through the porch, through the old mosaics, the mosaics of bathing, of cleansing, my mind was crusted with bitterness. I'd done what I had to do – and like our muskets with their plug bayonets, we looked hard, looked sharp – but I could not bring myself to think of him opening her legs, lying on top of her, making his flesh go hard, go where mine longed to go.

I remembered seeing him once with his breeches down – seeing his cock. Tiny, miserable little thing it was. And I remembered the jokes about it, the sly jokes: about it being too small and him not knowing what to do with it. They were wrong. Bloody wrong. He did know.

And if he didn't know she'd teach him. She'd show him her tits, her painted tits, and she'd play with his balls. Play the games of love.

And his fingers would part her hairs, make her moist, make her wet with desire, wet with wanting. And his belly would rub against her soft white belly. And his spotty little bum would bounce up and down and the long siege would be over. Virginity would fall. Blood would be shed. And that wretched little thing of his would fire a victory salute: one-gun, two-gun, three-gun – as many as he bloody liked, as many as he could manage.

And my cock would hang limp, hang dead.

I closed my eyes tight, clenched my fingers around the shaft of my halberd. The sun had heated the wood. It felt hot, felt hard, felt like my cock should feel – if I was standing in his shoes.

Then I couldn't bare the thought of it, the thought of him, doing what I should be doing and I booted the cobbles. But the side of my foot hit the side of my halberd, bounced it in the air, made it swing to the right, made it clatter on the cobbles.

Sergeant Owen looked at me and whispered: 'What the hell's wrong with you?'

I felt so low, so down, I blurted out the truth: 'She's marrying the wrong man.'

'Who should she be marrying?'

I looked at the ground and bit my lips.

He reached over, pulled my face towards his. 'Oh dear,' he whispered. 'Oh dear, oh dear.' Then he paused. 'Tonight, I think we're going to have to get you stinking rotten drunk. And tomorrow when you wake up you'll feel so bloody sick you won't be able to think about her.'

I watched her come out of the church, watched her white face drained of passion, drained of excitement, drained of the blush, the flush of pleasure.

I watched her father – withered now like the dry plants he keeps in his glass bottles – and I hoped the bastard was satisfied, hoped he'd got his price, his mattress of money.

I watched Wyndham, watched him standing beside her: pink-faced, spotty, wet-eyed and flush with excitement. I looked at his breeches, his flat empty breeches, and I couldn't imagine why she would want to take them off. To have a thing like that, when she could have had me, had mine, had the joys that used to make my lady in Rua de Carmo moan in the night, was against reason, against the desires of the flesh – the desires that should have drawn us together.

Then I began to think this marriage might be the price of ignorance. Or innocence. Or virginity. Whatever it was, it was bloody unfair, and it made me want to scream, want to pull down my breeches and show her what she could have had – if she'd had the courage to defy her father, to lie with me in carnal meadows and feel the butterflies, the blue butterflies that would have made her tummy tremble.

Afterwards, when the clapping had died away and the wind was stirring the showers of pink petals, blowing them into the gaps between the cobbles, de Colville said to me: 'That girl hasn't got a thought in her sweet little head. In a month's time when the novelty's worn off it will be like having a sack of flour. And they won't have anything to talk about.' He paused and smiled at me. 'That's what I used to like about you and me: afterwards. When we'd lie there – all sleepy and tired – and talk freely. With no inhibitions. No false posturing. I miss it. And I miss you. And I want you back.'

Then he walked away with long slow strides, sensual strides.

79

An hour later, in a haze of tobacco smoke, Sergeant Owen and I settled ourselves into The Broken Crutch: a small tavern in Avares Street, just behind St John's Square. It was run, as its name suggests, by an old soldier with a gammy leg, and he'd nailed his old crutch, his broken crutch above the fire. The fire was dead and we were counting our money, wondering if we could get anything to eat – anything hot – when the deep boom of the great cannon thundered through the room. Then the great bell in Peterborough Tower began to toll, began to signal the general alarm.

Owen slammed his tankard on the table. 'Bloody hell! What a way to start the New Year.'

I downed my beer, grabbed my halberd, and hurled out the door.

As we ran through the Market Place, ran with thirty or forty other men, I yelled to him: 'Do think Wyndham was hard up her when the cannon fired?'

He laughed. 'The cannon would have been like a shot up his bum. He would have exploded with fright. And thought his balls had been blown off.' And he laughed some more. Then his laughing turned to puffing, to panting, and he slowed to a trot and then to a walk. He waved me on. 'Go on. Go on. I'll catch my breath. And I'll be there in a moment.'

I ran through the Upper Castle – ran past the burghers, the townsmen, assembling on Stayner's Battery – ran up the steps and onto the great bastion that supports Peterborough Tower.

In the distance the Moors were gathering in their thousands – on foot and horseback. Then they began to encircle Henrietta and Charles. I could see spades flashing in the air and picks swinging arcs, catching the glint of the sun. Within a few minutes they began to raise mounds of earth. Henrietta and Charles opened fire with muskets and cannons. The Moors did not reply. They kept on digging.

Owen came up the steps, took one look, and said: 'Christ! The bastards are serious this time. Look at all those boards, the size of doors. And those bundles of straw – they must have been saving it for months.'

We watched the Moors mount the boards and the bundles on the mounds of earth. I couldn't hear the musket balls hitting the wood, lodging in the bundles of straw, but I could imagine the sound. It disturbed me, for this looked like a new form of warfare – no that's not true, it looked old, as old as the Romans – but it was new to the Moors, new to us. It felt ominous, felt like the start of the long-awaited attempt to besiege our two strongest forts: Charles, and Pole which some of the old soldiers still called Catherine.

At the moment Pole was safe. Close-up it was protected by Norwood, Bellissis and Bridges. But at the outermost lines, on the great arc that was guarded by Monmouth, James, Anne and Pond, and formed Pole's first line of defence, the Moors were edging closer. But here they were not digging. They were not entrenching, not preparing for a long siege.

Wyndham came panting onto the bastion, sweating and looking red-faced. Lockhart grinned at me, and yelled, in a voice that carried: 'You look fucked, sir!'

A spluttering of giggles ran along the bastion. Wyndham glared at him. It was a murderous glare, full of hate, full of daggers. Lockhart ignored it and yelled: 'From the running, sir. All that jogging up and down. They say it fucks you. If you're not fit. If it's your first time.' The bastion roared with laughter.

Wyndham – to his credit – smiled, then he laughed. But a few minutes later I overheard him say to Lockhart: 'Next time I'm looking for a volunteer, someone with verbal flux, I'll know who to pick. Won't I?'

I smiled to myself, and watched Lord Inchiquin and the members of his train, his staff, huddle, talk, and point. About twenty minutes later Captain St John double-marched his company – one lieutenant, one ensign, and seventy men – out the sallyport, along the communication line and into Charles Fort.

For the rest of the day the Moors dug trenches, and the men in Charles and Henrietta showered them with a hail of lead and red-hot iron.

Towards dusk we returned to our quarters, drank to Crabtree's version of married life, 'lots of little cock-ups', and fell into bed at midnight. My body was dead drunk, but my mind was fresh, was bright with life, was cold sober. It kept me awake, kept me wondering about the Moors in the trenches.

The dawn uncovered a night of work. The Moors were now entrenched between Charles and Henrietta – and from here they had dug a line back to Teviot Hill, the site of their old lines. They were also entrenched from Kendal to Pond, were close to the stockades, 'within a cast of a granado'. At Charles they were 'within half a musket shot'. But the trenches were too deep for musket shot, and the diggers were safe – apart from the granadoes that our men could launch from the mortar at Charles – and they continued to dig. On the 28th, the Sunday, we woke to find they'd cut the communication lines between Henrietta and Charles, and dug a trench from Pond to the foot of a little hill that lay close to Charles.

Captain Trelawny – the Captain commanding Charles and Henrietta – ripped out some of the large beams inside Charles and built a wooden tower, a 'cavalier'. It could hold nine men, and it altered the angle of sight, and hour after hour his men poured fire deep into the trenches. By day this hindered the digging but at night it went on – we could hear them when the air was still and their shovels or picks struck a rock – and in the morning the trenches had grown a little more. And so too had the mounds of stone, the blinds, they were now building to protect the trenches.

On the last day of the month, about an hour before I was due to go off guard at four o'clock, the Moors began to beat their great drum, 'to beat it like a cooper on a tub', and they planted eight flags in their trenches: three red, one green, and four with yellow stripes. In one sense they were colourful, gaiety flapping in the wind. In another sense they were an affront, an insult to Christian dignity, an insufferable arrogance – like claiming victory before the battle had begun.

The flags and the beating enraged Captain Trelawny. He turned his fire on the flags: shot down the green one, and was rewarded with loud bursts of cheering that echoed along the full length of our walls. Then his muskets tore holes in another flag, and the Moors pulled down the rest. It was a victory of lead over cloth. It lifted our spirits but there was no substance in it, no reality, and it altered nothing.

A few days later four companies of Lord Dunbarton's Regiment – Scotsmen in skirts – disembarked, and half the town rushed down to the Mole, lined the streets and clapped them into the Market Place. Lord Inchiquin inspected them in front of the Head Court of the Guard, pursed his lips at their infirmities, their hairy knees, their blankets – they were draped over their shoulders, were making them look like shawled women with beards – and called for 'three cheers'. That night we began to feel that we were not forgotten, not alone, not cast adrift from an England that often thought – if the papers could be trusted to convey the truth – that we were nothing more than a 'nursery for popery', and our fall might be 'in accordance with the will of Almighty God'.

The trenches began to curve around both sides of Charles, and on the afternoon of April the 8th, the day Sir Palmes Fairborne returned to take command of the regiment – and was greeted with delight, for he was possessed of a vigour, a strength of purpose, that had long departed Lord Inchiquin – the Moors cut through our lines of communication. On the following day the two arms of the trenches joined up. Charles was encircled. Henrietta was encircled. Both were isolated from us, and from each other. And Devil's Drop – out of sight, out of mind – was also isolated, but it had one advantage: it could be relieved from the sea, if Admiral Herbert was of a mind to risk his ships, risk his men.

The next day, Easter Sunday, a day that did not see the resurrection of our spirits, Captain Lacey cancelled the services for our company and ordered us to maintain the guard at full strength. He sent me up Peterborough Tower with a spyglass, and I could see the Moors had dug three separate trenches around both forts. The deepest looked to be about twenty feet and all of them were joined together. From the innermost trench, more trenches were making straight for the forts. These trenches looked like the spokes on a wheel: spokes that would soon lock into the fort, the hub, and squeeze it tight. Inside the trenches at Henrietta, the Moors were building wooden towers – fighting galleries – and they looked to be on wheels, looked as though they could be pushed along the spokes, pushed hard against the walls of the fort.

Two hundred and forty men were protecting the two forts. I knew they must be packed in tight, like salted herrings in a barrel, and they must have smelt like herrings that had been left in the sunshine for a couple of hours – for both forts were battened down tight. I couldn't see a single man, but I could see the flashes of light, see the granadoes exploding, and I could hear the thump of the mortar and the crackle, the endless crackle of their muskets.

As the day dragged through the heat of the afternoon, I saw myself in Henrietta. I saw the sweat running down the insides of the walls, felt it running down my back. I knew the air would be still, knew it needed the door wide open to create a draught. And I knew the air would be white, would be heavy with gunpowder, with the smell of sulphur and burning matches. I could see myself with my coat off, watching, waiting, firing when I saw the slightest movement. And knew my eyes would be watering, and I'd be coughing, choking, spluttering as the smell burnt its way into my nose, my throat, my lungs, and my belly – when it sauced the beef, the pease, that lay on my plate.

About eight o'clock, as the dark was beginning to mask the movements of the Moors, the air stilled, and the speaking trumpets relayed a message from Henrietta. I don't know what it said – it was in Irish because of the renegades who were known to be helping the Moors – but a few seconds later when the Moors attacked Henrietta, I guessed it was a warning.

The attack raged before our eyes, our impotent eyes, till about three o'clock in the morning. I thought I could see the galleries close to Henrietta, but I wasn't up the tower and I didn't have a glass, and the night was dark, and the firing, the flashes, from Charles masked my view.

The dawn brought our first sight, our first taste of victory. At Henrietta the galleries stood close to the walls. But the roof was intact. The Moors hadn't been able to break through, to drop stinkpots into the fort. But they had brought up long beams, propped them against the walls, covered them with faggots and straw and tried to tunnel under the walls, to lay a mine and bring them down. But they hadn't reckoned on the walls being fourteen feet thick: four of stone and brick, and ten of earth.

Five men ran down the walls on ropes and pulled away the beams, the faggots and the scaling ladders, and piled them against the galleries. A few minutes later when the men had been pulled back in the fort and the hail of covering fire had died away, they threw down fireballs. The galleries burnt like ancient funeral pyres, and when the smoke cleared, when the bodies of the fires was no more than heaps of red-hot ash, we saw a long pole sticking out from the top of Henrietta.

Two heads, the heads of brown-faced Moors, hung from the end of the pole.

Over the next few days the Moors changed the thrust of the siege: attack became defence, became containment. They extended their trenches, dug through the graves at the top end of the burying ground at Whitby and cut off the avenues, the approaches that could be used to mount a rescue.

Sir Palmes planted palisades around the revetments below Peterborough Tower, created a safe enclosure that could be used to assemble troops to mount a rescue or support a breakout. And we speculated that the Moors had gone underground: were digging tunnels under the walls of both forts and preparing to lay mines.

On the line guarded by Pond, Anne and James, there was no need to speculate: we could see the Moors and we could hear them. They were attacking – night after night – and it was obvious they wanted to break through the lines and lay siege to Fort Pole. This fort was the key to our whole system of defence. It sat on the high ground and it guarded the approach to the main gate: Catherine Gate. If it fell, we fell. It was as simple as that. For the hard truth, the truth that nobody wanted to face, was that the city walls had been neglected, been allowed to decay, to crumble, and what looked strong was not strong, and could not withstand a siege of more than two or three months. And so we were committed to fighting in the forts, to holding the forts, if we wished to hold Tangiers.

Sir Palmes strengthened Pole by covering the walkway that linked it to Norwood Redoubt, and he restored the lines that Lord Inchiquin had permitted, through indolence or lack of money, to fall into ruin.

The smaller forts – Stream, Sandhill, Palmes, Powel, and half a dozen others that never merited a name – were now bearing the brunt of the attack: night after night. Most of them were sighted within the arc of fire of a stronger fort and in theory they were supposed to strengthen the line and be protected by the stronger fort. In a moderate attack spread evenly along the line the theory held true. But when the Moors attacked the stronger fort with a large force, it was unable to help the small fort – it had to protect itself first, it had to survive the onslaught. In effect the small fort was isolated, was left on its own. And when the Moors brought up another force – often a larger force – and attacked the small fort, it could be overwhelmed. Two were abandoned: the men took fright and ran away. One was burnt down. Another was lost in the night and recaptured in the morning. And now Sir Palmes was asking for volunteers, for men who were prepared to hold the fort, prepared to die, if need be.

Late in the night, four or five hours after I first heard about this, I turned to Owen – our friendship was entering into the beery haze that solicits secrets – and said: 'You'd have to be fucking mad, bloody crazy, to volunteer for something like that.'

'Hmm,' he said. 'Depends.'

'Depends. What do you mean depends?'

'Depends if you want to live or die.'

'I can't imagine wanting to die.'

'That's because you're young, and healthy. And you could live for another twenty years. But when you're old like me – thirty-six – and you've done a lot of hard living' – he smiled into his mug of black beer – 'it doesn't matter any more.'

'You're wrong. It always matters. And I'd never want to volunteer. Not for that.'

'Don't be too sure. Sometimes life can be so hard, so cruel, so bloody unfair, you don't want any more of it. And you don't care what happens – don't give a fuck.'

I looked into his eyes – bleary now with sleep and drink – and shook my head.

About ten days later, as I was walking back from the Watergate and thinking about the siege – the Moors were still entrenched around Charles and Henrietta, and still attacking the outermost forts every night – I saw Mister Tate sitting on the steps to the Misericordia. He was holding his head in both hands and blood was seeping through his fingers.

I rushed over to him and tapped him on the arm. 'Are you all right.'

He blinked at me. His eyes looked empty, looked dead. Blood was pouring from his scalp, matting his white hair and running down his face. He looked at his fingers and sucked the blood off them, sucked them clean – one by one. I put my hands under his arms and helped him to his feet. 'They pushed me,' he said. 'Pushed me down the steps.'

'Who pushed you?'

'They did.'

'Who did?'

'They did,' and he pointed to the convent.

A woman came up to me, shook her head, and said: 'No one pushed him. I saw him fall. It happens all the time. He preaches with his eyes shut. Says it helps him to see the Lord. Sometimes he throws his arms in the air and runs along the step, that top step. And sometimes he forgets to open his eyes and falls off the end. And other times he throws his arms around so much he loses his balance.' She gave me a smile, a sad smile. 'And I'm tired of taking him home.'

'I can take him,' I said. I looked into his hair. The gash was about two inches long.

'He'll need some stitches in that,' she said. 'She'll stitch him up. She's done it before she has.'

'Who has?'

'His wife, poor thing. How she puts up with him I don't know. But then we all have our cross to bear don't we.' She pulled at the white apron that covered the front of her skirt, straightened an edge that was already straight. 'You'll need to tie something around his head, to staunch the flow. That white scarf of yours. That would be ideal.'

I undid the knot and tied my scarf around his head, and two or three seconds later red flowers began to bud, to unfold, to come into full bloom.

I pulled his hat over the scarf, pulled it down tight. 'I'm going to take you home.'

'I live at St John's. The church of St John. That's where I live now.'

The woman shook her head. 'He's still up there in St Barbara's Street. Do you know where he lives?'

'Hmm. I helped to repair the chapel, when he first arrived.'

'He should never have come. All he does is cause trouble. And upset the Fathers.' She leant towards him, put her face right up to his and yelled: 'Goodbye Mister Tate! This nice sergeant is going to take you home!'

I took his arm and guided him up the Market Place. When we came to the fountain he began to pull away, to try to walk towards St John's Street. I took a firmer grip and said: 'This is the right way.' He shuffled to a halt and looked at me. I smiled and it seemed to reassure him, then we walked to the top of the Market Place. When we came to St Barbara's Street, he appeared to know where he was. He shook off my hand and strode on ahead. He looked so confident, so full of purpose, I thought he had no need of me, thought my task was finished, when he stopped, turned round and looked back. I don't think he was looking at me. He was just looking, looking in wonderment. I walked up to him.

He blinked and said: 'Who are you?'

'Sergeant Fenton.'

He shook his head. 'I don't know you. Why are you talking to me?'

'I'm taking you home.'

'Home? I don't live here.' He looked up and down the street. 'I live in St John's Square. In the church.'

I gripped his arm. 'Then we can walk this way, walk down the street.'

He smiled at me. A second or two later I knocked on his door. He looked at the door, looked at me and said: 'This is my door. We don't have to knock on my door.' He slid the latch and walked in.

I took off my hat, followed him in, and laid my halberd on the floor. Mistress Tate hurried down the stairs holding up the front of her skirts. She looked from him to me and said: 'What's wrong? What's happened?'

I told her about the accident, about bringing him home, and needing stitches. She sighed to herself and kissed him on the cheek. 'Would you mind helping me?' she said. 'Usually I ask Mistress Westcombe but she's not well, and I can't do it on my own. He's too strong for me.'

I helped him up the stairs, took off his coat and his shoes and made him lie on the bed. It was a large bed, a marital bed covered in white linen, and wreathed with muslin to keep out the mosquitoes. I was thinking about the bed, thinking about her lying on it, lying naked, lying with her legs spread wide open, when she said: 'You won't be able to hold him down. You'll have to sit on his chest and use your legs and your bottom, to pin his arms down. And you'll have to hold his head with both hands.'

I sat on him, sat with my head in the muslin, and he smiled at me. She drew the two flaps of his scalp together and pushed the needle through them.

He yelped like a puppy and she made soothing noises, cooing noises, close to his ear and this calmed him. Then she tied a knot, patted his scalp flat and checked that the two flaps were lying edge to edge, would knit together. She smiled at her needlework, smiled at me, put in another stitch and then another, and I relaxed my grip – there was no fight, no resistance in the man. She pushed the needle in for the next stitch and he threw his head forward and brushed his scalp against her white blouse. I pushed him back down, held him tight, and saw her blouse, saw it was smeared with blood. The blouse was embroidered with tiny white flowers and white crosses, grouped in clusters, like stars. The blood was colouring the flowers, was making them red, was making me remember that first night when I fell down the stairs on the ship and she held me to her bosom and I bled, bled into her nightshirt and speckled the flowers with red. I remembered her smell, the sweet smell of summer flowers. And I remembered the closeness, the warmth, the softness of her bosom. And I wanted her.

I reached out and touched the flowers, the flowers that touched the stars and she jabbed me with her needle. I yelled with surprise, yelled like a boy stung by a bee, and I sucked at my finger. Mister Tate smiled at me with dreamy eyes, eyes of trust.

When his scalp was stitched and flattened, she washed his face and hands, and washed the blood out of his hair. Then she laid a cloth under his head and covered him with a blanket. She pulled the curtains across, changed day to night, and when she saw his eyes were closing, she pointed to the door and we crept out of the room.

Downstairs she washed my scarf and hung it on a rail close to the fire. Then she dried her hands, looked at me, and burst into tears. I took her into my arms, held her tight, and felt the soft curves of her body. 'Some days,' she said, 'I don't know what to do. Some days he's like a child. Some days he doesn't know me. Tells me to get out of the house. Tells me I don't belong here. Tells me he isn't married. Other days he knows who I am, and he calls me names. Vile names. Cruel names.' She sniffed, wiped at her nose. 'I'm sorry I shouldn't be telling you my troubles, should I?' She wriggled, tried to free herself.

But I didn't want to let her go. I wanted to comfort her. To be kind. To be tender. To be loving. I kissed her forehead, smiled into her eyes and held her tight. I felt her warmth. I ran my fingers over her neck, over her shoulders, down her back, round her bottom and back up the knobbles of her spine. We began to sway. I wanted her. I wanted her more than I'd ever wanted anybody in my whole life. I reached down, ran my hand under her skirts, up her leg and felt the softness of her hair, felt the warmth of her cleft, the wetness of her netherlands. 'No,' she said. 'No.'

I kissed her lips and she bit my lips. I tasted blood, tasted passion, tasted madness. I had to have her. I had to make her mine. The thought inflamed my mind, inflamed my body, and made me into an animal, a rabid animal.

I stepped out of my shoes, pulled down my breeches and eased her against a chest of drawers. I lifted her skirts, spread her legs and entered the wetlands, the lands of lust, the lands I had desired in my secret heart for so long.

For a moment I was filled with the most incredible feeling of satisfaction, of accomplishment. It was as if my whole life had come to a climax, had been waiting for this moment, this bonding of bodies. I took her face in my hands, looked into her eyes, into her pools of darkness, thrust once, thrust twice, thrust my whole being deep into her body and exploded.

She shuddered, grabbed at my arms and held me tight.

I kissed her forehead, smelt her perfume, smelt the faint whiff of roses, of summer love, of gentle days and gentle nights.

Then she screamed in my ear, pummelled my back, scratched my head, my face, tried to throw me off. I held on, held tight, pushed her hard against the chest of drawers. She kicked my legs, banged me with her knees. I bent down and bit her neck, and every time she hit me I bit her.

She burst into tears. Her crying, her fighting, hardened my desire – made it grow deep within her body – and I began to stir, to walk again in the wetlands. My steps were slow, deliberate, like those of a man setting out on a long journey, and I wanted her to come with me, to explode with delight, to shudder with pleasure. But there was a coldness, a chill on the wetlands, and my snowflakes fell in silence – like the first gentle flakes of winter.

In the frozen snow-blinding calm that followed she settled her skirts and knelt in front of the fire. I sat on the seat, a foot or two away from her. We stayed like that for twenty or thirty minutes. Then I knelt in front of her, ran my arm round her shoulder, laid my face in her bosom and burst into tears. 'I'm sorry,' I whispered in her ear. 'I'm so sorry.'

I helped her to her feet, tried to wrap my arms around her, tried to seek her forgiveness. But she pushed me away. Then she picked up my shoes and breeches, pulled my scarf off the rail, shoved them into my hands and said: 'Get out! And don't ever come back.'

That night I walked the streets alone in black despair. I hated her and I hated myself. Deep in my heart I knew what I had done but I could not bring myself to form the word – even in my mind. I can remember shivering, can remember sitting on the walls, can remember leaning over the parapet, looking into the blackness, looking at the rocks far below, and wanting to topple, wanting to fall head-first, wanting to be swept out to sea. To be dead. To be gone. To be no more.

The dawn uncovered the rocks far below: they edged the strand, close to the new redoubt. I could see myself lying on the rocks, waiting for the storm that would sweep them clean. My head was matted with blood; my coat was patched with stains, was gaudy with gold; my breeches were torn – sea-green waiting to return to the sea. My stockings were white, were imprinted with brown toes, brown soles. And my shoes were lying on their own, dead, like black gulls that would fly no more.

My life was spent. Was done. Was over. It was time to die.

I looked at the redoubt. Like all redoubts it lay in the shadow of a stronger fort – in this case Three-gun Battery – and it made me think of the small forts: the forts on the lines, the forts that were under attack, the forts that needed more men, men who were prepared to die.

There would be no glory in it. No honour. No recompense.

There would be oblation. Sacrifice. Atonement.

It would be private. Secret. Known but to God. And that would be right, just, proper.

I prayed that death would bring forgiveness.

Then the sun rose. The rays were yellow, bright yellow like butter that is full of sunshine. They filled my mind, expelled the black of the night, the gloom of the dawn, and I swam in a sea of yellow. Then the yellow took shape, took form, became a mass of tiny yellow flowers swaying in the wind. They formed themselves into fields, squares of bright yellow, and they nestled among the fields of green and quilted the land. I could smell them, could smell the smell that reminded me of cabbages. But they weren't cabbages. They were being grown for their seed, for the oil in their seed, for the wild seed that was called: rape.

I leant over the parapet. My head spun, my belly heaved and I vomited.

That afternoon I walked down to the armouries in York Castle and drew four boxes of granadoes, three boxes of lead balls, forty feet of match – cut into two-foot lengths, twelve barrels of coarse gunpowder, and one barrel of fine gunpowder. As I was about to leave, two cuirasses with backplates and leather straps caught my eye. They were hanging from pegs halfway up the brick wall at the back of the cellar and they were covered with cobwebs. I lifted one down. It was heavy, but not as heavy as I remembered. I wiped away the cobwebs, wiped away layers of dust, and yelled to the armourer: 'Can I have these?'

He stared at me for a moment. 'What the hell for?'

'If we can't get out, if we have to fight to the death, they might keep us alive for another hour or two. Might help us kill a few more of the bastards.'

He shrugged his shoulders. 'Make sure you take them off if you have to run for it. They'll slow you down too much if you leave them on. And when you bring them back, wash the blood off first, will you.'

In the morning when I knocked on Captain Lacey's door and told him I wanted to volunteer, to command a small fort, a fort that could fall at any moment, he sat back in his chair and looked at me for a long time. Then he said: 'Has this anything to do with Sergeant Brandon or Lieutenant de Colville?'

It sickened me to think he knew enough to couple them to me. I bit the insides of my mouth and shook my head. 'Or Jenny Bartholomew – Mistress Wyndham?' I shook my head again, kept my eyes fixed on the black surface of his table, and wondered who the hell had been whispering in his bloody ear.

Lockhart volunteered the moment I asked him. And so did Powel, and that surprised me. And so did ten other men from our company – six pikemen and four musketeers – and that surprised me even more.

I thought we'd have to wait a couple of days, but soon after midday Captain Lacey called me back to his room and said the men in Sandhill Fort – between Anne and James – were very low, 'dispirited' is the word he used, and he didn't think they could hold out for another night. I told him we'd be ready to leave in an hour. He mumbled, 'good', then he said he was still hoping to find some volunteers for Anne.

For a moment I didn't realise what he'd said, but then it sank in and I said: 'Christ! You're looking for volunteers for Anne, for a proper fort?'

He nodded. 'It could fall tonight. Or tomorrow. Or the night after. It won't last much longer than that.'

'Shit.' The word rushed out of my mouth without thinking – I hadn't realised the situation was so bad. 'But they've got a falcon. A bloody great cannon. It fires a two-and-a-half-pound ball.'

'Hmm. But there are too many Moors and not enough falcons. The truth is we could do with six falcons at Anne, and we haven't got them. And even if we did I don't think Sir Palmes would put them out there.'

I looked at him and blinked in amazement.

'We couldn't take the risk of them being captured and turned against us. One falcon could bring down Henrietta in two weeks – one week if they kept hitting the same spot and fatally weakened it.' He paused. 'Ensign Wyndham is going to escort you to the fort. He'll bring the rest of the men with him and they can help to carry everything you'll need. They're also going to take some more supplies up to Anne. I've told him to look over the ground and work out some fields of fire for you. He's quite good at that.' He smiled. 'And one last thing. No bloody heroics. When it's time to go. Get out. Get out as fast as you can. And blow the whole place up. Make sure you take enough powder to do that. And if you've got any granadoes over put them on top of the gunpowder. We don't want the Moors throwing them back at us, do we?' Then he smiled and held out his hand.

At Sandhill Fort the old guard rushed out the door and down the ladder – about a minute after Wyndham told them we were taking over the fort. Their faces were grey, their eyes were bloodshot, and they looked as though they hadn't slept in days. They might have said something to Wyndham, but they didn't say a thing to us. Not a bloody word. Not even 'good luck'. They just lined up and marched away, and I was left feeling I'd just seen the dead, the living dead.

We roped the barrels and began to pull them into the fort.

Wyndham sent the rest of the men off to Anne with their supplies, then he jumped up on the bank, peered between the pointed stakes of the palisade and yelled: 'There's a slight hollow, close up, to the right. You mightn't see it from the top of the fort, but it could hide—'

A musket fired.

Wyndham staggered, fell backwards, and rolled down the bank.

I slid down the bank, dropped my musket and fell to my knees. I turned him over. His face was a bubbling mass of red. His teeth were chattering and air was hissing out of his mouth. He began to twitch. To jerk. To throw his arms and legs around like a man with the palsy. I grabbed at him, tried to hold him, tried to calm him. His heels began to drum the ground, and I could feel his muscles cramping his legs, his arms, making them into rods of iron – then he collapsed, went limp in my arms.

Lockhart knelt down, looked into the face that was no longer a face, and whispered: 'Christ. The poor bastard's dead.'

I cradled him in my arms, and I thought of her, thought of her holding him in her arms, having him in her body, and I said: 'I wish it was me that was dead.'

Lockhart touched me on the shoulder. 'No, you don't wish that. You're worth three of him. Maybe more.'

I shook my head. 'In death we are all equal. And within a day, two at the most, we shall lie in the earth together. And we shall both be at peace.'

I shut my eyes, and they filled with tears. I cried for him. And I cried for her, for her of the blue butterflies – butterflies that were now veined with red, winged with red, touched with death.

83

The dark brought the Moors. They banged their drums and blew their trumpets. They screamed. They yelled. They fired their muskets. They came in waves. Soft-coloured waves tinted with darkness, frothed with white, the white of a hundred, two hundred, three hundred head cloths, banded with brown, with black, with the strands of the night.

We crouched down. Waited in silence. Waited till we couldn't miss. Then I yelled: 'Muskets! Pick your targets and fire. Granadoes! Wait till they're in range.'

I nodded to Lockhart. He gave me a big grin, rammed his cannon through the wooden battlement and fired. It spat nails into the night. In my imagination they were opening out like a fan, scything through the Moors who were gathering, were forming the next waves – a hundred yards away. But I couldn't see them, see them falling, and I yelled to Lockhart: 'Ram some wood under the back of the carriage and lower the elevation – to about thirty yards. If you can't see them bring it down to twenty yards. Lacey's ideas are a load of bloody crud!'

He looked at me and laughed. Lacey thought we should have three fields of fire: granadoes for close up; muskets for middle range; cannons for long distance. And all the cannons should be ranged and notched to know the elevations. It was a theory, was all right – I suppose – if I had a large fort and it wasn't dark, and I could see where the Moors were, could remember the notch-count, and see the marker lines on the floor. And as for Wyndham's hollow, the hollow that could hide a man, it was bloody farcical – it was swarming with men.

A ball slammed into the wood, just below my waist. I dropped to my knees, pushed my back against the parapet, spread my legs in front of me, lit a granado, waited till the fuse was half burnt, and tossed it over my shoulder. 'Have I got the range?' I yelled to Powel – as he reloaded his musket. 'I want to toss them high in the air, drop them over the palisade. Make them explode in the air.'

'Throw another one,' he said.

I lit it, waited, and threw it.

'Throw it a bit harder, a bit higher. Then you won't have to watch that fuse burn for so long. And you won't blow your balls off.' He laughed in my face and fired again – right in my bloody ear.

I counted to thirty, lit another granado and tossed it. I kept counting, kept lighting, kept tossing, kept yelling at the other three throwing granadoes: 'Spread them round! Cover as much ground as you can!'

High to our right, about a hundred yards away, flashes of bright light broke through the wreaths of smoke, the deep boom of the cannon and the hail of musket fire that outlined the top of Anne. About a hundred yards to our left James was coming under heavy fire. The two forts looked like a pair of twins, fiery twins. Below us, looking back towards the town lay the large field that we had smoothed with the rubbish, the rubble that came from St Barbara's. In the far corner of this field, about a hundred yards away, stood another fort. The name has slipped my mind at the moment, but it was about twice the size of Sandhill, and the lower part was built of brick and stone. It was standing mute, lost in the darkness. This was a good sign. It meant the Moors hadn't broken through the line from Anne to York.

I lit another fuse and was thinking we should have practised jumping out our door – it was about eight feet above the ground – practised running for the fort, when Powel grabbed my arm and said: 'I smell fire.'

I laughed and tossed the granado. The muskets fired another volley, and I yelled: 'There's fire everywhere.'

'No,' he said. 'This is straw. I can smell it.'

'Christ!' Lockhart yelled. 'They're running away.'

I stuck my head above the parapet and laughed. 'Raise your fire. Hit them in the bum.'

Then I could smell the smoke, smell the burning straw, and I saw the flames licking up the far side of the palisades.

The muskets fell silent. The cannon died. Anne and James calmed. For twenty, maybe thirty minutes, we watched the palisade burn. It lit the land – the moorland – and we could see every hollow, every hairy groin, every place a Moor could hide. The living were gone. The dead lay humped on the ground, like rocks, covered in cloth, wet cloth laid out to dry. Then some of the humps began to move and I yelled: 'Put a shot in every one of them. Start with the ones that are moving. I don't want those bastards jumping up and rushing at us the moment the fire dies.'

We shot the humps, shot the living, shot the dead, shot the three who jumped up and tried to run away. As the fire died their shadows grew longer, grew darker, and then they were lost to us. And so was fifty yards of palisade. We were like a virgin lying on her bed, with her skirts hitched up and her private parts twitching: we were about to be had. The only thing in doubt was the number of minutes we had to wait.

I tapped Lockhart on the shoulder. 'Raise the cannon to the extreme range and fire once every five minutes. Sweep an arc. Left to right, then hard back to the left and start again. We can't stop them if they get close. Our only hope is to keep them at a distance.'

We fired for two, maybe three hours. But nothing moved. Nothing came to take our virginity. In the dawn, in the soft grey light, in those few minutes of confusion when the night is melting into the day, I turned to Powel. 'I want to enrage the bastards. Get out there and chop all their heads off. And stick them on the palisades. Take four men. Crouch low. And work fast. Bloody fast. If they see you, they'll come in like madmen, and you won't last ten minutes.' And I smiled. 'We'll cover you. If we start to fire – run like hell.'

He grinned at me and then he was gone. About twenty minutes later, when the heads were stuck on the sharpened tops of the palisade, and I was telling Lockhart we'd have to make as many nail-bombs, 'Lockharts', as we could, he touched my arm and said: 'Christ! Look what the silly bastards have done.'

I looked down and my belly heaved. Powel had laid about twenty heads on the ground – about thirty yards in front of the ditch, in front of the black-stumped bank that was once our palisade – he'd laid them in the shape of a cross.

'Christ!' I whispered to Lockhart. 'They're going to murder us.'

He nodded. 'They'll come tonight, as soon as it's dark. And I reckon we'll last twenty minutes. If we're lucky.'

I pulled a face, looked grim. But in the depths of my soul, in the innermost reaches, in the places where secrets are safe, I was bloody delighted. I'd take the bastards with me, take them in their hundreds – hundreds of tiny little bits.

Then I would be no more. I would be in the depths of hell. I would be where I belonged – be where I longed to be.

84

Soon after midday we ate our last meal. Powel called it the 'Last Supper' and we all laughed. I never thought he had a sense of humour, and I was surprised. I was also surprised at the way the men would follow him, would do what he said. When his brother was alive the two of them were never apart, were like islands bound by the same reef. But now he was different, was like a man discovering himself, and I wasn't quite sure what to make of it.

I talked to Lockhart, talked about blowing up the fort. It was twenty-four feet high, double-skinned and filled with sand. It had two wooden floors: the first was level with the door and the second was another eight feet higher. Then came the roof and the parapet. In the chamber below the door, the earth formed the floor. In winter it was wet and damp, but now it was cold and cool, and it made the chamber a good place to escape the heat, to sleep – if we should be so lucky.

I remembered old Tattleton, in the quarries at Whitby, and I began to think what he'd do if he had to blow up the fort. I remembered the wedge-shapes we used to cut into the top of the tunnels to direct the force of the explosion upwards, to bring down the rock. But that wasn't what we wanted. We wanted the force to blow out the sides. To make thousands of wooden splinters that would kill thousands of Moors. I looked at Lockhart and said: 'If we put the barrels against the wall, put most of them on this floor' – the floor with the door – 'and a few on the next one that would blow out the sides.'

He kicked at the wall – most of the planks were an inch and a half thick – and shook his head. 'The blast would go straight up. The walls are too solid. The sand would contain the explosion.'

Powel looked up. 'Why don't we take out the sand? If you're right, if we're only going to last thirty minutes, we don't need it.'

Lockhart turned to me. 'And if we loosened some of the planks, inside and out, we could make musket holes.'

'And if we brought the cannon down here we could fire straight into them. And when it came time to go we could spin it round and fire through the door.' They both looked at me and laughed. 'And if we put the sand on the roof, that would weigh it down. And we could nail up the trapdoor.'

'And then they wouldn't be able to drop a stinkpot in on us.'

'Hmm,' I said. 'Make it difficult to throw granadoes.'

'We could make some big holes. Up on the next floor.'

'We need some sort of slingshot. A catapult.'

I shrugged. 'You've got to spin round for a slingshot. You need to be out in the open for that. And as for a catapult, we don't have anything that would stretch.' Then I turned to Lockhart. 'We need everyone this afternoon, but tonight' – and I hesitated – 'I don't think we need everyone. Five or six could go back.'

'We talked about it this morning, Sergeant,' he said in a quiet voice. 'And we're all going to stay. We think if you're fucking mad enough to do it, think you can get out alive – then so can we.'

I nodded and tried to smile. 'I want you to talk to every man. Talk to them one by one and tell them I'm going to be the last man out. Tell them I don't expect to get out alive. And if any man changes his mind, he can go back. No one will blame him. And no one will think the worse of him.'

It was harder to get the planks off than we'd thought. But once they were off, or half-off, or sprung a few inches, the sand poured out. We changed our minds about the barrels of gunpowder. We decided it was too dangerous to spread them over two floors, so we turned the top floor into a firing gallery and shifted all the gunpowder onto the floor with the door, and only made one opening down there – for the cannon. Then we prised open all the barrels, pushed them against the walls and half-covered them with sand. Lockhart took one look at them – I could almost see him thinking about the cannon recoiling, filling the air with sparks, with flames that would have to be swabbed out – and he said: 'We're going to have to cover them up with coats. And lay the trail at the last minute.'

We talked about opening the walls inside the bottom chamber, bleeding the sand, but it was getting dark and I was more concerned with making sure the men could get out when the time came. An eight-foot drop doesn't sound much but I knew it was enough to break an ankle. And a man with a broken ankle could never run a hundred yards. I looked at Lockhart and said: 'If they surround us, we could never get through. So, we have to get out that door before they get round this side.' He nodded. 'So we don't need this big drop. And if we made a heap of sand down there – four feet high, five feet high, something like that – nobody would break an ankle or twist a foot.'

He nodded, and for the next hour we sprung the last of the wallboards on the main floor – the floor we were now calling 'the gun deck' – and bucketed the sand out the door. Then we barred the door and I told Lockhart I wanted him to jump just before me; told him we'd be at greatest risk and I intended to wear a cuirass. He looked at me as though I'd gone bloody mad, and shook his head. He made me feel a fool, feel a coward. I picked up the two cuirasses and the two backplates, swung them backwards and forwards, and tossed them through the trapdoor into the chamber, into the darkness. The candle – it lived in a sooted lamp to the left of the ladder and never dispelled much of the darkness – made the four pieces of armour look like the discarded shells of a giant black beetle.

I climbed up to the next floor, thanked each man for coming, for volunteering, and I wished them luck. I told them we'd fire the cannon after they'd all jumped out the door. We'd fire it to the left – so they were to run to the right and then to curve down towards the fort. 'Any silly bastard who runs to the left will end up with a nail up his arse. And that mightn't be the sort of end you were hoping for.' They laughed, then we sat in silence with our matches fizzing, glowing in the dark, and we waited.

The firing from Anne and James warned us of their approach. Then we heard Lockhart fire. 'Wait,' I said, 'wait till you can see them.' Then Lockhart fired again. And again. Then I saw them: crouched low and running fast. There were bloody hundreds of them. I wanted to run. I wanted to run for my life. I closed my eyes. Took a breath. Gripped my musket and yelled: 'Fire!'

In the distance shapes crumbled. We reloaded. Fired again. And again. And again. Then they were in the ditch, on the bank, on the stumps of the palisade, were hurling towards us. We had thirty seconds. 'Out!' I screamed. 'Out now!'

They shot down the ladder, jumped into the sand, and ran. I grabbed Lockhart. We swung the cannon round, ran it to the door, swung it hard to the left and fired. Then he began to load again. I ran round the room, laid the trail of gunpowder over all the barrels, pulled my lighted match out of my musket and shoved it into the end of the trail. Lockhart fired again.

We heard screaming. Saw shapes fall. 'Come on!' he yelled. He grabbed his musket and jumped. 'Run!' I yelled. 'Fucking run!'

I slammed the door. Reloaded his cannon. Opened the door and fired. The Moors jumped for the door. I slammed it shut and dropped the bars. I could hear screaming, hear lead balls thumping into the wood. I ran to the trapdoor, took one last look, made sure the match was still in the trail, still burning, then I froze. All the granadoes were still on the next floor! We hadn't thrown them – not a bloody one! I tore up the ladder, dropped the two boxes down the hole and hurled back down. Poured the granadoes over the barrels, slid down the ladder, bounced on the earthen floor and crashed onto a cuirass. I looked at it for one moment – thought: what the hell – heaved it on and strapped it to the backplate. Then I pulled out my sword, ran to the wall and lay down. I could just see the other cuirass and the backplate. They had pulled apart. I grabbed them. Covered my balls and covered my face.

I waited for the explosion, waited for the Moors, waited to kill them with my sword.

Then I heard voices. Saw a flash of light.

The explosion thumped my ears, belted my head against the wall, and sucked the breath out of my lungs.

The earth shuddered and I heard beams falling.

I felt a rain of sand. A storm of hail, of grit.

Then came blackness, came smothering, came nothing.

85

I became aware of voices. They were coming from high above me and they were not speaking English or Irish. They were speaking the language of the Moors, making a melody that bubbled like water till it hit the hard notes, the rocky notes, and became harsh, discordant. Behind these voices came another voice, a shrill voice, keening death.

I tried to move, tried to sit up but I was pinned to the wall, locked in my prison of armour. I wiggled my fingers. I tried to wiggle my toes, wiggle my legs, but I couldn't feel them.

Then I knew I was entombed, knew it was time to die; and the blackness that was pressing on my body, on my eyes, seeped into the blackness in my mind, and the voices drifted away.

The light woke me. It was a muted light, a light made dark by shadows, by beams of wood, by waterfalls of sand. My head ached and my arms hurt. I could feel a weight pressing down on my legs. The voices were gone.

I struggled, tried to free myself. Then the thought of death, the thought of rotting and seeping into the earth, into the sand, maddened my mind and I screamed. I tried to kick, tried to batter my way out. The sand trickled onto my face, into my mouth. I wet myself. Then my mind exploded, flew to bits like a granado and I fell into the void, into the pit of darkness.

When I woke I was calm, and I remembered the prayer: Into thy hands O Lord I commend my spirit. I made the prayer my prayer. I said it in my mind, said it with my lips, and like the tincture of opium it soothed the pain, the ache, and I drifted through the cornfields, the fields of Elme; and the corn poppies, the red poppies were waving to me, were seeping blood, seeping life, were calling me home. And I was at peace.

I drifted through the lightness of the day and the darkness of the night that followed, and on the next day – when the edges of time were beginning to blur – I heard a voice, an English voice. It was far away, in another land. I did not want to respond to that voice. It disturbed the peace, my peace. I closed my eyes and settled into my grave.

Then the light came into my head. It was like a sunrise. I blinked and opened my eyes. Someone said: 'Bloody hell! He's still alive.'

I felt their hands lifting me up, passing me from hand to hand. Then I was sipping water and they were lying me on the ground. I felt them take off the cuirass and the backplate, felt the pain in my shoulders. Then I was on a stretcher, swaying up and down, feeling sick, seasick, vomiting over the side.

In the infirmarium, in the cool still darkness that is supposed to restore life, but is in truth a bringer of death, I heard Doctor Lawrence say to someone: 'No bones broken. But he's badly bruised on the legs and the feet. And the upper arms.'

Next morning Lockhart arrived, took one look at me, shook his head, and said: 'You stupid bastard.'

I shook my head, shook the pain that lurked behind my eyes, and felt it run down my neck. I tried to grit my teeth, to swallow the pain, but it escaped my mouth, came out soft, came out like a prayer: 'J-e-s-u-s.'

He helped me sit up. 'You tried to kill yourself. You bloody did – didn't you?'

I bit my lips and nodded.

'Well I told them you saw we couldn't get through. And you deliberately stayed behind and reloaded the cannon, cut a path through the Moors. And that's what you did. Everyone heard the cannon fire. It saved my life. No one can dispute that. I ran straight through the path. I can remember leaping over the bodies,' and he laughed. 'And everyone got to the fort.'

'Everyone?'

He nodded. 'They all think you're a fucking hero. So keep your bloody mouth shut and I won't say a word.'

I closed my eyes and lay back on the pillows. 'How many did we kill?'

'Anne counted sixty but I think it was a few more than that. Some of them were right on the fort, right up against the wall, on ladders, and they were blown to bits.'

We talked for a while, about Powel and how well he'd done, and how we might have held on a little longer if we'd had a mortar to fire granadoes, and then he said: 'You were lucky to get out yesterday. You wouldn't have got out alive today.'

I smiled, thinking he was going to say something stupid, something flippant, but he said: 'Anne was abandoned last night. Two died and most of them wounded, and they couldn't carry the falcon, so they spiked the touchhole. But they say the Moors will have it fixed in a couple of days.'

'Then God help Henrietta.'

He nodded. 'Did anyone tell you about Charles?' I shook my head. 'The Moors dug a tunnel under the walls and laid a mine. Then they called on Captain Trelawny to surrender but he wouldn't. They say he didn't believe them. So the Moors let two of his men go up the tunnel and it was full of gunpowder. They'd cut through solid rock – fifteen feet of it. And that's as good as we ever did with old Tattleton.'

'What happened?'

'They filled the trenches up with troops – big black bastards with oiled skins and curved swords, like the one that was in the fort at Whitby.' I nodded. 'And they sprung the mine. But it didn't bring the walls down. And they hanged the poor fool who dug the tunnel and laid the mine.'

I laughed. 'They can hang as many as they like as far as I'm concerned.'

'Hmm. But next time they dig a tunnel, it means they'll get it right. You can be bloody sure of that. But there is one consolation.'

'What's that?'

'They say the Moors haven't got enough gunpowder to lay another mine.'

It sounded like a reprieve, and I was wondering how we knew something like that, and thinking it would help Charles to hold out a bit longer, when he said: 'What did Captain Lacey say?'

'When?'

'Yesterday.'

'Yesterday?'

'He was at the infirmarium when you arrived. They say he helped to carry you up the stairs.'

I shook my head. 'I've no idea what he said. I don't remember much of yesterday morning. And I certainly don't remember him.'

Two days later I sat in a chair fixed to two long poles and two men, porters, carried me up Castle Hill, over the drawbridge and into the Upper Castle. Then they swung to the left and I said: 'You need to go to the right. We're round the front in the lodging houses by Peterborough Tower.'

'Our orders is to take you to the Governor's House.'

'What? What do you mean?'

'We mean to take you to the Governor's House. The orders were quite clear.'

'Whose orders?'

'Doctor Lawrence's.'

'But why would he say that?'

They both shrugged. 'We've no idea. We do what we're told, Sergeant.'

At the Governor's House, at the front entrance, they helped me out of the chair, slipped two walking sticks from under the chair and put them into my hands. I felt frail, felt tottery. And as I watched them pick up the chair, watched them swing it round, I felt stupid.

Then the door opened and a servant in a red coat hurried down the steps. 'Are you Sergeant Fenton?'

I nodded, and he extended his arm. 'Captain Lacey's waiting for you, sir.'

He helped me up the steps and into the entrance hall and he said: 'Everyone admires what you did, sir. May I offer you my congratulations.'

I blinked and looked at him. At first I thought he was joking, but there was no hint of fun, of humour, in his words and I said: 'It's what every man would do, if he found himself in the same situation.'

He shook his head. 'No, sir. If every man did something like that we'd have them traipsing through here in their hundreds. There was Sergeant Heathley, at Whitby. But he died, didn't he, sir. So that makes two. Two in twelve months.' Then he knocked on a door, opened it, murmured: 'And once again please accept my congratulations, sir,' and bowed me into the room.

Captain Lacey was standing beside the window. 'How are you feeling?'

My brow felt damp, my head was sending waves rolling across the floor, and my belly felt queasy. 'Not as well as I felt in the infirmarium, sir.'

He laughed. 'Most men say they feel better when they come out.'

I smiled. 'It must have been the chair, sir. It had a strange sway, a rolling gait.'

'Hmm. They say they take some getting used to.'

I nodded and was wondering what to say next, wondering what the hell I was doing here, when the door opened and Lord Inchiquin walked in. Captain Lacey bowed. I bowed, squinted out the corner of my eye, and made sure my head was down as low as his. It felt unnatural and it sent more waves rolling across the floor.

'You're Sergeant Fenton?'

'Yes, Your Excellency.'

'I do recognise you. Captain Lacey said I would. Said you worked here, sometimes, in the office next to my secretary. In your own time.'

'Yes, sir. I worked for two years in the clerk's office when it was in York Castle, sir. And I like the work. I like the change of company, sir.'

He waved his hand towards a group of seats. 'Let's sit down. I want you to tell me all about Sandhill Fort. Start from when you volunteered, start by telling me why you volunteered.'

I looked at the floor. I couldn't tell the truth and I didn't know what to say.

'I'm sorry,' he said, 'I didn't mean to embarrass you.'

'I was thinking, sir. I was trying to remember, to remember exactly. I'm afraid my head's still a bit woolly, sir.' He smiled. 'I knew we were short of volunteers. I knew somebody had to do it. And I thought if we were quick, were smart, we could get out alive.' I'm not sure how it sounded in his ears, but I rushed on before he could say anything, and I told him everything, as it happened, and why we did it, with one small exception

– Lockhart's exception: I stayed behind to fire the gun again, to make sure the others could get to the fort.

When I came to the end they both sat in silence for several seconds then His Excellency said: 'You are a very brave young man. Captain Lacey has recommended that you be promoted to Ensign. It is, as you know the first of the commissions His Majesty bestows on a man. It is a great honour and it carries many responsibilities. As part of my responsibilities, as part of my duties, I must make sure that a young man is fit to bear a commission. When a promotion is made from the rank of sergeant it is traditional for the man's commanding officer, for the captain of his company, to recommend him. In this case Captain Lacey, and that is what he has done.' He paused. 'It is also traditional for this recommendation to be supported by two others, and I have found that a man's first sergeant and his first lieutenant, are the two who know him best.'

'They are Lieutenant de Colville, sir, and Sergeant Brandon,' Captain Lacey said. 'I could have them here, if it's convenient to you sir, in two hours' time.'

He nodded, stood up and stretched out his hand. I stood, shook his hand and he said: 'I'm sure it will be a formality. So let me be the first to congratulate you: Ensign Fenton.'

I smiled, and through a daze I mumbled: 'Thank you, sir.'

Then Captain Lacey shook my hand, and said to him: 'May I remind you of the other thing, sir. The office.'

'Oh yes.' He turned to me. 'Doctor Lawrence says you'll not be fit to rejoin your company for another month, maybe two. But you will be fit for light duties. We're very busy here. We need more help. So, for the next month, two if need be, I'd like you to work here in my office.' And he smiled. 'And once again may I offer you my sincere congratulations.'

Captain Lacey guided me out of the room and as the door shut, reality hit me hard, hit me right between the eyes, blew my bloody brain away: Sergeant Brandon would never support me.

I was fucked. I was about to become the shortest-lived ensign in the whole history of the regiment: two hours, two and a half if they dithered.

86

Outside the Governor's House, Captain Lacey said to go back to the lodging house and rest, but that was the way of a fool. I knew I had to confront Brandon. I had to ask for his support. I had to grovel, to rub my nose in the dirt, if that was what he wanted.

A chance like this would never come again. I knew that.

I leant on my sticks, hobbled all the way to the warehouse and by the time I was at the stairs, looking up, the pain was roaring up my legs. I sat down for a couple of minutes and I knew I was wasting time, time that would not come again. I bit my lips, stood up, and eased myself up the steps: one by one.

On the landing I leant against the door – the sweat was pouring down my face, down my back – caught my breath and knocked.

Brandon was sitting at his desk. He was on his own. He looked up and said: 'Congratulations.'

'You know?'

'We all know.' And he waved at the empty desks. 'They've just rushed out to buy you something.'

'What are they going to buy?'

'I've no idea. They didn't tell me. It's supposed to be a secret.'

I shrugged, sat on the chair, wiped my brow, and said: 'Lord Inchiquin has asked to see you, in two hours' time.'

He looked at me, burst out laughing and said: 'He's never heard of me. He's never spoken to a sergeant in his whole bloody life. Why would he want to talk to me?'

I told him – in quiet measured tones – and when I finished, I said: 'I want to ask you to support me. To recommend me.'

He ran his fingers down his quill – broke open the feathered spines, ran his fingers back up again and closed them, locked them tight – and said: 'And why should I help you? What have you done for me?'

'I don't think I've done anything. I was a boy. A pikeman. I did as I was told. And that was what you wanted. You didn't have any rights to my arse. And you still don't. And I'm not going to bend over for you. Not today. Not tomorrow. Not ever. And the sooner you get that into your bloody head the better.'

'Not very gracious are you.'

I laughed. 'I'm sorry. Sometimes I still think I'm a child. Sometimes I fear you – in the night.'

He smiled. 'You still haven't told me why I should help you.'

'Why?'

'Yes why?'

'Because I've always wanted to be a bloody officer. No – that's wrong – since I realised I could do it better than Wyndham.'

'That poor bastard's dead. It didn't do him any good did it?'

'No.'

'So why do you want to be an ensign?'

I slumped in a heap. 'I don't know,' and I sighed. 'Because they eat better food. Wear better uniforms. Live in better rooms. Sleep in better beds. And get paid a hell of a lot more money.'

He roared with laughter. 'Those are the best bloody reasons I know. Hunger. Greed. Avarice. Pride. Self-interest. I approve of them all. Everything else is a heap of shit. Pious crud.' He narrowed his eyes and stared at me. 'Maybe there is some hope for you. Maybe I was wrong.' He paused. 'I don't want your arse. My cock doesn't do this any more.' He clenched his fist, pulled his forearm close to his upper arm and pretended to fuck the air. 'Not since that bastard belted off the wheel and tried to kill me.'

He looked out the window for two, maybe three minutes, then he said: 'Two questions. If you tell me the truth, I'll tell them what they want to know. I'll even tell them the sun shines out of your bloody arse if that's what they want to hear.' And he paused. 'It's about that day.'

'You were there,' I said. 'You know what happened. You saw it with your own eyes. You know the truth.'

'Hmm. But sometimes things aren't as clear as they could be. Things fade. And I don't remember. I want to hear it. I want to hear it from you.'

I looked around the empty room, the room with no witnesses and said: 'What's the first question?'

'Did he hit the wheel from the front or the back?'

I wet my lips and looked at the floor. 'From the back.'

'And you. Did you know he was going to hit it from the back?'

I swallowed hard. 'Yes.'

He rested his head in his hands for a moment, then he said: 'Get out!'

87

Twenty minutes later I knocked on de Colville's door.

The moment he saw me his face burst in a smile. He pulled me into his room, banged the door shut, flung his arms around my neck and hugged me tight.

Arrows of pain shot into my head and down my arms. I groaned.

'Oh God,' he said, 'I'm sorry.'

I swayed. My eyes filled with tears, and I tried to blink away the pain. He held me by the arms, my sticks splayed out to the sides like the legs of a dead beetle, and he said: 'I thought you were dead. We all thought you were dead. I even lit a candle for you, down in the cathedral, in front of Our Lady's altar.'

I smiled, remembered her statue – with the dark wood, the sad face and the peeling paint – and some of the pain seeped away. He helped me to sit down on his bed. I took off my hat and he stroked my hair – the way some people stroke a cat – and he said: 'I've missed you. I really thought I'd never see you again. Never hear your voice. Never touch you.' He came close, laid my head against his chest and held me close – the way a mother holds a child.

I felt a swelling of affection, of wanting. But I also knew it wasn't right, wasn't what I wanted, and I pushed him away – gently – with the tips of my fingers.

Then he looked into my eyes and said: 'Captain Lacey was here just a few minutes ago.'

'So you know.'

'Yes.'

'And what did you say?'

He moved away, pulled up a chair, sat down, and looked at the floor. The room stilled and the air froze. 'I told him, I'd like to consider it. I told him I'd never thought of it. And I needed a few minutes.'

'And what did he say?'

'He didn't say much at all. He was surprised. But it was obvious he'd been thinking about it for some time.'

'I had no idea.'

'No. Nor did I.'

We sat in silence for about thirty seconds – weighted down by our own thoughts – then he lifted his head, and I said: 'And what do you think now? Now you've had time to think.'

'I'm not sure. In my heart I still want you. I want things to be as they used to be: when you were afraid of Sergeant Brandon and needed me.'

I shook my head.

'I hated the way you ended it. The way you told me. You were so cold. So callous. So brutal.' He clenched his mouth and shook his head. 'You didn't think about me. About how I felt. About what I wanted. The moment you were safe, you didn't give a damn about me. And that's the truth.'

'It wasn't as simple as that.'

'Then you tell me how it was.'

'We've been through this before. You know how it was. You know I needed you. I never tried to hide it. I never thought we would become so close. And I never thought it was right. You know that. And when Brandon was injured, when we thought he was dying, that was the right time. The time to stop.' I bit my lips.

'I don't agree. But I've said that before haven't I? And you don't care for my feelings. Well – I don't care for your promotion. I don't think you'd make a good ensign. If you can't help me when I need you, you won't be able to help other officers when they need you. I think you've reached the right rank, Sergeant. And that's what I intend to tell Captain Lacey.'

I stared at him for a long time. I knew him well. Too well. And I knew he meant what he was saying. I reached out, touched him on the knee. 'What do you want?'

'To change my mind?'

I nodded.

'I want you. I want you in my bed.'

I sighed to myself, picked up the walking sticks, slammed my hat on my head and stood up. 'Michael' – the sound of his name softened some of the lines on his face – 'I can't do it. I'm sorry, but it's over. And you're going to have to accept that. And I'm going to have to accept that I'm a Sergeant. And that's all I'll ever be. But I won't forget this hour – when I thought I was an Ensign.'

I hobbled to the door. He made no effort to get up. No effort to open the door. I turned, looked at his back, slumped forward now as though his spine had rotted. 'I didn't expect this,' I said – almost in a whisper. 'I expected Brandon to block me. I never expected, never thought for one moment it would be you.' I swallowed hard. 'Is there anything that might make you change your mind? Anything that you might ask instead?'

'Martyn. I can't stop you. I want you too much to stop you. I want to see you succeed. I want to be proud of your success. I want to share it.

To be part of it. Not in public. That could never be. But in private.' He stood up and turned towards me. 'And yes, there is something.'

'Something that doesn't involve that bed?' I pointed to it with my stick.

'Yes. Something much more important than that.'

'What?'

'It will keep. I don't want to spoil your day. But you must promise me' – he walked up to me and took my hand – 'you must promise that you will do what I ask.'

'You want me to promise to do something, and you won't tell me what it is?'

'Yes. That's what I want. And that will make you an Ensign.'

I looked at the floor. Then I looked into his eyes, looked into those dark pools, those pools of longing, and I said: 'I promise.'

88

Late in the afternoon Captain Lacey called me into his room and handed me a partisan. It had belonged to Wyndham – the tassel below the spearhead was still wreathed in white ribbons, the ribbons the wind had fluttered on his wedding day. It was strange to hold it. It was a staff of office, of rank, and it made me think of him, think of the smug look he wore as he came out of the church. But then that look, that smug look was replaced by the bubbling frothing mass that was his face, in the last few seconds of his life. I looked at Captain Lacey, smoothed the long ribbons and said: 'I'm sorry I couldn't go to Ensign Wyndham's funeral. I've never held anyone in my arms before and watched them die. I would have liked to be there. To say goodbye.'

He shook his head. 'It was a dreadful funeral. Her father should never have let her go. Women have no place at funerals. They can't control themselves. That's why funerals are for men. Men can control their emotions.' He shook his head again. 'I blame her father.'

'I'm sorry, sir. I don't understand. Did something happen?'

He nodded. 'The poor woman lost control. Sobbed and screamed. Was quite hysterical. And most embarrassing. I didn't know where to look. And then at the end – it was raining and the ground was slippery – that stupid minister gave her some earth to throw into the grave. As she went to throw it she slipped and fell into the grave and screamed.' He paused. 'Some people say she didn't slip. They say she threw herself into the grave, but I didn't see that. So I don't know. But I do know two of our men had to get into the grave and pull her out – she didn't want to come. And her face and all the front of her dress, her shawl, were covered in black mud.'

He was silent for a few seconds, then he said: 'Your promotion will be published, made official, on May the 4th. I looked up the muster book, the one you signed on the day you enlisted. I'd forgotten I made you make an X, and then made you sign your name when I learnt you could read and write.' He smiled to himself. 'Officially you will be: Ensign William Martyn Fenton of Elme, in the County of Cambridge. A gentleman from The Fens, from the marshlands.' He smiled at me.

Then he was silent again, and I was thinking it was time for me to leave, when he said: 'I want you to do something for me. I want you to call on Wyndham's wife: Mistress Jenny Wyndham. I want you to tell her about him dying. Dying in your arms. We never told her about his face being blown away. We thought it better. So there's no need to mention that. And make sure you tell her his dying words.'

'But he never said anything.'

He shrugged. 'Make something up. Something appropriate. Something she'll treasure. Appreciate.'

'He might have murmured her name.'

'Hmm. That's a good start. Or a good ending. But it needs a bit more than that. Something to put her mind at rest.' He patted me on the shoulder. 'I'll leave it to you.'

I ran my fingers down one of the white ribbons – tried to straighten it – and he said: 'You should cut those off. Right away. Some people think white is the colour of death. Did you know that?' I shook my head. 'Not the right colour for a soldier, for a young ensign.' He laughed. 'And one last thing: Sergeant O'Sullivan is waiting for you. Down at the clerk's office. Him and that corporal . . .'

'Corporal Trigg?'

'Yes, that's the one. They've arranged a surprise for you,' he smiled.

A few minutes later, when the green tassels on my partisan were stripped of their white ribbons, I knocked on the door to the clerk's office. Trigg pulled open the door, flung his arms around me, and bloody near choked me. O'Sullivan pumped my hand and made my arm ache. I laughed, laughed with them, and then Brandon looked up and said: 'I hear it's official.'

I nodded and burst into a smile, a big beaming smile.

'Always thought you'd make a good officer. Bastards make the best officers. It's a fact. I've seen it time and time again. And you always were a sweet little bastard.' Then he laughed.

I laughed with him, and so did Trigg and O'Sullivan. Then O'Sullivan said: 'We knew you were going to need a new uniform so Trigg and I, we—'

'And Ives, don't forget Ives.'

He smiled at Trigg. 'And Ives. We put our money together and bought you a uniform. An ensign's uniform. The man's dead, and they say his wife's going back to England. And she needs the money, so' – he spread his hands, opened his fingers, as if to let the man's life escape – 'here we are.'

I took off my uniform, stripped down to my under-breeches, and O'Sullivan said: 'Dear God. You're covered in bruises. They look like black mushrooms.' He walked right round me. 'Do they hurt?'

'Only when I laugh or try to walk too far. And I can't take a deep breath. Doctor Lawrence thinks I've cracked all my ribs down this side.' I touched my left side, the side that took the weight of the falling beams.

My new shirt was white with an edging of lace and it matched the scarf they tied at my throat. My breeches, stockings, long waistcoat, top coat and hat were all soft grey – the grey they call dove-grey. The plum-pink ribbons on my hat, matched the ribbons that decorated the shoulders and the short sleeves of my coat. They also matched my garters, the bows on my shoes, the cord that tied around my waistcoat, and the baldric. The baldric was about six inches wide, made of cloth and edged with a ribbon ruffle, and best of all it had a buckle – it could be adjusted to my size and it wouldn't swing loose, swing round to the front like my old leather one used to do.

When I was dressed they all pretended to bow. I laughed and it hurt my ribs and brought tears to my eyes and they all thought I was overcome by the moment. They patted my back and made my ribs hurt even more, made my eyes water even more.

Then Trigg said: 'We have another surprise for you.' He reached under his desk and brought out an officer's sword. The hilt was finer than my old sword and so was the blade. The scabbard was covered with leather and tooled with gold.

'I don't know what to say,' I said.

He smiled. 'There's no need to say anything. We're all so proud of you. Now slip it into the baldric, and turn round. Let's have a proper look at you.'

I turned around and smiled at them. 'The coat's so light. So cool. Everybody should wear a uniform like this. It would stop all those bloody heat rashes that start under your balls, run round your bum and set it on fire.'

They laughed. I gave them both a hug, a gentle hug, and said: 'I wasn't expecting this. Any of this. I want to thank you. To thank both of you.' And I smiled.

Then I turned to Brandon. 'What do you think?'

'It suits you, sir.'

'Sir?'

'Yes, sir.'

I laughed. 'I'm sorry. I wasn't expecting to be called sir.'

He shrugged. 'Mister Fenton. Does that suit you better?'

I walked over to his desk and rested my hands on the edge of the tilted top. 'I was just surprised. I wasn't expecting it. Not from you. Not from anyone.'

He nodded. 'They say you get used to it.'

Then I was overcome by a strange feeling, a need to make a new beginning, and I held out my hand. 'Thank you for what you did today. I've been thinking, if you were agreeable, we could forget about the past. Draw a line under it – as they say – and start again.'

He stared at me for a long time. Then he took my hand and shook it. 'It would be for the best, it would—'

The door banged open. Ives hurled into the room, saw me, saw the uniform, and slammed to attention. 'Sorry, sir. I didn't expect to find – Christ! It's you!' He rushed over, thumped me on the back. My ribs collapsed, my head exploded. The pain roared through my body and tears ran from my eyes. I gripped the desk, gasped, and bloody near died.

'Oh God! I'm sorry. I forgot.'

I tried to nod but it hurt, and I said: 'Corporal. You haven't changed. Not one bloody bit.'

'And don't you change. Don't get a bloody swollen head like all those other bastards who call themselves officers. You be you. And the men will love you for it.' Then he walked right round me. 'It suits you. And it fits. It's just a pity we couldn't buy the gorget.'

'She wouldn't sell it,' Trigg said. 'Sold everything else, but not that. She says she's going to wear it, under her dress, next to her heart' – he touched his chest and smiled – ''till the day she dies.'

'I'll buy one,' I said, 'when I get some money.'

'No need to do that,' Brandon said. He got down from his stool opened up his chest – it sat under his desk and he used it as a footrest – pulled out a velvet cloth and unwrapped a gorget, an ensign's gorget: a flat half-moon shaped piece of silver, embossed with the Royal Arms. It was tarnished, blushed with black. 'I bought a uniform once, when I thought I was going to be made an officer. It was the biggest mistake I ever made. They thought it was an arrogance. An impertinence.' He paused. 'It's not an arrogance or an impertinence to want a commission if you can afford to buy one. But it is if you can't afford to buy one.' He shook his head. 'It's all gone now, apart from a few buttons, and this.' He held the gorget up in the air. 'I'd like you to have it.'

I didn't know what to say – I was so surprised. I walked back to his desk, took off my hat and leant forward. He slipped the chain over my neck and said: 'I've never been able to say sorry. It's not in my nature. But maybe this will do it for me.'

PART FOUR

89

On May 8th, four days after my promotion became official, the Moors hauled a cannon onto a small hill and began to bombard Henrietta. It chilled my soul and filled my mind with gloom, and that night in the Governor's House, Lord Inchiquin and Sir Palmes wore grave faces and spoke in hushed voices. It marked a change in the thrust of the war, a shift in the balance of power. It was like the death of a close friend or relative. It had been expected for so long, talked about so often, it never felt as though it would really arrive. But here it was, and it was a shock. And we were mourning what was, what used to be, and would never come again.

The Moors' aim was poor. Some of the balls were hitting Henrietta's walls and some were missing, were screaming over Charles, over our walls and landing in the town. We received a couple of reports of houses being hit and roofs shedding tiles and I entered them in the Governor's daybook. At about ten at night Captain Bastin arrived with a cannon ball. He'd dug it out of a house. It weighed two and a half pounds, and as we waited for him to go in to see His Excellency he said: 'We think it was fired by a falcon. By the one that used to be in Fort Anne. They say they spiked the cannon but it's obvious the Moors have repaired it. And now we're being attacked by one of our own cannon. And all because we didn't have enough bloody common sense to drag it out before Anne fell.'

Next morning the speaking trumpets brought a message from Henrietta. Sergeant Murphy, an Irishman from Cork, translated it for me and I entered it in the daybook: 'At Henrietta the shot is weakening the walls. The foundations are undermined. The fort could fall at any moment.'

A few minutes later I entered another message. This one was from Captain Trelawny and it made me feel sick: 'We will have to abandon both forts and fight our way back to Peterborough Tower. We can cover the retreat from Henrietta to Charles. But from Charles to Peterborough Tower we will need to be supported by four or five hundred troops from the garrison. We cannot break through the siege lines on our own.'

Lord Inchiquin called a Council of War. We sat and waited in the outer office. I thought there might be some orders to copy but there was nothing, and the hours dragged. His Excellency's Secretary recorded the decisions of the council and locked the book away. We went to bed, not knowing what they had decided.

But in the morning it was obvious. Lieutenant Fitzgerald, Lieutenant Westcombe and Mister Leddington set out under a flag of truce to negotiate with the leader of the Moors: the Alcaide. From Peterborough Tower – I was walking there and back twice a day as the rooms in the Governor's House were small and dark and they were making me feel as though I was trapped in the fort again, making me tremble, making me burst into cold sweats – I could see four, maybe five thousand Moors, and all of them were pressing close to Charles and Henrietta. To my mind there wasn't anything to discuss: we could fight or we could surrender. Late in the afternoon we heard the Alcaide was of a similar mind except for one thing: in place of surrender our men were invited to 'throw themselves upon his mercy'.

Next day Admiral Herbert assumed responsibility for the defence of the Mole. He landed a hundred seamen, mounted a new guard – all bearing muskets – and his gunners took over Mole Fort and all the batteries of cannon. It was strange to see blue and white, and black and white uniforms far below me on the Mole. But it was also reassuring to see the men from the moleguard and the gunners from the batteries, up on the walls by Peterborough Tower. But there was one thing that disturbed me, and to begin with I didn't notice it, didn't think about it.

When we'd been in Sandhill Fort and the Moors were running towards us in the dawn or the dusk, they were blurred, hard to see, and they blended into the sand, into the scrubby folds in the land. Down on the Mole, the seamen were blending into the stone, into the shadows of the buildings, and they were hard to see. But it was never like that with our men in their red coats. They were always crisp and clear, easy to see. I turned to Sergeant O'Sullivan and said: 'If they ever develop a new musket, one that shoots straighter than ours, is lighter and easier to hold steady, then our red coats are going to make perfect targets.'

He looked at me as though I'd gone mad, grunted, dipped his quill into the ink and wrote another line.

The following day the falcon battered Henrietta for hours on end, and in the evening at about ten o'clock Captain Trelawny signalled his intention to retreat at seven next morning. Lord Inchiquin wanted the retreat to be at six, but then there was a Council of War, and the retreat was delayed to give us time to prepare a sally. God knows why we couldn't have prepared it earlier on – there was ample time, too much time if the truth is known. Then came another Council of War – we waited in the office but once again we were not wanted – and the day dribbled away. Maybe that's a bit hard, a bit cruel, but that's how it appeared to me, sitting at my desk, waiting, watching, listening to the thump of the falcon.

Then we were told the retreat was to take place next morning – the

14th – and it was to be supported by four hundred and eighty troops from the garrison. The plan was simple: an advance party of eighty-six men – aptly named, Forlorn Hope – would rush the siege lines. They would be followed by the main body and strengthened by seventy-two men on both sides – like wings. The reserve of a hundred and twelve men was to stay a hundred yards behind the main body. The palisades below Peterborough Tower formed the first line of defence for the revetment or ravelin, and they were to be manned by seamen and commanded by two naval lieutenants.

Under the direction of Admiral Herbert – in the sloop *Bonetta* – two barkalongoes and a fleet of ship's boats were to attempt the rescue of the thirteen men trapped in Devil's Drop.

Captain Lacey was ordered to support the right wing, not as part of the formal order of battle, but as a second reserve, stationed on the Whitby Road, far below Peterborough Tower, in case the Moors made a sudden dash along the road and threatened the Mole.

Early in the evening I hobbled along to our lodging house. I only needed one walking stick and I was beginning to look less like a cripple, and as long as I didn't take a sudden deep breath or throw my arms around and splay my ribs, most of the pain had vanished. I was thinking I might be able to rejoin the company tomorrow – just for the day – for everything in the Governor's House had gone quiet, eerily quiet, as though the power, the authority to act, to decide, had passed to the captains commanding the various companies and there was now nothing for us to do. I said this to Captain Lacey and he said: 'It's the lull before the storm. The eve of battle, when everything that can be done has been done, and now we must wait. And that's all we can do.' He smiled. 'I don't think you're fit enough to join us tomorrow. It's not as if the war's going to end tomorrow. It's not. There will be more battles, more retreats – if Sir Palmes is right. And more chances to cover yourself in glory.'

'With due respect, sir, I would like to take part. I think I'm fit enough.'

He pursed his lips. Then he raised his arm and slapped me on the back with the flat of his hand. The pain exploded my chest, watered my eyes. I doubled forward, grabbed at the table, coughed and spluttered.

'That,' he said, 'was only a light tap.' Then he smiled. 'Do you still think you're fit enough to join us tomorrow?'

I tried to say something but the pain was roaring up my throat and my forehead was bursting into a sweat, and I shook my head.

He took my arm and said: 'Let's go up to the tower and walk the walls for a few minutes.' Then he turned to Lockhart. 'Sergeant. I'll be back in about half an hour.'

It was now about eight o'clock, and under cover of darkness the first of the soldiers who were to take part in tomorrow's rescue would soon be pouring into the Upper Castle. If they had come in during the hours of daylight the Moors would have seen them and been forewarned. I'd heard Sir Palmes say surprise was a weapon of war, was one of the few things we had in our favour, and the orders for tonight were specific: no one was to make any noise whatsoever. Secrecy – surprise – was to be preserved till the last possible moment.

For about twenty minutes we paced the walls – talked about Sergeant Lockhart being accepted by the men, and Powel needing 'more schooling' before he could be made a corporal – and then a message came from Charles. It was loud and clear, in stark English, and frightening in its simplicity: 'Henrietta has surrendered.'

We looked at each other. I felt sick in my belly, and he said: 'This is our fault. We did nothing. We abandoned them. We should have rescued them a week ago. Ten days ago. Before the Moors began to strengthen their lines.' And he shook his head.

For a long time we stood side by side peering into the darkness. We couldn't see anything but we kept peering, kept hoping for some sign, but there was nothing – apart from a few words in Irish and we couldn't find Sergeant Murphy to translate them for us.

We returned to the lodging house. Captain Lacey spoke to Lieutenant de Colville. I spoke to the men, and my gloom, my sense of loss, seeped into them, and for an hour or more, in soft tones, tones of mourning, we recalled our days, our nights, in Henrietta. It was hard to believe she was gone for the second time, and we couldn't help thinking, help wondering aloud what the Moors had done to the men who surrendered, who threw themselves upon their mercy.

I slept in Wyndham's old bed. It was narrow and it cramped my elbows, cramped my mind. I dreamt I was in a wooden coffin – a great rarity in Tangiers – and I was alive, was trying to get out, to elbow the sides away, when I felt the coffin hit the bottom of the grave. It thumped, thudded, shuddered. I sat up – sweating, heart-thumping. 'What the hell was that?' I yelled.

Half the room was sitting up, jumping up, rolling off their pallets. The room was trembling. 'Christ!' someone said. 'Was that an earthquake?'

'More like a mine,' someone else said.

'Under Charles?'

I put my feet on the floor. 'Lockhart!' I yelled. 'Where are you?' He grunted and waved to me – he was pulling on his breeches. 'Run up to the walls. Find out what's happening. Everyone else. Get dressed. Quickly.'

He was back within two or three minutes. 'They've blown up Henrietta. Charles is still safe. And you can hardly move out there. There are bloody men everywhere.'

Twenty minutes later, in almost total silence, Sergeant Owen marched the whole company out of the Upper Castle. To preserve the element of surprise, they went the long way: down to the Old Parade, out the

Watergate, along the quay, onto the Mole for a few yards, out Fort Whitby Gate, and along the Strand.

I walked past the ranks of waiting men, climbed the steps, and sat on the great bastion, just a few feet to the right of Peterborough Tower. It was cold and the air was damp. It had rained a lot in the past few days and some of the officers were saying the bottom of the Moors' trenches would be heavy with mud and deep with water, and this would make it difficult for our men to cross them. From my perspective it looked easy: the night still lay heavy on the earth and it was filling the trenches with black shadows, making them look shallow. It was also colouring the Moors, cloaking them with darkness, and making the trenches look deserted.

About an hour later, at about six o'clock, the land shook off the night and the dregs of the dawn, and a thousand Moors marched our men out of Henrietta and headed towards the camp of the Alcaide. For several minutes it was a parade of triumph, of victory, and they beat their drums and blew their trumpets, and their banners fluttered in the wind.

Then the drumming changed. It became urgent, became an alarm.

The Moors broke away from the parade, surged out of their tents, and they ran – they ran in their hundreds – towards their lines. In a few minutes, like a wave crashing upon a beach and filling a ditch scoured in the sand, they filled all their trenches, surrounded Charles, and destroyed any notion of secrecy, of surprise.

Sergeant Murphy came down from Peterborough Tower, made the sign of the cross, looked at me and said: 'Dear sweet Jesus. They are betrayed.'

'Betrayed?'

'They've found O'Reilly – our man in Henrietta, the one who speaks Irish – that's what they've done. And they've put a knife to his neck or a blade to his balls. And they've forced him to translate the messages from Charles to us. They know the breakout is going to happen at any minute. That's why they're running. And those poor bastards down there in Charles' – he bit at his lips and his eyes watered – 'they're dead. They don't have a hope in hell.'

90

A few seconds later the men in Forlorn Hope, the Dunbartons – Scots fresh from Ireland, fresh from blooding – advanced through the revetments, formed ranks, and double-marched towards Fort Charles and its one hundred and seventy-six defenders.

Then the fort doors opened and Captain St John jumped out. He was followed by a stream of men. They bunched together and doubled towards the inner trench.

The Moors opened fire.

Another mass of men poured out of the fort, bunched together and doubled towards the inner trench – banked high with earth.

A Lieutenant in Peterborough Tower, one of the few men with a spyglass, yelled: 'It looks as though they're all out! I can see Captain Trelawny and his young son – right at the back.'

Both groups of men hurled themselves into the inner trench and Charles blew up.

The blast stilled the musket fire, filled the air with smoke and made our walls shudder. The Moors shrieked, screamed, cheered, and the sound clutched at my heart like the talons of death.

Then the smoke cleared and the dust settled. Most of the fort was still standing: only one bastion was destroyed. Sergeant Murphy said to me: 'They should have blown up the four bastions. They couldn't have had enough gunpowder left.' And he shook his head.

Then the Moors swarmed over Charles: raised red and green banners; beat their drums and blew their trumpets.

Just a few feet from me, Mister Francis Povey, the new Comptroller of Ordnance aimed his mortar and opened fire. It splattered the Moors all over the stonework and sent a cheer along our parapet. Then his three gunners raised their cannons, checked the elevations and pushed burning matches into the touchholes. Cannon balls tore through the air, left long trails of white smoke and ripped through the Moors on horseback. The horses reared, galloped madly, and tossed their riders high in the air.

The men from Charles fought their way out of the inner trench, ran across the bare ground, up the bank, and plunged into the next trench. As they clambered out of this trench, hundreds of Moors pressed them from the flanks, pursued them from the rear, destroyed any thought, any hope, of retreat, of return to the fort, and chased them towards the outer trench.

Then the Moors were upon them.

They fought hand-to-hand: running, stumbling, rushing to reach the outer trench. They jumped into the trench, jumped down fourteen feet. The mud sucked at their feet, at their legs, and slowed them down. As they waded for the other side, waded across twenty-four feet of mud, the Moors lowered their muskets and began to shoot at them. The trench filled with smoke and masked our view, but we could still hear the muskets, hear the crackle of death.

Then the Dunbartons pounded up to the outer trench and opened fire. The volleys slowed the Moors and thickened the smoke in the trench.

The Lieutenant high in Peterborough Tower yelled: 'I can see a pikeman coming out of the trench! And there's another! And another!'

We let out a cheer and my heart raced. Just along from me one of the gunners yelled: 'If we had more cannons and more gunners we could have blasted shit out of the bastards.' I turned and smiled. 'And why you fucking officers didn't get us up here a bloody month ago when they were first building the trenches is bloody beyond me.' He laughed, jabbed his match at the touchhole, and I slammed my hands over my ears.

As the smoke parted I caught glimpses of the Dunbartons. Most were standing in three files: shuffling backwards and forwards, loading and firing. Behind them, men were lighting granadoes, tossing them high in the air, tossing them beyond the trench. In front of them, one man was kneeling and one was lying flat on the earth – both were reaching into the trench, reaching for a man.

I was thinking they might have pulled thirty men out, thinking they'd have to move faster, if they were going to get the rest out, when they began to edge away from the trench. 'Dear God,' Sergeant Murphy mumbled. 'They're coming back. That's all. That's all they're going to get.'

We looked at each other, and I felt sick. I couldn't believe what I was seeing, what I was hearing. I shaded my eyes, peered hard, peered long, but the trench was swarming with Moors – bloody hundreds of them – and they were coming out of the trench, coming after the Dunbartons and the men from Charles.

Then the Moors swarmed out of their side trenches, ran across our old lines of communication – formed giant crab claws – and tried to cut the Dunbartons off from the main body.

'What the hell's wrong with the main body? Why aren't they advancing?'

'Jesus!' I murmured. 'What are they waiting for?'

The main body advanced a little, like a cautious maiden, and through the smoke, the noise and the mutterings of the crowd that was pressing us close to the battlements, we could see faint stirrings – towards the front of the main body.

But then, instead of advancing, instead of attacking, instead of helping, the main body lost their balls: they panicked and fled. And so did the reserve. The Dunbartons and the men from the fort were left on their own, were left with the bitterness, the cruel irony of their name: forlorn hope.

The Moors scenting victory, scenting blood, and disdaining our cannon fire, our mortar fire, engulfed the Dunbartons in their claws of foot and horse.

For an hour or more, massed together and fighting at the front and the rear, they came towards us – like a snail spitting blood and smoke, and dragging its wounded entrails.

As they came closer, came within musket range, the wings of the main body – the wings that did not fly to their aid – closed around them and they were saved. In their midst I recognised a few of the officers from the main body – they had stood their ground, had waited for the Dunbartons and the men from Charles, and they had fought beside them, had helped them to return.

The cannons and the mortar continued to roar in my ears, and in the slices of silence, I heard the cries, the screams, the wailing of the wounded. They were being carried, being helped to walk, to hobble, towards the sallyport just below us.

Then the Moors fired one of the cannons in Charles. 'Christ!' Murphy muttered. 'We made a piss-poor job of spiking those.' After four shots they found the range and pounded the walls of Pole Fort. Then they unspiked another cannon and began to fire cannon balls into the town.

As the morning wore on they raised a platform of earth about a hundred and fifty yards to the south-west of Pole, protected it with palisades stolen from Henrietta, dragged over a cannon from Charles and opened fire. The balls slammed into the walls below Peterborough Tower, opened bloody great cracks – I could put two fingers into one of them – showered us with chips of stone and drove the crowds off the wall. Then they found the range of the Governor's House: smashed holes in the walls, shattered glass windows, cascaded tiles onto the great bastion and shredded his orange trees.

Lord Inchiquin and Sir Palmes, white-faced and grim, huddled a few yards away from me. I couldn't get any closer, couldn't hear what they were saying – they were surrounded by a dozen officers – but a few minutes later they sent a flag of truce to the Moors. And about an hour after that the Alcaide gave us permission to collect our dead.

In silence we filed down to the courtyards below Peterborough Tower and waited to receive the dead. I was used to death – it was no stranger to me. I'd seen many men die: in their beds and on the field of battle. But I was not expecting what I was about to see. Every single man was hacked and stabbed. Some had their breeches pulled down and a raw slash – haloed in hair – was all that was left of their private parts.

And every single head was chopped off.

We piled up the red-coated corpses, each bleeding from the stump that was once a man's neck. They made the courtyards into a charnel-house, and all I could think of was 'lambs to the slaughter'. Then I remembered the ancient prayer: 'Lamb of God who takest away the sins of the world have mercy on us . . . have mercy on us . . . grant us peace.' I made that prayer my prayer, and I repeated it over and over again.

The bodies attracted the flies. Their buzzing disturbed the silence, and heaved my belly, and for a long time, I could not bear to look, bear to think. Women and children were flocking into the Upper Castle, were crying, were wailing, were renting their garments, were clutching each other, were mumbling words that had no meaning.

Then I walked past the bodies – piled on top of each other – and I counted the feet. Some were stockinged, some were bare, and some were shoed. When I reached a hundred and one pairs, I gave up and my thoughts, my feelings died in a tomb of mind-numbing misery.

In the afternoon the Moors sent in the heads. We washed their faces, brushed their hair, laid them out in long lines, but we could not marry the heads to the bodies. The uniform of life had become the uniform of death and there was nothing to distinguish one man from another – with one exception: Captain Trelawny. Even in death the uniform of an officer stood out; and in the night the surgeon sewed the Captain's head back onto his body.

In the courtyards, shrouded by the dark, I stood between Lieutenant de Colville and Captain Lacey and we mourned the dead. After ten or twenty minutes of empty silence, the Captain said: 'Our company didn't do anything. Not a thing. Not a single solitary bloody thing. We weren't even allowed to help at Devil's Drop.' And he paused. 'Do you know what happened?' I shook my head. 'They couldn't get in close enough. They tried, but the musket fire was too hot, too accurate. And the seamen were sitting targets. So they yelled to the men in the fort to run for the water and swim. But only one man could swim, and the rest were captured, or they surrendered. I don't know which, and it doesn't matter. And now they're saying twenty-two seamen died to rescue one pikeman.' And he shook his head.

An hour later, in the Governor's House, as the wind blew through the holes smashed in the walls, I copied the 'Provisional Toll':

FORT CHARLES GARRISON
39 men escaped
14 men captured
1 boy captured – Captain Trelawny's son
123 men dead

FORLORN HOPE
Ensign Bayly dead
15 men dead

DEVIL'S DROP
1 Volunteer dead
22 seamen dead
12 men captured

OTHER FIGHTS
10 men dead
30 men captured

ORDNANCE CAPTURED
From Charles Fort
13 cannons – plus shot
3,300 granadoes – our mine failed to destroy them
1 mortar
From other forts
7 cannons

WOUNDED
Doctor Lawrence is tending 52 men and some are not expected to last the night.

MUSKET SHOT
This afternoon the Moors were observed scouring the lines around Fort Charles and picking up musket balls. They appear to have reclaimed several thousand balls and regrettably, most will be able to be reused. Those that are not reusable could be recast in less than 24 hours.

Around midnight I crawled into bed and for a long time I lay flat on my back staring into the crosses formed by the rafters. In my mind they became a graveyard of crosses, broken crosses, mutilated crosses, and through them drifted words, drifted a fog of phrases – spoken by others, spoken in muted tones: bloody incompetent; should have got them all out – if we'd done it right, done it earlier; at least they didn't capture any gunpowder; we can't hold out for more than three months; they can dig tunnels – can mine the walls; there aren't enough men left to man the walls; we can't hold Pole or Norwood. And every so often I heard the words of Major Boynton – he commanded the main body, turned and fled, and now the men were calling him Major 'Wheel-about' – and he was saying: 'Horses. Troops-of-horse. That's what we needed. Troops-of-horse.'

Next morning, as the great bell in Peterborough Tower tolled the passing of life, the passing of hope, we buried the dead in a common grave – it was like the trench in which so many of them died – and it cast a pall of mud-wet gloom over the town. Then we buried Captain Trelawny and Mister Wray – the gentleman volunteer from the boats off Devil's Drop – side by side in the garrison church, just a few feet from Lord Middleton. And the words of the prayer book, of the funeral service: 'The Lord gave, and the Lord hath taken away; blessed be the name of the Lord', tasted bitter, tasted like bile in my mouth.

Soon after midday Sir Palmes emerged from the Council of War hot for defence, for fighting to the last. He was, as they say, a tower of strength, and I heard him mutter: 'We have secured Pole with ten-foot-high rumbuts filled with earth, and these will preserve her for some time. They won't batter her down in a hurry.'

But over the next few days the Moors strengthened their first battery, built another battery near the ruins of Fort James, hauled some of our great cannons onto Teviot Hill – well out of our range – and bombarded Pole, Norwood, and the houses clustering to the west of the Market Place.

Mister Povey replied with cannon and mortar fire and 'sent some of the Moors to Mahomet' but the tide of war was against us. If Pole fell, another hundred and three men would be dead or captured, and from the top of the fort the whole town could be bombarded. It was the commanding height.

In the Council of War, Sir Palmes and Lord Inchiquin, concluded – with much reluctance according to the whisperings of His Lordship's secretary – that it would be better to destroy Pole and sue for peace than to allow Pole to be taken and used as a platform for bombardment.

On May 20th the Moors agreed to Lord Inchiquin's request for a truce. When the envoys returned to the Council of War and read the conditions they say they were met with silence, dead silence, and that night when I read the conditions, I too was wrapped in silence, in the great stillness that is defeat.

The conditions – in simple summary – read:

Pole and Norwood are to be abandoned within three days.
Cambridge, Fountain and Bridge Forts are to remain in our hands.
The batteries raised by the Moors are to be destroyed and all cannons threatening the town are to be removed within three days.
Our cattle may graze in the fields.
No new works or trenches are to be begun by either side.
The truce is to last four months – till September 20th.

In effect eighteen years of work was lost, was destroyed, and conditions were to be as they were 'in the time of the Portuguese', with one small exception: our three remaining forts would be able to protect our main water supply. If the summer was wet, it would be a concession of no importance; but if it was dry, if it brought a drought, the stream would become our only source of water.

Within a few days the town was rife with rumours of secret articles, secret conditions for the truce, for Lord Inchiquin would not permit any cannons to move around the walls, and nor would he allow the walls to be repaired. Not a single stone was to be touched. But we were still allowed to cut stone for the Mole. And in that concession lay a bitter message: the Moors wanted us to finish the Mole before they took the town.

Then Lord Inchiquin lost all sense of judgement, sense of proportion, sense of reality: the bloody fool – they are not just my words, they were, they are the words of every right thinking man – allowed the Barbary Jews back into the town. And they reported everything to the Moors. Nothing was to be kept secret, kept hidden.

On the 25th, Sir Palmes's son, Ensign Fairborne – from time to time he acted as his father's secretary and copied confidential documents for him – fell ill with a coughing fever. I didn't think much of it, coughs, colds and fevers blighted our lives every summer and they were to be expected; but just as I was about to finish for the night, to leave the Governor's House and go back to our lodgings, Sir Palmes called me into his room. He told me Lieutenant Fitzgerald was to take the mail boat to Tarifa, first thing in the morning. Then he was to gallop by day and by night through Spain and France, take the boat to Dover and gallop on to London with urgent letters, urgent pleas for His Majesty.

I could tell he was reluctant to use me, to trust me to do the copying his son used to do for him. He made me promise, made me swear an oath of secrecy, and then he said: 'How do I know I can trust you?'

I looked at my brown shoes and fiddled with my white cuffbands – smudged now with black ink – and I said: 'I trusted you sir, with my life, on that night in the cathedral, when you came to pay your respects to the four Irishmen. The ones who died in Whitby. In the landslide.'

He nodded his head. 'I thought you looked familiar.' And then he smiled.

As the dawn approached, and I was on to my eighth or ninth letter – some of them ran to a dozen pages – I came to the essence of his message: The situation is impossible. We need four thousand soldiers-of-foot and five hundred troopers. If they cannot be sent immediately, 'His Majesty had better resolve to quit and leave both the town and the Mole in a ruin'.

91

Next day Sir Palmes reviewed the whole garrison and announced his intention of sending home all old soldiers, and all soldiers who'd lost an arm or a leg or were maimed in any way. They were to go with the widows and the children of the men who died in the retreat from Fort Charles. I didn't give it a great deal of thought. The underlying reason was obvious: he was preparing for the fall of Tangiers, and that didn't bear thinking about. But when I wandered into the clerk's office late in the evening Sergeant Brandon and Corporal Trigg both looked glum, looked miserable – like men drowning in the depths of melancholy – and it was obvious they'd been thinking about it.

Neither of them stood up. Sergeant O'Sullivan did, but they didn't. It surprised me. I suppose it shouldn't have. I'd told them often enough not to stand up for me – when the four of us were on our own – but they hadn't taken any notice of me and they kept on standing up. In some ways I was getting used to it. Getting to expect it. Getting to think it was my right. And their not standing, not showing the proper degree of respect for my rank, grated hard, and I bit my tongue.

O'Sullivan looked at me and said: 'Trigg is going home.'

'Jesus,' I said – turning to Trigg and bursting into a smile. 'You lucky bastard.' I stretched out my hand to congratulate him.

He looked at my hand with disdain, sniffed, and shook his head. 'Have you ever been to the north of England, to Northumberland, where I come from?'

'No, but—'

'Well if you had you'd know it was cold. Bloody cold most of the time. And sometimes summer lasts for four weeks. Six if we're lucky. Here it last for six months. And my hands, they thaw out after a month – two if I'm unlucky – and then I can write for four or five months. But in England . . .' He slumped forward, cradled his head in his hands, and bit at his lips.

O'Sullivan put a finger to his lips and motioned me to be silent. I turned to Brandon. 'Are you going home?'

'I don't know. I hope not. I have to see Doctor Lawrence tomorrow. I've been told I can stay if he thinks I'll be fit for duty in three months' time. Otherwise I have to go home.'

'I'd go home if I were you. Go, while you have the chance.'

'That might be all right for you, but I don't have any relatives left. And I don't have a home any more. This' – he looked around the room – 'is my home. And my friends. They're all here. All the sergeants in this regiment.'

I remembered his friends. Remembered them pulling down their breeches. Remembered Oldfield sprawled over the stone wall, and I grunted.

I pulled the stool away from my desk – my head of Christ and my blue-butterfly broach still lived in the drawer, lived in a clutch of memories, and they signified possession, ownership – and I sat beside Trigg. 'I'm going to miss you. This office won't be the same without you.' He shook his head. 'I mean it. I truly do. I'll never forget those talks we used to have – the ones on Popery. Or how you taught me to think. To think logically. To test a premise and work from one conclusion to another. I always admired the way you could beat him, in an argument.' I nodded towards O'Sullivan but he was busy writing, and if he was listening, was hearing, he didn't acknowledge it. We talked for another twenty or thirty minutes and we both knew, without saying it, that he could be ordered to go at any moment. We relived the past, dug it up and then bedded it down again, and tried to bury our fears for the future, for the unknown that lay ahead. Then I gave him a hug, a wordless hug, wiped my eyes and left.

In the morning Brandon hobbled into our room in the Governor's House and laid the orders and the copybooks upon the table. I wanted him to go. I wanted him to get on the ship and be gone for ever. But something was niggling deep inside me. Maybe I was sorry for him. Maybe I was forgetting what he'd done to Oldfield. Maybe I was being a fool. I don't know. I stared at him for ten or twenty seconds, then I was conscious of him looking at me, looking hard, and he said: 'Were you wanting something, sir?'

I nodded. 'I heard a rumour last night, after I left you. About Doctor Lawrence and small casks of brandy-wine. They say he has a liking for it. Not for himself you understand, but for his patients. For the ones who are walking in the valley of death. They say it eases the pain, the pain of life, the pain of death.' I paused. 'And sometimes they say it eases his disposition, colours his judgement – is the way I heard one man put it.'

Within a few hours Trigg and a hundred and forty-five other men were gone, and apart from the ache in my heart there was little to show for his passing. A week later Lord Inchiquin was also gone, and to be honest, after the wind cleared the smoke from the farewell salutes, there was even less to show for his passing. He was in truth, a lazy prick. And I feared we were about to pay the price of his indolence.

Sir Palmes became acting Governor. Two days later he came into our room and said: 'I want you to stay in this office. I need someone I can trust. Someone who can write my letters for me.' I blinked hard, and he laughed. 'I don't mean the contents. I want you to write the words down for me, as I dictate them. Afterwards you'll have to make a fair copy and we'll send that. So if I change my mind when I'm dictating, and you have to cross out a few words it won't matter.'

'With due respect, sir, Captain Lacey was expecting me to rejoin his company as soon as I was well enough, sir.'

He looked at me, said: 'Hmm. I want you here. Arrange a bed for yourself in one of the offices. And have your meals with the household. And when the truce is over, when we've beaten the Moors – I'll think about sending you back to Captain Lacey.'

92

Far to the south of here, in the hot dry lands, in the deserts of our imagination, they say the vultures gather when a sick animal is about to die. They sit and wait for death. But sometimes hunger makes them impatient and they harry the dying: screech and squawk, flutter closer and peck at their eyes. In their dying the animals can see the beaks, see the claws that will tear the flesh from their bones, the entrails from their belly; and they are gripped with fear.

As June slipped into July and the Moors harried our old lines, shouted abuse, walked the hills within musket shot and stole our sheep – a hundred and fifty by one counting – we became the living dead, penned in walls of stone, and gripped with fear.

Our fear became more intense, became harder to bear when we heard rumours of the Moors making a treaty with the French and being supplied with gunpowder. It was the thing they needed most: with it they could fire our cannons, pound the town with our own cannon balls, and lay mines under the walls. It was hard to believe that a Christian country, a Catholic country, would support the infidel, would prefer them to Christian men, protestant men. And if they couldn't accept we were Christians, how could they allow the Moors to murder the Portuguese, the Irish – their fellow Catholics?

It didn't make much sense to me.

The next rumour was worse, was like Cain and Abel: brother killing brother. It came in two versions. The first claimed Englishmen had landed gunpowder in Tangiers, in our own harbour, and smuggled it to the Moors. The second claimed that English ships had evaded Admiral Herbert's blockade and landed gunpowder further up the coast at Salli. Sir Palmes feared both were true, called them treason, and late one night as I was resting my hand in a bowl of cold water and trying to ease the ache before he started dictating again, he said: 'As long as the enemy can be supplied with powder and other stores from England it will be impossible to reduce these people to reason.'

I nodded, tried not to think about this bleak prospect, and we went on to talk about Mamora. It was a Spanish city further along the coast, well into the Mediterranean Sea. It too was besieged by the Moors. 'The

Spanish,' he said, 'they see us as one of a chain of forts – holding back the Moors, the dark forces of Barbary.' He paused. 'Did you know the Moors once occupied Spain, for three, four hundred years – something like that?' I shook my head, I'd never heard of them till I was forced to join the regiment. 'The Spanish don't want them back. And they don't want Tangiers to fall. So they're prepared to help us.'

I looked at him in amazement. To me the Spanish were the enemy. The embodiment of evil. They were popery made man, made manifest. They were Bloody Mary, the Armada, the Inquisition and a hundred other evils rolled into one.

He smiled. 'It is a bit like getting into bed with the devil isn't it?' He smiled again. 'His Majesty has signed a treaty with the King of Spain and he's sending two hundred horses. Catalan horses. They won't be like our English horses but they will be used to the climate, and they will be able to be ridden right away. And they won't die in the heat like our English horses do, and that's the most important thing.'

I burst into a smile. It was the first good news I'd heard in months. 'And the men to ride them? The troopers?'

He nodded. 'They're coming with two hundred troopers. Spanish troopers.'

I felt my jaw drop.

He laughed. 'And we're going to be able to buy a couple of hundred horses for our own troopers.'

'They're coming? They're definitely coming?'

He nodded. 'And six hundred men of the King's Battalion under the command of Colonel Sackville. Plus another twelve companies of Dunbartons from Ireland. And they're raising a brand new regiment to serve in Tangiers. And best of all Lord Plymouth, the King's son, has been appointed to command it. And that means the King himself is committed to our success.'

I felt dizzy. 'I can hardly believe it, sir – after so many years with so few men.'

He smiled. 'I know how you feel. But in the meantime I want to dictate some instructions for Mister Sheres. I want him to build new quarters for all these men. I don't want them out in the rain, catching fevers and dying before the truce expires. And I want to write to London for more timber, more nails, more charcoal, more tools, more pots – more everything if I'm being honest.'

About an hour later when the letters were written he said: 'Did I tell you Lord Ossory has been appointed the new Governor.'

I shook my head. 'We all thought, sir, we all hoped, that you would be . . .'

He smiled. 'No. That's not to be.'

Lord Plymouth turned out to be about three years older than me and he looked like a Spaniard. He was tall, dark and swarthy – nicknamed

Don Carlos – and impatient for a fight. So impatient he came on ahead of his regiment, and when he found the truce still had another month or so to go, he invited himself onto Admiral Herbert's ship and went off to fight the pirates. Some thought him brave, others foolish, and others called him a 'silly bastard' and looked for a knowing grin.

Lord Ossory – if the papers are right – thought Tangiers was a poisoned chalice, a cup from which he had to drink. He took to his bed, raved in a fever, and died of fright. We prayed for him in the garrison church and tolled the bell but it was hard to disguise the sense of satisfaction we all felt: we knew Sir Palmes and he knew Tangiers – knew how to defend it.

The day after the service for Lord Ossory I found an old polishing rag, poured pink paste onto my gorget, and spent twenty minutes making it shine, making it glitter in the hot sunshine. Then I took my partisan and walked down to the Little Parade, opened the door to the apothecary's shop and rang the bell.

Mister Bartholomew shuffled into the shop, shaded his eyes and peered at me. His eyes were now white: circles of white layered on balls of white. 'Who are you?' he said.

'My name is Ensign Fenton, sir. I'm here at the request of Captain Lacey. I have a message for your daughter. For Mistress Wyndham.'

For a moment or two he stood and stared, and I was thinking he couldn't have heard, couldn't have understood, when he mumbled: 'Wait here.'

As she came into the shop I took off my hat, smiled, and bowed.

'It's you,' she said – waving her hand in a circle as if to encompass my new uniform.

I smiled again, then I let the smile die away. 'I've come to express my condolences. To tell you I'm sorry. To tell you he died in my arms.'

She nodded. 'They told me that.'

'And did they tell you what he said, in those final moments?'

'Said?'

'Hmm.' She shook her head. 'He said: Tell her I want her. Tell her I'll be waiting for her.'

Her face paled, she raised her hand and slapped me across the face.

I reeled back and banged into the wall. The top of my partisan pushed a bottle off the top shelf. It crashed to the floor and broke.

'You, sir, are a liar! I found out. I found the truth. Not at first. They wouldn't tell me at first. But then they did. They thought it would calm me. And now I know. I know the truth. His face was blown away. His mouth was a froth of bubbles. He didn't say a word.'

Then she put out her hand again and I tried to step back but the wall held me firm. 'What's this?' she said – lifting the ribbons that draped my left shoulder. 'These are my stitches. And these and these.' She ran her hand across my pocket. 'You're wearing his coat.' Then she grabbed at my hat. 'And that's his hat – I recognise the band. I straightened it, made it flat. Sewed those ribbons there.'

I didn't know what to say.

She walked to the back of the counter and laid both hands flat on the wooden top. 'He was my husband. Was the man I promised to honour and obey. And you come here, wearing his uniform, wearing his rank – pretending to be him – and telling me lies.' She shook her head. 'You are despicable. You are beyond contempt, and I don't want you in this shop. I don't want to set eyes on you ever again.' She bit her lips. 'My father was right about you.'

I opened my mouth. I tried to explain: my words tumbled out, tumbled over each other, and didn't make much sense.

She shook her head, raised her arm and pointed to the door. 'Get out, and don't come back.'

Her words echoed Mistress Tate's words, layered them with bitter memories – raped me of my dignity – and sent me stumbling out of the shop.

The peace came to an end a week earlier than we expected. The Moors calculate their months according to the moon and not according to the calendar – old or new – and before dawn on the morning of September 15th they removed the posts that marked the boundaries for our grazing, and soon after seven o'clock they opened fire – from the ruins of York Fort.

For us, that last week, when we knew the peace was dying and would not be renewed, was a time of frantic madness. There was no point in pretence, in a scrupulous observance of the conditions of the ceasefire. Seventeen cannons from the waterside walls were removed, hoisted onto the walls between Catherine Gate and Johnson's Battery, and mounted on carriages supplied by Admiral Herbert's ships. The walls between Irish Battery and Catherine Gate were strengthened and prepared to take another battery of cannon.

The *Swiftstakes* arrived on the 12th with provisions, stores of war and one hundred and thirty-five troopers. It was not the four, five or six hundred that had been requested, had been promised, but it was more than I'd seen in seven years. Some of the troopers were ill and their equipage was poor. All of their horses were unshod – to stop them slipping in the holds of the ship – and it took us a couple of days to fit them with new shoes and get them used to our climate.

The new troopers raised our spirits and changed the nature of the war that was to come: from now, instead of just watching and waiting, we could mount a fast-flowing attack, could take the Moors by surprise.

There was however one sour note and it niggled at us: the new men in the Dunbartons were paid up to the 25th of September and we were still eighteen months in arrears. It may not sound much, but it put them in the queues for the whore houses, put them in the taverns at night – and it put them on their backs with broken heads and empty pockets if they strayed into a dark alley on their own.

The Council of War resolved to wait till the Moors attacked. Sir Palmes told me we needed every day we could get and I found it strange to be copying instructions, preparations for a war that was still to be fought, and then, ten minutes later copying letters for London, letters that spoke of the peace that was to come, the peace that would need to be sealed with gifts to the Emperor of the Moors: 'pistols, fusils, fine watches, clocks, fine cambricks, fine Holland, fine broadcloth – in scarlet, green and violet – and two fine cabinets, table and stands, all of which is to be remitted by the first ship to be ready upon the closure of peace.'

As soon as the Moors broke the peace, the sentries on the walls from Irish Battery to Peterborough Tower returned their fire, and for several hours the thump of the great cannons echoed across the town and down the cleft of the old stream that is now the sewer. We stayed behind our walls, stayed tight, stayed safe, and the Moors stayed in their trenches. It was a strange day, a day of exuberance, a day that said goodbye to peace and left us celebrating the advent of war. It was not how I expected it to be. I'd imagined a solemn day. A day of prayer, of fasting, of people going in and out of church. But this was more like a carnival, a rejoicing, with the crackle of muskets replacing the crackle of fireworks.

Sir Palmes was determined to retake the high ground, to reclaim the ruins of Pole Fort.

Five days later, on the 20th, we paraded on the Old Parade at three in the morning. We were joined by Admiral Herbert and five hundred seamen. In silence, without the beating of drums, the blowing of bugles, the ringing of bells or the shouting of orders – without destroying the element of surprise – we listened to Sir Palmes, listened to his words of encouragement. Then we marched in muffled silence up to Catherine Gate and waited. The troopers rode to the front and waited in the portals of the gate. The seamen marched to the 'Old Gate' on the south-east side of the walls and waited.

At daybreak Sir Palmes and the troopers rode for Pole, found it deserted; rode for Monmouth, and found it deserted. Sir Palmes posted troopers between Pole and Monmouth and signalled for us to march out. Once again the advance party of two hundred men was called Forlorn Hope – this time with less cause. It included Lord Plymouth and the other gentlemen volunteers, and it marched straight to Pole. The King's Battalion – the Guards – marched to the right of the fort and positioned themselves on the skirt of the hill. We marched to the left: eight companies, a full battalion, under the command of Captain Giles. Further to our left, stretching towards Monmouth, two battalions of Dunbartons took up position. Major 'Wheel-about' Boynton commanded the reserve battalion: the eight other companies of our regiment. They remained behind the stockades in front of Catherine Gate and were to secure our retreat.

Admiral Herbert marched his seamen to Fort Cambridge and they began to dig trenches, to form the far left flank.

The Moors – soothed by our silence – slept on.

But then Major Beckman, the engineer, put his men to work. They began to dig trenches, to build a new Pole Fort – to bring timber, stone and brick up from Catherine Gate – and in a few minutes the sound of their carts, their digging, aroused the Moors.

In a confused, disbelieving manner they streamed out of their tents, down the hills, into the old trenches between Monmouth and James and opened fire. We returned their fire – began with what should have been three murderous volleys – but we were shooting at white-shawled heads, at little red caps that kept bobbing up and down, and the earth protected them, gave them the advantage.

To entice the Moors away from the men digging the trenches, Sir Palmes drew detachments from every battalion and sent them over to the ruins of Anne and Kendal. The Moors exploded in a frenzy of madness and the battle raged over an arc of a mile or more. Every hour or so the detachments-of-foot were being replaced, and towards noon I was doubling with ten men towards Anne. But the fire was too hot for us. I threw myself down on my belly and the others followed. We crawled for the ruins, for the gaunt ribs of timber and piles of sand that used to be Sandhill Fort.

It was strange to lie in the cup of shifting sand – the sand that was almost my grave – and I wished for my old cannon, for a box of granadoes and ten feet of height. For an hour or more the Moors pinned us down and every second or so a lead ball thudded against the wooden ribs and dropped into the sand. And in that weird way, when time expands and every moment is slowed, is made heavy with a tincture of opium, I began to look at the balls, to toss them up and down in my hand, to toss off the heat that was still within them, and to wonder if they were English balls, fired with English gunpowder.

Then the new troopers rode a fast sweep across the lines of battle, hacked hard at the Moors besieging us, and sent a dozen of them running: straight towards us. We stood and fired. And fired again. Two of them jumped into the ruins. I pulled out my sword and slashed at the one in white. Powel slashed at the one in brown, slashed from behind, chopped into his neck, into his shoulder. His head flopped, his neck spurted blood. He staggered against the white Moor, knocked him off balance. I brought my sword straight down, cleaved the white Moor's skull in half, saw his brains, saw the pink mass – veined and convoluted, just like a sheep's brain – and I thought they would taste all right: in a sauce of milk and onions, with a sprinkling of black pepper.

Then I saw the troopers were wearing cuirasses and backplates, and I was wondering if the ones that saved my life were still buried below me in their tomb of sand, when the field of battle stilled – time shook off the dregs of the poppy, sped up, returned to normal – and a strange calm settled on all of us. We looked from one to the other, realised we were still alive – not wounded, scratched in any way – and we began to laugh: wild mad laughs, laughs that betrayed fear, brayed relief.

I looked at the sun. It was past noon – maybe two o'clock. I was starving hungry. I shoved my hand into my pocket and discovered I'd eaten my bread and cheese. And there was nothing else: nothing to eat, nothing to drink. I tried to lick my lips, to wet them, but my mouth was dry.

Towards eight, as the Moors began to regain their courage, to pepper the air with musket shot, we were recalled. And so were the seamen who held the left flank, who fought their way through the sandhills – for four or five hundred yards – and secured 'Portuguese Cross': the old trading place.

The ground that used to be Pole was now entrenched and protected by a stockade – angled inwards to keep the Moors in our line of sight.

In the twilight we marched back to the town, left the new fort, the new Pole, to Lord Plymouth, Colonel Sackville and five hundred men of the King's Battalion – and hoped they would survive the night.

94

Next morning, in a dawn made wet by a night of heavy rain, we marched back to the lines of yesterday, and the battle began again. I use the word 'we' in a general sense for in truth our battalion swopped places with Major Boynton and we became the reserve for the day. For me it was a day of enforced idleness, of boredom and frustration, and I wandered up and down inside the stockades in front of Catherine Gate and cursed my luck. Late in the evening I copied Sir Palmes report for the two days: seven soldiers-of-foot were dead and eighteen were wounded; two troopers were wounded; two horses were killed and two more were wounded.

On the following morning, after another night of heavy rain, we marched back to Pole Fort, and Admiral Herbert's Grenadiers – famous for their long arms and granado-throwing skills – occupied the ruins of Fort Monmouth. The Moors attacked on horseback, directed the whole thrust of their attack against the Grenadiers. The Dunbartons advanced, the troopers charged, and the battle began. We loaded and fired and loaded again in blind unthinking madness. They came at us in waves – swords slashing the air, mouths screaming – and at times I thought they were going to overwhelm us. But at the end of the day, when the new walls for Pole Fort had risen a little higher, and we had preserved our lines of defence, had made them ours by right of arms, we abandoned them, gave them back to the Moors for the night, and prepared to march back to the town. But the Moors had observed this twilight-retreat – twice – and far down the hill they massed to the left and right of the lane, and waited. Major Hackett advanced with the reserve, drew the Moors to one side, and then, covered by cannon and musket fire from the city walls we doubled down the lane, passed through the stockades and the revetment, and entered Catherine Gate.

The toll for the day made grim reading: eight dead, twenty wounded.

Next morning as we took up our positions again, the Moors appeared in their thousands, slipped into their trenches and opened fire. We pinned them down for most of the day, but we couldn't dislodge them, couldn't make any impression on their numbers. In the twilight we left behind a garrison of six hundred men and marched back to the town feeling bitter, feeling thwarted.

This became the pattern of our days and little by little the walls of Pole grew higher, grew thicker, and the defences surrounding them grew more secure.

The Moors, recognising they could not take the town till they took Pole Fort, began to attack the fort by night.

On my first night in the fort, as the rain softened to a drizzle, the talk was all about Lord Plymouth: riding fast, riding hot all day; then up all night in Pole, mounting guard, getting drenched, getting cold and breaking out in a fever. And now he was fluxed, delirious, and confined to his bed in the Upper Castle. A day or two earlier I'd been admiring him, admiring his clothes, coveting his rank, his title, his wealth, but now – now I was glad I was me.

I was bloody tired and wet around the edges. My new winter coat – red, heavy, tight-fitting and bound with a sash – was warm inside, but the wind was blowing the rain, blowing it up my sleeves and down my neck and I could feel the cold seeping into my shirt, into my wrists, into my neck. My shoes were wet and thick with mud, and the damp was inching its way up my stockings. The cracks between my toes were squelching water, were itching, were trenched with pain – sharp, stinging pain.

Tents covered the ground in the centre of the fort. They were supposed to protect us, but the canvas was old, cracked and eaten with mildew, and the tents leaked: dripped water all the time. In the early evening it was almost wetter in the tents than outside because the water was ponding on the canvas and fattening the drips.

Towards midnight I joined Corporal Powel and Sergeant Lockhart on the east rampart. For a long time we stared into the dark – made shapeless by the black of the night – and then, just as he was saying: 'They won't attack. Not on a night like this,' the Moors fired a bloody great cannon. The cannon ball ploughed into the earth walls – fountained the earth into the air. Then the Moors rose from the mud. They'd been slithering along like black snakes – black on black, unseen by us – and now they were running towards the first stockade, waving their swords and screaming.

I opened the tarred box, took out a burning match and turned to Lockhart. 'Why do you think they scream so bloody much?'

He looked bemused. 'They say it fills them with courage, stops them being afraid.'

'I don't see anything to be afraid of.' I raised my musket, took aim, applied the fire, and shot a snake in the head.

'Fucking hell!' I yelled. 'Did you see that? Straight through his bloody head.'

He laughed and a musket ball screamed between us.

'Shit! That was close.' We both laughed. Then he rested his musket on the wooden edge of the parapet – steadied his barrel, improved his aim – and fired.

After an hour or so, the Moors slid away into the night and the cannon fell silent. I turned to Lockhart and said: 'When we were down there in Stream Fort and Sandhill, I used to get the shits. Used to wet myself when they got too bloody close. But here, with all this height and all these men, and bloody thick walls, it's almost too easy.'

'That's probably what they used to think in Charles.'

'I didn't know you were a bloody philosopher.'

He laughed. 'I'm a realist. And I don't have a death-wish.'

I pretended to laugh, but inside, deep inside I was hurting: hurting for the woman I had wronged; and hurting for the woman who had wronged me.

95

Over the next few days the Moors built another battery close to Pole, and began to pound the fort by day and by night, and we could not touch them.

The great cannons on the bastion below Peterborough Tower destroyed a cannon in the battery close to Charles Fort. This provoked the Moors – or offended their dignity – for they trained a cannon on Sir Palmes's house in the Market Place, blew great holes in it and 'frightened the ladies'.

Then the Moors did what we had always feared they would do: they built a battery of three cannons on the sandhills overlooking the harbour and pounded the Mole and the ships lying at anchor. But their aim was poor and the best they achieved was a shot on the Mole that 'battered a poor cook's broth off the fire'.

Sir Palmes, writing home to England, complained about being promised 1,000 matchlocks and 700 firelocks, and receiving none, and he ended by saying: 'there is never a day that fifty or sixty arms are not spoilt; so unless a speedy supply be sent I must give over fighting for without them nothing can be done.'

By the 7th of October Pole Fort was almost ready to mount cannons; Admiral Herbert was in Spain with a fleet of ships embarking our two hundred Spanish troopers; and the Storekeeper-of-ammunition was reporting on small shot: our muskets had fired two and a half tons of lead in fifteen days and our reserves had dropped to six tons. Sir Palmes dictated orders for the compulsory purchase of all lead stored in the town – it raised the reserves by one ton – and he sent a ship to Spain to purchase lead: 'ready-cast'.

In Irish Battery some of the wooden carriages were so rotten they collapsed in a heap the first time the cannons were fired. And on the walls to the left and right of Catherine Gate the great cannons – transferred from the waterfront walls – were defective, were the victims of years of neglect, of rust that bloomed in the salt air. Three of them burst, killed four men, hit Mister Sheres in the leg and wounded several other men.

Then the Alcaide sent in a letter under a flag of truce: he proposed peace, if we abandoned Pole Fort. Sir Palmes thought the letter was both 'insolent and impertinent' and the offer was rejected.

The siege continued and a few days later we observed the Moors digging a tunnel, a horizontal mine-shaft, and it was heading towards Pole Fort.

On the 17th Lord Plymouth died. In London and Plymouth they were still raising his regiment: the Second Tangiers Regiment-of-Foot. In common parlance they were to be called the Plymouth Regiment or the 'Plymouths' – it was traditional for a regiment to take the name of its colonel and at times this could be confusing: some were saying we were still the 'Inchiquins' and others were saying we were the 'Ossorys'. To me it didn't matter much, but I have to acknowledge that when I was up in the Governor's House looking through some of the old documents I had to keep reminding myself that the name changed when the Governor changed – the regiment did not change, the regiment remained the same.

Sir Palmes talked of the new regiment having sixteen companies – of sixty-five men and three officers – and when the siege is over, when the King's Battalion and the Dunbartons have gone home, the 'Plymouths' are to stay on, are to become part of the permanent garrison. It was strange to think that Lord Plymouth, the only man in the whole regiment who arrived in time, was dead, and the others were still a month away, and by then, as Sir Palmes confessed to me in a moment of gloom, of pessimism, the 'Plymouths' will have a new name and 'the war will be won or lost'.

Each day Sir Palmes rode our lines, went out with the dawn and came back with the dusk: encouraged the men, shouted advice, issued orders. Each day he rode the same horse, and each day the Moors recognised him: fired at him, and missed. Soon after seven on the morning of the 24th, Sir Palmes was directing the digging of emplacements on a rise to the left of Peterborough Tower. A hundred and fifty soldiers-of-foot and fifty Spanish troopers were guarding the diggers. The Moors, entrenched again in their old lines in front of Charles Fort, recognised Sir Palmes and opened fire. A shot smashed into his chest. He toppled forward. Then he fell from his horse. Dazed and in pain, he ordered the work to go on. The men made a stretcher and carried him back to the Upper Castle.

The Moors, encouraged by their success, swarmed out of the trenches. The troopers swept forward, chased them back to their lines, fired into the trenches, cut them down with their swords, slew their horses and chased their riders. As the troopers rode back, the Moors regained their courage, and swarmed out of the trenches again. The troopers, now reinforced by another troop of Spanish horse, charged again, carried them right back to the trenches and killed every man who didn't jump into the trenches and flee.

Then they trotted back to the ground they occupied at the beginning of the attack, and resumed their guard.

It was a display of might, of power, of bravery, of courage – the like of which we had never seen – and in the night a hundred toasts, maybe a thousand toasts, would be drunk to their success. And no one – least of all me – thought of them as Dons or papists. They were saviours, were a hint of what was possible.

As the day wore on Sir Palmes hovered between life and death and by early evening we all knew his wound was mortal. It tarnished the Spanish victory and it depressed our spirits, and no one was quite sure what would happen next.

I walked up to the Governor's House. Inside was still, dead still, as though it was already a tomb for Sir Palmes. There was nothing for me to do. Doctor Lawrence, Colonel Sackville and Ensign Fairborne were upstairs with Sir Palmes.

I wandered down to the Old Parade – the Castle Hill side was crusted with the new barracks Mister Sheres had built with the money that was supposed to pay for the next section of the Mole – passed through Middleton's Line and ambled along the Little Parade.

Standing in the dark, looking through the windows, I could see her in the shop cleaning the counter. She was on her own. I knocked, open the door, walked in and took off my hat. Her face froze.

'I wanted to explain,' I said.

She was wearing a blue dress with a white apron and a white lace cap. The gorget hung from her neck. On her it looked like a silver necklace, a silver moon. On Wyndham it had looked strange – like a dropped chin.

'I don't want to know,' she said. 'You have his clothes. You have his rank. You have his place in the regiment. You have everything he had except this.' She touched the gorget. 'And his name. You don't have his name. I have his name. That's all I have. His name.' And she paused. 'I know you want me. I've always known that. But you can't have me. That's all that's left. And if you took that, had that, he would be truly dead. And he would become you and you would become him. I want to keep his memory. To keep him alive in my mind.' She stretched out her hand and touched mine. 'Please don't come again.'

96

I left Jenny, walked past the Watergate and up Misericordia Street, and as the rise slowed my feet, a crack of thunder split the heavens in two and the rain poured down. It was like standing under a waterfall. Within a second or two I would be drenched. I ran for shelter, ran up the cathedral steps and into the porch. I took off my hat and shook it, shook my arms and legs, edged into the shadows, the shelter of the porch and waited. But the rain did not ease. If anything it grew worse. And it chilled the air.

I thought about Jenny, thought about the softness of her voice, the sweetness of her smile and the tenderness of her touch. To me she was a temptation, and I wondered if I was a temptation to her. The thought raced my heart, dried my mouth and stirred my flesh. I closed my eyes and fell into a soft warm dream: of having and wanting and having again.

Then the dream passed but the rain did not, and now it was driven by the wind and it was making me shiver. I walked up and down, rubbed at my hands, then I gave the cathedral door a gentle push and it opened. If I hadn't been in the cathedral before, hadn't mourned the four Irishmen, I would never have gone in, never have had the courage to set foot in such a place. But it seemed right, natural; and inside it was warm, and once again I smelt the smell of that first night: the sweet smell of stale incense. It was calming, beguiling in a strange way, and I sat down on one of the benches.

I counted twenty-three other shapes, other people, sitting, kneeling, praying. Most were on their own but one or two were huddling close together for warmth, solace – to share their faith? – I don't know. None of them had come in while I'd been in the porch, come in to get out of the rain. This was not like our church in Elme or the garrison church over the road.

They were cold and empty: no one ever went in to pray on their own. Our church was a formal place, a place for formal prayer, but this – this had a quiet sincerity, a soft wet-lipped mumbling, a rattling of prayer beads. People believed. People were here because they wanted to be, and not because they had to be. It was in truth a house of prayer. This disturbed me, for I knew, we all knew, truth did not reside in this church. But faith did: the faith of our fathers, the old faith, the faith that was encrusted with error – was evil, twisted, perverted, corrupt. So why did it draw people on a cold wet night? Were they naïve, shackled, blinkered, coerced into thinking they wanted to be here, had to be here? I did not know where the truth lay, but I did know that our church was shut, was cold, dead, empty – was locked for the night.

My thoughts drifted on to Sir Palmes. I'd come to like him, to respect him. He'd been in Tangiers for eighteen years. Tangiers was his life, and now it was about to take his life. I knew I'd miss him, miss his vigour, his enthusiasm, his thinking ahead, his trying to predict the future, to second-guess the Moors. I knelt and closed my eyes, prayed for him. Then my prayers drifted into memory, and I remembered the first time I spoke to him, in this church over by the side altar. He heard my confession – confession of truth – and he spared Oldfield, absolved him of death. In Oldfield's time of penance, of punishment, death returned to claim him, but the blame for that did not lie with Sir Palmes.

Then I became aware that the church had filled with silence. The heavy beat of the rain had passed away. I stood up, turned to walk towards the door and a voice said: 'Martyn. What are you doing here?'

My heart raced. I felt like a little boy caught with his breeches down, caught playing with himself. 'Sir?'

Lieutenant de Colville emerged from the shadows. He repeated his question: 'What are you doing here?'

'It was raining. I came in out of the rain.'

'I saw you earlier on. I didn't know it was you. I saw you on your knees – praying.'

'I was thinking about Sir Palmes. It seemed natural to pray for him in the hour of his death.'

He nodded. We walked out of the cathedral, stood on the steps, and smelt the clean air. 'I've been thinking about your promise,' he said, and I could catch the hesitation in his voice. 'Your promise to do what I asked you to do.'

I nodded. I'd let it slip my mind and as each day passed, I'd come to think it had slipped his mind. I turned, stared at him – eye to eye – tried to show he held no fear for me.

'I've always known what it should be, but I've hesitated to ask. But now, tonight, seeing you here, of your own free will, I know it's right. And this is what I'd like you to do.'

I listened to his words. They chilled my heart, froze my spirit, and exploded my mind. I shoved him against the wall, shoved him hard, and yelled: 'You must be bloody mad!'

Then I stormed down the steps and into the night. The rain returned in howling gusts and it wet my clothes – wet them right through to my skin – but it did not cool my anger.

97

Sir Palmes, in great pain, lingered on through the night and in the morning Colonel Sackville took command of the garrison and called a Council of War.

Captain Lacey, eager to know what was happening but unable to go up to the Governor's House himself – he was not a member of the Council of War – ordered me to go up to the Governor's office: in case I could be of assistance.

When the council adjourned for an hour, soon after midday, we could detect a new spirit, a new optimism. Major Boynton had lost some of his caution and I overheard him say: 'He's right. If we don't attack, Pole Fort will fall within a week, two at the most. We saw what happened to Charles. We know they have started digging a mine. And we know they're digging trenches. In a week the fort will be encircled and we won't be able to relieve it. And when it falls the town will fall.'

In the late afternoon they agreed a plan. Tomorrow was to be a day of preparation. The attack was to be launched at dawn on the following day: October 27th.

As the evening wore on, as officers came and went and we copied their orders, the outline of the plan became clear. The men in Pole were to be the advance guard, the Forlorn Hope. As soon as they attacked, the whole garrison was to march to Pole and attack. The strategy was to drive the Moors out of the trenches, to deprive them of the protection the earth offered, and then to fall upon them with troopers and soldiers-of-foot. As soon as parts of the trenches were taken and filled in, the troopers were to cross them, to pursue the fleeing Moors. The Militia was to make a diversion to the right, and the longboats from all the ships anchored in the Bay were to make one to the left, to distract the Moors, to stop them reinforcing the centre – the ground around Pole Fort.

Next day brought us a string of bitter disappointments. The pikemen from our company and Captain Philpott's company were to combine, to carry pikes and shovels. The pikes were to kill the Moors in the trenches, or to drive them out of the trenches – by standing on the edge of the trench and thrusting down – and the shovels were to fill in the trenches. I was ordered to go with the pikemen and carry a partisan. I'd been expecting to carry the ensign and in my mind I'd seen myself standing in the thick of the battle, and heard the musket balls screaming past my head as I kept the flag flying. But it was not to be, and Captain Lacey said: 'A partisan will be more useful than an ensign when you're in the trenches. Captain Philpott and I have agreed that all our pikemen and all our musketeers will rally to his ensign – so there's no need for you to carry ours.' Then he patted me on the shoulder. 'It's a disappointment I know, but we need every man we can get, and the men look up to you, they admire your guts. And after some of the bloody awful displays of leadership, lack of nerve, lack of courage we've seen in some of our companies in the last few days, we need a few more men like you.' He paused for a moment. 'One other thing. The musketeers from both companies will also be combining and their first priority will be to protect you, to make sure you get those trenches filled in as quickly as possible.'

At three in the morning, in total silence we assembled on the Old Parade: five battalions-of-foot, one battalion of seamen, seven troops-of-horse. In the dark it was hard to estimate the exact numbers, but remembering the orders, the estimates of yesterday, the seamen and the foot looked to number 1,300; the troopers 300; the Militia – strengthened by the volunteers and the molemen – 200, maybe a few more. In Pole we had another 150 men. Adding all these figures together gave us a force of about 2,000. To these we could add the seamen in the diversion. They were to make it look as though they were loading the longboats, were preparing to land at any moment, and with luck they would come under fire, would tie up hundreds of Moors and stop them attacking us.

And how many men did the Moors have? Depending on who I talked to, listened to, the numbers were as low as 8,000 or as high as 16,000. A lot thought 15,000, but to be honest we had no way of counting them, and rumours ebbed and flowed according to the state of the teller's bowels, or the richness of his imagination.

The dark made us into shapes, uniform shapes, and it took away our identity, and it was hard to believe that the dawn, the day that was soon to be, could take away our lives.

Colonel Sackville spoke to the whole assembly, then he walked over to our two battalions, lowered his voice a little and said: 'Your Colonel, Sir Palmes Fairborne, is still gravely ill and could die at any moment. Some of your actions in the last few days have besmirched his honour, and the honour of your regiment. You know what I'm talking about and I see no point in recalling each of these acts of cowardice right now. Or naming the companies involved.' He paused, gave us time for his words – words that were barbed with truth – to settle in our minds. 'Today you will have a chance to redeem yourselves. So take heart, take courage, and do your duty. And should any man run away again, dawdle, or refuse to fight, I shall have him shot.'

As he walked away Lockhart hissed: 'Bastard!'

Crabtree whispered. 'It's all right for him. Only been here a bloody month. Doesn't know what it's really like, year after bloody year. And I bet he's been paid; bet he's been stuffing food in his mouth all the time we've been bloody starving; and—'

I spun around. 'Be quiet,' I hissed. 'And stop your bloody bitching.'

We marched in sullen silence up to Catherine Gate, and in the still air the soft sound of the horses snorting came drifting over the walls. Then we filed through the gate and lined up behind the troopers. The King's Battalion formed the right flank, then came the Dunbartons – the mad bloody Scotsmen who didn't know the meaning of the word fear, then came us, and just as the battalion of seamen came through the gate to take up their position on the left flank, we were discovered.

The Moors beat their drums and blew their trumpets. The sound shivered my spine and froze my mind. I clenched my partisan and bit my lips.

Colonel Sackville signalled for the men in Pole Fort, in Forlorn Hope, to rush the trenches. They were followed by the reserves secreted in Pole. Then Major Beckmen and his men rushed out of Pole, rushed the mine shaft – to prevent the Moors exploding the mine.

The troopers galloped through the stockades in front of Catherine Gate and charged up the hill. The King's Battalion and the Dunbartons hurled after them screaming: 'Hurrah! Hurrah! Hurrah!'

We pounded after them – screaming and yelling – and behind us came the seamen: chanting obscenities.

We fell upon the Moors like a tidal wave crashing from the right, breaking, foaming along the full length of their lines.

Granadoes rose in the air, dropped deep in the trenches and exploded. The musketeers fired into the trenches. The Moors – hundreds of them, hundreds more than we were told to expect – jumped out of the trenches, screamed, and ran at us with swords held high in the air. We bunched together, lowered our pikes and charged – ran the bastards back into the trench and hurled our pikes straight down. Skewered them together. Speared them to the earth.

A Moor hurled towards me. I caught his eye, caught the wet brown globe of madness, of hate. I ran straight at him. He slashed at the shaft of my partisan, jarred my arms. I kept running, ran the spearhead straight through him. His eyes flared, then glazed, and he toppled – pulled me to the ground. I jumped up. Tried to pull my partisan free. It wouldn't move. I put my foot on him but it still wouldn't budge. I pulled out my sword, slashed at him, slashed at another Moor – took off his hand. He dropped his sword, fountained blood and sunk to the ground. I slashed at his neck. His head rolled off. I chased it. Booted it into the trench. Then I saw the trench was empty, the fighting had moved a few yards to our left and right and I yelled: 'Get your shovels!'

We dug into the embankment, shovelled the earth back into the trench and buried the Moors – buried the living and the dead – as the musketeers fired straight over our heads. Then we rushed to the next trench, shovelled earth like madmen, like demented gravediggers, gravefillers. I looked up and screamed at the Spanish troopers. They galloped towards us, laughing, slashing the air with their swords. In a couple of minutes, twenty or thirty of them crossed the first trenches and encircled the Moors.

In a moment of stillness, I saw, heard, the diversion in front of Peterborough Tower. Banners were flying, men were assembling, were marching up and down. Men were riding horses.

I laughed. They were the rockcart horses. Docile plodders. But from here they looked like another troop-of-horse, a reserve waiting to spring into battle. A reserve of old men. A Militia of withered limbs and boys with no hair on their balls. It was pathetic, laughable. But it looked real, and far to my right, beyond the ashes of Henrietta, I could see the Moors massing, waiting for this force to charge into battle.

Then the Moors on horseback charged the Spanish troopers, and the Moors in front of us rallied and fell upon our lines. We stood our ground – now red with blood and heavy with dead and dying men – and fought, hand to hand, man to man.

In a vague way, like being aware of a distant thunderstorm, I heard the cannons in Irish Battery pounding the sandhills.

Out of the corner of my eye I saw flashes of lightning – flashes from the mouths of the cannons by Peterborough Tower – and still the Moors waited, waited for the Militia to advance.

Hours later – that was how it seemed – we forced the last of the Moors out of the last of the trenches. The troopers rode them down, cut them down – and when they broke and fled – they chased them all the way back to their tents, a mile or more behind the lines.

I looked up, wiped the sweat of victory from my eyes, spat out the taste of gunpowder, slashed the head off a wounded Moor, looked at the sun and reckoned it must be about three o'clock.

I knew, we all knew, that without the troopers, the Moors would have regained their courage, regrouped, and by now they could have been charging us again, and we could have been staring defeat, staring death straight in the eye.

Far below me, to the right, well out in the Bay, the seamen were still in their longboats rowing, massing, preparing for a landing that would never come. In the sandhills above them, the cannons and the muskets fell silent, and the Moors began to drift away. Then the Moors on the slopes beyond Henrietta also began to drift away.

In the eerie calm that followed, we pushed the dead horses into the trenches, heaved the Moors on top of them, and buried them in the earth that was supposed to protect them.

Close to Pole Fort Captain Beckmen built a stockade around a spur of land to prevent the Moors returning to their old mine shaft and to stop them digging a new one. We filled in all the new trenches round Pole and all the old trenches between James and Monmouth, and we destroyed everything that could provide the Moors with cover – if they were mad enough to return.

In silence we carried our dead back to the town. We had redeemed our regiment's honour and no one would speak of our supposed cowardice, supposed fondness for retreat – ever again. But the price was high, too high: 34 of our men were dead; 124 were wounded. I helped to carry Sergeant Owen. He was dead – shot in the head by a lead ball. As I looked down at him, swaying as we walked, his mouth twisted and froze, and I knew it would soften no more, speak no more; and that Welsh lilt of his, that way of making words sound like music was gone, gone for ever. And so too was his advice, his help, his friendship, and my eyes filled with tears.

Crabtree was wounded: slashed in the calf, slashed to the bone. The wound was thick with blood, black with mud. We carried him back to the infirmarium, told him his leg could be stitched but feared it would have to be cut off.

We scoured the battlefield, cleared it of weapons, and dragged the four cannons we had recaptured from the Moors back to the town. In the quiet hollows of death we found the bodies of another forty Moors. Their heads had been hacked off. No one had been able to restrain our men, to curb their barbarity, their desire for revenge, for their memories – our memories – were fuelled by the headless corpses, the corpses of our friends: the men who died in the retreat from Fort Charles.

We laid their bodies on the ground, just outside the stockades between Catherine Gate and Fountain Fort. The Moors came for them and in return they brought four bodies, four more men for us to mourn.

In the evening, in a town caught between the excitement of victory and the sorrow of death, I walked up to the Governor's House. Sir Palmes was dead. He saw our victory, saw the victory he made possible. In his dying hours they carried him onto a balcony and sat him in a chair, and he watched the battle, watched us come home in triumph, bearing five of their colours, their standards of honour. They say his mind was lucid, say he talked about Alexander the Great and Julius Caesar, and the ebbs and tides of fortune, and he did not resent the victory that was denied to him but granted to Colonel Sackville.

The Governor's House became a house of mourning and in the silence, in the stillness of my soul – sucked empty by so much death – I copied the mortality tables: the cost of victory. They recorded the details regiment by regiment. I looked at the totals for a long time. They became engraved in my mind, became tombstones in the graveyard of my mind: officers – 14 killed, 32 wounded; sergeants, corporals and men – 98 killed, 334 wounded. In the months ahead I would read other totals, and maybe they included men who lingered and died of wounds later on – I do not know. These are the figures I copied. They are wreathed in my mind, and I will never forget them.

Our total casualties for the eight days, October 20th–27th, were estimated at six hundred and fifty. There were no accurate figures for the Moors. We heard they'd lost a thousand men, but we also heard they never include the Mountaineers, the Berbers, in their death counts, and Colonel Sackville thought the true figure lay somewhere between thirteen and fourteen hundred.

As I walked back to our lodgings, walked in the dark, the great bell in Peterborough Tower began to toll, to mourn the men who were no more.

98

Within a few hours, Omar the Alcaide of Alcazar, offered to restore the truce or negotiate a peace. Colonel Sackville chose peace. It was to last for six months and the conditions were to be much the same as before: no forts or lines were to be built or repaired outside the walls, but we could graze cattle, cut hay, cut wood, quarry stone, hunt wildfowl, and fish the sea from Jews River to the river by Old Tangiers. In return for peace the Moors were to sell us fruit, two hundred sheep, one thousand fowls and one hundred head of cattle – each month. We were to supply them with muskets, gunpowder and cloth. I do not know the exact quantities. Colonel Sackville preferred the clerks from his own battalion, the King's Battalion, and I was ordered to return to my company. I was no longer needed. And like a stream deprived of water in a drought, my sources of information dried up.

I must confess I did not understand the politics of war and peace till a few days later Colonel Sackville commanded all the officers in our regiment to attend him in the great hall, in the Governor's House. He began by saying that the gifts from the Alcaide, gifts of wild boar, venison and river-fish, were given and received as a mark of respect, as a tribute to the valour of our officers, and told us he had thanked the Alcaide for them on our behalf. To me it was strange to thank, to flatter a man who sent so many of our officers to their death. And like so many others in that long night when the bells tolled and the town wept, I was hot for pursuit, for revenge. But now as I listened to the Colonel, listened to his logic, I knew that other forces had to prevail.

He ended his speech by saying: 'Our engineers have surveyed the walls, and they have estimated that the cost of strengthening the walls and building new fortifications, will come to three hundred thousand pounds per year, for ten years. That makes a total of three million pounds.' We looked at each other and gasped in astonishment. 'To defend the walls we must hold the high ground. And to do that I believe we need ten thousand soldiers-of-foot, and eight hundred, maybe a thousand troopers. All these men, and the walls, would have to be paid for by His Majesty out of his own privy purse. Parliament, for reasons that are well known to most of you, will not contribute any money towards the up-keep of Tangiers. Not a penny,' and he paused. 'So – we are forced to conclude that such an undertaking is beyond His Majesty's purse. In these circumstances, the great prize is not a triumph of arms, a victory in the field – and in saying this I am not demeaning the great victory we won – the great victory, the great prize, is peace. Permanent peace.' He looked around the hall and we waited in hushed silence. 'To this end I have asked His Majesty to send a Royal Ambassador to Mulai Ismail: the Emperor of the Moors. It is an opportune moment, and may not come again. And I would ask you gentlemen to keep this man in your prayers, for in the months to come much will depend on him.'

A few minutes later I said to Captain Lacey and Lieutenant de Colville: 'I don't understand why the members of Parliament won't help us. Did we do something to offend them?'

The Captain shook his head. 'They fear the past. They know what Cromwell did with an army that was loyal to him. And they fear us. They think we're all papists.' He smiled at de Colville. 'They think the King could bring us back to England, suppress Parliament and rule on his own. And if he died, if the Duke of York – a papist – became King, he'd have a papist army to support him. Then he could restore popery and Parliament couldn't do anything about it – without another civil war, and nobody wants that.' He paused, said something to Major Boynton – our acting Colonel – then he came back to us. 'So I think Parliament will talk a lot, will pretend to look upon us with favour, but will never vote us any money.'

In late November, Sergeant Brandon returned to our company and reclaimed his old position of pike-Sergeant. Sergeant Lockhart became our musket-Sergeant. Crabtree – still learning to walk on one leg and one crutch – was ordered to work for Sergeant O'Sullivan in the clerk's office. It was my idea but I couldn't tell him that. He hated the thought of being a clerk, claimed it made him into a pensioner, made him old before his time. I told him it was warm and dry, had a fire and paid money, and he was bloody lucky he wasn't pushed out, given a tavern licence, and told to look after himself. But he couldn't, or wouldn't, see the thrust of my argument.

De Colville was being just as bloody stupid: he couldn't see the thrust of my argument either. It boiled down to this: I didn't care what I'd promised – or what he thought I'd promised – I wasn't going to take instruction from a popish priest. And that was that. He could call it what he bloody liked, dress it up in any words that suited him, but I still wasn't going into that popish convent. I wasn't going to learn about his religion. And no, I wasn't prejudiced. I knew what was right and what was wrong. And his church was wrong.

'But how do you know?' he said – exasperating me once again. 'If you haven't listened, haven't learnt.'

'I have! I've heard a hundred bloody sermons on the subject. And everyone came to the same conclusion. Popery was wrong. Was evil. Was corrupt. Was everything that was wrong with this bloody world.'

'But if you've never heard someone set out the arguments for Catholicism – someone who believes it's true – you're not in a position to judge. In many ways it's like a case in a court of law. You've only heard one side and you've made up your mind. But half the evidence is still missing, still to be presented.'

'As far as I'm concerned it can stay missing for the rest of my bloody life. I don't give a fuck.'

'I seem to remember you promised to do anything. Anything I asked. Except the one thing I really want you to do.'

'And I'm not bloody doing that either.'

'I wish you wouldn't swear so much. You're supposed to be an officer. It makes you sound crude and vulgar, like a pikeman.' He paused. 'I suppose you know they say swearing is the sign of a poor mind – or a poor schooling. It means you don't have a good command of English. Don't know enough words to express yourself correctly – every time.'

I stared at him. Inside I was seething. I clenched my hands, looked at his nose, stepped back and raised my fist.

'You won't win an argument by thumping me on the nose. You win an argument by using your brain.' He tapped the side of his head with his finger. 'And when you've finished this course of instruction, you'll be able to make up your own mind. No one's asking you to convert. No one's expecting you to convert. And after a while I think you'll surprise yourself. I think you'll enjoy talking to Father Francifo. He has a fine mind. He can teach you a lot. Maybe he can teach you not to swear.' And he laughed.

I shook my fist at him, clenched my teeth, and tore out of the room.

In mid-December the Second Tangiers Regiment-of-foot arrived on the *Newcastle*. The ship was overcrowded – it was built for half the number – and the holds were cold and wet. The storms of winter had battered the ship, and the voyage had taken too long. More than fifty men had died, had been buried at sea, and the rest were in a pitiful state. Lieutenant-Colonel Kirke and Major Trelawny came ashore and an hour or so later we drew stretchers from the infirmarium and began to carry the men who couldn't walk from the Queen's Steps on the Mole, to Mister Sheres's new barracks on the slopes of Castle Hill.

Within a few days our spirits were pummelled by the worst of rumours: we were to amalgamate with Colonel Kirke's regiment. In view of the number of men left in both regiments it was a sensible idea, but to us it would be a public humiliation, a public disgrace. Colonel Boynton petitioned His Majesty, 'in the name of the officers and men of the Old Regiment' and some months later His Majesty was 'graciously pleased' to allow us to retain our honour and our own identity. But in the meantime it soured our relations with Colonel Kirke and not one of our officers was inclined to trust him. His ambitions became a subject of much speculation and he evoked a deep sense of fear, of disquiet.

Colonel Sackville concluded a second peace agreement with the Alcaide and we were told it was going to last for a whole year. It was unbelievable – like a gift from the gods – and it lightened our spirits. But soon after that, when the King's Ambassador to the Moors arrived, and we escorted him in state to the Upper Castle, our spirits became heavy, became weighted with lead. The man was a veteran, an officer in the Tangiers Troop-of-horse and he'd acted as an envoy to the Moors many times in the past. Now he was back with a title, with a knighthood, and we had to call him Sir James – Sir James Leslie. We were expecting a Lord, a man of breeding, of high birth, and I think the Moors were expecting the same, and I could imagine them being surprised, being offended, feeling slighted when Sir James arrived. To them he would still be Captain Leslie: a common man, a man who rose through the ranks – a man whom fortune had favoured.

None of us could see what Sir James was going to do, now that Colonel Sackville had signed the treaty. There was talk of a letter from His Majesty to the Emperor Ismail, but it didn't need an ambassador to deliver a letter – and we were bemused by his presence.

A day or so later, with an escort of horse, mounted trumpeters and mounted drummers, Sir James passed through Catherine Gate and began the slow procession to the tents of the Alcaide – in the hills beyond the Marshan. I do not know what was said at this meeting or all the other meetings that ate up the last days of December and drifted into January. But I do know Sir James wore a grim face and Colonel Sackville looked most out of sorts – quite poorly, was the general opinion.

Then a letter arrived from the Emperor Ismail. It commanded the Ambassador to attend him at once. But Sir James could not go, would not go, and the Alcaide agreed with him: the presents Sir Palmes had requested so long ago had not arrived, and Sir James could not go without the presents. Protocol, diplomacy, demanded the presents.

Sir Palmes – lying now in cold silence below the flagstones in the garrison church – would have been disgusted. But not surprised. He wrote so many letters, made so many pleas for things that never arrived, I often thought it would break his spirit, but it never did.

I went to bed and dreamt about presents becoming the present, being lost at sea – being lost in the past; being carried into the future – becoming future presents, and thinking this sounded like a tense, a grammatical tense: we will be being. I was thinking I'd made a new discovery, thinking it would change our understanding of English, of grammar, and would rank beside O'Sullivan's book of words, when a loud voice screamed in my ear: 'Where are my presents? I want my presents! You have no presents?' The air chilled, grew a heavy frost, a whitening of death, and the voice said: 'No presents. No head.' A black-faced Moor stepped forward, eyed my neck, my long skinny neck, and swung his sword. The sword glinted, flashed in my eyes. Then I felt the blow, felt the cut, felt my head begin to topple. I sat up, woke up, jolted my head backwards and forwards.

Captain Lacey – half-greyed by the dawn – was bending over my bed. His hand slid from my neck to my shoulder.

My heart was racing, was beating in my ears. 'Jesus,' I whispered. 'You gave me a hell of a fright.'

'I'm sorry. I didn't mean to startle you.' He sat down on the end of my bed. 'I suppose you know about the presents – or should I say the lack of presents? – and Sir James, and the Emperor.'

'Yes sir.'

'I thought you would.' He smiled to himself. 'The Governor's Council has decided that the Ambassador cannot meet the Emperor till the presents arrive, but in the meantime, Colonel Kirke is to visit the Emperor in Mequinez. He is to act as the Ambassador's representative, and he is to present Sir James's apologies, to explain the reasons for his delay – with great formality. He is to be escorted by the Alcaide whom we now know lives in fear of the Emperor's wrath. The man's most anxious that Colonel Kirke leaves right away and we suspect he wants to write to the Emperor, to reassure him about our intentions.' He paused, looked out the window, looked at the sky that was beginning to grey. 'Colonel Kirke is to be properly attended, as befits a man of his rank and responsibility, and to that end he will be escorted by several officers from the garrison. In addition to these gentlemen, Colonel Kirke wants to take a clerk, a man he can trust to keep his mouth shut – a man with a fair hand. His own ensign-clerk died on the *Newcastle* and I have offered your services.' I blinked at him in amazement. 'And I want you to be ready to leave in an hour.'

99

From the camp of the Alcaide, early on the evening of January 10th, Colonel Kirke wrote to Colonel Sackville. I was expecting him to dictate his letters – I'd been told most of his letters were written by a secretary and then signed by himself – but he sat alone, sat with his thoughts and wrote.

I stayed in the shadows and waited till he finished, then I asked if he would like me to make a copy and I produced a new copybook. It was bound in soft brown leather and all the pages were waiting to be ruled. He shook his head. 'If the Moors search our tents, or go through our belongings, I don't want them to find anything that would give them a clue to our intentions. If you intend to keep a journal don't write anything in it that could offend them. Leave blank spaces, write a couple of words to jog your memory – if you have to – and fill in the spaces when you get back to Tangiers.'

Then he waved his letter in the air, checked the ink was dry, and handed it to me to fold and seal. As I took out the sealing wax and lit the candle, I managed to read the first sentence without appearing to do so. It read: 'I am among the most sevilised pepell in the worlde and iff ever I have a sone I will rather chose to send him hether for breeding than to the court of France.'

In my mind I gulped and swallowed hard. The spelling was dreadful, was an excuse for O'Sullivan's book and I knew if I had to copy it, I would have wrestled with his words, would have lost, would have been forced to admit that it would be an arrogance, an affront, to correct his spelling.

The Moors had flattered him for two days, courted him like a virgin. The haste of departure had slowed to a gentle dawdle, and now there was no hurry, no rush, and today he shot wild boars and antelope. Tomorrow they say he will hunt hares and partridges.

I have to acknowledge that these Moors were not like the mad savages who came screaming towards us in the great siege. These men possessed the most exquisite manners, and they were thoughtful, attentive. They brought scented water to wash our hands and faces. They left platters piled high with sweetmeats and dried fruit: sultanas, prunes, raisins, figs, dates, apricots and tiny black berries with a smooth skin. The fruit was moist –

not rock-hard like all the fruit that came from England – and I kept some in my pocket, chewed it when the walking tired me, made me feel hungry. I've never seen so much fresh meat. It was brought to our tents every night so that we could cook it in our own way, the way that suited our bellies. They also brought cooked meats. Some were cold and sliced. Some were hot, made hotter by sauces and spices. And some were bound in rolls, like sausages, and they tasted of garlic.

Only one thing disappointed me, disappointed all of us: they didn't drink beer, wine or fermented spirits. They squeezed oranges, lemons and limes, and drank thimble-shaped cups of strong black coffee. But the main drink, the drink that demanded much care and attention was water: cold water. It didn't loosen many tongues or make the company merry, but it did loosen my bowels and never once did I suffer the passage of a rock-hard stool.

In Alcazar we lingered for a week, then it grew to ten days. Colonel Kirke kept hoping Sir James would arrive but each day brought more eating, more shooting, more wandering through the narrow alleys of the bazaar and pacing the great walls – but no Sir James.

Colonel Kirke concluded with some reluctance, that the presents were still at sea, were caught in the foul storms that batter the Bay of Biscay at this time of the year, and nothing was to be gained by waiting any longer. And so, with a calm that belied the churnings in my belly, we set out for Mequinez.

Each mile brought the Emperor closer, enlarged his reputation. He'd been on the throne nine years and they say he celebrated his accession by defeating his nephew, beheading ten thousand of his followers and impaling their heads on the walls of Fez and Marrakesh. Their bodies were bound with rushes and used to make a bridge, and his army marched over it, marched to victory. Murder was his favourite pastime. He strangled slaves, speared negroes, tested the sharpness of a new blade on anyone who displeased him, and executed criminals with his own hands. Friday was his favourite day for death, and they say the colour of his robes betrayed his mood: yellow bespoke death. He was a descendant of the Prophet Mahomet; a man of prayer – private prayer and public prayer; and the Koran was carried in front of him at all times.

Through the defeat of his enemies all the forces of Barbary had been arrayed against us instead of each other: in victory he was the architect of our misfortunes. We were the infidel, and he was the defender of the faith. It was obvious we could never defeat him: the forces at his command were too great. It was also obvious that Captain Lacey was right: our mortal enemy, Oman the Alcaide, our guide to Mequinez, feared the Emperor, feared his displeasure, feared his wrath; and as we drew closer to Mequinez he became quiet, solemn, moody.

Mequinez was the Emperor's favourite palace. He lavished his wealth upon it, and as we passed through the walls, I remembered the stories of the slaves: buried alive, buried in the walls – for his amusement – and now the walls are their tombs, are bonded with their flesh, their bones. And the stones are gilded with gold.

Painted tiles paved the walks. Rows of orange trees scented the air. Water ran through narrow ducts, lay still in long watercourses, and fountained high in the air – caught the sparkle of the sunshine, filled the courtyards with glitter and dampened the air. I could not help thinking that this would be the most perfect place a man could ever hope for – in the heights of summer, when the sun had baked the earth and the wind had dried the air.

The Emperor received Colonel Kirke next morning. We bowed low, stayed at a distance, and the Colonel walked with the Emperor, walked in the gardens. We could not hear their words, but there seemed to be a closeness, a harmony, an affinity from almost the moment they met. A few minutes later the Colonel came back, came bursting with the most amazing news: the Emperor had agreed to four years of peace.

We couldn't believe it. Couldn't take it in. It was like being given the gift of eternity. It bubbled our spirits, almost made us drunk with joy. In this mood, this state of disbelief, we watched the Emperor exercise his troops-of-horse. They wheeled and trotted and thundered past us in their hundreds. I was impressed by their bearing, their speed and their fine breeding. I said this to Captain Johnson and he nodded, and I thought he was agreeing but then he said: 'They have no discipline. There's too much confusion. And you cannot hear the words of command. They could be conquered by troops-of-horse, English troops, if we broke their charge with a few troops, broke them into loose groups, and our main body stood their ground.'

I smiled to myself. In six months' time we'd be lucky to have a hundred horses and tactics would count for nothing: we would be overwhelmed by numbers. And as long as the Moors heard the first command, the command to charge – what else did they need to hear?

Next day at the invitation of the Emperor we journeyed on to the city of Fez. It was his capital and we thought it would be like his palace, but it was much decayed. We slept and ate in the house of the Governor; the furniture bore tiny carvings – motifs of flowers; the walls were covered with hangings; and Turkey carpets in reds, purples, blacks and pinks covered the floor; and like the palace in Mequinez, the cloistered arches, the Moorish arches, trapped the shade, the shadows, the smell of water and the scent of orange blossom.

In Fez we learnt the secret of the Emperor's horses: it lay in the stables. They were built of stone, were like a great cathedral with pillars fifty feet high, and they could hold two hundred horses. They were dark, restful for the horses; and more important they were cool – were cooled by cisterns of water, cellars of water, that chilled the stone floor.

Colonel Kirke was much taken with a small boy, a slave who could speak English. He was dark-haired, dark-eyed in the manner of the Moors, and fair-skinned like a child of England. The Colonel tried to purchase him, to redeem him from slavery, but his money was declined, was smiled away, and next day – to our surprise – the Alcaide presented him to the Colonel, made a gift of him. I suspect the Alcaide thought the Colonel desired the boy, but it was not so. It was an act of kindness, of Christian charity, and like so many things to do with the Colonel, it worked to his advantage: the boy became his personal interpreter.

On the night we returned to Mequinez, the night we began our long wait for Sir James, I stripped off my clothes and sank into a cistern of warm water. I stretched out with my neck resting on the tiled edge and closed my eyes. The water smelt of jasmine, and the hairs on my belly washed backwards and forwards like seaweed in a swell. The first time I lay in the water a man brought me a towel, poured more hot water into the cistern and left. This time two towels lay on a chair. I heard a noise, like a door closing, and I thought the man might be coming again with more hot water. I opened my eyes – made sleepy with warmth – retched with fright and slammed my hands over my groin. Two girls were standing on the edge of the cistern taking off all their clothes. They slipped into the water, smiled at me, let the water lap around the hair in their crotches, slid further down into the water, allowed the water to ripple round their nipples, and sat down. For modesty, or for some reason I could not understand, both still wore a tiny square of pink silk: it veiled their noses and their mouths, and made their eyes look like honey, dark honey – and I felt helpless, felt like a bear trapped in a honey pot.

They wriggled their toes, giggled, splashed the water, splashed it at me. I lifted my hands, wiped my eyes, laughed and splashed them back. They swam towards me, ran their hands up my legs, made me shiver, made me want them. One of them parted her legs and sat on my belly, then she eased herself back, eased my rampant flesh deep into her body. I reached up and touched her breasts. The other girl lifted me up, locked herself onto my back, kneaded my buttocks, fingered my spine, bit at my neck – and I exploded. Then still running their hands over me, making me feel like a slippery fish, they changed places and the three of us swayed to my gentle thrusting, and I felt the explosion – the discharge of love – run through me, through the girl at the front, through the girl at the back. It locked us together, seared us together, and for a long time we stood, eyes shut, arms wrapped around each other.

Then we slipped back into the water, and like nymphs that play with each other, they kissed, raised their nipples, fingered their crotches, splayed their legs, rounded their buttocks – and roused me back to life. They had me, and I had them. We had each other. Then they dried me, rubbed oil into my skin, made me smell like a garden of roses, and they led me into the other room, the room I had thought was mine and mine alone.

We slept together, slept on the bed. In my dreams we were locked in an endless embrace. When I woke it was dark, and they were gone, were like a mirage, a sweet smell in my memory.

I was late for the dinner the Alcaide gave to celebrate our return to the palace. He smiled at me. It was a knowing smile. I smiled back, bowed low, and sat on my cushion. I felt clean, felt calm, felt aware of my skin, of every inch of my body. And I wanted them, wanted to rest within them, to be part of them, to be locked in the vice of love.

February drifted into March. Sir James did not arrive, and I had no desire to go back to Tangiers. In truth I didn't care if he never arrived. But Colonel Kirke did. Frustrated, concerned that the mood of the Moors would turn sour, and that we might become prisoners, become hostages to the fortunes of war, or the victims of ill-will, he wrote to Colonel Sackville urging Sir James 'to make haste'.

My nymphs of the night, my ladies of the bath, came and went as the pleasure took them, and despite my many signings, my trying to talk with my fingers, trying to say I wanted them to come every night, I never knew if they would or would not come. And often I did not know the hour of their coming or the hour of their going, and some mornings I woke and I did not know if they had been – till I found the juices of the night, the juices of love, had matted the hairs below my belly.

But there comes a time when the fruit is ripe, a time when the apples fall off the tree – and go bad – and Adam can tempt Eve no more. It is the time when good things must come to end. And so in high season, a season I wished would never end, my ladies retired into the night, became part of my past, and Sir James arrived with a retinue of twenty-one.

The man was a fool. Dear God he was. His words were courteous, were couched in etiquette, in the language of the diplomat, but they spoke of forts, of lines and trenches, of taking in more land. They enraged the Emperor, and according to some reports, he threatened war.

It was a great sadness, and it hung over us like the black clouds of an approaching storm. And the truth, the unspoken truth, was that Colonel Kirke could have negotiated with the Moors, could have persuaded them that our fortifications, our strengths would be to their advantage – to our mutual advantage – of such was the smoothness of his tongue, the oiled perfection of his words.

The Emperor appointed the Alcaide to conduct the peace negotiations on his behalf, and what was agreed in the night was returned in the morning, cut, chopped, hacked. And we came to understand that we were deceived. Under the Alcaide's mask of politeness, of hospitality, lay a deep hatred, a loathing for us and all things English. In truth he wanted us to go, to abandon Tangiers: everything else was a compromise.

In the end – when they were unable to agree on their own peace terms – they modified Colonel Sackville's terms. The balance in points 1, 4, and 6 tipped in our favour.

POINT 1: Peace for four years.
POINT 4: To be allowed to repair the watercourse.

POINT 6: To be allowed to repair the four forts.

Points 3 and 10 were a recipe for disaster.

POINT 3: No fortifications to be built.
POINT 10: When Pole Fort is pulled down, leave to be given to cut stone for the Mole and the wall of city.

And then, as if this were not bad enough, the negotiations to release 130 English prisoners – 70 men from our own regiment were well known to Sir James – failed: the Emperor demanded 200 pieces-of-eight for every man, and he insisted on every prisoner being ransomed and released at the same time. Sir James had enough money for 70, but not for 130. And now we knew we would have to leave them all behind.

In all of this there was only one shard of hope: the Emperor wished to send an Ambassador to England, to King Charles, and maybe His Majesty would be more persuasive than Sir James.

On the last night the farewell dinner was wreathed in gloom, and I sat well away from the main party, well away from the useless retinue that had fawned on Sir James and failed. I sat next to a courtly old man in grey: a cleric, a man of God, a man of the Islamic faith. I'd sat next to him several times and we always smiled and nodded, but we had no words, no words in common. But this night the young boy, the Colonel's translator sat beside us, sat between us, and we talked through him.

We talked of many things, and he told me about his faith, about its oneness, its simplicity, its purity, and he said he believed it would spread throughout the world, would reach England, in the fullness of time. I smiled and let his dream, his pious hope, slip from my mind. Then he wanted to know about my religion and the religion of the Portuguese – wanted to understand the things that separated us, the things we held in common. I tried to explain, but I didn't make it very clear, and then somehow I was telling him about de Colville, about him wanting me to talk to Father Francifo. He said: 'I would sit at his feet. I would listen and learn. I would study. And if God gave me the wisdom to understand his faith, I would be able to refute that faith, through its own contradictions – and through the words of the Prophet.' He smiled. 'I think you have been offered a precious gift. It would be churlish to refuse it.'

Early in the morning the boy came to my room and unrolled a carpet, a prayer rug. It was patterned with the greens of spring, summer, autumn: the greens of Islam. He said: 'It is a gift, for you, from our friend of last night. And he said, I am to give you a message, and I am to ask you to kneel on the rug, and then I am to give you the message.'

I knelt, ran the palm of my hand over the pile, felt the softness, and the boy said: 'There is but one God. And through faith you will find him.'

100

Early in May Colonel Sackville – his health failing – returned to England, and Colonel Kirke became acting Governor.

The story of the Great Siege had drifted out of the columns of the journals and newspapers that came from London and littered the tables in our new rooms of refreshment. Since the demolition of Whitehall and the loss of our bowling–bare, these rooms at the market-end of Avares Street had become a focal point, a meeting place for off-duty officers.

I was sitting in the upstairs rooms, sitting on a settle with my feet on a footstool, reading the *London Examiner*. It was dated the 28th March: four days into the new year. The news was grim: Parliament had refused to supply the King with any money – raised through taxation – until he signed the Exclusion Bill: the bill to deprive the Duke of York of his rights to the throne. The King refused to sign and dissolved Parliament. From now on he intended to rule on his own. And no matter what the temper of Parliament might have been towards us, towards Tangiers – at some time in the future – if they could not meet they could not vote any money for our relief.

The columns of the paper recalled the King's final request for money for Tangiers; recalled the words of Sir William Jones – opening the debate in Parliament: 'Tangiers is a place of great moment, but I take the preservation of Religion to be much greater . . . Tangiers is no part of England and for us to provide for it, as things stand now, is to weaken our own security. Tangiers has a Popish Church.'

The feelings unleashed by these words ran through Parliament like a canker, and now Parliament was dead, would speak, would vote, would be no more. Like the flesh it was dissolved by death, laid in the grave, entombed in the past, and now, with an eerie shivering that chilled my soul, I began to suspect it had sealed our fate, had numbered our days.

The news from along the coast was just as grim: the Moors were still besieging the Spanish city of Mamora, and they had captured two small redoubts close to the coast. As the Emperor approached with another army the Moors issued an ultimatum: surrender immediately, or we will behead every man, woman and child when we take the city. The Spanish lost their nerve and kept their heads; and the Moors added a hundred

cannons, dozens of muskets, and huge quantities of powder and shot to
their armouries.

In the weeks that followed, the arrogance of the Moors became insufferable – every time we marched beyond the walls they closed on us like
clouds of mosquitoes; and we were beset by a rumour that had the ring of
truth: 'The Emperor had boasted that he could take Tangiers in one night
if he wished.' It did not fill us with confidence, and one evening, soon after
we were back from foraging and bringing in the grass the Moors cut for us
to make hay, de Colville and I walked into the refreshment rooms and we
heard the Colonel say: 'Although the Moors have made a peace for four
years, they are still Moors and not to be trusted too far, and the better the
condition of the garrison, the better they will keep the peace.'

We looked at each other and nodded, then we settled into our chairs,
picked up the papers and sipped black beer. De Colville laughed at me
when I said it would be nice if the beer was cold, ice-cold, and then the
words began to blur, to crowd together, and I closed my eyes. A few
minutes later I felt him shaking my arm, and he was saying: 'It says in here
Lord Plymouth was buried in Westminster Abbey, and Lady Fairborne is
to erect a memorial to Sir Palmes.'

'In the Abbey?'

'Hmm. It's to be a marble plaque with a poem by Dryden.' He was
silent for a few moments, then he continued: 'It's a dreadful poem.' And
he handed me the paper.

I read through it once at normal speed, then again at a more measured pace. He was right. It opened with high-flown nonsense, distorted
the truth:

> Ye sacred reliques, which our marbles keep,
> Here undisturbed by wars, in quiet sleep—

But the last lines, the last verse captured his spirit, and I read them aloud:

> 'More bravely British Gen'ral never fell,
> Nor Gen'ral's death was e're revenged so well,
> Which his pleased eyes beheld before their close.'

'Hmm. They sound better when they're read aloud. I'll grant you that.'
Then he paused, and like a Moor rising in ambuscade, he said: 'You still
haven't been to see Father Francifo.'

I swallowed hard, stilled the fright that was racing my heart, and
said: 'No.'

'Are you going to?'

'I thought I might wait.'

'You've already waited a year.'

'A year?'

'Yes.'

I hadn't realised so much time had slipped away. 'I was thinking, thinking I might, after my Test Communion.'

He smiled. 'So, when you've made your communion, taken the oath and signed the declaration; when everyone knows you're a Protestant, a member of the Church of England; when it's all official – it will be safe for you to be seen going up the steps to the convent.'

'I thought I'd go at night.'

He roared with laughter. Then he calmed and said: 'You're quite right. Not about the night but about the Test Communion. It will confirm your rank, your credentials, your right to be an officer. And that's important.' Then he smiled. 'I'll tell Father Francifo to expect you.'

101

In June Admiral Herbert transported the Spanish troopers back to Spain, and we were left with eighty mounts to be shared by four troops-of-horse: two hundred men. The other troops-of-horse promised by His Majesty in our hour of need had never arrived – would never arrive – and now we were sliding back into the old days, the old ways: the habits of static defence.

In July I made my Test Communion: on the Feast of Saint James the Apostle, and then, as July slid into August I knew I could not put it off any longer.

In the early evening I walked up to the clerk's office, sat at my desk and talked to O'Sullivan and Crabtree. I touched my green rug – now hanging on the wall beside my desk – and I fortified my spirits with brandy-wine. And then, just as I was about to leave, was closing my drawer, I saw Jenny's blue butterfly nestling close to my head of Christ. On an impulse, a whim, I pinned the butterfly to my coat and walked into the night.

I ambled through the Market Place, made light, made noisy by all the open doors, open windows of the taverns. I walked past the Preaching Cross, past the doors of the Misericordia – now shadowed with darkness – and walked up the steps to the Convent, to the door that led to perdition. I lifted my hand to knock, to fall into that abyss of error and my finger caught on the butterfly, caught on the pin. It felt like a bee sting. I sucked at it, sucked away the taste of salted-blood, and I began to wonder if it was a sign, a sign to turn away from temptation. Then I thought that was silly. Signs don't come in pin-pricks. They come in thunderbolts, come from heaven above. Then I began to think I might be able to talk to Jenny for just a few minutes before I talked to Father Francifo, and almost without realising it I was walking down the hill, walking towards the Little Parade.

She was standing in the shop, standing in a soft halo of light, like a plaster-saint. As I pushed open the door the bell jangled and her father slid into the shop with his hands outstretched. I took off my hat and smiled at her. She shook her head and pulled her lips into a thin line. Then the line softened, became creased with a slight smile, with a hint of acceptance. She put a finger to her mouth – stilled the words that hung on my lips – turned to her father, and said: 'It's a gentleman for some goutweed. He's been here before and I can help him.' She took his arm, led him to the front door and said: 'I'll be back in just a moment, sir. Just as soon as I've settled my father, next door in The Dappled Cow.'

I ran my eye along the bottles, read the labels: dill, fennel, St John's-wort, angelica, cowslip, foxglove, chicory, horseradish, sorrel and many more, but I couldn't find goutweed. I was trying to remember the names of the diseases, the afflictions they were supposed to cure, when the bell jangled and she rushed back into the shop. 'Sorry it took so long,' she said. 'But he likes me to get him a pint of cider and a pint of ale before I leave, and then he's happy for a couple of hours.'

'I noticed his eyes, last time, and . . .'

The smile slipped from her face. She nodded, as if distracted, as if reminded of something she would rather forget, then she said: 'He's gone blind. Those white growths on his eyes, they're cataracts, and there's no cure.'

'Can he see anything at all?'

'Shapes. Shapes in a fog, is the way he puts it.' She sighed. 'There's nothing wrong with his mind and he tries to tell the herbs by their feel. But so many feel the same, and sometimes I can't tell the difference, and he gets upset: his hands twitch and his face sweats. And now he's scared of giving someone the wrong medicine. He says we should go back to England. Says there aren't enough people left to make enough money. And now we can't afford to buy our herbs in England, and I don't know what we're going to do when these run out.' She waved her hand towards the bottles, to the wall of drawers with wooden knobs.

I looked away for a moment, she made me feel helpless, and I said: 'I couldn't find any goutweed.'

She smiled. 'That's the common name, the name we use all the time. The proper name is ground-elder. It's good for gout – as you'd expect – and it's also good for arthritis and rheumatism. I can make you a poultice for your hands and feet if you'd like.' She picked up a bottle. 'I've enough left for that.'

I smiled and shook my head. 'Why did you choose goutweed? What made you think of that, for me?'

She laughed. 'I don't know. It was the first thing that came into my head.' Then she saw the blue butterfly, reached out and touched it with the tips of her fingers. 'I used to love that butterfly.'

I took it off and handed it to her. 'I've been keeping it for you.'

She smiled, twirled the pin in her fingers, made it look as though the butterfly was alive, then she said: 'I was very rude to you last time, wasn't I?'

I shook my head.

'It was so unfair. Just a few days, a few nights, that's all we had. And he didn't even leave me a baby, a child who could bear his name, who could remind me of him.' She paused, sucked at her lips. 'It's been fifteen months. And I can't even remember what he looked like.' She shook her head and burst into tears.

I took her into my arms, felt the warmth of body. She rested her head on my shoulder. 'You feel different,' she said. 'Feel harder, stronger.' She ran her hands down my spine, let them rest in the small of my back. 'He was soft. Gentle. And he smelt different. He smelt clean. Smelt of lye. You smell of summer, dry grass and hay, and walking in the sunshine. And you smell of gunpowder.' She lifted her head and took my hands. 'And musket oil. And you—' She looked over my shoulder, looked out the window.

I turned, followed her gaze, saw two small noses pressed against two of the window panes. Above the noses two pairs of brown eyes, boys' eyes, leered at us. She rapped the window with her knuckles, tried to shoo them away, but they laughed, pressed their noses harder to the glass – made them look like squashed figs – and waited.

She shook her head, locked the door, picked up the candle and beckoned me to follow her into the back room. I was expecting to find a storeroom, a place where her father mixed ointments, ground seeds, made pastes, steeped herbs in raw spirits and filled tiny bottles with tinctures: killers of pain, draughts of sleep. Instead I found a small kitchen with a large table, three chairs, a dying fire, and a shelf of books. On the spines of the two fattest books, spines shedding flakes of leather, I could just make out the words: *Culpeper's Pharmacopoeia (1649)* and *Culpeper's Complete Herbal (1653)*.

She smiled at me. 'Mister Wyndham used to sit in this chair.' She pulled a chair away from the fire, pulled me forward with her fingers. I sat down, half-turned and caught her smile. 'No,' she said, in a soft way, as if recalling the past, running memories through her mind, 'he used to take off his coat before he sat down.' I stood up and slipped off my coat. She took it, held it to her face the way some women hold a baby's shawl. Then she ran her fingers over the ribbons on the shoulder and peered at the seam. 'My stitches have held. I made them very tiny, almost invisible, that's what he used to say.' She hung the coat on a peg. 'We used to drink a little wine, red wine, from Spain. Would you like some?' I nodded and she poured a little into two wine glasses. It was a light wine, watery, like a raspberry cordial. It tasted raw, flat and bitter, but I smiled and nodded – I sensed this was what she wanted.

She built up the fire, and as it caught, as it filled the hearth with flames, with warmth, I swilled my wine round the glass, filled it with the glitter of rubies, of blood-red desire. I held the glass up to my eye, saw her face fill with desire, saw the glitter of rubies in her eyes, and I smiled.

She hooked a small black pot onto a chain and lowered it into the flames. 'We used to have something to eat. Just a little something that was over from midday. With bread. He liked crusty bread.' She took a wooden spoon and stirred the food in the pot. 'It's a ragout. Fish, shrimps, lobster, and Barbary cockles in a milk sauce with peppers and spices. It's very hot. You might like some more wine.'

She poured some wine. And then, wrapped in a soft warmth, a warmth that asked, that demanded nothing, we ate the fish, broke the bread and wiped the last of the sauce off our plates.

'And when we were finished,' she said, 'my father would go upstairs, go to bed, and leave us on our own.'

I nodded, slipped off my shoes and wiggled my toes at the fire. 'I was surprised when I came into this room. I thought it would be a storeroom. Full of herbs and spices.'

She shook her head. 'You couldn't keep them in here. The steam from the cooking would settle on them. Make them damp. And they'd go soft, grow mildew and rot.' She paused. 'My father has a room upstairs. It catches the morning sun, and the midday sun. Three years ago he had a window put in the west wall and now it catches the afternoon sun – it means the room is hot and dry, all day. And he has heavy drapes. He pulls them just before sunset, traps the warmth in the room and keeps the herbs warm overnight. Of course in wintertime, in the rains, he has to keep a fire going in the room all the time, and he has to turn the sacks. He can't allow moisture to condense on the sacking.' She stood up and took my hand. 'Come and I'll show you.'

Upstairs she opened the door to his room. A wave of heat engulfed us and the smell of spice ran up my nose. It watered my mouth – despite the food, the feeling of well-being that rested in my belly. When my eyes grew used to the gloom I could see a bed, close to the hearth.

Then she said: 'I'll show you my room, our room.'

Her room was small: a bed for two, a single chair, a table, a shuttered window. She walked to the bed, picked up a long nightshirt – gathered around the yoke, like a yeoman farmer's smock – and handed it to me. 'He used to change out here on the landing, for the sake of modesty.' She smiled.

She walked into the room and half-closed the door. I took off all my clothes, dumped them in a heap and pulled on the nightshirt. It was too long. It swished the floor, ruffled my toes. I waited for her to get into bed, then I slipped in beside her.

She was lying with her back towards me. I cuddled in close, put my left arm around her, fondled her breasts, tried to find her nipples. But they were laced into her nightdress, laced tight, laced flat. She sighed and turned, rolled into my arms. 'They are for the baby,' she whispered. 'They're not for you. This is for you.' She pulled my hand down to the foliage of hair, to the garden of herbs that lay moist between her legs. My fingers walked in the garden, roused the herbs of desire, roused me, and I sat up to take off my nightshirt but she pulled at my nightshirt, and said: 'Modesty. In all things we must remember the Christian virtue of modesty; must remember the gifts of God and avert our eyes.'

And then, for some reason, my two ladies, my water nymphs, swam into my mind, swam stark naked. They had no need of modesty, of Christian virtues that hid the truth, hid the flesh. In my remembering of them, I wanted her, wanted them. I hitched up my nightshirt, slipped into the garden of herbs, and in a blaze of sunshine, the sunshine of Mequinez – made sweet by Moorish memories – it became a pleasure garden, became the place to raise my seed.

102

Father Francifo was not what I was expecting. In my mind I had painted a picture of a fat friar with a blubbery face, or a thin man, a Spanish aesthetic with a long face, yellow flesh tinged green and darkened with heavy black stubble. But he was ordinary: short, olive face – leathered by the sun, thinning hair and watery eyes. He could have been a pikeman. My fear of him ebbed away and we sat down, facing each other, on opposite sides of the table.

The room was small and the heavy drapes made it dark, made it look smaller than it was. A crucifix – the figure of the dying Christ was white, tinged brown, like old ivory – hung on the wall. It was the only ornament in the whole room.

He wore a long black robe, and when he slipped both hands – they looked white, soft, unused – into his sleeves, rested them on the table, his body, his robe, merged with the shadows, and his face, his eyes, appeared to hang in the air, at head-height.

'Lieutenant de Colville tells me you wish to take instruction. To learn the truths of our holy faith.'

'No,' I said, shaking my head. 'I don't want to do that at all.'

'Then why are you here?'

'Why?'

'Hmm.'

'Because Lieutenant de Colville made me promise.'

'And why did he do that?'

'I needed his support to be become an ensign, an officer. It was – it is – the price I have to pay.'

He shook his head. 'That is immoral. You cannot be held to that promise. You must be here of your own free will, your own desire. Otherwise you are not opening your heart to the Holy Spirit – to his ministrations.' He stood up. 'Maybe you should go away and think about it. And if you want to be here, want to learn, come and see me again. I'm always here.' He stood up and walked towards the door.

'But I'm here now, and I thought—'

He stopped and turned. 'We can talk. If that is what you want.'

I couldn't see what I had to lose. He looked harmless. I'd told Jenny I'd be an hour late. And if someone had seen me come in the door, had recognised me, it was too late now and I didn't really want to come back again. 'Maybe just this once.'

He made a gentle bow – the sort of bow the priests make in the sanctuary when they pass in front of the high altar – and he sat down again. 'What do want to talk about?'

'I don't know. I don't mind.'

'What do you fear? Hate? Don't understand about the Church?'

There were so many things – enriched by error and superstition. I didn't know what to choose. Then I remembered the Test Communion, the oath, the declaration, and I said: 'I don't understand how anyone can believe in transubstantiation.'

He nodded. 'Do you accept that Jesus was both man and God?'

'Yes.'

'And do remember on his last night, he took bread into his hands, blessed it, broke it, and gave it to his disciples saying: "This is my body"? And then he took the cup and said: "This is my blood."'

'Of course.'

'Then we must believe what he says. He is God. And God is the embodiment of truth. He would not, could not, lie to us.' He paused. 'It is the essence of faith: we believe what we cannot understand because Almighty God himself has said it is true.'

I didn't know how to argue against that. 'Hmm, but – it still looks like bread and wine. Still tastes like bread and wine. And the bread can still go mouldy, just like ordinary bread.'

'And if someone puts poison in the wine the priest will be poisoned, and he may die.'

'So the poison is still poison. But the bread and the wine, that still look and taste like bread and wine, aren't bread and wine. They are the body and blood of Christ.'

'Yes. And for hundreds of years men struggled to understand how this could be. And it's only in the last five hundred years, through an understanding of philosophy, of the forces of nature, that we know how God works this miracle.'

I sat back in my chair and waited.

'If you look around the room we see what philosophers call the accidents. These are the things, the surface things that make a table a table – wood, stain, oil, carved legs and so on. But hidden from our view, cloaked by the accidents is the real essence that makes a table a table. The philosophers call this the substance. Every single thing has it own substance, it's what makes bread bread, and wine wine. And it's the reason bread isn't wine and wine isn't bread. Can you follow what I'm saying?'

I nodded, and he continued: 'In the mass, when the priest says the sacred words, "This is my body" the substance of the bread is changed into the substance of Christ. It is a trans, a crossing of substance. And the same thing happens with the wine. But because Christ is now alive, is resurrected, is in heaven, and his body and blood cannot be separated from his Godhead, we have the living Christ present on the altar, under the accidents of bread and wine.'

It sounded good but it was like a greased pole – slippery – and I didn't believe a word of it. I bit my lips and said: 'If someone could prove the philosophers were wrong, prove there was no such thing as accidents and substance, it would prove transubstantiation was wrong.'

'Hmm. But through scriptures, through the traditions of the Church and the great Doctors of the Church, Saint Augustine, Saint Gregory, Saint Thomas Aquinas and so on, God has revealed these things to us. God would not lead his church into error. God desires us to find him, to find his salvation, to know his truth.'

We talked on for an hour or more, slid through the great mysteries of the Trinity and redemption. And as we approached the life-ever-after: heaven, hell and purgatory, he smiled and said: 'Perhaps another time?'

To my surprise, I found myself agreeing. I had warmed to the man, warmed to his frankness, and although I couldn't respect his beliefs, I could respect him.

An hour later when Jenny's father had gone to bed and his door was shut tight, I crept up the stairs, changed on the landing and slid into her bed, her body.

Afterwards, in the soft warmth, in the bunching of nightshirts, she talked of babies, of her desire for a child, her wish to be a mother. I'd never thought of being a father, having a child. It frightened me, chilled the air, and I began to tell her about Father Francifo. She went rigid, pushed me away, pushed me over to my side of the bed. I sat up and talked about accidents and substance. She said: 'Some women call it an accident when they find they're going to have a baby and they didn't want to have a baby.'

I laughed. 'I always thought it was in the hands of God.'

'Hmm. But he needs a helping hand. He needs us to do what we've just been doing.' She paused. 'I don't like it. I didn't like it with John – with Mister Wyndham – either. It's animal. Crude. Rude. But a woman must submit, submit to the will of God, if she wants to bear a child.' She sniffled, blew her nose, and snuggled into the bed covers.

I had often wondered why a child looks like his father or mother, and wondered how the peculiarities of their minds and manners could be seen again in the child. I began to think it might be something to do with substance, and I wondered how the substance that was me, was in my snowflakes, became part of her substance, became a new substance, a substance that had not existed before: a child of God. And the soul that this child would have: did it have part of the substance of my soul, her soul, or did God give each of us a brand new soul? Was there a storehouse of souls, in heaven, waiting to be born, to be implanted in the substance of each new child – when he or she quickened in the womb?

And what about original sin, the evil blackness that corrupted Eve's soul? She passed it to her sons, and they passed it on to us – through the generations of the cursed – and now through baptism it was washed away. But how did we get that evil, that blemish, that corruption of the spirit? Was it in my substance, my snowflakes, or did God paint it on, stain the unborn souls, in his storehouse? And if there was a storehouse what was it called? It wasn't limbo. That was where unbaptised souls went – the souls of children, the souls of the holy innocents. And I was thinking I must ask Father Francifo, when she reached out, took my hand, walked my fingers in the undergrowth, the shrubbery that edges the place of pleasure.

I possessed her again, possessed the memories of my water nymphs, for she lay still, lay calm, lay unresponsive. And later, as we lay together, lay blanketed in darkness, her voice came to me, like a soft swelling of the waves: 'My father says we are now betrothed, by the act of love, physical love. And in a year, when my time of mourning comes to an end, we may be married.'

103

As August slid into September and then into October my life fell into a gentle pattern, a blanket of comfort. I lay with Jenny two, three times a week. She had my essence, my substance, my snowflakes – the explosion of my being – but her womb was like the stones of summer: hot, dry, barren. Her wanting was of the spirit and not of the body and she continued to lie in her bed, our bed, like a marbled statue: cool, cold, rigid. Each night, before she would let me touch her, mount her, she said her prayers, long prayers, prayers of passion, prayers for the life she wanted to bear. They cooled my ardour, chilled my passion, my desire, and in frankness I have to confess, that if it were not for the two water nymphs swimming in my mind, my cock would have stayed limp, stayed dead.

Father Francifo became a friend and the Roman faith lost some of its horns – was less like the spawn of the devil – and one day he invited me to attend a mass, a sung mass. He was the celebrant, the chief minister. I thought it showy, theatrical. De Colville called it operatic – it was a word I'd not heard before, a word for O'Sullivan's book – but it was also something else, something that troubled me. It was like an affair of the heart, the emotions. My head, my brain, my intellect knew it was wrong, could prove it was wrong, but somehow my heart wasn't listening to my head, and the music, the costumes, the incense, the candles, the rituals were seducing me; and like a man in the arms of my lady from Rua de Carmo, I wanted to come again.

One day, as I was leaving the cathedral, I was accosted by the Reverend Mister Hughes and he said: 'I do not understand how an officer like you, a man who made his Test Communion and took the oath can be seen coming out of there.' And he pointed to the cathedral.

For a moment I didn't know what to say – his words had all the virtues of a sudden attack: surprise, preparation. Then I said: 'I think a man has a right to enquire. To look. To learn. To understand. To strengthen his faith.'

'Hmm. But that doesn't include taking instruction. Once a week if I hear right.'

'But understanding includes talking, listening, thinking.'

'And it's fraught with danger for weak souls, souls who cannot distinguish truth from error.' He paused, fixed his eye on me, and whispered: 'You are in grave danger. Mortal danger. Your soul is in peril. You need help. And God has sent me to help you.'

He took my arm, guided me across the street and into his house. We climbed the stairs and entered a large room. Books lined the lower half of the back wall, two small tables and four chairs stood in the middle of the floor. A pair of doors with small panes of glass opened onto a long balcony. Beyond the balcony lay the Watergate, the Old Mole, the Mole, and the waters of the Bay. It was a room full of light, full of sunshine. 'This is my library,' he said. 'These books can refute error, can illuminate the truth.' He pulled one from the shelves and handed it to me.

I read the spine: *The Mystery of Jesuitism.*

'You are welcome to come here whenever you want. To sit and read. To think. To study. And if you would like some help, would like to talk about anything, I'm downstairs. And I would like to help you.' He paused, laid his hand on my shoulder. 'I'll leave you here. Leave you on your own.'

I nodded and mumbled: 'Thank you.' I was overwhelmed by his generosity, his trust.

I walked around the room, looked at the pictures, the maps that hung on the wall, and I spun the two globes. Then I stopped one, traced the passage from England to France, Spain, Portugal and Tangiers, a distance of 1,100 miles – or thereabouts – and then I spun the globe again, spun any thought of retracing that passage out of my mind. I ran my fingers over his books and read the titles: Doctor Fuller's *Worthies of England*; An English Bible – printed in London in 1594; *The Works of King Charles the First*; *Charles Stuart and Oliver Cromwell United*. Then I found two books by John Milton, Oliver Cromwell's Latin Secretary: *Paradise Lost, Paradise Regained*. They made me think of my water nymphs: lost and never to be regained, except in my mind; and I felt sad, felt empty.

I flicked through the *Mystery of Jesuitism*. The words were cold, formal, and they did not move me. They had none of the warmth of Father Francifo's words. I slipped the book back on the shelf and settled down with *Paradise Regained* – it seemed to speak of hope, of optimism. After a while the measured cadences, the poetic echoes, filled my mind, and I was lost in wonderment, enchanted with the beauty of his words, the power of his language. I forgot all about Romanism and the passions it arouses in the hearts of those who have abandoned, have rejected its embrace.

In the evening, having nothing to do, and having no money – our pay had slipped again and was now two years in arrears – I wandered into the clerk's office. They were making copies of the latest Muster Roll. I read the totals:

King's Battalion 491
Governor's Regiment-of-foot 959
Dunbartons 1,176
Kirke's Regiment-of-foot 798
4 Troops-of-horse

Mounted 82
Unmounted 112
Gunners 33
Company of miners 44
Total 3,695

The totals included Corporals, Drummers and Sergeants, but they did not include the officers.

'God Almighty,' I said, 'look at our total: 959. If I walked round right now and counted every man in the whole company I'd be lucky to find 850.'

'Hmm,' Crabtree said. 'But that's always been true. If they stay on the Muster Roll for another six months, or twelve months, after they die, it means the Captain can draw their money. You know that.'

I grunted. 'But I thought it was just a few men: a dozen, a couple of dozen. Nothing like this.'

O'Sullivan looked up. 'We used to have a word for them when I was young: the undead.' He laughed. Then he paused, looked down at his desk and said: 'They tell me you're taking instruction. At the convent.'

'How the hell did you know that?'

He smiled. 'Everyone knows. They think you're mad. Bloody crazy is the way I heard one man describe it. And there was another who claimed, "that's what comes of having a papist up your bum for years on end". And they all knew who he meant.'

I slammed my hat on my head and walked out into the night air, took deep breaths, and tried to calm the fury, the sense of shame that was pounding my brain.

A few days later the Barbary Jews were saying the Emperor had arrested Omar the Alcaide, and a week after that we heard he was dead: poisoned by the Emperor – if the rumours were true. I wondered if he drank from a chalice, drank wine with a poison that could retain its accidents, its substance, its power to kill, when it was mixed with wine, as it did in the mass, in the miracle – the supposed miracle – of transubstantiation. But his spirit was not encumbered by such things – and may never have heard of such things – his was a simpler faith, a purer faith, and it did not need bread and wine to commune with God. It did not need miracles.

I remembered him alive, remembered he did not drink wine, and I found it strange to think of him as dead, buried in the sands, his grave swept by the winds, his resting place unmarked, known only to God: the God who spared us but did not spare him.

The Emperor appointed Omar's brother, Ali Benabdala, to be the new Alcaide of Alcazar. He too was hostile to us, would have liked to push us into the sea. But he needed muskets, gunpowder and cloth, and we needed beeswax, poultry, straw and cattle, and most days he allowed the traders to approach the stockades. And in the clink of money, the clink of satisfaction, the trade grew.

At the end of November, Colonel Kirke rode to Ali Benabdala's camp and escorted the Emperor's Ambassador, Alcaide Mohammed Ohadu into Tangiers. Pole Fort fired the first salute, and as they passed through Catherine Gate the great guns on the bastion below Peterborough Tower echoed the salute. Men from the Dunbartons and the second battalion of Colonel Kirke's Regiment lined the streets from the Gate to the Market Place and from there to the Little Parade. In front of the Town House the Mayor and the Corporation welcomed the Ambassador, and the Recorder delivered a speech. In the Little Parade, the Militia straightened their feeble limbs, held their pikes firm, and cheered.

On the Old Parade, we slammed to attention, and as the procession came through Middleton's Line we caught our first glimpse of its grandeur. It was led by four troops-of-horse – made skittish by all the cheering and clapping, fifty Grenadiers from the Dunbartons, thirty gunners in their new coats and caps, and thirty negroes in painted coats. Colonel Kirke was escorted by six men carrying long muskets and twenty gentlemen on horseback.

Then came the Ambassador and twenty Moors bearing gifts for His Majesty: four jewelled caskets, wooden chests bound with brass, two caged lions, and twenty ostriches – on long reins.

As the procession wound up Castle Hill they passed Colonel Kirke's first battalion – drawn up at the castle gate – then they walked through lines of Grenadiers with bayonets fixed in their muskets. On the forecourt in front of the Governor's House, the King's Battalion and the troops-of-horse from the escort, saluted the Ambassador and he entered the House.

About twenty minutes later Colonel Kirke and the Ambassador appeared on the open gallery, and we fired – every regiment fired – three volleys to welcome His Excellency.

In the evening the Governor presented the senior officers to the Ambassador and they dined in the Great Hall. At about nine o'clock the first of the fireworks climbed high into the sky, exploded, lit up the town and filled the air with cascades of stars: green for the Moors and the Irish, red for the English, blue for the Scots, and gold for peace, for the great prize that lay at the end of the rainbow.

Two weeks later the Ambassador and Sir James Leslie boarded the frigate *Hampshire*, and with the *Golden Horse* as an escort, they sailed for England. They left with our hopes, our prayers; and as the seas began to mount, to brew the storms of December, my belly heaved for them, and the lions deep in the hold.

Captain Lacey sailed with them, as a gentleman of honour, an officer in attendance. Colonel Kirke appointed Lieutenant de Colville acting Captain, and refused to allow him to buy a Captain's commission to make the appointment permanent. He said it was because he was a papist, a practising papist, but as the weeks drifted by it became obvious that the Colonel had other motives, and they could mean the end of our company.

104

I lay in bed, cuddled into Jenny's back and held her tight. She was wrapped in misery. She was bleeding from her private parts. Pain wracked her belly, cramped her legs and her mind, and we knew my seed had not taken. Her womb, like pantry shelves in a time of hunger, a time of famine, would stay bare, stay empty.

Outside, through the muffling of rain, the bells were ringing out the old year, ringing in the new. It was the 25th March 1682, and the blood lay between us like a reproach, an admission of failure, of private shame.

My balls still ached, throbbed with a dull pain, like the pain of a boil, an abscess. When I climbed into bed, she reached under my nightshirt, grabbed them hard, yanked them, tried to tear them off. I grabbed her wrists but she wouldn't let go, and she screamed: 'They're no good! No good! They can't make a baby!' She twisted them, wrung them like wet washing, sent the pain roaring through my belly, made my eyes water.

Then she fell back on the pillow, saying: 'I've seen bigger balls, better balls on a dog.' She turned over, began to sob, to wail, like a child in distress.

When sleep was approaching, when her sniffles were beginning to calm, I heard her mumble: 'It's a punishment. A punishment from God. We should have waited, waited for his blessing, waited for marriage.'

I slipped into the dawn, and walked back to our quarters.

In the afternoon we paraded in front of the Head Court of the Guard, and Colonel Kirke's warrant, the formal document appointing him Governor in his own right, with the 'style, title and dignity of His Excellency', was proclaimed to 'all and sundry'. Then the warrant was processed to the Town House to be viewed, to be acknowledged as lawful, by the Mayor, the Corporation and the Recorder – meeting in formal session.

As night gathered, blurred my face and masked my features, I knocked on the Convent door. For Father Francifo this was not New Year's Day or Lady Day, the day when new leases, new rents, new indentures began. It was just another day, a day for quiet, for reflection, for prayer, for helping men like me. We had fallen into the habit of talking for an hour or so, once a fortnight, and I had come to respect him, to like the measured calm he brought to every problem, every discussion. The contrast between him and Mister Tate, the fiery Mister Tate of nine years ago, inflamed my sense of amusement, and I often wondered what Mister Tate would make of Father Francifo, what they would say to each other – if Mister Tate could bear to sit with him, to suffer his presence.

We began the night talking about confession and my belief, the Protestant belief, that a priest is an obstacle, that man does not need him, can talk to God on his own – and can be forgiven by God without the mediation of a man, a priest. Then we drifted on to dogma, and the way it keeps developing, and he said: 'Some truths, you call them dogmas but there is no difference, were there in the early church, were growing, developing, becoming known – in much the same way that children grow and develop. Now, in the years of their maturity, we know all about them, can understand them, can appreciate why God let them unfold gradually.' He paused. 'Sometimes I think of them as flowers, opening in God's garden.'

For a moment or two I walked in that garden. It was heavy with dead flowers, flowers that needed pruning, needed composting, and I said: 'Lieutenant de Colville was telling me about the Assumption, the belief that the dead body of the Virgin Mary flew up into the sky and is now reunited with her soul in heaven.'

'Hmm. That is a pious belief. I believe it's true, but it's not essential to faith. To salvation.'

'Might it ever become a dogma, an article of faith – something you must believe?'

He ran his hands over his head. 'I don't think so. But then, I don't know what's in the mind of God, do I?' And he smiled.

'What about the Pope? I've heard them say he's supposed to be infallible.'

He shook his head. 'If you become a student of history, the history of the church, you'll soon learn that popes are men just like us. They sin, they make mistakes, they fall into error.' He paused. 'It is possible that the whole church, speaking through all its bishops, meeting in one of the great councils of the church, might be infallible. But not one man. No, that's not possible.'

I nodded. 'There's something else I wanted to talk about.' He sat back in his chair and waited. 'When I used to work in the Governor's House I saw a copy of the treaty between England and Portugal: the treaty that gave Tangiers to England. It said – these aren't the exact words just the spirit of the words – there were eighteen Portuguese Fathers, priests, and when they died they were not to be replaced. But in the last census I copied I remember there were still eighteen Fathers. And some are young, no older than me, and it's obvious they are being replaced.'

'That was a treaty made between Portugal and England. It was not a treaty made between the Church and England. It is the work of man, and the Church of God is not bound by the works of man. It is man who is bound by the works of God – made known through the Church. But we do, in the interests of law and order, of good government, cooperate with the civic authorities, the secular governments, but we are not bound by their dictates, their treaties. We are bound by the will of God.'

'And eighteen, the figure in our man-made treaty, is that the will of God?'

'Discretion is a virtue. And virtues lead us to God. So maybe yes.' He smiled, stood up, and showed me to the door.

Early in May another warrant arrived for Colonel Kirke: this one appointed him Colonel of our regiment, and in common parlance we now boasted four names: the Old Regiment, the Governor's Regiment, the First Tangiers Regiment-of-foot and Kirke's Regiment. Colonel Trelawny took over the command of the Second Tangiers Regiment-of-foot.

Within a few days we knew the worst. Captain Lacey had pleaded ill-health and resigned his commission. He would not be returning to Tangiers and our company was to be disbanded. Sickness, the siege, old age, had cut our numbers to just under thirty. We were the smallest company. Captain Rowes was next with forty, and after him came Captain Talbotts with forty-two. All the companies needed more men and we agreed there was a logic, a brutal logic that demanded our death, and their reinforcement.

In addition to being Colonel-of-the-Regiment, Colonel Kirke also commanded our First Battalion and the First Company of that battalion, the 'Governor's Company'. In his absence this company came under the command of the Captain-Lieutenant. The Second Battalion was commanded by Lieutenant-Colonel Boynton who also commanded that battalion's First Company. When Colonel Kirke was absent – this was now proving to be most of the time – Colonel Boynton took command of the regiment. De Colville and I were appointed supernumerary to Colonel Boynton's Company – in effect we became reformadoes on full pay. Sergeant Lockhart and Corporal Powel were given temporary postings in the same company without any loss of rank or pay. We managed to keep the men in twos and threes to maintain their friendships – to maintain the bonds that were in many cases closer than the bonds of marriage – and despite the feeling of gloom, of arranging our own funeral, there was a high degree of satisfaction, with one exception: Sergeant Brandon. His legs had weakened and he needed a walking stick. Colonel Boynton was adamant: he could not remain on active service. On the morning of our final parade, we watched him march off the ground: no walking stick, back straight, halberd held high. He wet our eyes, brought lumps to our throats, and it was impossible not to admire the old bastard, to feel for him. And later, to feel for O'Sullivan and Crabtree who would have to live, to work, to clerk with him, till the day he was discharged from the regiment.

At the end of May we guarded Pole Fort for a week, and there was talk of another week in August or September. It was one of the unexpected benefits of having a garrison of over three thousand men and only four forts to guard.

Nobody in our regiment decried the new regiments, or our need for them, but they did – in an unwitting way – rouse in us a sense of resentment, a sense of shame. The fault, the blame, lay not with them. It lay with the King. His Majesty had decided on an order of precedence, a ranking for his regiments. His own Guards, the King's Battalion came first. Then came the Scots, for they were his second oldest regiment; then came all his other regiments; then came us – with the Trelawnys right at the end. It meant that we, who had always marched onto the Old Parade first, or led the way into the Market Place, had surrendered pride of place, and now we were always third – second to last was the way we put it. This precedence manifested itself in subtle ways and the one that used to rankle most was the new set of signals, the call to run to our alarm posts. Each signal began with the firing of the great gun on the Governor's Bastion and then the bastion-bell was rung: 10 strokes for the King's Battalion, 20 strokes for the Dunbartons, 30 strokes for us, 40 strokes for the Trelawnys.

In June after practising the new signals for a week, the general alarm sounded. It was signalled by one cannon from the the Governor's Bastion followed by the tolling of the great bell in Peterborough Tower. For a moment we looked at each other in stark amazement – we'd been given no warning, no intimation of a practice. We grabbed our muskets and ran. Everybody ran. It was like a mad streaming of sheep, or maybe goats would be more apt for they run faster than sheep, and for once there was no thought of precedence, no waiting, no counting of strokes. For once we were all equal.

But in the Governor's inspection, in the confirmation that this was just another practice, the order of precedence was restored and we stood in the sunshine and waited for about an hour. After the inspection and the dismissal, I walked down to the Little Parade, to see Jenny, but the burghers, the Militia, were still lined up close to Councillor Earlesman's door, and they were blocking the door to her father's shop. I knew they'd have to wait another twenty minutes before Colonel Kirke arrived, and I didn't want them peering into the shop, pressing their noses against the panes – like the boys on the first night Jenny took me into her bed – and wondering why she let me go into the back of the shop. So I turned around and walked back to the Market Place and then on to St John's Square. Our new lodging house was just off the square and I was feeling hungry, feeling thirsty, when I saw Mister Tate.

He was wearing a white shirt, black breeches, black stockings and black shoes. He didn't have a hat, coat, neckscarf or walking stick – the accoutrements of dignity, of a gentleman. He looked bewildered. His face and his hands looked grubby, and finger-lines of dirt smeared the front of his shirt.

I hesitated to approach him, but then I remembered his kindness when I fell down the steps, fell into his cabin and needed his help. I smiled and said: 'Mister Tate.'

He looked at me and blinked, then he turned away.

'Can I help you?' I said.

'Help me? Why do you want to help me?'

'You're a long way from home. And I thought – I thought you might be lost.'

'I live there.' And he pointed to the house that used to be the church of Saint John.

'I'm sorry, I didn't know you'd shifted. You must forgive me.' Then I realised I hadn't seen him, or her, for two years, maybe more. 'I haven't seen you preaching outside the cathedral for a long time.'

He blinked. 'What cathedral?'

'The Catholic cathedral.'

'Why would I want to do that?'

I burst out laughing. Why indeed? I looked into his eyes. They were awash with innocence, with the blue-eyed sparkle of a newborn baby. I smiled and sighed for the man that was, and I said: 'I'll knock on the door for you.'

I knocked. Then I heard a voice yelling down at me: 'What do you want?'

I stepped back, looked into a pinched face aged by the sun, and said: 'He wants to come in.'

'He's always wanting to come in. He can't get it into his silly head that he doesn't live here.' She closed the shutters, closed off the questions I wanted to ask.

I turned to him.

He smiled. 'Shall I knock on the door?'

I sighed to myself and took his arm. 'I'll walk you home.' Then memories flooded into my mind. Memories I had tried to forget, tried to ignore, and they chilled my soul.

As we turned into Saint Barbara's Street a boy ran past and I yelled: 'Will you take him home for me.'

He laughed, and still running he called back to me: 'He's bloody mad he is. And I ain't going nowhere near his door.'

I walked down the street, kept hoping someone would come out of a house, but no one came. I knocked on his door and stood back.

Mistress Westcombe – from a few doors along – opened the door. She saw me, saw him, and a look of relief crossed his face. 'Thank God,' she said. 'We were so worried. He escaped.' She took his arm and as she led him inside, I stepped back, half-turned to leave.

Then a little boy toddled to the door and looked up at me. I looked into his face, into his eyes. They were my mother's eyes: burnt chestnuts speckled with sparks of fire.

105

A moment or two later Mistress Tate came to the door. We looked at each other then I lifted my hands in the air, as if to make her keep her distance, and I backed away. 'I'm sorry,' I said. 'I didn't intend to come. I wouldn't have come if I hadn't found him, in Saint John's Square. He looked so helpless. So confused. And I couldn't find anyone else to bring him back.'

I looked again at the child, at my Mother's eyes, the same eyes I had known as a child, then I turned and began to walk away, to walk up the street. I broke into a sweat, a sweat of confusion, of bewilderment.

She came running after me. She touched my arm, and whispered: 'Please don't go away. I've been waiting for you to come back. I've been waiting so long. Please.' She took a firm grip on my arm.

'But last time,' I swallowed hard, 'last time, I shouldn't have done what I did. It was wrong. And I'm sorry. I know I can't undo the wrong I did to you, but I can stay away, stay out of your sight. I can give you a chance to forget me, to forget what I did to you.' I slipped away from her arm and strode up the street.

She hurried after me, grabbed my arm, pulled me towards her bosom. 'I wanted you. I wanted you the night you fell down those stairs in the ship. I've always wanted you. And that's the truth. And I'm so ashamed.'

'Ashamed?'

'Whenever Mister Tate took me, took his marital rights, I thought of you. You were the one in my arms, in my body. You were the one in my heart. The one I wanted.'

'But that day when we . . . you were so cold. And I was like an animal. I forced you.'

She wiped a tear from the corner of her eye. 'You forced my body. It was like a frozen lake: iced over by the laws of man, and the laws of God. You broke through the ice. You did what you had to do. What I wanted you to do. And now my spirit, my heart are free to love you.' She paused. 'I know it wasn't wrong. God would never have given me a child if it was wrong. I know that in my heart. In my whole being.'

I looked at her and my eyes filled with tears. 'And the boy?'

'The boy is your son. A late flowering. A gift of God.'

I shook my head. It didn't seem real, seem right. 'And what did Mister Tate say?'

She sighed to herself. 'Mister Tate has lost his mind. Some days he doesn't know who he is, or who I am. He's never asked about the child. Just accepted it. The same way people accept a stray cat into their homes and never question where it came from.'

I followed her into the house in a daze. The little boy smiled at me, wiggled his fingers – I wiggled mine at him – then he lost his courage, ran behind his mother and snuggled into her skirts.

Mister Tate was sitting in a chair close to the fire. A rope bound his arms and legs to the chair.

Mistress Tate caught me staring at him. 'I know,' she whispered. 'It's looks wrong. And it is wrong. But we can't stop him running away. He doesn't know he's running away. He thinks, well, in truth, I don't know what he thinks any more. One day we found him walking down the road with no breeches. And everybody could see between his legs. It was so humiliating. Having to take his hand. To lead him home.' And she burst into tears.

I put my arms around her, held her tight, waited for the sobbing to die. Then I began to feel a warmth for her, a wanting – it was like blowing on hot ashes in the dawn, rekindling the flames of yesterday – and I could not trust myself. I let go, slid my hands down her arms and stood back.

She wiped her eyes, wiped away the past.

Mistress Westcombe picked up the child and said to him: 'I think it's time for your sleep, don't you?'

He mouthed noises. They didn't mean anything to me but she said: 'Yes I know. And if you get into bed on your own, I might be able to tell you a story.'

As she carried him up the stairs he leant over her shoulder and waved to us. We both waved to him, and I wanted to pick him up, to hold him, to feel that he was real. 'What's his name?'

'Charles. Charles Tate.'

I felt a pang of sorrow, of regret for what might have been. She seemed to sense this, and she reached for my hand, cupped it in hers. 'I know. I would have liked Fenton. Would have preferred it. But it cannot be.' And she smiled.

I nodded. I still couldn't accept the evidence of my eyes. And there seemed to be no relationship between what we did, what I forced – what I thought I forced – her to do.

Mister Tate tried to stand up in his chair, tried to shuffle it closer to the fire. She rushed towards him, gripped the back of the chair, patted his shoulder, whispered in his ear, and calmed him. She came back to me. 'A week ago he fell in the fire. He doesn't understand about fire any more – can't remember that it can burn him.'

I looked around the room. It hadn't changed since the days when we pulled the wattle and daub off the walls, left the frames, and made three rooms into one. The boards with the Ten Commandments still hung on the wall. The communion table was pushed hard against the wall, like an altar, and long ago that would have offended Mister Tate. Now it was just a table covered with books. In the left-hand side of the room, in what used to be the main room of the other house, the fire was dead and a bed sat close to the wall, blocked the old front door. 'Why don't you restore the wall' – I pointed to the left-hand wall – 'and make that part into Mister Tate's room? It would make it harder for him to escape.'

'Hmm. But he needs a fire. He feels the cold. I'd have to have a fire in both rooms and I couldn't afford that. And I wouldn't be able to see him if he fell in the fire. And besides, he needs to go into the outside chapel. We have his privy out there.'

'Hmm. Then why don't you fill in the lower part of this wall.' I pointed my toe at the bottom of the right-hand wall. 'And add more studs to the top section, enough to stop him crawling through. And if you put his bed in there, he'd be close to the Commandments, and close to the door to St Barbara's Chapel. And the warmth from the fire in the other room would go through the top of the open wall, and you'd know he was warm, and safe.'

'I thought of doing something like that once. But I didn't have any money then and I don't have any at the moment. Our money from England, our money for the mission, it hasn't arrived.' She gave me a smile, a sad, helpless smile.

'I could do it for you. I know one of the carpenters and I'm sure he'd help.'

'But the wood would be dear, too dear for me.'

I shook my head. 'When we pulled down the forts we brought back all the wood. I know where it's stored, and I think we could have it built in two, maybe three days.'

She smiled and gave me a big hug.

Then Mistress Westcombe came down the stairs saying: 'He's fast asleep. I've a few things to do for myself now. I'll be back in a couple of hours, and then I'll be getting him something to eat.'

When she was gone we looked at each other with shy embarrassment, then she took my hand. 'Come up stairs. He looks like an angel when he's asleep. And every time I see him he reminds me of you, on that first night on the ship, when your skin was soft and your face was covered with down.'

I touched his skin, touched his hair – it was black like mine – and I was filled with wonderment. I still couldn't think of myself as a father. But here was the proof. The living proof.

Then she wrapped her arms around me, and for a long time we watched him sleep. Then she whispered: 'I want you.'

106

The Ambassador returned from England with the new treaty – the Treaty of Whitehall – at the end of August, and two weeks later, after recovering from the rigours of the sea, he left to present it to the Emperor. He took with him all our Moorish slaves. They numbered sixty or seventy and under the terms of the treaty they were to be exchanged for all the Emperor's English captives without payment of any ransom by either side.

In private Colonel Kirke was much against the treaty. One provision rankled him more than any other: thirty Moors were to be allowed to live in the town. In the past we tolerated the Barbary Jews, accepted the benefits of their intercourse with the Moors, but this would be worse. This would be like bubbling secrets in the soft warmth, the gentle glow that lulls a man to sleep when he has had a woman.

For me the treaty brought a sudden and unexpected consequence. Our men were now expected to do the work the slaves used to do. And each day, for the next month, Sergeant Lockhart and I took twenty men down to the cliffs below York Castle, to the stretch that fronts the Strand, and loaded stone onto the rock carts. The quarrymen were shaping the cliffs – cutting the stone they could not cut at Whitby – making them vertical, making them harder to scale, and using the stone to repair the holes the sea kept tearing in the raw ends of the Mole.

Then the most incredible rumour swept through the town. For a long time I couldn't believe it, didn't want to believe, but by the following morning it had congealed, had set like a pot of hot fat and we knew it was true. The Ambassador had been arrested and paraded before the Emperor in chains, in disgrace, and they say, if it was not for the great compliment His Majesty paid to the Ambassador – when he raised his hat to welcome him to London – the Emperor would have had him executed. What the Ambassador is supposed to have done, or not done, I do not know. But they blame it on the Barbary Jews. They say they followed him to Oxford, Cambridge, Newmarket and Windsor. They spied upon him, reported his every word, his every doing, and unlike the English, they were not impressed by his displays of horsemanship in Hyde Park.

Somewhere, behind all of this, if the rumours are right, lay the hand, lay the money, of his mortal enemy: Ali Benabdala.

The Emperor refused to ratify the treaty, refused to acknowledge he had given the Ambassador the powers of a plenipotentiary: the right to negotiate, to sign a binding treaty on his behalf. And worse still he refused to free the English prisoners – claimed we still had another four hundred Moors in the city and he couldn't free our men till we freed these men. They might have existed in his imagination but they did not exist within our walls.

Then the Emperor invited the King to send him a new ambassador, a man 'of great quality'; a man who would bring him more gifts. His words appeared to offer fresh hope, to offer settlement, but in our hearts we knew that he would never sign a treaty that led to peace, permanent peace. It was an illusion, a mirage in the desert.

My talks with Father Francifo slipped to once every three weeks, and then once every four weeks. In his heart I think he was expecting, was praying, I'd be like Saul of Tarsus – Paul the Apostle – on the road to Damascus; and I'd see a blinding flash, make a miraculous conversion, and believe in popery. But the fibre of my being was not the fibre of the apostles, the martyrs, and besides I was dreading the day when he might want to talk about swiving. He wouldn't use that word, it was too rough, too coarse for him. But he would find a word, or a phrase with subtle insinuations of meaning, and we'd both know what he was talking about. So far, I'd been honest with him – as honest as I could be. And I didn't know what I'd say if he wanted to talk about men like Michael, and what they do. In my heart I kept hoping he wouldn't know about such things. But he'd know about swiving. I was sure of that. And how the hell was I going to tell him I was sleeping with two women? And one of them was married, and I was breaking the Seventh Commandment: three, four times a week.

I tried to ease myself out of Jenny's bed, but my courage failed me. In truth it was easier to have her body, to swim again in the waters of Mequinez with my nymphs, than it was to tell the truth or tell a lie, and be gone from her bed. In her loving, her lust for a child, she locked her legs around my bum and held me tight. Some nights I was so deep in her, I felt she was going to possess every inch of my being, to drain me of the essence of life, and through the death of my body, the fleeing of my spirit, she would be seeded with life – my life.

In the wildness of her new-found passion, the frantic possession of my staff, the staff of life, she made my balls ache: two or three times a week.

Lieutenant de Colville and I sometimes walked down to the early morning mass: the one that praised the Lord, offered the sacrifice of bread and wine, and shared the Body of Christ – with those who could believe in miracles – and then allowed us to slip away into the gloom, unrecognised. De Colville drew strength from them but I found them empty. To me they were a ritual, performed by one man, performed by rote. A mumbling of Latin. In essence they were the same as the high mass, but they were stripped of all their music, colour, ritual, ceremonial. They were the bare bones: the core of belief. All the rest were trappings. And what I couldn't bring myself to tell de Colville or Father Francifo was this: I liked the trappings, but I didn't like the core, the bones of belief.

107

In July of the following year, as the sun dried the land, dried the water courses and locked us into the hot days of summer, days of drought, Mistress Tate – Elizabeth – gave birth to a boy.

When he was less than an hour old, I held him in my arms. He was so tiny, so light, so fragile, it didn't seem possible that he could grow into a boy and then into a man. And I was thinking he was mine, thinking I was the father, the man who gave him life, when he opened his eyes. They were blue. They were Mister Tate's eyes. I stared at them in horror. The man was now raving mad. Wetting his bed. Pooing in the hearth. Crying in the night, screaming with pain, scratching at his flesh, unable to rest his limbs, rest the aches in his joints. It wasn't possible for him to be the father. But I was looking into his eyes, sky-watered eyes. I felt my jaw sag. Elizabeth raised herself from the bed and said: 'What's wrong?'

'His eyes. They're blue.'

She lay back on the pillow. 'All babies have blue eyes. His will change in about six weeks.' She smiled and held out her hand.

Ten days later, in the garrison church, the Reverend Mister Hughes christened him: James Fenton Tate. I gave him two pieces-of-eight and he thanked me. Then I asked if he'd turn back the pages of the Baptismal Register and find the entry for Charles Tate. He looked at me with knowing eyes, disapproving eyes, then he found the entry and I said: 'I would like, we both would like' – I turned to Elizabeth and smiled – 'to insert the name Fenton. To call him Charles Fenton Tate.'

He shook his head. 'It's done. It's in the past. This is a legal record. I cannot alter it.'

I took a piece-of-eight out of my pocket and laid it on the stone rim of the baptismal font. It was worth four shillings and sixpence in common currency, but when we were paid the treasurer valued them at four shillings and nine pence – so we were cheated out of threepence every time he handed us a piece-of-eight.

He drew back. Looked offended, affronted.

I laid another piece-of-eight on the rim. It was minted in silver. One side bore the crown of Spain and a coat of arms. The other side bore the two Pillars of Hercules and a smaller version of the crown of Spain.

He sucked at his lips, stared at the two coins.

I laid my last piece-of-eight on the rim – sometimes they're called Dollars or Pillar Dollars – and I waited.

He hesitated for a moment, then his hand swept them off the rim and into his pocket, and altered the register. The writing was the same, was his writing – was a little cramped – but when the ink dried it looked as though it had always been there.

Then he said to me: 'I'm glad you brought the child here. I was fearing you might take him over the road.'

Elizabeth looked at him, looked at me. 'What does he mean – over the road?'

I opened my mouth, stammered, swallowed my words.

He said: 'To the cathedral.'

A look of horror swept over her face.

He touched her on the arm. 'I'm sorry, I thought you knew.'

108

Elizabeth said I was mad, 'stark raving mad'. And by the tone of her voice, the scorn that wracked her face, I knew she thought my illness was worse than anything that was afflicting Mister Tate. I tried to explain the unfolding of faith, the blooming of the roses of truth in my mind, but she would have none of it. I was 'gripped with evil, seduced by the devil'.

In my mind I feared she was right. It was easy to prove parts of popery were wrong. It was also easy to prove the reformers had discarded some of the old truths, some of the wisdom of the ages. And the Church of Rome was not the Church of the Reformation: it was reformed, made new, made clean by the Council of Trent. She admitted, I admitted, we did not understand, did not agree with some of the things that lay at the core of our own faith. But we were forced, were required, to accept on faith things we did not understand. And it was the same for the papists.

It was an argument that left her unmoved. She had listened to Mister Tate for too long, had absorbed his wisdom, his errors, his stiffness of faith. She opened the Prayer Book, turned to the '39 Articles': the articles of religion, the articles that are the flesh and bones of our faith. 'Listen to this,' she said. 'This is article 22:

"The Romanish Doctrine concerning Purgatory, Pardons, Worshipping and Adoration, as well as of Images as of Relics, and also invocation of Saints, is a fond thing vainly invented, and grounded upon no warranty of Scripture, but rather repugnant to the Word of God."'

She let the words sink into my mind, then she said: 'What do you have to say about that?'

'It is based on a simple error. In the beginning the Church did not have the scriptures. It had the living word. Then it had the written word and the living word: the two great pillars of revelation. At the time of the Reformation the reformers pulled down the pillar that was the living word – the oral tradition of the Church. But it is still valid, as valid as it was in the very first days of the Church. To deny this is to deny that the early Church was the repository of faith, of truth.'

She looked at me and shook her head. 'Dear God,' she whispered, 'they have corrupted your mind.' Then she beckoned me to follow her.

We climbed the stairs, walked into her bedroom, our bedroom. It was dark. I opened the doors, walked out onto the balcony and look down into the chapel. It was cool, it had trapped the morning air, and the leaves of the grapevines that now crossed from one side to the other were dappling the flagstones with shadows. I heard her opening and closing drawers, then she was beside me thrusting a journal into my hand. It was old. It bore the date August 1678. It told the story of the 'Popish Plot' – the plot to kill the King and put the Duke of York on the throne. It appalled me. It appalled every right-thinking man, but I didn't see it's relevance. 'How does this affect faith?'

'A man is judged by what he does. By the company he keeps. These men were papists. This was popery – popery plotting murder. They were condemned by their actions, and through their actions they showed us the true nature of popery. These were deeds, not words. And deeds speak louder than words.'

I hung my head in shame. She was right. Popery had led them to think, to plot murder, but the actions of a few men did not condemn the many. Did not destroy hundreds of years of faith, of searching for truth. I was about to say this when she said: 'And I agree with Colonel Kirke. I think he was right to arrest the priests.'

I shuddered. Her words brought back painful memories. The Governor did not throw them into prison, he confined them to the convent – placed them under house-arrest. The problem was of their own making. I said this to Father Francifo but he shook his head, and whispered: 'It will pass. In the fullness of time the will of God will prevail.'

The fullness was yet to arrive, and at the moment the will of the Governor prevailed. It was a question of authority. The Fathers claimed the right to exercise a spiritual jurisdiction over our Irish soldiers. To my mind that could be justified as right and proper. But the Fathers were not content with that, and they strayed into temporal matters. The Governor would have none of it, was hot for closing the cathedral and sending them all back to Portugal. But such things were beyond his power, and mindful of the patronage of Her Majesty, her concern for the prosperity of her dowry, he allowed the Fathers to imitate the Moors: to settle into a truce that decided nothing.

A day or two later when the silence between us was still heavy with frost, the frost of ice-cold words, words that neither of us had retracted, I found her sitting at the table, writing a letter. I sat down and smiled. She glanced at me then dipped her quill in the ink and returned to her letter.

Her writing was bold, well formed, and easy to read. But it was also the writing of a child. It had not matured, taken on the character, the style, of an adult hand. O'Sullivan, Trigg and Ives would have poured scorn upon it – called it youthful – but to me it was a wonder to behold:

never before had I known a woman who could write. I watched for several seconds, then I said: 'Who are you writing to?'

'Lord Extonmouth.'

The name screamed in my mind. It was the name on the Commandment Boards, the name of de Colville's father. 'Why do you want to write to him?'

'He was a friend of Mister Tate. And when he learnt we were coming to Tangiers he asked Mister Tate if he would write to him. Once every three months. And in return he would send us money for our mission.' She laid down her quill. 'And since Mister Tate's illness I've been writing on his behalf.'

'But what do you write about?'

'I tell him about his son: Lieutenant de Colville. And I tell him about Tangiers, the regiment, the Moors, our chapel. Almost anything that comes into my mind.'

'But why doesn't de Colville write himself?'

'His father was horrified when he converted – became a papist. Didn't want to have anything to do with him. Couldn't bear the disgrace, the shame. So he bought him a commission and sent him here. Hoped he would see popery for what it really is. And he refused to have anything to do with him till he came to his senses.'

'Then why does he want to know about him?'

She smiled. 'No parent can abandon a child. It's not in their nature. There's always a thread, a cord, a bond of birth that ties a child to his mother, to his father. And it can't be broken.'

James began to cry. She walked over to his crib, lifted him up, and let him suckle her breast. Then she turned to me.

'The sad thing is that Tangiers has strengthened his faith. Being able to go to church, to go openly, has confirmed the error of his ways. And now there is no hope for him.'

'Does his father ever reply?'

She shook her head. 'Not once. Not once in nine years. He told Mister Tate the money would suffice. Would be our only recompense.'

It seemed a strange correspondence. It was like spying, like shadowing a man through the days of his life. Then I began to wonder if I was in those shadows, and I said: 'Did you ever say anything about me?'

'Once long ago. Mister Tate told him you were his friend – his only friend if I remember the words right.' She hesitated. I looked at her and she looked at her letter, fiddled with the corner of the sheet of paper. 'And now I'm telling him about you. About him corrupting you. Filling your mind with the evils of popery and making you think it's true.'

'If it's true, if most of it's true, we don't have a choice. We must follow the will of God. We must trust him. And if trust means popery, we must accept it. We must embrace the truth. We must convert.'

She shook her head, the colour drained out of her face, and she turned away from me.

From his bed Mister Tate screamed with laughter, screamed as though he'd understood every word we said.

109

In August, soon after five in the morning, I took half our company and twenty prisoners – chained to each other by the ankles – up to the junction of Catherine Street and Saint Barbara's Street, and we dug two trenches right across the street. We were hoping to find an old water course. We didn't know if one existed, but last year Colonel Kirke, after questioning a couple of old men who lived here in the time of the Portuguese, had found a long-forgotten water course. And then he'd been able to reopen forty or fifty garden wells and relieve some of the water shortage. And now, enamoured of the suggestion that other old water courses might lie below the streets, we were digging trenches, day after day.

At three feet we found nothing – not even compacted back-fill – and I ordered the men to go down another three feet. Yesterday was an easy day: we stuck solid rock at two feet and that was the end of the digging.

The drought had made water more precious than ever before and now the watersellers were waiting at Catherine Gate, every morning, long before the dawn. The price of their water had risen to tuppence a pail, and as we dug, one of them came towards us yelling: 'Fresh water! Fountain Fort water! Drinking water! None of your old rubbish in this water.'

I smiled, watched him go down the street, swaying as his buckets swayed, not spilling a drop. We were scared of the water. Not his water, the water in the fountain in the Market Place. It had lost its sparkle. It looked brown, looked muddy when it flowed, and there was a rumour – more than a rumour, a certainty: the Moors were poisoning our water. The evidence lay before our eyes: four hundred men were lying sick – many of them in the infirmarium – heaving their bellies and passing blood. It was never like this in other years, when the water flowed, when women didn't have to push the cattle away from the trough in the Market Place to fill a pail of water.

And there was more evidence: the Moors were now camped on the Marshan, camped on the springs, the headwaters that fed our water courses. And they were there in their hundreds, shitting in our water.

Colonel Kirke thought the Moors were assembling to attack. He said we were lucky to have had almost three years of peace. He doubled the guards on the wall from Peterborough Tower to Irish Battery, and sent extra men to Pole Fort. He said we could never hold Fountain and Bridges, and when they went, when our only supply of clean water went, we could pray for rain, or leave.

August burnt itself out at last, and early in September, when there was still no sign of rain, and Colonel Kirke was predicting the Moors would attack within the next ten days, a ship arrived. To me it was just another ship, but next day Colonel Kirke wore a sour look, and soon after that the seamen came ashore and we all knew a great fleet was on the way, and it was bringing a new governor: Lord Dartmouth.

The ship unloaded the latest journals from London and they carried the most appalling news: in April a plot had been discovered to murder the King and his brother the Duke of York when they paused for refreshments at Rumbold's Rye House, on the way back from Newmarket. The traitors – that is what the papers were calling the three lords who plotted the royal murders – were planning to put the Duke of Monmouth on the throne and they were to be supported by insurrections in London and the West Country. Unlike the earlier plot, the Popish Plot that aimed to put a papist on the throne, this one aimed to put a Protestant on the throne, and this time the noble lords, the noble plotters were Protestants, not papists. It was a strange twist, a twist that appalled the whole garrison, and it gave men like de Colville, men who had to suffer, had to endure sneers of contempt at the time of the Popish Plot – because they were papists and were assumed to be secret sympathisers – a great sense of satisfaction.

Rumours about the fleet ran wild: the ships were packed with new soldiers-of-foot; with troops-of-horse; with enough provisions to withstand a siege for three or four years. Other rumours claimed the ships were empty and we were all going home. Others said Colonel Kirke was in disgrace and he was the one going home. And others said they were loaded with treasure to redeem the captives. In truth no one knew why they were coming.

On the 13th we caught sight of the fleet, but the winds blew it south, right across the mouth of the Straits, and it dropped anchor off Cape Spartel.

Next morning the ships clawed their way into the Tangiers Roads, exchanged salutes with York Castle and the battery on the Mole, and dropped anchor.

I counted twenty-one ships. It was the biggest fleet to arrive in ten years and there had to be a reason. To me most of the ships looked to be riding high, riding empty, and I favoured going home. When I said this to Lockhart, he pulled a face and said: 'Can you imagine anybody pulling all this down?' Then he waved his hand at the two castles, the town and the Mole. I gave him a grin, a sheepish grin. It was wishful thinking. Home was the burying ground beyond Catherine Gate – that's what we used to say in our darker moments, our beer-soaked moments when truth shook off her cloak of lies and stared us in the face: naked, raw, unadorned.

The sailors rowed Colonel Kirke out to the *Grafton*, to the flagship, to meet the new Governor.

Then nothing happened – apart from the emergence of two more rumours: we were going to invade Spain; and we were showing the Alcaide we had enough ships to supply Tangiers with enough men and enough supplies of war to ensure his defeat.

On the morning of the third day His Excellency came ashore and rode in state to the Upper Castle. We saluted him on the Old Parade and heard the formal reading of the King's Commission – it appointed him Admiral, Captain-General, Governor and Commander-in-Chief. He looked younger than I thought he would, and to my surprise he was not the focus of attention. Maybe I've put that wrong. He was the focus of attention to begin with, but then our interest, our curiosity shifted to three of the men in his train. It did not stay long on the first man, Doctor Kenn: Lord Dartmouth's personal chaplain. He was slight, with a crooked frame and they say he has a penchant for hymn-writing. He didn't impress me at all, but then, in truth, no cleric ever has – with the sole exception of Father Francifo.

The next man was a London lawyer: a Doctor Trumbull – white-faced and gaunt, like a man still ravaged by the swellings of the sea. He looked fussy, impatient, in need of the trappings of the law, the dignity of a courtroom. In short, he looked out of place.

The third was a Mister Samuel Pepys. His face was pocked with mosquito bites and he was wearing a full-length wig. In the heat it must have been like wearing a fleece. It flushed his face and every few seconds he was mopping his brow. I felt for him, and I felt for myself – since being commissioned I've had to grow my hair. I've had it cut and curled, just below my ears, to let the air flow round my face, round my neck, but it's still too long, too hot and it does not suit our weather. But at least I wasn't suffering like Mister Pepys. They say he suffered in the Tower of London. He was arrested for conspiracy, for involvement in the Popish Plot. His wife was a papist, and that was enough to put him in the Tower. Before that they say he was the Secretary of the Admiralty, and I can remember when I was in London, can remember Rutherford from A.J. Woodgate & Sons saying he used to bribe someone called Pepys – to get him to sign contracts to provision the ships in the King's navy – but whether or not this was, is, the same man I do not know.

Kenn was not a mystery. He was a believer in mysteries.

But Trumbull and Pepys were a mystery – a mysterious presence. None of us could fathom what they were doing in Tangiers.

Within a few hours a new spirit ran through the garrison. Lord Dartmouth did not want war. He wanted peace. And unlike Colonel Kirke he was prepared to meet the Moors, to extend to them the hand of friendship. He began by sending them presents: three dozen bottles of cider – they made me wonder if anyone had told him the Moors don't touch strong drink; twelve barrels of fine gunpowder – the most expensive kind; cambric – the finest white linen; bolts of cloth and lances ornamented with brass. The Moors, seduced by the presents, agreed to meet Lord Dartmouth on the 28th.

On the 19th Lord Dartmouth solved the mystery of Trumbull and Pepys. By public proclamation he created a special commission and instructed it – instructed them – to examine and determine the title to every single property in the whole of Tangiers. It was a mess. Everybody agreed. But nobody had ever thought it would be sorted out. Those with title from the time of the Portuguese were required to submit their documents, their proof of ownership. Those with leases were required to submit their leases and provide proof of renewal, proof of expiry, and proof of the annual rental. Everyone was required to declare any repairs or additions that had been made to their property at His Majesty's expense. Tiles, wood, tarras, stone, brick, nails or any items used in these repairs were to be declared; and any work done by the carpenters, the blacksmiths or the soldiers of our regiment, at any time since the regiment arrived in Tangiers, were also to be declared.

The proclamation upset Jenny's father. To begin with he didn't know where he'd put the lease and then he was thinking it mightn't be able to be renewed. He knew it still had two years to run, but he couldn't remember all the repairs. He'd paid for some. He could remember that. But in the early days when he first arrived, when Jenny was a child, the house, the shop, had no tiles, doors and shutters – the Portuguese took them when they left – and if the troops hadn't fixed them for him, who would have? And why did they want to know? What was the point of it? That's what he wanted to know.

I didn't know the point of it. None of us knew the point of it. The proclamation spoke of the 'better ordering of our public affairs', and it would do that. It would establish a base, a legal platform for the buying and selling of property, and the transferring of leases.

It also did one thing I hadn't expected: it killed off all the rumours about leaving, about abandoning Tangiers. But for some reason when one rumour died it fertilised another and now everyone was saying the King was going to demand compensation for the work done at his expense, and he was going to put a tax on property. And he couldn't do that till he knew the true owners, the true values. I told Jenny's father he should forget about all the repairs, but he said: 'I cannot tell a lie.'

I offered to help him but he shook his head. 'These are family matters. And you're not one of the family – not yet.'

I looked at Jenny and we both shrugged.

Later that night, as I lay in her bed drifting in a soft haze with my two nymphs, I said: 'You'll have to help him.'

'But I don't know anything about leases and the law. And I don't remember the repairs. I was too young at the time. And I can't read – you know that – so I can't help him.'

'I could read it for you.'

'He'd never let you read it. You saw what he's like.'

I looked into the wooden beams, watched the shadows flit from one to the other – the window was open and the curtain was swaying, was cross-hatching the shadows – and I said: 'Then I think you should take the lease when he's asleep some time. And show it to a friend. Get him – or her – to read it to you. And have it back before he wakes up. And when he goes to the Commission, go with him, and you'll be able to help him.'

She nodded, mumbled, 'I'll have to go with him anyway. He could never walk that far on his own,' and drifted off to sleep.

In the morning I rushed up to the clerk's office – intending to find out what they knew – but the office was deserted.

I ambled down to Elizabeth's. Her eyes were red and puffy. Her cheeks were drawn. I took her hands in mine and said: 'What's wrong?'

'Doctor Lawrence was here a few minutes ago. He says Mister Tate is very poorly. He says,' she hesitated, 'he only has a short time to live. Two, three weeks at the most. And he's left this.' She picked up a bottle and looked at it. 'It's to ease the pain. And he says we should give him some brandy. He says that will help. I told him Mister Tate disliked strong drink. But he said, for him it wouldn't be strong drink, it would be medicine.' She sniffled and wiped her nose. 'Do you think that's right, for a man who thought – who thinks – strong drink leads to sin, to eternal damnation?'

I nodded and she gave me a weak smile, a smile tinged with sadness.

A few minutes later we were talking about the leases and she said: 'I can't do it. I can't go down there. Not with the children I can't.'

'I could go with you.'

'I don't want to go. Mister Tate should go. It's his place to go. But he can't go.' She looked towards the bed, towards the sleeping shape. 'He can't stand any more. And he screams with pain when we carry him out to the privy.'

I touched her face, looked into eyes. 'I could go for you.'

A smile crept over her face. She rushed upstairs and came back with three documents. The first was the lease for the main house, the old priest's house. It was granted by Manuel Don Prego. It was for fifteen years at fifteen pounds per year and it still had four and a half years to run. Mister Tate was entitled to renew it for another five years 'at his own discretion'. The next lease was for the small house we opened up to make the chapel. It was for fifteen years at five pounds per year and it still had five years to run. It did not contain the right of renewal. I turned to Elizabeth and said: 'Why's this one so cheap?'

'It didn't have a roof and the outside walls were starting to crumble.'

I nodded. 'I'd forgotten all about that.' Then I smiled. 'And it will stay forgotten. And so will all the tiles we laid on the roof. And so will all the other things we did.'

'No,' she said, making her voice sound stern, 'you must declare it. The King paid for it. He has a right to know what happened to his money.'

Christ! I thought. Another one with no bloody common sense. But I smiled and nodded, pretended to agree, and read the last lease, the lease for Saint Barbara's Chapel. The term was for fifteen years at one penny per year. Title for the land and chapel was vested in His Majesty the King of Portugal, as the 'Protector and Guardian of the rights of the Most Holy Catholic Church in Tangiers'.

'I wouldn't be surprised,' I said, 'if the Commission finally settles all the Catholic Church's claims for compensation – for its old churches and chapels.'

She nodded. 'And that means they'll have a lot more money to spread their evil message.'

I bit my lips and sighed.

Then she took my hand and said: 'I've been thinking about what you said the other night. About you and popery. And I have to tell you that if – when – Mister Tate passes on, I will not be able to marry you, if you become a papist.'

110

Next morning I walked into the Town House to present Mister Tate's leases. I was still in a state of shock. I'd never thought of marrying Mistress Tate. She was seven years older than me – maybe a little more – and besides I was betrothed to Jenny. She expected me to marry her. It was understood. It wasn't official, or legal, or announced in church like the banns of marriage, but it was a moral obligation. To put it bluntly: fucking her demanded a price. And that was it. That was what she wanted, what her father wanted. And to be honest, in the days before Charles toddled into my life, it was what I wanted. Now I wasn't so sure.

And then of course there was the matter of religion. What would Jenny say if she knew about my feelings for popery? Would she also threaten to toss me out of her bed, out of her life?

I could be left with neither. Left on my own. Left with my nymphs, with my hand, with storms of snowflakes, seeding my hairy belly. And then there was de Colville – Michael the archangel – and his desire for me. But I did not want him, that was clear, was fixed in my mind. The past was done with. And I wasn't going to unearth it.

Inside the Town House, I was surprised to find O'Sullivan, Brandon and Crabtree seated behind a long table checking documents. 'What are you doing here?'

'We're clerks,' O'Sullivan said. 'And they need clerks.' He nodded towards Mister Pepys and Doctor Trumbull, sitting at small tables at the end of the room. 'So here we are. For the next week. The next ten days – whatever it takes.'

I leant over the table, put my face close to his. 'Do you know what it's all about, know the real reason?'

He pulled back from me. 'Mister Pepys has told us, confidentially, that it's to determine ownership. To determine rights. He says it should have been done years ago.'

Crabtree looked up. 'Doctor Trumbull says it's a disgrace. Says no self-respecting English city would have put up with it for ten minutes.'

Eight or nine Portuguese men came into the room talking at the top of their voices. Brandon walked over to them and I heard him say: 'If your documents are in Spanish we have to translate them, and you need to talk to that man over there.' He pointed to another clerk on the other side of the room, then he came back and said to me: 'What do you want? Why are you here?' His tone was brisk, almost abrupt, but I let it pass, and I told him I'd brought Mister Tate's leases. He pointed to Mister Pepys. 'He sees them first, and if he's satisfied he sends you back to us.'

Mister Pepys read the first lease – the one for the Priest's House – looked up and said: 'Was any work done on this house by any men from the regiment?' I shook my head. 'Anything by the King's carpenters, masons, tilers or smiths?' I shook my head. 'You asked Mister Tate – specifically?'

'He's dying, sir. He can't recognise anybody. And he can't answer any questions. But I have his wife's word on it. She says nothing was done at the King's expense. Mister Tate paid for everything.'

'Clergymen don't usually have any money.'

'I remember them taking up a collection for him in the garrison church when he first came, sir. And Lady Middleton was his patron.'

He nodded and read the next one. 'And this one, what about this one?'

'Nothing was done on that house either, sir. Some of the men did help when they were off duty. Pulling down the inside walls and making a private chapel. But that was all.'

He read the lease for the chapel. 'And this one?'

'A lot was done on that one sir. Clearing rubbish. Making new doors and windows. We were going to construct a new roof but the Fathers wouldn't agree to it, and it was never built.'

'Hmm. Well. That saved the King some money – I suppose.' Then he told me to take the leases over to the clerks, to have them entered into the records.

That night I walked from Elizabeth's house to the Market Place and sat in the cathedral, sat on my own, sat for an hour or more. I did not pray, did not make a prayer of my own or read one from a book, but I felt I was in the presence of God. I felt he was real, felt he was there in the tabernacle on the high altar, under the accidents of bread. And I felt I could talk to him, like a friend. Then Father Francifo came into the church. He recognised me and smiled. I told him about these feelings and he said: 'We often talk about the Real Presence. We mean God, Jesus, is really present on the altar, and you can come to him at any hour of the day or night.'

He knelt, and for ten maybe fifteen minutes he was wrapped in prayer, wrapped in union with God. Then he said to me, almost in a whisper, as if it were a secret: 'If you can now sense these things, sense the presence of God, you are ready to join the Church. Follow your senses. Follow the dictates of your heart. And in the years to come, your mind, your intellect will follow; and your belief, your faith will be well-founded.'

I sat in silence. I wasn't expecting to hear this. It was too soon. I wasn't ready. I hesitated, then I said: 'I've been thinking. Lord Dartmouth is going to hold a great parade, next week, outside the walls, to impress the Alcaide. They say he's going to ask for another treaty. For the peace to be continued.

And we're all going to take part – even the Militia. There's talk of the seamen coming ashore and taking part. There's also talk of a survey of the walls and the strong points, and the cost of putting them right. And there's more talk about the Mole, surveying it, cutting stone and finishing the right arm. And now it's obvious we are going to stay. Obvious the rumours were wrong. We are making a new beginning. And I feel if I'm going to be here for the rest of my life, here in the Real Presence, the presence of God, I would like to embrace the truth, to accept the faith and be received into the church.'

He touched my hand.

'If we were going back to England, protestant England, where the Catholic churches are closed and priests are persecuted – hung, drawn and quartered if they are found saying mass – I could not, would not make this decision.' I hesitated. 'That is a measure of my faith. My lack of faith. I do not have what Lieutenant de Colville has. What the Duke of York has. I'm being honest. Frank. And you must accept me for what I am.'

He nodded and we understood each other, understood the limits of faith, and we agreed to set a date – some time in the next two weeks.

In the night I woke up screaming, sweating. I was being hung, drawn and quartered, by Jenny and Elizabeth, and I could not go back to sleep. In truth I was afraid to go back to sleep, afraid of what they would do to me.

In the cold light of the morning – when there were no shadows to fudge the edges, to blur reality – I was afraid of what this decision was going to cost me.

Two days before the great parade, rumours became facts and we knew, knew for sure, that a thousand seamen were to start coming ashore next morning. Under the command of Sir John Berry they were to form four battalions. Two battalions were to wear their normal linen – white with blue stripes – and carry 'muskets, pikes, pole-axes and four Union flags'. The other two were to wear the new red coats Lord Dartmouth had brought for the Scots and the Trelawnys. The coats were to make them look like soldiers-of-foot, make them look like a new regiment that had just arrived. And to complete the disguise, they were to carry muskets, eight of the Trelawny's colours and four of the old Irish colours.

As an ensign, as the official bearer of our company colours, I'd always felt we were slighted when our company was told to rally to Captain Philpott's colours on the day we defeated the Moors and lifted the great siege. The reasoning was sound but it didn't stop me feeling hurt, feeling slighted. To me the parade was an opportunity to redress this wrong, and now that I knew Lord Dartmouth was more interested in mounting a show of strength and impressing the Moors than he was in the niceties of regimental correctness, I presumed to approach Colonel Boynton and ask 'if I could parade Captain Lacey's colour for the last time? To honour the memory of the company, and the men who died.'

For a moment or two he was a little diffident, then he smiled and called it 'a fine sentiment'.

A few minutes later, as I walked down the steps in front of the Head Court of the Guard, the Town Crier rang his bell and yelled: 'Hear ye! Hear ye! A special proclamation! Tomorrow is the last day to submit your claims, your titles to the Commission on property. Hear ye! Hear ye!'

With a sudden jolt I realised Jenny still hadn't taken her father to the Town House to register his lease. I rushed down to her house but the shop was shut. I banged on the door, shouted at the open window on the upper floor, but nobody answered.

I wasn't sure what to do next, and as I walked back up the hill, walked towards the Market Place, I saw the cathedral. Jenny slipped from my mind and I knew I had to set a date: to embrace the faith that embraced the truth. It was what I wanted. It was what I had to do.

Father Francifo welcomed me into the convent, smiled that sad weak smile of his and we agreed he would receive me into the Church on the evening of October 4th, and after the ceremony I would make my first confession. Next morning, at a Low Mass – a mass stripped of all its theatricals, a mass that demanded faith – I would make my first communion.

I walked back up to the Head Court of the Guard and asked de Colville if he would come with me on the 4th and 5th. He said he'd be honoured. Then we began to talk about confessions and I said: 'Did you tell him everything when you made your first confession?'

'Hmm. We went right back to about the age of seven, the age when a boy can start to sin. Can be held responsible for his actions.'

'Was it difficult?'

'To begin with. But he was very helpful. And he asked a lot of questions. Jogged my memory.'

'Father Pio's going to hear my confession. I don't know him. But Father Francifo says I'll find it easier, confessing to a stranger in the dark.'

He nodded. Then I began to think about him making his confessions in the cathedral, two or three times a year – ever since we arrived – and I said: 'Did you ever tell the priest about us? About everything we used to do?'

He looked down and sighed. 'Yes, I did.'

'And what did he say?'

'He said it was wrong. A mortal sin. Said I'd go to hell if I didn't stop.'

'And you promised to stop? To give it up? To give me up?' I laughed. I didn't intend to – it just burst out of me.

He gave me a sour look. 'Yes.'

'But you never tried to give me up did you? And that means when you made your promise, you didn't mean it. And that's' – I hesitated, then I lowered my voice to a whisper – 'hypocrisy.'

'I intended to stop, at the moment I said it. And that's the important thing.'

'Father Francifo told me to make a valid confession, to receive absolution, I'd have to repent my sins; to make a firm intent not to sin again; and to accept my penance.'

'Hmm. It's easy to repent. And it's easy to say a few prayers, to do your penance. But when it comes to not sinning again, that's very difficult. And despite all your good intentions, and your high-mindedness when it comes to my sins, I think you're going to find it very difficult. I know about you and Wyndham's wife. It's common gossip. And I used to wonder about you and Mister Tate's wife, till I saw her little boy for the first time the other day – saw he was the spitting image of you.' And he smiled.

I was shocked. I thought a few might know about Jenny. But not about Elizabeth. We'd been so careful. So conscious of her honour. Her dignity as the wife of a clergyman.

I looked at my shoes – black leather speckled with mud – and I knew they were the image of my soul. And I knew this was going to be even more difficult than I'd ever suspected.

About half an hour later I walked up to Elizabeth's. Our orders for the afternoon were to pitch the tents on Parson's Green for the seamen who were coming ashore tomorrow. I knew it would take bloody hours, and after that we had to check the lodgement houses below Irish Battery – to see they were also ready for the seamen – and I didn't think I'd be able to see her in the evening, to help with Mister Tate. She was finding it hard to move him. To wash him. To change his nightshirt. To get him on and off the commode that now stood close to his bed and stank out the whole room. And it seemed natural, seemed right, that I should help him. And besides it wasn't the sort of thing a woman should be doing. It infringed on her dignity and stripped him of his.

I knocked on the door, and walked straight in as I always did. Elizabeth and Jenny were sitting together at the table. Elizabeth was reading a document, reading aloud, reading the details of the lease. She stopped, stood up and smiled.

Jenny frowned.

Charles came running towards me, with arms outstretched, yelling: 'Da-da! Da-da!'

I picked up Charles. He threw his arms around my neck and gave me a big hug. I smiled at him, but my heart was thumping, thumping like mad.

Charles twisted round – lined our heads up side by side – looked at Jenny and Elizabeth and waved.

The colour drained from Jenny's face. I knew she'd seen the likeness, seen we were father and son.

She stood up, snatched the lease out of Elizabeth's hand, and rushed towards me.

I let Charles slide out of my arms.

'I trusted you. I gave you everything. I didn't hold back. I didn't ask you to wait. You had what you wanted. And this' – she waved towards Charles, and James sleeping in his crib – 'this is how you repay me.'

Her eyes filled with tears. She bit at her lips. Then she swung her arm and slapped my face.

I reeled backwards. She came after me slapped my face again. Then she pushed me hard against the wall. 'Bastard!' she screamed. 'Bastard!'

Then she spun round and yelled at Elizabeth: 'Did you know about this?'

'She didn't know,' I said.

She glared at Elizabeth. 'I shan't be back. I don't want any more of your help. Thank you very much.'

Then she screamed: 'Ahhhhh!' Spun round, slapped my face again, banged the door open and tore out of the room.

I wiped my lips with the back of my hand, wiped away the blood.

I walked over to the table, slumped in the chair and looked at Elizabeth. She didn't say anything. Not a single word. She just waited. When the heat drained out of my face, when my heart stopped thumping, I whispered: 'She thinks we are to be married. It is understood. Like a secret betrothal. But I do not want her. I want you. And Charles. And James.' I closed my eyes and I felt sick, felt as though I was about to lose everything I wanted, needed – loved.

'Have you been sleeping in her bed?'

'Yes.'

'Since James was born?'

'Yes.'

'And before he was born?'

I nodded. 'It began soon after Ensign Wyndham was killed. Soon after I tried to kill myself.'

'What do you mean – tried to kill yourself?'

'That's what I tried to do. After – after I forced myself upon you. And they thought I was a hero and they gave me this.' I touched my gorget, felt the cold chill of the silver. I'm sorry. Maybe I should go . . .'

'Yes,' she whispered. 'Maybe you should.'

The following afternoon as the seamen came ashore and began to mount guard on Parson's Green, I walked down to the Little Parade. Jenny was in the shop, working at the counter. I tried to go in but the door was locked. I knocked on the door. She came to the window, saw me and yelled: 'Go away!'

I tapped on the glass. 'I'm not going till you talk to me.' And I tapped on the window again.

For a few minutes she ignored me, then my tapping grated her patience, and she flung open the door. 'Go away!'

'I only want to talk to you.'

'Well I don't want to talk to you. There's nothing to talk about. And do you know what hurts? What hurts the most?'

I shook my head.

'She's old Martyn. Old. And you know what else hurts?'

I shook my head again.

'You gave her a baby. Two babies. And you couldn't give me one. Not one.' She burst into tears.

I walked up the steps – intending to comfort her – but she pushed me away.

'I've told my father. Told him you're not coming back. Told him there will be no wedding. And you know what he said?'

I waited.

'He said, he was right not to trust you with the lease. That's all he said.' She took my blue butterfly out of her pocket and held it out to me. 'Remember this?'

I nodded.

She dropped it on the stone step, raised her foot and stamped on it. Then she walked into the shop, closed the front door, walked through to the room at the back, and closed the door.

I picked up the butterfly. Its wings were broken, were shedding tiny splinters of blue enamel. And like my dreams for her, for us, my dreams of so long ago, they would fly no more.

Next morning as the last of the seamen came ashore and changed into their red coats, the Militia replaced the guard on the walls from Peterborough Tower to Irish Battery. One battalion of the Trelawnys, carrying eight of their company colours – a red cross with gold rays laid on a field of red – mustered in front of the walls overlooking Parson's Green, Cambridge Fort and the beach where the meeting was to take place. The gunners loaded the great cannons in Irish Battery, hauled an extra battery of seven small cannons into place, and trained them on the sandhills where the Moors lay in strength. And then, assured that the cannons and the reserve force were ready to come to our aid if the Moors betrayed their word and launched a surprise attack, we marched out of Catherine Gate.

The King's Battalion led the column. They stopped by the stream close to Fountain Fort, made a right turn and faced the Moors in the sandhills. We halted and turned, and so did the the Dunbartons behind us, and we formed a long line back towards Catherine Gate. More soldiers-of-foot marched up the old lanes towards Pole Fort, halted and turned to the left. Between us we contained the Moors – in a large zig-zag formation – and protected our line of retreat, our port of safety: Catherine Gate.

The seamen marched onto the beach. The battalion of men in blue and white formed ranks in the deep shade below the cliffs of Parson's Green. The three battalions in red coats made a line at the water's edge and guarded the long sweep of beach. Behind them, the Governor's Galley and thirty-seven longboats filled with men 'armed with blunderbusses and hand granadoes' drifted with the tide. And behind them, eight ships clawed their way deep into the Bay, dropped anchor, and trained their cannons on the sandhills.

The combined battalion of Miners and Grenadiers carrying lighted matches, marched onto the hard sand and dressed ranks just in front of Fountain Fort. Then an officer, a Cornet-of-horse bearing a red pennant with a gold crown, led two troops-of-horse past our lines and onto the beach. One troop stopped by the sandhills, close to the Grenadiers and the other stopped right opposite – in front of the last battalion of red-coated seamen. Between them the troops-of-horse could close off the beach and protect the seamen and the Grenadiers if the need arose. Beyond them lay a stretch of empty sand: the formal place of meeting.

A line of Moors on horseback guarded the far end of the beach. Behind them came three lines of Moors on foot. The lines followed the contours of the sandhills and they streamed to the water's edge. At first glance they looked impressive, but the men were few and the distance between each line varied – in some places it was pinched and in others it ballooned – and I realised the Moors were doing what we were doing: spreading their men, trying to make them look more impressive, look stronger than they really were.

We shuffled our feet on the sloping ground under Irish Battery, and waited for an hour or more. The sun was beginning to lose the burning heat of high-summer but the wind was gusting, was flapping the ensign in my face. In each battalion-of-foot the ensigns were grouped in the middle of the front line. Behind us came the pikes, making thickets, spiking the air and casting shadows on the ground. The musketeers formed the ranks on both sides of the pikes, and in front of them came the drummers, standing in pairs.

As His Worship the Mayor, Alderman Smith, and all the members of the Corporation – wearing their robes-of-state to enhance the dignity of the occasion – walked towards us, we came to attention. They raised their hats, saluted the colours, and behind them, clustering close like an honour guard, came the burghers. Most were merchants, traders, made wealthy by selling goods imported from Spain, Italy, and France, and all of them, if the mutterings of the men in the ranks behind me were right: were too old, too fat, too greedy, too lazy, to serve in the Militia. In truth I think most of them coveted a seat on the Corporation, saw themselves as aldermen-in-waiting, and knew there was more to be gained by attending the Mayor and witnessing the meeting between His Excellency and the Alcaide Ali Benabdala, than there was from mounting guard on the walls.

The waiting closed my eyes and made me yawn. I blinked hard, took a deep breath and wriggled my toes. Then I remembered somebody saying: 'Count to ten. Count backwards. That's the best way to stay awake.' I counted backwards but it didn't make much difference, then I looked round, blinked again and started to count all the men in our ranks. I didn't have a clear view of everybody. The need to keep all the seamen together, to keep them close to their reserves in the longboats so they could fight as one force if they had to fight, had guaranteed us a poor place, a poor view. I made some quick counts, some estimates, added in a figure for the Trelawnys on Parson's Green – my back was to them and the figure was a guess, was a dredging of memory – and after a couple minutes I arrived at a rough total: four thousand. It was more than double the number we needed to end the great siege.

The Moors were much easier to count, and by twisting to the left I could see most of them. They appeared to number about two and a half thousand. But then of course there was the element of surprise, of trickery. How many men had the Moors hidden? In the valleys below the ruins of Charles Fort they could conceal a thousand men and we'd never see them, not even from the top of Peterborough Tower.

But once again the balance of power did not lie in the numbers of men on foot, it lay in the horses; and putting aside the Moors we could not see – the Moors of our imagination – they still had more horses than we did: hundreds more. If the war was renewed, we would be forced to look to Spain again.

I remembered the Spanish troopers coming out of the cathedral, making the sign of the cross with holy water – in the days when I heaped scorn upon such practices – and I remembered the peace they won, the peace that was worth a thousand blessings: self-blessings. And I remembered Colonel Kirke's peace: the four years the Emperor promised. That peace still had over a year to run, but now it was like a desert flower that had wilted and died in the sun: nothing would revive it. We needed a new bloom, a new flowering of peace.

At eleven o'clock, about an hour before the sun would stand straight overhead and shorten the shadows – wilt the flowers of the desert – ten mounted trumpeters and two mounted kettle-drummers played a fanfare, and Lord Dartmouth and the officers of his staff, Colonel Kirke, Mister Pepys, and an escort of gentlemen volunteers rode out to meet the Alcaide.

The Dunbartons saluted them with a roll of drums and they lowered their colours: the blue and white-crossed colours of Scotland. As they came close to us, our drummers repeated the roll, and I lowered the colour – in time with the other three ensigns – and held the end about four inches above the ground. The fabric was thin but the paint hadn't faded, and as it flapped and rippled in the wind the sun filled and emptied the ripples, made them darker, then lighter, like sea-green waves swallowed by a falling tide. Fragments of the red cross curled and surfed the waves, and every so often one of the golden rays appeared to rise, to skim the waves like a golden flying fish.

Lord Dartmouth and his entourage acknowledged our salute and rode on. We raised the colours, stood at ease and waited. About ten minutes later they stopped at the far right-hand corner of the beach. A group of Moors bearing one red flag embroidered with a golden crescent, rode down from the sandhills and for twenty minutes the two groups mingled, became a jostling of colour. Then the groups drew apart and we had no idea if we were looking at success or failure: peace or war.

Then the seamen on the beach fired three volleys, and the men leaning over the battlements in Fountain Fort began to cheer. The men at the top of Cambridge Fort, and the Trelawnys on Parson's Green joined in the cheering. One by one each battalion from Fountain to Catherine Gate, and from Pole to Catherine Gate came to attention and our musketeers fired three volleys high in the air.

The Moors responded by firing into the air, by racing the length of the meeting place and firing out to sea. It was wild, undisciplined, like the crackling that led to the fall of Charles and Henrietta.

As Lord Dartmouth raised his hat to the Alcaide, made his final farewells, the cannons in Irish Battery, and the battery on Parson's Green fired a salute. A second or two later the ships in the Bay and the fort at the end of the Mole repeated the salute, and clouds of smoke began to roll across the water. Then the great cannons on the bastion below Peterborough Tower thundered the salute over the remains of Charles, Henrietta and Devil's Drop. And high above us Pole Fort saluted the Moors; and if the soldiers up there in that eminence of blood, were like me, the salutes also mourned the chain of forts, the men who were no more.

A few seconds later Colonel Boynton ordered both battalions of our Regiment to make a right turn, and we double-marched towards the spur of land below Peterborough Tower – the spur that cost Sir Palmes his life. We spread ourselves along the foot of the walls, just in front of the great ditch. High above us, from a mast at the top of the tower, the union flag – the flag of Scotland overlaid by the red cross, the cross of Saint George, of England – flapped defiance.

On the beach, in the meeting place, the Moors were displaying their horsemanship: charging, wheeling, drilling with lances.

Then the Alcaide rode into the sandhills – we followed his banner, followed the other banners that were now riding in his train – and we knew if he looked back, looked across to the town, to the citadel that would never be his, he'd have seen it girded with men, with red coats who were prepared to give their lives, their blood, to hold him at bay.

Half an hour later we marched past the Master of Ordance. He was demonstrating a new contraption, a mechanical instrument of war. In the evening I would learn to call it a cup-discharger, but at that moment I'd never seen one before and had no idea what to call it. Both Colonel Kirke and Mister Pepys had dismounted to take a closer look. It was tossing flaming granadoes high in the air, then they were falling to the ground three hundred yards away and exploding. If I'd been told about it I would never have believed it. I would have argued the distance was too great, or the speed would extinguish the flame, or the granado would explode too early. But here it was in front of my eyes, and I looked at Lockhart in amazement. 'Imagine,' he said, 'if we had three of them on top of Sandhill Fort. And one was set at three hundred yards, one at two hundred and one at one hundred. We would have killed the bastards in their hundreds. And the fort would still be ours.'

It was three years too late. Hundreds of deaths too late. And in peace there would be no place, no need, for the instruments of war.

We marched back to the Market Place. Colonel Boynton stood us at ease and said: 'I have spoken with Colonel Kirke, and he confirms what most of you suspected from the moment the seamen fired the first salute. The Alcaide has agreed to a new peace treaty. The details will be settled over the next few days. What you won't know is that the Alcaide and Colonel Kirke have shaken hands, publicly, and that means the Alcaide is committed to peace. He cannot withdraw his agreement.'

Lockhart looked at me and whispered: 'A few granadoes up the Alcaide's arse – at a distance of three hundred yards – would be a better guarantee of peace. A handshake doesn't mean a thing. Not a thing. And if Lord Dartmouth thinks he's got peace, real peace, he's a bloody fool.'

115

Four days later, in the cool of the evening, I wandered into the clerk's office. O'Sullivan was sitting at his desk writing. He said the others were still down at the Town House and Mister Pepys was complaining about the leases: the titles were full of 'imperfections and would not be worth sixpence in Westminster Hall'; and he was despairing of having everything finished by the 4th, by Thursday – the day after tomorrow.

For me the 4th was looming fast and every so often my belly rumbled and I felt queasy, felt as though I was walking on quicksand, was about to be sucked into a morass, a bog of superstition. O'Sullivan smiled as I told him about these fears, and he said: 'In a few months you'll wonder why on earth you were afraid, wonder why it took you so long to see the truth.'

His words were like a crutch, they supported my faltering spirit, my hesitant steps. But then I remembered Trigg, remembered he had converted, had recognised his error, his 'act of gross stupidity' and returned to the Church of England, penitent and contrite. It soured his spirit, made him bitter, twisted; and in all the time I knew him, he could never compare the two faiths in an objective, dispassionate manner. In a subtle way he was always preaching, expounding the truth – as he saw it – and decrying Rome.

We talked about Trigg. O'Sullivan called him an apostate and said: 'He was given the gift of faith. The most precious thing a man can be given and he threw it away. He thought his intellect, his reasoning was superior to the gift of God. It was pride. Arrogance.' He shook his head. 'A man must approach God with humility. He must seek the truth. Sometimes the truth hurts. And sometimes it surprises. But at all times it is the truth. It is the embodiment of God.' He picked up his scissors, trimmed the wick on his candle – it was too long, it had curled and was making wisps of black smoke – and he said, in a much quieter voice: 'I shall be thinking of you, praying for you on Thursday night. I shall ask God to bless you. To give you courage. Strength. For when this becomes public knowledge, I'm afraid you're going to need it.'

For a minute or so we sat in silence, then he said: 'Those rumours were right.' I looked at him. I didn't know what he was talking about. 'The ones about surveying the walls and the Mole.' I nodded. 'Lord Dartmouth signed the orders today, so now it's official. But they've already made a start, and this morning I copied some of their findings.' He paused. 'There's something strange about them. Something I don't understand.'

'What do you mean strange?'

'I'll give you a couple of examples. They're talking about building a new fort at the end of the Strand, just below Peterborough Tower, and running a new wall up to the great bastion. And there are plans to widen some of the existing walls, to repair others, and strengthen the Forage Gate. They're estimating the cost for every single thing. I added some of them up in my head and they came to over two hundred thousand pounds. And I doubt if that's a tenth of what they're talking about.'

'It has to be done. Everybody knows that.'

'Hmm. But it doesn't seem real. Everyone knows the King doesn't have any money. Not getting paid is proof of that. And Parliament still hasn't been recalled, so they won't be giving him any money. So why are they wasting their time doing a survey, writing a report, when everyone knows the things will never be done?'

'Maybe the King is going to give it back to the Portuguese. Or sell it to the French. And they want to know what has to be done.'

'I hadn't thought of that.' He sucked at his lips. 'If that's true then tell me how you explain this. The survey of the Mole isn't a survey in the traditional sense of measuring the length and width, and calculating the volume of stone that's still needed to complete the arm. It is a survey of opinion. They're asking the ship's captains what they think about the Mole, the anchorage, and the Bay silting up. I get the impression they want the captains to say it's no good. To say the Straits are some of the wildest waters in the whole world and nothing we ever do will make them into a safe anchorage.'

'But why would they want to say that, when ships have anchored here for a long long time?'

He shrugged. 'I don't know. And when I said some of the opinions were very bad – almost lies – I was told to shut my mouth. To remember my oath of secrecy and get on with my work.'

I told him I thought they were both right and wrong. For most of the year it was a good anchorage, but there were times when the ships had to up anchor, to put to sea to ride out a storm. And if we wanted to keep the fleet here: to provision it, to keep the Barbary pirates locked in the Mediterranean, to stop them raiding the Kent coast and make the seas safe for trade, English trade, we needed a port controlled by England. A port we could rely on in a time of war. We also needed a port for ships that came down to this latitude to catch the trade-winds to and from the Americas. In short: we needed Tangiers.

Lord Dartmouth's representatives had met the Moors, were now meeting them every day, and the peace would soon be confirmed in writing. Then the future of Tangiers, our future, would be assured. In peace we didn't need new walls, new forts, new lines of defence. We needed money in our pockets, beer in our bellies, meat on our plates, and women in our beds: obliging women. That's what we needed.

Then Elizabeth came into my mind. I knew I had to tell her, had to be frank, had to be honest. She had a right to know before I knelt in the cathedral and made my profession of faith.

A few minutes later I knocked on her door and waited. Mistress Westcombe opened the door. Her face was flushed and her brow was damp with sweat. 'Thank God you've come. We can't control him.' She grabbed my arm. Pulled me into the room.

Mister Tate was lying on the bed, flat on his back, thrashing the air with his arms and legs, and yelping like a dog. Elizabeth was standing with her back to the open wall, her hands to her face.

I put my arms around her and she burst into tears. 'Go upstairs,' I whispered in her ear. 'I'll look after him for you. I can stay the night. I don't have to go back till half an hour before the parade tomorrow morning.'

She smiled like a wet-eyed child, bit at her lips and rushed upstairs.

I picked up his prayer book, and began to read to him, to read the words of my childhood, the words that readied us for Evening Prayer: 'When the wicked man turneth away from his wickedness that he hath committed, and doeth that which is lawful and right, he shall save his soul alive.'

Then I read the confession, the Lord's Prayer and the Magnificat: 'My soul doth magnify the Lord: and my spirit hath rejoiced in God my Saviour . . .'

The words calmed his soul, stilled his arms and legs, soothed the twitchings in his fingers and toes. His eyes closed and after a while I thought he was asleep. I closed the prayer book but he reached out and touched my arm. I opened the book again and read the rest of the service. Then he opened his eyes and smiled.

I washed him, combed his hair, and fed him a thick soup with bread dipped in brandy.

When he lay quiet I tiptoed upstairs.

His crying, his whimpering, cut the night into slices of darkness, and I left her bed four, five times. In the dawn, in the ebbing of darkness I told her I was committed to the fullness of the faith, to the richness that had been denied to us by the reformers. She wanted to know how I came to believe, to accept the things she found most abhorrent. I told her I thought it was through the ritual, the re-enactment of the life of Christ in the liturgy: the progression of his miracles; his preaching; the making real of his birth, life, death and resurrection. She said: 'I'm sorry. I don't understand. I can't understand. In some ways this is worse than the illness, the madness, the dying of memory that is affecting Mister Tate.' She sat up. Pulled her knees close to her breasts – bound firm to support the weight of her morning milk – and rested her chin on her knees. 'I know I need you. I know Mister Tate needs you. But I do not want a papist in this house. And I know Mister Tate would not want a papist looking after him.' She sighed to herself. 'I'm sorry, but from Friday morning you are not welcome in this house, this bed.' She burst into tears, and she would not let me touch her.

Two, maybe three hours later, as we were marching off the Old Parade after an hour of drill and five minutes of formal prayers – prayers that were drained of life, drained of meaning – the Town Crier came towards us ringing his bell and crying: 'Hear ye! Hear ye! A public meeting is proclaimed. In the Town House tomorrow afternoon for all burghers. For all who wish to know the findings of the Commission. Hear ye! Hear ye! The meeting will be addressed by His Excellency Lord Dartmouth.'

Lockhart looked at me and whispered: 'What the bloody hell is that all about?'

I shrugged. 'New taxes on property. Repaying the King for the repairs done in his name. Who knows? It won't concern us.'

But in the afternoon the mystery deepened: all officers were summonsed to hear an address by Lord Dartmouth – tomorrow evening, after the public meeting finished.

I couldn't think what it would be about. In truth I didn't think much about it at all. I returned to Elizabeth's house, helped with Mister Tate, tried to encourage her to attend tomorrow's meeting – and failed – and cuddled into her, held her tight, held her for the last time. I felt the warmth of her body, her secret places, and in my mind I said goodbye. But in my heart I wanted her. I wanted her with every sinew, every fibre, every ounce of my being.

The 4th dawned clear and cold. We said goodbye with a silent embrace, with a wrenching of body and soul, for we belonged together, fitted together like one person, one body, one entity. I wanted her as much as she wanted me.

But it could not be. She was an 'occasion of sin' – according to Father Francifo. To me she was no such thing. She was tenderness and compassion. A madonna with child, my child, and I did not want to give her up.

In the chill of the day I was tempted. My resolve weakened. My desire for her grew. My need for Charles and James haunted my mind, like their crying in the night. I needed to talk, to be reassured – to waylay the forces of doubt – and in the afternoon I wandered up to the clerk's office, intending to sit, to talk with O'Sullivan. But he was busy. And so was Crabtree. And so was Brandon. They didn't want to talk and they resented my presence. I could feel it. For a while I stared out the window then I sat down at my desk and started to copy one of the letters from O'Sullivan's pile. The act of writing, the flow of words, the curling loops and the flowing tails emptied my mind, filled it with faith. In the peace and the quiet of the work I knew so well, a hour or two drifted away.

Then the door slammed open, Ives rushed in and screamed: 'We're going home! We're going home!'

We stared at him in shocked silence. In my soul I felt the chill of winter, the icy blast that can freeze a man to death, if he's made a mistake, if he's dressed his soul for the warmth of Romanism, the warmth of Barbary, and must now face England – face the cold bleak winter that is the faith of the protesters, the faith of his father.

Ives grabbed me. Shook me. 'Didn't you hear? I said we're going home! Going back to England. All of us.' He pulled me out of my seat and danced me around the room.

116

Ives spun me to a halt, roared with laughter and yelled: 'Isn't it fucking marvellous!'

O'Sullivan shook his head. 'Who told you we're going back to England? I haven't read anything about it. Not a word. And I haven't seen the slightest hint in anything I've copied.'

'Lord Dartmouth told the meeting. In the Town House. All the burghers can choose where they want to go: England, Ireland, Portugal, Spain, France, Italy. They can even go to the Plantations, to Virginia if they want to. And it's not going to cost them a thing. They have to go in the next two or three weeks and then we're going to pull down all the houses, blow up the walls, and destroy the Mole. And after that we're going back to England. Christ! I can't wait.'

Brandon looked up from his desk. 'I don't want to go home. This is my home. Why would I want to go back to England? I don't have any friends left in England and my uncle was a daft old fool and his wife was no better. And as for their two children, my cousins, I don't care if I never see them again.'

'I suppose they'll tell me I'm too old,' O'Sullivan said. 'And they won't want me any more. And they'll ship me back to Ireland, and all that bloody rain.'

'And what about me?' Crabtree said. 'They won't want a man with one leg. There are hundreds of clerks in England. And they've all got two legs.'

The grin slipped off Ives's face. He looked from O'Sullivan to Crabtree to Brandon. 'What a heap of misery you three are.' He turned to me. 'I suppose you want to stay too?'

I wanted the cathedral. The bastion of faith. I wanted it to be in England. But Catholic cathedrals, churches, chapels are banned, with one exception: Queen Catherine's private chapel in Saint James's Palace. And I wouldn't be going there. I wouldn't be able to sit in the quiet of the night and feel His Presence, the Real Presence of Him who made us, who will come again, will judge us for what we are, what we were. I looked into Ives's expectant face and said: 'No, I don't think I do.'

He shook his head, picked up the pot of ink from my desk, tossed it in the air, caught it without spilling a drop, and hurled it at the wall. It smashed.

Black ink splattered the wall. 'Well I'm bloody delighted. And I'm not going to let you bastards spoil it.' He rushed out of the room, thumped the door shut, and thundered down the wooden steps.

We looked at each other in soulful silence. Brandon picked up his quill and began to write. Crabtree stood up and looked out the window. O'Sullivan closed his eyes, sat rigid, white-faced, like a corpse with rigor mortis. I crept out of the room, paced the walls by Stayner's Battery, and looked at the town, allowed my eyes to wander along the streets I knew so well, and it didn't seem real, seem possible, that it was about to die, to be destroyed, to be no more.

In the evening I stood beside de Colville in the great hall, and as we waited for Lord Dartmouth I caught snatches of conversation: 'we could never make the town secure' . . . 'overlooked by too many hills' . . . 'trade hasn't flourished' . . . 'the harbour isn't commodious' . . . 'the Moors will always be hostile' . . . 'the walls are in a ruinous state' . . . 'it's cost too many lives' . . . 'would cost more lives' . . . 'would have cost a fortune' . . . 'the King doesn't have the money'.

I turned to de Colville. 'If Lord Dartmouth knew we were going, from the day he arrived, from before he arrived if the truth is known, why did he arrange a survey of the walls and the Mole?'

He shrugged. 'Maybe it was a ruse. Or maybe he was told to confirm what they suspected in England before he made – or announced – the decision.'

'Hmm. And the parade? The meeting with the Moors? And this peace that is supposed to last for two or three years? Why did he go to all that trouble when it won't matter in a couple of months?'

'There's been a lot of talk about that in the last hour or so. Most officers are convinced it will be easier to withdraw if we don't have to fight the Moors at the same time. And on the last day when the walls come down, we'll be able to destroy both the castles, and we won't have to fight our way down to the Mole and clamber into the boats under fire. And that will save lives.'

After a while our talk drifted to Mister Pepys and the Commission. Now we knew it was a ruse, an excuse to determine the true value of all the leases and all the titles. And if what we'd heard so far was true, almost everyone was going to be compensated. Freeholders were to receive the equivalent of four years' rent. Leaseholders with ten or more years still to run on their leases, were to receive three years' rent. The remaining leases were to be divided into four groups and compensated on a declining scale: the last group was for leases with two to four years still to run, and for these the leaseholders were to receive one year's rental. The figures for compensation would therefore vary from property to property but all had one thing in common: any repairs that were done at the King's expense, or any materials that were provided at the King's expense, were to be deducted from the compensation. And any property that had encroached upon the King's land – in the way of buildings, gardens, orchards or walls – was to have the value of the encroachments deducted from the compensation. These deductions were to be called defalcations, and as we waited this word seemed to float above the noise of all the other words – it sounded as if it was being stressed, being given a heavy slant, an italic of bitterness.

In my head I worked out Elizabeth's compensation. Both her leases came in the second to lowest group, so both were to receive one and a half years' compensation:

$$1^1/_2 \times £15 = £22–10–0$$
$$1^1/_2 \times £5 = £7–10–0$$

The figures added up to £30 and there were no defalcations: thanks to Mister Pepys and my poor memory.

For a moment or two I wallowed in the thought of being given £30. It was an enormous sum of money. More money than I'd ever seen in my whole life. And I was thinking it was enough to start a marriage, for Elizabeth and I to become man and wife in England – a year or so after Mister Tate was laid in the ground – when de Colville said: 'Did you see the latest journals from London?'

I shook my head.

'There's more about the Rye House Plot, the plot to kill the King and the Duke of York. Lord Russell's been executed. The Earl of Essex has killed himself in the Tower – some are saying it wasn't suicide, it was murder. And Algernon Sidney, the son of the Earl of Leciester is to be tried in November. They're all Protestants. Whigs. Dissenters. Not a papist among them. So why do they continue to persecute . . .'

A hush came over the great hall and we turned towards the door. Lord Dartmouth strode into the room, walked up the steps, laid a sheet of paper on a wooden lectern – it looked like the one from the garrison church and might have been borrowed for the occasion – and began to read:

'I need not repeat to you the reasons that necessitated His Majesty's resolution to part with this Garrison – having given them already to the Corporation and the inhabitants – nor need there be any excitement about your obedience to his commands, for I am confident you are as ready by inclination as duty to obey. But you have a more peculiar happiness than the rest of this place, that after all the devilish designs, the implacable malice, and the strange restlessness of the late associations for the assassination of His Majesty's Royal Person, and his Royal Brother, and the universal destruction of all his faithful subjects; you are remanded from this place, where you can no longer be capable of doing His Majesty further service here abroad, and chosen to be instrumental in the safeguarding of himself and his Kingdoms at home.

I have only therefore, to remind every one of you, in your proper stations, to perform your duty diligently, and to act vigorously, that this service may be so well and so speedily performed that you may return for the safety, and to the favour, protection, and maintenance of the King our Master, whom God preserve; and then you will be able to assist him against all the damnable designs of his enemies.'

Twenty minutes later de Colville and I slipped away, We walked down Castle Hill and through the narrow streets made light by open doors and windows, and made noisy by people bustling from house to house, chattering, laughing, singing at the top of their voices. In the Market Place men and women were milling about, children were running in and out of the houses. Drunks were leaning out the tavern windows, whistling, waving, yelling at the young girls. It was like a carnival. In some places it reminded me of New Year's Day – of the drunken happiness it brings. In other places it was like May Day – full of dancing and quiet lechery. And in others it was like the Autumn Festival that follows a good harvest – full of thankfulness.

The cathedral was a solemn contrast: dark, empty, silent. It awakened my old doubts, and it made me remember the words that netted me to the faith. They were qualified by words of slippage, words that presumed I'd be staying in Tangiers till the day I died. But now the staying was not to be. We were going back to England, protestant England. I began to think this could not be, this conversion of mine. But somewhere in my mind, in my heart, in the blending of mind and heart – the blending that makes me what I am – I still wanted the truth and the truth lay here, lay in this darkness. And despite my words of slippage, words of escape, I still wanted to have the faith in England. I wanted what I could have here. But at the same time I feared I was being foolish and should not have what I wanted to have, for I knew England, and England did not want to know popery.

In this confusion of mind, spirit, body, in this faltering of resolution, de Colville and I sat down in the pew in front of Our Lady's altar. The flame was flickering behind the blue glass, would flicker for two maybe three weeks more, and then it would go out. Go out for ever.

Father Francifo was late.

I heard a door open and shut. We both stood up, but it was not him, it was Father Pio, the Father Confessor.

'I'm sorry,' he whispered – like a child trying to keep a secret from God. 'But Father Francifo has been unwell all day, and he'll be here in a few minutes.'

He knelt beside us, back straight, head bowed, for about ten minutes. Then he eased himself onto the seat. De Colville said: 'We were surprised to hear we're going home, going back to England. We had no idea. We thought the rumours were just rumours – vain hopes, imaginings.'

He nodded. 'It's been a secret for several months. We didn't believe it. Not at first.'

For a moment I couldn't make sense of what he was saying. Then I said: 'Did you know?'

He nodded. 'I don't suppose it matters now. But yes, we did know.'

I remembered talking to Father Francifo, remembered the words of slippage, words that were a measure of my faith, words that presupposed Tangiers would be my home, my place of faith, place of worship, place of burial.

De Colville turned to him. 'How did you know?'

Father Pio smiled. 'Queen Catherine told her chaplain and he wrote to Father Prior. And he told his counsellors, his most trusted advisers.'

'And Father Francifo – he knew?'

He nodded.

'But when I told him I couldn't convert if I ever thought I was going back to England, he didn't say anything.'

'He couldn't tell you. He was sworn to secrecy.'

'But he knew. Knew the premise on which I was basing my faith, my acceptance, was a lie.'

'Not a lie in the sense of telling an untruth.'

'It was a lie. He knew it was a lie.'

'The best you can say – the worst you can say – is that it was a lie of omission. He was sworn to secrecy. He couldn't tell you the truth.'

A lie of omission. I savoured the word, the idea, the subtlety of truth and untruth, the blurring of subterfuge. But to me a lie was a lie. And my conversion, my acceptance of the faith, his faith, was based on a lie. And if he'd lied to me about this, what else had he lied about? Had forgotten, had declined to tell me?

I felt cold, felt alone. And I knew I had to be ruled by mind and not by heart. A lie was a lie. Omission was like trying to cross a chasm with no bridge, no walkway, no struts of faith.

I looked at Father Pio, at the innocence, the naïvety, that kept his face young, unlined – like an omission of life, a life unlived.

I stood up and said: 'Would you please tell Father Francifo, I'm sorry. I'm not ready. And I fear I'll never be ready.'

I walked into the night, walked the streets, walked the walls: alone. And my faith that had been like an hour glass, had been running smooth, running strong, cracked and broke; and one by one the grains of dogma, the sands of belief, of faith, ran away, ran free – rejoined the mica of discontent, disbelief.

Towards morning, long before the dawning of the new day, I walked back to the cathedral, sat in the arches of darkness, heard the words of the mass, the words that changed nothing, nothing of substance, and I knew my faith was dead.

117

An hour later I took Elizabeth into my arms and said: 'I couldn't do it. I wanted you and Charles and James too much.' I shivered and my eyes filled with tears and I cried for her, for the friend I almost lost. And I cried for the friend whose presence in the cathedral had once been real, the friend who was now dead and gone, who would walk no more in the cloisters of my soul.

Towards the end of the morning Colonel Kirke invited us to witness the senior officers signing an address, a Petition of Gratitude. It repeated the arguments for abandoning and destroying Tangiers and it concluded with the words 'We shall never use unworthily those swords which your Majesty has been pleased to put into our hands, but employ them for the preservation and honour of Your Majesty's Sacred Person and your Royal Service to the last drop of our blood.'

They were fine sentiments and I would have signed if I'd been invited to sign, but I have to confess that like most of the men in our company I was more interested in signing for my pay. Lord Dartmouth had brought it with him, and once every two weeks his paymasters were handing out our arrears in small amounts. I'd told the men in our company it was to make their money last, but they were suspicious: they kept thinking they wouldn't be getting any more, kept thinking they were going to be cheated out of their money. The truth was much simpler as they were well aware: having a pocket full of money meant getting drunk for a week. And if the nights were hot and sticky, quarrels would grow into fights and fights would become riots, become orgies of bloody madness. On the other hand cold wet nights – like the ones that lay ahead – would keep the drunks inside, keep them in small groups, and the fights would not spread down the streets, engulf one tavern after the other and grow into a riot. It was a way of buying peace. It was also a way of buying their cooperation, their hard labour, for now the talk was about destruction, about how long it would take to wreck this bloody place, and how soon we'd be going home.

The prospect of leaving, of going home, filled Elizabeth with terror. She kept saying James was too young and if she couldn't buy fresh milk, couldn't drink fresh milk to make her own milk, how was she going to feed him? And who would stop Charles running around the deck and falling over the side? And what about Mister Tate? He was losing weight. His muscles were wasting, and his skin – mottled with pinks and purples and tinged with green – was hanging in great folds from his legs and arms. His eyes were losing their wet sheen and his lips were beginning to crack. I held his hand and read Morning Prayer to him, but he made no response. I washed him, removed the towel Mistress Westcombe had tied between his legs. It was stained bright orange and filled with black pellets that looked like sheep shit. I wrapped another towel between his legs, brushed his hair, soften some bread in a gruel of chicken and tried to spoon it into his mouth. But he wouldn't open his mouth. I prised his teeth apart, pushed in the spoon and dribbled the bread and gruel down his throat. I repeated it again and again, and I thought he was doing well, thought I was doing well, till the mush began to fill up his throat and wash around his mouth. Then Mistress Westcombe arrived and she said: 'He's forgotten how to swallow. You have to sit him up and rub his throat. Coax him to swallow.' She smiled, took the spoon from me and squeezed the muscles around his Adam's apple.

Two days later, in the early afternoon, we heard a knock on Elizabeth's front door. I went to answer but she shook her head and gestured for me to stand in the corner by the front window where I would be hidden by the door when it opened. A man's voice said: 'Good afternoon. I was wanting to speak with Mister Tate.' Elizabeth said something but her words were too soft for me to catch. Then the man's voice said: 'Would you tell him the Mayor, Mister Smith, has prepared a loyal address, and tomorrow he intends to ask His Excellency to present it to His Majesty on behalf of all the citizens of Tangiers. It thanks His Majesty for his wisdom, his kindness, his thoughtfulness in delivering us from the Moors. There are as you know about five hundred families here in Tangiers, and Mister Smith thought if forty or maybe fifty of our leading citizens, our most influential family-heads, also signed the address it would convey to His Majesty the gratitude of all our families.'

Elizabeth said something, but once again her words were too soft for me. Then she closed the door. 'The children are the ones who'll be most grateful in the years to come. They say there are four hundred of them. Did you know that?' I shook my head. 'And they say we're going to have to look after our own children on the boat. There should be one adult for every child, that's what Mistress Westcombe thinks. And how can I look after Charles and James if I also have to look after Mister Tate?'

She seemed to have forgotten that Doctor Lawrence had only given him two or three weeks to live. He was slipping towards death, slipping a little more each day, but it felt wrong to remind her, and I said: 'What about Mistress Westcombe? Can't she go with you?'

'I was told this morning we're to go on the *Saint David* with the Mayor and the Recorder and the other people of quality. It's because of Mister Tate. Because he's a clergyman. And Mistress Westcombe is to go on the *Swallow*.

Her husband was a blacksmith. She'll be going a week before me, and what am I going to do without her?'

I wrapped my arms around her. 'I'll be here.'

'But you can't be here all the time. And you won't be on the ship.'

'Why don't you go down to the Town House with Mistress Westcombe? Go now and I'll stay here. I'll look after Mister Tate. Tell them you want to be together. Tell them you have to be together.' I lowered my voice. 'Tell them you could soon be a widow and you cannot manage on your own. And if she could take Mister Tate's place on the *Saint David*, they won't have to allow for an extra person. If they won't listen, tell them you'll have to go on the *Swallow*. Tell them you'll have to lower your dignity, have to go with the smiths and the artisans. Tell them they won't leave you with any choice.'

She put Charles to bed, blew me a kiss, and left with James in her arms.

Three hours later she came with a long face. 'I had to wait in a queue. The whole place was heaving with people. And when it was my turn the clerk was so rude. He didn't have a seat for me to sit down on, and he pulled a face when James woke up and I had to feed him. And do you know what he said?'

I shook my head.

'He said people were trying to get onto the *Saint David*, not off it. And I wouldn't like it on the *Swallow*. It would be too cramped for a lady like me. And I should find out who else was going on the *Saint David* and ask if they could help me.'

'But what about Mister Tate?'

'He said Mister Tate was still alive and as long he was alive he had to retain his place on the *Saint David* and I was not entitled to change his allocation. A wife does not have that right. Only he could do that.'

'But Mister Tate can't even—'

'I know. But he wasn't interested in that.'

I kissed her on the forehead. 'We'll think of something.'

Next morning Colonel Boynton handed me a list with twelve names and said: 'Everyone on this list is a head-of-family. I want you to take two Sergeants and twenty men, and make sure every name is on board the *Unity* with all their dependants and all their possessions by the afternoon of the 15th.' He paused. 'Most of them will want to dither around till the last minute, saying goodbye to friends they may never see again, and that's understandable. So make sure all their heavy possessions – furniture, chests, boxes and so on – are loaded by the 13th. And when they go on board they should only be carrying the things they'll need on the voyage.'

I ran my eye down the list and my heart did a thump. The last name on the list read:

P.T. BARTHOLOMEW, APOTHECARY, The Little Parade

I dithered for an hour or more, decided I'd leave Jenny and her father till last, and that meant I wouldn't have to see her for another couple of days. But she kept coming into my mind and I could feel myself getting more and more nervous – I was making little farts and for me that's always been a bad sign – and I began to think it might be best if I called on every family on my list and told them what was going to happen.

In the late afternoon I knocked on her door, walked into the shop, and waited by the counter. Her father opened the back door, stared at me with white-blinded eyes, and said: 'Yes. What do you want?'

'I'm ordered by Colonel Boynton, sir, to help take your things onto the *Unity*.'

His mouth gaped. I knew he'd recognised my voice. He backed away from the counter, felt for the back door, pushed it open and yelled: 'Jenny! Jenny! It's that man!'

She rushed into the shop, saw me, and smiled. Her face was flushed and her bosoms had swollen and she'd put on a little weight around the middle, but she looked younger, looked more beautiful.

I wanted her. I wanted to lie in her bed. I wanted her for herself and I did not need, did not want my ladies of Mequinez. For several seconds we stared at each other without saying a word. Then she led her father into the back room, closed the door behind him and said: 'I thought you had a right to know that Mister Wyndham and I are going to have a baby – your baby. I've told my father and we've agreed not to tell anyone else, but I had to tell you. When we're back in England and settled in Bristol, we're going to tell everyone Mister Wyndham was killed by the Moors. Shot in the face, just a few days before Lord Dartmouth arrived to take us home.' She looked at the floorboards, looked like a young girl caught in a moment of mourning, a moment of loss. 'If it's a boy we're going to call him John, after his father. And if it's a girl we're going to call her Jane, after my mother.'

Then she reached under the counter, pulled open a drawer, and handed me a blue butterfly. The enamel was a little darker than our butterfly and it made this butterfly look older, look more mature, and maybe that was a reflection on both of us. 'It's for you,' she said with a soft smile. 'To help you remember me, help you remember us.' And she laid her hand on her belly.

For the next few days we worked in the houses, took down doors and shutters and made them into chests. When they were packed with goods, were nailed down tight, we carted them down to the Mole and loaded them onto the *Unity*. At the same time another company was loading two hundred tons of tarras – it had been intended for the Mole, now it was going to be used to rebuild the fort at Tilbury, close to the mouth of the Thames.

The *Unity* was a hospital ship. Her holds ran from side to side like great caverns and from the beams hung a hundred hammocks. In the gloom they looked like spiders' webs, and every time I came on board more of the webs were holding old soldiers. Some were lame, some were blind, some had lost an arm or a leg, and some had lost their minds – were shouting, were screaming profanities. Some were covered in sores, in ulcers that wept and bled, and most of them were waiting for Mister Bartholomew, waiting for his herbs, his lotions, his potions – for the soothing, the calming that lay in his tinctures.

There was much talk of a hospital that was being built on the banks of the Thames, two or three miles to the west of London at a place called Chelsea. It was to be for old soldiers, was to be a place where we could live out our last days, could sit in the sun and dream of other times, other places. And there was talk of a herbal garden, a Physic Garden, where men like Mister Bartholomew could gather plants from around the world, could grow them, could use them to ease the aches and the pains that will sear our declining years.

The nature of Mister Tate's illness was changing. He was racked with spasms and hot with fever. He couldn't bare anyone to touch him. It made him scream. It made him into an animal. He kept throwing off the bedclothes. It was as though they were too heavy for him, were weighing him down. But the relief – if it was relief – was short-lived for in a few minutes he would be shivering, would be covered in blue goose-bumps and when we tried to warm him, to cover him, he began to scream again, to throw off the bedclothes.

I slipped down to the infirmarium. It was dark and cold inside, almost deserted. I talked with Doctor Lawrence and he said: 'Mister Tate is too ill to go on board the *Saint David*. He'd only last a day. Two at the most. It would be cruel to put him through that. If he's still alive, when it comes time to sail, he should come here. We can look after him for a few days.'

I told him that would please Mistress Tate, would ease her mind, and then we talked about Mistress Westcombe and how she could help with the children. He liked the idea of her going in Mister Tate's place, and he said: 'We need to have her shifted from the *Swallow* to the' – he looked at a list – 'to the *Dartmouth*. She's due to sail about the 1st of November.' He found a sheet of paper, picked up a quill and wrote for a minute or so. 'Give that,' he said, 'to the Major at the Town House and he'll transfer Mistress Westcombe.' He smiled. 'Don't look so worried. They're used to my notes. And when it comes time for the *Saint David* to sail I'll give you another one to get her on board. We'll call her a nurse.' He smiled again. 'And now about the tincture of opium, I think it should be stronger than last time. And I suggest you build a frame over his bed. Something light. It could be made of canes. Cover that with blankets and it'll take the weight off his body, and it'll keep him warm.'

On the 16th, as the tide turned, the *Unity* dropped its sails, caught the wind and began to edge away. I watched for an hour or more, watched those wind-filled sails become smaller and smaller, and I knew they were taking my child away. A child I would never see, would never hold in my arms, and tears flooded my eyes, and I wanted him, wanted her. And I wanted Jenny. I wanted to float with the blue butterflies, to be lost in the blue, the endless blue that is the sky, but the sky was clouding, was wet with rain, wet with tears: my tears.

For the rest of the day I felt drained of life, and I plodded through my next list – of people sailing on the *Oxford* on the 23rd – with leaden feet, made heavy by a leaden heart. There was no one I could tell, no one who could help me close the door to this part of my life that was gone for ever, and would not, could not, come again. I mourned on my own, mourned in the silence of my soul.

Three days later, as the dawn was unwrapping rows of half-gutted houses, I walked to the cathedral with de Colville. In a moment of weakness, of fondness for what might have been, I agreed to attend the last mass. It was to be a sung mass, a requiem mass – a final farewell to the dead who could not come with us, who would lie in this earth, this foreign earth, and wait for the resurrection, for the gift of eternal life.

The cathedral was packed. All the side altars were stripped bare and all the statues were gone. It felt as if the Puritans had arrived and torn out all the symbols, the conduits of faith. On the high altar three candles burnt on either side of the great crucifix. The priests, vested in black, bowed low to the altar and the singing ebbed and flowed, like the sobbing of a lamentation. The bread and the chalice rose from the altar for the last time, and they were saluted by the ringing of bells, the bells of parting. In shuffling silence a dozen women and eighty, maybe ninety men approached the altar, knelt, and received the communion bread for the last time.

When the mass was finished, when there were no more prayers to be said, Father Francifo walked down to the altar rail and said: 'I know this is not the feast of Saint John the Baptist, but if you took communion today and you do not have an Agnus Dei, you are invited to come forward and accept one now.'

Two women, and twenty, maybe twenty-five men went forward and Father Francifo pressed the badge, the Lamb of God – the lamb who takes away the sins of the world – into their hands.

Then we stood and the priests left.

De Colville and I sat down, waited for the crowds to go. One of the priests returned and snuffed out the candles. Then my eyes were drawn to the tabernacle doors on the high altar. They were wide open. The repository was empty. The consecrated bread, the bread of the mass, the accidents that hid the Real Presence, the presence of God, were gone. In effect the heart of the cathedral had been torn out, and now the building was a shell, a dead place, a place waiting to be destroyed. And I began to understand that the Requiem had also been for the cathedral.

As we stood up, bowed to the cross, to the empty tomb, the tomb that would never again hold the body of Christ, Father Francifo came into the cathedral touched me on the shoulder and said: 'I was hoping you'd still be here.' He pressed an Agnus Dei into my hand. 'One day, if God grants you the gift of faith, you will earn the right to wear this. In the meantime, keep it, treasure it, and pray for God's grace.'

Outside I looked at the Lamb – it was enclosed in a circle and made dull by a casting of tin or lead – and de Colville said: 'Did you know the men in the other regiments are calling us Kirke's Lambs?'

I turned to him and laughed. 'It's true,' he said. 'Most of our men are Irish – as you know very well – and most of them are wearing the badge on their hats. And sometimes it almost looks as though it's meant to be a way of distinguishing us from other regiments. A sort of regimental badge.'

'But the linings of our coats are green and we have our own ensigns, and we don't need any other form of recognition or identity.'

'I know. But that's what they're saying.'

I looked at my hat, looked at the badge, and I knew I could never wear it. It would be like a cattle brand. It would denote ownership, allegiance to another power, a spiritual power; and in England where the Test Act demanded public allegiance, public communion with the Church of England, it would be viewed with suspicion. And suspicion could lead to resignation – my resignation. And then what would I do?

I walked back to Mister Tate's and as I lifted my hand to open the door I realised no one had thought of Saint Barbara. Her marbled face was still looking down the street, her street, and I remembered Mister Tate wanting to take her down, to be rid of her, to be rid of all the symbols of popery.

I turned round, walked to our lodgings, brought back six soldiers-of-foot, and chiselled her off the wall. We packed her in straw, boxed her in timber and carried her down to the Mole. Then we rowed her across the Bay and loaded her onto the *Centurion*.

Next morning, soon after the engineers exploded the first mine on the Mole, the *Centurion* weighed anchor, and Saint Barbara and the priests headed through the Straits, picked up the deep Atlantic swell, and vanished in a cloud of rain.

In the evening I sat with Mister Tate. I told him Saint Barbara was gone, was on her way back to Lisbon with all the priests. I told him the chapel was now his, was now a protestant chapel and he could do what he liked with it, and no one would complain to the Queen, no one would interfere.

A flicker of a smile came and went on his lips. Elizabeth said it was wind, said he needed burping like a baby, but I liked to think, wanted to think, he understood.

On the night of the 24th the pain made Mister Tate scream and yell, and every time I spooned the tincture into his mouth and massaged his throat, made his Adam's Apple bob up and down, the tincture dribbled out of his mouth. He could not swallow – even with our help – and now nothing could go down, could sooth the pain. He began to kick, to writhe, to jerk like a man being pulled to and fro. Towards midnight Elizabeth came downstairs but I told her she needed her sleep, told her I would sit with him.

From time to time he whimpered and drummed his feet. I wiped his face, wiped away the sweat, then he opened his eyes and whispered: 'Help me. Help me to go.'

His words tore at my soul. I hadn't heard him say a thing in weeks – nothing that made any sense. And now here was this plea, from the edge of the grave, and I knew I had to help him, help him to embrace death.

I found a funnel and I rubbed it with olive oil. I sat him up, slid the stem of the funnel into his throat, tilted his head and poured all the tincture down his throat. I held him upright for about ten minutes, gave the opium time to send him to sleep, then I took away his wooden frame, covered him with a blanket and gave him back his dignity.

I moved the candle closer to his bed. The soft light filled the room and everywhere I looked there were shadows and secret places. In them I could sense the presence of those who worshipped in this room when it was a chapel. They had come to be with him, to pray with him, to help him on his way.

Then I prepared for his final service.

I shifted the things off his communion table and covered it with a white linen cloth. I found his Bible – the old one with the large print and the leather cover that had split and pealed from the spine. I opened it and laid it in the centre of the table. I would have liked to put the candle close to it, liked to read in the halo of light, but I remembered he did not approve of candles on the communion table, and as this was his service, his service of departure, everything had to be as he would want it to be.

Then in a loud clear voice, I said: 'The reading comes from the Gospel according to Saint John. Verse twenty-four. Verily, verily I say unto you, He that heareth my word, and believeth on him that sent me, hath everlasting life, and shall not come unto condemnation; but is passed from death to life.'

Then I turned to the psalms, found the hundred and sixth psalm, the psalm that graces evening prayer, and I began to read: 'Give thanks unto the Lord for he is gracious: and his mercy endureth for ever.' In the silence I felt as though I was reading the words for the first time, was seeing them with fresh eyes, and this feeling, this sense of wonderment stayed with me verse by verse; and then I came to the last verse, the forty-sixth verse, a verse I had sung many times in my youth, and I closed my eyes and said: 'Blessed be the Lord God of Israel from everlasting, and world without end: and let all the people say, Amen.'

Then I paused for a moment, knelt beside the bed, took his pillow, placed it over his face and held it firm.

I closed my eyes and I wanted to pray, wanted to join the hidden mourners, but I could not form the words. I looked up and there above the table was the board with the Lord's Prayer. The board had begun to crack and warp and pull apart. The paint was peeling, was rolling up into tight little curls. And the letters, in red and black, had faded, had become pale and dull. But the words could still be read, and I wanted to make them mine, make them my private prayer. But as I began to say the words in my mind, I realised he would want to hear them for the last time. I began again. I read them aloud:

'OUR FATHER, WHICH ART IN HEAVEN,'

My thoughts intruded into the words of our Lord and became part of the prayer: To me Mister Tate you were like a father, more real than my own father. And I'll always think of you, sitting up there in heaven. You'll be at home. And you'll see God and you'll sing with the angels, with the choirs of heaven.

'HALLOWED BE THY NAME.'

Will they hallow your name, speak of you in hushed tones and remember you with reverence, when they tell the story of Tangiers? Or will you drift out of their minds and be forgotten, as the sands drift over your grave? I fear you will drift, we all will drift, will be lost in the sands of time.

'THY KINGDOM COME.'

You prayed for this, for sixty, seventy years. You talked as if the kingdom would come today, if not today, then tomorrow. And now it is tomorrow and the kingdom hasn't come, and I see no sign of it – despite all our prayers. And that is the truth, the hard truth that beggars belief.

'THY WILL BE DONE IN EARTH, AS IT IS IN HEAVEN.'

You did his will and you tried to get us to do his will. God knows, you tried long enough, hard enough. And what did we do? The truth is we ignored you. We laughed behind your back. That's what we did. And now we are sad, are sorry for what we have done, have left undone.

'GIVE US THIS DAY OUR DAILY BREAD.'

He began to struggle, I pushed harder on the pillow, held him firmer by the nose and the mouth.

'AND FORGIVE US OUR TRESPASSES,'

His head twisted from side to side.

'AS WE FORGIVE THEM THAT TRESPASS AGAINST US.'

His hands reached out to beat me, to push me away. Then his body heaved up and down, tried to break free.

'AND LEAD US NOT INTO TEMPTATION;'

I fell on him. My chest covered the pillow – smothered it – and my hands grabbed at his arms, grabbed at his hands.

'BUT DELIVER US FROM EVIL:'

He shook and twitched and bounced me up and down. His feet thrashed the end of the bed. I held him firm, held him down, forced him into the dip in bed.

'FOR THINE IS THE KINGDOM,'

Then I felt him weaken. Felt his strength ebb away. His hands flopped onto the blanket.

'THE POWER, AND THE GLORY,'

He became calm, became still.

'FOR EVER AND EVER. AMEN.'

I lay my head on his pillow and went to sleep. I might have slept for an hour or more – it was hard to tell – but when I woke the dawn was beginning to creep in the window. His candle had gone out and the unseen mourners had paid their last respects and departed.

He stank. He'd wet himself, and his bowels had opened, had soiled his night shirt. I washed him and tied a ribbon round his cock, tied it tight to stop any more pee leaking out. Then I changed his bedclothes and placed the pillow under his head. I closed his eyes and his mouth, brushed his long grey hair and curled the ends around my finger. The colour had drained out of his face. His frowns had softened, and he looked relaxed, looked at peace. He looked younger, much younger. He looked like the Mister Tate who rescued me on the *Salisbury*. I remembered that night, remembered he did not ask any questions. I leant over, kissed him on the forehead and whispered: 'Thank you for that night. And goodbye. Goodbye, old friend.'

I closed his Bible, then I looked up, looked at the boards with the Commandments and read: THOU SHALT NOT KILL.

The words stunned my mind and heaved my belly. They made no allowance for compassion, for charity, for words of mitigation, for the plea of a dying man. They were harsh and unforgiving; and in their chiselled perfection, their marbled eloquence, they captured the spirit of Moses, Mount Sinai, and the God of the Jews, the God of the Old Testament. He was a cruel God, a God of sacrifice, a God who was not satisfied till he had witnessed the death, the immolation of his own son on the cross at Calvary.

He was a God I did not want.

I touched Mister Tate's hands, the hands that had touched Elizabeth, and I knew what I wanted. I wanted her to be to me, as she had been to him: I wanted her to be my wife.

120

I went upstairs and lay on the bed beside Elizabeth. When she woke I told her Mister Tate had died in his sleep. For a long time she held me tight and I could feel her sobbing, feel the heaving of her breasts. Then she dried her eyes and said: 'I'd like to be alone with him for a few minutes.'

I listened to her feet going down the stairs. Most of her things were packed, were ready to go on board the *Saint David*, and her feet made an empty echo, an echo that would once have been dulled by mats, wall-hangings, curtains and cushions.

She came back about twenty minutes later with red eyes, and she said: 'He looks so peaceful. He looks like a man who has seen the face of God. And I'm so happy for him. I'm so glad there's no more pain. No more suffering.' She gave me a weak smile. 'I told him his name would live on in the boys. And when they had children, his grandchildren, they too would bear his name. And he would not be forgotten.' She touched my hand and looked into my eyes. 'Thanks to you.'

I gave her a gentle smile and took her in my arms. I did not want Charles and James to have his name for their surname, their family name. I wanted them to reverse their last two names, to have my name for their surname and his for their middle name. I wanted them to be Fentons, to be men of The Fens. And I wanted them to know my Mother, my Father – and then I realised I hadn't thought of either of them for years and years and I had no idea if they were dead or alive. I felt empty, felt as though their lives had been stolen from me, and I remembered them, remembered the days of my innocence, the days I should have had with them and I burst into tears.

She hugged me tight, ran her hands down my back, made soothing noises and whispered: 'It will be all right. He was an old man. And he wanted to go. He wanted to be with the Lord.'

I felt embarrassed, ashamed, but I could not tell her the truth. I smiled, a wet weak smile, and she dried my eyes.

A few minutes later we heard a knock on the door. I waved her back into her chair, opened the door, and stared straight into Sergeant Lockhart's face. Behind him eight soldiers-of-foot waited for his orders. They were all unarmed and I knew at once they'd come for Mistress Tate's things.

But before I could say a word, he gave me a grin, a filthy lecherous grin and said: 'Been entertaining ourself have we, sir?'

I shook my head. 'Mister Tate died in the early hours of this morning.'

The grin slid off his face and he stammered: 'I had no idea, sir. I'm sorry. Maybe we could come back later. This afternoon?'

'Just wait here. I'll talk to Mistress Tate and she can decide.'

I took Elizabeth's hands and I told her they could come back, but she said: 'No. They're here now. And Mister Tate did not approve of waste, and it would be wasting their time if they had to come back.'

'Then we should wrap him in a shroud first. We should prepare him for the grave.'

'He didn't mind the sight of death. He used to say it fixed our minds on the life that was to come. And he didn't think it should be hidden away. He was a practical man. He was always saying "in the midst of life we are in the midst of death", and that is why those two little square boards and the four long boards' – she pointed to the boards with the Commandments, the Creed, and the Lord's Prayer – 'are to be nailed together to make his coffin.'

My face must have been a picture of disbelief, for she smiled and nodded – as if to reassure me – and she said: 'The text is to go inside. In death he is to be surrounded by the words he loved in life.'

I took her upstairs and said: 'I'll send for Mistress Westcombe and when we're ready to close the coffin you can come down and we can leave you with him for a while.'

She gave me a gentle nod and sat down on the bed with James and Charles.

I sent two men down to the garrison church for the handcart, and two more to the burying ground to dig the grave. Within half an hour we had the boards off the wall and nailed together. We wound a sheet around Mister Tate and lifted him into the coffin. His limbs had stiffened and his mouth had twisted. He didn't look right and I slipped a cushion in behind his neck and this made him look a little more natural. Then we splayed the sheet over the top end of the coffin and tucked the other end around his legs and his feet – made it look smooth, look neat.

Then I went upstairs and I said: 'We can wait till tomorrow. We can take your things today and we can have the funeral after you've gone on board the *Saint David*.'

She shook her head. 'I'd like him to go first. To leave from his home. I don't want him to leave from an empty house, from a shell that was our life. It wouldn't seem right.'

Mistress Westcombe brought her downstairs and we all went outside and waited in the street. The men with the handcart arrived back with a bunch of red flowers. They were the wild flowers, the star-shaped flowers men with pox used to bring to Saint Barbara. I took them into her and she broke each flower off its stem and scattered them all over the white sheet. Then she kissed his forehead and pulled the sheet over his face.

Then she stood bewildered, not knowing what to do, what was expected of her. I nodded to Mistress Westcombe and she led her upstairs.

We nailed down the lid. The dull thumping filled me with gloom and it reminded me of sods of earth thumping onto a coffin lying deep in the earth, in the hole we call a grave.

We shut the door behind us, strapped the coffin onto the handcart, and began to make our way up the street. Twenty, thirty people, stood on both sides of the street, stood bareheaded, stood silent in the face of death.

At the end of the street as we turned to go up Catherine Street, I had a sudden idea, and I said: 'I want to take him down to the cathedral.'

Lockhart gave me a strange look and said: 'But he wasn't one of them.'

I nodded. 'I know that. But he did most of his preaching down there, and I thought he might like a last look.'

He shrugged and I heard some muttering, but I let it drift over my head.

We stopped in front of the cathedral. Men were up on the roof, straddling the beams, stripping off the tiles. The doors were gone. The wind was blowing through the empty windows, blowing away the smell of stale incense, stale prayers. Someone had taken a sledge hammer to one of the walls by the empty arches, but the walls were too thick and now they were pitted, and it looked as though they'd been hit by an exploding mortar.

I banged on the coffin lid with the flat of my hand and I said: 'If you can hear me, if you can see me from up there' – I pointed a finger at the sky – 'this is the day you've been waiting for. They're tearing the whole place down. It's what you wanted. What you prayed for. And now it's happening. Your prayers have been answered. And from what I've seen of this world very few men ever get their prayers answered. You're a lucky man Mister Tate. A very lucky man.'

An hour later, in the burying ground, long after Sergeant Lockhart and his men had gone back to Mister Tate's house, I stamped the damp earth into his grave – settled it with my feet – then I scuffed the surface flat, found a leafy twig and swished it backwards and forwards. The outline of the grave vanished, became one with the earth, and I whispered: 'When we're gone, when the Moors are tramping this land, your grave will be a secret place, a sacred place, a place where your bones will lie undisturbed till the last day, the Day of Judgement when regiments of men will rise from this earth, and the Lord will come in glory, come from the east, from the land of the rising sun. Till then dear friend may you rest in peace, and may the Lord bless you and keep you.'

A few minutes later, in the infirmarium, in the tomb of silence that death had vacated, Doctor Lawrence signed the pass for Mistress Westcombe.

She was expecting the pass. She knew it would come. She had packed her chests, her boxes, her memories of the life she shared with her dead husband and she was ready to go. But the sight of the pass, the sight of officialdom flustered her, and she rushed back to her house, and a stranger could have been forgiven for thinking everything had to be packed, to be made ready in less than an hour.

I gave her twenty minutes, time to collect her wits, time to sip a glass of bandy-wine, and I said to Lockhart: 'Get another half-dozen men and empty her whole house. Leave some food and some bedding, and a small chest for her personal things, but take everything else. And be gentle with her. This was her home and she chose not to go back to England when her husband died, and now I'm hoping she'll live with Mistress Tate – will help her to look after the boys.'

In the night Elizabeth and I slept on the floor – the bed was dismantled, was gone – and we possessed each other in a madness of passion, of wanting. I feared, and I sensed she feared, that this could be the last time we were united in love, and for a long time we clung to each other, like children who are scared of the unknown.

In the dawn, as the time of our parting approached, I opened the balcony doors, the doors to our private place, to the chapel that used to belong to Saint Barbara, and I said: 'If God had been willing I would have liked to marry you here in the chapel, under the stars, in the sight of the angels. But it cannot be.' I took her hand. 'In England, when you have mourned for Mister Tate, when you have laid him to rest in your heart, I would like you to be my wife – if you will have me to be your husband.'

She leant forward and kissed my forehead.

121

Early in November, a few days after the first of the great chests that backboned the end of the Mole was blown up, the last of our French men, women and children boarded the *Swan* and set sail for Marseilles. And now, with the exception of a few families from the Mole and a few others who were staying on to prepare food, wash clothes and housekeep for some of our senior officers, we were a town of men: 3,700 according to the clerks in the Upper Castle who tallied the muster lists from the ships and the regiments.

Our company was ordered to destroy the houses close to the common sewer. And day by day, in the pouring bloody rain we sawed and chopped beams of wood for the fire and salvaged roof tiles, floor tiles, panes of glass, iron bars – anything that had a value and could be reused in England – and lumped them down to the quay. Out on the Mole the houses and the warehouses had been demolished, and most days – most nights when the moonlight was bright enough – two and a half thousand men were picking at the rock, drilling tunnels, laying mines, loading stone into boats and dumping it in the Bay.

To us who had been in Tangiers for ten years or more there was a bitter irony in the scene: more men were being used to destroy the Mole than had ever been engaged on its construction at any one time. There was much talk about how easy it would be to destroy the oldest part of the Mole – once the seawalls were broken down – because it was all loose-fill and the sea would wash it away. But by a perverse twist of fate it soon became obvious that the new chests were going to be easier to destroy because the loose-fill had compacted, had become solid stone. And it was also obvious that it wasn't going to take two or three weeks as everyone first thought, and within a few days we were hearing estimates of two or three months.

The heavy rain slowed the work, drowned our spirits and sapped our strength, and the infirmarium began to fill up again with men who coughed and spat, and died in a fever. Provisions ran low and herrings, butter and cheese replaced our salt-beef. The men's mood turned sour, became mutinous, and it didn't improve till the Moors agreed to honour their promise and four hundred head of cattle crossed the drawbridge – in truth it was more like a bridge for the chains had rusted and it was never drawn up – and passed through Catherine Gate.

Day by day the Moors watched the destruction and they did nothing. We kept thinking they might rush the walls, try to take the town, the Mole, while there was still something left to take, but they did not make a move. Some thought they held us in awe – remembered our numbers, our strength from the great parade – and others thought they were prepared to bide their time, and stay out of the rain. Still others thought Lord Dartmouth had bribed them, and some thought he was making promises, trying to redeem the English captives, and the prospect of gold was keeping them snug in their tents. Whatever the truth Lord Dartmouth was taking no chances, and every night he doubled the guards on all the walls.

Late November brought high winds, high seas, and for days on end the storms of winter kept the seamen on their ships – twenty-eight were now riding at anchor – and they could not work on the Mole, row their longboats or load their ships, and the work of demolition, of salvage almost ground to a halt. The storms had another effect, an effect we had not foreseen: as the height of the Mole sank towards the high-water mark, the storms surged over the Mole, turned it into a reef, a wild foaming of water that swept men to their death and limited the number of hours that could be worked each day.

The storms also raised the level of the common sewer, flushed it clean and washed away the stench of summer. But within a couple of days water was pouring over the top of the banks, flooding the rubble, flooding the cellars we'd filled with stone. For a week we knocked down walls, worked in a foot or more of running water. The chill ran up my legs and froze my balls, and at night I couldn't warm myself and I was wracked with a hacking cough, a chill that wouldn't leave, and I longed for Elizabeth – for the warmth of her body.

Early in December Colonel Boynton sent us down to the waterfront to clear the coalyard, and for four days we shovelled coal into sacks and humped them down to the longboats. To me it would have been better to burn the coal, to warm the men, but old habits, habits of thrift, habits of parsimony die hard – if they die at all – and it provoked a bout of grumbling. I closed my ears to it – it helped the men vent their anger, their frustration – and in truth I couldn't see much point in taking the coal all the way back to England. We could have dumped it in the Bay, and it would have helped to block the harbour, would have stopped the Moors and the Barbary Pirates from using it as an anchorage.

Through all of this, through everything that was happening, ran a common thread, a common gripe, and it could be summed up in a few words: why the hell didn't we destroy Tangiers and leave in the summertime, when the days were fine and dry, and the work could have been done in half the time?

In the evenings our thoughts were beginning to turn to home, to the life that lay ahead of us. In addition to the old and the sick, the *Unity* was also carrying the wives and the children of the men in our first battalion,

Colonel Kirke's battalion. By now we knew they should be at Pendennis Castle on the shores of Falmouth Harbour. And we knew each wife was to receive an allowance of threepence per day and this had eased the pain of parting. We also knew the castle was in ruins and our men would have to rebuild it, and they had been chosen to do this because they were 'used to labouring'.

Our second battalion – Colonel Boynton's battalion, my battalion – was going to be stationed in Tilbury, to rebuild the fort, but then this was changed and now we were going to Plymouth. By sea the distance between Plymouth and Falmouth was about fifty miles, by land it was a little more than this. To us it was wrong to split the regiment in two and then separate the two halves by fifty miles. It boded ill, and it induced hours of endless speculation, and the common wisdom, the common consensus told us that the King did not need all the soldiers who were coming home. And in time, our numbers would be reduced, the battalions would be amalgamated, and if a war did not loom over the horizon in the next two years, the regiment could wither and die.

We also knew Colonel Kirke was talking to each officer one by one and although most officers were tight-lipped, nothing we heard contradicted the common wisdom.

I did not know when he'd be talking to me, but I did know he was talking to de Colville some time this morning. I wandered along to his men – they were stripping marble out of the old cathedral – but he wasn't there and I wandered back to the quay. My men had formed a long line and they were passing cannon balls from hand to hand and loading them into the longboats. The sea had picked up a chop and the seamen were only taking small loads and the loading seemed to be taking for ever. I was thinking of sending some of them back up to Three-gun Battery for more shot when I saw de Colville sitting alone on the stone terraces high above the quay.

I bounded up the steps and sat beside him. He looked white and drawn.

He looked at me, pulled his lips into a tight smile.

'What did he say?'

For a long time he stared out to sea, to the Bay that was now gorged with rocks, then he said: 'I have to resign my commission. He says tolerance is a mistake and should not have been permitted here. It is not permitted in England. And even if I made a Test Communion and signed the oath and denied the truth of transubstantiation, he would regard it as hypocrisy and he would not accept it.' He paused, looked at me, and blinked away the tears. 'I told him nothing would induce me to take the Test Communion. And he told me there was nothing else to say. And I have to resign my commission on the day we arrive in England.'

I reached out and touched his arm. 'I'm sorry.'

'It's the price of faith. It was why I came here. Why I couldn't be an officer in England.'

'And what are you going to do?'

'I was half expecting it, and I've written to my father, Lord Extonmouth. I've asked him to write a letter on my behalf.'

'But, I thought you didn't get on with your father.'

'As a man, as a person, I like him, and I do get on with him, as you put it. But he doesn't like my religion. That's the only thing we disagree about.'

'Will he write this letter for you?'

'Yes. I think he will. If it was successful it would appeal to his vanity. And he'd like the thought of it.'

'What's he going to say in the letter?'

He smiled. 'I can't say at the moment. But if I'm accepted everyone will know. It will be public knowledge and they'll print an announcement in the journals. But in the meantime . . .'

I nodded, but in truth I was none the wiser. 'And what about the regiment? What about all this talk of amalgamation, less men, less officers?'

'I'm sorry. I didn't ask. It didn't seem to be relevant.'

We sat together for about half an hour, I watched my men and he watched the sea. Then the seamen signalled that the water was too rough for any more loads.

I left him still watching the sea. I told my men to be ready at dawn tomorrow, then I walked up to the clerk's office. I knew the King's Battalion was going to pull the roof off the warehouse in the next day or so, and I wanted to take one last look, to clear my things out of my old desk. O'Sullivan was sitting at his desk. Brandon and Crabtree were packing their things into wooden boxes. I took my green rug off the wall, rolled it up and tied it with a cord. It wasn't my intention, but somehow O'Sullivan and I began to talk about de Colville and I told him what had happened. He nodded. 'It's to be expected,' he said. 'He's not the only one. And if you'd been a bit braver, had the courage of your convictions, as they say, you too would have had to resign your commission on the day you arrived back in England.'

I nodded. I'd been aware of it, in a vague way, and maybe it was one of the things that had niggled in my mind, had crushed, had bruised, had destroyed the fragile flower that was my faith.

I sat at my desk for the last time, ran my finger tips down the inked edge and pulled open my drawer. Ives walked into the room, took off his grey surtout and shook water everywhere. He tossed his hat onto a peg and it dripped water onto the floor. A splattering of black ink, the ink of temper, of tantrum, still defaced the wall. He looked at me, looked hard, then he turned to O'Sullivan and said: 'I am right. It does look like him. They're about the same age.'

O'Sullivan nodded.

'Have you shown him?'

O'Sullivan shook his head. 'I haven't had time. He's only just arrived.'

I looked from one to the other. They weren't making any sense.

O'Sullivan opened his drawer, pulled out a small parcel and began to untie the string. 'This arrived a couple of days ago. It's a portrait. A picture of my late uncle. He left it to my mother but she didn't want it. She never forgave him for going to England, for pretending he was a Protestant and enlisting in Cromwell's army, the Model Army.'

He unwrapped the paper and held up the painting. It was a picture of a young man in a buff leather coat, the coat that protected a musketeer in Cromwell's army. It was painted in oils, was dark, oppressive. The man's face was light-skinned, might once have been white. His hair was black and his eyes were green, a bright pond-green. He looked like an Irishman, like any number of our young soldiers-of-foot, and in my mind I could see him wearing an Agnus Dei on his black felt hat. I looked at O'Sullivan and I looked at the young man. 'He doesn't look much like you.'

'No, he doesn't. They say I take after my mother. But Ives says he looks like you.'

'Me? He doesn't look like me.'

'I can see a resemblance,' Brandon said.

'And so can I,' Crabtree said.

I looked from one to the other and burst out laughing. I couldn't see any resemblance. 'He doesn't look like me. He doesn't look like anyone I know.'

I took the picture from him and peered at it. Then my blood ran cold. 'Dear God,' I whispered. 'In the background. That church . . .'

'Hmm.' O'Sullivan said. 'Most unlike him to have a church painted in the background. I don't recognise it. Brandon thinks it's English, but I don't know.'

'It's English,' I said. 'It's Ely cathedral.'

'Ely? Where you come from?'

I nodded. I knew who he was. I could see my Father in him. Could see the shape of his neck. The way he held his head. The way he used to look at me, when he wanted me. I shivered. For a moment or two I couldn't trust myself to speak, then I took a breath, a slow deep breath, and said: 'Long ago I once asked you about a man. A man called Patrick O'Sullivan. The man who was my Father's father, his real father. And you said . . . you said, you didn't know anyone called Patrick O'Sullivan. But you did know a man by the name of Seamus, Seamus O'Sullivan, if I remember you right.'

O'Sullivan leant back on his stool. 'I don't remember talking about him. But then we used to talk about so many things didn't we? And you are right about his name. It was Seamus. Seamus O'Sullivan.'

I turned the painting over and looked at the back, but there was nothing to see. I looked again at the man, held him up to the light, and I could feel the frame was loose, was beginning to slip away from the canvas. I tapped it with my fingers and it came away in my hands. At the bottom of the portrait, in bright red letters, running over a clean slice of buff coat, I read: SEAMUS PATRICK O'SULLIVAN.

I broke out in a sweat. My heart raced and my hand shook.

O'Sullivan reached out, took the frame and the picture, and said: 'Good Lord. His middle name was Patrick. She named me after him and she never told me. She kept it a secret.' He stared at me for a long time. 'You do look like him. I can see it now. And you say he was your father's father. Your grandfather. So you are Irish – part Irish.' He laughed. 'Who would have believed it? The man who used to hate the Irish, used to think we were bloody stupid – if I remember it right.' He laughed again. 'If you'd had the courage to trust your instincts, to accept the faith, you would have been one of us – in body and soul – been the very man you used to despise.' He smiled, and looked bemused for a moment. 'And this means you and I are related.'

I nodded, and looked from Ives to Brandon to Crabtree and back to O'Sullivan. In the depths of my soul I'd always known I was tainted by the Irish, but I'd pushed it out of my mind and tried to pretend that it was not so. But now it was back, and I felt as though my soul had been seared, had been branded at birth, and in a strange way, a way that defies the power of words, the power of understanding, I now knew why I'd been attracted to the old faith. It was in my blood. It was a birthright – an inheritance – and now it was spent, was gone for ever. And I was demeaned by its passing.

122

Towards the end of January when the Mole was no more than a reef at low tide and the Bay was clogged with stone, with rubbish from the town and sand from a hill we had levelled to hasten the shallowing, the whole garrison marched out to Pole Fort. And then with the perfection of a formal parade, with dressed ranks and ensigns fluttering in the wind, we watched the engineers explode the mines in Pole Fort. We felt the blast and heard the sound – it rolled down the hill in one gigantic boom and filled the air with clouds of mushrooming dust, flames and smoke. And like a mortar bomb exploding, it showered the hill with hundreds of stones. The Moors – assembled in the distance – cheered and whooped and danced. The victory was theirs but the dignity was ours; and as we retired in good order with our drums beating and our ranks aligned, the wet sun was making our pike-heads and bayonets glint, and Lord Dartmouth's words were running through my head: 'We are leaving of our own free will. We are leaving without allowing the Alcaide any false pretences, pretences of being sainted for driving the English out of Barbary.'

As we thinned the walls of cannons, trundled them down to the quay, hoisted them into the air with our sheerlegs and lowered them into the longboats, the engineers mined our last three forts, the guardians of our water supply: Fountain, Bridges and Cambridge. And deep in the tunnels below the city walls, in the cellars of York Castle and in the great bastions of the Upper Castle, the miners stacked barrels of gunpowder, and they told us the Moors would never be able to use them to mount cannons, to bombard ships as they passed through the Straits.

The last of the horses were loaded onto the ships. They were to be sold in Spain, at the Bay of Bulls because the troopers thought they would never adapt to the cold, to the rains, to the soggy marshes of England.

By early February everything in the town lay in ruins, with the exception of our lodgings and the Head Court of the Guard. We paraded in front of the Head Court for the last time – for a service of thanksgiving – and afterwards, as the last of the cannons came off the walls I was called into Colonel Kirke's room. He invited me to sit down, then he said: 'You will have heard the rumours about amalgamation, about reducing the number of companies, the number of men, the number of officers.' I nodded. 'I have not received His Majesty's commands and I do not know what is in his mind, but Lord Dartmouth has indicated that this is the most likely course of action, and we should prepare for it. In such circumstances, I regret to tell you that we will have too many ensigns. And since your old company, Captain Lacey's company, was disbanded, and you have in effect been a reformado for the past two years, I'm sorry to have to say that there will not be a place for you in the regiment.' I stared at him in disbelief and swallowed hard. 'I've been told of your gallantry and I admire the way you earned your commission, but in confidence I must tell you I have to protect the investment of those officers who purchased their commission. They must come first.' He paused. 'There could be a place for a Lieutenant. Have you ever thought of purchasing a Lieutenant's commission?'

'I don't have any money, sir.'

He nodded. 'I thought as much. And it's a pity, a great pity because I could have kept you on then, on half-pay as a reformado, till a place became available. But I'm sorry . . .'

I looked at my shoes and they reflected the blackness that was seeping into my mind.

'The best I can do is to make you a sergeant, a senior sergeant, and I would value your experience. But if you want to leave the regiment when the time comes to resign, I will respect your decision.'

123

February 5th, our day of leaving, day of abandonment, dawned cold but
fine; and in the grey gloom, in a greyness of spirit, Fountain, Bridges and
Cambridge exploded, and announced the signal for retreat.

The Union Flag came down for the last time, and for a few minutes
Peterborough Tower, looked naked, looked undressed. Then the tower
exploded, crumpled in a heap, and the cheers of the Moors rolled over
the walls.

In a fever we demolished our lodgings and the Head Court of the Guard,
and rushed everything that could be salvaged down to the quay. As the
tide uncovered the reef that was once the Mole, the troopers, the miners
and the first of the soldiers-of-foot marched onto the rocks and formed
long fingers that stretched to the right, stretched into the shallow water.
Then the longboats edged up to the end of each line and the men began
to clamber on board.

At midday, the Grenadiers and both our battalions formed a line of
defence through the middle of the ruins. High on Castle Hill I could make
out the ruins of de Colville's old house – the house of the angels. Down
by the lower walls, the Little Parade was outlined with heaps of rubble
and I could trace the remains of Jenny's house. But Rua de Carmo and
most of Saint Barbara's Street were now covered with rocks, with waves
of rubble, and Elizabeth's house and my Lady's house had fed those waves,
had become part of them and now they were gone, were houses of love,
places of lust, in the streets of my memory.

For twenty, maybe thirty minutes we waited, and I walked the streets of
my memory, the streets that brought me to manhood, then the engineers
fired the mines along the top wall and in the Upper Castle. Some of the
mines in the castle failed to explode. The Moors swarmed over the rubble.
We screamed and yelled, tried to wave them away, but the madness of
victory had gripped them and they waved their banners, jumped up and
down, and shrieked with glee. Then the mines that failed to explode blew
up, blew eight of them to bits. The Moors retreated and the Grenadiers
marched to the foot of the sandhills, and with granadoes in their hands and
matches burning, they kept them away from the explosions.

As the day wore on and the long walls from the Upper Castle to York

Castle, and from Irish Battery to the sea came down, section by section, we edged closer to York Castle, closer to the final farewell. Just before dusk, Saint George's flag, the flag of England was lowered in the tower above York Castle, and then the reality of the moment gripped me: this was farewell. This was the end. The end of England in Barbary. And we would not be coming back. Tears flooded my eyes, embarrassed me with sentiment, and I turned away, hid my eyes in the black-brimmed darkness of my hat.

For the next two hours we sledge-hammered the sides of the cistern on the quay and let the water run free, pulled down the sheerlegs and loaded them onto a longboat, and smashed anything that had to stay behind. Then in the darkness as we shuffled down to the Mole, made our way onto the rocks – into the water and waited for the longboats – the sea walls came down and the dust, the coal that was tramped into the sand in the coalyard began to burn.

Then the engineers fired the mines in York Castle, and the tower that had watched over my life for ten years blew apart and fell in a heap. Through the flash of exploding gunpowder – as the last of the castle walls came down – square-cut stones flew through the air, fell on the terraces, shattered, and filled the air with shards of stone.

Then the old galley that had acted as a pontoon – had been moored beside the quay that crossed the beach – was set on fire. It had been filled with tar and wedged into the legs of the wooden fort that had become the Lazaretto, the place of isolation, the place where infectious men had lived and died. As the flames licked up the legs, the Lazaretto became a torch of fire, a burning pyre, a place of cleansing. It also became a torch and it lit up the rocks below it, the beach, the gaunt remains of the city walls, and the last remaining fort: Fort Whitby Gate.

Towards midnight as the Grenadiers came onto the Mole and we clambered into the longboats, Lord Dartmouth fired the last mine and Fort Whitby Gate blew up. And now the Strand, the way to Whitby, lay open, lay unprotected, lay ready for the Moors who in all this time had not fired one single shot.

As we passed the rocks that marked the end of the Mole, and our longboat came into the wind, into the chop of the waves and made for the *Centurion*, the Lazaretto fell into the water and the flames licked at the sea, made it burn with fire. Then the waves put out the flames, restored the darkness, the sanctity of the night, and in the swell, in the crest of the waves, in the wind-blown spray, we caught the soft sounds of singing. The words were words of sorrow, words of parting and they came from the old lament, the Lament for Tangiers. I let my fingers drift in the water, drift in sadness, and we picked up the words, sang the words of the final refrain:

Farewell, farewell
Farewell to Barbary.

124

Next morning in a dawn made queasy by the swaying of the *Centurion* we mustered on deck and watched the ruins emerge from the darkness. In the night they had been old friends, familiar shapes that exploded, flashed with light, showered rocks in the air, contorted, and fell in heaps. Now they were strangers in a strange land, a landscaping of rocks on foreign hills, foreign earth. They were wrapped in silence and softened with smoke – a thin gauze of smoke that looked like sea-fog and would blow away in the first stirrings of the wind – and they presented a picture of desolation, of abandonment.

Then the sun hardened the picture, fixed the soft images in my mind, and made the edges of the rock look raw, look like stone that had just been cut in the quarries at Whitby. In my mind's eye I could see these stones rising again, see them shaping a new town, a new Tangiers. I wondered if the Moors would build on our foundations, follow our walls, our streets; and my eyes drifted down the outlines of Catherine Street, through the Market Place, over the rubble that was the Watergate and down to the beach, where the waves were crashing on the sand, throwing foam in the air.

Then I heard a noise, a tidal wave of noise, and I looked up. The Moors were clambering over the rocks by Catherine Gate, pouring down the street in their hundreds, and spreading out, spreading through the ruins, waving banners, screaming, laughing, yelling, calling to each other, skipping from rock to rock. It was a moment to savour – they had waited for this moment for hundreds of years. The infidel was gone, had taken fright and run away, and now the land was their land, was returned to the Prophet and the One True God, the God who could be worshipped from a prayer mat, a green prayer mat. And I wondered what they would build on our places of prayer, places of sacrifice.

Then they were swarming over the rubble that was York Castle, yelling, jeering, dancing in circles and shaking their fists at us. Their triumph was complete.

Many of the men on deck began to go down below, they had no stomach for the Moors and no stomach for the sea, and I was thinking I might follow them, when a mighty explosion shattered the ruins and hurled rocks high in the air. For a moment there was silence, then the Moors began to scream, to run, to flee in terror. The men leaning against our rails began to cheer and a mighty roar ran right round the fleet. De Colville turned to me and said: 'Must have been a mine that didn't explode. They must have disturbed the fuse somehow.'

I remembered Oldfield and the fuse he disturbed. The fuse that cost him his life, and I nodded.

Later in the morning Lord Dartmouth sent ashore barrels of gun-powder. It might have been some sort of tribute, or a sign of goodwill, or maybe he was trying to tempt the Moors into releasing the English prisoners. I don't really know. But it did provoke a lot of muttering in our company, and in truth we couldn't see the point of it.

Throughout the day the seamen shifted soldiers from ship to ship – in the darkness many of the longboats had made for the closest ship, unloaded the men and gone back for more. Our regiment was spread over five ships. Colonel Kirke's battalion was on board the *Montague* and the *Dragon*. Captain Giles's company was on the yacht *Ann*, Captain Chantrell's company was on the ketch *Deptford*, and the rest of our battalion – six companies totalling 253 men – was on the frigate *Centurion*.

I thought we would up-anchor next day or maybe the day after that, but the winds were contrary and in the next week only seven of the troop-ships – moored well out in Tangiers Road – were able to set sail and beat their way through the Straits.

On the 14th – nine days after the walls came down – the Moors released fifty-five English prisoners. Some had been held captive, made slaves for many years, and I have to confess that when I saw Lieutenant Wilson – captured at the fall of Fort Henrietta – I did not recognise him. His features were gaunt, his limbs were spindle-thin, and his shoulders were bowed like a man at prayer. As they rowed him round the fleet, we leant over the rail, cheered, clapped, yelled. He waved – his hand made a bony claw in the sky – and then he sank back into his posture of prayer. When they reached the *Greyhound*, the seamen threw nets over the side and helped him onto the boat. In the evening we heard that one of our men, a soldier-of-foot by the name of Thomas Nicholls had been held for twelve years, and a seaman – George Tegor – had suffered eighteen years. In a moment of remorse, I wished I'd been able to see their plight with greater clarity, had given something to the work of the Redemption Fathers.

Next morning Colonel Boynton returned from the *Grafton*, from paying his respects to Lord Dartmouth, and we weighed anchor and set sail for the Bay of Bulls. A few minutes later the *Tiger* and the *Dover* followed, and one by one we saluted the ruins that had been our home for so long. Mister Pepys had gone on before us to buy provisions, to resupply the whole fleet, and as I watched the hills of Barbary become smudges on the horizon my thoughts turned to fresh meat, fresh fruit, vegetables and the sweet wines that taste of summer.

De Colville and I were sharing a hold. It was small and cramped but it gave us a measure of privacy. It also gave us a measure of isolation – like a Lazaretto – and in some ways this reflected our situation. It was now common knowledge that he was to resign and it was assumed, with varying degrees of tact, that I too would be resigning and retaining the dignity of rank. In private I talked with Colonel Boynton and he advised me to swallow my pride, to be a sergeant again and enjoy what he called 'a secure income'. My mind was confused. In truth I couldn't make up my mind, didn't want to make up my mind, and as I lay in my hammock I looked at the mementoes that marked my life: a green prayer rug; a crushed butterfly; another butterfly that still glittered blue, glittered with life; an Agnus Dei – a symbol of what might have been; the head of Christ – still crowned with thorns, still wracked with sorrow; O'Sullivan's painting of his uncle – he insisted I have it, insisted a grandson had more right to it than a nephew; and my gorget – the gorget that would soon lose its power, its authority, and become a trinket, a silver trinket, a plaything for a child – Jenny's child?

In the night the wind freshened, blew us south, separated us from the *Tiger* and the *Dover*, and drove us straight into a storm that seemed to suck the sea into the sky and froth it to madness. It heaved the ship and heaved my belly. After about an hour the darkness was shattered by a large bang, by running feet, by thumping, by yelling. A mast had split, had broken at the top and draped the deck with ropes.

In the dawn the seamen chopped the ropes, freed the masthead and rerigged the sails. As the storm passed to the south – pulling a rolling sea in its wake – we limped back to Tangiers and dropped anchor close to the *Grafton*.

The seamen stepped the mast, heated iron hoops, shaped a spar and bound it to the top of the mast – restored the full height. By early March, when most of the fleet had left for Spain, we were ready to sail. On the morning of the 7th, when the wind came round, came off the land, came off the ruins the Moors were now rebuilding, the *Grafton* hoisted the signal to sail.

As the seamen unfurled the sails and we began to edge towards the middle of the Straits, a small boat came out of Tarifa. It was flying the Union Flag, the flag that signalled it was carrying dispatches from London and was under English protection. We heaved too and waited – for them the winds were on-shore and they forced them into a long tack. As they came close we threw down a line, pulled a leather bag on board, and saluted the last post, the post that would never come again for an English Tangiers.

A ship's Lieutenant handed the bag to Colonel Boynton. I leant on the rail, watched the boat draw away, watched the Spaniards take down the Union Flag, and felt the *Centurion* catch the wind, roll the deck to an angle and head for the open sea. A voice yelled: 'A letter for Ensign Fenton! A letter for Ensign Fenton!'

I turned round in a daze, walked forward and took the letter. I recognised the writing. It was from Elizabeth. It was an 'Express' and I knew she must have written it within a few days of arriving back in England. It set my heart thumping and I couldn't trust myself to open it, to read it in public. I slipped it into my coat, into the inside pocket, patted it smooth, and feared the worst.

Then the voice called again: 'A letter for Lieutenant de Colville! A letter for Lieutenant de Colville. A letter from His Royal Highness the Duke of York.'

I froze. A hush came over the whole deck. I turned, we all turned and looked at de Colville. He walked forward and held out his hand. As he went to walk away, to put the letter into his pocket, Colonel Boynton said: 'Are you going to open it? Are you going to tell us why His Royal Highness is writing to you?'

De Colville flushed, took the letter out of his pocket, broke the seals and read the words. 'It is not from His Royal Highness, sir. It is from his secretary, writing on his behalf, and it says: I am commanded by His Royal Highness to invite you to wait upon His Royal Highness, to become a member of his household and to enjoy the style, title and dignity of a Gentleman of the Bedchamber.'

A sour look crossed the Colonel's face. 'And why would he choose you?'

'My father, Lord Extonmouth, went into exile when King Charles was executed. He became a member of the Duke's household and he served him for many years. Some say he paid some of the Duke's debts, his Dutch debts, but I don't know if that is true or not.'

The Colonel nodded. 'And in those days the Duke was a Protestant and your father – is he a Protestant?'

'Yes, sir.'

'And now you are a papist and the Duke is a papist and he is surrounding himself with like-minded men. He is courting trouble, and I don't like it and nor do the English people. If his brother dies they won't have him for King. They've had enough of popery, and if you're smart, you'll thank him for the honour and tell him you're not well. Tell him you have a fever, a foreign fever, and you dread the thought of passing it on to him.' He sucked at his lips. 'But then you're not smart are you? If you were smart you wouldn't be a papist. The two are a contradiction.' He shook his head and turned away.

In the quiet of the hold I lit a candle, crawled into my hammock, and read Elizabeth's letter. It said:

My dear Mister Fenton,

Since we parted I have given much thought to your proposal of marriage, and it is with a heavy heart that I must tell you that circumstances do not permit me to accept your kind offer.

Mister Tate, as you well know, was a Cannon Emeritus of the Cathedral Church of Saint Mary and Saint Peter in Exeter. As his widow the rights and privileges that were his now devolve on me, and as a consequence we are living rent-free in an alms-house. This entitlement will remain with me for the rest of my life, or till I remarry.

Both the boys as the legitimate heirs of Mister Tate are entitled to be educated in the Choir School and in the Grammar School at no cost to me. But once again this privilege would come to an end if I remarried. It would become the responsibility of my new husband.

I am also entitled to a small pension, a gratuity that recognises his life's work. This would also come to an end if I remarried.

Conscious of the restraints that will be placed upon your purse in the years to come, and knowing that you, or you and I between us, could never afford to purchase a Lieutenant's commission, and knowing also that I must put the welfare of my two sons before my own happiness, I have, with great reluctance and many tears, decided that we cannot marry.

I know this will be a bitter disappointment for you, but I would ask you to do as I am doing: to think first of Charles and James.

With many thanks for the great honour you did to me through your most generous offer of marriage,

I remain, your most affectionate friend,

Elizabeth Tate

Relict of the late Reverend Mister Tate: Cannon Emeritus.

I let the letter slip from my hands, blew out the candle, lay back in my hammock, and let the darkness swallow my tears, my sorrow, my disbelief.

An hour or two later, de Colville came into the hold, lit the candle, picked up her letter and said: 'Can I read it?'

'If you want to.'

He read it and handed it to me. I read it again. This time I found it harder, harsher – cruel in its rejection. It was a letter without hope.

He climbed into his hammock and blew out the candle. A few minutes later he said: 'If you were a Lieutenant would she change her mind?'

'She might. The extra money would compensate. And when I left the regiment and sold my commission it would replace her pension. And the boys could bear my name. That's what hurts the most, the thought of them being Tates. The thought of never being able to publicly acknowledge that I am their father, and they are my sons.'

For a long time I listened to the sounds of the ship, the creaking, the gentle slosh of water, then he said: 'I have a proposition, a proposal I'd like to put to you.'

I looked into the black-beamed darkness, the darkness that was drowning my soul. 'Do you want to pay for their schooling? And their bed and board?'

'In a way, yes.'

'What do you mean?'

'I would like to sell you my commission, for one pound. And in a year or so, when you have a place in the regiment, I'm sure you'll be able to persuade her to marry you.'

'And what do you want in exchange?'

'I want you. I want you and I to be as we were – for however long this voyage takes.'

I rolled out of my hammock, went up onto the deck, and breathed in the cold damp air. And I knew that my life had slipped ten years, and once again I was faced with that most dreadful choice: the choice that is not a choice.

Sources of reference

QUEEN'S ROYAL SURREY REGIMENT MUSEUM
Clandon Park, West Clandon, Guildford. This regiment traces its foundation back to the Tangiers Regiment-of-Foot. Over the years it has been known by several names – the most common abbreviation was 'The Queen's'. In 1685 the regiment fought at the Battle of Sedgemore which ended the rebellion of the Duke of Monmouth. The unflinching courage (some would say harshness or brutality) of the men in this battle confirmed or encouraged the use of the nickname 'Kirke's Lambs', and this has led to the assumption that the men were now wearing the badge that would later become their official regimental badge: the Lamb of God (the Paschal Lamb). It is the oldest badge in the British Army, and the earliest known regimental representation appears on cut-outs of soldiers that were used in recruiting depots in 1715.

BOOKS
The Second Queen's Royal Regiment, Volume I, Lt-Col. J. Davis (1887)
Tangier, England's Lost Atlantic Outpost 1661–1684, E.M.G. Routh (1912)
Tangier at High Tide: The Journal of John Luke 1670–1673. Luke was Secretary to Lord Middleton – Governor of Tangiers.
Tangiers Journal 1683, Samuel Pepys In London, Pepys was a member of the Tangiers Committee.
The British Army 1660–1704, J. Tincey and G. Embleton.
The English Civil War 1642–1651, P. Haythornthwaite (Arms and Armour Press, 1996) (For military organisation, equipment and tactics.)

THE BRITISH LIBRARY – MAP LIBRARY
The etchings of R. Thacker. Maps and other etchings.

THE BRITISH MUSEUM – PRINTS AND DRAWINGS
STUDENTS' ROOM
The original watercolours of Wenceslaus Hollar (1669). Also the etchings that were made from them and sold in London.

NATIONAL MARITIME MUSEUM – GREENWICH
The Lord Dartmouth Collection which includes: plans, surveys, maps, letters, written orders, watercolours and the documents of the valuation commission. These are held in the library. Two large oil paintings by Dirck Stoop are held in the Reserve Collection.

THE NATIONAL ARMY MUSEUM – CHELSEA
Stoop's oil painting of Lord Dartmouth's parade in Tangiers 1683 – from the Lord Dartmouth Collection. This is the first painting of the modern British Army on parade.

HAMPTON COURT RESERVE COLLECTION
Danckert's painting of Tangiers.

THE PUBLIC RECORD OFFICE – CHANCERY LANE AND KEW

THE COMMUNION SILVER FROM
THE TANGIERS GARRISON CHURCH
This is held in the private treasury in Portsmouth Cathedral and was used by naval officers making their Test Communion up to the abolition of the act in 1828.

THE MEMORIAL TO SIR PALMES FAIRBORNE
This is fixed to the right-hand wall of the nave in Westminster Abbey – close to the choirscreen. It features a poem by John Dryden.